PRAISE FOR

THE LEGION OF FLAME

"With this series, [Ryan] has the characters, world building and magical system to deliver, and now, thanks to *The Legion of Flame,* he has all the characters positioned for a fiery conclusion."　　　—Fantasy-Faction

"Because of the amazing characters, seamless blend of fantasy and steam-punk, exciting adventures, page-turning plot and killer use of dragons, *The Legion of Flame* is *perfection.*"　　　—The Obsessive Bookseller

"Ryan does a masterful job in writing this complex story that intensifies the further we delve into the horrors we witness in a world that is falling apart."　　　—The Reading Cafe

PRAISE FOR

THE WAKING FIRE

"A marvellous piece of imagination with plenty of twists, a refreshingly different setting and excellent world building. A great read."
　　　—Mark Lawrence, international bestselling author of *Grey Sister*

"*The Waking Fire* is part *Indiana Jones,* part *Pirates of the Caribbean* and part *Mistborn.* It's got wonderful, memorable characters and great action . . . I loved it."　—Django Wexler, author of *The Infernal Battalion*

continued . . .

THE
LEGION
OF
FLAME

BOOK TWO OF THE DRACONIS MEMORIA

ANTHONY
RYAN

ACE
NEW YORK

ACE
Published by Berkley
An imprint of Penguin Random House LLC
375 Hudson Street, New York, New York 10014

Copyright © 2017 by Anthony Ryan
Excerpt from *The Empire of Ashes* copyright © 2018 by Anthony Ryan
Penguin Random House supports copyright. Copyright fuels creativity, encourages diverse voices,
promotes free speech, and creates a vibrant culture. Thank you for buying an authorized edition
of this book and for complying with copyright laws by not reproducing, scanning, or distributing
any part of it in any form without permission. You are supporting writers and allowing
Penguin Random House to continue to publish books for every reader.

ACE is a registered trademark and the A colophon is a trademark of Penguin Random House LLC.

Ace trade paperback ISBN: 9781101987919

The Library of Congress has cataloged the Ace hardcover edition as follows:

Names: Ryan, Anthony, author.
Title: The legion of flame / Anthony Ryan.
Description: First edition. | New York : Ace, an imprint of
Penguin Random House LLC, 2017. | Series: The Draconis memoria : book 2
Identifiers: LCCN 2017005849 (print) | LCCN 2017014642 (ebook) |
ISBN 9781101987902 (ebook) | ISBN 9781101987896 (hardcover)
Subjects: | GSAFD: Fantasy fiction.
Classification: LCC PR6118.Y3523 (ebook) | LCC PR6118.Y3523 L43 2017 (print) |
DDC 823/.92—dc23
LC record available at https://lccn.loc.gov/2017005849

Ace hardcover edition / June 2017
Ace trade paperback edition / June 2018

Printed in the United States of America
1   3   5   7   9   10   8   6   4   2

Cover illustration © Larry Rostant
Cover maps © Anthony Ryan
Cover photographs: lace trim © antipathique/Shutterstock;
fire frame © Alexander Chernyakov/iStockphoto; smoke © Honchar Roman/Shutterstock;
sextant © Morphart Creation/Shutterstock
Cover design by Judith Lagerman
Book design by Laura K. Corless
Interior maps by Anthony Ryan

For Robin, Norman and Nick,
because once upon a time we fought the good fight.

2

ACKNOWLEDGMENTS

Once again, thanks to my proofreader, Paul Field; my agent, Paul Lucas, for his diplomatic skills; and my US and UK editors, Jessica Wade and James Long, for their valuable input on the first draft.

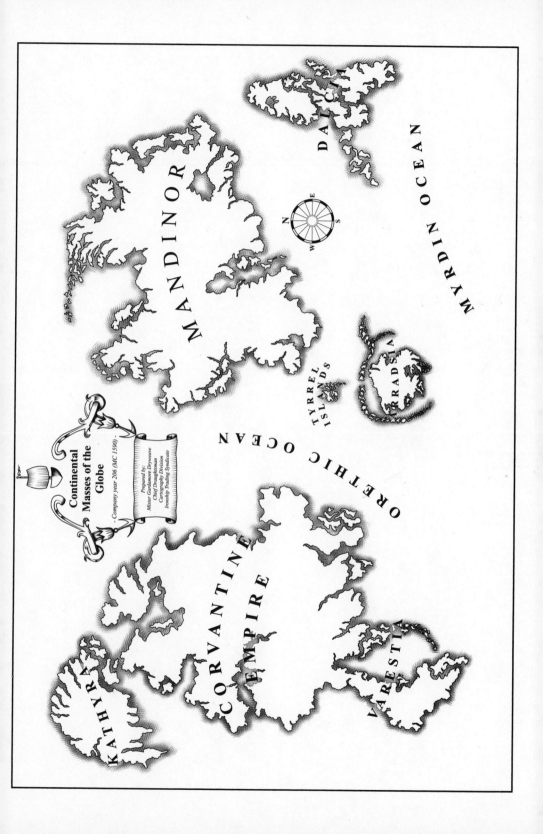

DALCA

MYRDIN OCEAN

MANDINOR

ARRADSIA

TYRREL ISLANDS

ORETHIC OCEAN

Continental
Masses of the
Globe

– Company year 206 (MC 1590) –

Prepared by:
Mister Gardamore Dryweave
Chief Draughtsman
Cartography Division
Ironship Trading Syndicate

CORVANTINE
EMPIRE

KATHYRA

VARESTIA

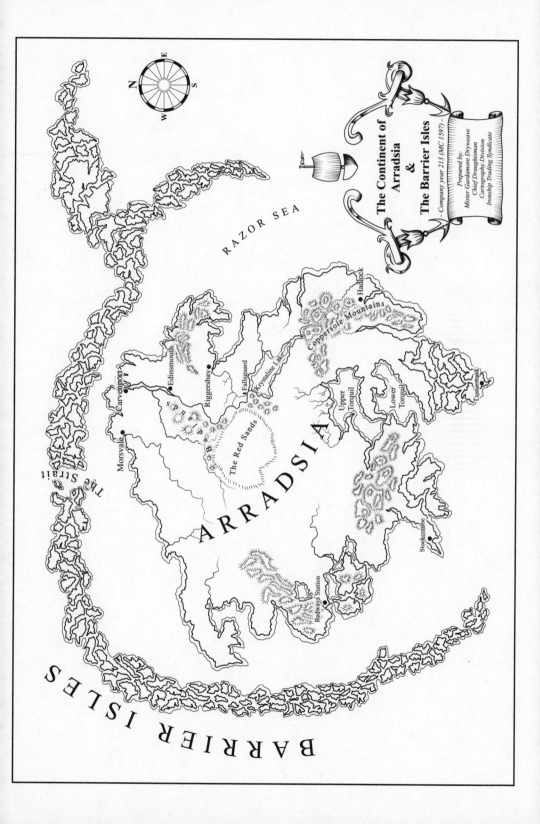

The Continent of Arradsia & The Barrier Isles

- Company year 213 (MC 1597) -

*Prepared by:
Mister Gardamore Dryweave
Chief Draughtsman
Cartography Division
Ironship Trading Syndicate*

RAZOR SEA

ARRADSIA

The Strait

BARRIER ISLES

Coppersole Mountains

Hadlock

Tussenvault

Upper Torquil

Lower Torquil

The Red Sands

Crystaline Lake

Fallsguard

Riggersbay

Edinsmouth

Carvenport

Morsvale

Redways Station

Stockcombe

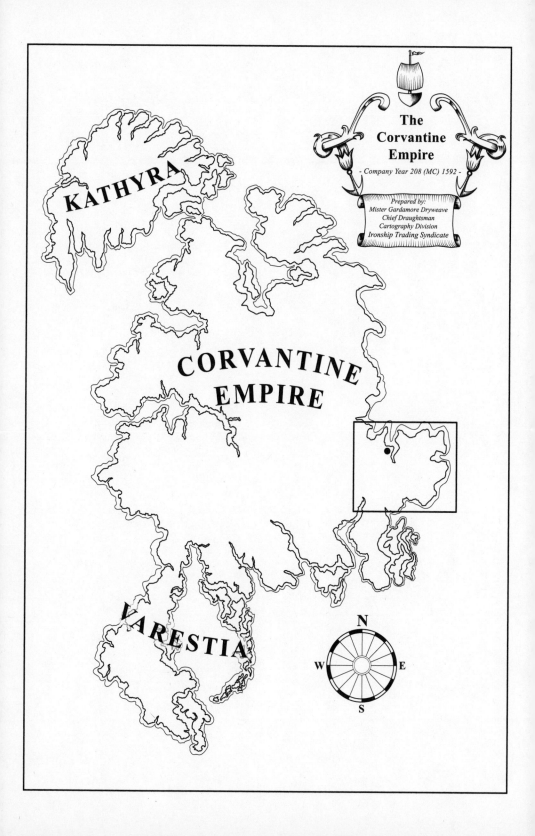

KATHYRA

CORVANTINE
EMPIRE

VARESTIA

The
Corvantine
Empire

- Company Year 208 (MC) 1592 -

Prepared by:
Mister Gardamore Dryweave
Chief Draughtsman
Cartography Division
Ironship Trading Syndicate

N
W   E
S

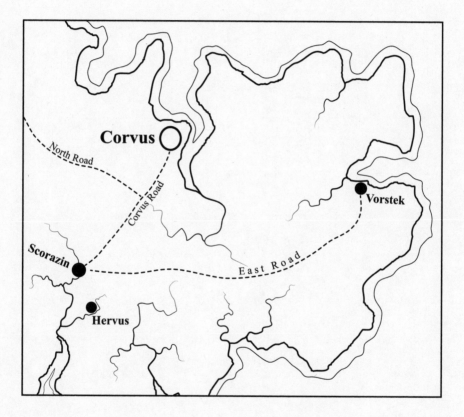

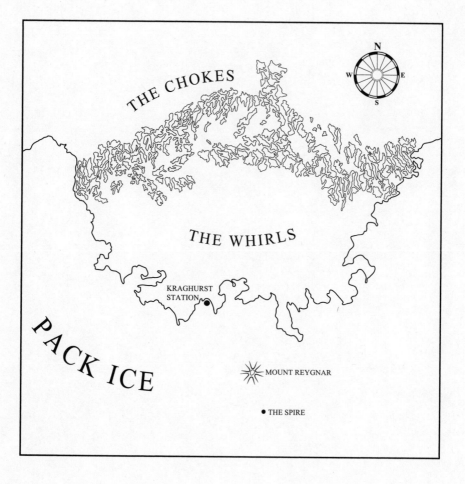

I

THE REAPING

FAMED SOCIETY BEAUTY PERISHES IN ASYLUM INFERNO

Widespread Mourning for "Queen of Mandinorian Society"

Charmed Life Ends in Madness and Flame

The wealthy Dewsmine family is in mourning today after the tragic demise of their most celebrated daughter—the once-beautiful and -charming Catheline, aged twenty-five. It scarcely seems credible that less than four years ago this very periodical named Catheline Dewsmine as the uncrowned Queen of Mandinorian Society. A glittering and vivacious presence at any ball or managerial gathering, Catheline garnered many admirers, and not a few sharp-tongued enemies, in her meteoric rise to societal eminence. This humble correspondent has heard her described as both "a soul of celestial grace and boundless generosity" and "a venomous, razor-taloned harpy whose back never met a mattress it didn't like." Whatever the truth, it is plain that, with her passing, Mandinorian society will be a much less interesting place.

The Dewsmine family dates its prominence back to the days of empire when the family fortunes were largely derived from various landholdings granted by Queen Arrad III in recognition for service in war against the Corvantines. With the advent of the Corporate Age the family was one of the first aristocratic dynasties to purchase shares in the then-nascent Ironship Syndicate. Over the succeeding decades their fortunes prospered thanks to ever-increasing profits derived from the Syndicate's Arradsian holdings. Not content to simply enjoy the fruits of a sound investment, the family have never shirked their managerial responsibilities. Every son or daughter bearing the Dewsmine name is expected to enter the Syndicate at a junior level on the assumption that their inherent gifts of ambition and intelligence will see them rise to a more suitable station. Several such scions have even risen to occupy a seat on the Board.

Catheline Dewsmine was to prove a spectacular exception to this rule, much (it is rumoured) to the dismay of her parents. No family, be they ever so grand, is exempt from the Blood-lot, and the Blessing is no respecter of station. Whereas, amongst those families of less fortunate rank the identification of a Blood-blessed child is invariably seen as a route from gutter to prosperity, for a child of the managerial class it is often regarded as a curse that will inevitably sever their links with family, friends and a share of dynastic wealth. However, subsequent to the Blood-lot revealing her true nature, this was not to be the case with Catheline. When called upon to pack her things and travel to Arradsia for enrolment in the Ironship Academy of Female Education she promptly refused and threw what a former employee of the Dewsmine mansion described to this correspondent as "the great-grandfather of all screaming fits." Although every entity in the corporate world is bound by the accords regulating the education and employment of the Blood-blessed, the Dewsmine family, thanks to a good deal of expensive legal counsel and an inventive interpretation of Company Law, were able to secure an "exceptional release" from standard regulatory practice on the grounds that Catheline was of too "delicate a disposition" to cope with such a savage wrenching from the bosom of her family.

So, instead of spending years learning the proper employment of her gifts under the expert eye of the renowned Academy's staff, Catheline received a private education at home from various Blood-blessed tutors. Although she would rarely display her gifts in public, many accounts speak of Catheline's particular facility for the use of Red, one servant relating how she could light a candle from fifty yards away whilst another described an incident in which she incinerated an entire orchard during a fit of pique. It should be pointed out in the interests of balanced reporting that the Dewsmine family denies this latter incident ever took place.

Catheline's unique position was sure to arouse interest from press and public alike and her progress through adolescence became a novelty item in many a periodical that saw fit to print recurring—and recurrently denied—tales of roasted kittens, eviscerated puppies and maids being propelled through upper-floor windows. Since no legal action ever arose from these supposed incidents their veracity cannot be ascertained. However, this correspondent has noted that several former employees of the Dewsmine mansion do live very comfortably in retirement despite disabilities arising from long-term injury.

Catheline's status as an interesting if unimportant curiosity was to change with her first appearance at a prominent managerial gathering. Aged just seventeen but already blossomed into what a fellow correspondent described as "the near perfection of womanly loveliness," Catheline simply enchanted all who attended the annual Introductory Ball at the Sanorah Banqueting Hall. Rumour has it she received no less than six marriage proposals in the course of the following week, all from notable executives of impressive standing, one of whom was apparently already married. However, Catheline was not to be so easily wooed and her glittering if brief career as the pinnacle of Mandinorian Society was marked by a complete absence of any engagement or serious romantic entanglement (rumours of less-than-serious entanglements abound, but such gossip is beneath the pen of this correspondent).

Within the space of a year Catheline had become *the* required guest for any serious gathering and garnered a considerable income from endorsements for various fashion houses and cosmetic concerns. Soon her photostat appeared everywhere, although the images often failed to capture the near-ethereal nature of her beauty, something which could only be appreciated if one were fortunate enough to find oneself in her proximity. More than simply the conformity of feature to accepted notions of beauty, Catheline exuded a sense of otherness. At the risk of laying oneself open to charges of hyperbole, this correspondent is of the opinion that, through some agency of her Blood-blessed gifts, Catheline had somehow transcended mundane humanity. More than one witness has commented on the addictive nature of her company, the sense of being transfixed whenever her gaze fell upon one's eye, the near-desperate desire to remain in her presence and the bereft lurch of the heart upon separation.

Sadly, it was all to end much too soon. The first sign that all might not be well in Catheline's world came during her twentieth birthday party, a truly lavish occasion funded entirely by the Clothing and Accessories arm of the Alebond Commodities Conglomerate. By all accounts Catheline remained her usual compelling, enchanting self for much of the evening, despite an ugly incident when one of her suitors became overly insistent on pressing his case and had to be forcibly removed. Whether it was this episode that upset her, or some previously hidden malady of the mind, none can say. In either case, towards the end of the evening Catheline Dewsmine began to speak gibberish. It started as a mutter, low and guttural, the words indistinct but the tone of it still retains the power to chill this correspondent's bones some five years later. That this was not the first such incident was made plain by the alacrity with which Catheline's family began to usher her from the ball-room, something that seemed to unhinge her completely. Her mutters became screams, her perfect face an ugly, crimson mask. She flailed, she spat and she bit as they dragged her away, her words echoing in the shocked silence left in her wake. I have never forgotten them: "He calls to me! He promises me the world!"

Catheline Dewsmine was never seen in public again. All enquiries regarding her condition were sternly rebuffed by her family though servants later related a horrible interval during which her parents attempted to care for her at home. Doctors of both mind and body came and went, various concoctions were administered, novel and experimental distillations of Green applied. All to no avail. Reliable witness accounts agree that by this stage Catheline was completely and incurably mad. By the advent of her twenty-first birthday she had been committed to the Ventworth Home for the Emotionally Troubled, an Ironship-sponsored institution specialising in the care and treatment of those Blood-blessed suffering mental affliction. Soon Catheline faded almost completely from the public mind, save as a vehicle for the occasional cruel witticism or unkind cartoon, and perhaps would have been forgotten completely but for the terrible events of two days hence.

The origins of the fire that engulfed the Ventworth Home are yet to be established. For reasons that should be obvious not one drop of Product is ever permitted on the premises and all patients are subject to close monitoring. What is clear is that at approximately two hours past midnight an intense conflagration broke out in the building's west wing and soon spread to all parts of the structure. Only six members of the staff and three patients escaped. Tragically, Catheline was not amongst them. An initial report by the Ironship Protectorate Fire and Safety Executive confirms that the blaze began within the building but no cause has as yet been ascertained. Also, a full count of the dead is not possible due to the condition of the remains.

And so, Catheline Dewsmine, once a Queen of sorts, and an unparalleled beauty, leaves this world in as ugly a fashion as can be imagined. Her light no longer shines upon us, and in the opinion of this humble correspondent, the world is a much darker place as a consequence.

Lead article in the *Sanorah Intelligencer*—35th Verester 1600 (Company Year 211)—by Sigmend Talwick, Senior Correspondent.

CHAPTER 1

Sirus

He awoke to Katrya weeping again. Soft whimpers in the darkness. She had learned by now not to sob, for which Sirus was grateful. Majack had threatened to strangle her that first night as they all huddled together in the stinking torrent, Katrya pressed against Sirus, holding tight as she wept seemingly endless tears.

"Shut her up!" Majack had growled, levering himself away from the green-slimed sewer wall. His uniform was in tatters and he had lost his rifle somewhere in the chaos above. But he was a large man and his soldier's hands seemed very strong as he lurched towards them, reaching for Katrya's sodden blouse, hissing, "Quiet, you silly bitch!"

He'd stopped as Sirus's knife pressed into the meaty flesh below his chin. "Leave her be," he whispered, wondering at the steadiness of his own voice. The knife, a wide-bladed butcher's implement from the kitchen of his father's house, was dark red from tip to handle, a souvenir from the start of their journey to this filthy refuge.

Majack bared his teeth in a defiant snarl, eyes meeting those of the youth with the gory knife and seeing enough dire promise to let his hands fall. "She'll bring them down here," he grated.

"Then you had better hope you can run faster than us," Sirus told him, removing the knife and tugging Katrya deeper into the tunnel. He held her close, whispering comforting lies into her ear until the sobs faded into a piteous mewling.

There had been ten of them that first night, ten desperate souls huddling in the subterranean filth as Morsvale died above. Despite Majack's fears their enemies had not been drawn to the sound of Katrya's sobs. Not then and not the night after. Judging by the continuing cacophony audible through the grates, Sirus suspected that the invaders had found sufficient sport to amuse themselves, at least for the time being. But, of course, that didn't last.

Ten became nine on the fifth day when hunger drove them out in search of supplies. They waited until nightfall before scurrying forth from a drain on Ticker Street where most of the city's grocers plied their trade. At first all seemed quiet, no piercing cries of alarm from a disturbed drake, no patrols of Spoiled to chase them back into the filth. Majack broke down a shop-door and they filled several sacks with onions and potatoes. Sirus had wanted to head back but the others, increasingly convinced by the continual quiet that the monsters had gone, decided to take a chance on a near by butcher's shop. They were making their way back along a narrow alley towards Hailwell Market, laden with haunches of beef and pork, when it happened.

A sudden rattling growl, the brief blur of a flashing tail and one of their number was gone. She had been a middle-aged woman from some minor administrative post in the Imperial Ring, her last words a garbled plea for help before the drake dragged her over the edge of the roof-top above. They hadn't waited to hear the screams, fleeing back to their grimy refuge and dropping half their spoils in haste. Once back underground they fled deeper into the sewers. Simleon, a stick-thin youth of criminal leanings, had some familiarity with the maze of pipes and tunnels, leading them to the central hub where the various water-ways converged to cast effluent into a great shaft where it would be carried out to sea. At first the roaring torrent had been filthy, but as the days passed the water grew ever more clean.

"Think there's anyone left?" Majack muttered one day. Sirus reckoned it to be a month or more after their abortive foray, it was hard to keep track of the days here. Majack's dull-eyed gaze was lost in the passing waters. The soldier's previous hostility had subsided into a listless depression Sirus knew to be born of hunger and despair. Despite the strictness with which they rationed themselves, they had perhaps two more days before the food ran out.

"I don't know," Sirus muttered, although he had a strong suspicion these nine starving souls were in fact all that remained of Morsvale's population.

"Wasn't our fault, y'know." The listlessness in Majack's gaze disappeared as it swung towards Sirus, his voice coloured by a plea for understanding.

"There were so many. Thousands of the bastards, drakes and Spoiled. Morradin took all but a handful of the garrison to fight the corporates. We had no chance . . ."

"I know," Sirus said, adding a note of finality to his voice. He had heard this diatribe before and knew, if left unchecked, Majack's self-pitying rant might drag on for hours.

"A hundred rounds each, that's all we had. Only one battery of cannon to defend a whole city . . ."

Sirus groaned and moved away, stepping carefully over the damp brickwork to where Katrya huddled on a ledge beside one of the larger pipes. She held her hand out to the water gushing from the pipe, slender fingers splayed in the cascade. "Do you think it's clean enough to drink now?" she asked. They had perhaps a bottle and a half of wine left, their only remaining source of uncontaminated hydration.

"No." He sat down, letting his legs dangle over the ledge and watching the water disappear into the vast blackness of the shaft. He had considered jumping several times now, but not out of any suicidal impulse. According to Simleon the shaft conveyed the water to a vast underground tunnel leading to the sea. If they survived the drop it might prove a means of escape. *If* they survived the drop . . .

"You're thinking about *her* again, aren't you?" Katrya asked.

Sirus fixed her with a sharp glare, a harsh reminder of her status coming to his lips. *Please be good enough to remember, miss, you are but a servant in my father's house.* The words died, however, when he met her eyes, seeing the mixture of defiance and reproach. Like most of the servants in his father's employ Katrya had taken a dim view of his embarrassing but irresistible obsession. However, he thought it strange that she should care about such things now.

"Actually no," he said instead and nodded at the shaft. "Simleon says it's about eighty feet to the bottom."

"You'll die," she stated flatly.

"Perhaps. But I increasingly fail to see any alternative."

She hesitated then shuffled closer to him, resting her head on his shoulder, an overly familiar action that would have been unthinkable only a few weeks before. "It's awful quiet up there now," she said. "Could be they've all gone. Moved on to Carvenport. Some of the others think so."

Moved on. Why not? Why stay once they've slaughtered everyone else? The notion was almost unbearably enticing but also dangerous. *Alternatives?* he asked himself, the absolute gloom of the shaft filling his gaze once more.

"Your father would have at least gone to look," Katrya said. The words were spoken softly, free of malice or judgement, but they were still enough for him to push her away and get to his feet.

"My father's dead," he told her, the memory of his last interrogation looming large as he stalked away. The Cadre agent sitting at the foot of his bed, shrewd eyes on his, somehow even more frightening than the men who had tortured him in that basement. *"Where is she? Where would she go?"* And he had no answers, save one: *"Far away from me."*

In truth he remembered little of Tekela's escape. The hours that preceded it had been full of such agony and fear his memory of it remained forever ruined. His arrest had swiftly followed Father's demise, a half-dozen Cadre agents breaking down the door to drag him from his bed, fists and cudgels the only answer to his babbling enquiries and protestations. He woke to find himself strapped to a chair with Major Arberus staring into his face, expression hard with warning. Arberus, Sirus soon realised, was also strapped to a chair and, positioned off to Sirus's right, so was Tekela. He remembered the expression on her doll's face, an expression so unlike anything he had ever expected to see there: deep, unalloyed guilt.

"I'm sorry," she'd mouthed, tears falling from her eyes. It changed then, the obsession he had chosen to call passion, the delusion that had compelled him to pen verse he knew in his heart to be terrible and make an unabashed fool of himself at every opportunity. Here she was, his one true love, just a guilt-stricken girl strapped to a chair and about to watch him die.

Their attendants were two men in leather aprons, both of middling years and undistinguished appearance, who went about their work with all the efficiency of long-serving craftsmen. They started on the major first, Sirus closing his eyes tight against the awful spectacle and Tekela's accompanying screams. They turned their attentions to Sirus when Arberus fainted and he learned for the first time what true pain was. There were questions he couldn't answer, demands he couldn't meet. He knew it all to be meaningless, just another form of pressure, added theatre for Tekela's benefit. How long it took to end he never knew, but it seemed an eternity before his heart began to slow, transformed into a softly patted drum in his chest and he became aware of his imminent departure from this world. The basement disappeared into a fugue of distant sound and vague sensation. He heard shouts and thuds at some point, the sounds of struggle and combat, but assumed it to be just a figment of his fading mind. Despite the confusion he still retained the memory of the precise moment his heart stopped. He had read of those who returned from the brink of death to tell of a bright beckoning light, but he never saw it. There was only blackness and the dreadful pregnant silence left by his absent heart-beat.

The Cadre brought him back, though it had been a close-run thing as his doctor had been happy to tell him. He was a cheerful fellow with a lilting accent Sirus recognised as coming from the northern provinces. However, there was a hardness to his gaze despite the cheeriness, and Sirus sensed he knew as much about taking life as saving it. For days they tended him, generous doses of Green and careful application of various drugs until he was as healed as he could ever expect to be and the numerous scars on his chest reduced to a faint web of interconnected lines. Sirus understood this to be only a respite. The Cadre were far from finished with him.

The man who came to question him was of diminutive height and trim build. He wore the typical, nondescript dark suit favoured by Cadre agents, though the small silver pin in his lapel set him apart. It was a plain circle adorned with a single oak leaf that matched those of the Imperial crest. Sirus had never met anyone wearing this particular emblem before but all Imperial subjects knew its meaning well enough. *Agent of the Blood Cadre.*

"She left you behind," were the agent's first words to him, delivered with a tight smile of commiseration. "Nothing like misplaced love to harden a man's heart."

The agent went on to ask many questions, but for reasons Sirus hadn't yet fathomed the Cadre's more direct methods were not visited upon him again. It could have been due to his fulsome and unhesitant co-operation, for his experience in the basement had left no lingering pretensions to useless bravery. "My father and Burgrave Artonin worked together on their own projects," he told the agent. "I was not privy to their studies."

"The device," the agent insisted, leaning forward in his chair. "Surely you must know of the device? Please understand that your continued good health depends a great deal upon it."

Nothing, Sirus thought, recalling the way his father would jealously guard those artifacts of interest to his precious circle of select scholars. *I know nothing.* For a time Sirus had entertained the notion that such circumspection had been for his protection, the less knowledge he possessed the less the Cadre's interest in him. But he knew such concern was largely beyond his father's heart. It had been simple professional secrecy. His father had happened upon something of great importance, something that might transform their understanding of this entire continent and its history. Like many a scholar, Diran Akiv Kapazin did not relish the notion of sharing credit. Sirus had only ever caught glimpses of the thing, and indulged in a few snatched glances at his father's notes. It remained a baffling, if enticing enigma.

"I was privy to . . . certain details," he lied.

"Enough to reconstruct it, perhaps?" the agent enquired.

"If I . . ." He had choked then, the lies scraping over his parched tongue. The agent came to his bedside and poured a glass of water before holding it to Sirus's lips. "If I had sufficient time," he managed after gulping down the entire contents of the glass.

The agent stood back, lips pursed in consideration. "Time, I'm afraid, is both your enemy and mine at this juncture, young sir. You see, I was sent here by a very demanding master to secure the device. I'm sure a fellow of your intelligence can deduce to whom I refer."

Unwilling to say it aloud, Sirus nodded.

"Very well." The agent returned the glass to the bedside table. "I'm going to send you home, Sirus Akiv Kapazin. You will find your household largely unchanged, although sadly my colleagues felt obliged to arrest your father's butler and he failed to survive questioning. All the papers we could find in his offices at the museum are awaiting your scholarly attentions."

So he had gone home, finding it bare of servants save Lumilla, his father's long-standing housekeeper, and her daughter Katrya. It seemed the Cadre's visit had been enough to convince the others to seek employment elsewhere. He spent weeks poring over his father's papers, compiling copious notes and drawing diagram after diagram, making only the most incremental progress. The agent came to the house several times, appearing less impressed with every visit.

"Three cogs?" he enquired, one eyebrow raised as he looked over Sirus's latest offering, a simple but precisely rendered diagram. "After two weeks of effort, you show me three cogs."

"They are the central components of the device," Sirus told him, his voice imbued with as much certainty as he could muster. "Establishing their exact dimensions is key to reconstructing the entire mechanism."

"And these dimensions are correct?"

"I believe so." Sirus rummaged through the pile of papers on his father's desk, unearthing a rather tattered note-book. "My father wrote in a short-hand of his own devising, so it took some time to translate his analysis. I am convinced the dimensions of these cogs is directly related to the orbits of the three moons."

He saw the agent's interest deepen slightly, his shrewd eyes returning to the diagram. "I suspect you may well be right, young sir. However"—he sighed and set the diagram aside—"I have a Blue-trance scheduled with our employer in a few short hours and I fear he will be far from dazzled by your achievement. I regret I must anticipate his likely instruction to en-courage you to greater efforts." He moved to the study door. "Please join me in the kitchens."

They found Katrya scrubbing pans at the sink whilst Lumilla prepared the evening meal. Sirus had known her for most of his life, a lively woman of plump cheeks and a ready smile, a smile which froze at the sight of the agent. "Which are you least fond of?" the agent enquired, plucking a vial from his wallet and gulping down a modicum of Black.

"Please . . ." Sirus began, then choked to silence as an invisible hand clamped around his throat. Katrya began to move back from the sink then froze, limbs and torso vibrating under the unseen pressure.

"I'd hazard a guess the pretty one's probably your favourite," the agent went on, pulling Katrya closer, her shoes dragging over the kitchen tiles until he brought her within reach. "I always find it curious," the agent mused, raising a hand to stroke Katrya's cheek, "how pleasing to the eye the gutter-born can be despite such lack of breeding."

Katrya's mother, displaying a speed and resolution Sirus would never have suspected of her, snatched a butcher's knife from the chopping-board and charged at the agent. He let her get close before freezing her in place, the tip of her knife quivering an inch from his face.

"It seems the choice has been made for you, young sir," he remarked, allowing Katrya to slip from his unseen grip. She collapsed to the floor gasping, flailing hands reaching out for her mother as she was lifted off her feet.

"Now then, good woman," the agent said, angling his head and lifting Lumilla higher, the knife falling from her hand to ring like a bell as it connected with the tiles. "I'm not a needlessly cruel fellow. So, I'll just take an eye for today. But which one . . ."

He trailed off as a boom echoed outside, loud enough to rattle the glass in the windows. The agent's head jerked towards the sound, a twitch of irritated alarm playing over his bland features. For several seconds nothing happened, then another boom just as loud as the first, quickly followed by two more. Despite his panic Sirus managed to recognise the sound: *Cannon fire*.

"How curious," the agent said, still holding Lumilla in place as he stepped towards the window to peer out at the street. People were running, dozens of them, all casting pale, terrorised glances up at the sky. Then came a new sound, not the flat boom of cannon but something high-pitched and sufficiently piercing to provoke an ache in the ears. Sirus knew it instantly, his sole childhood visit to the Morsvale breeding pens had left an indelible impression. *Drake's call*. Pen-bred drakes invariably had their vocal cords cut shortly after birth, but in the interval the infants would scream out their distress. As a child his tearful reaction had been enough to earn a judgemental cuff from his father, but now he couldn't help regarding it as a potential deliverer, for the agent clearly had no idea what he was witnessing.

"What in the name of the Emperor's countless shades . . . ?" he murmured, watching as more and more people fled past the window.

It was at this point that Katrya snatched the fallen butcher's knife from the floor and plunged it deep into the agent's back. The reaction was instantaneous and near fatal for all concerned, the agent's reserves of Black seeming to explode in one convulsive burst. Sirus found himself hurled against the far wall, plaster cracking under the impact as he subsided to the floor. It took seconds for him to shake off the confusion, stumbling upright to find the agent on his knees and screaming, his body contorted like a circus performer as he pulled the knife from his back.

"You . . . fucking . . . little slut!" he yelled at Katrya, now lying semiconscious several feet away. The agent gave a final shout of agony as the knife came free of his back. "You vicious whore!" His voice had taken on a strangely peevish edge, like a child who had been hit for the first time. He staggered to his feet, sobbing as he fumbled for his wallet, blood covering his chin as he babbled hate-filled threats. "I'll rip out your mother's guts and make you eat th—"

The iron skillet made a dull sound as it connected with the back of the agent's head, sending him to all fours, vials scattering as the wallet flew from his grip. He glanced over his shoulder at Sirus, now raising the skillet for a second blow. The agent's brow formed a frown of aggrieved betrayal. "I . . . let you . . . go . . ." he sputtered.

"No," Sirus replied, "you didn't." He brought the skillet down with all the force he could summon. Once, twice, a dozen more times until the agent's head was a pulped ruin and his legs finally stopped twitching.

Lumilla was dead, her neck snapped by the impact with the wall. Sirus left Katrya weeping over her body and went to the window, where he saw the first full-grown wild drake in his life. The Red landed in the middle of the street, pinning an unfortunate Morsvale resident under its claws. It was at least twenty feet long from nose to tail and stood in stark contrast to the emaciated, wingless wretches from the pens; muscles bunching beneath its crimson skin and wings beating as it gave a small squawk of triumph before beginning its meal. Sirus jerked his gaze away then saw another impossible sight, more running figures but, judging by their completely unfamiliar garb, not townsfolk. One paused outside the window, a tall man dressed in what Sirus instantly recognised as hardened green-leather armour near identical to an exhibit in the museum's Native Arradsian collection. His suspicions were instantly confirmed when the man turned his head. *Spoiled* . . . The scaled, spine-ridged visage and yellow eyes left no doubt that the creature he beheld was a living breathing member of the deformed indigenous tribal inhabitants of this continent.

He ducked instantly, hoping the Spoiled had missed him, scuttling towards Katrya's side and retrieving the knife on the way. "We have to go!" he told her.

So they fled through street after street of horror and chaos. Confusion reigned, drake and Spoiled killing with little or no attempt at resistance from the scant few constables and soldiers left in the city. They were just as panicked and terror-stricken as the civilians and it was obvious this attack had come with no warning.

Sirus's first hope had been to make for the docks but the surrounding thoroughfares were choked with people all beset by the same delusion that they might find a ship to carry them away. Such a throng proved an irresistible target for the scores of Reds flying above. He dragged Katrya into a doorway as the massacre unfolded, dodging a rain of corpses and limbs. It had been her idea to make for the sewers, one they shared with a few others possessed of well-honed survival instincts. Ten at first, then nine and, as Sirus discovered when he was woken by Katrya's soft weeping, only two.

"They took a vote," Katrya said. "Didn't wake you cos they knew you'd talk them out of it, I s'pose. Majack's idea."

"But you didn't go with them," Sirus said.

She said nothing, fidgeting and glancing at the tunnel that led to the outlet near the docks.

"How long since they left?" Sirus asked her.

"Hours ago. Haven't heard anything, could be a good sign."

"Or they're all dead."

He saw her face bunch in frustration as she battled to contain an outburst. "There's nothing here!" she exploded finally, water sloshing as she stamped her foot. "You wanna stay and starve amongst shit, then fine! I'm going!"

With that she turned and disappeared into the tunnel. Sirus cast a glance back at the shaft and its eighty-foot drop, gave a tired curse then ran after her.

The outlet ended at the western slip-way, affording a view of the harbour where Sirus was greatly surprised to find at least twenty vessels still at anchor, though he could see no sign of any crew. Some of the ships bore signs of damage or burning but for the most part had been left intact. Beyond the ships the tenements that stood atop the great harbour wall were a ruin, some destroyed down to their foundations, others roofless and burnt so that the whole edifice resembled a blackened saw-blade. Sirus found the complete absence of any sound save the faint keening of gulls more troubling than the absence of people. He motioned for Katrya to stay put then inched closer to the opening, darting his head out for a quick glance in all directions. Nothing, just silent docks and, due he supposed to the drakes' appetites, no bodies. He paused then took another longer look, concentrating on the sky this time and finding only patchy cloud.

"Told you," Katrya said, giving him a hard nudge in the ribs. "They've all gone. Ages ago, prob'ly. We've been starving for weeks for no reason."

"Wait," Sirus said, reaching for her arm as she stepped free of the pipe, face raised and eyes closed as she bathed in the sunlight.

"Get off!" She shook herself free and trotted out of reach. "I'm going to find something to eat. You coming or not?"

Sirus watched her march determinedly towards the nearest warehouse then ran to catch up, all the while casting repeated glances at the sky, one hand on the knife in his belt. The warehouse was mostly empty apart from a few crates stacked in a corner of the cavernous interior. Katrya gave voice to some protracted profanity when Sirus used the knife to lever off the lids to reveal only crockery. They moved from one warehouse to another until they finally uncovered some food, a shipment of fruit preserved in brandy.

"Slowly," Sirus cautioned as Katrya gulped down half a jar of tangerines. "Too much at once and you'll make yourself sick." She just stuck her tongue out at him and kept eating. In the event it was the brandy that had more of an effect than the fruit and Sirus was obliged to half carry her to the quayside, a sack full of jars slung over his shoulder.

"My Auntie Sal lived there," Katrya slurred, gazing at the ruined tenements.

Sirus's gaze roamed the wharf until he found the smallest craft, a fishing-boat about a dozen feet long with a single narrow stack rising from its guard-box-sized wheel-house. He had no experience of piloting a vessel and reckoned the smaller the better.

"Shouldn't we find the others?" Katrya enquired as Sirus led her to the boat. He didn't answer, feeling the weight of the silence more heavily with every passing second. All his instincts led to one conclusion; they had to get away from here, and soon.

"What about the door?" Katrya pressed as he threw the sack onto the boat and used a mooring rope to pull it closer to the quayside. Sirus raised his gaze to the great door positioned in the centre of the harbour wall. From the level of detritus and algae building up where the metal met the water it was clear it hadn't been raised in weeks.

"We'll just have to fire up the engines," he said, nodding at the wheel-houses on either side of the door. "I've seen it done, once. My father took me to . . ."

He trailed off as he saw the expression on her face, wide-eyed and pale, staring fixedly at something that had banished her drunkenness in an instant. Fighting a sudden paralysing dread, Sirus pulled the knife from his belt and followed her gaze.

The drake sat atop a near by goods cart, head cocked at an angle as it regarded them with a curious gaze, its tail coiling idly like a somnolent snake. Two very salient observations immediately sprang to Sirus's mind. Firstly, the drake's size. It was far smaller than any he had seen before, little bigger in fact than an average-sized dog, forcing him to conclude it must be an infant. Second was its colour. Not Black, not Green, not Red. This drake was entirely White.

The drake stared at them both for a long moment and they stared back. Sirus would later consider that they might have gone on staring at each other forever if Katrya hadn't voiced a small, terrified whimper. The drake started at the sound, tail thrashing and wings spreading as it opened its mouth to issue a plaintive screech. The cry echoed around the docks and through the empty streets beyond, a clear clarion call.

"Have to shut it up!" he said, starting forward, knife at the ready. The drake's cries redoubled in intensity and volume as he came closer, causing it to hop down from the cart and scuttle away, casting baleful glances at him as it did so, like a spiteful child fleeing a bully. Enraged by its continued screeching Sirus charged towards it, deaf to the warning Katrya screamed after him.

The drake had begun to clamber up a warehouse wall by the time he got to it, claws scrabbling at the stone, screeching all the while. It bared small, needle-sharp teeth at him, hissing as he drew the knife back, all the horror and suffering he had endured adding strength to his arm. *You did this!*

Something looped around his neck and pulled tight, jerking him off his feet an instant before the knife would have pierced the drake's hide. He found himself dragged backwards across the flagstones, trying vainly to suck air into a constricted throat. He could hear Katrya screaming and lashed out with the knife, the blade finding no purchase before something hard cracked against his wrist and the weapon fell from his grip. Hands closed on him, seizing his limbs and head, pressing him down with unyielding force. Faces loomed above him, spined and deformed silhouettes against the sky. *Spoiled.*

Knowing death to be imminent, Sirus tried to spit his defiance at them but the cord about his neck permitted no sound. As one the faces loomed closer and he was flipped onto his stomach; impossibly strong hands bound his wrists with more cord before he was jerked to his feet. He staggered, gasping for breath, finding that the cord about his neck had been loosened slightly. He was able to make out his captors now, a dozen or so, clad in a variety of garb that indicated different tribal origins, though he doubted that would make much difference to his eventual fate. *Should have risked the drop,* he thought.

His gaze paused on one of the Spoiled, marked out by his clothing, fabric instead of leather or coarse woven hemp. Looking closer Sirus saw it to be the ragged and besmirched tunic of a Corvantine infantryman. He assumed it must have been looted from the bodies of the slaughtered garrison, then he saw the face of the wearer. This one's deformities were not so pronounced as the others, the scales about his eyes and mouth barely noticeable and the ridge on his forehead scarcely more than a series of small bumps in the flesh. Also, his eyes, black slits in yellow orbs, regarded Sirus with a clear expression of recognition.

"Majack?" Sirus said.

The Spoiled gave a short nod before he and his companions stiffened in response to another cry, not the screech of the infant but something far deeper and more commanding. They raised their gaze to the sky as a very large shadow descended. *A Black?* Sirus wondered, squinting upwards as the shadow obscured the sun. The notion died when he saw that this drake had a wing-span greater than any drake known to science, but it did match one known to legend.

CHAPTER 2

Lizanne

She was dreaming of the evacuation again when the noise of her father's latest invention woke her. *She bobbed in the chilly swell as the Blue rose above her, water cascading from its coils, eyes bright with malicious intent as it lowered its gaze to regard her as one might regard an easily caught fish, and spoke,* "Can't you make him stop? Just for a few hours."

She groaned, blinking bleary eyes until the drake's visage transformed into the red-eyed, tousled-haired and annoyed face of Major Arberus. She grimaced, shaking her head and sinking back into the bed-clothes. "He's *your* father," Arberus went on.

"And you're a guest in his home," she replied, closing her eyes and turning away. "If he has one principal occupation in life it's in the generation of noise. If you could bottle it and sell it we would have been a much richer family."

Whatever retort Arberus began to voice was drowned out by a fresh upsurge of rhythmic thumping from downstairs. Lizanne bit down a curse and opened an eye to view the clock on the bedside table. Fifteen minutes past ten, and she had a very important meeting at twelve.

"Go on," she said, nudging Arberus's naked form with her foot. "Back to your own room, if you please. Appearances must be maintained."

"Surely he knows by now. Your aunt certainly does."

"Of course she knows, and so does he. It's a matter of respect. Now"—she gave a more insistent shove—"go!"

She felt the mattress bounce as he got out of bed, heard the rustle of hastily donned clothes. She heard the click of the latch, then a pause as he hesitated at the door. "You don't have to go," he said. "It's not as if you owe them anything, after all."

"I have a contract," she reminded him. "I like to think that still means something in this world."

She turned onto her back as he slipped out, less quietly than she would have liked, and stared up at the ceiling. It was decorated with a spiral pattern made up of birds and dragon-flies, her aunt's work. The colours were a little faded now but the swirling mass of flying creatures remained mostly unchanged from childhood. She would stare up at them every morning in the days before the Blood-lot saw her shipped off to the Academy. The notion stirred memories of Madame Bondersil and the lingering pain of her betrayal. *She had a contract too.*

She found Tekela at the kitchen table eating an oversized breakfast under Aunt Pendilla's supervision. "Not healthy for a girl your age to be so thin," Pendilla said, pouring tea and nodding at a plate of buttered bread. "Eat up now. Never catch a husband looking like a stick."

"I don't want a husband," Tekela responded in her now-near-perfect Mandinorian. "Lizanne appears to get along perfectly well without one. And so, I notice, do you, Miss Cableford."

Seeing her aunt's face darken, Lizanne moved quickly to relieve her of the tea-pot. "Allow me, Auntie."

"This girl is of too sharp a tongue for her own good," Pendilla stated.

"An observation you are not the first to make." Lizanne sat down next to Tekela and poured herself some tea as Pendilla disappeared into the larder.

"She's obsessed with making me eat," Tekela murmured. "It's unnerving."

"She's obsessed with making everyone eat," Lizanne returned. "Something many in the incomers' camp would appreciate. I'm sure I could find one who would be willing to swap places with you."

A slight vestige of her old pout came to Tekela's lips before she caught herself and returned to her breakfast with renewed enthusiasm. "Wasn't complaining."

Lizanne sipped her tea and winced as a fresh round of thumping came from the direction of the workshop. It continued for about thirty seconds before stuttering to a clanking halt. "I see they still haven't fixed it," she observed.

"Jermayah says it's the intake valve," Tekela said. "The Professor says the combustion chamber."

"Which means they'll be tinkering with the bloody thing for weeks to come whilst more pressing work remains incomplete."

"We're keeping up with orders," Tekela pointed out. "Producing up to six Thumpers a week now. I believe I could probably assemble one myself without assistance, if anyone would let me. I think I have a way to do it faster too."

Lizanne hesitated before telling her to stick to their established piece-meal manufacturing methods. The three weeks since their rag-tag refugee fleet arrived in Feros had taught her that a bored Tekela was a very trying Tekela. "You can demonstrate when I return this afternoon," she said, moving back as Aunt Pendilla returned to set a heavily laden plate before her. "Thank you, Auntie."

"You're wearing that, are you?" Pendilla asked, her somewhat critical gaze playing over Lizanne's rather plain dress of light blue fabric adorned only with a shareholder's pin on the bodice. "It hardly reflects your current status."

Current status? Lizanne had puzzled over this particular question since stepping onto the Feros quayside. What was she now exactly? A hero to many. The saviour of the Carvenport Thousands to some. The refugees still called her Miss Blood, showing a sometimes annoying deference in her presence, as if the authority she wielded in fending off the drake and Spoiled assault still held true. In fact, whatever titles or respect they chose to bestow upon her she was officially a suspended agent of the Ironship Exceptional Initiatives Division, an agent currently awaiting the findings of a Board-sanctioned inquiry.

"Sober dress is expected at Board meetings," she told her aunt, glancing at the clock above the range. *An hour to go, and it would be best not to be late.*

"Good morning, Major," Pendilla greeted Arberus with a bright smile as he descended the stairs. She bustled over to pull a chair out for him. Lizanne had noticed before how her aunt tended to do her best bustling around the major. Lizanne assumed Pendilla was worried Arberus would decide to take himself off without marrying her ruined niece first. Both her aunt and her father retained some tiresomely outdated notions.

"You do look smart today," Pendilla said, patting the shoulder of the overly expensive suit Arberus had insisted on buying to replace his tattered cavalryman's uniform. Lizanne often thought it strange that a man of fierce egalitarian convictions should care so much about appearance. "Doesn't the major look smart, ladies?"

"Green suited you better," Tekela muttered around a mouthful of bacon.

"I thought I should make the effort." Arberus forced a smile at the veritable mountain of food Pendilla placed before him. Unlike Tekela, he retained a strong Corvantine accent, though his syntax was flawless. "It's not every day a man steps into the lair of the corporatist cabal, after all."

"You're staying here," Lizanne told him, glancing at Tekela. "The contingency."

She saw him about to protest before a grimace of reluctant acceptance showed on his face. Their contingency consisted of a bag filled with all the Ironship scrip and exchange notes they could spare, plus a pair of revolvers. There was also a sympathetic Independent ship's captain in the harbour willing to take them to a friendly port. "You think it might be necessary?" he asked. "The entire expatriate Carvenport population will riot if they lay a hand on you."

"Desperation may force them to extreme measures." Lizanne reached for the toast. "I must confess I haven't the faintest idea of how this day will turn out. But, if there's one lesson we learned in Arradsia, it's the value of contingency." She buttered the toast and took a sizable bite. "There are two Exceptional Initiatives agents in the house opposite and another two playing the role of vagrants in the alley behind the workshop. I believe only one is Blood-blessed, a woman posing as one of the vagrants. If I fail to return by six o'clock and the agents at the front make themselves visible it means I've been arrested. You'll need to kill the Blood-blessed first. Jermayah's prototype portable Growler should suffice for the task. Assuming the refugees oblige us with a riot, it will provide sufficient cover to make it to the docks."

She finished her toast and glanced at the clock once more. "Forgive me, Auntie," she said, rising from the table. "It appears I shan't have time to finish breakfast."

"Don't you want to see your father before you go?"

Lizanne looked at the door to the workshop, hearing the rising pitch of voices as her father and Jermayah commenced yet another argument. "As ever, he appears to be preoccupied with more important things."

Although the Ironship Trading Syndicate had never been overly fond of ostentation in its architecture the early Board members had felt compelled to make an exception for their Feros Headquarters. The building stood five stories tall and had a castle-like appearance, being formed of four corner towers linked by recessed walls. The archaic impression was alleviated by the many tall glass windows behind which countless clerks, lawyers and accountants laboured to maintain the bureaucratic machinery of the world's largest corporation. Lizanne's visits here had been infrequent over the years, the nature of her employment requiring that she minimise any risk of identification by agents from the Corvantine Empire or one of the syndicate's many competitors. Of course, such concerns were now largely irrelevant. She was, after all, quite famous.

Before making her way to the main entrance Lizanne took time to note the building's enhanced defences; Thumper and Growler batteries placed on the towers and also the roof-tops of surrounding ancillary offices. Despite Arradsia being a considerable distance away it seemed the Board had not been entirely deaf to the warnings contained in her initial report.

Normally she would have been required to report to the main desk and spend a tedious half-hour pacing the foyer before being granted entry. To-day, however, things were very different. Two Protectorate officers, both with side-arms, met her as soon as she stepped through the revolving door and she was conveyed to the Board's private, steam-powered elevator after only the most cursory greeting. They made the journey to the Board-Room in total silence and Lizanne took care to note the pale patches of skin on the hands of her two escorts, the legacy of the Blood-lot. The Board, it appeared, were unwilling to take any chances today.

She had only been granted access to the Board-Room once before, the day she received her shareholder's pin. It had been a formal affair shared with a dozen other young managerial types summoned to receive their reward for exceeding predicted profits or, in her case, successfully stealing the designs of a competitor. Incredibly, that had been less than a year ago and now here she was, called to suffer their judgement.

She was surprised to find all but three of the Board's ten members in attendance, unusual for a body that could rarely count on half its number at any given meeting. Ironship's truly global reach meant that those appointed to lead it were often called to far-distant climes and would receive a full recording of the Board's deliberations via Blue-trance before a final vote on any major matter was taken. For practical reasons the day-to-day decisions were made with a quorum of no less than five members. Today, however, was a far-from-mundane matter and it appeared most of the Board preferred to hear her testimony in person before casting their vote.

The Board sat at a semicircular table in front of a large stained-glass window featuring the Ironship company crest. The window's predominant colour was blue, which gave the ambient light in the cavernous room a strangely surreal cast, reminding Lizanne of a Blue-trance she had once shared with a fellow agent on the brink of death following an encounter with a Corvantine assassin. It wasn't an encouraging portent. She took her place, a spot where the blue light from the window disappeared to form a small white circle. A chair had not been provided and the two Protectorate officers took up station on either side of her, just far enough back to evade her eye-line.

Her gaze swept over the Board members, recognising them all but searching for one in particular. She found him seated at the extreme left of the semicircle, a large, bearded man of notable girth dressed in a slightly shabby suit Arberus wouldn't have been seen dead in. Taddeus Bloskin, Director of the Exceptional Initiatives Division, who this day could prove to be either her best ally or worst enemy. She truly had no idea which; he had never been an easy man to read.

"State your name and employment status."

Her eyes snapped to the Board's Chairperson. The position changed hands every year and was currently occupied by a small woman of deceptively fragile appearance. Madame Gloryna Dolspeake had spent the bulk of her career in Mergers and Acquisitions, an arm of the Syndicate that tended to foster both a predatory mind-set and a fierce attachment to company loyalty. She stared at Lizanne over a pair of half-moon spectacles, pen poised over her papers with what seemed to Lizanne to be a dagger-like anticipation.

"Lizanne Lethridge," she stated. "Shareholder and lifetime contracted agent of the Exceptional Initiatives Division, currently under suspension."

A few pens scratched on paper but otherwise silence reigned until Madame Dolspeake spoke again, "For the sake of the record please confirm that you are the author of this report." She held up a bundle of papers bound with a black ribbon, the one-hundred-page report Lizanne had compiled on return to Feros. "Board file number six-eight-two, submitted on the second of Harvellum, Company Year two hundred and eleven. Title reads: Report on operations undertaken and events witnessed by Shareholder Lizanne Lethridge during deployment to the Arradsian Continent."

Before replying in the affirmative Lizanne made a mental note to come up with a more compelling title should she ever decide to publish the report in book form. "I authored that report, yes."

"All members present and not present having read this report, certain salient points are considered worthy of further discussion." Dolspeake began to make her way down a list scrawled on her papers. "One: the apparent betrayal of company interests and collusion with Corvantine agents undertaken by the now-deceased Lodima Bondersil, formerly Director of Arradsian Holdings. Two: the dispatch and progress of the 'Torcreek Expedition' to the Arradsian Interior and its apparently successful discovery of the previously legendary White Drake. Three: the successful recovery and subsequent loss of an artifact containing potentially valuable information said to have been produced by the so-called 'Mad Artisan.' Four: the attack on Arradsian Holdings by what this report describes as, quote: 'a combined army of drake and Spoiled I believe to be in thrall to the White by virtue of means unknown,' end quote."

Lizanne maintained a placid expression as Dolspeake fell into an expectant silence. "What else is there for me to say?" she enquired as the silence wore on. "You have my report. I have also submitted to Blue-trance interrogation by Internal Security, who I believe confirmed its veracity."

One of the other Board members spoke up, a gruff older fellow she recognised as the Director of Manufacturing and Procurement. "Memories can be falsified. A skilled Blood-blessed can plant lies in another's head."

"Only the head of another Blood-blessed," Lizanne pointed out. "And there are thousands of former Carvenport residents in the incomers' camp who can attest to the truth of my report. I would suggest that a brief reconnaissance of the Arradsian coast will also bear out much of my account."

She saw the Maritime Protectorate Admiral who chaired the Sea Board exchange a brief but guarded glance with Dolspeake. As commander of the body that exercised control over all Ironship war vessels, he would be responsible for ordering any such mission. "I see such action has already been taken," Lizanne went on. "Might I enquire as to the outcome?"

Dolspeake waited a full ten seconds before giving a barely perceptible nod of assent to the admiral. "We sent three fast frigates, all modern blood-burners," he said. "Only one returned, having lost half its crew. They barely had time to glimpse the Arradsian shore before coming under attack by both Blues and Reds."

"Then the crew are to be commended on a considerable feat of arms," Lizanne told him before returning her gaze to Madame Dolspeake. "Since you are fully aware of the accuracy of my report, might I enquire why I'm here?"

The woman's gaze flicked to the far end of the table where Taddeus Bloskin was shaking a match as he puffed on a newly lit pipe. "Your report makes mention of a Corvantine woman," he said in his decidedly non-managerial accent. Director Bloskin did not owe his position to privileged birth. "A Blood-blessed."

"Electress Dorice Vol Arramyl," Lizanne said, suspecting an imminent accusation of corporate treason and moving swiftly to head it off. "She survived the siege and the evacuation, if you would care to question her."

"We have. She was very forthcoming." Bloskin regarded her with steady eyes behind the rising pall of pipe-smoke. "You permitted her to trance with the Blood Imperial."

"Morsvale had fallen to the drakes and the Spoiled. Given the circumstances I decided news of events in Arradsia might forestall further Corvantine aggression."

"Thereby exceeding your authority in the extreme," Madame Dolspeake stated.

"We were all very likely to die in the near future," Lizanne replied. "I had little time or concern for the trivia of syndicate regulations."

"It worked, in any case," Bloskin broke in before Dolspeake could retort. "Hostilities with the Corvantine Empire have ceased. Partially, one suspects, due to the fact that they no longer possess a fleet in Arradsian waters, but then"—he turned to favour the admiral with a thin smile—"neither do we."

The admiral glowered at the spymaster but evidently retained sufficient wisdom to remain silent.

"Although no formal treaty has as yet been agreed with the Corvantines," Bloskin went on, "we have received an approach via unofficial channels. Apparently they want to talk."

"Negotiation would seem a sensible course at this time," Lizanne said.

Bloskin's grin broadened into a smile, smoke seeping between his teeth. "I'm glad you think so, since it's you they want to talk to."

Lizanne took a long moment to survey the Board members, eyes tracking over a variety of faces, men and women of middling years or older. Some dark-skinned, others pale like her, and all sharing a singular attribute she once imagined to be beyond those who have risen so high. *They're all terrified.*

"Me?" she asked Bloskin, feeling a warm flush of confidence building in her breast.

He shifted his pipe from one corner of his mouth to the other and she saw a twitch of resentment crease his heavy brow. Of them all he was the least afraid. "It appears the Imperial Court was impressed with your boldness," he said. "Not to say honesty. The Emperor, or more likely his senior ministers, seem to think they can trust you." He leaned back in his seat and cast an expectant glance at Madame Dolspeake.

"Lizanne Lethridge," the Chairperson began in formal tones, extracting a fresh sheaf of papers from her stack, "you are hereby reinstated as a fully contracted agent of the Exceptional Initiatives Division. In recognition of your actions in the recent Arradsian Emergency you are awarded two additional company shares. You are also hereby appointed Special Executive Liaison to the Corvantine Empire and instructed to sail to Corvus at the earliest opportunity in order to establish terms for a shared undertaking aimed at recovering the Arradsian continent . . ."

"No."

Madame Dolspeake's eyes snapped up, blinking in surprise. "I beg your pardon?"

"No," Lizanne repeated. "I refuse your appointment."

"You have a contract, young woman . . ."

"Hereby dissolved under my own initiative as per section thirty-four, clause B." Lizanne paused, finding she couldn't keep the smile from her lips as she enjoyed their shock and outrage. "You . . ." She laughed and shook her head. "All of you, ruling half the world for over a century with paper, ink, ships and guns. Did you really think that's where your power lay?" She held up her arm, drawing back the sleeve of her dress to reveal the veins in her wrist. "Here is where your power lay. In me." She jerked her head at the two Blood-blessed Protectorate guards behind her. "In them. And now it's gone. The product has stopped flowing and your syndicate is a bloated corpse that hasn't yet acknowledged its own death. My advice to you is to immediately dissolve all company holdings and form a military alliance with any and all willing to join. Forget profit, forget loss. They no longer have meaning. The White is not done, and it will be coming. Survival is the only currency now."

She gave a formal bob of her head before turning to go. "I hereby resign from the Ironship Trading Syndicate. Good day."

They let her leave, not that she was overly surprised. Ultimately they were just a roomful of scared people at a loss for what to do next. Besides, Arberus was probably right, had they tried to apprehend her the reaction of the former Carvenport refugees would have been highly unpredictable.

It had become her habit to visit the camp most afternoons, compelled by a sense of duty mingled with a masochistic guilt, for the people she had done so much to save now had very little. A minority, those lucky enough to have relatives across the sea who might take them in, had chosen to sail for other ports shortly after arrival. The majority had stayed for the simple reason they had nowhere else to go or no funds for passage elsewhere. The camp covered several acres of nonarable land a mile or so north of Feros, tents and makeshift shelters sprawling across a series of low hills beneath a pall of smoke and dust. Ironship continued to supply food and fuel, but only enough to forestall an upsurge of trouble and in spite of a rising tide of resentment amongst the native Feros population. Protectorate patrols were scrupulous in hounding any incomers from the port's environs and only a few refugees had found regular employment.

She made her way through the rows of tents and shacks, greeted by the usual nods of respect or calls from those she remembered from the siege, and many she didn't. However, she noticed as the days went by respect was often replaced by anger.

"Tell those bastards we need more milk!" a woman called to her from one of the shacks, hefting a skinny toddler in her arms to emphasise her point. "Or d'they want us to starve? Is that it?"

"I no longer work there, madam," Lizanne told her, forcing a sympathetic smile before moving on.

She found Fredabel Torcreek at the makeshift clinic, engaged in tutoring Joya in the correct method of applying a bandage. Clay's aunt had taken a protective interest in the girl since the evacuation, partially motivated by the years Joya had shared with her nephew as they lived out a perilous childhood in the Blinds. Their patient was a young woman wearing a clownish mask of white make-up and swearing constantly as they tended the wound in her upper arm.

"Been fighting again, Molly?" Lizanne asked, moving to her bedside.

"Them that don't settle their bill deserve punishment." Molly Pins winced as Joya tied off the bandage. "You sure you ain't got no Green? I can pay."

"Sorry, Moll." Fredabel shook her head. "Last of it went three days ago." She handed over a small wrap of paper. "One half-spoonful in a tincture of clean water twice a day. You get a fever or feel sick at any time you come right back, you hear?"

"Yessum." Molly swung her legs off the bed, nodding thanks as Lizanne helped her to her feet. "Cralmoor sends his regards, Miss Blood," she said. "Should I see you, told me to say they saw off another press-gang t'other night."

Lizanne smothered a sigh of frustration. The Maritime Protectorate had become somewhat desperate to replenish its ranks recently. Pressing vagrants into service was permitted under company law, but the practice had long fallen out of use, until now. "I'm sorry to hear that," she said. "However, I'm afraid my influence will be even less effective these days."

Molly shrugged. "He says they didn't kill any sailor boys this time, but they come round again it'll be a different matter. If you got anybody to tell, then you'd best tell 'em that."

Lizanne had long given up trying to educate the refugees in her true status. For many of these people she remained Miss Blood, their great Blood-blessed saviour. The notion that she was in fact little more than a minor functionary, and now not even that, didn't seem to have penetrated the collective consciousness. "I will," she said instead.

After Molly had taken her leave Fredabel brewed coffee in her small canvas-walled office-cum–living space. "What happened to her customer?" Lizanne asked.

"Didn't make it," Joya replied. "Some managerial type fallen from grace. Liked to take his frustrations out on the girls from the Blinds. Should've known better than to welch on Molly's bill though. Don't worry, he won't be missed. Cralmoor took care of it."

Lizanne stopped herself delivering another lecture on the parlous effects camp violence had on the refugees' reputation. She was now essentially powerless after all and in no position to be lecturing anyone.

"You have news?" Fredabel asked, passing her a mug of coffee. Lizanne was impressed by her self-control in not asking the question sooner. Thanks to Lizanne Fredabel knew her husband, daughter and nephew had survived the search for the White, but the interval between trances no doubt made for a nerve-wracking wait.

"I tranced with Mr. Torcreek three days ago," she said. "He and the Longrifles are aboard the Protectorate vessel and making for Lossermark. The captain is insistent on replenishing supplies. Also, he remains undecided about the next course of action."

"Can't say I blame him." Fredabel sank onto a stool, clasping her hands together. "But I guess my husband's attitude remains unchanged?"

"He and the other Longrifles remain committed to this course of action."

"It's madness," Joya stated. Lizanne had noted before how her managerial origins tended to overcome her Blinds accent in moments of stress. "Sailing south through an ocean full of hostile Blues . . ."

"The Blues seem to be concentrated in northern waters," Lizanne said, recalling the admiral's words at the meeting. "They have a good chance of making it."

"If this captain agrees to take them," Fredabel pointed out.

"Quite so." Lizanne paused and pulled a bundle of scrip notes from her dress pocket. "For medicine, and whatever you deem fit," she said, handing the notes over.

Fredabel's eyebrows rose as she counted the bundle, which comprised a quarter of the profits from the newly established Lethridge and Tollermine Manufacturing Company. "You ain't making yourself poor on our account, I hope."

"Business is booming," Lizanne assured her. "We should be able to take on some more workers soon."

She stayed for a time, catching up on the camp news, which often made her consider that this place was simply a transplanted if much-reduced version of Carvenport. Although many social barriers had disappeared under the pressures of siege and evacuation, others lingered with surprising tenacity, and the camp had soon evolved a neighbourhood structure that reflected prior allegiances. The former denizens of the managerial district proved the most strenuous in maintaining a certain exclusivity in their wood-and-canvas dominion, though Lizanne felt there was something pitiable in their attempts to cling to lost eminence. They could strut around in their fine but increasingly threadbare clothes all they wanted, in the end they were all just beggars now.

Emerging from the clinic a short while later, she drew up short at the sight of a tall, large-bellied man in a shabby business suit. "A little overdramatic, don't you think?" Taddeus Bloskin asked her.

"What do you want?" Lizanne said, acutely aware she had neither product nor weapon on her person, though she took some comfort from the fact that Bloskin had chosen to come alone.

"I want what I assume your little tantrum was intended to achieve."

Lizanne forced herself to remain still as Bloskin reached into his inside pocket to extract a bundle of papers bound with a black ribbon. "I believe, Miss Lethridge," he said, proffering the papers, "it's time to renegotiate your contract."

CHAPTER 3

Hilemore

"Lighthouse in view, Captain," Steelfine reported, glass raised to his eye as he peered through the early-morning mist. "She's still lit."

Someone's alive here, at least, Hilemore thought, his relief tempered by the suspicion that the Spoiled, or whatever commanded them, were not beyond mounting a ruse to lure them into an ambush. "Best take no chances, Number One," he said. "Sound battle stations. Split the riflemen into two sections and spread them along both rails."

"Aye, sir." Steelfine saluted and strode from the bridge as Lieutenant Talmant sounded three long blasts from the steam-whistle.

"Captain Torcreek," Hilemore said, turning to the tall man in the green-leather duster. "If you would care to oblige me, I believe your eyes will be best employed in the crow's nest."

The Contractor's leathery features betrayed a slight smile as he inclined his head, presumably in recognition of the respect Hilemore had continued to show him throughout the voyage from Hadlock. "Glad to, Captain," he said, hefting his rifle, a .422 Silworth from the ship's armoury. "I'll take Preacher too. Ain't much his eyes'll miss, even in this fog. Lori and Mr. Skaggerhill will take their place with your riflemen. Don't want it said we don't earn our keep."

"Also," Hilemore added as Torcreek moved to the hatch. "Your nephew's presence would be greatly appreciated. Captain Okanas is required in the engine room should we need to make a rapid escape."

He saw a shadow pass over the Contractor's face before he replied with a slow nod. "He's . . . resting. But I'll make efforts to rouse him."

"Very good, Captain."

By the time the Lossermark lighthouse came fully into view the ship was ready for battle, a demonstration of hard-won expertise that stirred a small glimmer of pride in Hilemore's breast. Despite everything the *Viable Opportunity* remained a battle-worthy ship of the Maritime Protectorate, although he had reason to believe she might be the last such ship in the entire Arradsian region.

The lighthouse was of less impressive dimensions and design than the curve-sided wonder that guarded the approaches to Hadlock, having been constructed much longer ago by engineers lacking the insights of modern science. It rose from a cluster of wave-battered rocks to a height of little more than sixty feet, a plain octagonal tower painted red and white to draw the eye, though the colours had faded over the years. The light, however, remained strong and bright. Hilemore blinked moisture from his eye as he trained his spy-glass on the tower's apex, picking out two faint figures through the glare. He took some comfort from the fact that the figures were waving, but whether in warning or welcome he couldn't say.

"Lamp signal, Mr. Talmant," he said. "Send in plain: 'Is this port safe?'"

"Aye, sir." Talmant relayed the order via the speaking-tube and Hilemore heard the clacking shutter of the *Viable*'s signal lamp through the wheelhouse roof. However, the only response from the two lighthouse keepers was yet more waving. Hilemore tried to pick out their faces but the lingering mist was too thick. Spoiled or human, he had no way of knowing.

"I could take a boat over, sir," Talmant suggested. "See what's what."

"No," Hilemore replied, lowering the glass after a moment's consideration. "Can't wallow about so close to these rocks. Helm, maintain course."

He went out onto the upper works, gazing ahead at the faint outline of the south Arradsian coast. It had taken six days to get here, mainly due to his desire to husband as much Red as possible. With the loss of Carvenport the flow of product into corporate holdings would have been reduced to a trickle, perhaps halted completely, meaning there was no certainty of procuring more. Before that they had been obliged to spend three tense weeks in Hadlock whilst Chief Bozware repaired the *Viable*'s many wounds and the crew gleaned what supplies they could from the ruined port. It hadn't amounted to much, sundry small arms, some powder barrels, which went only partway to replenishing their stocks, and a few dozen cans of preserved vegetables. More concerning than the meagre pickings, however, was the fact that amongst all the rubble they hadn't found a single survivor.

"Should be more bodies, Captain," one of the riflemen told him as they picked over the remains of the Ironship offices, hoping to find some product secreted away in the vaults. Instead they uncovered nothing more than a mound of blackened scrip notes.

"More?" Hilemore asked.

"Yes, sir," the man insisted. "Been in and out of this port more times than I can count. Always a lively place, must've been home to nigh on twenty thousand folk, not counting all the sailors coming and going."

A brief check of the ship's books had confirmed the man's reckoning, though he had under-estimated Hadlock's population by some three thousand. Unwilling to impose the grisly task on the crew Hilemore had personally conducted a count of the corpses, though he was obliged to estimate the number they had found floating in the harbour on arrival as most had now subsided beneath the water. When added to the rapidly putrefying remains littering the ruins he came up with a figure of only eight thousand. It was a singular puzzle and he knew of only one person who might hold an answer.

"Spoiled took 'em," Claydon Torcreek told him simply. He sat regarding Hilemore from across the ward-room table, wearing the same vaguely interested expression that had dominated his prematurely aged features since that first meeting with his Contractor company.

"Where?" Hilemore pressed. "Why?"

"I'm guessing the White has a use for 'em."

"What use?"

"I don't imagine it's anything good."

Hilemore resisted the officer-born impulse to shout. This man was not technically under his command after all. "Mr. Torcreek," he said in as patient a tone as he could manage. "I have listened to your story in exhaustive detail, and, whilst I find it convincing in many respects, your continual attachment to cryptic responses does little to further your cause."

Clay's face momentarily lost its preoccupied cast, instead forming something that resembled an amused and insolent adolescent. "None of this matters, Captain," he said. "Don't matter if you believe me. Don't matter where all those poor townsfolk went or what the White's doing to them. Don't matter how many days we spend in this dump fixing doohickeys and scraping shit from the hull." He leaned forward, the insolence fading into a regretful certainty. "You and me, we're going south to the ice. And there ain't nothing gonna change that."

"To save the world," Hilemore said.

Clay reclined, shrugged and sighed, "Just repeating your words."

"Words I have no memory of speaking."

"Not yet. But you will."

The White's blood. Hilemore still wasn't sure he believed it, this man had been gifted a vision of the future by drinking the blood of a White Drake, a creature once thought a legend. It was the stuff of fables, not the rational reality of the modern world. *There's a place,* Clay had said that first night in Hadlock as they wandered the empty, wrecked streets together. *A place where we'll get answers, perhaps the biggest answer of all. How do we kill it?* He went on to describe the spire he had seen in his vision, and Hilemore's presence there. There was a strong temptation to dismiss it all, offer these Contractors a berth on the *Viable* in return for service and sternly forbid any more nonsensical talk of visions and saving the world. But he hadn't. He told himself it was the corroborating testimony of Torcreek's uncle and the other Contractors that swayed him, but in reality it had been the look in Clay's eyes when they first met. The absolute sense of recognition on the man's face was undeniable. *He knew me.*

They stayed only a few more days until Chief Bozware reported he had done all he could to return the *Viable's* engines to their previous level of efficiency.

"Could do with a lot more grease," he said. "And more product. *If* we're really going south, that is. She's a tough old bird, Captain. But she ain't built for the ice."

"Can you make it so she is?"

"Maybe, with sufficient iron to buttress the bow and stern. It'll slow her down a good deal though."

"The Eastern Conglomerate owns a shipyard at Lossermark," Hilemore remembered. "It's where they build most of their Blue-hunters, as I recall."

He saw a glimmer of anticipation creep in the Chief's gaze. "And fine ships they are, sir."

He smelled Lossermark before he saw it, the familiar coal-fire scent mingling with the sickly stench he knew came from the port's harvesting plant. Despite the unpleasant aroma seeping through the mist he took it as an encouraging sign that this town retained some vestige of a human population.

"Seer's balls, that stings," Clay said, face bunching and eyes blinking rapidly against the smell. He had finally chosen to grace the bridge with his presence, even going to the trouble to arm himself with a revolver.

"I'm told you get used to it," Hilemore said. "But it takes a year or so."

The dark curtain of Lossermark's harbour wall resolved out of the mist a few minutes later. It was of unusual construction in that it lacked a central opening. Instead it was formed of a series of huge copper doors suspended from an iron frame that stretched between the two rocky cliffs forming the harbour mouth. Each door was broader than two ships side by side and could be raised individually. Today, however, they were all firmly lowered.

"All stop," Hilemore commanded, tracking his glass along the top of the wall. He could see a knot of people clustered around a bulky apparatus he recognised as a signal lamp. After a short delay the lamp began to blink out a series of bright, rapid flashes. The message was sent in plain code so he had no trouble reading it: "This port is closed. State your business."

"Reply Mr. Talmant," he said. "'IPV *Viable Opportunity* seeking leave to enter in order to procure supplies. Our intent is peaceful.'"

He watched the light from their own signal lamp flickering on the greenish copper then trained his glass on the knot of people, watching them engage in an animated and lengthy discussion before apparently deciding on a reply. "'Contact with other stations lost one month ago. Do you have news?'"

"'Affirmative,'" Hilemore sent. "'Will share after making port.'"

More commotion and gesticulation, then another message. "'Do you have a Blood-blessed aboard?'"

He glanced at Clay, who seemed to be regarding this whole palaver with only mild interest. *Don't matter . . . We're going south.*

"'Affirmative,'" Hilemore replied. "'We have contact with Feros. Willing to negotiate services in return for safe anchorage.'"

He watched the people at the signal lamp discussing their options. He sensed more resignation than enthusiasm in their demeanour, evidenced by the hesitancy with which the next message was delivered. "'Leave to enter granted. Be advised, Corvantine vessel also at anchor here. You are reminded this is a neutral port.'"

"Trouble?" Clay enquired as Hilemore exchanged a sharp glance with Mr. Talmant.

"I thought it didn't matter," Hilemore said, moving to the speaking-tube. He called down to Steelfine to convey the news and issue strict instructions that no weapons were to be fired without his explicit instruction. "Just one shot and I'll hang the man who fired it."

"Understood, sir."

A great grating squeal rose from the door directly in front of the *Viable*'s bows, steam billowing atop the wall as the engines that drove the door laboured to raise it.

"How much Black do you have?" he asked Clay.

"Two full vials," he replied. "No Red, though. Your Islander wouldn't let me have the smallest drop."

"On my orders." He nodded at the door, now grinding itself free of the sea. "There's a Corvantine ship on the other side of this. I doubt their reaction to our presence will be friendly, however I'm determined not to fire the first shot. Should they do so, I'll need you to ensure they miss."

"Diverting a shell in flight." Clay's eyebrows rose in consideration, face free of any particular alarm. "Miss Lethridge did it. Might tweak her nose a little if I could match the feat."

"Can you do it or not?" Hilemore demanded, patience wearing thin.

"Maybe." Clay gave a mock salute and turned towards the hatchway. "Guess we'll find out in short order." Hilemore watched him descend the ladder to the deck and make his way forward. He took up position beside Skaggerhill, the Longrifles' harvester, and extracted a vial from his duster as the door reached its apogee fifty feet above.

"Ahead dead slow," Hilemore ordered, gaze fixed on the revealed harbour ahead. He could see a line of Blue-hunters moored along the quay but no sign of a Corvantine warship as yet. The *Viable* slipped through the opening at a crawl, Hilemore forcing himself to appear as calm as possible though the tension was clear in the bead of sweat he saw trickle down the helmsman's cheek.

"Steady, lad," Hilemore told him. "If their whole fleet couldn't sink us in the Strait, I'll be damned if just one of their tubs will sink us now."

"Enemy vessel twenty degrees to starboard, sir!" Talmant snapped. "One of the new ones by the look of it."

Hilemore soon saw he was right. The Corvantine ship sat high in the water, sleek lines bare of paddles and a single stack angled back towards the stern. Her length and the number of guns singled her out as a frigate, smaller than the *Viable* and not so heavily armed, but probably almost as fast thanks to her screw propeller, even faster if she proved to be a blood-burner. She had clearly been in the wars, her paint-work blackened and hull dented in several places. It also appeared the rear section of her upper works had been wrecked, though the bridge remained intact. It took Hilemore a moment to pick out the Eutherian letters embossed aft of the forward anchor chain: INS *Superior*.

"I count only six crew on deck, sir," Talmant reported. "Her guns are unmanned and she's not making steam."

Hilemore's gaze was drawn to the frigate's mast as a flag was hauled up, unfurling in the wind to reveal a white circle in a black background. *Truce-flag. Too much to expect them to surrender, I suppose.*

"Mr. Talmant, run up the truce pennant," he said. "And tell Mr. Steelfine to stand down from battle stations."

A small pilot tug guided the *Viable* to her anchorage, a length of quay at the extreme western end of the harbour, as far from the Corvantine frigate as they could get. Despite the exchange of truce signals it seemed the port authorities didn't want to chance a clash of warships within the confines of the harbour. A platoon of twenty soldiers were waiting to greet them on the wharf, all clad in the grey uniform of the Eastern Conglomerate Levies, the name given to that company's version of the Protectorate. They were an irregular force, a hard core of contracted professional officers augmented by sailors and shipwrights called to the Levies in times of crisis. From the state of their uniforms and the lack of cohesion in their line Hilemore concluded it had been some time since they had faced a proper inspection. Nevertheless, there was a hard-eyed wariness to their gaze and he noted that, whilst their uniforms could have benefited from a thorough laundering, their rifles were clean and held by experienced hands.

"Major Ozpike." The platoon commander greeted Hilemore with a precise salute as he stepped onto the quayside. "Commander Lossermark Defence and Security Levies." The major was a South Mandinorian of sturdy build, his clean and pressed uniform contrasting markedly with the appearance of his men.

Hilemore came to attention and returned the salute. "Captain Corrick Hilemore, Ironship Protectorate Vessel *Viable Opportunity*." He glanced around at the surrounding buildings, seeing no sign of damage. "Glad to find you in such good order, Major."

Ozpike blinked and cast a cautious glance at his men, regarding the exchange with a uniformly keen interest.

"So that ain't the case elsewhere?" one of them asked, a diminutive fellow of Dalcian heritage as were many Eastern Conglomerate sailors.

Hilemore scanned their faces, seeing a great deal of fear and uncertainty. "You truly have no notion of recent events?" he asked Ozpike.

"Only what the Corvies told us," the Dalcian replied before the major could answer. "Said a great mass of Blues rose from the sea around Carvenport and tore their fleet to pieces. That true, Skipper?"

"Matters for discussion with the Comptroller," Ozpike barked with a military authority that seemed to carry little weight.

"I got family in Carvenport," the Dalcian went on. "The mail packet is three weeks late and not a single Blue-hunter's returned to port in all that time. We got a right to know, Major."

"And you will," Ozpike said, forcing what Hilemore judged to be an unaccustomed note of conciliation into his voice. "But the Comptroller needs to speak to this officer first."

A growl rose from the rest of the platoon and their already loose formation turned into a cluster of angry men, all demanding answers.

"Stand fast!" Hilemore shouted, his voice apparently compelling some vestige of discipline for they all froze as one. Their obedience may also have been informed by the sudden appearance of Steelfine at the *Viable*'s rail along with the full complement of the ship's riflemen. Hilemore allowed a few seconds to pass before speaking again, seeing the soldiers' anger vie with their trepidation.

"Carvenport was overrun by a combined force of drakes and Spoiled over a month ago," he told them, pausing to allow the shock of his words to sink in. "However, most of the population was successfully evacuated to Feros. Make a list of any loved ones and pass it to my first officer. Our Blood-blessed will trance with his contact in Feros to ascertain if they are amongst the evacuees."

"Hadlock?" one of the other bondsmen asked, face ashen and eyes pleading. "My wife . . ." He trailed off, seeing Hilemore's expression.

"I'm sorry," Hilemore told him. "Hadlock is gone. There were no survivors."

He turned to Major Ozpike as his men sagged into disconsolate disorder, the widower weeping openly as his comrades made lacklustre efforts to comfort him. "I believe you intended to take me to your Comptroller?"

"This was supposed to be my retirement posting," Ozpike muttered as he led Hilemore up the steps to the Eastern Conglomerate Headquarters, a spindly three-storey structure that must have dated back to the earliest days of the port's existence. "Fifteen years in the Ironship Protectorate and the pension wasn't enough to keep the wife in her accustomed style. You a married man, Captain?"

For the first time in weeks Lewella's face sprang into Hilemore's head, as lovely and fascinating as ever. *It is with a heavy heart I write these words* . . . "No," he replied. *Nor will I ever be.*

"Good for you, sir," Ozpike huffed as they came to the door and made their way inside. "Take my advice and stay that way. After long consideration on the matter, I have concluded that a military career and marriage are fundamentally incompatible."

The Comptroller's office was on the top floor of the building, necessitating a climb up several flights of rather rickety stairs. The Comptroller proved to be a Dalcian woman of perhaps forty years in age, possessed of a high-cheekboned, austere attractiveness accentuated by her plain business suit and severely-tied-back hair. "Madame Hakugen," Major Ozpike greeted her with a short bow. "I present Captain Hilemore of the IPV *Viable Opportunity.*"

Hilemore stepped forward to offer a bow of his own; Dalcians were notorious for their attachment to formality. He hesitated in mid-bow upon noticing that there was a fourth occupant in the room, an athletic young man in the uniform of the Corvantine Marines. His gloved hand rested on the hilt of a sword but he wore no revolver. The man's face remained rigidly expressionless as he offered Hilemore a very slight nod.

"Captain," Madame Hakugen greeted him in perfect Mandinorian. "Welcome to Lossermark."

"Thank you, madam," Hilemore replied, tearing his gaze from the Corvantine. "It seems you and I have a great deal to discuss."

"Yes." She glanced at the Corvantine. "Forgive my rudeness. Allow me to introduce Lieutenant Myratis Lek Sigoral, acting captain of the INS *Superior*."

"Lieutenant," Hilemore said with a stiff nod, memories of the Strait crowding his mind.

"Captain," the Corvantine replied in heavily accented Mandinorian, Hilemore noting the stitched scar tracing across his forehead. The scar did much to enhance the man's authority but Hilemore realised he couldn't be more than a year or two older than Mr. Talmant. *Just a boy, yet he commands a cruiser. What tribulations brought them here, I wonder?*

"I had hoped you would see fit to bring your Blood-blessed," Madame Hakugen said. "As per our agreement."

"I thought it appropriate to discuss terms first," Hilemore replied. "Though I must confess my surprise that a port of this size doesn't contain at least one Blood-blessed."

"We had two, until recently." A thin line appeared in her brow. "Our long-serving contract agent sadly expired of a heart attack during a Blue-trance with our Hadlock office. Whatever he witnessed in his final trance appears to have been too much for him. His colleague, a less experienced and even less diligent character, tried to re-establish communication, to no avail. Trances with other Conglomerate offices revealed only ignorance of unfolding events. Sadly our sole remaining Blood-blessed then decided to smuggle himself aboard an outgoing vessel, one of the last to leave port actually, the ECT *Endeavour*. We know they were intending to make for Dalcian waters. I had hoped you might have news of them."

"I do," Hilemore replied, recalling the grisly contents of the life-boat they found shortly before docking at Hadlock. "She didn't make it."

"A pity." Madame Hakugen gave a regretful grimace. "The captain was my cousin." She permitted herself a small sigh before quickly regaining her composure. "And Hadlock?"

Hilemore related the destruction of Hadlock before going on to describe the loss of both Morsvale and Carvenport.

"It appears your war has been superseded by more pressing matters, gentlemen," Madame Hakugen observed when he had finished, inclining her head at Lieutenant Sigoral.

The marine maintained his expressionless visage and confined his reply to a short, "Indeed, madam."

Hilemore decided it was time to get what he came for. "Our Blood-blessed will be at your disposal for the duration of our stay, madam," he said. "However, in return we will require product, all the Red you can spare. Also, coal and provisions sufficient for a lengthy voyage."

"A hefty price, Captain."

"Necessitated by the importance of our mission."

"The details of which you are not at liberty to share, no doubt."

"I compliment you on your insight, madam."

She barely acknowledged the praise, lapsing into silence, the line once again reappearing in her forehead.

"Might I enquire," Hilemore began as the silence stretched. "If this port has suffered any attacks, as yet?"

Madame Hakugen nodded to Major Ozpike, who reported, "Not directly, but the first Blue-hunters failed to return at their allotted time six weeks ago. Contractor companies stopped arriving at the north wall with product to sell. A few days ago just one man came stumbling out of the hills, a Headhunter, half-mad and raving. It took hours of coaxing to get the tale out of him. All of his company wiped out by Spoiled and Greens. Would've liked to get more information from him but he hung himself shortly after, not before assuring us we were about to die. You can imagine the effect this has all had on the people. You saw my men and they're the hardiest souls in this port. The air is thick with fear."

Well it might be. Hilemore fought down a spasm of guilt. His best advice for these people was to arm their ships with every gun they possessed, cram as many people aboard as could be carried and sail for Varestian waters. Even then he entertained serious doubts they would escape the attentions of marauding Blues. But what chance of securing his supplies and product in the midst of a panicked evacuation?

"I wish I had better news," he said instead. "Hopefully the trance-communication will provide sound orders from your home office, once I have your agreement to our offer . . ."

They provided ten vials of Red, five Green and two Black, a fifty percent down payment on the final amount dependent on Mr. Torcreek performing to expectations. Surprisingly, Madame Hakugen had been more parsimonious with the other supplies, limiting the amount of food he could purchase and demanding a near-extortionate price for the iron plate needed for Chief Bozware's modifications. By the time the contract was agreed he had been obliged to promise half the contents of the *Viable*'s safe.

"I suspect the people of this port will shortly have need of every scrap of food and fuel," she stated. "And my contract stipulates that every opportunity to enhance company profits is to be exploited to the full. I see no reason to abandon the values of the corporate world, even in such alarming times."

Hilemore made his way back to the port under escort, the two guards steering him through little-used alleyways to avoid encounters with townsfolk desperate for news. He didn't relish the impending conversation with Clay, unsure of how he would react to an abrupt return to contracted status. For all Hilemore knew he might simply look on this as something else that didn't matter. *Perhaps he thinks this ship will make it to the ice-cap under the power of destiny alone.* It occurred to him that the supposed gift contained in the White's blood was in fact the cruelest curse. To have the sensation of discovery taken away, banishing curiosity or anticipation, seemed an awful fate.

He found the crew hard at work on return to the *Viable*, a dozen or so hanging from ropes to replenish the paint on the hull whilst others scrubbed the deck or polished the fittings. "Glad to see you haven't left them idle, Number One," he told Steelfine on ascending the gang-plank. "But the paint will be wasted. Chief Bozware needs to make modifications to the hull."

"Captain's orders, sir," Steelfine replied, voice coloured by a poorly suppressed tone of extreme reluctance.

"Captain . . . ?" Hilemore began, then trailed off as understanding dawned.

"He woke up an hour ago," Steelfine muttered before stiffening to attention. "Lieutenant Hilemore, Captain Trumane has ordered you be relieved of all duties immediately. I am to escort you to his cabin." He hesitated then held out his meaty hand. "I require your sword and side-arm, sir."

CHAPTER 4

Lizanne

"An impressive sight, isn't it?"

Lizanne's gaze swept over the broad spectacle of Feros harbour. The sky was cloudless today and the great mass of ships seemed to shimmer in the sunlight, particularly the warships with their polished guns and scrubbed decks. The bulk of the Protectorate High Seas Fleet was now at anchor here: battleships, cruisers, frigates and gunboats initially summoned from their various ports to do battle with the Corvantine Navy. Now, of course, they faced a much more formidable enemy.

"It's a great many ships," Lizanne replied to Taddeus Bloskin. "But it won't be enough."

The Director of Exceptional Initiatives settled his bulk on one of the benches arrayed alongside the old war memorial and began his endless ritual of reigniting his pipe. At his invitation she had followed him here to Signaller's Mount, the highest point on the southern shore of this island. The war memorial rose above them to a height of eighty feet, an example of the ostentatious masonry typical of the late Mandinorian Empire with its numerous relief carvings and superfluous filigree, the great column topped by a statue of Lord Admiral Fallmoor in overly dramatic pose. The Liberator of the Tyrell Islands stood in straight-backed and stern resolve, sword raised above his head as he pointed out to sea. The impression of martial heroism was spoilt somewhat by the fact that his finger had dropped off at some point in the one hundred and twenty years since the monument's construction. The fact that no one had bothered to replace that missing finger summed up the regard with which the corporate world held the trappings of the empire it had displaced.

"Really?" Bloskin asked as he puffed. "Over a hundred ships and forty thousand soldiers, the cream of the Protectorate, armed with ever more of your infernal modern guns. You really think a rabble of Spoiled and drakes could stand against such a force?"

"Yes. And, since the fleet remains in port, apparently so do the Board."

"In fact the Board is divided on the issue."

Bloskin flicked a spent match away and reclined on the bench. His tone was one of affable conversation rather than that of a Board member committing the heinous act of revealing their private deliberations. "Admiral Heapmire continues to lobby hard for an immediate invasion, supported by most of the Sea Board despite the fate of their three frigates. Madame Dolspeake is of more cautious mind, wishing to seek alliance with the other corporations and formulate a joint strategy before embarking on any military adventures."

"And your thinking, Director?"

"I think," Bloskin replied with a faint smile, "it is a great shame the Mad Artisan's device was lost in the evacuation. Who can say what more we might have learned from it?"

Lizanne suppressed a sigh. Bloskin evidently knew exactly where the device currently resided or he wouldn't have raised it. Also, the fact that he had made no efforts to recover it indicated he was content for it to remain under her father's studious care. However, people in their profession did enjoy their games. "It was certainly a regrettable loss," she said, deciding to indulge him.

"Especially after the progress made by Mr. Tollermine in deciphering its mysteries. Still, wasted are the tears of those who weep over spilled wine. Just pour yourself another, I always say."

Lizanne said nothing. Now they were alone her earlier sense of vulnerability was slowly morphing into a simmering anger. Evidently, she was out of practice in masking such things for he frowned upon reading her expression. "I know you have questions for me," he said. "Please do not feel constrained. We are no longer manager and employee, after all. Just two former colleagues enjoying the view."

"Madame Bondersil," she said. "Did you know?"

His face bunched a little in irritation at an unwelcome topic and he took a long drag on his pipe before replying. "You wonder how her unfortunate choices could have evaded my notice."

"I do."

"Then I regret to inform you that your estimation of my abilities is overly generous." He gave a small grunt as she continued to stare. "There were . . . certain irregularities," he admitted after a short but uncomfortable silence. "Small things, really. Slight inconsistencies in reported expenses, a few unexplained absences. I'll admit I had concluded she was probably up to something, assuming her to be engaged in some intrigue or other aimed at furthering her status and finally ascending to the Board. Not an uncommon pursuit for a senior manager. Still, in light of the ever-increasing problems in maintaining a steady supply of quality product, it was . . . concerning."

"And yet you still approved her request for my deployment."

"It seemed likely that whatever scheme she had hatched was approaching its final phase, especially if it required your particular talents. I suspected she would seek to exploit the secrets contained in the Corvantine device, keeping them to herself whilst she enhanced her position. Having a living, breathing White in her grasp would have meant swift ascension to the Board. Of course, I had no notion of the true scale or nature of her deception."

"And I was to be the agent of discovery."

"To find a queen you have to break apart the hive. You have always been something of a catalyst, my dear. Wherever in the world I send you, noteworthy events are sure to follow. Though none as yet so noteworthy as the loss of Arradsia."

"It would have happened in any case."

Bloskin gave a non-committal shrug and once again retrieved the bound bundle of papers from his jacket, placing it on the bench. "You haven't yet asked to see your new contract."

Lizanne glanced at the bundle, making no move to pick it up. "Why do you imagine I want one?"

"Curiosity," he said, leaning towards her and dropping his voice into an exaggerated conspiratorial whisper. "There's more than just a contract in there, Lizanne. Don't you want to see?"

"Not if the act of seeing it places me in danger."

He reclined and turned his gaze towards the sea. "It seems so peaceful today. The sea becalmed beneath a summer sun. But it does make me consider that one day we may awake and find something very unwelcome on the horizon. I think you and I both know that very soon there could no longer be anywhere in this world free of danger."

He kept his gaze on the sea as she stepped closer, retrieving the papers and untying the ribbon that bound them. The first few pages were a standard employment contract amended with the very specialised additional clauses unique to those recruited into Exceptional Initiatives. Also, she noted, a doubling in salary and enhanced allotments for nominated beneficiaries in the event of her death. Beyond the contract, however, was something else entirely. A sketch, or more accurately, a design rendered in clean precise lines on a piece of cheap parchment. It showed some form of bulbous con- traption, rather like an elongated balloon, with several attachments that resembled the Corvantine's screw propulsion system she had first glimpsed beneath the waters of Morsvale harbour. But this was no ship, as evidenced by the Eutherian letters inscribed along the sketch's edges. The words were formed with florid lettering and an archaic sentence structure, though she had little trouble translating it: *Rapid and easily navigable passage through the very air lies within our grasp.* There was more, mainly consisting of a list of dimensions and projected velocities, plus a brief calculation entitled: *Projected atmospheric resistance relative to forward velocity.*

Lizanne detected a certain similarity in the lettering, stirring recollec- tions of the scraps she had seen in Burgrave Artonin's cache of documents.

"Yes," Bloskin said softly. "It is indeed the Mad Artisan's handwriting."

Lizanne held the parchment up to the light. It was thick and coarse but lacked the speckling or stiffness of truly aged paper. "This is too recent to be genuine," she said. "A copy of one of his designs, perhaps?"

"Perhaps. However, it has been examined by the finest graphologists and scholars, discreetly of course, and they all agree this is either the work of the Artisan himself or that of someone who can mimic his hand with absolute precision. Furthermore"—he tapped a yellow-stained finger to the calculation—"this particular formula was previously unknown to science prior to the discovery of this document. It has been thoroughly checked by experimentalists in the Research Division and it works."

Lizanne's gaze roamed the design again. "This can't be more than five years old."

"Our experts estimate three."

"He died centuries ago."

"Indeed he did, and yet here we have evidence his genius lives on, as real as you or I." A smile returned to Bloskin's lips and Lizanne could have sworn she heard the hard snap of a trap closing on her wrist. "Would you like to know where we got it?"

*I*t's impossible. Over the Blue-trance, Clay's dust-devil swelled into a rendering of his face, the particles assuming a scornful expression.

Is it? Lizanne asked, summoning the whirlwind that contained the memory of his encounter with the White. *You saw many wonders beneath that mountain, as I recall. We know the Artisan went there once. We know that those crystals have the power to change us. What if they changed him?*

A shudder ran through Nelphia's surface, raising the moon-dust into a facsimile of the domes he had seen in the subterranean city and the light shining from them: white, red, blue and green, but no black. *Green,* she said. *You saw what the blue crystal did to the Briteshore Minerals people, transformed into Spoiled by the power of its light. What if he found a green crystal? Green blood is a panacea and a restorative. If these crystals possess the same power as the product they represent . . .*

Which means, Clay mused, his scepticism diminished but only slightly, *the Artisan made it into the city and back out again. Might explain why he went crazy. You say your boss got this from the Corvantines?*

Handed to him personally by an old adversary in the Blood Cadre. They meet every now and then to reminisce, apparently. There was no explanation as to its origins but they did request it be shown to me.

It's bait. They want you on this diplomatic mission of theirs.

Obviously. The question is why.

You stole the Artisan's solargraph, killed a cart-load of their agents and held off their army at Carvenport. I doubt they're gonna greet you with flowers and candy.

She let her thoughts settle, her whirlwinds becoming more placid and losing the red tinge of frustration that stemmed from the much-detested sensation of ignorance. *You have docked at Lossermark, I assume?*

Day and a half ago. Things've gotten a little confused since this tub's original captain woke from his coma. He's pretty trying company, I must say.

If he proves a barrier to our objective it'll need to be dealt with. The time for scruples is behind us.

Hopefully it won't come to that. My uncle's got a notion of how to proceed. Looks like the future's gonna need a helping hand.

There was a pause before he conveyed his next thought, several nascent dust-devils sprouting then fading before he found the right words. *The White's coming. You know that. When it does there'll be a lotta people in Feros needing your help. Our people.*

He didn't need to share a memory for her to discern the object of his concern. *Joya and Fredabel.*

I can help them more if I can find the Artisan, she said eventually, conjuring the image of the design Bloskin had shown her. *If he's still somehow alive he possesses knowledge far beyond our own. I have to take the chance.*

The domes he had raised turned to instant powder as another shudder rippled through the moon's surface. *You're really gonna do this? Place yourself at their mercy?*

I have never been at anyone's mercy, Mr. Torcreek. I don't intend to start now.

The late-afternoon shift was winding down by the time she got to the workshop, the industrial cacophony not quite at its usual bone-shuddering pitch. Tekela and Arberus were overseeing the final assembly of a Mark II Thumper, an even more fearsome beast than its predecessor with lengthened barrels for greater range and a higher rate of fire thanks to the more efficient gearing her father had designed. Their work-force of twenty former Carvenport artisans laboured away at the production line, an array of work-benches snaking through a recently constructed extension to the shed which had been the birthplace of the Lethridge family's often wondrous, if rarely profitable innovations.

Jermayah was engaged in yet another heated discussion with a tall man in a long, heavily besmirched white coat. The tall man stood with his arms crossed and gaze raised in stubborn dismissal as Jermayah expounded at length on the correct arrangement of fuel lines for the bulky yet complex confection of iron and copper sitting on the bench between them. From the recent scorch-marks on the bench Lizanne deduced yet another test had ended in failure. The tall man glanced over as she went to a neighbouring bench, ignoring his questioning glare and extracting a roll of blue design paper from a near by bin. Taking up a thick pencil she weighted down the paper's edges with some discarded knick-knacks and began to draw. As expected it took only moments before the pair of them forgot their argument and came to scrutinise her work.

"A balloon," the tall man said in a determinedly neutral tone as the diagram began to take shape on the paper, Lizanne reproducing the image from memory with practised ease. "The envelope shaped so as to be navigable through the air. Hardly an original idea."

Lizanne kept drawing, completing the sausage-like shape and the ribs tracking along its length, before going on to set out a much neater Mandinorian translation of the original Eutherian notes.

"Interesting," Jermayah said, leaning closer to read the words. "'Fashion the structure from a composite of tin and zinc.' Of course, lightness and strength combined. Remarkable." His stubby finger tapped the calculations. "Have these been verified?"

Lizanne didn't reply, completing the diagram by adding the propelling apparatus to the body of the main structure. "A parting gift, Father," she said, looking up to meet the tall man's gaze. "I'm going away for a time."

Professor Graysen Lethridge stiffened and turned his eyes towards the lumpen collection of iron and copper resting on the neighbouring bench. "I have little time for flights of fancy. The Lethridge Tollermine Mark One Caloric Engine nears completion. And when it does the world will change for the second time in a generation . . ."

Unwilling to suffer through another speech, Lizanne tossed the pencil aside and walked away. "Build it or don't," she said, striding off towards Tekela and Arberus. "I have good-byes to make."

"Wait!"

She paused, turning to regard his flustered visage. As long as she could remember she had possessed the gift of turning this occasionally brilliant man into a barely coherent picture of paternal rage and disappointment. Today, however, there was at least an attempt at restraint in his demeanour. It took a moment of jaw clenching and needless coat straightening before he said, "Might your father know your destination? Or have you once again sunk yourself into the mire of Ironship's covert intrigues?"

"A public intrigue, in fact." She looked at Jermayah expectantly, adding a few insistent eye-flicks before he took the hint and retreated to tinker with the caloric engine.

"I now hold the respectable post of diplomat," she said, returning to the bench. "They're sending me to Corvus, ostensibly to help negotiate an alliance. In fact"—she gestured at the diagram—"I am tasked with finding whoever designed this."

The professor's eyes roamed the design with a new intensity then narrowed in recognition. "The same hand that crafted the baffling box you brought me, if I'm any judge."

"Quite so, Father."

"The Corvantine Empire is vast. How could you hope to accomplish such a thing?"

"There are . . . lines of enquiry," she said, unwilling to divulge anything that Bloskin might take exception to. "Will it work?" she asked, nodding at the diagram.

"Perhaps, with a sufficiently light-weight means of propulsion . . ." He trailed off and glanced at the as yet lifeless caloric engine. "I see my daughter's gift for improvisation hasn't deserted her."

She smiled. "I have every confidence in you, Father. Also . . ." She pulled a sealed contract from her pocket and placed it on the bench. "I was able to negotiate a new agreement on your behalf."

His gaze darkened and he made no attempt to retrieve the contract. "I want . . ."

". . . nothing to do with that band of thieves. I know."

She sighed and broke the seal, unfolding a document signed by all Board members currently in Feros. "'The Ironship Trading Syndicate (hereinafter referred to as "The Syndicate"),'" she began, reading aloud the opening paragraph, "'hereby acknowledges, without prejudice to any preceding legal decisions or agreed contracts, that Professor Graysen Lethridge is the sole inventor of the Mark I thermoplasmic engine (hereinafter referred to as "the engine"). Furthermore, the Syndicate agrees to pay a restitution fee of ten million in Ironship Trading Scrip in lieu of incurred royalties. The Syndicate also agrees to pay a further twenty million in Ironship Trading Scrip for the exclusive right to use, manufacture, sell or otherwise exploit for commercial gain any and all original designs contained within the engine for a period not to exceed fifteen years from the date of this agreement. At the conclusion of this period both parties undertake to engage in reasonable negotiations for the renewal of this contract.'"

She leaned across the bench to place the document in front of him. "There's more, mainly relating to termination rights and confidentiality. It requires your signature but you should have a lawyer look it over first."

He said nothing for a long time, staring down at the words on the page with a stern, almost resentful frown. "It doesn't mention your grandfather," he muttered eventually.

"At my insistence," she said. "He was the real thief, after all. The thermoplasmic engine was yours, not his." She moved to his side, plucking a pen from the ink-stained pocket of his coat and holding it up in front of his nose. "Just sign it, Father. It took me almost five minutes of hard bargaining." She stood on tip-toe and pressed a kiss to his cheek. "I leave in the morning. I'll understand if you're not there to see me off."

The IPV *Profitable Venture* was the largest ship she had ever sailed on, a Tempest class battleship of eight twelve-inch guns and enormous, sail-sized paddles secured within armoured casements the size of castles. A small army of sailors were busy about the deck as she came aboard to be greeted by the ship's First Officer, who ordered her trunk carried to her cabin before requesting she accompany him to the ship's ward-room. "The rest of the delegation is already aboard, miss. We sail within the hour."

"A moment, please." Lizanne turned and cast her gaze down the long gang-plank to where they stood on the quayside. Jermayah waved, Aunt Pendilla awkwardly hugged the shoulders of a half-sobbing Tekela whilst her father stood apart, for once not dressed in that dreadful white coat but a reasonably smart if unfashionable business suit that probably hadn't seen the outside of a wardrobe in decades. There was no sign of Major Arberus. Of them all, his reaction to her news had been by far the least sympathetic.

Lizanne watched her father give a stiff nod of farewell then turned briskly about. *No distractions,* she told herself, summoning a lesson from her training, though, like much of her education, the words had a somewhat hollow ring these days. *An agent must accommodate their character to solitude. Friends, family and lovers are not within the scope of your employment, except as cover.*

"Lead on, if you would, Commander."

"Ah, Miss Lethridge, excellent." A grey-haired man in civilian clothes came forward to greet her as she entered the voluminous ward-room, the expression on his lean features considerably more welcoming than the carefully bland one he had shown her the day before. "Director Bloskin advised us of your change of heart."

"Director Thriftmor." She inclined her head at the Board member responsible for Extra-Corporate Affairs. She knew him by reputation only, a renowned negotiator who had overseen the successful end to the Dalcian Emergency, though his task had been made easier by the near-complete destruction of Sovereignist forces at the hands of the Protectorate.

"I believe you know the Ambassadress." Thriftmor turned to an elegant young woman in a finely made dress of black-and-white silk, her hair done up in a pleasing arrangement of golden curls.

"Electress Dorice Vol Arramyl," Lizanne greeted her in Eutherian, employing the full nomenclature as required by Imperial Court etiquette.

"Miss Blood," the Electress replied in her slightly accented Mandinorian, lowering her head in a shallow bow. Lizanne found her expression difficult to read, alternating between suppressed resentment and reluctant gratitude. Difficult as it might be to admit, this woman had to know she would have perished at Carvenport but for the evacuation.

"Just Lethridge these days," Lizanne said. "And I find you elevated to ambassadress no less. How our fortunes have changed."

"The Blood Imperial advised me of my new title only yesterday," the Electress replied. "The Emperor thought it only fitting."

"The Electress has been educating me in Imperial history," Director Thriftmor said. "A fascinating subject. Did you know the Arakelin dynasty has held the throne for over four centuries?"

"Four hundred and seventy-six years," Lizanne said. "To be precise."

"Quite a remarkable feat, don't you think? For one family to hold on to power for so long."

A family of blood-soaked inbreds and tyrants who barely survived the last bout of revolution, Lizanne restrained herself from saying. Diplomacy required circumspection. "Indeed, very impressive."

"Come." Thriftmor turned and gestured at the gaggle of Ironship functionaries standing near by. "Meet the rest of our delegation."

There were ten of them altogether, a collection of economic advisers and managers with Corvantine expertise. There were also two senior Protectorate officers, one an admiral, the other a general. They socialised for an hour or more, drinking wine served by the ship's immaculately turned-out orderlies, the conversation lively with corporate gossip and amusing anecdotes. Lizanne found their collective joviality somewhat unnerving, as if none of them truly understood the import of this mission. But then, of the entire delegation, only she and the Electress had been in Carvenport.

"Did they really call you 'Miss Blood'?" one of them asked, a young economist from the Strategy and Analysis Division who had called for his wine-glass to be refilled several times now. "It seems," he went on, eyes tracking over her with undue scrutiny, "such an *inappropriate* title."

"She killed over a hundred Corvantine soldiers in a single day," Electress Dorice put in, speaking in slurred Eutherian before downing the contents of her own glass and beckoning to an orderly for more. "Plus half a dozen Blood Cadre agents. Her title would in fact seem to be fairly inadequate." She raised her glass in a mocking toast. "Miss Slaughter would suit you far better."

"Whereas a willing spectator to a slaughter is, of course, to be admired," Lizanne returned. "I don't believe anyone forced you to embark upon your little jaunt, Electress. And I apologise if the reality of war failed to meet your expectations."

The Electress flushed, composure slipping away as she flourished a hand at Lizanne, displaying several pale Green-healed scars on the palm. "See these. The legacy of slaving in your filthy manufactory. Forced to labour like a slattern in a workhouse, never knowing if each day might be my last."

"On behalf of those not born into a life of useless indolence, I bid you welcome to adulthood."

"Adulthood? You imagine all of this horror has somehow improved me?" The Electress reached up to jerk down the collar of her dress, revealing another scar, this one broad and not so well healed. "From when a Blue breathed fire over the length of our ship during the evacuation. I shielded a baby in my arms. She died anyway."

"Ladies!" Director Thriftmor broke in, dismissing the now-acutely-embarrassed economist with a jerk of his head. The Director smiled, spreading his arms in warm placation. "We stand on the verge of an historic peace. Why sully the occasion with needless acrimony?"

Lizanne realised the rest of the party had fallen silent whilst the volume of their argument rose. *Too long out of the shadows,* she berated herself. *I need to do better.*

"Quite so, Director," she said, setting her wine-glass down on an orderly's tray before offering Electress Dorice a bow. "My apologies. Your actions were very brave and are still well remembered among the Carvenport refugees." She nodded at Thriftmor. "I believe I'll take a turn about the deck before retiring."

The *Profitable Venture*, it transpired, had no less than three upper decks. The largest sat level with the edge of the hull and encompassed an area equivalent to three playing-fields. The next two encircled the ship's command centre and officers' quarters, a great iron island bristling with small-calibre cannon and newly installed batteries of Thumpers and Growlers, many no doubt bearing the crest of the Lethridge and Tollermine Manufacturing Company. Lizanne's quarters were located on the middle deck, where she had been advised to confine her evening wanderings. She spent some time leaning on the starboard rail watching the sea pass by beyond the bulk of the paddle casement. The *Profitable* had recently been fitted with two of the latest mark of thermoplasmic engines and ploughed a north-westerly course at close to thirty knots. It was, she knew, a necessary expense of increasingly scarce product. The faster they could get to Corvus the sooner this alliance could be formalised, though she harboured serious doubts as to the Corvantines' sincere desire for an agreement. After spilling so much blood and treasure it seemed unlikely the Emperor would willingly forfeit his cherished ambition to control the source of wealth in this world.

She made her way forward, finding herself replaying the final conversation with Tekela. "If you go there, you'll die," she had said, tears swelling in her eyes. "The Cadre never forgets and never forgives. Every Corvantine learns this from an early age."

She was right, of course. The vindictiveness of the Cadre had been hammered home to Lizanne throughout her training. On several occasions over the past century long-retired Exceptional Initiatives agents had been targeted for assassination or abduction. It didn't bode well for any reception she might receive.

On nearing the forward-facing section of deck she became distracted by the sight of a Growler crew struggling to free the loading mechanism of a jammed cartridge. Deciding to offer some words of advice she started forward when two strong hands reached out from the hatchway behind. One clamped onto her mouth, the other encircled her neck to drag her from sight. Lizanne didn't bother to struggle, instead remaining limp until the assailant revealed his intentions.

"Now then," a voice breathed in her ear. "What's a tasty morsel like you doing wandering about above decks of a night?"

Lizanne bit the hand over her mouth, her captor withdrawing it with a soft curse. "Your accent is abysmal," she told Arberus.

"Seems good enough to fool my shipmates," he muttered, inspecting the bite mark on his hand. Lizanne looked him over, finding his uniform a little too neat for a recently press-ganged ordinary seaman.

"How did you get up here?" she asked. "Bloskin said you'd be assigned to the lowest deck."

"Indeed I was. Been swinging buckets of bilge-water all day. Finding my way here wasn't overly difficult. It's always the same with military folk, move with a purpose and they tend to leave you alone." He flexed his hand, wincing. "Quite the powerful bite you have."

"Stop pouting, I didn't break the skin." She sighed and stepped closer, raising a hand to stroke his chin, speaking softly. "This is foolish. We can't be seen together, not if you're going to be of any use in Corvus."

"I wanted to see you," he said with a shrug, hands encircling her waist. "Where exactly is your cabin?"

"Oh no." She put a hand on his chest and gently pushed herself away, not without some reluctance. "Our relationship will remain strictly professional for the duration of this mission. I need to . . . re-acclimatise myself to this role."

"It could take weeks to find the Artisan," he said. "If the bugger actually exists."

"I was thinking more in terms of months, actually." She stood back and pointed an imperious finger at a wrought-iron gangway descending into the lower decks. "Now be off with you, and don't let me catch you pestering your betters again."

He huffed out a small laugh and began to climb down, pausing before his head disappeared from view, face completely serious now. "You know I still think this whole enterprise is insane."

"We're living in an insane world." She extended a foot and tapped the toe of her shoe onto his head. "Now get out of my sight, you unkempt bilge rat you."

CHAPTER 5

Hilemore

"Collusion with the notorious pirate Zenida Okanas. Unauthorised pardoning of said pirate. Gross misuse of Protectorate equipment and personnel. Failure to adhere to standing orders in time of war. Allowing Syndicate interest to be usurped by informal contract with independent civilians spouting fairy stories." Captain Trumane's voice took on an increasing tremble as he spoke, his red-rimmed eyes seeming to glow with fury in the pale, hollow-cheeked mask of his face. He paused, staring up at Hilemore from behind his desk, a much-diminished version of the man who had greeted him only a few months before. Though never a physically imposing presence the captain had nevertheless possessed an energetic, if frequently petty air. Now the collar of his tunic hung loosely around a reedy neck and his hands shook so badly he was obliged to keep them clasped together on the desk. His faculty for pettiness, however, seemed as strong as ever.

"Please, Lieutenant," he said, baring his yellowed teeth in something that might have been intended as a smile but in fact appeared more of a snarl. "Feel at liberty to correct me if I have omitted anything."

"You were incapacitated, Captain," Hilemore replied, standing at attention and keeping his voice as mild as possible. "The fleet had been destroyed in the Strait. Difficult choices had to be made."

"There's a difference between a hard command decision and outright betrayal of Syndicate interests . . ." Trumane's tirade was interrupted by a bout of coughing, his reduced form convulsed by a series of deep, wracking heaves.

"Are you alright, sir?" Hilemore asked, stepping forward. "I can send for Dr. Weygrand . . ."

"Stay where you are!"

Trumane took a kerchief from his pocket and wiped at the pinkish moisture on his lips. "Rest assured, Lieutenant," he rasped after a short period of heavy breaths. "If we were in a Syndicate port I would file formal charges obliging you to account for your actions in a court martial. As it is, all I can do is demote you to third mate pending future enquiries by the Sea Board. My first order to you is to get that rag-bag bunch of Contractors off my ship. And"—he levelled a shaking finger at Hilemore—"you can forget any lunatic notions of sailing south. Once reprovisioned, the *Viable* will sail for Feros."

Hilemore clenched his teeth together to cage the unwise words churning in his thumping chest. "Captain Okanas," he managed after a moment, the words clipped and precisely controlled. "Might I enquire as to her status?"

"Since she seems to be the only means of firing the blood-burner, I have little choice but to honour your contract with her."

"She will not wish to sail for Feros."

"She'll do as she's told or she and her whelp can stay here and take their chances. We'll sail north on auxiliary power only, if necessary. Now get out."

"He simply doesn't believe it," Hilemore said. Zenida Okanas glanced back at the *Viable* where a work party of sailors were carrying the newly arrived supplies aboard under Steelfine's supervision. The captain had made it clear that, once fully loaded, she would depart with the evening tide. "Then he'll need to be made to," she said. "I will not take my daughter anywhere near Feros."

"He didn't see what we saw," Hilemore pointed out. "He awoke to a changed world and doesn't yet know it."

"When the Blues rip his ship apart, he'll know it quickly enough."

"It's not just the Blues." Hilemore shot a glance at Clay, standing near by alongside his uncle. The rest of the Longrifles waited a short distance along the wharf, packs heavy with their belongings and the rations Hilemore had quite illegally provided from the ship's stores. "Mr. Torcreek's story proved too outlandish for him to accept."

"So you're just gonna let him leave us here?" Braddon asked.

"He's the captain of my ship," Hilemore said, a certain heat creeping into his voice. "As appointed by the Sea Board and confirmed fit for command by the ship's doctor. My duty is clear."

"Balls to your duty," Clay said. "We got us a place to be and it's far from here." He turned and nodded towards the ship where an unusually vocal Steelfine harried the work party to greater efforts. "Seems to me there's plenty in your crew ain't too happy he woke up. The Islander in particular."

"Mr. Steelfine knows his duty as well as I," Hilemore snapped. "And I'll thank you not to make mention of such dishonourable allusions in future."

"Your captain don't believe it," Braddon said, adopting a more conciliatory tone than his nephew. "But you do, Mr. Hilemore. You really want to risk us not making our destination due to the jealous arrogance of a sick man? I see it if you don't. This ain't about broken regulations or deals with pirates. He knows when the only Protectorate ship to survive the Strait makes it to Feros, the laurels won't be his. Lest he can find some way to discredit you, that is."

Hilemore fell silent, turning away to wander to the quay's edge. *Mutiny will never be forgiven,* he knew. *Regardless of the justification. They'll hang me and any who join me.* He closed his eyes as memories of recent weeks crowded in: the destruction of the INS *Imperial,* the great northward migration of Blues, the bodies littering the ruins of Hadlock. *If we're gonna save the world . . .*

"The crew won't be with me," he sighed eventually, voice barely above a mutter. "Most just want to get back to the safety of a familiar port, however illusory that safety might be. In truth, it was my intention to ask for volunteers when it came time to sail south. I thought perhaps half might step forward, now not even that. Taking a ship is one thing, sailing her shorthanded is another. Then there's the question of Chief Bozware's modifications. The *Viable* won't last a week in southern waters without them."

Braddon moved to his side, longrifle cradled in his arms as he stared out into the harbour, a thoughtful frown on his brow. "Seems to me there's more than one warship in this port," he said. "One that won't require so large a crew. And I ain't no sailor, sir, but that looks like a pretty thick hull to me."

Hilemore followed his gaze, straightening as his eyes lit on the sleek shape of the INS *Superior.* The Contractor captain was right about her hull, built strong enough to withstand the forces unleashed by driving through the heavy seas of the northern oceans at high speed. *Which means she must be a blood-burner.*

"Had Preacher and Lori keep watch on her since we got here," Braddon went on. "They reckon there's no more than ten sailors aboard. Seems they had a bad time of it up north. Reckon you can muster more than ten men, Mr. Hilemore?"

Hilemore straightened further, clasping his hands behind his back as if a military posture might alleviate the enormity of what he was about to do. "The harbour wall," he said.

"Best leave that to me," Clay said. "You're forgetting we got another ally to call on."

"You wanna sail the Chokes, eh?" the sailor spoke in a grating rasp that told of a throat beset by decades of grog and tobacco. His name was Scrimshine and he appeared to be of mixed heritage, the wiry build and high cheekbones speaking of some Dalcian blood, though his blue eyes and accent indicated a North Mandinorian birth. According to Major Oz-pike the man was a recently captured smuggler about to embark upon a lengthy sentence in the Lossermark gaol. What made him of interest to Hilemore, however, was his previous service aboard Blue-hunters sailing the southern seas. Hilemore's attempts to recruit a pilot from amongst the numerous seafarers in port had proven fruitless, mere mention of the southern seas bringing an abrupt end to all interviews. It left them with only one other option. Ozpike had demanded a hefty bribe to allow them access to the inmates, and the promise of yet more once he signed the parole orders in the event they found a suitable candidate.

"Indeed we do," Hilemore replied. "And then on to the Shelf."

The sailor's eyes widened a fraction, though his voice betrayed only a cautious self-interest. "What's at the Shelf that needs a Protectorate warship to fetch it?"

"Mind your own Seer-damn business," Clay said. "You want out of this shit-pile or not?"

Clay ignored the warning glare Hilemore gave him, instead matching stares with the smuggler. "I know this brand of fellow of old, Captain," he said after a moment's narrow-eyed inspection. "He's like to cut our throats the moment we clear the harbour. You'd best throw him back."

"You do that you'll be sailing to your deaths," Scrimshine promised. He had been chained to the table, which itself was bolted to the floor of his cell.

The iron links rattled on wood as the sailor shifted, fixing his gaze entirely on Hilemore. "This one don't know shit about the sea, do he, Skipper? But you do. There's salt in your veins just like me. Ever see the price the Chokes extracts from a foolhardy captain? Ain't pretty. If the rocks or the bergs don't rip the hull out from under you, the ice on the rigging might just get thick enough to tip you over. Then there's the Blues, a'course."

"The Blues are all up north," Clay said. "Or didn't you hear?"

"I heard," the sailor said, gaze not shifting from Hilemore. "Blue-hunters been scurrying into this dump for weeks now, and they tell a different story. There's still Blues aplenty down south, Skipper, you can bet a year's worth of prizes on it. And it's a dead-on certainty you'll find Last Look Jack amongst 'em."

"Who in the Travail is Last Look Jack?" Clay enquired of Hilemore.

"A legendarily monstrous Blue," he replied. "The dock-side taverns are rich with dire warnings about the great beast and his ravenous appetite for ships and sailors. Though, curiously, no one has ever actually seen him."

"How'd you think he got his name? They call him Last Look Jack, 'cause you see him once chances are you won't be seeing nothing again. He was vicious even before the drakes rose against us, now they say he's got a hunger that can't be sated."

"Guess that means you'd rather stay here," Clay said, turning in his seat to face the door. "I'll call for the next one . . ."

"Didn't say that!" Scrimshine spat. "I'd sail the length of the Travail and back to get my carcass clear of this place. Just wanna make sure the good captain is aware of the risks." He revealed a far-from-complete set of teeth in a strained smile. "And you won't find a better pilot for the Chokes, Skipper. Sailed 'em for a dozen years or more, and it's all up here." He tapped a finger to his temple. "Might forget me old mum's maiden name, but every course I ever set is still in here."

"And the Shelf?" Hilemore asked.

"Been there too, not so often, but I can navigate a safe passage there and back."

"What about farther south? Across the ice."

The sailor's chains rattled as he reclined in his seat, a deeper caution creeping into his gaze. "Once. Had a captain a bit touched in the head, convinced there was some old pirate treasure buried south of the Shelf.

Never found it and the daft old sod froze to death on the journey back, along with four others."

At Hilemore's nod Clay pulled his book of sketches from the pocket of his duster, filled with his inexpert but legible drawings of what he could remember from the vision contained in the White's blood. He flipped pages until he came to the image of the great spike rising from the ice, placing it in front of the sailor, who peered at it in evident bafflement.

"Guess you never saw this on your travels," Clay observed.

The sailor gave a despondent groan and shook his head, slumping back in his seat. "Nah. Meaning you got no use for me, right?"

"Right." Clay retrieved the book and turned to Hilemore. "The major's got another dozen or so might fit the bill . . ."

"Saw the mountain though," Scrimshine broke in.

"What mountain?" Hilemore asked him.

"The peak in the background of that scribbling. That's Mount Reygnar. Named for some old god or other by the first Mandinorians to make it to the Shelf. I only ever saw it at a distance, right enough."

"But you can guide us there?" Hilemore asked.

"Surely. But truth be told, it don't take much guiding. Only high ground for miles around. Moor up at Kraghurst Station then keep true on a south-south-west heading for sixty miles, you'll see it soon enough. That's the easy part, Skipper." He gave another gap-toothed smile, this one possessing some real humour. "Hard part is getting anywhere near Kraghurst in the first place. But you got me for that." He turned his smile on Clay. "Right?"

"The debt between us is long settled," Hilemore told Steelfine, watching the Islander cross his thick arms as he lowered his head in stern contemplation. "You should feel no obligation to join me in this."

They were in the armoury, the thick walls offering protection against prying ears. Steelfine's bulk took up most of the space, obliging Chief Bozware to squeeze himself into the gap between rifle racks. His agreement had been offered without hesitation. If anything, he seemed a little aggrieved it had taken Hilemore so long to approach him. "We'd be at the bottom of the Strait if not for you, Captain," he said with a shrug. "Far as I'm concerned, you set the course and I'll make sure we'll get there."

Steelfine was another matter. The fortunes of war had seen him rise higher in the ranks than a seaman of his station could normally expect, except after a lifetime of service. Hilemore was asking him to give up a great deal. In fact there was a small corner of Hilemore's heart that hoped the Islander would march straight to the captain and report his crime. The man had repaid Hilemore several times over for saving his life during that first near-fatal meeting with Zenida, but it appeared some debts were never settled.

"Twelve," Steelfine said after a long moment's consideration. "Perhaps fifteen if their mates persuade them. Mr. Talmant and the juniors too, of course."

Hilemore swallowed a sigh of equal parts relief and regret. He wanted to ask Steelfine if he was sure about his choice but knew it would be taken as a stain on his Island honour.

"Talmant and the other lads aren't part of this," Hilemore said. "I'll not blight their future, assuming they have one." He turned to the Chief. "You'll speak to Dr. Weygrand?"

Bozware shook his head. "He won't come, sir. Not with patients still in need of his care."

"Very well. We'll need a short delay to get properly organised. Tell the captain there's a problem with the engines, something minor but it'll take until tomorrow to fix."

"Might be better to sabotage them. Stop him coming after us."

"No. I've no desire to leave this ship marooned here." He rested a hand on the bulkhead, feeling the thrum of the auxiliary engines turning over as Bozware's stokers prepared for the impending voyage. Of all the ships he had sailed on he knew he would miss the *Viable* the most. "She'll have a hard enough time being left in Trumane's care as it is."

He pulled his watch from his tunic, the two men following suit and synchronising the time on his mark. "The operation commences at four hours past midnight, gentlemen. To your tasks, if you please."

Hilemore spent the rest of the day going about his duties with typical efficiency and ignoring the nervous winks or grins offered by Steelfine's chosen co-conspirators. He left the surreptitious gathering of arms and provisions to the Islander and, aware of Trumane's continually watchful eye, confined his first act of outright mutiny to retrieving two-thirds of the ship's product from the safe. Luckily, the captain's distrust hadn't extended to relieving him of the keys. He briefly considered taking all of the Red but decided there was a possibility, however faint, that Trumane might find a Blood-blessed at another port. *Once you've decided your course you can never falter.* Another of his grandfather's lessons popping into his head as he regarded the contents of the safe, wondering what the old man would have made of this. *Mutineer and now thief. Hanging will be too good for me.*

He found the Chief waiting at the port rail with Zenida and her daughter. Akina seemed unusually cheerful, her usual scowl replaced by a bright-eyed excitement and she fairly bounced on tip-toe as the first boat was lowered over the side. Steelfine had ensured the night watch consisted entirely of his trusted crewmen, numbering sixteen men in total, mostly riflemen and stokers. They were further aided by Dr. Weygrand, who, despite refusing to join them, had contrived to add a soporific to the captain's nightly dose of medicine.

"Doc says he'll be dead to the world for at least eight hours," Bozware reported. "Even if there's another who raises the alarm, I doubt there's a man aboard with the heart to fire on us, sir."

Hilemore nodded and glanced over the rail to confirm the first boat was now in the water. "Captain," he said, handing Zenida a small draw-string oilskin bag containing a good supply of their stolen product. "I would prefer no fatalities, if possible."

She nodded and paused to kneel and embrace her daughter, speaking in soft Varestian. "Stay with the grease-rat."

Hilemore swung himself over the rail and began to climb down, making the boat without undue difficulty and taking up the oars. Zenida joined him a moment later, taking the tiller whilst he began to propel them towards the dark bulk of the *Superior.* Behind them came the clinking of chains through the davits as Steelfine's party lowered three more boats over the side. Hilemore concentrated on rowing the boat, working oars with a smooth, even rhythm to avoid tell-tale splashes, the squeal of the rowlocks muffled by a liberal application of grease and canvas. Zenida kept mostly to the shadows cast by the other ships at harbour, steering through the curving cliff-like hulls for several long minutes. Finally, she nodded for Hilemore to halt alongside an Alebond Commodities freighter some fifty yards from the *Superior's* anchorage.

"We could get closer," Hilemore whispered, judging the remaining distance too great for his liking.

"Too risky." Zenida stood up and began to strip. Hilemore expected her to stop at her underthings and found himself instinctively averting his gaze when instead she removed every scrap of clothing. "It'll just slow me down," she said, crouching to retrieve the bag of product. "Besides, I've noticed men are often reluctant to shoot a naked woman."

"I wouldn't be," he muttered. "If my ship were under threat."

"But you are a very singular fellow, Mr. Hilemore." It was too dark to see her face but he could hear the smile in her voice. She extracted three vials from the oilskin bag, presumably Red, Green and Black, and drank them all in quick succession. Drawing the bag's string tight, she hooked it over her head and slipped over the side into the water. "If I die . . ." she began, the dark silhouette of her head just visible in the gloom.

"I'll see her safe," Hilemore promised.

A short pause and she was gone, her disappearance betrayed only by the softest slap of water against the boat's hull. Hilemore turned his full attention to the *Superior* and waited. The mist that seemed to greet every morning in this port was beginning to gather as night faded towards day, a thin veil of vapour lingering over the still waters. It took perhaps two full minutes before he saw her pale form appear at the base of the frigate's forward anchor chain. She ascended to the deck in seconds, moving with the strength and swiftness of a Blood-blessed fully dosed with Green. On reaching the deck she disappeared from sight, though he caught a brief glimpse of her through the upper gun-ports as she sprinted for the ship's command deck, a white blur in the gloom almost too fast to follow. Hilemore counted ten seconds before the first shout of alarm sounded, followed by two rapid pistol-shots. He took up the oars and began to row as fast as he could, glancing back to ensure Steelfine's party were following suit.

Two minutes of strenuous effort later the prow of the boat butted against the *Superior*'s hull and Hilemore shipped oars before reaching for the coil of rope at his feet. He swung the attached grapple with practised precision, the iron-barbed hook looping over the rail and snaring a firm purchase at the first attempt. Some skills were beyond the ability of his body to forget. Like most warships the *Superior* sat lower in the water than a merchant vessel and the climb was short, though made somewhat agonising by a fresh salvo of pistol-shots from above.

Grunting in frustration, he hauled himself up the last few yards and clambered onto the deck. The first sight to greet him was the body of an unconscious Corvantine sailor. He lay on his side near one of the starboard guns, his faint groans indicating that Zenida had so far managed to avoid any killing. Hilemore drew his revolver and ran for the ladder leading to the upper works. He passed another Corvantine on his way to the bridge, a stocky middle-aged man bent double and retching whilst a steady stream of blood flowed from his nose. He raised his head to gaze blearily at Hilemore, but returned to his retching when it became apparent he wasn't about to be shot.

Hilemore found another Corvantine on the bridge, little more than a boy and presumably equivalent to an ensign in rank. He glared at Hilemore in helpless outrage, both his wrists firmly knotted to the helm by a length of rope. Hilemore's Corvantine was poor but he detected more than a few choice obscenities in the invective flowing from the boy's mouth. Hilemore gave the boy a quick salute and moved on, drawn towards the stern by the sound of a fresh commotion.

Lieutenant Sigoral stood amidst a section of poorly repaired superstructure, sword in one hand and revolver in the other, as something pale and very fast moved around him in a wide circle. He tracked the pale thing with his revolver and pulled the trigger, cursing when the hammer clicked on a spent cartridge. Sigoral then performed some impressively timed and well-practised strokes of his sword, each failing to connect with his tormentor, causing him to swear with increasing volume. This time Hilemore picked out the word "bitch" amongst the tirade. He tapped the barrel of his revolver against an iron railing, calling out, "Captain!" When Sigoral failed to respond, still swinging away with his sword, though with an increasing lack of finesse, Hilemore sighted the revolver an inch or two from the Corvantine's foot and fired a single round. It proved sufficient to capture his attention.

"Captain," Hilemore repeated, raising his sights to aim at the man's forehead. "Look to starboard, if you would."

Sigoral glared up at him, eyes blazing beneath a sweaty brow, then did as he was bid. He cursed again at the sight of Steelfine's party now within ten yards of the ship, the Islander standing tall at the prow of his boat with grapple in hand.

"You raised the flag!" Sigoral hissed through gritted teeth, once more glaring up at Hilemore.

"Yes," he said. "I did. But I am a mutineer who has forsaken all honour."

He glanced over to where Zenida had come to a halt, shuddering as the product faded from her veins. He experienced a moment of pride at the fact that he managed not to allow his gaze to linger on her moistened and heaving breasts before returning his gaze to Sigoral. "Are your colours struck, sir?"

"What a lump of shit." Bozware's lip curled as he regarded the monstrous collection of boiler plate and piping that comprised the *Superior*'s blood-burning engine. Even to Hilemore's inexpert eye it appeared a stark contrast to the compact wonder that drove the *Viable*. The Corvantine vessel's engineering compartment was cramped compared to the *Viable*'s, her coal-burning auxiliary engine taking up even more space than the blood-burner. It was also markedly less clean and well-ordered than Bozware's domain, with the beginnings of rust showing on several fittings.

"Will it work?" Hilemore asked.

"Can't see any damage," Bozware mused, circling the engine with a critical eye. "Stupidly over-engineered though. Also looks like she's been cold for a good few weeks. Needs a proper clean too."

"Lost your Blood-blessed, did you?" Hilemore asked a stiff-backed and white-faced Sigoral. He had surrendered his sword and pistol but refused to be paroled, obliging Hilemore to allot two riflemen to guard him. "So did we," he went on when Sigoral refused to answer. "At the Strait. Were you there perchance?"

Sigoral met his gaze squarely, a humourless smile coming to his lips. "Yes. What a great and glorious day it was."

"A remarkable victory," Hilemore agreed. "If, as I'm given to understand, somewhat short-lived. And, as you saw, we found another Blood-blessed. Do you have any product on board?"

Sigoral's only response was a weary glare.

"Give us a few minutes, sir," one of the riflemen said, moving closer to the Corvantine. "We'll get him singing soon enough."

"No," Hilemore said. "Take him aloft and put him with the others. Tell Mr. Steelfine to prepare a boat to put them ashore when we're ready to sail."

He saw surprise flicker across Sigoral's face for a moment. It seemed plain he had expected either execution or a lengthy tenure in the ship's brig. "And give him his sword back when you cast them off," Hilemore added as the marine was led to the engine room's exit.

He moved to where Zenida sat, dressed in liberated Corvantine overalls and sipping a restorative mixture of rum and warmed milk. "Are you alright?" he asked.

She gave a tired nod and turned her gaze to Akina, who had joined the Chief in his examination of the Corvantine engine. In contrast to the engineer her small face betrayed fascination rather than professional distaste. "My daughter has always loved mechanicals," Zenida said. "Could never get her out of the *Windqueen's* engine room."

"Good," Hilemore said. "I have a sense we'll need every hand during the voyage ahead, and the Chief could do with an apprentice."

"Mr. Steelfine's compliments, sir," a rifleman called from the hatch. "The Contractors' boat just came alongside."

"I'll be there directly." Hilemore handed Zenida the leather satchel containing the rest of the stolen product. "We raise anchor as soon as the Chief gets the engines on-line. Are you . . . ?"

"More than capable, thank you, Captain." She took the satchel and got to her feet. "The Corvantine," she added as he started for the hatch, making him pause. "He called me some very unfortunate names. I let him live as a favour to you."

This wasn't a trivial matter, he knew. Varestians, particularly the women, were renowned for their violent intolerance of insult. "Your restraint is appreciated, sea-sister," he told her in his coarse Varestian.

She smiled and turned back to the engine. "A small matter."

The mist was lit by the faint but growing rays of the morning sun, a thick concealing blanket covering the harbour and obscuring the top of the wall from view. "Your nephew seems a little tardy, Captain Torcreek," Hilemore observed. He stood with the Contractor at the *Superior's* narrow prow, gaze fixed on the wall and ears straining for the sound of a lifting engine springing to life. The Longrifles had come aboard a quarter hour ago, having collected Scrimshine from the Lossermark gaol. The smuggler regarded the unfolding preparations with a nervous suspicion, causing Hilemore to ask the young gunhand to keep a close watch on him.

"If he tries to jump over the side, shoot him in the leg," he told Loriabeth. "We need him alive."

"Clay'll be along," Braddon said, his voice absent of doubt, though Hilemore noted his gaze was as keen as his own. He checked his watch, finding them a full five minutes behind schedule. *Much longer and the tide will be against us.* "I'll get the prisoners away," he said, hurrying towards the stern.

He found Sigoral and his nine crewmen under guard amidst the section of wrecked superstructure. Hilemore's attention was immediately drawn to one of the guards, a young man in an ill-fitting seaman's uniform who seemed at pains to keep his face shaded by his cap. "Mr. Talmant!" Hilemore barked.

The youngster froze then snapped to attention. "Sir!"

Hilemore bit down on a tirade and stepped closer. "What are you doing here?"

Talmant's response was immediate and clearly rehearsed. "Following my captain, sir. As per my oath. I left a letter on Captain Trumane's desk resigning my commission and providing a full explanation of my actions."

Hilemore was not overly fond of corporal punishment, except where demanded by necessity, but now experienced a near-irresistible desire to beat the naïvety from this boy in full view of prisoners and crew alike. However, Talmant's statement gave him pause. "You left him a letter?"

"Indeed, sir. Honour required no less."

At that moment the shrill pealing of a ship's steam-whistle cut through the mist. The *Viable* was concealed by the fog but Hilemore knew the sound like the voice of an old friend.

"Dr. Weygrand said he'd sleep for hours yet," Talmant said in a thin voice.

"Captain Trumane always had a love of confounding expectations," Hilemore muttered before turning to meet Talmant's eye. "Get to the bridge and take the helm. Signal Chief Bozware to start whichever engine he can make work."

"Aye, sir." Talmant saluted and sprinted off.

"Lieutenant Sigoral." Hilemore strode towards the marine. "Please muster your men. Time for you to take your leave."

One of the Corvantine sailors growled something at that, the tone of stern refusal requiring little translation. The rest of them all quickly echoed the sentiment, bunching together in a tight defensive knot. "This is our ship," Sigoral stated. "Thanks to the townsfolk, my men are fully aware of recent events. They do not wish to stay here, and I find I cannot argue with their reasoning."

"They'll find berths on other ships," Hilemore said.

"Not warships. And I doubt your captain will make room for us."

Hilemore looked in the direction of the *Viable*'s mooring as the faint chug of her auxiliary engine drifted through the mist. "The voyage we are about to undertake," he began, turning back to Sigoral, "will bring more danger than anything you'll face aboard a Blue-hunter in northern waters."

"This is our ship," Sigoral repeated. "The Imperial Navy is not the Protectorate, Captain. These men are bonded to their ship by sacred oath. Would you give up your home so easily?"

The *Viable*'s whistle sounded again, three long blasts accompanied by the swish of her paddles stirring into motion. "I require your parole," Hilemore told Sigoral. "And you'll be accountable for these men. I cannot tolerate even the slightest suggestion of trouble."

The Corvantine glanced at his remaining crew, jaw bunching as he fought long-instilled instinct. Finally he gave a strained rasp, "My parole is given."

Hilemore looked up at the *Superior*'s single stack, noting the absence of smoke. "You have engineers in your party?" he asked.

"Shopak! Zerun!" Sigoral barked and two Corvantines stepped forward, both clad in the besmirched overalls typical of those who toiled amidst mechanicals.

"Take them to the engine room," Hilemore ordered. "They are to help my Chief Engineer get this ship underway. You will translate. The rest of your men will raise the anchor."

Sigoral nodded but didn't move immediately, instead extending his hand to the rifleman who had hold of his sword. Hilemore nodded and the man handed it over. Sigoral buckled his sword about his waist then turned to his men and barked out a series of orders that sent all but the two engineers scurrying to the forward anchor mounting.

"I look forward to learning our destination," the Corvantine told Hilemore as he led the engineers towards a hatch and disappeared below.

"The lads won't like this, sir," said the rifleman who had offered to torture Sigoral for information. "Lotta bad feeling after the Strait."

Hilemore began to snarl out a command for the man to shut his mouth but hesitated. He had already asked a great deal of these men and clinging to normal proprieties seemed foolish in the circumstances. "We don't have enough hands to work the ship properly," he said instead, adding, "Any who don't want to serve with them can take a boat and get gone, but they'd best be quick about it."

He made his way forward, covering half the distance to the bow before the deck began to thrum beneath his feet. A glance at the stack confirmed that Bozware had at least managed to get the auxiliary engine on-line. He paused to watch the Corvantines haul the anchor clear of the water then went to stand alongside Braddon, still maintaining his vigil of the wall.

"I should've just bribed the harbour-master," Hilemore muttered, picking out the hazy bulk of the lifting engines atop the wall.

Braddon stiffened then grinned as a shout of alarm rose from the Corvantines. All eyes snapped upwards at the panicked shout, "DRAKE! DRAKE!"

"Apologies for the delay, Captain," Braddon said as a large shadow cut through the thinning mist above. "My nephew was obliged to climb the highest spire in the port. And his pet gets less obedient by the day."

Hilemore watched the shadow glide towards the wall then flare its wings for a landing. A piercing scream sounded through the mist followed by a brief but fierce gout of flame. "It takes a brave man to deny the request of a Blood-blessed riding a drake," Braddon commented. After a short delay the two lifting engines guttered into life and the door ahead of the *Superior* began its squealing rise.

"Sir!"

Hilemore turned at Steelfine's shout, finding him pointing to a familiar shape resolving out of the fog, the *Viable* coming on at full auxiliary speed. "Man the guns, sir?" Steelfine asked as Hilemore started for the bridge.

"I thought there wasn't a man aboard with the heart to fire on us?" Hilemore asked.

"Captain Trumane's a forcefully persuasive fellow," Steelfine replied.

"And, to be honest, sir, there's a few lads left aboard who'd gladly see us both dead."

"A lie, Number One?"

"Thought you needed a little prod, sir."

Hilemore sighed and shook his head. "I won't fire on my own ship, not that Trumane knows that. Load powder only, give us a smoke-screen."

"Aye, sir."

The *Superior* had already begun to move by the time he got to the bridge, finding Talmant working the wheel with accustomed hands. "She's a real beauty to handle, sir," he said.

"Good to know, Lieutenant. Keep her straight and true, if you please." Hilemore went to the starboard gangway, watching the *Viable* close to within a hundred yards, her signal lamp blinking furiously: "'Heave to. Prepare to be boarded.'"

He saw with dismay that the forward pivot-gun was manned and in the process of being loaded, though not with the kind of urgency he would have expected. Perhaps the remaining crew liked him more than Steelfine thought. Nevertheless, the time for subtlety was over.

He returned to the bridge, scanning the various instruments before he found the engine telegraph, though the lettering on its dial was completely indecipherable. "The red one for full ahead, sir," Talmant said.

"Thank you, Lieutenant." He pushed the lever to the red dial and waited. Ahead the door was at least ten yards short of being fully raised and the *Viable* was closing by the second. *Come on, Chief,* Hilemore prayed inwardly. *It can't be all that different.*

From outside came the flat boom of a cannon followed by the instantaneous whine of a shell slicing the air. The shot impacted a few yards to the right of the bow, a trifle too close for a warning shot. Either the pivot-gun crew had missed on purpose or they were worse shots than he remembered. Steelfine didn't wait for the order, the *Superior's* three starboard guns barking out a response in quick succession, the resultant smoke mingling with the lingering mist to craft an impenetrable fog.

A shrill bell sounded from the engine telegraph, the dial swinging away and then back to the red portion of the dial. The *Superior* gave a now-familiar lurch, not as violent as that produced when the *Viable's* blood-burner came on-line, but still enough to make him stagger. The *Superior* surged forward, sweeping through mist and cannon-smoke thick enough to momentarily obscure the door, but luckily Talmant proved capable of holding the course. They exited the harbour at fifteen knots, rapidly rising to twenty as Talmant steered them through the channel to the open sea.

"Steer true south, Mr. Talmant," Hilemore said. "Keep her at full ahead until further notice."

"Aye, sir."

Hilemore went outside and slipped down the ladder to the deck, making his way aft where the Longrifles stood in vigilant expectation. They didn't have long to wait. The great shadow of the Black rose from the misted channel and closed the distance to the ship with a few lazy beats of its wings. Hilemore heard a few near-hysterical shouts from the Corvantines and a hushed Dalcian prayer from Scrimshine as the drake flew closer. Lutharon spread his wings and landed on the aft deck with a skittering thump as his claws found the boards, folding his wings and crouching to allow Clay to climb down from his back.

"Well," he said, glancing around, "this tub's hardly an improvement on the last one."

CHAPTER 6

Sirus

It killed Simleon first, reaching out to enclose the boy in one of its claws before tearing him in half with a quick snap of its massive jaws. It tossed the pieces to the squalling clutch of infants scrabbling about near by. Their Spoiled captors had dragged Simleon from the ranks of prisoners and pushed him towards the White, using comparatively little force due to the boy's placidity. He just trotted along obediently, shoulders slumped and head lowered. It seemed to Sirus as if Simleon had lost the last vestiges of himself in the sewers and all that remained was an empty shell awaiting execution. Sirus wanted him to scream and struggle, at least then there may be some scrap of sanity amongst all this horror. But Simleon hadn't screamed. He just stood, not even looking up as the legendary beast dipped down to sniff him, issuing a faintly satisfied rumble. Katrya, unlike Simleon, had plenty of screams left in her. Sirus tried to shush her, fearing a silencing blow from their captors, but she kept wailing on. The Spoiled, however, seemed content to let her scream, Majack's deformed features barely glancing down at them before returning his yellow-eyed gaze to the impossible beast that now ruled this city.

The White had coiled itself around the statue of the Emperor Voranis occupying the centre of the plaza at the heart of the Imperial Ring. It should have been majestic in its size and evident power, like something stepped from the pages of myth. But the inescapable realness of the beast made it dreadful rather than awe-inspiring. There were scars on its hide in several places, and red veins could be seen pulsing in its wings as it wrapped them around the bronze effigy of long-dead Voranis. He had been the first of the Arakelin line to sit the throne, his bronze effigy now partly unrecognisable thanks to recent melting. The cause of the vandalism became apparent when

Sirus saw the infant drakes casting their flames at it, wings fluttering and tails whipping as if engaged in a delightful new game. Those not preoccupied with turning the statue into slag were busy gathering up the many bones that littered the plaza, jaws laden with blackened sticks that had once been limbs and balls that had once been skulls. They appeared to be fashioning a stack from this ghastly detritus, fusing the bones in place with some kind of steaming bile heaved up from their stomachs. Sirus's gaze swept the plaza, counting five completed stacks arranged in a circle around the White. Before vomiting, Sirus noticed most of the bones were too small to have been adult remains.

There were about forty other captives in their party, presumably the last survivors to have been scoured from the ruins of Morsvale. Sirus was surprised to find so many, but the city had been large and its antiquated architecture provided many nooks and crannies where desperate souls might conceal themselves, but not, apparently, forever. The captives were greatly outnumbered by their captors, Sirus estimating that at least three thousand drakes had gathered in this plaza. As the captives were dragged through the silent crowd, arms bound, expecting death at any second, he noticed that many of the Spoiled were clad in the clothes of the townsfolk: soldiers, constables, servants and shopkeepers. Like Majack their faces were not so deformed as those clad in tribal garb, although they all shared the same expression of faintly interested scrutiny.

The White spent a few moments watching the infants squabble over Simleon's quickly diminishing remains then turned its gaze to the ragged line of kneeling captives. Katrya's screams finally stopped as the beast's eyes swept over them, choking into a final terrorised exhalation. Sirus wanted to look away but found himself captured by the White's gaze. Its eyes were narrowed and its brows bunched in calculation and Sirus realised he had a yet deeper well of fear in him as the realisation hit home: *This animal can think!*

The White's gaze tracked across them all several times before halting to focus on one captive in particular, Sirus noting how its brows deepened as if in recognition. The captive was a small man of at least fifty years of age, dressed in a filthy set of overalls typical of those who worked at the docks. He knelt with his head lowered, lips moving in a silent prayer. Sirus wondered if he was beseeching the Emperor's divine intervention or, more likely given his age, casting his hopeless entreaties at one of the older, sup-pressed gods. In either case he had to know there was no prayer that would rescue him now.

A low rumble issued from the White and two Spoiled immediately dragged the man to his feet. His prayers trailed off as they pushed him towards the White, whatever lingering faith he possessed replaced by abject terror as he stared up into the beast's critical gaze. The White angled its head, its scrutiny deepening. The docker could only stand and tremble under the examination, Sirus noting how his bound hands spasmed at the small of his back, one of which, he saw, featured a pale circle in the otherwise olive-hued skin. *A Blood-blessed,* he realised, understanding how the man had managed to survive until now. But without product, a Blood-blessed was just another meal for their conquerer.

Abruptly the White jerked its head back from the docker with a growl that contained a clearly discernible note of frustration. Whatever it had hoped to find in this unfortunate apparently wasn't there to be found. Sirus finally looked away when the White's claws closed on the fellow, talons piercing his torso like spears. From the resurgence of squawking from the infants it was clear they had been given a new toy to play with.

When he looked again he saw that the White had uncoiled much of its bulk from the part-melted statue, revealing two objects that had previously been hidden by its wing. Sunlight glittered on two huge crystals about the size of a man, one green and one blue, both pulsing with some kind of inner light. Sirus found his gaze immediately caught by the pulsing, both the green and the blue crystal flaring and fading in steady, synchronised rhythm, oddly soothing in its ability to entice the eye. Sirus felt the sicken-ing chill of his fear fade as he continued to stare at the crystals. The many aches and pains of his strained and part-starved body slipped away along with all sense of time. There was only the light, the wonderfully soothing light . . .

"No!" He never knew where he found the strength or the will to look away, clamping his eyes shut and jerking his head to the side. The crystals' gifts were intoxicating, and he longed for the absence of fear and pain, but some primal instinct screamed a warning in his mind: *This is taking more than it gives!*

Strong hands clamped on his shoulders and head, forcing it forward, whilst implacable fingers prised his eyelids apart. Sirus tried to shout but the sound was muffled by the hands holding his jaw and he could only spout angry spittle as the Spoiled held him in place and let the crystals' light flow into his mind. After only a few heart-beats, he found that the desire to look away had vanished.

. . . still sleeping. Probably dreaming about her *again . . .*

Sirus groaned as Katrya's voice banished the dregs of slumber, her tone more sullen and bitter than he remembered. He shifted, blinking rapidly as a confusion of images greeted his eyes. It took some time before he could make sense of what he saw. There were so many colours, as if he lay in a room bathed in light from a multitude of stained-glass windows. More blinking and things became marginally more comprehensible. The colours, just confused smudges at first, soon resolved into people. They were outlined in some kind of red haze, like the glow of a lantern, but still recognisably people. *No,* he corrected himself as their features came into focus. *Not people. Spoiled.*

They lay or sat on a collection of beds or mattresses arranged in a loose order that resembled a barrack room, albeit one occupied by soldiers with scant regard for military order. The floor was littered with various refuse, from discarded bones to empty bottles. A closer look at the Spoiled brought an instant of sickening recognition. These were his fellow captives, though their faces now featured the same nascent deformities as Majack's.

Sirus fought down panic and reached up to place a tremulous hand along the new ridge of dome-like protrusions extending from the centre of his brows into his hair. They followed the line of his skull to the base of his neck where they grew yet larger, proceeding down his back in parallel to his vertebrae. A quick inspection of his face confirmed the presence of soft but scaled skin around his eyes and mouth. Had he a mirror he knew he would now be staring at the visage of a yellow-eyed monster.

Isn't so bad, Katrya said. *Doesn't hurt any more, at least.*

His gaze snapped towards Katrya, finding her sitting on the next bed, her face betraying the same deformities as the others. As he tried to overcome the shock provoked by her appearance another realisation came to him. She hadn't spoken, and yet her words sang clear in his mind.

He saw her scaled mouth twitch in faint amusement. *Clever, isn't it? Like magic or something. I think it, you hear it.*

Sirus recalled the silence of the Spoiled in the plaza, the way their captors had moved with a shared purpose despite not exchanging a word. *The crystals,* he thought, remembering the pulsing light, the way it had seemed to flow into him. *They did this . . .*

That's what I think too, Katrya agreed, smiling wider as he started.

This . . . His hands came up to paw at his face, fingers exploring the scales and the ridge of bumps with fevered disgust. *It's horrible . . . I can't . . .*

He got to his feet, casting about wildly for some kind of weapon, anything with a sharp edge capable of opening a vein. He spied a discarded bottle near by and snatched it up, raising it high to smash the glass. *I will not be this!*

STOP!

The command rang in his head like a bell, implacable and inescapable. He froze in place, the bottle slipping from suddenly numb fingers. It hadn't been just one voice this time, though he heard Katrya's in there amongst the multitude. Looking around their makeshift barracks, he saw the rest of the former captives all staring at him intently. He could feel their thoughts in his head like the low buzz of a disturbed beehive. Words began to form out of the buzz, jumbled for the most part but some leaping out with sufficient force of will to make him wince: *. . . needed . . . He needs us . . . This one is smart . . . He will be valuable . . .*

More than the jumble of voices was the sense of something beneath it, something spurring them on, a will far greater than all of them combined.

Sirus reeled under the onslaught and fell to his knees, clutching his head in pain. Then came a new sensation, something softer, kinder, subduing the commanding babble and its overwhelming accompaniment. *Best if you don't fight it.* Katrya knelt to gently pull his hands away from his temples. Her slitted eyes met his and a fresh wave of sensation rushed forth. The voices faded to a whisper as a collage of images ran through his head.

A small boy in a garden, seen through the eyes of someone whose head didn't yet come level with an old sun-dial which the boy studied with complete attention. A small but insistent hand reached out to place a ball on the sun-dial, drawing an irritated scowl from the boy that soon softened into a smile, and then a laugh. The image shifted and Sirus saw the same boy, older now and glimpsed through a half-open doorway. He stood at stiff attention, fighting tears whilst his father harangued him for a lack of attention to his studies. Sirus could feel the sympathy that coloured this memory, the desire to comfort. The vision blurred again, swirling into something different, something tinged with a dark stain of hurt and jealousy. The boy is perhaps eighteen now, standing with head bowed in the garden of his house, stuttering through some poorly written verse as a bored girl with a doll's face regards him with ill-concealed contempt. When the boy has finished his poem the girl simply rolls her eyes and walks away without a word . . .

Sirus shuddered as the images faded and he found himself back in the warehouse, on his knees and staring into Katrya's remade eyes. *It's wonderful, isn't it?* her mind said. *Now we can share everything.*

Sirus stifled the impulse to recoil, clamping down on the disgust and fear mingling in his breast. He could feel something in Katrya's thoughts, beyond the affection she had hidden for so long and now felt no compunction in sharing. It was like touching a jagged bone shoved through sundered flesh. Something had been broken in Katrya, probably in all of them when the crystals' light flooded in. Somehow it had reached inside them and snapped the cord of reason and humanity that should have made them hate this transformation. He had it too, he could feel it, a throbbing persistent desire to surrender to this new body with its marvellous gifts. Katrya no doubt had more memories to share, as did the others . . .

You are needed. Sirus's gaze snapped to the warehouse entrance, finding Majack regarding him in placid expectation. *At the docks.*

Sirus could sense no affection in Majack's thoughts. In fact the soldier exuded little of anything beyond a blind sense of purpose as he led Sirus to the docks. Katrya followed along behind, skipping a little. Her thoughts conveyed a tone of childlike contentment that made Sirus wonder why such acceptance remained beyond him. They passed many fellow Spoiled on the way, all labouring to gather what provisions could be looted from the city into several great mounds along the approaches to the quayside. After a moment's concentration Sirus found he could sense their purpose amongst the unspoken hum of shared thoughts. *He commands that we prepare . . . The sea is broad and the way long . . .*

The sea is broad . . . Sirus felt his simmering fear rise a notch at what that might mean but the sight that greeted him at the docks banished further consideration. Spoiled were at work aboard every ship in the harbour, hauling cargo or repairing damage with a concentrated, near-feverish energy. But what commanded his attention most was the presence of the White, perched atop the deck of a large freighter moored directly ahead. His attention was concentrated even more by the fact that it was looking at him.

Come . . .

The voice invading his mind was instantly recognisable; possessing the same note as the compelling undercurrent that ran through all their thoughts. It was soft, far from the booming echo Sirus might have expected from this beast. But its power to command was undeniable. He marched straight to the ship and up the gang-plank without hesitation, coming to a halt in the shadow of the White's wing as it curled its snake-like neck to regard him.

Different . . . The voice mused as Sirus felt a sharp series of stabbing pains at the front of his skull, causing him to stifle a gasp as a thousand memories ran through his head in a scant few seconds. *More,* the White mused as it rummaged through his mind, Sirus sensing a note of increasing satisfaction. *Thinks more . . . Knows more.*

Abruptly the pain stopped and the White huffed out two twin circles of smoke from its nostrils. Once again the beast's voice sang in Sirus's mind, a single word but this time completely unintelligible, resembling no language that Sirus spoke or could recognise. However, the word was accompanied by a brief image, a man in white clothing reading a book, the page rich in complex diagrams and calculations.

Scientist, he thought. *Scholar.*

The White's wings gave a small jerk, knife-length teeth bared in sudden annoyance. Sirus discerned a clear note of frustration in its shared thoughts as it swung its gaze away.

No, Sirus realised. *I don't understand.*

After a few seconds the White's wings settled and it swept its head round in a long arc that encompassed the whole harbour, Sirus following suit in response to the urge it placed in his head. *Thirty-three ships,* he counted obediently. *Capable of carrying a force of perhaps four thousand.*

He felt the White's anger flare, visions of rent and burning bodies filling his mind.

We can build more, Sirus replied, the thoughts rushing forth in a panicked torrent. *Simple craft . . . Barges that can be towed. A tactic first employed by the Emperor Hulahkin in the First Regency War . . .*

He stopped as the White's anger, and the dreadful encouraging images, receded to be replaced by a single word. *Build.*

I will . . . All that you need.

The White turned away, raising itself to gaze towards the east. Feeling a keen sense of dismissal, Sirus retreated to the gang-plank and returned to the wharf. A group of Spoiled had already begun to gather, presumably summoned by the White. They were all former townsfolk, clad in the tattered regalia of their station: carpenters, artisans, shipwrights, labourers. Sirus could feel their expectation and obedience; the White had given him a work-force. After a moment's calculation he focused his mind on an illustration he recalled from one of the older tomes in the museum library: Marschenik's *History of the Regency Wars.* The illustration showed an armada of oar-driven war galleys approaching the then-independent city-state of Valazin, each one towing two barges behind, all heavily laden with troops.

Draught's too shallow for the Arradsian seas, a heavy-set man in shipwright's garb responded before providing an image of his own, a longer craft with a narrower beam and a deeper hull. *Troop barge from the Imperial Fleet,* the shipwright explained, his thoughts rich in craftsman's certainty. *With enough timber we can build fifty in a month.*

Timber? Sirus sent the thought out to all of them, receiving a chorus of responses. *Plenty of trees beyond the wall . . . Tear down the houses . . . Break up the smaller boats . . .*

Sirus nodded and glanced back at the White, still maintaining its eastward vigil. He summoned the memory of its command and conveyed it to his new work-force: *Build, fifty in a week.*

The first barge was completed by nightfall, with another ten already under construction in the Morsvale yards. Sirus couldn't help but feel an absurd pride at the sight of the barge descending the slip-way to the harbour waters, greeted by a wave of satisfaction from the onlooking work-force.

His fear hadn't abated, nor had his disgust at what he had been fashioned into. But the power of what the White had wrought here was undeniable. The ability to take an entire city of individuals and transform them into a cohesive whole, free of rivalry, greed or envy, and capable of working in absolute concert. Added to that were the physical changes. Sirus had never been a particularly athletic youth but now found himself lifting burdens previously beyond him, working for hours on end with scant need for all but the briefest rest. He was quicker too, moving about his new domain on swift and nimble feet. Then there were the skills. Sirus had never hammered a nail or chiselled a length of wood in his life, but now found himself working timber with the hands of a master craftsman, and it wasn't just him. Every Spoiled under his command now possessed the same skills. Somehow the shipwright's knowledge had been passed to all of them.

They worked through the night with only two hours' break for sleep. Sirus was grateful to find his rest untroubled by the dreams or night terrors that had often plagued him since the basement. The White, it seemed, decreed that its army must have an undisturbed slumber. They launched the third boat a few minutes after dawn, Sirus shooting a cautious glance at the White. It had shifted its perch to the tallest remaining structure atop the harbour wall and now crouched silhouetted against the rising sun, still gazing east. Any sense of satisfaction at their achievement was absent from the faint torrent of its thoughts, which now held a dominant note of impatient expectation.

Sirus shuddered as the White straightened, every Spoiled within sight wincing in unison at its sudden shift in mood. Flaring its wings, it gave a loud but thankfully brief roar then launched itself into the air. It circled the harbour until a fresh sound greeted Sirus's ears with piercing force. *Drake calls,* he realised, shifting his gaze from the White to the eastern sky, which had grown suddenly dark. *A thousand drake calls.*

They came in a screaming crimson mass, swirling around the harbour and churning the surface of the water with the beat of their wings. The White fanned its own wings and hovered as the Reds flocked around it. Another roar, far louder and longer than the first, issued from its gaping jaws. Sirus could still hear its thoughts but the sensation was different now, reminding him of the untranslatable word it had tried to teach him. This event, he knew, was beyond human understanding. The drakes were sharing something he and the other Spoiled could never hope to experience.

Are they gods now? he wondered. *Will this be the entire world when they're done?*

After several more roaring sweeps the White descended to the quayside, landing a short distance from the slip-way. The sky gradually emptied as the Reds descended into the city, save one that glided down to land opposite the White. It was the largest Red Sirus had seen so far, as large as a full-grown Black, but still of course dwarfed by the White. The left side of the Red's face was pock-marked with deep scars and its hide bore the signs of recent battle. Sirus noted that it alighted on three legs instead of four and assumed it had been injured, but then saw it held something in its claw. Sinking low, the Red gave a subdued rattling growl as it extended its claw to deposit an offering at the White's feet. The White sniffed the gift then prodded it with its toe, drawing forth a groan that made Sirus realise this tribute was in fact a man. He lay immobile for several seconds before raising his head, revealing craggy but unspoilt features. He gazed around at his surroundings for a time before getting slowly to his feet, a large, barrel-chested man of middling years who betrayed absolutely no fear at all as he gazed up at the White.

"Chew well, you fucker," Sirus heard the man say in coarse Eutherian. "I'm likely to choke you."

It was one of the soldiers who recognised the man, the knowledge spreading through the onlooking horde of Spoiled in short order as the memory spread from mind to mind. Sirus had never seen this man in person but every Corvantine alive knew his name. Grand Marshal Morradin had returned to Morsvale.

CHAPTER 7

Lizanne

Electress Dorice came to find her on the last day of the voyage, appearing at Lizanne's side as she paused during her morning constitutional around the mid-deck. The noblewoman's handsome face was pale this morning, unadorned by rouge or paint, and she wore a simple gown of plain muslin.

"Miss Lethridge," she said, her voice lacking any of the usual condescension or resentment. They had tended to avoid one another during the voyage, save for the evening meals, which Director Thriftmor insisted be attended by all members of the delegation. Lizanne assumed he was trying to cement some form of bond between them whilst also providing a talking shop from which a "nuanced strategy" would emerge to guide their impending dealings with the Corvantines. Director Thriftmor was full of phrases like "amicable concordance" and "synergised outcomes," but "nuanced strategy" was by far his favourite. Lizanne had contrived to limit her presence at these soirees with some inventive imaginary ailments and artfully constructed euphemisms such as "the feminine regularity." She found the prospect of their imminent arrival in Corvus oddly attractive in that it would at the very least spare her the company of her fellow diplomats.

"Electress," Lizanne responded with a formally respectful nod then turned her gaze to the prow where the sea broke white against the iron hull of the *Profitable Venture*. "Grey skies and grey seas," she said. "It seems we are to be denied fine weather for our last day aboard."

"Quite appropriate, I assure you. Corvus is a fairly dreary city, truth be told." The woman fell silent and Lizanne saw a new distance in her gaze, the eyes sunken and ringed with dark circles.

"Are you well, Electress?" she asked.

Unexpectedly, the woman smiled, though it was brief and her perfect teeth remained hidden behind unpainted lips. "I am as well as I will ever be," she said, her smile fading completely before she continued. "I should like to tell you something, about the siege." She hesitated, the distance in her gaze becoming yet more pronounced. "The child . . ." she began, the words soft and formed with a forced precision. "The child I failed to save in the evacuation. I found her the night the Spoiled came over the wall, wailing away in a ruined house, her parents gone or slaughtered. I was going to leave her. I was so terribly afraid, you see. I was at the barricade when the Spoiled and the Greens came charging out of the flames . . . And I ran. As far and as fast as I could, I ran and I ran. But I stopped when I heard that child crying."

"You saved her," Lizanne said.

"I picked her up, swaddled her as best I could and tried to find somewhere to hide until morning. A Red found us before I could. I had a small amount of product left. Luckily, it proved sufficient, though the beast put up quite a fight, I must say. In the morning I took the child to Mrs. Torcreek's hospital, intending to leave her in the care of more experienced hands. But the place was in such a terrible state, and what better hands to protect her than mine?" Her lips formed another smile, her face brightening with a cherished memory. "So I kept her, and I named her Aledina, my grandmother's name. It was my intention to formally adopt her on return to the empire, should we survive the evacuation . . ." The emotion drained from her face as she trailed off, taking several moments before continuing. "It wasn't the flames that killed her. I shielded her from those. But the heat sucked all the air out of the cabin, just for a few seconds, and her lungs were too small . . ."

Electress Dorice turned her face out to sea, eyes closed and expressionless save for the tear that trickled from the corner of her eye. Lizanne lowered her gaze, suppressing a grimace as memories of Carvenport's fall crowded in. "I'm sorry . . . " she began.

"No," the Electress said. "Do not be sorry. I came to thank you. You were right, I came to Arradsia in search of excitement. I was so terribly bored in Corvus. Life amongst the Imperial elite is an endless drudge of gossip and petty rivalry. I barely knew my own parents, so distant and wrapped up in their own prestige were they. I have had several lovers, none of whom I have loved. Only amidst war and horror did I discover what it feels like to love. A life without it is a barren, wasted thing, Miss Lethridge. Thanks to you, that fate, at least, has been denied me."

She took a small silver jewellery box from the pocket of her dress. "I would like you to have this," she said, offering the box to Lizanne. "I believe it may be of use in your future endeavours."

Lizanne accepted the box, opening it to find a small circular pin of plain silver adorned with the oak-leaf symbol of the Imperial crest. "This was yours?" she asked, unable to keep an incredulous note from her voice. "*You* were an agent of the Blood Cadre?"

"A mostly honorary position," the Electress said, apparently unruffled by Lizanne's scepticism. "But one that involves certain inescapable responsibilities." She met Lizanne's gaze before continuing, her expression intent and, as far as Lizanne could tell, completely sincere. "I tranced with the Blood Imperial this morning. He instructed me to acquaint you with certain facts regarding the Imperial Court. Firstly, everyone you will meet there is a self-serving liar, although I assume that won't come as any great surprise. Secondly, since infancy Emperor Caranis has suffered from a very unusual malady. For extended periods he will appear to be of an entirely rational, if somewhat coldly practical frame of mind. However, throughout his life there have also been periods when his behaviour could best be described as erratic. I am instructed to inform you that the Emperor's most recent erratic episode began three days ago."

"You mean he's mad?" Lizanne asked. She had assumed, given the Emperor's warmongering, that his character must possess some delusional elements. But the fact that he was truly unhinged had so far escaped the notice of Exceptional Initiatives.

"It means," the Electress said, "that your prospects of securing an alliance with the Corvantine Empire are now extremely remote."

"Is there no regent or proxy we can negotiate with?"

"For centuries the empire has run on one simple principle: all power rests in one man. Be assured, whatever order Caranis gives during his madness will be followed, and to the letter. During his last episode he ordered every remaining temple to the elder goddess Sethamet be destroyed and her followers purged from the empire. When some of his chamberlains pointed out that there had never, in fact, been an elder goddess named Sethamet, Caranis had them disembowelled for treason. So, the understandably unnerved surviving chamberlains set about creating the cult of Sethamet from scratch, building temples and hiring poor folk to worship her, even employing a group of theologians to pen a body of scripture. She had actually begun to build up a genuine following by the time they unleashed the purge. Hundreds died and the newly built temples were destroyed as per Imperial Dictum. When Caranis returned to sanity, he professed no knowledge of any such orders."

"Then this mission is hopeless," Lizanne said. "We may as well turn the ship about and go home."

"The Blood Imperial is very keen for you to continue the mission. He has something of considerable importance to share, but only with you."

Lizanne's thoughts returned to the design Bloskin had given her, and the curious tale of its origins. Had the Blood Imperial been behind it? A device to lure her here for purposes unknown. For an operative accustomed to relying on her own resources, the sense of being a piece in someone else's game was an unpleasant one. It reminded her too much of Madame Bondersil. "Can't you share it now?"

"I am not privy to it. Besides"—Electress Dorice nodded at the box containing the silver pin—"my tenure as a Blood Cadre agent has now come to an end. The Blood Imperial feels I am not best suited to the work. A judgement I find it hard to argue against."

She moved back from the rail, then paused. "I buried Aledina in the graveyard at the Church of the Seer near the bluffs east of Feros. It would ease my mind to know the grave will be cared for."

"Come back with us and care for it yourself," Lizanne said. "You are an ambassadress, after all."

The Electress gave another small smile and shook her head, turning to go before lingering awhile longer, as if compelled to share something further. "Did you know," she said, her voice soft and reflecting the sadness in her smile. "My family once ruled a kingdom even greater in size than the entire land-mass of Arradsia. When the empire swallowed it up they allowed the ruling house to keep its titles, even though they were now utterly powerless. And so I am permitted to call myself an Electress, a figure who once held sway over millions. Now, regardless of what titles I possess and all the finery with which I adorn myself, I am in fact no different from any other subject of the Emperor, and he has given me a command."

She inclined her head at Lizanne and walked away, leaving Lizanne to contemplate her gift. The pin sat in the box, a small piece of silver catching a dim gleam from the muted sunlight. *A token of esteem?* she wondered. *Or a marker for some nefarious design of the Blood Imperial?* She was decidedly unsure if she wanted to accept a gift from the most highly ranked Blood-blessed in the Corvantine Empire, fearing acceptance might signal some form of compliance. Diplomacy, it seemed, could be just as aggravatingly complex as espionage.

Sighing, Lizanne returned the pin to the box and gazed once more at the sea, glimpsing the first hazy shadow of land on the horizon. She had always suspected her profession would bring her to the Corvantine capital, though hardly under such odd circumstances. She had no target to assassinate, no secrets to steal. Just a tantalising clue to the existence of something impossible.

The *Profitable Venture* docked at Corvus the following morning. Lizanne joined the rest of the delegation as tugs pushed the ship towards the docks. A complement of riflemen was arrayed along the length of the port rail in impeccable order and the warship's every fitting gleamed with fresh polish. Lining the length of the docks was a full brigade of Imperial Household troops, complete with a musical band playing a bombastic interpretation of the Ironship Syndicate Anthem.

"Quite an effort they've made," Lizanne observed to Director Thriftmor, nodding at the three thousand or more troops arrayed up on the wharf.

"A demonstration of strength rather than welcome," he said in an unusually subdued voice. Lizanne noted the grim set of his features, an expression shared by the rest of the delegation, save one who appeared to be absent.

"Where is the Electress?" she asked.

"A steward found her in her cabin this morning," Thriftmor said. "The ship's doctor identified the poison as arsenic mixed with laudanum, presumably to dull the pain."

I am as well as I will ever be . . . Lizanne's hand went to the small box in her pocket. *A parting gift, apparently.* She clamped down on the upsurge of guilt and regret, choosing instead to regard the Electress's death as a useful reminder. She had resumed the role of an Exceptional Initiatives agent, a role that had no place for sentiment. "Was there a note?" she asked.

He shook his head. "There was ash on the port-hole in her cabin. It seemed she burned any papers in her possession."

Commanded to suicide either to silence her or at the whim of her mad Emperor? As yet, there was no way to tell which, but Lizanne fully intended to find out.

"She told me something yesterday," Lizanne said, seeing little point in concealing the information. "The Emperor is mad and this mission is a waste of time. I suggest you proceed with the formalities as quickly as possible then sail for home at the earliest opportunity."

He turned to her with a deep frown, his usual air of affable authority replaced by a certain cold calculation. "Thank you, Miss Lethridge," he said. "But I will decide how best to proceed, the Board having given me full authority in this matter."

"Not over me, Director."

From fore and aft came the distinctive rattle and splash of anchors dropping into the harbour waters. Sailors swiftly hauled the gang-plank into place and the ship's duty officer stepped forward to blow a piercing note from a whistle. An honour guard of Protectorate riflemen trooped down the gang-plank to the wharf. They lined up opposite a company of very tall Imperial Guardsmen flanking a clutch of Corvantine dignitaries in various garish finery.

"Whatever Bloskin sent you here for," Thriftmor said in a soft murmur as he took a step towards the gang-plank, "if it results in any disruption to this mission, rest assured I will not hesitate to disavow any knowledge of it and let the Corvantines have their way with you."

"I would expect nothing less, sir."

They were conveyed to the Imperial Sanctum in a convoy of ornate carriages, each gilded in gold and drawn by a team of white horses. The Sanctum was a sprawling complex of palaces, parks and temples occupying a full one-fifth of the capital. Their route was lined with yet more soldiers, standing two ranks deep in places, usually where the onlooking crowd was thickest or the surrounding buildings less opulent. Lizanne noted clusters of cheering people where the soldiers' ranks were thinnest, but in the more heavily guarded portions of the route the crowds were quiet and suspicious. Her gaze also picked out the tell-tale signs of recently repaired damage to several houses: patched up roofs and freshly painted walls that failed to conceal the scorch-marks beneath. *There have been riots here,* Lizanne mused. *And recently too. Military failure is never conducive to civil order.*

Naturally, it all changed when they entered the Sanctum. It was ringed by a wall of ancient appearance, twenty feet high and fifteen feet thick. The gatehouse through which they gained entry was in fact a fortress equal in size to anything produced during the Mandinorian feudal age. Once inside they were greeted by broad fields of neatly kept grass and copses of maple and cherry blossom.

"The Imperial Gardens," explained the plump man seated opposite Lizanne. She had been guided to the last carriage in the convoy where the fellow had introduced himself as Chamberlain Avedis Vol Akiv Yervantis. The quatra-nomina indicated he was both scholar and hereditary member of the ruling class, evidenced by the biased historical commentary he delivered during the journey. "Here we see the statue of General Jakarin, victor of the Second Great Rebellion, tragically and treacherously slain by the rebels to whom he had granted mercy on the field of victory."

Lizanne knew that, in fact, General Jakarin had been stabbed to death in a whore-house. It was an act of revenge undertaken by a prostitute who had seen her brother publicly tortured and executed on the general's order the day before. The chamberlain was the only other passenger in her carriage and Lizanne couldn't decide if he was simply the effete, over-privileged fool he appeared to be or might, in fact, be a particularly skilled Cadre agent in disguise.

"This may be hard to believe, my dear," Yervantis went on, as if her half-raised eyebrow had been a sign of deep interest, "but the gardens, and the entire Sanctum, were constructed on swamp land. Construction of the whole complex was commenced by Emperor Larakis the Good, who decreed that he would not rob his people of valuable land. Instead, the swamps, which had been a source of fever for generations, would be drained. Thereby, glory and duty would both be served."

"Wasn't Larakis the one who married his twelve-year-old sister?" Lizanne enquired. "And later had her poisoned when she failed to produce a male heir?"

The chamberlain blinked, managing to maintain the smile on his pear-shaped face. However, she did notice a beading of sweat amidst the sparse hair on his head. "I see you are something of a scholar yourself, Miss Lethridge," he said with a chuckle of forced joviality.

"Not particularly," she replied. "But I've often found a knowledge of Corvantine history to be useful. Tell me, Chamberlain, did you ever have the good fortune to meet Burgrave Artonin?"

The man's eyes widened before he blinked again, his eyelids performing several rapid flutters as fresh sweat broke out on his scalp. "Artonin?" he replied in a small voice.

"Yes. Burgrave Leonis Akiv Artonin, late hero of the Imperial Cavalry and a scholar of impeccable repute. I thought, given your shared interests, you may have corresponded with him at some point."

Yervantis said nothing, his now-unsmiling features wobbling as he shook his head.

"A pity," Lizanne said, turning back to watch the gardens pass by, knowing she would now enjoy a quiet journey. "I think you might have learned a great deal from him."

Beyond the gardens lay the Blue Maze, an intricate series of interlinked canals encircling the small city of palaces and temples that lay at the centre of the Sanctum. From her studies, Lizanne knew the maze to be as much a defensive fortification as an aesthetic feature. Its many bridges and ornately statued artificial islands were certainly pleasing to the eye, but she could see how no two bridges were aligned and the walkways constructed so as to funnel a large body of people into narrow and easily defended channels. Also, the number of Imperial Guardsmen in sight grew as they drew nearer to the Sanctum proper.

Chamberlain Yervantis found his voice again when they had begun to wind their way through the outer ring of temples. There were dozens of them, some grand and opulent, others barely more than a marble box, all built to honour the former emperors who had risen to godhood by the simple act of dying. "If I might draw your attention to a point of particular interest, my dear," Yervantis said, then coughed to clear the quaver from his voice.

Lizanne raised another eyebrow at him but he ploughed on valiantly. "The temple to the Emperor Azireh is now passing by on your left. I think you'll find the statuary particularly interesting."

She glanced out of the window, frowning at the sight of the temple. It was of average size compared to the others, but set apart by the fact that the crowning statue was female, whereas every other temple featured a male figure. "Azireh is a woman's name," she said, surprised.

"Quite so," Yervantis confirmed, an eager note creeping into his strained voice. "However, as a result of the massacres that marked the end of the third and final Regency War, she found herself the only surviving member of the Imperial dynasty."

"But no woman has ever sat the throne," Lizanne said.

"Indeed." Yervantis shifted his plump self on the carriage seat, leaning closer, close enough in fact for Lizanne to smell the lavender-scented oil mingling with the sweat on his skin. It wasn't a pleasant aroma. "As ordained by the first emperor," the chamberlain went on. "But, with no other possessing the Divine Blood left alive, she was able to negotiate this obstacle by having the Arch-Prelate of the Imperial Divinity declare her the living embodiment of Great Arakelin himself, essentially a man in a female body. Consequently, she was able to rule quite successfully for the better part of two decades."

Lizanne's gaze lingered on the statue. If the sculptor's eye was to be believed, Azireh had been slightly built with a fairly prominent nose and chin, but there was a certain implacable resolve in the gaze she cast out at her fellow rulers. "She must have been quite a formidable woman," Lizanne commented.

"Oh yes." Yervantis shifted closer still, causing Lizanne to respond with a warning glare. The Chamberlain gave a weak and entirely non-amorous smile before continuing, his voice now little more than a murmur. "And fond of riddles too. It's said there's a great treasure hidden somewhere in her temple, a treasure that can only be revealed under Nelphia's light. Many have tried to find it, at risk of death I might add, as the Imperial family has always guarded well the sanctity of their ancestors. But, after so many centuries, the treasure remains undiscovered." There was a weight to his gaze and voice now; a man attempting to convey meaning beyond his words, and in spite of a deeply felt fear.

Nelphia's light, Lizanne thought. *Nelphia is the only moon visible tonight.* "I've spent a surfeit of my life hunting for hidden treasures," she told the chamberlain, meeting his gaze and holding it for a second longer than necessary. "I must say, it's a mostly fruitless enterprise."

He gave a barely perceptible nod and leaned back, taking a silk handkerchief from his top pocket to mop his face. "Unseasonably hot, today. Ah!" He pointed to his right as another temple came into view. "See here, the monument to Emperor Hevalkis. Note the aquatic theme to the relief carvings, for Hevalkis was known as the Scourge of the Seas . . ."

One of the Sanctum's minor palaces had been given over in its entirety to housing the Ironship delegation. According to Chamberlain Yervantis it had been built three centuries before for the then-emperor's favourite concubine. Lizanne couldn't help but wonder if there wasn't some subtle insult in the current Emperor choosing to place his corporate guests in the home of a courtesan. A plainly attired servant guided her to her suite in the palace's eastern wing, no less than four spacious rooms arranged around a central pool complete with ornate fountain of somewhat erotic design. "The original occupant?" Lizanne asked the servant, nodding at the bronze woman at the centre of the carnal tableau.

"It's Yesilda, my lady," the serving-woman replied with a deep bow. "An elder goddess of passion and fertility."

"I thought images of the elder gods were frowned upon."

"Only those beyond the Emperor's sight, my lady. Those within the Sanctum dare not impugn his divinity, this being the centre of his holy power."

Lizanne searched the woman's face for some sign of mockery and smothered a laugh upon realising she was entirely sincere. "I . . . see," she said, glancing around. "My luggage?"

"It will be here momentarily, my lady."

After a thorough search, no doubt. Lizanne went to the fountain, resting on its rounded edge and playing a hand in the water.

"I can have it warmed, my lady," the serving-woman offered. "If you would like to bathe before dressing. The Welcoming Ball will commence in less than three hours."

"No, this is sufficient, thank you. But I would be grateful if you would fetch some tea."

Her bags arrived shortly after the tea, a rich blend of leaves from the empire's western mountains. Lizanne made no effort to sniff its aroma or display hesitancy in drinking it. The Emperor, even if in the throes of madness, would hardly summon her all this way for a mundane poisoning. In any case, it suited her for the serving-woman, who was much too keen of eye and toned of muscle for her station, to think Lizanne unworried for her safety.

After enjoying her tea she bathed in the fountain for a time. It was deep enough for her to float free, arms spread wide and eyes closed as her hair trailed in the water. Despite the water's soothing caress she found herself irked by the constancy with which Electress Dorice's face lingered in her mind. *Pampered, indolent and useless for most of her life . . . until the last few months.* The thought birthed a simmering heat in her chest, the same sensation that had gripped her when the Cadre had taken Tekela in Morsvale. *Anger is a distraction,* she reminded herself. *Vengeance is for amateurs.* But still, the heat continued to simmer.

After bathing she checked her luggage, confirming the tiny threads she had glued in certain places had been broken. The fact that whoever had performed the search hadn't bothered to replace the threads was more concerning than the search itself. *They don't care if I know.* Fortunately, whilst the search had evidently been thorough, it hadn't been expert. She touched a satisfied hand to the cosmetic and jewellery cases nestled in her chest, before casting a reluctant eye at the ball-gown Bloskin had insisted she bring. *A certain degree of finery will be expected,* he had said, before handing over the frilly monstrosity. *I'm told this is all the rage in Corvus, and it wouldn't do to disappoint the Emperor. By all accounts, he's quite taken with the legend of Miss Blood. Try not to disappoint him.*

CHAPTER 8

Clay

Silverpin smiled as she bled, uncaring of the dark red torrent rushing from the hole he had blasted through her. *He called me here for a reason,* her voice spoke in his mind, calm and rich in certainty. *A very old but very necessary design has been interrupted, and will now be resumed.*

"I didn't mean to," Clay said, reaching out for her as she collapsed, her blood spreading across the chamber floor to form the now-familiar crimson wings. But this time it was different, because she didn't die. Instead she stared up at him, face serene and accepting.

I was a monster, Clay. I deserved this . . .

"No . . ."

Millions would have died. Millions more enslaved. You saved them, for a time.

A great hiss of drawn breath drew his gaze and Clay found himself face-to-face with the White, its eyes full of malice and anger, mouth opening to reveal a haze of heated air as it summoned the flames from its guts. The fiery stream rushed forth, enveloping him in screaming agony. His skin blistered and peeled, his body twisted and deformed in the heat and through it all he heard a deep, grating rumble he knew was the sound of the White's laughter . . .

"Dammit, young 'un, wake up!"

Clay shuddered as the dream faded, blinking until Skaggerhill's broad, leathery features came into focus. The cabin they shared was still dark save for the dim moonlight streaming through the port-hole. "Ain't even morning yet," Clay groaned, pushing the harvester's hand from his shoulder.

"That pet of yours is acting up again. Your uncle's already had to stop one of the Corvies shooting it."

Clay muttered a curse, swinging his legs off the bunk and reached for his clothes.

He found Lutharon in the aft section, lowered into a defensive crouch amidst the circle of accumulated driftwood and purloined barrels he had crafted into a nest. Uncle Braddon, Preacher and Loriabeth had formed a cordon in front of the drake, facing down a half-dozen Corvantine crewmen. They were all armed with a variety of edged weapons and seemed disinclined to heed the placating words of their young officer. To his surprise, Clay found he could understand much of their babble despite never having spoken Varsal in his life. *Must be the trance,* he concluded. *Miss Lethridge knows it, so I know it.* It was a strange but welcome facet of Blue he hadn't known existed.

"The bugger nearly roasted me, sir!" one of the Corvantines said, the burliest one amongst them, brandishing the scorched arm of his jacket at Lieutenant Sigoral. "Ain't natural having that beast aboard. Blasphemous even."

Clay paused, deciding to experiment with his new-found ability. "You were told to stay away from him for a reason," he said in heavily accented but reasonably-well-phrased Varsal. "He doesn't like to be gawped at."

"Threw him some grub is all!" the burly man bridled, stepping forward with a sea-axe in hand. Sigoral moved into his path, snapping out a curt order to stand fast as the fellow's mates gave an angry murmur that bespoke imminent violence.

"Doesn't like to be fed, either." Clay stepped through the line of Contractors and moved slowly to Lutharon's side. The Black gave a low rumble of discontent but allowed Clay to touch a hand to his flank. "Like to hunt, dontcha, old fella?" he said, slipping back into softly spoken Mandinorian.

Lutharon's hide twitched under his palm and Clay sensed he was fighting an instinctive desire to flinch away. This was behaviour he had never exhibited in Ethelynne Drystone's company, but then she had practically raised him from an orphaned infant. During the first few days following Ethelynne's demise, Lutharon had followed Clay without question. He seemed fully capable of understanding his new master's moods and responding to his unspoken wishes thanks to whatever bond Ethelynne's final command had instilled. They had spent days ranging out over the

Coppersoles whilst Captain Hilemore oversaw the repairs to the *Viable Opportunity*. Clay's former fear of flight soon disappeared as they wheeled and soared above the mountains, the temporary joy a welcome respite from their shared grief. But since leaving Hadlock, Clay felt their connection fading with every passing day. Lutharon was becoming less placid in the presence of humans, more inclined to threatening growls or warning puffs of smoke whenever anyone but Clay came close. He had tried to strengthen the bond, spending as much time with the beast as he could, even drinking Blue and attempting to establish the kind of trance connection he had briefly shared with Silverpin. It didn't work, their bond continued to erode and Clay had an intuition as to why.

"Heart-blood," he murmured, smoothing his hand along Lutharon's ebony scales. "That's what I need, isn't it, old fella? And we ain't got any."

He stayed with Lutharon for several hours. Eventually the drake had calmed enough for the Corvantine officer to persuade his sailors to return to their duties. The Longrifles went back to bed when it became clear they weren't likely to return, though Braddon handed Clay a revolver just in case.

"Would've preferred the captain leave that lot behind," he said.

Clay shrugged and strapped the gun-belt around his waist. "Reckon so will they before this is done." He watched Braddon rest his arms on the aft rail, staring out at the passing ocean. It was calmer tonight, though the air grew colder with every southward mile they sailed and Captain Hilemore had assured them rougher seas were ahead.

"I don't know what's down there," Clay said. "All I know is what I saw in the vision, and that ain't much. Could be good. But the way our luck's been lately, I think we both know it's gonna be bad."

"The whole world's gone bad, Clay. You're the only clue as to how to make it good again." Braddon paused, lowering his head as if gathering resolve for his next words. "It was my fault," he said finally. "Silverpin . . . I knew something wasn't right. The hunger I had for the White. She did that to me."

"She did a lot to all of us," Clay said, hoping the flatness of his voice would forestall further discussion. He didn't relish the memories, or the dreams that might be stirred by talking about Silverpin.

"Took her into my home," his uncle reflected softly. "Treated her like my own daughter. All the time, she was waiting . . ."

Her blood, spreading out like wings . . . "Yeah," Clay muttered. "Well, now she's dead. Her, Scribes, Miss Foxbine and thousands of others, with a damn sight more to come. Just don't want you and Lori counted among 'em. Best you stay on the ship when we get to the Shelf."

His uncle had stiffened, turning to fix him with a hard stare. "Your cousin's a grown woman now. Seasoned gunhand too, and she knows her own mind. Just like her father. You ain't getting shot of us, Clay. Best get yourself accustomed to that."

Lutharon remained restless after Braddon returned to his cabin, the Black's claws dragged along the deck as his narrowed eyes constantly roamed the ship as if in fear of attack. Furthermore, Clay could feel a tremble beneath his skin that had nothing to do with fear. *Blacks don't mind the cold as much as Greens and Reds,* Skaggerhill had advised. *On account of them nesting in the mountains. But there's cold and then there's southern seas cold. And that's a whole other order of business.*

"I can't keep you," Clay said, giving Lutharon's hide a final pat before moving back. The drake gave a quizzical grunt as he swung his gaze towards Clay, sensing the change of mood. "Miss Ethelynne would've wanted you kept safe," Clay told him, hoping that speaking the words aloud would convey some meaning to the beast. "How long's it gonna be before this thing between us is gone for good? Then I won't be able to stop them shooting you, that's if the cold don't kill you first. 'Sides which, how you gonna hunt so far from land? You gotta go, old fella."

Lutharon became very still, staring at Clay with steady eyes that betrayed little understanding or reaction. Clay sighed in frustration. *Can't exactly shoo him away.* He searched his memories of Ethelynne for some clue as to how to sever their connection, then realised that she was the connection.

"You know she died," Clay said, filling his mind with visions of Ethelynne battling the White, her last few seconds of life as her small form vanished amidst the whirlwind of infant drakes.

Lutharon gave an abrupt growl, jerking as if prodded by a sharp blade.

"She died," Clay repeated, raising his voice and pointing at the northern horizon. "And you can't be here no more!"

Lutharon bared his teeth in a short growl, shifting from side to side, his claws raising more splinters from the deck.

"Go on, damn you!" Clay drew his pistol and fired a trio of shots into the air, causing Lutharon's growl to transform into a challenging roar. His wings flared as he lowered himself in preparedness for a lunge, tail coiling so that the spear-point tip pointed at Clay's chest.

"That's right," Clay told him. "I ain't friendly." He drew back the revolver's hammer for another shot but Lutharon whirled about, his great body transformed into a shadowy blur, tail whipping out to wrap around Clay's chest. It squeezed tight, forcing the air from his lungs, the pistol falling from his grip as the drake drew him closer.

The vision, Clay thought, more in hope than certainty. *Ain't my time yet.*

Lutharon's breath was hot on his face, hot enough to birth an instant sweat. The drake's growl subsided into a curious rattle, nostrils flaring as he sniffed Clay, breathing deep. For a second their eyes met, and Clay saw no anger in the beast's gaze. The slitted irises narrowed then widened, conveying a sense of understanding.

The tail uncoiled in an instant, leaving Clay gasping on all fours. A scrabble of claws on deckboard then the thunder of wings and Clay looked up to see Lutharon climbing into the night sky. The slender moonlight caught a gleam from his scales, outlining the great wings in silver for the briefest second, then Lutharon turned towards the north and was lost to sight.

"Captain's still awful mad at you," Loriabeth observed, joining him at the port rail. It was a week since Lutharon's departure, an event that had seen his stock with Hilemore fall several notches.

"The beast would have been very useful where we're going," he said, Clay noting how his voice grew softer the angrier he became. "I will thank you to consult me before taking such a drastic decision in future."

"He wasn't yours to command, Captain," Clay had replied with an affable shrug. "Nor mine for that matter. Besides, I owed the greatest of debts to his mistress, now it's paid."

Hilemore had let the matter drop, though it was clear Clay's continual lack of deference was a sore point. The succeeding week had been notable for the captain's keenness to avoid Clay's company.

"The sailors say this is where the Myrdin Ocean meets the Orethic," Loriabeth said, gazing out at the grey, choppy waves of the southern seas. "Supposed to make for a lotta storms, though we ain't seen one yet."

Clay wasn't particularly knowledgeable about maritime matters but judged the *Superior*'s current speed as far in excess of any coal-burner. "Looks like the captain's keen to get us to the Chokes as quickly as possible."

"So we just fetch up at this big spiky thing of yours and this whole mess is over, huh?"

"I don't rightly know, Lori. Doubt it'll be that simple, though."

"If Mr. Scriberson had made it out of the mountain . . ." she began, then trailed off as her face clouded.

"He'd surely have had some smart things to say about all this," Clay assured her. "I guess I miss him too."

Loriabeth turned her gaze out to sea and thumbed something from her eye. "Stupid," she murmured. "Barely knew him for more than a few weeks."

"It's long enough," he said, thoughts crowding with unwanted images of Silverpin. *Don't worry*, she had promised. *He'll let me keep you. His kind always had their pets.*

"You see that?" Loriabeth asked, now standing straight and alert, eyes fixed on the waves.

"See what?" Clay followed her gaze, seeing only the continual chop of an unsettled sea.

"There was something," she said. "Maybe a hundred yards out. Something rose up, just for a second."

"A Blue?"

"Maybe." She squinted. "Could've been back spines, I guess."

Clay stared at the ocean for a long moment, but whatever she had seen failed to reappear. He knew these waters were rich in whales of various breeds, but Scrimshine's warnings made him cautious. "You better go tell Mr. Steelfine," he said. "Just in c—"

His words died as the deck shifted beneath their feet, sending them both tumbling against the bulkhead. Clay cried out as his bruised back connected with an iron buttress, but Loriabeth's cry of distress dispelled any pain. The ship had shifted again, this time tipping to port at an alarming angle and sending Loriabeth skidding towards the rail. She hit hard and clung on as the ship continued to heave, her feet dangling over the edge. Clay could see the waves below, frothed into white by the *Superior*'s disturbed wake, then exploding upwards as the very large head of a Blue drake broke the surface, jaws gaping wide.

CHAPTER 9

Lizanne

"Miss Lizanne Lethridge, Ambassadress of the Ironship Trading Syndicate!" The Imperial Herald, resplendent in a long white coat adorned with gold braid, thumped an ebony staff on the marble floor, announcing Lizanne's entrance in ringing Eutherian. She stood in her appalling dress at the top of the ball-room steps, trying not to squirm as all eyes turned to her. Being noteworthy was not a sensation she enjoyed, chafing as it did on her long-instilled need for anonymity. The murmur of conversation died as the guests, at least three hundred of them, all spent a moment in silent contemplation of the fabled Miss Blood. Despite the Corvantine dead she had piled up at Carvenport, she could detect no obvious signs of enmity amongst these Imperial worthies. Most faces exhibited a keen, near-predatory curiosity, whilst others affected an amused air or even a blatantly lustful glance or two.

Everyone you will meet there is a self-serving liar, Electress Dorice had warned and one glance told Lizanne she may well have been right.

"My dear Miss Lethridge." Director Thriftmor politely detached himself from a gaggle of Corvantine ladies to greet her, offering his arm, which she duly took and allowed herself to be led down the steps. "How lovely you look," he said, making her wonder if he might be taking some pleasure from her discomfort.

"Thank you, Director," she replied. "It has long been my ambition to attend an Imperial function in the guise of a bedraggled flamingo."

"Oh tosh," he scoffed. "Though I would have chosen a darker shade of red. It would have done much to enhance your legend. Our hosts are always greatly impressed by symbolism."

"Vapid as it may be," she muttered.

"Well, quite." He steered her towards a group of courtiers near the centre of the dance floor, switching smoothly into Eutherian. "A very important personage has avowed a keen interest in meeting you."

The group all offered formal bows as they approached. There were four men of chamberlain rank and one woman, standing tall and elegant in a dress of crimson silk. The dress matched the woman's colouring perfectly, complementing her pale skin and dark red hair to impressive effect. Lizanne knew her name instantly, having seen her face in many a photostat over the years. However, she contrived to display the correct amount of surprise when Thriftmor made the introductions.

"Countess, I present Miss Lizanne Lethridge, late of Carvenport and Feros. Miss Lethridge, please greet Countess Sefka Vol Nazarias, Noble Commander of the Imperial Cadre."

Lizanne gave a curtsy of the appropriate depth and lowered her head in respect. "Countess."

"Miss Lethridge. How wonderful to finally meet." The woman's voice had a surprising warmth to it, the words spoken in the kind of Eutherian that came only to those raised in the Imperial Court. "Please rise," she said, extending a crimson-gloved hand.

So close, Lizanne mused, taking the offered hand and rising, her practised gaze lingering on the countess's bare neck and the vulnerable kill spots it contained. *Has any operative ever come this close, I wonder?*

"This must be very frustrating for you," Countess Sefka said, as if reading her mind.

"Countess?"

"Balls, meetings, parades and such. All terribly tiresome for those of us engaged in more practical pursuits, don't you think?"

"I'll happily suffer them all to win the Emperor's agreement. This mission being of such import to us all."

"Oh, well done." The countess glanced at Thriftmor with a raised eyebrow. "Have you been coaching her, Director?"

"I assure you, Miss Lethridge knows her own mind."

"Of that, I need no assurance." She hooked her arm through Lizanne's and led her away. "Let me rescue you from these dullards. Male company becomes tedious after a while, I find."

She guided Lizanne to a set of tall windows opening out onto a veranda, Lizanne's eyes instinctively picking out any shadowed alcoves which might conceal an assassin. "We're quite alone, I assure you," Countess Sefka said, once again intuiting her thoughts with irksome precision. "Come, let me show you the view."

She released Lizanne's arm upon reaching the veranda's balustrade, resting her hands on the marble to gaze out at the broad ornamental lake below. It stretched away from the palace's west-facing wing for at least two miles, the surface broken here and there by artificial islands bearing yet more temples. Each one was lit by a cluster of lanterns, giving the impression of a swarm of fire-flies frozen above a mirror.

"Beautiful, isn't it?" the countess asked, turning to Lizanne with a smile.

"What do you want?" Lizanne replied, removing the formal respect from her voice. Without witnesses present continued artifice seemed pointless, even a little insulting.

The countess gave a brief laugh, apparently immune to any offence. "Cannot two professionals share a pleasant view and exchange an anecdote or two?"

"You've been trying to kill me for years. Now you want a chat?"

"Certainly." Countess Sefka leaned closer, lowering her voice to a conspiratorial whisper. "The Sanctum is full of the empire's worst imbeciles. Centuries of inbreeding will do that, I suppose. You have no idea how long it's been since I had a truly interesting conversation."

"I'm sure any of your agents who made it out of Morsvale had many interesting things to say."

"Actually, none of them managed to escape the great calamity. But the reports I received prior to their demise made for interesting reading." She turned to rest her back on the balustrade, the humour on her face fading into a judgemental frown. "You compromised yourself to rescue a spoilt girl."

"I rescued a Corvantine turncoat with contacts who could get me out of the city. The girl was his price for co-operation."

"You're lying." Countess Sefka gave a regretful grimace. "You allowed yourself to be guided by sentiment. How very disappointing."

"I have not the words," Lizanne responded, the heat she had felt earlier returning to colour her voice, "to describe the level of my indifference to your disappointment."

"You should be more appreciative, for I speak only in friendly guidance. Sentiment is not just a luxury for those in our profession, it is in fact a debilitating disease. Take myself, for example. There was a young woman in Morsvale, a member of the Cadre of the Blood, so not under my direct control. But nevertheless, we had formed a close personal attachment prior to her deployment." The countess paused to smile in fond recollection before continuing in the same affable tone, "After your visit to her safe house, they told me there wasn't enough of her left to fill half a coffin. And yet, here I stand, without your still-beating heart clutched in my hands."

The dressmaker, Lizanne recalled, failing to find much cause for regret in the woman's demise. "From what I saw, you were well suited to each other."

"Sentiment *and* moral superiority." The countess pouted. "Upon finally meeting you I had expected to look upon my own reflection, only slightly younger. The record of your accomplishments paints a very different picture."

"Nothing I have done compares to anything in your career."

"Really? Torture and murder are the same, are they not? Regardless of the quantity."

The memory of that last visit to Burgrave Artonin's house sprang into Lizanne's mind; the scholar lying dead in his study, the servants sitting at table, each with a bullet blasted into the back of their skulls. "It depends on the subject," she replied, her eyes once again fixing on the countess's neck. *It would be so easy, even with no product in my veins.*

"Don't be silly!" Countess Sefka snapped, more irritated than angry.

Lizanne took a deep breath and turned away, shifting her gaze to the lake and its many glittering islands.

"Director Bloskin should have dismissed you," the countess said. "You have clearly been too . . . modified by your experiences. Whatever mission he sent you on is already doomed, you must know that."

"My mission is the same as Director Thriftmor's. Both the empire and the corporate world stand on the brink of destruction . . ."

"Oh yes, your army of drakes and deformed savages." Countess Sefka shifted her slim shoulders in a shrug. "Just another storm to assail this empire. We have stood against all manner of threats for centuries."

"Not like this. You imagine this great tyranny to be eternal, immutable. What's coming cares nothing for history."

"This great threat of yours is an ocean away, probably busy eating its own followers."

"You are not foolish enough to believe that," Lizanne said. "Otherwise, why spend so much time and energy pursuing the Mad Artisan's device?"

"Largely thanks to Madame Bondersil's increasingly deranged insistence. Was it you who killed her, by the way? The circumstances of her demise are a little vague."

"She was eaten, by a Blue drake." Watching a faint amusement play over the countess's face, she added, "Tell me, were you really going to allow her to govern Carvenport independently?"

"It was not a decision I was privy to. All aspects of her co-operation were handled by the Emperor in concert with the Blood Imperial."

A loud upsurge of martial drumming sounded from the open windows, soon joined by a chorus of trumpets. "Perhaps His Divinity will explain it all himself," Countess Sefka said, Lizanne noting how her jovial tone suddenly seemed a little forced. "It seems he's about to join us."

She started back towards the ball-room, then paused, offering Lizanne a smile. "Despite it all, I am glad we finally met, Miss Lethridge. Please accept a word of caution; whatever it is the Blood Imperial wants of you, tell the old vulgarian bastard to piss off and sail home. It's only going to get you killed."

"Emperor Caranis Vol Lek Akiv Arakelin!" the page boomed out and every person in the ball-room sank to one knee. "First of his name. Divine Emperor of the Corvantine Empire, High Admiral of the Imperial Fleet, Supreme Marshal of the Imperial Host . . ."

It took at least two minutes for the herald to recite the full list of the Emperor's titles, by which time Lizanne's knee had begun to ache quite painfully. When the titular litany finally ended she couldn't conceal a groan of relief as she rose to watch Emperor Caranis descend the ball-room steps at a sedate pace. He was a tall man, resplendent in a marshal's uniform of an ivory hue and a long cloak of black fur. The thorn-like barbs of his silver crown glittered as they caught the light from the chandeliers above. Corvantine propaganda often spoke of the Emperor's handsomeness, court-appointed poets penning lengthy verses praising his impressive physique and athletic accomplishments. Looking at him now, Lizanne concluded it might not all be exaggeration.

An elderly chamberlain stepped forward as the Emperor strode onto the ball-room floor, the man bowing and gesturing towards Director Thriftmor, who stood near by. "Divinity, might I crave the honour of presenting . . ."

"Where is *she*?" the Emperor cut in, his gaze roaming the ball-room. In contrast to his appearance, his voice sounded weak to Lizanne's ears. Deep but also discordant, as if he had trouble maintaining an even tone. "Where is the one they call Miss Blood?" he went on, tongue lingering on the final word as if tasting it.

The chamberlain gave another bow and turned towards Lizanne, beckoning her forward. "Miss Lethridge, Divinity," he introduced her. "Ambassadress . . ."

"I know what title they gave her," Caranis snapped, causing the chamberlain to blanch and take an involuntary backward step. The Emperor's attention, however, was entirely fixed on Lizanne as she approached and offered a deep curtsy.

"Yes . . ." Caranis said in a thin hiss as his eyes roamed Lizanne from head to toe. She tried not to return his stare, finding the awe on display highly disconcerting. "It is her. Sethamet's Bane made flesh."

Sethamet. She recalled Electress Dorice's warning. *His imaginary dark goddess.*

"Rise!" the Emperor commanded with an elevating wave of his hand. "And walk with me." With that Emperor Caranis turned about and strode back up the ball-room steps, leaving a vast silence in his wake. Lizanne's eyes flicked towards Director Thriftmor, who replied with a minimal shake of his head. *I cannot help you.*

Smothering a sigh, Lizanne raised the skirt of her ridiculous dress and followed the mad Emperor out into the night.

She found him striding across a gravelled path on the bank of the ornamental lake, obliging her to adopt an undignified trot in order to come to his side. A platoon of Household Guards patrolled the grounds, each armed with a repeating carbine and never more than thirty yards away.

"An impressive form you've chosen," Caranis said, sparing her a brief glance as he continued his purposeful march. His voice now possessed a brisk, business-like tone, as if greeting a trusted colleague rather than the servant of a long-standing enemy. "Pleasing to the eye, but not ostentatiously so. I suppose it must be useful."

He doesn't think me human, she realised. *Rather, some manifestation of his invented religion.* She had dealt with the deluded and outright insane before. Some required lies in order to become useful, whilst others responded best to the harsh, unalloyed truth. But none had possessed the power that rested in the hands of this particular madman.

"I have often found it so, Divinity," she responded, deciding bland agreement would be the best course.

"Does it age?" he enquired. "The shell you wear."

"It . . . ages as do all others, Divinity."

He grunted and nodded in acceptance. "Of course. Unnaturally prolonged youth would attract undue attention."

"My missions often require anonymity, Divinity," she said.

"Enough pretence!" he grated, coming to an abrupt halt and rounding on her. Lizanne kept all emotion from her face as he came closer, merely blinking as he spoke in a harsh, rapid whisper, "I'll have no more of this mummery. I am no more your superior than a bug is superior to the sun. Sethamet has set her beasts loose upon this earth and the Guardians have sent you as our deliverer."

Although she tried to conceal it, some measure of confusion must have shown in her expression, for he frowned, face darkening in uncertain suspicion. "You are sent by the Guardians, are you not?"

Realising the time for half-measures had passed, Lizanne straightened and met his wide-eyed gaze before replying in as flat and certain a tone as she could manage. "*We* know them by a different name."

He gave a sharp intake of breath, eyes flicking to the sides to ensure no one was listening. "Am . . . am I permitted to know it?"

"You will be, in time. Such knowledge must be earned."

"Of course," he murmured. "I do not . . . presume to overstep. But you must realise how much I have already sacrificed. My best troops sent to die by the thousand, little more than bait for Sethamet's horde. This I did because the Guardians commanded it, plaguing my dreams every night until I complied, risking yet more rebellion. I realise the import of drawing out her minions, but do they not know how vulnerable my position is?"

"The whole world is vulnerable to Sethamet's horde," Lizanne replied evenly. "This they know."

"Yes. Do not think I question their commands. When word reached me that you had arisen in Carvenport, I knew I had chosen the correct course. Who else but Sethamet's Bane could have defeated both my army and her vile horde?"

"Your insight does you credit. But we are far from done."

He nodded, face grave. "To prevent the Dread Goddess from seizing this world, I will give all I have."

"The Guardians will expect nothing less. However, at this juncture they require only two things. First, you will sign the treaty with the Ironship Syndicate, allying your forces with theirs to defend against the hordes of the Dread Goddess. They will push for an agreement to launch an immediate invasion of Arradsia, but this you will refuse. Their actions are driven by greed, keen as they are to restore the source of their wealth. Whereas your actions, Great Emperor, are motivated by compassion and love for humanity. It is for these virtues that the Guardians chose you."

He lowered his head in a servile bow, making Lizanne cast a cautious glance at the surrounding troops. An Emperor would never bow to a corporate underling.

"Stop that," she told him in a soft hiss. "Others must never know of your true role. They would not understand."

He straightened, features resuming a regal mask, though she saw tears shining in his eyes. "Forgive me," he whispered. "It is just . . . I am so humbled."

"Humility will not save us. But strength and wise leadership might. From this point on you must be Caranis the Great, the Warrior Emperor who will save the entire world. You will speak no more of Sethamet, for merely giving voice to that name renders power unto her."

He straightened further, blinking the tears away. "Yes. That . . . that makes things clearer to me now. It seemed strange that her power grew with every warning I gave." He met her gaze, features stiff with resolve. "What is the second thing?"

"Merely information. You must impart to me all the information you hold concerning the man known to history as the Mad Artisan."

A mystified frown passed across the Emperor's face. "The old legend Kalasin used to witter on about? One of his many obsessions." Caranis gave a rueful grimace. "In truth, I think my Blood Imperial may be a little touched in the head."

"Touched or not, the Artisan is of interest to Sethamet's minions, and also, therefore, to us."

"Then it pains me to confess I have little to tell you. Kalasin comes to me every now and again with his arcane stories, begging funds for expeditions or scholarly investigations. Usually, I endeavour to indulge him, his other qualities being so useful. I will have his archive seized and conveyed to you forthwith . . ."

"No," Lizanne cut in. Even in his madness the shock on the Emperor's face indicated this may have been the first time anyone had ever interrupted him. Lizanne maintained her composure, meeting his gaze with an unwavering stare until he recovered. "We must be circumspect," she went on. "There are far too many distrustful eyes in your court. Countess Sefka, for one."

"You think she plots against our purpose?" Caranis's voice held little sign of surprise. "She wouldn't be the first Cadre Commandant to succumb to treasonous intentions. I suppose a quiet disappearance would be preferable to public trial and execution. Rest assured, all intelligence will be extracted from her first."

Vengeance is indulgence, Lizanne reminded herself, though not without a pang of regret. "Best to leave her in place, for now," she said. "Under careful watch. She may lead us to other plotters in time."

He nodded and smiled in admiration. "Clearly the Guardians chose well."

"I wasn't chosen, I was made." She glanced back at the palace from where an orchestra could be heard playing an old waltz. "We should rejoin the ball."

"But what of the information you require from Kalasin?"

She dropped into a deep curtsy, head bowed low as if acknowledging dismissal. "Leave him to me, and know well how much the Guardians favour you." She looked up, meeting his gaze and colouring her voice with a harsh note of command. "Remember; never again speak her name. Now return to your court and prepare to save the world, oh Caranis the Great."

She lingered at the ball for another hour, noting how the other guests made scrupulous efforts to avoid her gaze and the only invitation to dance came from Director Thriftmor. Countess Sefka was also conspicuous by her sudden absence. It appeared holding the Emperor's favour made Lizanne something of a dangerous acquaintance to make.

"I'm afraid I find myself tired by the day's events, Director," she said to Thriftmor at the conclusion of their first and only dance. "I believe I shall retire."

"Of course," he said, offering a respectful smile that failed to alleviate the concern she saw in his eyes. "In the morning we must converse fully regarding your interaction with the Emperor."

"There's little to say," she replied. "Except that he's every bit as mad as we were told. However, I have a sense he will be amenable to your diplomacy. I bid you good night, sir."

Upon returning to her suite of rooms in the concubine's palace, her first act was to render the keen-eyed, well-toned servant unconscious. It required only a well-placed blow to the back of her head as the woman offered a respectful bow of incautious depth. Lizanne dragged the senseless woman to the bedroom, leaving her face-down on the bed with her head correctly positioned so she wouldn't choke to death whilst aslumber.

Quickly divesting herself of the appalling dress, she clad herself in nondescript dark cotton trousers and blouse. Knowing she would need to change later, she filled her waterproof pack with garb typical of that worn by a Corvantine woman of middling station. She then turned her attention to the case of cosmetics the now-unconscious serving-woman had helpfully placed on her dresser. Like the rest of her belongings the case had been thoroughly searched. Luckily, Countess Sefka's operatives had proven to be less than familiar with Jermayah's ingenuity, missing three separate hidden compartments, each opened by pressing certain key points in the correct sequence.

She opened the compartment in the lid first, extracting a set of metal components and a slim leather strap, which were swiftly assembled into a device of spidery appearance. This was Jermayah's refined design, achieved after a short but productive collaboration with Lizanne's father. It was less weighty and more easily broken down into concealable components, whilst also featuring a more efficient injection mechanism and expanded vials.

Lizanne strapped the Spider onto her left forearm then turned her attention to the large bottle sitting in the centre of the case's perfume rack. The Cadre had undoubtedly checked all the bottles for the presence of product, paying closest attention to the four smallest. At first glance, the larger bottle appeared no more than a pleasant but unremarkable concoction redolent of roses and cinnamon, the clarity of the liquid a pale and unintriguing contrast to the more opaque and colourful smaller bottles. Bloskin had assured her of the efficacy of this new trick from the Ironship plasmologists, but Lizanne couldn't suppress a lingering pang of worried scepticism as she opened another compartment and extracted a stoppered vial containing a dark, viscous substance.

It's all to do with molecular weights, apparently, Bloskin had said back in Feros on the day of her departure. *Bind them with a correct mix of chem-*

ical agents and they combine into an inert, colourless liquid, though I'm told it's a bitter brew so don't be tempted to drink it. Simply add a little something to dissolve the binding agents and all four colours will instantly revert to their original state.

Has this been used in the field before? she had asked and saw with some surprise that Director Bloskin was a poor liar.

Of course, my dear, he said, lighting another cigarillo. *I'd hardly send my best agent off with an untried compound, now would I?*

So it was with some relief that she saw the liquid in the bottle change as soon as she added the contents of the vial. After a short interval of confused swirling the four colours duly arranged themselves into layers. Taking a long pipette from the compartment Lizanne began to carefully extract enough product to fill the Spider's vials. It was frustratingly delicate work but, as she had no intention of facing the approaching encounter without product, there was no alternative.

Upon completing the task she opened the case's third compartment and extracted a slender dagger, the seven-inch blade encased in a leather sheath, which she strapped to her ankle. Jermayah had offered to modify the case to accommodate his redesigned Whisper but there hadn't been time. He offered a number of miniature fire-arms but Lizanne had always eschewed such weapons; they were too noisy and lacking in effectiveness to make the risk worthwhile, leaving the dagger as her only realistic alternative.

Lizanne paused briefly by the bed to ensure the serving-woman's breathing remained regular, then proceeded to the upper floor, emptying the remaining contents of the perfume bottle into the fountain on the way. She made her way to a balcony before clambering onto the roof, crouching low and injecting a burst of Green to allow for a thorough examination of the surrounding palace grounds. It made for a depressing view; numerous Household troops patrolled the environs and even with a full dose of Green and Black she doubted she could make it across even two of the bridges in the Blue Maze before being discovered. There was the option of proceeding across the maze and methodically killing or incapacitating the guards en route, but that would exhaust her product in short order, not to mention having a parlous effect on Director Thriftmor's upcoming negotiations.

Lizanne gave a soft groan and moved to the roof's edge where she began to clamber down the north-facing wall of the palace. She didn't relish the task ahead but there was nothing else for it; she had a very long swim to make.

She climbed free of the maze some two hours later. The swim through the labyrinth of canals had been both mentally and physically taxing, forcing her to inject repeated small doses of Red to stave off the water's chill as she followed the map she had memorised aboard the *Profitable Venture*. The patrolling guards had also been a considerable nuisance, frequently appearing to scan the water-ways with commendable if annoying scrutiny, forcing her to remain submerged for several minutes at a time and further denuding her stocks of Green and Red.

She wasted no time on clearing the maze, injecting yet more Green to enable a sprint into the concealing marble jungle of the temple ring. It took only a short while to find the tomb of Empress-cum-Emperor Azireh, Lizanne having marked its location thanks to Chamberlain Yervantis's clumsy hints that morning. She made a wide circuit of the structure before approaching, finding no sign of anyone else in attendance. Lizanne read the archaic Eutherian inscription above the tomb's entrance as she came closer: *Greatness can rest in the most fragile vessel.* Pausing to take in the sight of the Divine Azireh's marble features in all its hawk-nosed imperiousness, Lizanne doubted this woman had ever exhibited a moment of fragility in her life.

Touching a tentative finger to the solid oak door covering the tomb's entrance, she was unsurprised to find it unlocked. *Got here early,* she surmised, flexing her fingers over the Spider's buttons before pushing the door fully open. For a second she saw only blackness, until the faint moonlight illuminated enough of the interior to reveal the curved bulk of Azireh's sarcophagus and the pale grey cascade of hair crowning the head of a stooped man leaning heavily on a walking-stick. The long grey tendrils shifted as the man turned to her, his features lost to the gloom. There followed a moment of mutual scrutiny, seeming to last quite some time to Lizanne though in fact it couldn't have been more than a few seconds. Finally the grey hair swayed again as the stooped man gave a short, irritated wave with his stick.

"Close the fucking door, love," the Blood Imperial told her, speaking in Varsal, his accent coarse, aged and distinctly lacking in nobility. "And let's get on with it, eh?"

CHAPTER 10

Sirus

Fire!

The volley crashed out in a single, jarring blast, each bullet fired at exactly the same instant. The targets, wooden man-shaped facsimiles positioned one hundred yards from the line of Spoiled marksmen, each received a simultaneous hit dead centre of the chest. Sirus watched the Spoiled reload their rifles with an uncanny, synchronised uniformity. At first their contingent of riflemen had consisted of former soldiers and constables, all possessed of an ingrained familiarity with fire-arms. Now their number had swollen to over six thousand and included Spoiled-born tribesfolk as well as converted townspeople. They fired as one, reloaded as one and marched as one, all guided by the expert, if often tortured mind of their new general.

Grand Marshal Morradin had reacted badly to his conversion, emitting a rising howl of rage and disgust as his fingers explored his remade features before launching himself at Sirus. The marshal's large, vise-like hands came close to crushing Sirus's windpipe before the collective will of the other Spoiled closed in. Sirus had seen the change in Morradin's eyes as his hands slipped to his sides, the murderous intent drowned under a barrage of invading thoughts. But still he resisted, Sirus sensing a ball of rage and defiance simmering away at the core of his mind.

That is unwise, Marshal, Sirus warned him. *He will expect complete obedience.*

The marshal's eyes flashed at him, the deadly promise shining clear and bright for a brief second before his rage subsided once again. Sirus felt the reservoir of defiance diminish further, subsiding into a fluttering spark, weak but not yet completely extinguished.

Very good, Sirus told Morradin. *Now, it's time for you to begin your task.*

Thanks to his father's influence Sirus had avoided conscription into the Imperial army, but his extensive historical knowledge told him that successfully training a body of soldiers required months, if not years. Grand Marshal Morradin, however, managed it in barely two days. The ability to convey orders directly without use of subordinates or messengers greatly accelerated all aspects of the process. The abilities of their most expert marksmen were instantly communicated to every soldier. The gunners allotted to their small collection of cannon had learned the art of gunnery from the sole artilleryman to survive the city's fall. They all now also possessed deadly hand-to-hand combat skills thanks to the knowledge shared by the tribal warriors amongst them.

However laced with self-loathing it might be, Sirus could feel Morradin's pride at what he had accomplished. They stood together on a raised dais overlooking the Morsvale garrison parade-ground, watching the mass of Spoiled soldiery perform a sequence of manoeuvres. They formed companies, squares and skirmish lines with a swiftness and precision that would have shamed even the Household Guards

An army to conquer a world, wouldn't you say? Sirus asked him.

A flare of anger coloured the marshal's reply along with a grudging if inescapable expert recognition of the power of what he had created in so short a time. *Trained the Household Division myself,* he mused. *Years of drill, route marches and floggings. Made them the best three legions ever to march under an Imperial banner. But this . . .* He waved a clawed hand at the unnaturally even ranks of the companies on the parade-ground, his scaled lips twisting into a mirthless grin. *This is a kind of legion never seen before. A legion of flame, with which our monster-god will burn the world to cinders.*

Sirus had initially tried to caution Morradin's thoughts but soon gave it up as the White appeared utterly indifferent to their personal exchanges. Every task it demanded of them was done, swiftly and completely. If those it commanded chose to hate one another, so be it. Sirus often wondered at the level of their master's ambivalence towards its slaves. *Are we no more than useful beasts of burden? Does it look on us as we looked upon its kind?*

Don't flatter yourself, boy, Morradin growled in his mind. *We're lower than maggots to that thing.*

And yet it needs us. Sirus nodded at the mass of troops as their ranks split apart then came together again in response to the marshal's unspoken commands.

For now, Morradin replied. *Makes you wonder what it'll do with us when it's done.*

They launched the last barge two days later. The initial quota of fifty had been increased to a hundred, far more than necessary to transport their entire force. *It's expecting reinforcements,* Morradin explained. The marshal was still on the parade-ground whilst Sirus now stood on the wharf watching his Spoiled work-force secure tow-lines from the ships to the barges. He had come to understand that the power enabling them to share their thoughts was not limited by distance, but the connection was stronger with some than others. Katrya's mind was like an open box, every emotion and memory there for the taking. By contrast, Majack remained a largely blank vessel filled with the White's purpose, as did most of the Spoiled, especially the tribesfolk. The memories of the native Arradsians were a best-avoided mélange of unfamiliar custom, violence and hardship. Strangely, despite their mutual antipathy, his strongest bond besides Katrya was with Morradin. It was as if dislike, or more truthfully, hatred, could breed as much closeness as love.

The marshal's memories were a curious mix, blazing bright when they touched on his many victories, brighter still at the unfolding spectacle of slaughter. However, they dimmed whenever they turned to the personal. An arranged marriage to a woman he barely knew, who soon grew to despise him. The children they produced, a son and daughter, growing into disappointing, rarely acknowledged shadows of his greatness. Morradin's cruel indifference to his children caused Sirus to wonder if his resentment of his own father had been entirely justified. He had been harsh at times, certainly, but when contrasted with this war-loving monster it became apparent to Sirus that his father had merely been a widowed man trying, in his own faltering way, to raise a son as best he could.

A loud and familiar cry sounded over the docks as the White came soaring out of the sky. A gaggle of Reds followed in its wake, led by the huge drake with the scarred face. Sirus had taken to calling this one Katarias, the darkest of the elder Corvantine gods. Legend had it that Katarias had ruled the whole world with depraved malice for a hundred years before his fellow gods cast him into the fire beneath the earth. This Katarias possessed all the cruelty of his divine namesake, having killed at least a dozen Spoiled in as many days, picking out the weak or infirm with a predator's expert eye. Whereas the shared connection permitted some sense of the White's mind, Katarias and the other drakes under its sway remained closed to Sirus and the other Spoiled. But, although he couldn't hear his thoughts, the enmity with which Katarias viewed the formerly human inhabitants of this city was plain in its every, baleful glare and the evident glee it exhibited whenever it feasted on a meal chosen from amongst their ranks.

The White settled on the part-ruined building atop the harbour wall where it made its nest. The clutch of infant Whites screeched out a greeting as it landed amongst them, crowding round to nuzzle its flanks, wings flapping in excited adoration. The White enclosed them all in its wings, issuing a low growl of paternal affection. After a moment it moved back, glancing up at Katarias circling above. The Red obediently folded its wings and descended to deposit something in the nest, something with two legs and two arms that managed to issue a plaintive, hopeless scream before the infant Whites tore it to pieces.

Another unfortunate from Carvenport, Sirus decided. *Or some wayward Contractor found in the Interior.* He wondered if there was any significance in the fact that the infant Whites only ever fed on human prey. He had seen the other drakes feed on livestock as well as humans, but not the White's brood.

It's training them, Morradin told him. *Making it so that's all they'll ever want to eat. When we go forth from here, they'll eat the whole world, boy.*

Katrya came to him after dark, as had become her nightly ritual. Their couplings, performed in full view of the other Spoiled since privacy was a meaningless concept now, seemed an inevitable consequence of joining minds so deeply. As they coiled together he could feel those other Spoiled similarly occupied throughout the city, their lust mingling to make the experience ever more compulsive. He knew he should have been disgusted by this, repelled by the spines and scales that marked Katrya's face and body, violated by the fact that every sensation was shared with so many others. But the intoxication of it was overwhelming, irresistible.

Did it made us like this for a reason? he pondered later as they lay entwined, finally spent, Katrya's contented slumber a low hum in his mind. *Something else to keep us bound to its will?*

Katrya gave a faint moan of distress as his thoughts turned to Morradin's words that day: *They'll eat the whole world.* He had learned that sober reflection tended to mute the interest of the other Spoiled, the lack of emotion partially masking his thoughts. But draining his mind of feeling was never easy, especially when the marshal's prediction led inevitably to thoughts of Tekela. He knew it was likely she had perished by now, if not during her flight from Morsvale then in Carvenport along with so many others. But a nagging sense of hope convinced him otherwise. She lived, somewhere beyond his sight, but not beyond the scope of the White's ambition.

He drifted into his dreamless sleep picturing her face, as caustically indifferent as he remembered, but this time drenched in blood.

The reinforcements arrived the next afternoon, emerging from the jungle beyond the southern wall in their dozens, then hundreds, then thousands. More Spoiled-born summoned from the Interior. The disparate tribal origins were evident in the wide variety of clothing they wore. Some had feathers in their hair, whilst others had skin etched all over with decorative scars. They were all men and women of fighting age, Sirus finding not a single child or old one among their ranks. Touching their minds briefly brought an explanation: children trotting in the wake of silent and indifferent parents marching steadily north, cuffed or cut down when they became a hindrance. Soon all the children were left behind to fend for themselves. The White had no use for those too small to fight.

By nightfall the White's horde had grown to ten thousand, rising to twenty come the following morning. Morradin absorbed them all into his army with typical efficiency and soon they were drilling with the same uniform precision as the others, though only about half possessed fire-arms. The fleet of ships and barges were loaded with provisions and ammunition, their cannon hauled aboard and every engine turned over in preparation for an imminent voyage. Sirus could feel the excited anticipation of the others, even sharing it to some extent though the prospect of what lay ahead stirred his dread in equal measure. He also sensed a change in Morradin's mood, the self-recrimination lessening as the prospect of conflict loomed. For a man whose soul appeared to be stirred only by triumph in war, the coming tribulation was as irresistible as Sirus's nightly surrenders to lust.

The White watched the preparations in silence until the last Spoiled had trooped aboard barge or ship, then raised its head and gave a vast cry. Its command spread through them all in an instant, the most powerful and implacable urge it had yet birthed in its horde of slaves: *North*.

CHAPTER 11

Lizanne

"What did that bitch Sefka tell you?" the Blood Imperial enquired, long-nailed fingers twitching on the curved head of his walking-stick. His entire bearing was that of an old man struggling to maintain posture despite a host of aches and pains. However, his eyes were bright and steady behind the veil of lank grey hair. "Said you should tell me to stuff it, didn't she?"

"Why don't we sit down?" Lizanne suggested, nodding at an alcove towards the rear of the tomb.

The Blood Imperial gave a faint huff before making a slow progress to the alcove, Lizanne casting a cautious glance at the door as the brass tip of his cane drew an echo from the flagstones.

"Nobody's coming, love." The old man sighed as he sank onto the narrow bench set into the alcove. "You can be sure of that."

Lizanne perched herself on the edge of the plinth supporting Empress-cum-Emperor Azireh's sarcophagus, taking a moment to scan the tomb's interior in greater detail. "So, have you ever found it?" she asked. "The great treasure revealed only by Nelphia's light."

"Years ago," he said, rubbing his knee. "Wasn't really treasure. It was a scroll hidden in the lintel. Some of the letters are carved to a different depth, only becomes obvious when Nelphia's at the right elevation. Took me years to work out the correct sequence to press. When I did, a scroll popped out of a hidden compartment. Clever old cow, Azireh."

"What was on it?"

"A list, all the people she'd killed over the years. Not the executions, you understand, because Azireh was renowned for her mercy. No, this was all the noble shit-eaters and trouble-makers she'd had poisoned or arranged to fall victim to an unfortunate accident. It was a long list. I suppose it was some sort of confessional, unburdening her soul before making the final journey into godhood. Would've transformed our understanding of her reign completely, if I hadn't burned it."

"Why do that?"

She saw his mouth twitch behind the grey veil. "You met our Divine Emperor tonight. Mad as a Blue-addled monkey, isn't he?"

Lizanne maintained a neutral tone as she replied, "He had some interesting notions to impart."

"Let me guess, you're some sort of holy incarnation sent to help him defeat Sethamet's demon horde." The Blood Imperial shook his head. "Every time he slips into this state his delusions get a little more complex, but at least they're consistent. His father always said we should've drowned the little fucker, and he wasn't exactly the straightest arrow in the quiver, either. It's how it is in this empire, love. The mad and the inept become gods. It's an absurd and ancient pantomime, and it works, but only if everyone stays in character. Azireh, the only woman ever to sit the throne, was a wise and magnanimous ruler who founded a dynasty that would one day produce our current beloved Caranis, and that's how she'll stay."

Lizanne noted that his hands had stopped twitching, making her wonder as to the true state of his infirmity.

"You killed a lot of my best people," he said. "The Blood Cadre is a bit like a family, there being so few of us, comparatively speaking. They look on me as a father of sorts, and many of my children want justice for their murdered brothers and sisters."

"Killing in war isn't murder," Lizanne replied. "And I lost plenty of good people in Carvenport, if you want to compare butcher's bills."

"Oh, don't mistake me." He shrugged and gave a dismissive wave of his stick. "Been many a year since I took any of this stuff personally. Just a word of caution, not all my kiddies can be counted on to help in our endeavour."

"And what exactly is our endeavour?"

"The defeat of the White Drake and its terrible minions, of course. With the help of the Mad Artisan, or whoever it was set down that marvellous design I sent to Director Bloskin. How is the old bastard, by the way? Still smoking too much?"

"Considerably. Since you sent the design, I assume you can point me to its creator."

"Wish it were that simple. Got it by a roundabout route, y'see. Passed through a dozen hands before one of my kiddies chanced upon it when she was doing a little job for me up north. It was in a box of documents the former owner no longer had a use for. An investigation of tedious length eventually tracked it back to a retired member of the Imperial Constabulary who, after some gentle persuasion, explained that the design had been amongst a number of keepsakes he'd helped himself to during his last posting."

"And where might that be?"

The Blood Imperial smiled, revealing oddly white teeth for a man of his age. "Scorazin, love. You'll find whoever drew it in Scorazin."

She stared at him for a long moment, watching his smile fade and eyes narrow in expectation.

"You expect me to infiltrate the Emperor's prison city," she said.

"Indeed I do."

"You have your own agents. Use them."

"Already tried it. Sent my two best. The first one lasted three days, the second managed four. You may not have heard, but Scorazin isn't a very nice place and getting product through the gates is practically impossible. But, if anyone can get in there and find the Artisan, it's you. Why else d'you imagine I sent the design to Bloskin?"

"I'll have the Emperor scour the place. He'll do anything for Sethamet's Bane, after all."

"Won't work, love. It's fair odds he'll have returned to sanity by the morning and won't even remember meeting you. Even if he hasn't, you must have realised by now that not everyone in this court shares my desire to preserve the current state of affairs. Countess Sefka's been plotting my downfall ever since she took control of the Cadre, and she isn't alone. Certain long-standing interests don't like a gutter-born upstart like me having so much influence over the Emperor. Nor do they appreciate so much power resting in the hands of a Blood-blessed. They'd much prefer it if we went back to being the slaves of the elite, and that I won't have. You might persuade Caranis to tear Scorazin apart in order to find the Artisan, but would he even be findable amidst so much chaos? Besides which, it'll be a clear signal to Sefka and her cronies that something of great value to me resides in that city, intelligence I've so far managed to keep from her. No, my dear

Miss Lethridge. You want the Artisan, you'll have to go in there and get him."

"And having done so, just hand him over to you, I assume?"

"Better in my hands than Sefka's, believe me. She looks upon the drake threat as a minor inconvenience. You and I know better. You do have my firm assurance, however, that whatever useful information he provides will be shared with the Ironship Syndicate."

He's probably lying, Lizanne decided, but knew it didn't really matter since she had no intention of taking the Artisan anywhere but Feros, assuming she could even find him. Everything she had heard of Scorazin told of a seething cesspool of degraded humanity forced to work in the mines beneath the city for scraps of food. However, her career had taken her to many terrible places and none had yet managed to kill her, or thwart her various missions.

"Very well," she said.

The Blood Imperial's hair parted as he nodded in satisfaction, revealing eyes, as bright and steady as a youthful soldier's, bespeaking an intelligence undimmed by age or frailty. "You'll need this," he said, taking a folded piece of paper from his pocket and handing it to her. "Can't go to prison without a crime."

Lizanne unfolded the document, finding a formal judgement from the Corvus Magistrate with a long list of charges, each one stamped with the word "guilty" in red ink. "Prostitution?" she asked him, raising an eyebrow.

"And extortion. You are an expensive courtesan who unwisely took to blackmailing a client, a senior official in the Imperial Treasury. Tragically, he'll be taking his own life about an hour from now, leaving a suitably incriminating suicide note. The Corvus Magistrate will deal with the matter in circumspect fashion to avoid embarrassment to the family. I have an escort standing by to take you directly to Scorazin." His bony hand disappeared into his pocket once more, coming out with a small vial of product. "Once we have established our connection . . ."

He fell silent as Lizanne slowly ripped the magistrate's judgement in half and let the pieces fall to the floor. "Understand me," she said in a low and controlled tone, matching his purposeful gaze with her own. "I do not work for you. I will make my own way to Scorazin and have no part of this amateur farce of a cover story. And if you imagine for one second I would ever trance with you, you're as mad as your Emperor."

She rose and moved to the door, making it to the top step before the tip of his stick rang loudly on the flagstones. She paused as the harsh grate of his voice, now sounding far from aged, filled the tomb. "And you imagine I will simply let you loose in this empire?"

She turned to face him, fingers poised over the Spider. "You will if you want the Artisan."

He was just a dim shape in the gloom now, though she could see his pale hands clenching the walking-stick in barely controlled fury. After a moment he calmed, the hands relaxing, though she knew this to be artifice. *I do believe this man intends to kill me when I'm done,* she thought, taking perverse comfort in the realisation. With one such as he, the choice was either subservience or deadly antipathy, and she preferred the simplicity of the latter.

"As you wish, love," he said, voice receding into the same uncultured rasp. He got slowly to his feet and hobbled towards her, the anger stripped from his gaze. "But, before you go, do me the favour of settling an old man's curiosity."

She put a hand on the door and pushed it slightly ajar, gazing out at the silent tombs. He would have some of his people out there somewhere, all Blood-blessed and apparently riven with a vengeful impulse. She could only hope they wouldn't act without his explicit instruction. "What is it?" she asked.

"The expedition Madame Bondersil sent in search of the White. I assume one or both of you were in trance communication with their Blood-blessed, the boy, Torcreek was it? My last intelligence on their whereabouts came from an operative in Edinsmouth, shortly before he had his head blown off. Director Bloskin was kind enough to elucidate on their eventual success in discovering the White, but I do wonder what became of them in the aftermath."

"They were attacked by Spoiled during the journey south from the mountain. My last trance with Mr. Torcreek indicated his companions were all dead and he had suffered a mortal wound."

"Ah." She could tell from the way he averted his gaze that he didn't believe a word of it. "What a pity. One who had actually met the White face-to-face and lived would have been very valuable."

Hence my desire to keep him very far away from your pestilent influence. "It's time I left," she said, pushing the door fully open and sparing him a final glance. "You'll hear from me when I have the Artisan."

"And if you fail?"

"Then you'd best hope your mad Emperor can marshal sufficient force to stop what's coming." With that she injected a burst of Green and sprinted off into the gloom.

Escaping the Sanctum took the rest of the night and the sun was climbing over the roof-tops by the time Lizanne made her way into the city proper. Several double-backs and sudden changes of direction revealed no sign that the Blood Imperial's operatives had managed to track her. Either that, or they were too skilled for her to detect them, which she thought unlikely. Even so she took every precaution before proceeding to her destination. She had changed into her nondescript clothing after scaling the Sanctum's outer wall and affected the tired, stooped walk of an underpaid worker released from a night-shift in the manufactory or cotton-mill. There were many such folk about in the small hours, providing useful camouflage as she made her way to the tea-shop.

The woman behind the counter was of pleasingly plump proportions and smiled affably as Lizanne said good morning. The woman's apple-cheeked cheerfulness slipped somewhat when Lizanne asked if she had any Sovereign Black. It was a spicy and expensive blend from northern Dalcia and virtually impossible to find since the Emergency. Meaning very few customers would be likely to ask for it.

"We have none," the tea seller replied, eyes flicking towards the window and the street outside. *She's not best suited to this,* Lizanne judged, seeing how the woman's hands fidgeted on the counter. "We, ah." The woman frowned as she struggled to remember the correct response. "We do have Red Drake's Breath though."

"That would be very acceptable."

The woman glanced at the street once more before raising the flap in the counter and beckoning Lizanne through to the store-room. "Wait here," she said in a whisper before proceeding ahead into the gloomy interior.

Lizanne heard the sound of a coded knock, two quick raps then three more, followed by the scrape of wood on wood as something heavy was hauled aside. A brief, quiet exchange of voices and the shop-woman reappeared. "Go on in," she said, moving past Lizanne and returning to the outer shop.

She found Arberus waiting at the entrance to a hidden room, a small lantern glowing at his back as he stood holding a concealing stack of shelves to one side. "You found it then?" he asked, speaking in Mandinorian and grinning a little.

"Varsal only," she admonished him, coming closer. "The shop-lady seems a little too nervous for a revolutionary."

"Nervous or not she's fully committed to the cause. The Cadre killed her fiancé for owning a printing-press. Her parents own this place but are thankfully too elderly to visit much. Plus, the local constabulary are appreciative of the free tea she provides."

Lizanne paused to press a kiss to his cheek before proceeding into the hidden alcove. It was of typically orderly appearance. Arberus would probably never shake off the military habits of a lifetime, even if it had all been artifice.

"This room is well soundproofed," he said, a slightly hopeful note in his voice as he slid the concealing shelf-stack back into place.

"I made my position on that matter clear aboard ship," she replied. "I assume your desertion was accomplished without difficulty?"

"The Director's man had me conveyed ashore in an empty rum cask. By now I expect he's expunged my name from the ship's rolls."

"And your contacts in the Brotherhood?"

"Diminished but still active. I'm afraid I've had to make certain promises to secure their co-operation."

"Presumably they know the importance of our mission? If this world falls then all their deluded ambitions will be meaningless."

"Arradsia is thousands of miles away, and the Brotherhood's crusade has spanned generations. Rest assured, the revolution will always come first."

Lizanne gave a small sigh of discomfort. Dealing with people steeped in dogma was never something she relished, but time was short and she had no other allies at hand. "Arrange a meeting," she said. "I'll need all the information they can provide on Scorazin."

He stared at her in unblinking silence for several seconds. "Scorazin?" he asked finally, a hard edge to his voice.

"The Artisan is most likely there. So that is where I need to go."

"Or I could just shoot you now and save time."

"We are faced with a distinct lack of alternatives." She undid her shoes and took them off, lying back on the bed with an arm across her eyes. All vestige of product had faded from her veins and her body was beginning to feel the exertions of the previous night. "I need to rest, Major. Please go and do as I ask."

"One million in gold, not exchange notes or Imperial currency." The young man spoke in soft but strident tones. He was of slight build with pale, freckled skin and a shock of red hair Lizanne's tutors would have ordered him to dye black had he been recruited to Exceptional Initiatives. Arberus had introduced him as Korian, a code-name borrowed from Corvantine antiquity. Korian had been one of the seven divine brothers fabled to have built Corvus after being cast out of the gods' heavenly abode. If Lizanne recalled rightly, Korian had been murdered by his brothers for the crime of coming to love the mere mortals who laboured in their service. His death sparked the revolt that brought down the brothers' dominion and established the first ruling Corvantine dynasty. Historians considered the whole tale a fanciful myth but it had provided inspiration aplenty for Corvantine subversives for centuries.

"Plus twenty thousand rifles with two hundred rounds apiece," Korian went on. "We will also require all intelligence the Ironship Protectorate holds on Imperial military deployments."

Yet another uprising in the offing, Lizanne concluded. *Don't they ever get tired of this?* "Done," she said, suppressing a grin at the youth's surprised frown. Evidently he had expected some hard bargaining but Lizanne saw little point in it. Although she was technically negating the good faith of Director Thriftmor's negotiations by agreeing to fund and arm these rebels, she suspected that by the time she got the Artisan on a ship the empire's internal problems would be superseded by more pressing concerns.

"You will simply hand all of this over without demur?" Korian asked.

"Crisis breeds urgency," Lizanne replied. "And I am fully empowered by my employers to make whatever agreements are necessary to achieve my objective."

Korian glanced at Arberus, who stood guarding the entrance to the store-room. The major smiled tightly and gave a firm nod, which seemed to alleviate the revolutionary's unease. "What do you require?" he asked.

"A capable forger," she said. "Plus, Imperial Cavalry uniforms in sufficient quantity to clothe a full company together with men to wear them and the requisite number of horses to carry said men. I shall also require a ceramicist skilled in delicate work."

She paused, regarding his puzzled expression with a raised eyebrow. "I assume these requirements are within the Brotherhood's capabilities. If not, perhaps there are other groups I should be speaking to. According to my employer's files, the Republic First Alliance is more effective when it comes to infiltration . . ."

"Republic First," Korian broke in, "lost all claims to Bidrosin's legacy during the revolution. They are little more than thieves posturing as radicals. Any other group you might approach are shadows of their former selves, cowed dreamers who do nothing but endlessly rehash the grand epic of failure. Only the Brotherhood still stands for the people. Our struggle will never be done, not until the old order is scoured from this land and Bidrosin's vision made real. Much as I despise the corporatist world and all it stands for, I'd crawl through the foulest sewer if it will win this struggle."

Lizanne always found radical invective jarring, especially when delivered without a trace of irony. "How noble of you," she said, unable to keep the weary tone from her voice. "Can you do this or not?"

CHAPTER 12

Clay

Clay skidded across the deck, staring in fixed horror as the drake's jaws began to close on Loriabeth's legs. He had no gun, no product and lacked even the strength to prevent his headlong tumble. Therefore, it was an overwhelming relief to hear the ear-jarring clack of the Blue's teeth snapping on empty air as Loriabeth swung herself clear. The ship righted itself just as Clay collided with the rail, a shout of pained frustration issuing from his mouth. He flailed on the deck, hands scrabbling on the boards as he tried and failed to haul himself upright.

He looked up at the sound of Loriabeth scrambling to her feet with both pistols in hand, firing a rapid salvo at the Blue's head as it darted forward for a second try. The beast flinched as the bullets tore at its snout, drawing blood but failing to dissuade it from making another lunge at its prey. Loriabeth dived to one side, rolling clear of the snapping jaws then whirling to empty both revolvers into the drake's face at point-blank range. The Blue reared back as if stung, blood trailing from a ruined eye. Its mouth gaped wide once more, infuriated growls fading and a haze of heated air blossoming from its throat. Then it froze.

Clay stared at the immobile head of the beast, seeing how the rest of its snake-like body coiled and thrashed in the water below. His gaze snapped to the walkway above, finding the Varestian pirate woman standing there, eyes fixed on the Blue. Her face was set in the hard concentration that told of intense use of Black as she held the drake in place.

Something landed on the deck in front of Clay: an open wallet containing two vials of product. Clay looked up to find Hilemore regarding him with a hard, commanding glare. "Hurry up!" he snapped, nodding at the wallet.

Clay fumbled for the vials, finding that his fingers lacked the strength to remove the stoppers. With a curse, Hilemore crouched to help him, thumbing the stoppers away and jamming both vials none-too-gently into Clay's mouth. The combined product, full doses of Green and Black, burned on his tongue before making a fiery progress down his throat. The effect was immediate, the Green banishing his weakness in an instant. He sprang to his feet, seeing the Blue's head was now shuddering as the Varestian woman's Black faded, flame seeping through its teeth as its jaw began to widen.

Hilemore moved away, barking orders as Clay focused his gaze on the Blue, its jaw clamping shut once more as he summoned the Black. A loud thud sounded from the starboard side as the beast's body thrashed against the hull. Clay could feel its strength, vastly more powerful than any man he had ever frozen, forcing him to drain product at an accelerated rate.

"If you've got a mind to do something," he told Hilemore through clenched teeth, sweat bathing his skin as the Green thinned in his veins, "it better be soon!"

He heard Hilemore shout some more orders before his voice was drowned by the booming roar of a cannon. Clay felt a hard rush of air as the shell whooshed by less than two feet to his left, quickly followed by a thick cloud of smoke. The last of the product faded as the smoke cleared, leaving him collapsed on the deck once more and staring up at the curious sight of a headless Blue. Blood geysered from the ragged stump of its neck as the body continued to coil and thrash, Clay hearing a scream as a jet of undiluted product found an unfortunate crewman. The drake's writhing corpse slithered along the *Superior*'s side before coming to rest on the aft deck, still coiling as its blood left a red stain in the ship's wake.

"All stop!"

Clay turned to see Hilemore standing alongside one of the starboard cannon, smoke streaming from its muzzle. The gun appeared to have been hastily drawn back and aimed by Steelfine and Lieutenant Talmant, the Islander providing the required elevation by the simple expedient of wedging himself under the barrel and lifting it with his back.

"Mr. Skaggerhill," Hilemore called to the harvester, who was crouched at Loriabeth's side, applying a salve to a small blood-burn on her wrist. "Ever drained a Blue before, perchance?"

Exhaustion had forced Clay back to his bunk, where he slept for several hours, drained by the day's events. He awoke in late evening, emerging onto the aft deck where Skaggerhill and Scrimshine were at work harvesting the Blue. Apparently the former smuggler was the only other hand aboard with enough experience to assist. The Blue's headless corpse lay on a bed of oilskins, a huge, grisly red-blue crescent. Skaggerhill's usual method of tapping the jugular was of little use here since the cannon shot had already rent the vessel open, denuding the body of at least half its remaining blood. The harvester had let the corpse settle for a while then made a series of deep incisions where it bulged the most, capturing the outrushing product in steel buckets provided by Chief Bozware. Meanwhile, Scrimshine was hard at work retrieving the valuable organs.

"Best hold your nose, now," he said, voice muffled behind the welder's mask he wore and, like Skaggerhill, clad head to toe in thick leather. "This is where we find out what the bugger had for dinner." With that he sank a broad-bladed knife into the lower section of the drake's belly and sliced deep and long. The resultant stench had Clay gagging even though he sat on a crate a good fifteen feet away. Scrimshine stood back as a steaming collection of guts spilled out onto the deck, then took a moment to poke through it with his steel-shod boots, commenting, "Seems we weren't the first ship he happened across in recent days."

He kicked something free from the mound of guts, something pale and round that rolled to a stop at Clay's feet. The skull had been mostly denuded of flesh but one of the eyes remained. The blank, milky-white orb stared up at him provoking an unpleasant memory; another dislocated head once gifted to him in a bag.

"Have some Seer-damn respect," Skaggerhill growled at Scrimshine from behind his mask, receiving only a shrug in response.

The sailor turned to rummage through the drake's abdomen, prising the lips of the cut apart and reaching inside, muttering, "Let's be having yer bile duct then, y'bastard."

"Is it him?" Clay asked. "Is it Last Look Jack?"

"King of the Deep's arse it is," Scrimshine replied, still rummaging. "This is a tiddler, lad. If old Last Look'd found this tub it'd be him harvesting us."

Clay watched Skaggerhill apply a hand to the Blue's hide next to the

final incision he had made, squirting a few more drops ı
"Well, that's about all the easy money we'll make," he said, s‹
"Have to render him down to the bone to get full value and we ꞈ
gear for that."

"Folk at Kraghurst'll take what's left," Scrimshine said, emergiı
the body holding a dark object roughly the size and shape of an apple, ꞈ
he plopped into a large pickle jar. "Even a rotted Blue's got value."

"What about the heart?" Clay asked.

Skaggerhill turned to him, moving clear of the pooling blood and pushing his mask back from his face. "What about it?" he asked with a cautious
frown.

"Can you get to it?"

"I guess so. Take a while to saw through his ribs though." The harvester's gaze narrowed further. "Why d'you ask, young 'un?"

Clay levered himself off the crate and started back to his cabin. "Just
curious," he said.

That, Lizanne told him, her whirlwinds twisting a little in agitation, *is
a very bad idea.*

Miss Ethelynne told me she drank the stuff twice, he pointed out. *And
she was fine.*

*You aren't her. Heart-blood is a highly unpredictable and barely under-
stood substance. Plasmologists have been attempting to refine it into a usable
state for decades, enjoying a singular lack of success. I urge you, Mr. Torcreek,
to put such notions aside and concentrate on the task ahead.*

As you wish. He hoped his insincerity didn't show in his mindscape.
Although he had become ever more adept in controlling it, he knew he
lacked her expertise when it came to fully concealing his thoughts. This
time, however, it seemed his growing abilities paid off, for her whirlwinds
settled into their usual contained orderliness.

Your position? she asked.

*Three days north of the Chokes. Captain's stopped burning Red on account
of the bergs. Must say I ain't liking the climate much. I knew it'd be cold but
this is hard to take.*

*I'm sure it'll be harder still when you reach the Shelf. Best keep some Red
handy for emergencies.*

Surely. Where you at now?

Halfway to Scorazin. He saw her whirlwinds darken again at the prospect ahead and found it unnerving; fear was usually absent from these trances.

Bad place, huh?

The worst in the empire, some say. Prisoners have been known to commit suicide upon being sentenced to life in Scorazin.

Anyone ever escaped?

Her whirlwinds twitched as a faint ripple of amusement ran through them. *Not to my knowledge, but I come from a long line of innovators.*

You could wait. See what we find beyond the Shelf. Could be, you don't have to do this.

I have a sense time is very much our enemy, Mr. Torcreek. Her thoughts took on a brisk note, indicating an imminent end to the trance. *There may be little opportunity to trance once I gain entry to Scorazin. If you fail to connect with me after a month, assume I'm dead and proceed at your own discretion. And put any notion of drinking heart-blood out of your head.*

He borrowed tools from the engine room and spent over an hour hacking away at the Blue's sternum with an axe. It had been two days since the trance with Lizanne and he felt an odd sense of pride at having resisted this impulse for so long. But the farther south they sailed, and the deeper the chill in the air, the more the Blue's heart seemed to call to him.

He grunted and swung the axe once more. The blade sank into the fibrous gash he had made in this slab of bone. It was as thick as an oak door and almost as hard. He gave a satisfied sigh as the sternum finally cracked open, reaching in with his thick-gloved hands to pry the sundered bone apart. Through the pink-grey gore he could see the Blue's rib-cage had compressed, the arcs of bone pressed together to conceal the prize within. Lifting a saw, he set to work, forcing down his rising gorge at the stink of the drake's decomposing innards. It required another hour's work before he cut a decent-sized hole in the wall of ribs, by which time the morning watch were coming on deck.

"What are you about, Mr. Torcreek?"

Clay glanced over his shoulder to see Hilemore standing near by, his blocky features rich in suspicion.

"Claiming my prize, Captain," Clay replied, tossing some bone fragments into a bucket.

"This animal is the ship's prize," Hilemore informed him. "Profit derived from it will be shared among the crew."

"I doubt they'd want any part of what I'm after." Clay lifted a lantern and shined the light into the gap he had created, seeing something glisten as it caught the glow. Closer inspection revealed it to be at least as big as his head and secured to the rest of the Blue's inner workings by a huge vein as thick as his forearm.

"Spare me some Black and this'd go quicker," he told Hilemore. "Miss Ethelynne once tore a heart right out of a Red's chest after drinking Black."

"You've had all the product you're getting, for the time being."

"Oh well." Clay reached for the large knife sitting amongst his array of tools. "Guess I'll have to do it the traditional way."

He half expected Hilemore to stop him. Instead, the captain just stood and watched as he cut the heart free and carefully extracted it from the rib-cage. "Might want to stand back a mite farther," he told Hilemore, carrying the heart towards a steel bucket. "I'm given to believe just a drop of this stuff on un-Blessed skin can have ruinous results."

Hilemore stared at him for a moment before taking two slow and deliberate backward steps. "Are you really intending to drink from that?" he asked.

"You intending to stop me?" Clay placed the heart in the bucket then took up the knife once more and made two deep cuts, forming a cross in the organ's surface that immediately swelled with blood.

"I find myself curiously ambivalent on the matter," Hilemore replied.

Clay watched as the blood dripped sluggishly from the cuts to form an inch-thick pool around the heart. It was darker and more viscous than the product Skaggerhill had harvested, and a distinct contrast to the paler, diluted substance Clay was used to. *How much?* he wondered, striving to recall every word Ethelynne had spoken on the subject, which he was depressed to realise amounted to no more than a few words. *She had command of Lutharon because she drank the blood of his mother,* he remembered. *So, stands to reason he was right there when she did it. Ain't no Blues here now.*

He reached for the empty spice jar he had purloined from the galley. It was double the size of a standard product vial but still small enough to carry in his pocket. He sank it into the bucket and let it fill to the brim, then fixed the lid in place and washed the excess product away with water from his canteen.

"Finally," Hilemore said, turning and striding towards the bridge. "A modicum of common sense."

The Chokes came into view the next day. At first they appeared as a long jagged saw-blade on the southern horizon but soon resolved into a series of narrow rocky islets, each rising to a height of at least eighty feet and topped with a thick cap of ice. At Scrimshine's urging, Hilemore had reduced speed to one-third during their approach in order to allow the tidal currents to raise the sea to the required height. "Need at least a two-moon tide to sail the Chokes," he advised.

Clay kept a close eye on the former inmate as he worked the wheel. He knew his undimmed distrust of the man was most likely the result of Blinds-born prejudice, but it was an instinct he had learned to trust. *Blinds don't wash,* he reminded himself, watching Scrimshine expertly spin the wheel to counter a sudden current.

"Gotta keep a watch on the eddies here," he said, glancing at Hilemore. "Best tell your lookouts that, Skipper. They need to sing out if they see a big swirl ahead."

Hilemore nodded to Steelfine, who relayed the command to the crow's nest via the speaking-tube.

"We're too far east," Scrimshine went on, squinting through the wheel-house window before tapping a finger to the compass. "Gonna have to tack west for a bit."

"We followed the heading you gave us," Hilemore pointed out.

"Chokes've never been mapped for a reason, Skipper." Scrimshine grinned and spun the wheel to starboard. "They change. Sea wears at the rock whilst the ice carves new channels and closes others. It's almost like they're a living thing that eats unwary ships."

They followed the northern edge of the Chokes for another two hours. Clay quickly gained an appreciation for Hilemore's insistence that they find a pilot before coming here. Through the gaps in the outer chain of islets he could see many more, too many to count easily, forming a close-packed maze several miles thick. He also saw how the chain of islets described a great curve, disappearing into the distance where a thin white line could be seen on the horizon.

"That's the Shelf, huh?" he asked Hilemore, who gave a short nod, his own gaze fixed on their helmsman, who, Clay noted, now had a sheen of sweat on his cheeks despite the chill.

"Something wrong?" Hilemore asked him.

Scrimshine didn't answer for a long moment, eyes feverishly tracking over the parade of passing islets. "It's, um," he began, swallowed then spoke on, his voice betraying a hoarse nervousness. "It's gone. The channel I was aiming for. See?" He pointed through a gap between two islets, beyond which a large iceberg could be seen twisting slowly in the current. "Looks like it's suffered a tumble since last I was here."

"I told you to throw this one back," Clay said to Hilemore.

The captain ignored him and took a step towards Scrimshine, looming over him and speaking in precise tones. "You are here for one reason. I have no room for useless hands aboard this ship."

"There's maybe another way," Scrimshine said, voice even hoarser. "Farther west, where the Chokes meet the Shelf. It's, uh, right treacherous though. Not to be risked lightly."

Hilemore stared at the perspiring convict for a long moment. "It seems we have little choice," he said eventually. "I hope for your sake you don't once again prove my trust to have been misplaced."

It took the better part of the remaining daylight to reach the Shelf. Progress was slow due to Scrimshine's need to compensate for the shifting and powerful currents flowing into the Chokes. As the light began to ebb the Shelf grew from a thin white line into a massive pale green-blue wall that towered over the *Superior* by at least fifty feet.

"Well, that's really something," Skaggerhill said, gazing up at the frozen cliffs with ice beading his bushy eyebrows. The Longrifles had gathered on the fore-deck as the ship drew ever nearer to the frozen edifice. They were all wrapped in a variety of clothing looted from the unneeded belongings of the *Superior*'s fallen crew, Loriabeth appearing somewhat comical in her voluminous collection of thick coat and seal-fur hat. It all seemed a very long way from the jungles and badlands of Arradsia.

"You were hoping for an interesting journey," Clay said. He was wearing a heavy coat that had belonged to the *Superior*'s coxswain, but still his teeth chattered as he spoke.

The harvester turned and nodded to the south. "That seems a damn sight more interesting than I was hoping for."

Gazing at the passage ahead, Clay couldn't help but share his trepidation. The channel between the Chokes and the Shelf was barely twice the *Superior*'s width and the water seethed as the energetic currents battered against the ice. As he watched, a chunk the size of a house detached itself from the Shelf and plummeted into the roiling waters. He had gained a grudging appreciation for Scrimshine's piloting abilities but found it incredible that any helmsman could successfully steer such a course.

Preacher said something, the first words Clay could recall him uttering since Hadlock, a soft recitation of scripture almost lost to the numbing air. "'Ware the safest roads, for they lure the slothful towards the Travail.'"

Clay saw that the marksman had a serene cast to his face, as if he looked upon the coming trials with calm acceptance. *He always was crazy,* Clay reminded himself, seeing the sharp glance his uncle shot at Preacher and knowing they shared the same thought. *Probably should've left him in Lossermark.*

"Ain't gonna attempt this tonight are they?" Loriabeth asked, casting a wary eye at the darkening sky.

Clay turned towards the bridge. Through the glass he could see Scrimshine engaged in some animated gesticulation as Hilemore loomed over him once more. "Seems it's a matter under discussion," he said, starting back towards the mid-deck.

"It'll be fully dark within the hour!" he could hear Scrimshine saying as he climbed the ladder to the bridge. The sailor's voice possessed a curious tone that mixed stern refusal with wheedling solicitation. "You take us in there, this ship'll be scrap come the morning."

"It's a two-moon night," Hilemore said, his own tone absent any inflection save command. "Bright enough to see by without lights and I'll not anchor here."

"We could draw back a mile or two to calmer waters," Scrimshine said, fighting a catch in his throat. "Steam in a slow circle until midday on the morrow. Should be able to get her through then."

Clay paused at the entrance to the bridge, watching Scrimshine stare at Hilemore in desperation. Clay clamped down on the urge to add his voice, knowing the captain's reaction to unasked-for advice, especially from him, was unlikely to be pleasant. After a moment's consideration, Hilemore shifted his gaze to the Varestian woman standing at the rear of the bridge, arms folded and face rigid as she witnessed the discussion. She met Hilemore's gaze and gave a short, barely perceptible nod that had Clay wondering if he wasn't in fact sailing on a ship with two captains.

"Very well," Hilemore said, moving back from Scrimshine. "Bring us about. Mr. Talmant, signal the Chief to take us to one-fifth speed."

"One-fifth speed, aye, sir."

"Mr. Steelfine, double watch tonight. I'll take the first one."

"Aye sir . . ."

"BLUE TO STERN!" the shout cut through the Islander's words, dragging every set of eyes towards the rear of the ship where a lookout stood pointing at something a good distance off. At first Clay saw what he thought was another collision of waves born of the region's unpredictable currents. Then he realised it was in fact a wake, a great swell of displaced water that spoke of something far larger than the rotting corpse lying on the aft deck. He could see a spine at least the height of two men rising from the centre of the swell, with a long row of others twisting behind as whatever created the wake made an unhurried progress towards the *Superior*.

"Oh fuck me to the Travail and back again," Scrimshine breathed. "It's him."

CHAPTER 13

Lizanne

"Hyran," the young man introduced himself, voice wavering a little and his large eyes averted. She put his age at somewhere around eighteen, though his thin frame and gaunt features made him look younger. Pale skin and dark hair meant his family was of northern origin, though his accented Varsal held a depth of street-born coarseness it was hard to fake. *Hyran,* Lizanne thought. *Another code-name from Corvantine myth. The mystical messenger who walked the dark paths between the divine and mortal worlds. Quite apt, really.*

Korian had introduced the lanky youth, nudging him into the secret refuge in the tea-house store-room with an impatient slap to the shoulder. "Haven't got all day, citizen."

"You can go," Lizanne informed Korian in tones that didn't invite discussion. "Close the entrance."

Left alone with her the boy squirmed under her scrutiny, though she saw how he resisted the urge to conceal his hands as her gaze tracked over them, finding no marks. "You never sought the Blood Imperial's Token?" she enquired, referring to the Corvantine equivalent of the Blood-lot.

"My ma and pa didn't like it," he muttered, eyes still downcast. "Godly reasons, they said."

"Are they aware of your current . . . activities?"

He shook his head. "Only if they're looking down from the heavens they was always going on about. Last purge but one. Emperor didn't like their holy books, see?"

"I'm sorry."

He shrugged, continuing to shuffle in nervous expectation.

"You've never done this before, have you?" she asked.

"Brotherhood don't let their Blood-blessed trance. Too worried the Cadre might be listening."

She pointed him to a stool next to the bed. "Please, sit."

After some hesitant fidgeting, he duly sat on the stool, though his eyes remained fixed on the floor.

"It won't hurt," she assured him. "Though the first time is confusing."

He clasped his hands together, hard enough to make the knuckles turn white. "Ma and Pa's cleric told of how the trance steals part of your soul," he said in a strained murmur. "Said you lose a piece of your soul then the gate to the heavens is barred to you. S'why they wouldn't take me to try for the Token."

"I thought the Brotherhood eschewed such notions," Lizanne said. "Didn't Bidrosin call religion the 'triumph of delusion'?"

"She did. But it ain't easy setting aside all you learnt from a young age, miss."

"I'm sure it isn't. But we have a mission, you and I, a mission that requires mutual understanding, and trust." She reached for the Spider and disconnected the vial of Blue it held, removing the stopper and holding it out to him. "You can trust me, Hyran."

After some more fidgeting he took the vial, eyes flicking up to meet hers for the first time. "How . . . How much?"

"Just a sip will suffice for today," she said.

"Aren't we s'posed to talk awhile first? Become friends or some such?"

"A brief acquaintance will suffice for basic communication." She gave him an encouraging smile. "Drink up."

He did so, grimacing at the burn before handing the vial back to her. "They said you'd try to take all I know," he said, watching her raise the vial to her lips. "Korian said it's a good job I hardly know anything."

Lizanne smothered a laugh and drank a small amount of Blue. *We all see more than we know, my lad.*

A rberus slipped back into the role of cavalry commander with practised ease, though the addition of an eye-patch and spear-point moustache did much to reduce the chance that a fellow officer might recognise a disgraced major of Imperial Dragoons. His dark green uniform and black cap marked him as a lieutenant in the 18th Light Horse, an undistinguished regiment often called upon to assist the constabulary in matters of internal security. He rode at the head of a dozen men, all members of the Brotherhood with sufficient military experience to pass for soldiers. Lizanne rode in a prison wagon of sturdy oak construction with barred windows and a slat in the floor for her bodily needs. She wore only a rough woollen smock and her unwashed and unbound hair was tangled with several days' worth of grime and sweat. After two weeks on the road she must look quite frightful, which was all to the good. Also, thanks to a painful but necessary procedure undertaken before leaving Corvus, she had a persistent and acute pain in her lower jaw.

They met other travellers on the road, mostly traders carting their goods to the capital's markets who were quick to shuffle onto the verge and lower their gaze at the sight of Imperial soldiery escorting a prison wagon. Occasionally they happened upon a constabulary check-point which invariably required Arberus to exchange curt pleasantries with their commander before proffering his forged orders. The sight of the Interior Minister's crest was usually enough to discourage further questioning but not all members of the constabulary were so easily cowed.

"Can't take any chances, Captain," one particular check-point commander said. "What with all the trouble in the capital." His boots thumped on the wagon's rear step as he climbed up to peer at Lizanne through the barred window on the door.

"A traitor, eh?" he asked Arberus. "Sure she's not a whore too? I can see her as one, but not the other. Though I wouldn't give more than a few pins for a gobble off that mouth, the state she's in." He moved back, glancing to the side. "Unless you're offering a free go?"

"Don't let appearances fool you, Inspector," Lizanne heard Arberus reply in a commendably mild tone. "You'll likely find yourself short a few inches."

The inspector grunted, looking down as he read something. "No name on the warrant," he observed, without any particular surprise. "Another one for the ranks of the disappeared, eh?"

"My orders come directly from the Interior Ministry." Arberus's voice had taken on a clipped, cautionary note. "Experience teaches me the folly of looking too closely at the particulars."

"Quite so, Captain." The man's brutish face lingered behind the bars a moment longer, Lizanne staring back at his predatory lust with studied indifference. *More than a few inches,* she decided. *I'll take his balls too.*

"Very well." The inspector disappeared, his barked commands audible through the wagon's sides. "Raise the barrier!" The oak planking next to Lizanne's head gave a loud thump as he pounded a fist against it. "Enjoy your time in Scorazin, my dear!" he shouted with a laugh. "I hear a whore can last at least a month if she's generous enough!"

"I'll stop by and kill him on the way back," Arberus said. They had halted for the night, allowing her the chance to engage in the daily stretching exercises she employed to prevent her muscles atrophying during the journey. He stood at the wagon's door, face framed in the barred window. She had forbidden any temporary liberations during the journey lest such a conspicuous breach of procedure attract attention.

"No you won't." Lizanne groaned a little as she raised her torso, keeping her legs straight and arms outstretched. "Much as I appreciate your chivalry, personal vendettas are a barrier to successful mission fulfilment."

"I hate it when you talk like that."

She looked up at the harsh tone in his voice, finding his face set with suppressed anger. "Really?"

"Yes, really. It's like you step back from being you, becoming . . . someone else, someone Exceptional Initiatives made you into."

"They didn't make me into anything. They only refined what was already there." She arched her back, sweeping her arms over her head so her body described the shape of a drawn bow. "And if they hadn't, I doubt either of us would be here now."

He said nothing, watching her hold the pose for several seconds before she relaxed. She sank into a sitting position and began working her neck muscles with a series of slow revolutions. "He said there was trouble in the capital," she said.

"There were riots when the Emperor announced the treaty with Ironship," he replied. "Relatives of those lost in the Arradsian campaign joined with traditionalists who despise the notion of allying their once-great empire with the hated corporatist enemy. The authorities were obliged to turn out the entire city garrison to restore order. It seems the Emperor has been even more industrious than usual in signing the resultant execution orders."

"So he's still mad," Lizanne mused. "For the time being, at least. We can but hope it lingers long enough for his forces to be of some use when the White comes north."

"So our fate is dependent on the continuing madness of an inbred fool."

"If we accomplish our objective perhaps it won't be necessary. How much longer?"

"A day and a half." She watched his face take on an even more grim expression. "Once I hand you over, there will be nothing I can do to assist you."

"On the contrary," she said, offering a smile which he failed to return. "You will continue to gather intelligence and prepare for my return, and contingencies in the event I do not. Your Brotherhood must be made to understand the danger we face. Seek them out, as many as you can, tell them what you saw in Arradsia. Tell them yet another hopeless rebellion will only hurt our cause, and theirs."

He sighed and gave a reluctant nod. "I suppose it's better than simply waiting at the rendezvous for you to trance with Hyran."

"Be sure to leave clear instructions with your people at the rendezvous. If I fail to trance within four weeks, assume me lost and try to convey word of the mission's failure to Director Bloskin. Also . . ." She hesitated, closing her eyes. "In such an event I would *request* that you return to Feros."

"You brought me here because of my useful allegiances. Now I'm back, you can't expect me to abandon them."

"Tekela is the daughter of your closest friend and comrade. Isn't she more deserving of your protection than these hopeless dreamers?"

He met her gaze through the bars, the eyes harder and more unyielding than she had seen before. "If you're expecting a solemn promise in that regard, you will be disappointed. I'll not deprive you of yet another incentive to survive that benighted pit. If you wish to safeguard Tekela, stay alive and do it yourself."

With that, he was gone, leaving her to ponder the folly of intimate relations for one such as she.

S he smelled the smoke a good while before the wagon trundled up to the walls of Scorazin. It was faint at first, the mingled scent of burnt coal and wood mixed with a sulphurous tinge. Soon the scent thickened into a cloying, acrid miasma. It wasn't quite as bad a stench as the green-leather tannery in Carvenport, but certainly came close. She heard the muffled exchange of military greetings as the wagon came to a halt, then the thump of boots on the step before keys rattled in the lock.

"Out!" Arberus commanded in an impatient bark.

Lizanne checked to ensure the manacles on her wrists were properly secured then got slowly to her feet. "Hurry up, you traitorous bitch," Arberus said with weary brutality as she emerged, blinking into the light. She gazed around with a blank expression that conveyed the impression of a woman unable to comprehend her changed circumstances. The walls of the prison city towered above her, at least three times the height of the barrier that had ultimately failed to protect Carvenport. She couldn't see the top of it through the pall of yellowish smoke escaping the confines of the city beyond. Before her stood the gatehouse, which was in fact a substantial fortress protruding from the wall like an ugly brick-and-wood tumour.

"Do you think I want to loiter in this stink a moment longer than necessary?" Arberus said, yanking Lizanne from the wagon with a hard tug. Her bare feet met mud-covered cobbles and she slipped, collapsing with a scared sob.

"Can't see any scars on her," a man said, the voice muffled. Lizanne shot a fearful glance up at a blocky Senior Constable, eyes dark and curious above the mask he wore, presumably to assuage the foul humours that brought a sting to her own eyes. "When the Cadre sends us a traitor they're usually marked up something frightful."

"Apparently, she was very co-operative," Arberus told him. "Sold her friends out in return for her life. They barely had to touch her."

"Life?" The constable laughed. "Weren't you sold a lame horse, love. Alright, get up."

He was surprisingly gentle as he brought her to her feet and she experienced a moment's disorientation upon reading the expression in his eyes: deep, unalloyed pity. "No name, I take it?" the constable enquired of Arberus.

"Number only: Six-one-four."

"Duly noted." The constable scribbled something on the document he held and handed it to Arberus. "Transfer complete and witnessed, Captain. I wish you a pleasant journey. Right, love." The constable turned away, taking hold of Lizanne's arm and leading her towards a small door in the base of the fortress-like gatehouse. "Let's get you sorted."

Lizanne didn't look back at Arberus as she was led away, and hoped he had the good sense to just close up the wagon and ride off. Somehow, though, she knew he had lingered to watch her disappear into the doorway.

The Senior Constable led her through a series of guarded doors, unlocked and then locked behind them as they passed through. Her escort hummed a faint but jaunty tune behind his mask as they made their way deeper into the maze of corridors and holding cells. He paused every now and then to exchange a word or two with the other guards, usually drawing a laugh with some witticism or shared gossip. He appeared to be a popular fellow. Lizanne kept the shocked, blank expression in place whilst her practised mind recorded the route they took and any names or other intelligence revealed by the guards. It seemed that the Warden Commandant, a new appointee of questionable judgement, had an unwise habit of actually venturing beyond the confines of the barracks.

"Came back covered in shit yesterday," one of the guards told the Senior Constable with a smirk.

"He's lucky it was just shit."

"True enough. Seems he didn't make it more than two streets before they ambushed him, Wise Fools mostly. Had his squad shoot three of the buggers by way of recompense."

"Wonderful," the Senior Constable groaned. "Makes it more likely there'll be another bloody riot on Ore Day."

They moved on, eventually coming to a small tiled room which contained a chair and table, both bolted down. On the table a pair of plain but sturdy shoes sat alongside a folded set of overalls and a cake of soap. In the centre of the room a bucket of water sat close to an iron-grated drain. "Sit down, love," the Senior Constable told her, pointing to the chair and closing the door. He removed his mask as she sat, revealing a broad, fleshy face set in a grimace of habitual sympathy.

"Your prisoner number is Six-one-four," he told her, unlocking her manacles and setting them on the table. "Remember it. You'll need it on Ore Day, otherwise you don't get fed. Understand?"

Lizanne stared up at him blankly for a moment before giving a hesitant nod.

"Good." His grimace deepened. "Need you to strip now. Best if you don't give me any trouble. Don't worry, I've seen everything you've got a thousand times and never been tempted once."

She briefly considered throwing a hysterical fit of some kind, but decided meek acquiescence would better suit her current persona. The constable was patient as she stood up and slowly pulled the coarse woollen smock over her head, placing it on the table and standing hunched with an arm across her breasts and a hand over her crotch. "You'll find the water's cold," the constable said, pointing to the bucket and handing her the soap. "Sorry about that. Be sure to be thorough."

So she washed, gasping at the chill of the water and dragging the cheap, odourless soap over her skin as he looked on with professional scrutiny, his eyes lacking any vestige of lust. She was unsure whether to find this reassuring or not. She deliberately prolonged the washing, knowing what came next and a lack of hesitancy would be sure to arouse suspicion.

"That's enough," he said, finally. "Rinse off."

He had her stand facing the wall with her hands raised and legs parted. "Alright then, love," he said as she shivered and bit down on a whimper. "You got anything hidden, now's the time to tell me and it'll stay just between us. But if you don't tell me and I find something, well, that's a different matter. Last lady who tried it got put through the gate with no clothes and no blanket. Trust me, you don't want that."

"I-I've nothing!" Lizanne babbled. "I swear!"

"Well, let's hope so, eh?"

The subsequent inspection was brief but thorough enough to provoke an involuntary shudder or two.

"Good," the constable said in brisk satisfaction. "Let's get you dressed, shall we?"

"It's better if you don't think of Scorazin as a prison," the constable told her a short while later. She walked ahead of him, her overalls chafing as they descended a series of stairwells into the bowels of the gatehouse. The garment was fashioned from thick, tight-woven cotton and, despite a recent laundering, retained a faded but recognisable blood-stain on the midriff. "It's a city, really," he went on. "And like any city it has rules. The precise details change according to whoever's enforcing them, but for the most part it boils down to two basics: don't take what you're not strong enough to keep and don't fight anyone you're not strong enough to kill."

They reached the bottom of the last stairwell where a heavy iron-braced door waited. The constable put a hand on her shoulder, turning her around, his gaze rich in the same pity she had seen outside the gatehouse. "Few words of advice, love," he said. "Make friends fast, and don't be picky about it. You'll need protection. There's a place you might want to make for. A tavern of sorts. When you get through the grate find Sluiceman's Way, it's the widest street in the eastern quarter. Follow it until you come to Pick Street. Keep to the sides and don't speak to anyone that speaks to you. If they press their case, start running. The place you're looking for is called the Miner's Repose but the sign's long since faded. You'll know it 'cause it's by far the largest building in the street. Ask for Melina." He cupped her chin in a gesture that was almost fatherly. "Tell her Constable Darkanis sent you."

Lizanne coughed, drew breath and asked in a small voice, "It's . . . It's a whore-house?"

He lowered his hand and gave a heavy sigh. "Trust me, love, it's far better than the mines."

He turned and worked a key in the heavy door, hauling it aside to reveal a tunnel. "Before I got here," Constable Darkanis said, hefting an oil-lamp to illuminate the tunnel, "they used to send the new arrivals in through the main gate at the start of each week. One big parcel of the poor sods served up like feeding time at the menagerie, 'specially if there were any women in the bunch. Started having a bad effect on the size of the work-force, so we've got a more civilised way of doing things these days."

He stepped aside, gesturing for her to go ahead. Lizanne gave a start at the sight of a rat scurrying away from the light, then clutched her blanket tighter and entered the tunnel. They sloshed through an inch of foul-smelling water, rats fleeing ahead of them as the constable kept up an advisory monologue she assumed he had delivered hundreds of times before. "It'll be dark soon. Best to wait a good couple of hours before you poke your head out though, gives the taverns time to fill up and clears the streets of those who've come off the day shift."

After a hundred yards or so the tunnel split in two and he pointed her to the opening on the left, advising that it would take her closer to the Miner's Repose. Fifty paces on Lizanne came to a sturdy iron gate; the bars spanned the tunnel from floor to ceiling and were set deep into the brick-work. Beyond the gate she could see a thin stream of light descending through an opening in the tunnel's roof.

"There's a few dozen entry points for you to choose from," Darkanis said, stepping forward to unlock the gate. "Just lift the grate and crawl out, but choose carefully cos it'll lock behind you. Avoid the one near the river, there's always some mud-slingers hanging around regardless of the hour."

He had crouched a little to unlock the gate, turning his exposed neck to her. Even without a drop of product in her veins, rendering him uncon-scious or dead wasn't a particularly difficult prospect. His keys and whatever valuables he had in his pockets might well come in handy in the days ahead, and the garrison was hardly likely to scour the whole city for his assailant. *The risks are too high,* she decided, telling herself the decision had nothing to do with sentiment. *Rare to find a decent man in so terrible a place.*

"Best of luck, love," Constable Darkanis said, swinging the gate open and standing aside.

Lizanne allowed a few seconds to pass before stepping through the gate, turning to watch as he locked it behind her. "Remember what I said about waiting for a while," he told her with a wink before turning to go.

"Thank you," she said. The constable paused and turned back with a puzzled frown that told her these were words none of his charges had spo-ken before. "Your . . . compassion does you credit, sir. For which I thank you."

"You're welcome, love," he said in a flat tone. It was clear to Lizanne he wasn't accustomed to going off script.

She nodded and turned to go.

"Wait."

Turning back, she saw him fishing in his trouser pocket for something. "This is against regs," he muttered. "But sod it, I'm retiring in three months." He held the object out through the bars, Lizanne recognising it as a penknife perhaps four inches long. "Isn't much of a weapon, I know," he said with a shrug. "But it's something. And"—his sympathetic grimace returned for a second—"as there's only one way out of Scorazin, it may come in handy if you feel in need of an . . . early release."

Lizanne reached out and took the penknife. She began to voice her thanks once more but he had already begun making his way back down the tunnel, humming his jaunty tune as the lamplight faded, leaving her in darkness.

CHAPTER 14

Hilemore

"Battle stations!" Hilemore barked, Steelfine pulling the steam-whistle's lanyard before the words had fully escaped his lips. Hilemore tore his gaze away from the sight of the huge spine knifing through the waves and turned to Zenida. "To the engine room please, Captain." She nodded and ran for the ladder. "Mr. Talmant," Hilemore went on. "Signal Chief Bozware: full ahead at two vials!"

"Full ahead at two vials, aye, sir!"

Hilemore fixed his gaze on Scrimshine, who stood with his back to the wheel, staring at the view through the bridge's rear window in bleach-faced, wide-eyed shock. "To your duty, Mr. Scrimshine," Hilemore ordered in an even voice.

"Can't . . ." Scrimshine gaped at him. "Can't go in there at full ahead. It's suicide."

"On the contrary." Hilemore drew his revolver and pressed the muzzle into the centre of Scrimshine's forehead. "Failing to obey my orders is suicide. Perhaps, if I toss your corpse over the stern, a tasty morsel might slow our friend down a little."

Scrimshine's feverish gaze swung from Hilemore to the approaching monster then back again before he turned and set his hands on the wheel. "He's too fast for us, even at full ahead," he said.

Hilemore felt the deck shudder as Zenida lit the vials Chief Bozware had added to the blood-burner. Within seconds the needle on the speed indicator ticked past twenty knots and continued to climb. "Allow me to worry about that," Hilemore said. "Mr. Steelfine!"

"Sir!"

"Muster the riflemen and toss the Blue carcass over the side. Then run up the stern-chasers. Fire as she bears."

"Aye, sir!"

"Mr. Torcreek." Hilemore turned to the young Blood-blessed, who stood clutching the jar of heart-blood he had harvested from the Blue's corpse, eyes narrowed as he regarded the huge wake beyond the *Superior*'s stern. There was none of Scrimshine's horror on the younger Torcreek's face, more a sense of indecision.

"Mr. Torcreek!" Hilemore repeated, finally capturing the fellow's attention.

"Captain?"

"One of Red and one of Black." Hilemore handed him the wallet of product. "Keep that beast away from my ship. And ask your uncle and that mad cleric to take their rifles aloft."

"Surely will." Clay inclined his head and made for the ladder, sliding down to the deck with a practised ease which said much for his time aboard ship.

Hilemore focused his attention on the channel between the Shelf and the Chokes as it loomed ever larger in the bridge window. A glance at the speed dial indicated the *Superior* had now surpassed forty knots and still had more to give. Scrimshine kept muttering to himself as he steered them towards the channel, profanities and sailor's curses for the most part but with a few Dalcian prayer-spells thrown in for good measure.

"Steady as she goes, Mr. Scrimshine," Hilemore told him, holstering his revolver and clasping his hands behind his back. "You're doing splendidly."

"Gonna fucking die . . ." the smuggler intoned, spinning the wheel to align the *Superior* with the centre of the channel. "May the ancestors bestow their protection upon a fallen son . . ."

Dual cannon shots sounded from the stern, Hilemore glancing back to see a pair of waterspouts rising from the waves just behind the enormous wake. Perhaps in response, the great spine descended below the surface and the swell faded as the huge body beneath sought the depths. "Perhaps we scared it off, sir," Lieutenant Talmant suggested, which drew an immediate, near-hysterical cackle from Scrimshine.

"Scared . . . Stupid little shit," he muttered before returning to his superstitious pleading. "Great-Grandfathers, Great-Grandmothers, look kindly upon this wayward wretch . . ."

Despite his terror, Scrimshine still retained enough presence of mind to safely steer the *Superior* into the channel, the wheel blurring in his hands as he countered the roiling currents. Despite his efforts, Hilemore soon appreciated that the man's warnings had not been exaggerated. Some fifty yards into the channel, a tall wave surged out of the Chokes to slam into the *Superior*'s port side. The ship swayed towards the Shelf as the deck tipped at an alarming angle. For a moment it seemed the frozen massif came close enough to reach out and touch before Scrimshine angled the bows to ride the wave rebounding from the ice, bringing them clear.

"Heavenly cousins show mercy to this dishonoured fool . . ." Scrimshine hauled the tiller to starboard, the *Superior* swerving away from the rocky shoulder of an islet as the speed indicator nudged forty-five knots.

A flurry of rifle-shots drew Hilemore's attention back to the stern. The riflemen were at the rail, firing furiously at the swell building up just fifty yards short of the stern. Steelfine was harrying the gun-crews to reload their pieces but Hilemore judged it likely that the beast would be upon them before the battery was ready. The tall spine was once again jutting above the waves, its height even greater now and he fancied he caught a glimpse of the Blue's head beneath the water. Perhaps it was a trick of the fading light but he detected a certain reddish glow to the animal's eyes. The signature crack of a longrifle sounded through the ceiling of the bridgehouse as the elder Torcreek or the mad cleric tried his luck. Hilemore saw the bullet impact just short of the spine but whatever effect it had on the Blue was so negligible that its course didn't alter in the slightest. Hilemore saw Clay step between two cannon, hand still clutching the jar of heart-blood.

"Oh, fuck me!"

Hilemore turned to find Scrimshine spinning the wheel to port. A glance through the bridge window revealed the source of his distress. The uneven but otherwise unbroken line of the Shelf had abruptly altered, a huge, blade-like promontory jutted into the channel leaving a greatly reduced gap.

"Won't make it!" Scrimshine shouted, eyes wide and pleading as he turned to Hilemore.

"You have to," Hilemore told him, his own gaze focused on where the promontory met the water, noting how it was thinner at the base than the top. He checked the situation at the stern, seeing how the Blue had shortened the distance between them to little over twenty yards; too close for the cannon to depress sufficiently for a shot. Steelfine was busily engaged in getting the gun-crews to move their pieces to the edge of the deck, so their muzzles could be lowered. The drake's head was clearly visible through the swell now, eyes seeming to glow even brighter.

"I'm going forward," Hilemore told Talmant, inclining his head at Scrimshine. "If he removes his hands from the wheel, shoot him and take over."

"Aye, sir!"

Hilemore slid down the ladder and sprinted for the pivot-gun on the fore-deck. "Solid shot loaded?" he asked the lead gunner.

"Loaded and ready, sir." The man was somewhat pale of face but kept a commendably straight posture as he glanced over Hilemore's shoulder at the stern. "Need a change of heading if we're going to get the bugger though."

"You have a different target." Hilemore pointed at the base of the promontory looming ahead. "Just above the water-line where it joins the Shelf, if you please."

"Sir?" the gunner asked with a frown.

"Just do it, man!" Hilemore snapped.

The gunner nodded and barked out a series of orders to his three-man crew, who swiftly brought the piece on target. The shot impacted on the Shelf a few feet above the waves, sending a cascade of shattered ice into the sea. Hilemore took out his spy-glass and trained it on the promontory, seeing a small fissure where the shell had struck home. *Not enough*, he mused. *Like firing a pistol at a mountain.* "Again," he ordered the gunner. "Same spot. As many as you can whilst she still bears. I'll be back directly."

He ran for the starboard batteries, ordering each gun primed and lowered to the correct elevation. "Fire on my order," he told the crews. The pivot-gun managed another two rounds before the *Superior* slipped into the gap between the promontory and the closest islet. The ugly, high-pitched groan of iron on rock sounded from the port side, indicating Scrimshine had slightly misjudged the course. The ship shuddered from bow to stern but kept on, the promontory looming overhead like a poised axe. *Let's hope it's sharp enough*, Hilemore thought before barking out his command to the starboard guns. "Fire!"

The four cannon fired at once, the range was less than fifteen yards meaning they were obliged to shrink from a hail of shattered ice as the shells slammed home. Hilemore stared up at the great frozen wedge, hoping Scrimshine's ancestors might hear his prayers for he had no reason to expect this to work. After several seconds of fervent hoping, it had become clear that the scoundrel's ancestors were indeed deaf today.

"Hit it again!" Hilemore called to the pivot-gun before switching his gaze to the stern as the chasers fired again. He saw the resultant waterspouts deluge Steelfine and the others, hoping to see the flash of red that would indicate a hit, but it appeared Last Look Jack was either too skilled a pursuer or just too lucky. A vast, ear-piercing screech sounded as the beast finally revealed itself, the great, red-eyed head surging from the waves a few yards short of the stern. It slowed a little as it reared up, falling behind but still staying close enough to cast a jet of flame at its prey. The men at the stern scattered as the flames swept down. Hilemore was unable to contain a shout of frustration at the sight of two men tumbling over the side, both wreathed in flame. A flat crump erupted as an ammunition stack caught light, the explosion sending one of the cannon high in the air.

"Mr. Torcreek!" Hilemore called, sprinting towards the carnage. He found the Blood-blessed on his knees, coughing in the smoke, and dragged him upright. "I said to keep it back!"

"He's too strong," Clay replied, staring at the beast as it slipped below the waves once more. "Only one chance now." Clay raised the jar of heart-blood and removed the stopper. "If I die, Captain," he said, raising it to his lips, "be sure to speak well of me."

His words were drowned by the vast, booming crack that filled the air above their heads. Hilemore's gaze snapped to the promontory, following the line of a fissure that had suddenly appeared in its flank. "That may not be necessary," he said, putting a restraining hand on Clay's forearm.

Last Look Jack had begun to raise himself once more, Hilemore gaining a true impression of the beast's size for the first time. It towered over them to a height of twenty feet with most of its body still beneath the surface, jaws widening to cavernous dimensions and its red eyes alive with what was unmistakably a deep, unquenchable hatred.

The promontory detached from the Shelf with another booming crack, the immense blade of ice plunging down so that its edge caught the monster just behind the head. Last Look Jack disappeared in an explosion of spume as the promontory met the water. The *Superior* rose high as the resultant wave swept along the channel, Hilemore fancying he heard a scream from the bridge as Scrimshine performed miracles to keep them on a true course. Beyond the stern the new-born iceberg sank to two-thirds of its length before grinding to a halt, wedged between the Chokes and the Shelf, firmly blocking the passage for years to come.

*C*asualties: *three dead, four wounded.* Hilemore dipped his pen in the inkpot and added a final few lines to the log. *The Blue known as Last Look Jack assumed dead, though not confirmed. Expect to clear the Chokes by morning.*

He added his initials to the entry and leaned back from the desk. Surveying the log, two-thirds of which was written in Eutherian and the remainder in Mandinorian, it occurred to him that this ship's story would provide ample evidence to future historians of the dramatic changes wrought on the world in a short space of time. He was sure the rest of the log would have made for interesting reading if his Eutherian hadn't been so poor. Half of the entries had been set down in the spidery script of the *Superior*'s original captain, later replaced by the less accomplished, and often barely legible, penmanship of the ship's first mate following the Battle of the Strait. A few weeks on and this hand was in turn supplanted by Lieutenant Sigoral's smooth-flowing calligraphy. Although the commentary was lost on him, the casualty lists were unmistakable. It appeared the *Superior* had lost over a third of her crew at the Strait and then even more at Carvenport. Sigoral's description of these calamitous events, set down several days later, was surprisingly brief but Hilemore was able to translate the phrase "entire fleet destroyed."

And yet, he mused. *Somehow he managed to sail her all the way to Lossermark with a skeleton crew, without suffering another casualty.* Hilemore decided a more thorough debrief of the marine was in order when circumstances allowed.

The cabin door opened and Zenida came in, closing it behind her and slumping into the seat opposite. Such niceties as knocking or requesting permission to sit were evidently beneath her. She was, after all, a fellow captain even without a ship.

"You look tired," he told her, noting the red tinge to her eyes.

"Took over the wheel from that bilge-scum for a few hours," she said around a yawn. "He was ready to drop. Navigating this course takes a toll. Mr. Talmant has the wheel. The channel's far wider now and he's a sure enough hand."

Hilemore saw her press her lips together, her slumped form betraying a slight tension despite her fatigue. "You have something to discuss, Captain?" he enquired.

"Joining you on this venture was a mistake," she said. "Even though I knew the risks. We had already survived so much, I couldn't imagine it might be worse. And I owed you a debt. But I have a daughter to think of."

"She may well have been no safer fleeing Lossermark," he pointed out. "And leaving you both in the hands of Captain Trumane was not acceptable to me."

"Even so, that Blue . . . I never suspected such a thing might even exist. It leads me to wonder what else we could find in these climes."

"I cannot turn back."

"And I would not ask you to." Zenida averted her gaze and Hilemore realised she saw this conversation as a shameful episode. Admission of fear was never an easy thing for a Varestian. "But," she added, voice heavy with reluctance, "when we reach Kraghurst Station, I will not be accompanying you across the ice."

In fact he had been worrying over how to persuade her to stay behind, fully expecting an outburst of rage at the implied dishonour. "I see," he said, deciding a tone of sombre acceptance rather than relief was appropriate. "Your skills will be missed."

She nodded and got to her feet, moving to the door.

"Sea-sister," he said in Varestian as she reached for the handle, making her pause. "The ship will be yours whilst I'm gone. You will wait four weeks. Not one day longer. In the event we don't return, consider the ship as payment for prior service and sail where you will."

"You think the crew will accept that?"

"I have every confidence in your ability to persuade them."

Her gaze narrowed a little in realisation. "You're saying this because you think it's of no consequence who holds the ship. You think if you fail to return everything will be lost, so what does it matter if you hand your vessel over to a pirate?"

"Privateer," he reminded her, which drew a brief smile from her lips.

"Four weeks then, sea-brother," she said, opening the door. "Not one day longer."

By morning the *Superior* was steaming through what Scrimshine called the Whirls, a fifty-mile-wide stretch of clear water between the Chokes and the Shelf. Hilemore assumed the name came from the swirling eddies disturbing the otherwise placid water. He had ordered the ship to dead slow upon clearing the channel, partly to conserve product but also due to the need to steer clear of the icebergs which slid across their path with worrisome regularity. He had also doubled the watch, ensuring as many eyes as possible were engaged in scanning the sea for the reappearance of Last Look Jack, despite Steelfine's confident assertion that the drake must be dead. "A fearsome beast to be sure, sir," the Islander said. "But still just flesh and blood."

Except there wasn't any blood, Hilemore didn't say, recalling the sight of the ice descending on the giant Blue's neck. He also took note of the fact that Scrimshine's terror remained at a high pitch and his gaze darted about with near feverish energy whilst at the wheel. Fortunately, his entreaties to his ancestors had tailed off into an occasional mutter.

"Ship ahead!" came an excited shout from the speaking-tube to the crow's nest. "Twenty degrees to port!"

Hilemore went out onto the walkway and trained his spy-glass on the given heading. A fine mist lingered over the water and it was a few seconds before he focused the lens on the dark, wide-beamed shape of a mid-sized Blue-hunter. He recognised her as an older ship from the hybrid configuration of paddles and sails. Her stacks were free of smoke and her mainsail swelled sluggishly in the listless morning air.

"Twenty degrees to port," Hilemore called through the bridge window. "Increase speed to one-third. Mr. Steelfine, run up the Yellow Black, let's say hello."

Steelfine had the flag raised in less than a minute, the yellow-and-black pennant that all ships recognised as a peaceful greeting. Hilemore trained his glass on the Blue-hunter once more, grunting in relieved satisfaction at the sight of an identical signal ascending her mainmast. He could see some of her crew clustered on the aft deck, all waving in excitement. Soon the *Superior* drew close enough to make out the Mandinorian letters painted on her hull: SSM *Farlight*.

"A South Seas Maritime ship." Hilemore turned to find Zenida had come to join him. She stood regarding the approaching vessel with a somewhat predatory cast to her gaze. "They were always my favourites. Holds fat with product and crews disinclined to fight. The captains could usually be counted on to come to a reasonable settlement."

"Let's hope they're as accommodating today," Hilemore said. He could see the faces of the *Farlight*'s crew now, taking grim note of the joyous relief on every face. *They think we're their salvation,* he realised, suppressing a momentary urge to simply sail on. *They may have useful intelligence.*

The Blue-hunter's captain was a tall South Mandinorian with a grey beard that reached halfway down his chest. He stood amidst his crew at the *Farlight*'s starboard rail as the *Superior* drew alongside, failing to join in their chorus of cheers. Lines were duly thrown and the ships slowly hauled closer. The *Superior* sat higher in the water than the Blue-hunter, meaning the bearded captain was obliged to stare up at Hilemore as the hulls bumped together. The man inclined his head as Hilemore offered a respectful salute, then barked out a command of sufficient volume and authority to instantly silence his crew. Hilemore noted their emaciated appearance, reckoning it had been several days since they had enjoyed a full meal.

"Remarkable vessel you have there, Captain," the *Farlight*'s master observed. "Never seen the like before."

"We live in an age of wonders, Captain," Hilemore told him, seeing how the fellow's eyes lingered on his face, an unmistakable glimmer of recognition lighting his gaze. "Have we met, sir?" Hilemore asked him.

"No. But I fancy I once served under a relative of yours. Name of Racksmith."

Good old Grandfather, Hilemore thought. *There's isn't a corner of the world where I won't find an old comrade of yours.*

"Then you were in the Protectorate?" he asked, summoning a smile.

"For a time." The man straightened a little, introducing himself in formal tones. "Attcus Tidelow, Master of the SSM *Farlight*."

"Corrick Hilemore, Commander of the IPV *Superior*, en route to Kraghurst Station on company orders."

The smiles lighting the faces of the *Farlight*'s crew faded abruptly, and Captain Tidelow's already stern visage took on an even grimmer aspect. "Then you'd best turn about, Captain," he said. "For there no longer is a Kraghurst Station."

"I always thought he was a myth, myself." Tidelow paused to take a long draw on his pipe, the bowl filled with leaf from the *Superior*'s stocks, then exhaled a thin stream of smoke towards the ward-room ceiling. "Hunted Blue in these waters for the better part of two decades and never caught even the smallest glimpse of him. Sailors do like their tales, the taller the better, and every tale of Last Look Jack I heard came from the lips of those who'd never actually set eyes on him. They'd always heard it from someone else who'd heard it from someone else." His teeth clamped on the stem of his pipe for a second, mouth twitching a little. "Now, I've got a story of my own, one I saw with my own eyes. Though I'd give my soul to the King of the Deep to take the memory away."

"Last Look Jack attacked Kraghurst Station?" Hilemore said.

Tidelow nodded. "'Bout three weeks ago now. Came out of the sea without warning one evening. And he wasn't alone. Him and at least a dozen Blues, all intent on our destruction. Kraghurst had a garrison of sorts, mostly sailors between berths. Did their best I s'pose but they had only rifles and a few cannon. Us and some of the other Blue-hunters tried our luck with harpoons, got a few of the smaller drakes, but not old Jack. We managed to put a steel-headed twelve-foot spike in his hide but it was like sticking a horse with a toothpick. Took maybe a half hour at most and the whole place was up in flames, docks all gone along with most all the ships too. Lucky for us Last Look had turned his flames on the dwellings carved into the Shelf."

Tidelow fell silent, lips twitching once more. "We made all the steam we could and sailed away. I know there's some who'll call us cowards, and maybe they'd be right, but staying to fight it out would've been suicide."

"You did the right thing, Captain," Hilemore assured him.

"Since then we been sailing up and down the Chokes looking for a course that'll take us to open sea. So far, we've found all the usual routes blocked by bergs, almost like we're being sealed in here on purpose. With food running low I made for the channel 'twixt the Shelf and the Chokes, though it's called the Madman's Rush for a reason. But what choice did we have with food running lower by the day and Last Look about to pop up at any moment? And now you're telling me he's dead." Tidelow gave Hilemore a sceptical frown. "Must say, I'm bound to confess a reluctance to believe that."

"Understandable," Hilemore conceded. "But he is certainly wounded, at the very least. Perhaps enough for him to leave us be whilst we complete our mission."

"You're still determined to go on to Kraghurst? There ain't nothing there."

"Destroyed or not, it remains our destination."

"Be that as it may, Captain, I can't go with you. My crew's been loyal so far, but ordering a return to the Shelf is most likely to earn me a mutiny, and I wouldn't blame them."

"I appreciate your position, sir. However, I believe there is a course that would benefit us both. Tell me, do any of your men have knowledge of explosives?"

Talmant stood rigidly at attention on the fore-deck, the set of his features revealing barely controlled emotions. It was a strange sight to witness, Hilemore never having seen him angry before. "I . . ." Talmant began, faltered then started again. "I must object to these orders, sir. My place is on this ship."

"Your objection will be noted in the log, Mr. Talmant," Hilemore said. "But the exigencies of our mission require you to undertake a new posting."

"If I might point out, sir," Talmant said, voice quivering a little. "I followed you on this course at no small risk to my person and my future prospects . . ."

"Also duly noted and appreciated, Lieutenant," Hilemore broke in, putting an edge to his voice. "But you made an adult decision, one worthy of the rank you hold. Questioning your captain's orders and failing to put aside personal preferences, however, are not."

Watching Talmant bite down on some more unwise words, Hilemore was struck by how much older he appeared now. The earnest ensign from several months ago had been much changed by all they had seen and done, but still a vestige of the boy remained. Sighing, Hilemore took a step closer and lowered his voice. "I cannot entrust this to anyone else. Your personnel file shows advanced explosives training at the Academy. Added to that, your navigation skills make you the perfect choice for this mission. Besides"—he glanced over at the group of crewmen transferring half of the *Superior*'s powder stocks to the *Farlight* via the gang-plank strung between the two ships, "I'll need someone to ensure Captain Tidelow keeps his end of the bargain. Why do you think I'm sending four gunners along?"

Talmant took a moment to reply with a stiff nod, though Hilemore detected a faint glimmer of pride amidst the anger still shining in the youth's eyes. "Once we have blasted a channel through the Chokes," he said, "these men will have no desire to linger."

"I'm sure they won't," Hilemore agreed. "However, it is your duty to ensure that the course is marked for our return. I will leave the means to your best judgement."

Talmant stood a little straighter. "Very good, sir," he said, snapping off a fine salute.

Hilemore returned the salute then extended his hand. "Good luck, Mr. Talmant."

The youth hesitated before taking Hilemore's hand, a small grin coming to his lips as Steelfine came forward to clap a large hand to his shoulder. "If it comes to it," he said, leaning closer, "shoot the bosun before the captain. Every mutiny I ever knew of started with the bosun."

"I'll bear it in mind, sir."

An hour later Hilemore stood at the stern watching the *Farlight* sail north, paddles turning swiftly thanks to the coal he had provided. He had also been obliged to hand over a quarter of their food as well as sundry other supplies. Captain Tidelow drove a hard bargain and it was fortunate the *Superior* had been so well-stocked when they seized her. However, Hilemore had drawn the line when the old captain demanded five vials of Green in addition to everything else.

"I shall require all we have to complete my mission," Hilemore told him. "But we find ourselves with a surplus of Blue, which I'm sure will earn a hefty price in any civilised port. You're welcome to two-thirds of it."

The old man's annoyance was palpable but he ceded the point after some protracted wrangling. "Your grandfather was a penny-pincher too," he grumbled. "Take the skin off a man's back just for going a drop over his rum ration."

"I happen to know my grandfather never flogged a man during his entire career," Hilemore returned.

"Tell you that himself, did he?" Tidelow's beard bunched in a grin. "Looks like he had a few tall tales of his own then. Got the stripes on my back to prove it if you want to see."

Hilemore had never been quick to anger but an insult to the memory of Commodore Jakamore Racksmith was bound to make him bridle, probably because it was such a rare occurrence. "No thank you," he told Tidelow in a low voice barely above a growl.

"Oh, don't get all prickled, Captain." Tidelow's grin broadened as he touched a match to the bowl of his pipe. "He was better than most, and the finest fighting sailor I ever saw. But wars aren't won by kindly men." He took an appreciative puff on his pipe then turned towards the rail, placing a foot on the gangway. "I'll take care of your lad," he said, pausing to touch the stem of his pipe to his forehead. "And you can be sure he won't be needing any fire-arms to ensure my adherence to our bargain."

"I know," Hilemore replied.

"Then why send him off with me?"

Hilemore said nothing, clasping his hands behind his back and raising his chin.

"Oh well." Tidelow shrugged and started along the gangway, casting a few final words over his shoulder. "Best of luck with whatever it is brought you here. And take heed of what I said about wars and kindly men."

CHAPTER 15

Lizanne

Beyond the gate the tunnel branched off in three directions. Lizanne chose the one in the centre, reasoning that most new arrivals would instinctively opt for right or left. She had a notion that it would be wise to choose the least used entry point. The gloom was partially alleviated by the light trickling through narrow holes in the tunnel roof, the scant illumination fading as the day wore on. The central passage branched off again after fifty paces and once more she kept to the straight course, following it for another hundred paces until it ended in a junction with another passage. Pausing, Lizanne saw that this tunnel extended left and right in a broad circle that probably encompassed the centre of Scorazin. She chose the leftward direction on a whim and soon came to the first entry point. It consisted of a cramped channel sloping upwards to a slanted iron grate. The prison city's fetid air was thicker now, the patch of light beyond the grate dim with drifting smoke. Lizanne crawled along the channel until she was a foot shy of the grate then cautiously raised her head for the first view of her new home.

Initially, it seemed just an unremarkable alley, no different from the many such alleys her career had taken her to over the years. Certainly the cobbles hadn't been swept for some time and the plaster on the surrounding walls was patchy, revealing weathered brickwork that gave the buildings a slightly diseased appearance. However, she had seen far worse places in her time and a brief scan revealed no obvious threats. Then she saw the corpse. It lay huddled against the walls, so shrunken and wasted she had taken it for a bundle of discarded rags. Now she saw white bone through the threadbare overalls that clad the remains and a matted clump of long dark hair obscuring the skull. The hair and the smallness of the corpse made this unmistakably the body of a woman. Lizanne wondered if she had been a new arrival like her, venturing forth only to be cut down within feet of the grate. It was equally possible that she was a veteran of this place, used up and left to wither in this alley. In either case, Lizanne decided to seek another entry point.

She was even more cautious when peering out from the next grate, having detected raised voices as she crawled along the channel, loud in argument and slurred with drink. Amongst the grunting babble she discerned two distinct accents, one with the broad vowels of the northern empire and the other the more clipped, nasal tones of the western midlands.

"'S your fault, y'fucker," the midlander said in a tense growl. "Had to open y'shitty mouth. Two sacks by morning. How in the name of the Emperor's balls are we s'posed to manage that?"

"Lick my arse," the northerner replied, his tone rich in aggression but also possessed of a certain weariness. "You're the one gave her the wrong count. Y'know what she's like with numbers. Never forgets. I told you that your first day." A short pause then. "Gimme that, you've had plenty."

"Fuck off!"

Lizanne raised herself as the sounds of a scuffle came through the grate. This entry point was positioned near an outflow pipe, which cast a steady stream of yellow water into a muddy channel leading towards the river. The stench was a gut-stirring blow to the senses, forcing her to swallow a gag and blink tears from her eyes. She could see the river-bank thirty yards or so off to the right, a bar of thick mud where dim figures were visible through the drifting haze; the mud-slingers Constable Darkanis had warned her about. Two men were engaged in a struggle beneath the pipe, stumbling around in a parody of dance with a bottle clutched between them.

"Give it, you greedy sot!" the northerner grunted, tugging hard on the bottle. He was the larger of the two, with a mane of shaggy dark hair and the reddened, bloated features of one who had been lost in indulgence for several years. His opponent was of roughly the same height but with a gaunt aspect and, despite the disparity in build, proved staunchly unwilling to give up his bottle. Lizanne took note of their clothing, standard overalls like hers, worn under knee-length jackets which appeared to have been stitched together from sackcloth. Her interest was piqued by the fact that they both had identical emblems stitched on the shoulders, a red-and-yellow symbol she couldn't quite make out.

"Hah!" The northerner gave a triumphal laugh as he finally managed to wrestle the bottle from his opponent. The gaunt man lunged for him but fell face-down in the mud, drawing a delighted bellow from his companion before he raised the bottle to his lips, then froze as Lizanne got to her feet and stepped up to the grate. She clutched her blanket tight and peered out at him, eyes wide and apparently uncomprehending, unlike his, which had abruptly narrowed in vulturine calculation.

"Gizzit!" the gaunt man snarled, darting closer to snatch the bottle from the northerner. He drew back in guarded puzzlement at his adversary's lack of a reaction before turning to regard the object of his interest. They exchanged a brief glance of mutual decision then slowly began to advance towards the grate. The gaunt man attempted a smile which would have failed to instill trust in the most addled fool. His companion seemed incapable of such artifice and kept his features free of expression though his eyes shone with hungry interest.

"New arrival, eh?" the gaunt man asked. Lizanne maintained her unblinking, blank mask as they drew closer. To her slight annoyance they both stopped a foot short of the grate, crouching to peer at her through the iron bars. "Aren't you lucky, dearest one," the gaunt man said, his inexpert smile broadening to reveal an incomplete set of rotted teeth. Even amidst the fetid stink from the river Lizanne could still smell his breath. "Finding us here to greet you, I mean," he went on, inching closer. "Decent folk are hard to come by within these walls."

Lizanne said nothing, continuing to stare and bunching her fists in her blanket.

"It's alright, dearest," the gaunt man said. "No need to be feart of us, is there Dralky?" He glanced at his comrade, who gave an unsmiling shake of his head. Lizanne didn't like the keenness of the larger man's gaze, having hoped to find it more dulled by drink.

"The . . ." she began, adding a shake to her voice, "the constable said I need to go to the Miner's Repose."

The northerner gave a grunt of smothered laughter whilst the gaunt man managed to conceal a smirk before replying with an assured nod. "O'course he did, dearest. We know the place well. Work there most days, in point of fact. No mining for the Furies. See?" He turned to tap a finger to the yellow-and-red patch on his shoulder, Lizanne seeing it clearly now: a flaming match. "It's like a club," he continued. "A club for those with skills. You got skills, dearest?"

"Yes." Lizanne's eyes flicked from one to the other as she drew back a step or two. Appearing overly trusting too early was unwise. Men such as these might spend most of their lives several sails to the breeze, but they invariably shared an innate cunning and instinctive nose for danger. "I'm a seamstress," she said, drawing back farther.

The larger man's arms twitched as he restrained the impulse to grab at her through the bars, earning a warning glare from his friend. "Good," he said, once again revealing the awful spectacle of his teeth. "That's good. Skilled folk got value in here, y'see? You come on with us to the Miner's Repose and we'll introduce you to a nice lady who knows best how to make use of your skills." He extended a bony hand through the bars, beckoning. "Come on now, dearest." He was unable to resist the impulse to lick his lips as she edged closer. "Come on with me and Dralky."

Lizanne crouched, reaching out towards the bars, making ready to push the grate aside, then stopped. "On second thoughts," she said, returning the gaunt man's smile, "I think not. You stink so much I'm amazed your friend here can stand to stick his cock in your mouth."

As ever with the more low-rent thug, anger always outweighed cunning. They both lunged in unison, Lizanne dancing back as their hands shot between the bars to claw at her. The blanket unfurled in her hands with a snap, looping over their wrists before they had time to snatch their arms back. She exerted her well-honed muscles to good effect, drawing the knot tight with sufficient force to extract a pained shout from both men. They had time to voice a few expletive-laden threats at her before their shouts turned to screams as she stepped closer, jumping as high as the tunnel would allow to bring her weight down on their trapped limbs. She had never been particularly gifted in body-weight, so it took two attempts before she was rewarded with the satisfying crack of breaking bone.

"Now then, gentlemen," she said, unknotting the blanket from their wrists and allowing them to collapse in sputtering agony, "let us have a little chat."

Lizanne encountered little trouble finding the Miner's Repose. She had followed Constable Darkanis's advice and waited for darkness before exiting the tunnels, choosing another entrance well away from the river. True to his description, the sign hanging above the door was an illegible, mud-spattered square offering no clue to the name of the raucous tavern it guarded, but the directions provided by her two greeters had been sufficient to guide her steps. She lingered outside for a short while, listening to the loud but largely laughter-free babble seeping from the lit windows. It consisted mostly of the raised voices of men engaged in competition or argument. Cards, drink and women were always a potent combination. Amidst the general din she detected the faint sound of a pianola being played with unexpected artistry, recognising the tune as the Mountain Breeze Cadenza from Illemont's third concerto, a classic of North Mandinorian composition.

I wonder if they know the full piece, she thought, hefting her sackcloth-wrapped bundle and making her way inside. *It would be nice to hear it again.*

The interior of the Miner's Repose was thick with the scent of cheap tobacco and hazy with smoke from a poorly maintained chimney. Overall-clad men stood around in thick clusters, earthenware tankards in every hand as they jostled and exchanged dull-voiced conversation. Thanks to Dralky and Jemus she knew the ground floor of the establishment was for drinkers only, those who either couldn't afford or had no interest in the entertainments found on the upper floors. Predictably, the conversation grew more muted as Lizanne made her entrance, many falling silent to regard her with various expressions of lust, some desperate, others resentful as it was never pleasant to want something you couldn't have. One man, a stocky fellow with a jaundiced tint to his skin, took a large gulp from his tankard before starting towards her, then coming to an abrupt halt as a strident female voice rang out from the bar.

"Y'know the rules, cock-brain!"

The stocky man hesitated a moment, teeth bared in a grimace of frustration as his gaze roamed Lizanne from head to toe before he retreated back into the crowd.

"Eyes on your drinks, lest you want me to fetch Anatol down here," the female voice continued, the crowd parting to allow a tall woman in a red skirt and surprisingly clean lace blouse to make her way through. She approached Lizanne with a confident stride, coming to a halt to tower over her by at least ten inches. She stood in silent appraisal for a long moment. Lizanne took note of the burn-scar marring the flesh around the woman's right eye, the socket filled with some kind of smoothed yellow crystal. She had the fine bones and length of limb that would have made her a sought-after fashion model in a corporate holding, but for the scar.

"Constable sent you, I'm guessing?" she asked, Lizanne recognising a Corvus accent, though not as coarse or thick as Hyran's. "Which one?"

"Darkanis," Lizanne replied.

The woman gave a satisfied nod. "Good. He doesn't charge as much as the others. I'm Melina." Her good eye went to the sackcloth bundle in Lizanne's hands. "What you got there?"

"It's for Electress Atalina. May I see her please?"

A twitch of puzzled amusement passed across the tall woman's lips. "That's not how it works, love. She'll see you when she decides it's time."

"It's from Dralky and Jemus. They said it would settle their debt."

Melina's brow creased into a frown. "How d'you know those two cock-brains?"

"They were kind enough to give me directions."

They stared at one another for some time. Lizanne had known this to be a dangerous woman at first glance, her eyes detecting the outline of a concealed knife beneath her blouse. It was also safe to assume she had more secreted about her person. But Lizanne also judged her smart enough to recognise someone equally dangerous.

"If you waste her time," Melina said finally, "she'll make you work the first week with no pay and no wash-bucket."

"Understood."

"Your funeral." Melina turned and started towards a staircase at the rear of the bar, Lizanne following and paying scant heed to the many eyes tracking over her. "What's your name, love?" Melina asked as they climbed the stairs.

"Six-one-four."

"Forget that shit. Need a name if you're gonna work here. Doesn't have to be your real one, not that it makes a difference either way. Best make it pretty though, customers prefer it. No Grubnilas or Egathas in the Miner's Repose."

"Krista, then," Lizanne said. A name she had used before but those still alive to relate the tale were far away.

"Bit ordinary," Melina said. "Get more clients if you go for something noble. It's where I got mine. Princess Melina. It's from an old tale about some silly tart who agrees to marry the King of the Deep."

"I know the story," Lizanne said. "And Krista will do."

They ascended to the first floor where men clustered around the gaming tables in various states of excitement or despair. In the corner a slender young man sat playing a pianola, the tune now far more simple and jaunty than the cadenza she had recognised outside. Despite its simplicity, the player still managed to convey an effortless artistry as his hands floated over the keys. Most of the surrounding tables were given over to the traditional Corvantine card and dice game of Pastazch, with a couple of spinwheels for those who preferred a more random method of losing money. Bets were placed using wooden chits, the length of which determined the value. After some judicious questioning Jemus had been particularly helpful in educating her on the system of currency adopted in Scorazin. One sack of mined minerals formed the basis of exchange, the length of the chit reflecting the value of the contents. Copper, being the most valuable, earned a five-inch chit, whilst pyrite earned four, sulphur three and coal two. Chits could be subdivided into shorter sub-units; half-sack, quarter-sack and so on. It was all surprisingly logical and, according to Jemus, worked well as long as you had the ore to back up the chits. "Anyone caught faking a chit will find himself tied to a pole with his guts around his neck on Ore Day," he had said, offering a desperate and ingratiating laugh which had singularly failed to stir any sympathy in Lizanne's breast.

"Welcome to the Sanctum of Earthly Bliss," Melina said as they ascended to the top floor. It consisted of a circular chamber with a seating area of velvet-cushioned couches surrounded by a series of rooms. About a third of the doors were closed and a few employees lounged around in various states of undress. They were all heavily painted with rouged lips and cheeks, making it hard to judge their age, though Lizanne put the youngest at no more than sixteen and the eldest at close to fifty.

"New meat, Mel?" one asked, a chunky woman with a mass of auburn curls sprouting from her head in the manner of an unkempt bird's-nest. She stepped closer to Lizanne, cigarillo dangling from her lips and an open steel flask in her hand. "Do yerself a favour and sod off to the mines, darlin'," she advised. "I can tell you ain't got the backbone for this."

"Shut it, Silv," Melina snapped, staring hard at the chunky woman until she averted her gaze and retreated to the couches. "This way," Melina told Lizanne, moving to a corridor opposite the staircase. "Don't mind Silvona," she said. "She just doesn't want the competition."

A large man rose from a chair beside a door at the end of the corridor as they approached. He stood tall enough that his head was only an inch or two shy of the ceiling and had the broad, irregular features of a prize-fighter. The impression was heightened by the concave nose he revealed as he turned and bent to press a kiss to Melina's cheek.

"This is Anatol," she said, clasping and releasing the large man's hand in a sign of genuine affection. "He's mine, so hands off."

Lizanne took careful note of Anatol as he looked her over, finding none of the dull-eyed desperation that had been writ so large in the faces of Jemus and Dralky. "She's no whore," he said to Melina in a soft voice that nevertheless retained a certain rumbling quality.

"Darkanis sent her," Melina replied with a shrug.

"Then he should have looked closer." Anatol angled his head, eyes narrowing as they tracked from her face to the bundle she carried. "What's that?"

"It's for the Electress," Lizanne repeated.

"Jemus and Dralky's debt," Melina elaborated. "So she says anyway."

"Need to see it before you see her," Anatol said, extending a shovel-sized hand.

A quick glance at his face told Lizanne the folly of arguing the point so she handed the bundle over. He pulled the sackcloth open and peered at the contents for a moment, his only reaction a soft grunt of satisfaction. He closed the sack and once again extended his hand, staring at Lizanne in expectation until she handed over the knife she had taken from Dralky and the weighted leather sap she had taken from Jemus. "And the rest," Anatol said.

"This was a gift," Lizanne said, handing him Darkanis's penknife. "I'd like it back when I leave."

"And you'll get it," he said, turning and knocking on the door, "*if* she lets you."

After a short delay an irritated voice sounded through the door. "For fuck's sake, Anatol, it's late."

Anatol turned the handle and opened the door a fraction, dipping his head through the gap to speak in carefully respectful tones. "New arrival, Electress. Says she's here to pay off Jemus and Dralky."

A short pause then a sigh. "What the fuck," the voice said, the tones clearer now. Lizanne was surprised to find it largely free of an accent, almost cultured in fact. "Bring her in. Never too late in the day for a good laugh, I always say."

Anatol opened the door and stepped aside, gesturing for Lizanne to enter. "Hands in view at all times," he warned as she passed by. The room was large and striking in its contrast to everything Lizanne had seen of Scorazin so far. A bookcase stood against the far wall and velvet drapes hung over the windows. An extensive mahogany desk sat in the centre of the room, behind which one of the largest women Lizanne had ever seen reclined in a leather armchair, her bare and impressively broad feet propped on the desk. She was leaning forward to run a metal rasp over the feet, grunting a little with the effort.

"Pardon me," she apologised as Lizanne came to a halt before the desk. "I'm a martyr to me corns."

Lizanne noted again the incongruity of her words and her accent. *Like a countess speaking the words of a street-walker,* she thought. She said nothing, keeping her hands at her sides and watching the large woman file powdered skin onto the desk. Lizanne put her age at somewhere past fifty, brows heavy and shoulders broad. She wore a sleeveless dress of violet-hued silk, the flesh on her arms wobbling as she went about her ablutions. Despite the excess weight Lizanne could see the innate strength in her, reckoning she might even pose a challenge to Anatol in a test of brute force.

"When did you get in?" the Electress asked, the rasp still filing away.

"A few hours ago."

"A few hours, eh? And you've already managed to extract payment from the worst two shit-stains in the Furies. Impressive." She turned to Anatol. "What's she got?"

The huge man moved to the desk and placed the bundle before her along with the knife and the sap. The Electress groaned as she removed her feet from the desk and set the rasp aside before unwrapping the bundle. She took a moment to view the revealed contents in expressionless silence before raising her gaze to Lizanne. "One but not the other. Where's Dralky?"

"He had a thicker neck," Lizanne replied. "My arm got tired and it was getting late."

"Then how do I know he's not still out there somewhere?"

Lizanne turned to Anatol. "I need to reach into my clothing."

He exchanged a glance with the Electress, who gave a nod of assent. "Slowly," Anatol said.

Lizanne undid the first three buttons on her overalls then reached inside to undo the cloth she had wrapped around her midriff. Unlike Jemus,

Dralky had possessed a full set of teeth, although about half had been fashioned from gold. The Electress gave a huff of satisfaction as Lizanne placed the teeth on the desk. "Was going to make him pull them out himself with pliers," the Electress mused. "Or get him and Jemus to fight to the death. Hadn't quite decided."

She leaned back in her chair, keeping her eyes on Lizanne but speaking to Anatol. "Get her a seat. Then leave us alone."

Lizanne tried not to enjoy the comfort of the padded leather chair as she sank onto it, the first time she had experienced the sensation since leaving Corvus.

"What's your name?" the Electress asked.

"Krista."

The large woman's mouth twitched a little. "No it isn't."

"Melina said it didn't matter."

"Not for most of the new arrivals who fetch up on my door, but I'm sensing that you're a special case." She reached for a silver-plated box on the desk and extracted a cigarillo. "Get these from the guards," she said, striking a match and lighting up. "One of several favours they do for me, 'cos of what I do for them. Wanna know what that is?"

"I would assume you bribe them," Lizanne replied.

"I do." Smoke billowed as the woman smiled. "And a greedy bunch of bastards they are, apart from Darkanis, but he still expects to wet his beak now and then. You'd be surprised how much an off-the-books sack of sulphur ore will sell for. But it's not just that. I enjoy certain privileges because I understand the need to keep this place orderly, or as orderly as a place filled with the worst scum in the empire can be."

She paused to turn the box towards Lizanne, raising a questioning eyebrow. "No thank you," Lizanne declined.

"Worried I might have added something to the leaf?" the Electress asked.

"I try to avoid indulgence at times like these."

The Electress rested her elbows on the desk, one hand on the other with the cigarillo smoking between her broad fingers. "What did you do on the outside?" she asked after a long pause. "And don't try telling me you were a fucking governess or some such."

"I stole things and I killed people."

"For who?"

"Whoever paid me."

"The Cadre ever pay you?"

Lizanne shook her head. "They couldn't afford me. Besides, I doubt they'd find me a suitable recruit."

A soft chuckle escaped the Electress as she took another draw on her cigarillo. "So that's it. Another child of the revolution."

"I'll confess I suffered from some naïve notions in my youth. I assure you any political allegiance is all behind me now. But the experience did leave me with a particular set of skills, skills I'm prepared to offer to you."

"How generous of you. But you may have noticed that this is a prison. I want a thief or a killer I can throw a rock in any direction and find one."

"Not like me you can't."

The Electress nodded at the grisly prize on the desk. Jemus's head lay on its side, face towards Lizanne, a vestige of that final desperate smile frozen on his lips. "You think you're the first to bring me some fucker's head and demand a favour?"

"I'm not demanding anything," Lizanne said. "Merely offering my services. If you find them unacceptable I'll be happy to leave."

"And offer yourself up to one of my rivals, no doubt. I assume you extracted a list of likely candidates from this bastard before you killed him."

Lizanne said nothing, knowing confirmation would be taken as a threat. "I chose to come here," she said instead.

The Electress gave Lizanne another long look of examination before shaking her head in consternation. "Got a lot going on behind those pretty eyes. More than I'd like. And, being honest, you'll probably live longer as a whore. I treat my girls well."

"I'm sure you do. But it's not my line of work."

The Electress shrugged and stubbed out her cigarillo. "You know how to deal Pastazch?"

"Corvus Twist and Varestian Draw-down."

"We play our own rules here, Scorazin Two-roll. It's basically the same as Corvus Twist with three more wild cards. I'm sure you'll pick it up."

"You want me to be a croupier?"

"For now. Since you're so averse to mattress-work. Can't have you just hanging around the place. People would talk." She turned to the door, raising her voice, "Anatol! Find this bitch a room!"

CHAPTER 16

Clay

Kraghurst Station was served by a floating-timber dock arranged along a series of buoys. The whole structure was tethered to the ice by huge chains, so as to allow it to rise and fall with the tide. Clay thought it must have been an impressive sight before Last Look Jack came by for a visit, a fine example of the human facility for ingenuity in even the worst climate. Now, however, it was a ragged thing of splintered and burnt wood, held in place by blackened chains, which had failed to burn in the fires cast by the drakes.

He sat at the front of the launch, Loriabeth huddled close to his side. She was finding the cold harder to bear by the day but reacted with fury to any suggestion she stay on the ship. Captain Hilemore had kept the party as small as possible. In addition to the Longrifles and Hilemore himself, the expedition consisted of the hulking Islander and four of his most trusted riflemen along with a predictably miserable Scrimshine and, to Clay's surprise, the Corvantine lieutenant and two of his men. Clay suspected that Sigoral's presence might be due to concerns over what mischief the man might foster in the captain's absence.

Beyond the ruined dock Clay could see dark, shadowed openings carved into the Shelf where Scrimshine said the inhabitants of Kraghurst Station made their home. "They have their own company," he explained before they set off. "The Kraghurst Trading Co-operative, they called it. Bunch've reprobates who'd been thrown out of the larger corporations for various misdeeds, but they certainly made a good go of it. South Seas Maritime has been trying to buy them out for years." His gaze darkened as he looked at the ruined dock. "Guessing they won't have to bother now."

The launch rounded the western edge of the dock and made for the Shelf where a number of iron ladders had been fixed into the ice. "Ship oars!"

Steelfine said as the launch came within the last few feet of the Shelf. "Fix a grapnel on that ladder, if you'd be so kind, Mr. Torcreek."

Clay flexed his fingers, numb despite the thick gloves he wore, and hefted the rope and grapnel at his feet. The water was placid and the launch close enough to make it an easy throw, the iron hook snagging on one of the lower rungs at the first attempt. Preacher and Braddon helped him haul the launch to the base of the ladder where Clay began to climb up.

"Belay that!" Hilemore barked. "Mr. Steelfine and Lieutenant Sigoral will go first."

"I ain't one to shirk a risk, Captain," Clay told him, finding his pride piqued a little.

"You're our only Blood-blessed," Hilemore reminded him. "Without you this mission is over."

He nodded at Steelfine, who shouldered his way past Clay and onto the ladder, ascending with a sailor's customary swiftness, Sigoral close behind. The marine had a repeating carbine strapped across his back whilst Steelfine carried a sea-axe and a pistol. The two men reached the top quickly, climbing up onto the ledge and drawing their weapons before disappearing inside. Steelfine's head reappeared after a few moments. "All clear, sir!"

At Hilemore's insistence Clay and the Longrifles were the last up the ladder, having spent some time fixing hauling lines to the supplies. Following Scrimshine's advice, the captain had ensured the food consisted mainly of salted meat plus a crate of preserved limes to stave off scurvy. There seemed to be much more than they would ever need but the convict had been insistent. "When a man's out on the ice," he said, "he'll eat twice what he usually would and still find his belt looser by the day. At these climes the cold wears at you like a grindstone."

When Clay finally ascended the ladder he found himself confronted by a broad, rectangular cavern with dozens of side tunnels in the walls. Hilemore and Steelfine stood regarding what appeared to be a pile of blackened sticks at the rear of the chamber as the rest of the party went about unpacking the supplies.

"They must have clustered together at the end," Hilemore commented as Clay drew closer. He could see the pile for what it was now, fleshless skulls grinning up at him from the mass of part-melted bone.

"How many?" he asked.

"Hard to tell," Steelfine said. "At least twenty here. Lieutenant Sigoral and I found another dozen in the next chamber."

"A sustained stream of fire," Hilemore said, glancing around at the glassy smoothness of the surrounding ice. "Last Look Jack was very thorough, it seems."

"So no survivors," Clay muttered, turning away from the burnt monstrosity. "At least you gave them some revenge, Captain."

Hilemore merely glanced at him before turning his gaze to the cavern opening and the *Superior* sitting at anchor beyond. Clay knew he was wondering if he would ever see it again and wished he could offer some assurance. But the closer they came to their goal, and the fulfilment of their shared future, he found himself increasingly lacking in certainty. *We were always going to be here,* he reminded himself. *But where next?*

He saw Hilemore blink before removing his gaze from his ship, striding off, voice raised to cast out a series of orders. "Let's get these packs filled, lads. I want to be gone from here before nightfall."

Clay's judgement proved to be grimly accurate. Their journey through the tunnels and chambers of Kraghurst Station revealed only more corpses in various states of immolation, as well as a wealth of incinerated furniture and supplies. They found only one unburnt body, a large man of middling years huddled in a side tunnel, his hair and skin frozen solid and his eyes two blank orbs in a desiccated leather mask.

"Cold got him," Scrimshine judged. "And right quick too. Tends to happen when a fella loses all hope of deliverance."

"He saved himself," Braddon said. "Found a corner where the fire couldn't reach."

"Truly," Scrimshine conceded. "But what to do next? No ships to take you away. All the food burned up and the open ice the only place left to go." He crouched to rummage through the dead man's stiff, frosted clothing, pocketing a small roll of exchange notes. "Won't do him much good will it?" he said in response to Braddon's disapproving frown.

They pressed on, the air growing colder the deeper they went. Scrimshine called to Hilemore to halt when they came to a large chamber where daylight could be seen through a narrow opening at the far end. "Looks like we've finally had some luck, Skipper," he said, moving towards a tarpaulin-covered mound. He pulled the tarpaulin aside to reveal a collection of narrow objects, each about seven feet long. They were constructed from a wood-and-wicker frame set atop a pair of iron runners.

"Guessing the dogs went the way of everyone else," Scrimshine observed. "Not that I mind. Vicious bugger, your sled-dog. Have your fingers off if y'don't handle him proper."

"What use are they without dogs to haul them?" Clay asked.

"Man can haul a sled too." Scrimshine bent to retrieve a harness from atop the nearest sled. "Less you want that bundle weighing on your back all the way to the mountain."

They dragged five of the sleds out onto the ice and piled on the supplies. Hilemore divided the party into teams and allocated each a sled, sparing Loriabeth, who, for once, didn't voice an objection. She stood apart as they donned the harnesses, staring at the vast expanse to the south. The ice stretched away towards the misted horizon beneath a dark blue sky where stars were already glimmering. Not since the Red Sands had Clay seen anything so completely devoid of life or feature. He saw how Loriabeth's expression alternated between reluctance and determination now she stood confronted by the enormity of their task. *All the guts and skill in the world can't put any more meat on those bones,* he thought, wondering if it might have been better to chain her to her bunk before disembarking the ship.

"Won't be much use this far south, Skipper," Scrimshine advised as Hilemore flipped open a small compass. "You'll find the needle dances about too much to gauge a heading."

"Then how do we fix our course?"

Scrimshine jerked his head at the stars beading the darkening sky. "The mountain sits betwixt Southern Jewell and the Crossed Swords. Reckon we got us maybe two more hours of daylight."

Hilemore glanced around to ensure they were all buckled in then waved a hand before starting off, the three other men in his team marching in step as he led the way. "Then we'd best make good use of it."

They covered a little over five miles before nightfall. The ice was a deceptive surface to traverse. Apparently thick snow-banks often transformed into loose piles of powder concealing slippery patches that left more than a few of the party with a painful rump. Elsewhere the surface rose into large jagged mounds several yards wide, necessitating long diversions from their course until they found a way around. Added to the aggravating terrain was the all-consuming cold, which Clay found sapped his strength with every step. It seemed a tangible thing, pressing in on all sides and making every breath feel like an inhalation of tiny needles. Like the others he had been quick to tie a cloth over his mouth and nose but it provided only minor relief.

At Scrimshine's urging they made camp by upending the sleds and arranging them in a circle. They then strung tents between the sleds to form a roof with a gap in the centre where Steelfine used lamp oil to light a fire. The evening meal consisted of boiled salt-beef washed down with black coffee dosed with a hefty portion of sugar. True to Scrimshine's word, Clay found his stomach still growling after wolfing down his meal though he resisted the urge to ask for seconds. He sat with his arm around his cousin's shoulders as she cradled a tin mug of steaming coffee with trembling hands. Scrimshine sat close by, using a small knife to whittle on a piece of bone from the Blue corpse he had helped Skaggerhill harvest.

"What was it?" Clay asked him, recalling his tale from their interview back in the Lossermark gaol. "The great treasure you came here to find?"

Scrimshine kept his attention on his carving, though his bony face betrayed a certain sheepish reluctance as he muttered a reply, "Bledthorne's Hoard."

On the far side of the fire, Clay heard Steelfine give voice to a rarely heard chuckle, one that was soon echoed by the other sailors. Hilemore turned to the smuggler, raising an amused eyebrow. "Did you, perchance, have a map showing you the exact location? Possibly a map that had been hidden for years?"

"Wasn't my idea," Scrimshine said, scowling a little. "And it was a long time ago, before the story was so widely known."

"Story?" Clay enquired.

"You mean to say you've never heard of Arneas Bledthorne?" Hilemore asked in mock surprise. "The Red Scourge of the Eastern Seas. A pirate so fearsome Queen Arrad herself offered a million gold crowns to anyone who could bring her his head. For ten years or more the Royal Fleet hunted him hither and yon, but always he eluded them, taking ships at will and casting their crews into the sea for his vile amusement. So great was his fortune, it's said his ship, the *Dreadfire*, nearly sank under its weight. Eventually, with all ports closed to him, he sailed south and hid his treasure somewhere in these frozen wastes, then murdered his crew lest they betray the location. Maddened by his crimes and his greed, and lacking any hands to sail his ship, he was unable to leave and died raving amidst vast wealth."

"Quite a story," Braddon observed.

"Indeed so," Hilemore said. "And for many years unscrupulous cartographers made good money selling maps purporting to show the very spot where Bledthorne's Hoard could be found. Eventually the story attracted the attention of a Consolidated Research Company scholar who traced it back to a novel from the late Imperial Era. It transpired the tale was mostly fiction. There had been a minor pirate named Arneas Bledthorne, who disappeared along with his ship somewhere in the southern seas. But in his short career his list of prizes amounted to the grand total of three ships, none of them laden with treasure. Also, there is no documentation confirming that Queen Arrad had ever even heard of him, let alone offered a reward for his capture. However, this doesn't prevent the foolish or deluded occasionally risking their lives on the promise of an aged parchment they won at the card table."

"Captain Sturwynd wasn't a man to cross," Scrimshine said, grimacing at the memory. "Especially when he had a firm notion in his head. He spent a great deal of loot on that map and wasn't about to be told he was a fool for doing so."

"I'm guessing you never found anything," Clay said.

"Just a lotta ice, lad. And poor mad Captain Sturwynd found his death." Scrimshine gave a sorrowful sigh. "Crazed and cruel though he was, he'd saved my skin on a bundle of occasions, so when he finally gasped out his last I wouldn't let the others eat him. It got ugly for a time, a right old knife party. Still, plenty more food to go round when it was done."

The nascent atmosphere of humour in the shelter faded quickly. "Your crew ate their dead?" Steelfine asked, staring hard at Scrimshine.

The smuggler shrugged, not looking up from his work. "You'll be surprised how fast a man starts to resemble a side of pork when you've tracked across the ice on an empty belly for days on end."

A few voices muttered in judgemental disgust but fell silent at Hilemore's sharp glare. Scrimshine, apparently oblivious to any offence he may have caused, kept on whittling. Clay drifted off to sleep a short while later to the steady scrape of Scrimshine's blade on drake bone.

It took five days before Mount Reygnar came into view, rising above the morning haze and dispelling Clay's weariness with the sheer novelty of looking upon something that broke the endless monotony of the ice. They reached the lower slopes by evening, making camp amid a cluster of massive boulders part-submerged in the encroaching glacier. Reygnar loomed above, stirring unwelcome memories of the narrow peak that had concealed the White's lair, though the two mountains were very different. The Nail had been a giant rocky spike whilst Mount Reygnar was a flat-topped mound that resembled the snow-speckled hide of a sleeping monster. But still, Clay couldn't suppress a shudder of unease as his gaze tracked across the slopes.

"Wondering what might be inside?" his uncle asked, coming to his side.

"Maybe," Clay replied with a shrug.

"The smuggler says it's a volcano, though it's stayed quiet for years. Nothing inside but molten rock."

"There was a whole lotta molten rock beneath the Nail. I think the folks that built the city chose it for that."

"Something you saw in your visions?"

Clay closed his eyes as the collage of memories crowded in. He had tried sorting through it all more than once, but so many images had been pushed into his head that making sense of it all was never easy, the effort inevitably leaving him with a pounding headache. "Just a guess, Uncle," he said.

Hilemore and the Longrifles climbed the peak the next day. Loriabeth wasn't among them, Braddon having ordered her to stay at the camp and eat all the food Steelfine prepared for her. She was growing more emaciated by the day and Clay knew it was only a matter of time before she would have to be placed on a sled and dragged along. Seeing the guilt dominating his uncle's face, Clay thought better of voicing any concern.

Mount Reygnar wasn't a particularly tall peak in comparison to the steep giants of the Coppersoles, but still the cold made the going hard. Thankfully, the mountain's flanks consisted of black, hard-packed ash that was largely free of ice so the route wasn't overly treacherous. A four-hour climb interspersed with numerous rest stops got them to the summit where the ground dropped away into a crater some fifty feet wide. The bottom of the crater consisted of a pile of boulders that appeared to have been undisturbed for many years.

"Guess she's lost her spark," Skaggerhill observed in a ragged gasp, slumping down onto the ash.

"Sometime ago, I'd judge," Hilemore said, casting a critical eye over the crater. "Otherwise, I suspect we would be looking out on a stretch of open water." He turned to the south and extended a hand to Clay. "The sketch, if you please, Mr. Torcreek."

Clay took the paper from the depths of his heavy overcoat and handed it over. "I'd judge the viewpoint to be some miles south-east," Hilemore said after a moment's study of their surroundings. "Given the shape of the peak as depicted here."

"Just over twenty miles south-south-east," Preacher said, standing with his longrifle cradled in the crook of his arm as he pointed out the bearing.

"You can see it, sir?" Hilemore asked with a sceptical frown.

"An eagle's got nothing on Preacher, Captain," Braddon said. "He says he sees it, he sees it."

Hilemore extended his spy-glass and moved to Preacher's side, following his extended arm to find the target. "Impressive eyes," he said with a faint smile of satisfaction. "Mr. Torcreek, I believe we have our destination."

Clay came to his side as Hilemore handed him the glass. It took a moment to bring the thing into focus, the great twisted spire seeming little more than a malformed thorn at this distance. But it was unmistakably the same structure from the vision. He felt no joy at this validation, the confirmation that his visions weren't simply the conjuration of a traumatised mind. If anything the sight stirred a sinking sensation in his gut; a sense of helplessness in the face of the vision's commands. *We were always going to be here.*

The ice became easier to traverse south of the mountain, covered by a thin blanket of powdery snow and the going more even. The sleds skidded across the surface easily and they made good progress, covering the distance to the spire in the space of three days. The size of the thing became more evident with every passing mile, towering above the haze to such an altitude that they had to crane their necks to see the top. The base came into view halfway through the third day, Clay estimating it to be over a hundred yards wide where it met the ice. From the slanted flanks it was clear it grew to even broader proportions beneath the surface. At the sight of it the entire party came to an unbidden halt, standing in silence as their breath misted the air. Clay could understand their awe. The vision hadn't done justice to the scale of the spire, nor captured the sensation of insignificance engendered by being so close to it.

His eyes tracked over the spire's surface, finding it dark and mostly featureless. As he looked closer he saw that the shade varied a little, straight lines and hard angles forming a pattern that confirmed this thing to be unnatural. Someone, some thing, had made it. As his gaze ascended, the spire's flanks took on a definite twist, becoming more acute near the top where it narrowed to a sharp point.

"They'll have someone's eye out with that," Skaggerhill said, which drew only muted laughter.

Clay tore his gaze from the spire at the sound of boots crunching across the snow towards him. He found himself shuddering as he turned to face Hilemore, a fresh ache lurching in his head as the vision and present reality became one.

"So," Hilemore said, "this is where we save the world, Mr. Torcreek."

II

Beneath a Starless Sky

"BLESSED DEMON" STRIKES AGAIN

Death Stalks the Marsh-Wold

Rogue Blood-Blessed Suspected

"Protectorate Constabulary Incompetent"
Claims Voter Agitator

Inhabitants of the Marsh-Wold Holdings were yesterday thrown into a fresh state of terror by the advent of another grisly discovery amongst the normally placid fields of their pastoral refuge. The victims on this occasion were the entire Shrivemill family, numbering three adults and six children, together with several employees at the family estate located in the heart of the Wold. Loyal readers will know this to be the fourth such outrage in this holding in as many weeks, bringing the total number of victims to thirty-six, at least half being of the managerial class.

The terrible events at Shrivemill Manor closely follow the same pattern of previous massacres; the main residence and lesser buildings reduced to cinders whilst those who had escaped the fires are found strewn about the grounds in various states of evisceration. Most of the injuries suffered by these unfortunates are too gruesome to detail at length but one witness to the aftermath of the Shrivemill atrocity described to an *Intelligencer* correspondent "a tree, made up of bodies, all smashed up and twisted together . . ." At this point the witness became so distressed by their recollections they were obliged to disgorge their breakfast.

The nature of these crimes has inevitably led to assertions that they are the work of a rogue Blood-blessed, a figure quickly grown to the status of dark legend in the vicinity, having earned the grim pseudonym of the "Blessed Demon." The suspicion that these atrocities may be the work of a Blessed hand is given further credence by the fact that all the high-status households so far targeted for destruction were known to keep private stocks of product on their premises—a fairly common habit amongst the managerial class since refined product does not spoil and can be counted on to retain its value regardless of the vicissitudes of the market. Could it be that this foul agent of death is as intent on thievery as they are slaughter? The Protectorate Constabulary have been quick to play down such suspicions with several officers—who did not wish to be named—voicing allusions to foreign-born brigands or members of the labouring class banding together under cover of darkness to pursue a bloody vendetta against those of managerial status. So far, however, no suspects have been arrested and such theories continue to arouse scorn from the Protectorate's critics.

Miss Lewella Tythencroft, recently elected Chair of the radical Voters Rights Alliance, has dismissed the notion of low-born agitators as "utter tripe of the worst kind." In a letter to the editor of this periodical Miss Tythencroft stated: "The Protectorate Constabulary is attempting to avoid the consequences of its own incompetence whilst fostering fear and discord between the social orders. It should be plain to even the most addle-brained buffoon that the people of the Marsh-Wold have become targets for at least one insane Blood-blessed, most probably some poor wretched soul driven to delusion by service in one of the Ironship Syndicate's ceaseless wars, the recent Arradsian disaster being the most likely." Miss Tythencroft goes on to demand the appointment of experienced detectives from one of the constabulary's urban precincts and the deployment of specially contracted Blood-blessed to capture the elusive "Demon."

In the interest of balance, it is this correspondent's duty to point out that Miss Tythencroft's views may be influenced by the tragic news that her fiancé, Lieutenant Corrick Hilemore, an officer in the Maritime Protectorate and decorated hero of the Dalcian Emergency, is currently listed as missing, presumed dead following the recent unfortunate events in the southern hemisphere. It should also be noted that the constabulary has doubled the number of officers in the Marsh-Wold and instituted regular mounted patrols. Their task is not an easy one, the Wold being a difficult terrain to police with its myriad water-ways and culverts. Added to these obstacles is the fact that witness reports have provided scant clues as to the true culprit's identity.

As ever, it is the nature of cases such as this to generate a plethora of false reports and unlikely tales from the erratic or drunken mind. This correspondent has been gravely assured that the atrocities are the work of a wild drake somehow transported from Arradsia and set loose upon the Wold by Corvantine agents. A more spectral suspect arises in the form of "Billy the Burner," a famed arsonist hanged for his crimes some two centuries ago and now apparently risen from his grave to wreak vengeance. Added to this are various fables regarding resurrected gods from the Shadow Age and the curious figure of "Scarecrow Annie," a more recent addition to the canon of local ghosts said to take the form of a skeletal woman in a burnt dress many swear to have seen wandering the marshes at night whilst spouting a continual diatribe of gibberish.

Whatever the truth of these fables, it is clear that the danger posed to the people of the Marsh-Wold is very real and, given the holding's proximity to Sanorah itself, the prospect of even worse carnage cannot be discounted. The *Intelligencer* urges all its readers to remain vigilant and report any relevant suspicions to the constabulary forthwith.

Lead article in the *Sanorah Intelligencer*—13th Rosellum 1600 (Company Year 211)—by Sigmend Talwick, Senior Correspondent.

CHAPTER 17

Sirus

The Islander screamed out a war-cry as he swung his axe. Like most who made their homes among the Barrier Isles he was tall and fair of complexion, long blond hair trailing as he sprinted into battle, blood streaming from the many cuts to his muscular torso. Sirus's first impulse was to shoot him, as he had shot three other Island warriors this morning, but he could sense the White's growing dissatisfaction with the death toll. Dead enemies were of no use if it was to build its army.

So, as the axe came round in a blurring arc towards his head, Sirus ducked under the blade and brought the butt of his rifle up to slam into the Islander's chin. His new Spoiled-born strength was enough to lift the attacker off his feet, sending him to the sand, limbs limp and face slack in unconsciousness. Sirus crouched, touching a hand to the man's chest to ensure he still breathed before binding his arms and legs with a length of cord. His first live capture of the day and his tenth of the week.

He straightened as Morradin's thought-command reached him, as terse and grating as any spoken word: *They're massing at the village. Circle round to the north.*

Sirus relayed the orders to his company, a three-hundred-strong contingent drawn mostly from the Morsvale survivors. Majack and Katrya had taken on the role of senior lieutenants, though the strictures of military hierarchy were often irrelevant in an army where all soldiers could hear every order instantly. Even so, the chaos of battle often made centralised control impossible and Morradin found it easier to communicate with select individuals once the fighting began in earnest.

Sirus took a moment to ensure the beach had been secured, ordering the badly wounded Islanders littering the sand to be finished off. He left a dozen Spoiled to stand guard over the survivors and the barges, then led the remainder into the jungle at a steady run. As they moved Morradin's mind conveyed a stream of images showing the island from above. A large group of warriors had organised a barricade around their village and were doing an impressive job of keeping Morradin's main force at bay. The Islanders' weapons were a mix of fire-arms, cross-bows and axes, and they were all raised as warriors from birth. A lifetime of ingrained martial skill made them fearsome enemies, but also valued recruits. Consequently, Morradin's assault force refrained from firing their rifles as they attacked, keen to preserve as many warriors as possible. If the battle wore on for too long, though, Sirus knew the White would convey enough impatience for such restraint to be abandoned and the struggle would quickly descend into a massacre.

On reaching the northern edge of the village, Sirus organised his company into a tight formation and led them in a charge against the point where the Islanders were most thinly concentrated. The defenders they met were all women, mothers guarding their clutches of infants against the onslaught of deformed monsters. The Island women fought with scant regard for their own safety, cutting down a dozen of Sirus's Spoiled before they were overcome. Most displayed such maternal savagery that capturing them proved impossible and Sirus allowed them to be shot down, leaving the children to fight on alone. They had learned quickly that Island children could be as formidable as their parents, especially if they had sufficient numbers to swarm over their assailants in a biting, scratching mass, as was the case here. Sirus lost another five Spoiled before the last child fell. There was no need for restraint in dealing with the children, the White having no use for them.

Watching his Spoiled bayonet the small twitching bodies, Sirus wondered at his lack of revulsion. He knew on a conscious level that he was now more of a monster than he could have ever imagined being, that whatever soul he might possess was forever stained and beyond hope of redemption. And yet he stood and regarded the massacre of innocents without the faintest stirring of nausea. He knew, or rather hoped, that this was the White's doing, that somehow the conversion process had eroded his capacity for trauma. Or it could simply be his mind adapting to new conditions. He was, and would remain, a prisoner in his own body, so what use compassion or guilt now?

We've broken through, Morradin told him. *Runners coming your way.*

They caught most of the runners. They numbered only about thirty and were easily overwhelmed and clubbed down. Inevitably, a handful slipped through to escape into the jungle. They would be left for the Reds and Greens to hunt down over the coming days whilst Morradin reorganised his forces for the next assault. Three islands taken in less than five days, but the next would not be so easy. It was time to face the Shaman King of the Northern Isles.

*W*hy do you think about them so much? Katrya's thoughts were coloured by a faint annoyance as she rifled through the images crowding his head; the piled bodies of the Islanders, old people, warriors they hadn't managed to capture, and the children. *So many children.* They had been dumped on the beach in two large mounds, one for the Reds circling above and one for the Greens baying loudly in the barges bringing them to shore. The White was ever keen to reward his drake kin, even when the victory rightly belonged to his Spoiled army.

We were them once, he replied. *Or they were us.*

Not any more. She snuggled closer to him, rubbing her spines against his, something that always seemed to give her pleasure though Sirus found the sensation somewhat dull. They lay together in one of the village huts, spent in the aftermath of a frenzied coupling. She was like this after a battle, as if the slaughter stirred her lust to greater heights.

We'll make one of our own one day, she told him, her thoughts betraying a sleepy contentment. *I can feel that he wants us to. Not quite yet though. We have so much to do . . .*

He felt her mind subside into sleep, a sleep he knew would be free of any nightmares born of what they had done today. His own sleep, however, would not be so untroubled. *She* would be there, her doll's face drenched in blood and her eyes bright with scorn. Sometimes she laughed at him. Sometimes she simply stared and ignored his pathetic pleas for forgiveness. But never would she speak to him.

Unwilling to surrender to another night's torment, Sirus disentangled himself from Katrya and rose from their stolen bed. He dressed in the stevedore's overalls he had found at the Morsvale docks. The White's Spoiled soldiers had little use for uniformity and wore whatever scavenged clothing took their fancy. Katrya went about in the uniform of a cavalry colonel; she thought the gold tassels were pretty.

He left the hut and wandered the darkened village for a time, trying to shut out the sounds drifting in from the beach where the Reds and Greens gorged and squabbled over their glut of meat. He often found it strange that, despite his remade body, the drakes aroused just as much fear and repulsion in him now as when he had been fully human. The thoughts seeping from his fellow Spoiled made it clear that such feelings were widely shared. For their part, the drakes regarded the Spoiled with either indifference or wary aggression. The vile Katarias was something of an exception, appearing to delight in feasting on those Spoiled too badly injured to be of further use.

"*Shiveh ka.*" Sirus turned at the sound of the voice, finding that his wanderings had brought him close to the prisoner pens. There were about sixty of the Islanders lying bound within the confines of a makeshift stockade, awaiting the morning when Sirus knew the White would unveil his crystals and add yet more recruits to his horde.

"*Shiveh ka,*" the voice came again, Sirus finding the source quickly. The Islander lay on his side close to the fence, staring up at Sirus through a gap in the planking. He was older than the other prisoners, his long blond hair turned silver at the temples and his face bore the scars of old battles. He was also taller and more muscular than his fellow Islanders. *A chief perhaps?* Sirus wondered as the man repeated the same words, more urgently this time, his eyes shining with desperate entreaty. "*Shiveh ka!*" Sirus was surprised to find he couldn't translate the meaning. He had absorbed the language of the other Islanders following their conversion, but they were finding the various tribes to be rich in unfamiliar dialects.

He wants you to kill him.

Sirus glanced up to see Morradin standing near by. The Grand Marshal had an Islander's drinking-horn in one hand and what appeared to be a cigarillo in the other, though the aroma spoke of something more potent than Dalcian leaf. *Still has an effect,* Morradin told him before taking a hefty gulp from the drinking-horn followed by a deep draw on the cigarillo. *A trifle dulled though.* Sirus could sense a certain fuzziness in the marshal's thoughts, although his usual desire to guard his memories had diminished somewhat. The recent battles loomed large, the scenes of slaughter all coloured by a note of reluctant triumph. It appeared that Morradin was beginning to enjoy his work.

Must be the shame of defeat, Morradin said, moving closer to peer down at the pleading Islander. *Very strict honour code amongst these savages, you know.*

He'll feel differently tomorrow, Sirus returned.

Perhaps. Or perhaps our drake god will toss him to his brood. Though it would be interesting to see what he knows about the Shaman King. Morradin crouched, leaning closer to the fence and speaking aloud, his modified throat making the words guttural and rasping, like a snake attempting human speech. "Ullema Kahlan," he said, a name that seemed to hold the same meaning on every island they took.

The Islander's face hardened at Morradin's words, the desperation abruptly replaced by defiance. He muttered something in his own language then lowered his gaze and squirmed away from the fence, rolling over and lying in hunched defeat. *See?* Morradin asked, straightening. *Loyal to the death. These tribes feud and fight for generations but forget it all when the Shaman King calls for unity. He'll have word of us by now, boy. It's an even bet he'll be gathering his warriors.* A cheery note crept into Morradin's thoughts as he took another puff on his cigarillo. *I suspect we might actually have us a real battle next time.*

And you relish the prospect?

Morradin shrugged. *Easy victory is boring. Carvenport.* He bared pointed teeth in a nostalgic grin. *Now, that was quite something. I'd've taken it in three days if it wasn't for those confounded mechanical guns, and their Blood-blessed.* He pushed a memory into Sirus's head, the images vague and out of focus until Sirus realised he was viewing a fierce struggle of some kind through a spy-glass. Figures leapt to unnatural heights, pistols blazing as they shot and lashed out at one another whilst the air around them shimmered with blasts of heat.

Blood-blessed in battle, Sirus realised, a sight he had never seen before. It was a grim spectacle, but a spectacle nonetheless.

Yes. Morradin's memory was rich in warm satisfaction. *The day I sent in the Blood Cadre to punch a hole in the Protectorate defences. Didn't work, of course. They threw in their own Blood-blessed, as you can see. Only a half-dozen Cadre agents made it back. But it was a fine old show, and I had the satisfaction of watching so many of Kalasin's beloved children die. The city would have been mine the next day . . .* His thoughts darkened, crowding with scenes of slaughter, the horde of drakes exploding from the jungle to tear his army to pieces.

Morradin drained his drinking-horn in a few gulps, the memories becoming more indistinct under the weight of alcohol. *Emperor's balls, that stuff is rank,* he observed, tossing the horn aside and turning to walk away on unsteady legs.

They say he's a Blood-blessed too, Sirus thought. *The Shaman King. The only one born to the Isles in six generations. Perhaps that's why they revere him so.*

Then I hope he's drunk his fill of product, Morradin replied, continuing to stagger away. *Because I'm hoping for another fine old show.*

CHAPTER 18

Lizanne

Makario's fingers danced over the keys as he favoured Lizanne with a grin, eyes twinkling behind the long dark hair that hung over his slender face. "Well?" he asked, raising a quizzical eyebrow and removing his hands from the pianola allowing the last few notes to fade.

"The prelude to Huberson's Second Symphony," Lizanne replied promptly. "A little pedestrian for my tastes, though I noticed you added a flourish or two."

His gaze narrowed slightly. "I, my dear, am an artist, not an automaton." He returned his attention to the keyboard, face set in a determined frown. "This one is bound to flummox you."

This tune was far more dramatic, a series of low, prolonged notes followed by a sudden, almost jarring lurch to the other end of the scale. Makario's hands usually floated across the keys but now they darted, fingers splayed and spider-like. The tune was complex and unfamiliar, conveying a sense of melancholy counterpointed with an angry urgency. It was also undeniably one of the most affecting pieces of music Lizanne had ever heard and she winced in annoyance as a loud rhythmic pounding sounded from above.

"Give it a rest, for fuck's sake!" came the Electress's muffled cry through the ceiling. "My head's splitting!"

"It seems our little game must be postponed," Makario said, closing the pianola's lid. "Did you get it?"

Lizanne smiled and shook her head. "At first the arrangement reminded me of Illemont, but the melody is . . . strange."

"As ever, you prove to have an excellent ear, dearest Krista. It was indeed composed by the great man himself. The pianola solo from his unfinished symphony, the composition of which is said to have driven him to suicide."

"The 'Ode to Despair,'" Lizanne recalled. "I thought the whole thing was lost. He burned all his papers before drinking poison, or so the story goes."

"And the story is true. But Illemont had a student with a keen ear and a penchant for listening at keyholes. In time he made his way to the empire and, keen to impress a handsome youth in his charge, taught him this lost masterpiece, or rather a fragment of it. I've been trying to fill in the blanks ever since, but then, I'm no Illemont."

Lizanne turned at the sound of Melina's strident step. The tall woman dumped a bag of chits on a card-table and began to count them out. "Time to cough up your tips," she told Lizanne. "And don't hold out, she'll know."

Lizanne went to her room to retrieve the bag containing the unimpressive haul of gratuities she had collected over the previous week. "Is this all?" Melina asked, fixing Lizanne with a sceptical frown.

"They tend to save their favours for the upstairs ladies," Lizanne explained. "And not all gamblers take kindly to a dealer who can tell they're going to cheat before they even try."

"Wouldn't hurt you to smile more," Melina muttered, counting out half the spoils and handing the rest back to her, along with a full-length copper chit. "Bonus," she explained. "Your table brought in a third again as much as the others. Don't expect the rest of the dealers to appreciate it though."

The reason for the relative profitability of her table was simple: she never stole, unlike her colleagues. Lizanne was sure the Electress knew of the petty graft indulged in by the other croupiers, but appeared to tolerate it. A discreet enquiry to Makario regarding this curiously forgiving attitude had revealed a simple answer. "Sooner or later she'll need an excuse to get rid of them," the musician said with a shrug. "It happens every couple of months. In all honesty, dear, you're the only dealer whose name I've bothered to learn for years."

"Will I be needed today?" Lizanne asked Melina.

"No, she wants you in the shadows as much as possible. You standing close by on your first Ore Day will draw too many eyes. Make your own way there with the girls, but be sure to go armed."

"Are you expecting trouble?"

"It's Scorazin, we're always expecting trouble. But the Scuttlers have been a bit antsy lately, so keep a keen eye out."

The Scuttlers, Lizanne knew, were the gang with the strongest hold on Scorazin's three deep-shaft coal-mines and holders of third place in the hierarchy of near-tribal groupings that ruled this city. She was learning that the internal politics of Scorazin were a fascinating if brutal microcosm of the power games played out beyond its walls. The various gangs existed in a perpetual state of flux, feuds and alliances came and went as the balance of power shifted. Currently, it seemed ascendancy lay with the Verdigris, the oldest gang in Scorazin, who ruled over the only copper mine, their position stemming largely from the fact that their ore commanded the highest price. The Furies, under the Electress's astute but ruthless leadership, were currently ranked second in terms of wealth and membership, a position achieved through complete control over the two sulphur mines. The fourth tier was occupied by the Wise Fools, by far the least well-organised, but most violent gang, who had recently managed to seize governance of the three open-cast pyrite pits after an ugly massed free-for-all known as the Battle of Pitch-Blende Square.

"Am I looking for anyone in particular?" Lizanne asked.

"Oh, all the luminaries will be there," Makario put in. "Failing to promenade on Ore Day is a terrible social mis-step." He rose from his stool and came over to loop his arm through Lizanne's. "Don't worry, dear, I'll guide you through the cast of rogues. Probably best if you don't mix too closely with the ladies, anyway." He leaned closer to add in a whisper, "They're jealous enough to claw your eyes out as it is."

The Ore Day Promenade began on a patch of muddy ground known, without apparent irony, as Apple Blossom Park. Makario led her to a row of chicken-coops abutting the park to witness the drab spectacle of Scorazin's population gathering together for the weekly ritual. The principal gangs all seemed to arrive at exactly the same moment. Lizanne had yet to catch sight of a timepiece in this place but all the inmates seemed to share an ingrained knowledge of the routines that underpinned their existence. The four groups moved in dense masses, clustered around the hand-carts which bore their precious ore. The largest gangs moved to occupy four corners of the field, each leaving a considerable gap between the other and allowing Lizanne to gain an appreciation for their numbers.

"Which are the Scuttlers?" she asked Makario. They were crouched in the gap between two coops, ignoring the annoyed clucks of the scrawny, mange-ridden hens on either side.

"Off to the right," he said, pointing. "The ones with the black patch on their shoulders. It's supposed to be a coal scuttle, not that you'd know. Embroidery is a rare skill in here."

Lizanne estimated the Scuttlers' number at perhaps three hundred, though the musician assured her their true number was closer to twice that. "Have to leave some behind to guard the mines, lest someone takes advantage of the truce," he explained. "Their friends will collect their share. See the dumpy fellow at the front?" Lizanne followed his pointed finger, picking out a ruddy-faced man who appeared to be little over five feet tall but with an impressively broad stature. "Devies Kevozan," Makario said. "Current Coal King. Got the job when he strangled the last one. It was a fair challenge, so no one minded too much. He's short on brains as well as height, but his untrusting nature means he's not an easy fellow to plot against, and he's far too ambitious for the Electress's liking."

Lizanne's gaze rested on the Coal King for a moment before being drawn to a taller figure standing to his left. He was younger than Kevozan by several years, pale of complexion for most Corvantines and possessed of unscarred and undeniably handsome features. However, it wasn't his face that piqued Lizanne's interest, more the way he maintained an unmoving posture whilst his eyes roamed the crowd in unceasing scrutiny. "And him?" Lizanne asked. "The tall man?"

"Ah." Makario's grin returned. "Quite the peach isn't he? Sadly, his only lust appears to be of the bloody variety. He calls himself Julesin. You might say he's the means by which King Coal services both his suspicions and ambitions."

Ex-Cadre perhaps? Lizanne wondered, her gaze lingering on the pale-faced man and deciding the suppressed violence in his posture was a little too obvious for one of Countess Sefka's servants. Yet, Cadre or not, she had little doubt she was looking upon the most dangerous individual she had yet encountered in Scorazin.

"Oh, she does like to bait him so," Makario sighed. Lizanne followed his gaze to see Electress Atalina lowering her bulky frame in a parody of a curtsy as she matched stares with the Scuttlers' leader. Her features had an uncanny ability to convey both contempt and solicitation in the same expression. Lizanne saw the redness of King Coal's face take on a deeper shade as he glowered in response. "I'm not sure that's altogether wise," Makario added.

An angry player is prone to revealing his hand, Lizanne thought, watching Kevozan turn and mutter a few terse words to his pale-faced subordinate. *Something every croupier learns on their first day.*

After the four principal gangs had taken their places the smaller factions arrived, standing in the no man's land between the larger groups in tight, wary clusters. Makario named a few, the Red Blisters, the Forgotten Sons and so on, but it was the last group to arrive that interested Lizanne the most. There were about thirty of them, and they stood out due to the dozen women in their ranks, the other gangs all being overwhelmingly male. Although their clothing was as ragged as the other inmates' they held themselves with a bearing that was almost regal, regarding the surrounding multitude with a stern defiance. "The Learned Damned," Makario named them.

"Learned?" Lizanne enquired.

"Comparatively speaking. Whereas most of us find ourselves confined here for our unfortunate mercenary or violent inclinations, the Learned Damned owe their incarceration to more lofty pursuits."

"Revolutionaries," Lizanne realised.

"Yes." There was a palpable disdain in Makario's voice as he regarded the cluster of political inmates. "Republicists, Co-respondents, Neo-Egalitarians, all the varied shades of malcontent. For all their pretensions, they're as dangerous as any of the others and not lightly crossed. Revolution tends to breed dangerous people, which is why they're generally left alone."

He fell silent as a fight broke out among the ranks of the Wise Fools. They were a mostly bare-chested bunch with shaven heads, heavily tattooed skin and, apparently, scant sense of discipline. They quickly formed a circle around the two combatants, both crouched in readiness with knives in their hands and fresh scars on their arms.

"Isn't that against the rules?" Lizanne asked.

"The Wise Fools fight amongst themselves all the time," Makario replied. "As long as it doesn't spill over into anyone else's garden, why care? However," he went on as the ranks of the Wise Fools parted to make way for a very large figure, "it *is* frowned upon."

The two combatants straightened at the sight of the huge man striding towards them, both dropping their knives. He was even taller than Anatol, his shirtless chest covered in a collage of multi-coloured abstract ink and honed to the kind of muscular perfection usually found only in classical statuary. The image of masculine perfection was somewhat spoilt by the man's face, most particularly the shiny metal nose, which was secured in place by a leather strap.

"Meet Varkash," Makario said. "Famed Varestian pirate. Rumour has it his nose was bitten off by a Blue drake, though you'd be wise not to mention it if you happen to find yourself in his company. He's apparently under the sincere impression that no one's noticed he's wearing a nose fashioned from solid pyrite."

Lizanne watched the huge Varestian as the two men babbled excuses at him. He nodded, rubbing his chin in apparent consideration then, moving faster than it seemed possible for a man of his size, his trunk-like arms lashed out left and right, delivering a full-force punch to the heads of both men that left them lying senseless in the mud.

"He doesn't like to be shown up," Makario explained. "Varestians were ever a prideful lot."

The honour of leading the promenade went to the Verdigris, the largest and most amply attired group present. They signified their allegiance by wearing copper bands around their necks. According to Makario they never took the bands off, making the source of their name obvious in the dull green stains that marked every neck. The leader of the Verdigris was a rotund man of average height and a cheery, apple-cheeked visage. He wore a long frock-coat and a tall, narrow-brimmed hat that were both at least a decade out of fashion but nevertheless made him the best-dressed figure Lizanne had yet seen in the city. He doffed his hat at Electress Atalina as he led his people from the park, Lizanne noting that this time there was no open mockery on her face as she nodded back.

"Chuckling Sim seems affable enough, doesn't he?" Makario said. "To look at him you'd never know he ran the Corvus gambling dens for the better part of a decade and, I'm reliably informed, always did his own killing and he wasn't quick about it. The more he chuckled, the longer it took."

They waited until the park had emptied out and the grand procession filled much of Sluiceman's Way as the inmates progressed towards the main gate. It rose to approximately half the height of the city walls and, according to Makario, no convict could remember it ever being opened. The gate lay behind a secondary inner wall curving out from the great stone enclosure in a semicircle to form what Makario called the Citadel. It was from this stronghold that the constables made occasional forays into the city or launched heavily armed incursions whenever levels of disorder began to affect productivity. However, its main purpose was policing the division of supplies on Ore Day.

Lizanne and Makario fell in with the few hundred non-affiliated stragglers at the rear of the procession. They were a ragged and desperate lot, mud-slingers from the river-banks, shit-pickers from the refuse piles, some so thin and haggard it was scarcely creditable they could still walk. All clutched small bags containing whatever scraps of ore they had managed to scavenge or trade for over the preceding week, plodding towards the gate with a uniformly slow gait, eyes fixed on the Citadel and the promise of sustenance it held. Lizanne and Makario carried no sacks, having surrendered a portion of their chits to Melina, who would exchange them for the requisite amount of ore and allot the received supplies accordingly.

One of the mud-slingers fell out of the procession halfway along Sluiceman's Way, a stoop-backed man of middling years with long tendrils of grey-black hair hanging over his face. He seemed slightly sturdier than the others to Lizanne, but his despair seemed to have overcome him. "Fuck it all," she heard him sigh as he sank down next to a stack of empty ale barrels outside the Miner's Repose, his mostly empty sack between his knees. Lizanne had time to note the old burn marks on his arms and the fact that he had two fingers missing from his right hand before Makario hustled her along.

"No point in stopping, dearest," he said, taking her by the elbow. "There's no help to be given and none to be had, not in here."

Were you always so callous? Lizanne wondered. The musician was the only inmate she had met so far to display even a basic level of compassion or civility. She assumed he owed his continued survival largely to his skills, the Electress appreciated the value he could bring to a clientele mostly devoid of music. But she also knew his presence here indicated a dark past,

for there were no petty criminals in Scorazin. She had resisted the temptation to simply ask what crimes had seen him confined within these walls,
such things were ever a touchy subject for a convict.

Makario guided her to a roof-top where they could watch the unfolding
ritual. He scaled the listing wall of a hollowed-out shack with a skilful
alacrity that reminded Lizanne of Clay and made her wonder if the musician's path to Scorazin might have lain in burglary. The distribution of
supplies proved to be an orderly if protracted affair. The ore was placed in
a dozen large iron buckets waiting at the base of the citadel walls, each one
attached by chains to a crane jutting out from the parapet above. Teams of
constables hauled the ore aloft then filled the buckets with a commensurate
amount of supplies. According to Melina, a number of smaller additional
sacks would be included amongst the overall haul and swiftly pocketed by
the constables in return for adding a few luxuries to the pile: soap, tobacco
and narcotics being the most common. Lizanne had surrendered her full
copper chit for a bar of scented soap and a comb.

It took the better part of an hour for the Verdigris to complete their
exchange whereupon Chuckling Sim raised his antique hat to the constables
and led his people away, hand-carts piled high with bounty. The Furies were
next and Lizanne soon formed the impression that Electress Atalina was
deliberately prolonging the affair, scrupulously inspecting each consign-
ment before it was hauled up and making sure Melina made a careful note
of every item received in turn.

"She's really bringing him to the boil this time," Makario observed,
nodding at King Coal, whose complexion now resembled an unripe beet-
root. He stared at the Electress with fists bunched as the Wise Fools grew
more fractious, grumbles turning to shouts as time wore on.

"She does this every time?" Lizanne enquired.

"Only since Kevozan ascended to kingship. Her way of testing his met-
tle, and he's failing."

It took another quarter hour before the dumpy king finally boiled over,
face stoked to a scarlet hue as he burst out, "GET A FUCKING MOVE ON
YOU POXED-UP OLD SOW!"

Silence reigned in the aftermath, Kevozan standing in quivering rage
whilst the assembled Furies fanned out behind the Electress, hands disappearing into the meagre clothing to clutch knives and cudgels. The Scuttlers

bridled in turn, massing behind their king in readiness. The Electress, however, betrayed scant sign of alarm, merely glancing over at Kevozan in bland acknowledgment before returning her attention to Melina's ledger.

An angry growl rose from the Scuttlers as Kevozan took a step forward, then stopped as a rifle bullet shattered the muddy cobbles a yard to his front. Both King and Scuttlers froze, all eyes snapping to the Citadel as a loud voice swept down from above. "Remember what day it is!"

Lizanne soon recognised the source of the voice: Constable Darkanis, standing atop the parapet with a bull-horn raised to his mouth. On either side of him a platoon of constables had lined up, rifles at their shoulders and trained on the crowd below. "Keep it civil!" Darkanis continued before aiming the bull-horn at the Electress. "You've had long enough, Eighty-Six! You've got ten minutes to get the rest of your ore up here or you don't get another bean!"

The Electress responded with a graceful bow and soon the exchange was proceeding at an accelerated rate. When it was done she led the Furies back along Sluiceman's Way, walking past a still-glowering King Coal without a glance as she chatted with Melina. There were some catcalls and insults exchanged between the two gangs but, with the rifle-bearing constables still watching, the simmering violence failed to erupt.

"Not much more to see now," Makario said, getting to his feet and offering Lizanne a hand. "We'd best get back. She'll expect us to lend a hand unloading the ale."

Lizanne took his hand and rose, pausing as her gaze swept over the Miner's Repose and well-honed instincts sounded a warning bell in her head. "He's gone," she murmured, eyes lingering on the stacked ale casks.

"Who?" Makario asked.

Lizanne tore her hand away and started across the roof-top at a run. "The man with the missing fingers."

She sprinted to the edge of the roof and leapt. With Green in her veins it would have been an effortless jump, but in her current state she barely made it to the next roof, her midriff connecting hard with the edge and legs dangling as she clung on. She grunted and hauled herself up, running across patchy tiles towards the next building. She could see the Electress up ahead, less than thirty feet from the piled casks. Lizanne forced more speed into her legs and leapt again. Fortunately this gap was shorter and she landed on her feet, rolling to absorb the shock. She was only a short distance behind the Electress now, the casks barely twenty feet away. The next roof-top was too steeply sloped to run across so this time she landed painfully on her rump before sliding down the tiles to the street below, landing squarely atop the Electress's shoulders. The big woman staggered but proved too substantial a person to collapse under the additional weight.

"Get down!" Lizanne shouted before performing a back-flip and sweeping the Electress's legs away with a round-house kick.

"You two-faced little cunt!" the Electress roared, glaring up at Lizanne with baleful promise. Lizanne threw herself across the large woman's head and shoulders, covering her own head with her arms, eyes closed tight and mouth open to spare her ears.

The explosion was larger than Lizanne expected, accompanied by a blast of sound that seemed to cut through her from head to toe. A wave of heat swept over them a split-second later, accompanied by a swarm of splinters from the shattered casks. Lizanne rolled clear of the Electress as the heat faded, swatting at a flame on her sleeve and scooping water from a puddle to smooth through her smoking hair. All around her people lay on the ground, most pierced with splinters or blackened with flame, some still, others writhing. Fortunately the ringing in Lizanne's ears spared her the screams.

Anatol came lurching towards her out of the lingering smoke, face pale but for the blood streaming from a cut to his brow. He held a large cosh in one hand and a curve-bladed knife in the other. The grim purpose in his gaze made Lizanne crouch in readiness, her hand going to the sheathed knife at the small of her back. Anatol's advance halted as the Electress rose between them. Lizanne couldn't hear the order she gave but it was enough for the body-guard to return his weapons to the folds of his coat. The Electress turned to regard Lizanne, face expressionless. She had a large splinter embedded in one meaty shoulder but exhibited no sign of pain as she considered her saviour. Lizanne could almost hear the gears churning in her head. *How did she know? Was it a ploy to gain favour? Should I kill her and have done?*

Finally the Electress grunted and turned towards the Miner's Repose. She paused for a moment to take in the sight of the shattered windows and blackened timbers before striding towards the entrance on steady legs, waving for Lizanne and Anatol to follow.

"The Scuttlers," Melina said. She used scissors to snip off the thread trailing from the final stitch in Anatol's forehead, then traced an affectionate hand over his mis-shapen face before turning to the Electress, face and voice hardening. "It has to be. We should kill every one of those fuckers."

The Electress sat behind her desk, a large blood-stained bandage on her shoulder and a cigarillo poised before her lips. There were a dozen extinguished cigarillos in the ash-tray on her desk and she barely seemed to hear Melina's words, heavy brows drawn in thought as she smoked.

"It was too clever," Anatol rumbled, sinking back into his chair and smiling thanks as Melina passed him a cup of brandy. "King Coal hasn't the wit for something like this."

"Julesin might," Melina replied.

"Julesin's a killer to the core, true enough," the body-guard agreed. "But not a bomber. A bomb requires a whole other set of skills." His gaze flicked to Lizanne. "Skills an insurgent might possess."

"She was with me the whole time," Makario spoke up. He sat in the corner fiddling with an old viola, occasionally plucking a discordant note from the strings. "Besides," he added, nodding at the Electress, "I think she demonstrated her loyalty well enough."

"There are other revolutionaries in this city," Melina pointed out. "Wouldn't put it past the Learned Damned to hire themselves out for the right price." She looked at the Electress expectantly, suppressing an annoyed grimace when she received no response. "I'll take a dozen lads round to that manor of theirs," she prompted. "See what they know."

Electress Atalina's eyes flicked to her, narrowing in dismissal, holding the stare until Melina took a step back from the desk. The Electress stubbed her cigarillo into the ash-tray before fixing her gaze on Lizanne. She had been instructed to sit on a small couch resting against the wall, too far away from the window or the door to offer a swift escape. "How's your ears?" the Electress asked.

"Not so bad I can't hear," Lizanne replied.

The Electress stared at her for a long moment, gears still grinding behind her eyes. "So," she said finally. "What do you know?"

"There seems to be a dearth of timepieces in this city," Lizanne said. She said nothing else and the puzzled silence lasted several seconds.

"So?" Melina demanded.

"It was timed," the Electress said.

"Yes," Lizanne said. "I imagine the constituent ingredients for an explosive compound aren't hard to accumulate within these walls. Sulphur and charcoal would be easy to come by. Saltpetre would be more difficult but there are alternatives, dried bird shit for example makes for an excellent oxidiser. However, the scale of the blast indicates a bomb-maker with extensive experience and expertise. As does the use of a timing device."

"Which would require a clock," the Electress said.

"Or the skills to make one from scratch."

Lizanne watched the Electress exchange glances with Anatol and Melina.

"He wouldn't," Melina said, Lizanne noting the defensive note in her voice. "He'd never hurt a fly, you know that. More likely, someone slipped the constables an off-the-books sack in return for a pocket-watch."

"Which would attract attention," the Electress said. "After all, who'd spend so much just to tell time in this pit?" She switched her gaze back to Lizanne. "Still haven't told us how you knew."

"Burns on his face and fingers missing from his left hand," Lizanne replied. "Hazards of the bomb-making profession. My guess is he designed the device and mixed the powder, but he would need help to adapt a timepiece and connect it to the detonator."

Melina stiffened a little, stepping closer to the desk. "Electress . . ."

"I'm not rushing to any judgements, Mel," Electress Atalina told her. "But, at the very least, I think you should have a little chat with the young fellow." She returned her gaze to Lizanne. "Take our new employee, see what she makes of the Tinkerer."

CHAPTER 19

Clay

"So you really saw it?" Scrimshine asked, one of many questions he had voiced over the preceding hours. The revelation of their purpose here had left the old smuggler's weathered features drawn in fascination, as well as engendering a bothersome curiosity.

"Yeah, I really saw it," Clay muttered in response, eyes fixed on the seam between the ice and the spire. He had wandered this section of the base a dozen times now, pick in hand, finding no sign of anything that might be called an entrance.

"And drank its blood?" Scrimshine persisted.

"That too."

Clay crouched and chipped away at the ice with the pick, chiselling out a small depression in the surface. Hilemore had already organised his sailors to hack out a deeper hole on the spire's south-facing side, getting down to five feet before he called a halt. So far, all their efforts had revealed no way into the spire and no clue as to its origin. Steelfine had tested the surface of the structure with a few hammer-blows, leaving no impression except on the hammer. Attempts to chip out small pieces for close inspection proved equally fruitless. Whatever material had been used to construct the spire was far beyond their knowledge or experience.

"How'd you manage that?" Scrimshine asked.

"I shot it." Clay gave a small grunt of frustration and got to his feet. "It didn't die."

He sighed out a foggy breath and raised his gaze to the top of the spire, seeing the stars twinkling in the darkening sky beyond its pointed summit. *What are you?* he asked it, once again churning over the alien images in his head. During the journey here he had assumed the fulfilment of his vision would uncover a plethora of answers, a trove of enlightenment to banish his perpetual confusion. Instead, there was only this vast monument, which he increasingly felt was somehow taunting him with its indifference.

He lowered his gaze and trudged back to the camp. Steelfine stood at the stewpot, overseeing the evening meal whilst the rest of them huddled around their fires. The cold had worsened since they got here and Scrimshine was of the opinion that they had perhaps one more week before the chill became severe enough to force a return journey. Although their respective professions made them a hardy bunch, it was clear the party was beginning to succumb to the depredations of the climate. Eyes were bright with a weariness that bordered on exhaustion and their movements exhibited an increasingly sluggish lethargy. Loriabeth was by far the worst off having been reduced to a near-immobile state, swaddled in thick layers of clothing and rarely venturing far from the fire. Judging by the persistent shudders that wracked her and the increasing gauntness of her face Clay was unwilling to wait another day, never mind a week.

"We have two barrels of powder," Hilemore said as Clay slumped down next to the fire. "Blasting our way in seems the only viable option."

"Powder won't even dent that thing," Clay replied, accepting a bowl of stew from Steelfine. He gulped down a few mouthfuls before meeting Hilemore's gaze. "We got only one real option now, Captain. I think you know that."

"How much can you tolerate at one time?"

Clay took the flask of Red from Hilemore and removed the stopper. They had five flasks altogether, enough to power the *Superior*'s engine for a full week at maximum speed. "Don't rightly know," he said, raising the flask to his lips and taking a large gulp, quickly followed by another. He staggered a little as the product slid into his belly then immediately began to spread throughout his veins. Miss Lethridge possessed plenty of knowledge about how drake blood affected the body but he hadn't felt any particular need to ask her to share it, something he now had occasion to regret. "Guess we'll find out."

He forced down another gulp, then focused his gaze on the semicircular depression Hilemore's sailors had hacked at the base of the spire. He unleashed the Red slowly at first, the air misting with steam that billowed high before being caught by the wind. The cloud drifted off to the left for a few yards then turned to snow, piling up into a sizable drift as Clay continued to melt the ice. By the time he had exhausted all the Red in his body, the depression had deepened by at least ten feet and widened to twice its former width.

"Still nothing," Hilemore said, peering down at the revealed surface of the spire. Clay saw that ice had already begun to form on the rising pool of melt-water at the base of the depression and once again raised the flask to his lips, draining it completely. "Best get a chain of buckets going, Captain," he told Hilemore. "I'm guessing this is gonna be a long day."

They worked in relays for the next hour, Clay melting the ice then pausing to let the sailors bail out the melt-water. After three flasks he began to feel decidedly woozy and found his focus slipping, Scrimshine scuttling away amidst a babble of profanity when Clay's heat-stream strayed from its target to singe the toe of his boot.

"Alright," Hilemore said, reaching out to steady Clay as he staggered. "That's enough for now."

Clay shook off his hand and moved to the edge of the depression. It had grown into a smooth-sided bowl some fifteen feet wide and at least twice that deep. "Still got a few drops left." He slid down to the bottom of the bowl then crouched to peer at the spire beneath the ice. It was less opaque now, rendered glass-like by the heat, and he could discern the way the spire broadened the deeper it went. Also, another dozen feet deeper from where he crouched, he could see a dark circular shape in the spire's surface.

"We got something," he called over his shoulder. "Bring me another flask."

Clay was ready to drop by the time night began to fall. Using up so much Red so quickly drained his energy at a faster rate than the cold, but he refused all entreaties to stop. It took another two flasks to burn his way down to the upper edge of the circle he had glimpsed through the ice. It proved to be a deeply recessed and, judging by the curve, perfectly circular interruption in the otherwise featureless surface of the spire. Clay could poke a hand through the gap between the ice and the edge of the circle, but the interior proved too gloomy to make out any detail.

"One more should do it," he said, extending a hand to Hilemore.

"We only have one left," the captain replied with an emphatic shake of his head. "And who's to say when we'll need it."

"We came too far to quit now," Clay said, fighting a wave of fatigue.

Hilemore crouched, eyes tracking over the ice and the revealed aperture in critical appraisal. "We know the powder won't hurt the spire," he said. "But it should shatter enough ice to allow access, if there's any to be had."

Braddon rigged the fuses with Steelfine's assistance. They hacked a hole into the bottom of the small cavern that Clay had crafted, placing both barrels side by side and inserting the fuse-wire before climbing out and retreating to a safe distance.

"W-won't it shatter the ice b-beneath us?" Loriabeth chattered, breath misting from the narrow hood that mostly covered her face.

"Take more than a few barrels for that, missy," Scrimshine told her, baring his few teeth in an attempt at a reassuring grin. "Ice goes down a long ways here."

"Everybody hunker low as you can and cover your ears," Braddon said, striking a match and touching it to the fuse-wire. Clay watched the ball of sparks dance across the ice before disappearing into the cavern, then lowered his head and clamped his gloved hands to his ears. The blast came two seconds later, the force of it enough to lift him clear of the ice for a second and cover them all with a fine dusting of displaced snow. Before the boom faded, Clay rose and hurried towards the cavern, sliding down its walls to the bottom where a three-foot-deep fissure had been blasted into the ice. The floor of the cavern was also cracked all over. He called to Hilemore for a flask of Black and used it to clear away the icy boulders and prise up the shattered chunks, casting them away into the darkening sky as he dug deeper. He had always found Black far less taxing than Red and he made rapid progress, adding another five feet to the cavern's depth by the time he was done.

The others slid down to join him as he stood staring at what he had uncovered.

"What in the Travail is that?" Skaggerhill asked. They could only see the upper half of what appeared to be a giant cog sitting within a circular recess. With the light failing, Hilemore ordered lamps lit before they moved in for a closer inspection.

"Part of some engine, maybe?" Braddon wondered, running a hand over the thing's surface. It seemed to be made from the same material as the spire, but of a darker hue.

Clay checked the seam between the cog's teeth and the surrounding wall, straightening in surprise at what he found. "It's buckled," he realised, lifting a lamp to illuminate a large indentation in the cog. It looked as if it had been punched inward by some impossibly huge fist.

"What could be capable of that?" Skaggerhill asked, eyes wide and round beneath his bushy brows.

"The ice," Hilemore said. "The pressure of it. But it must have taken centuries to have such an effect."

"There's a gap," Clay said, his lamplight revealing a space between the cog and the wall. It was a few feet above his head so they would need ropes to reach it, but it was wide enough for a grown man to gain entry. "Looks like we got us a way in."

Hilemore insisted they wait for morning before venturing inside. The decision grated on Clay's burning desire to know what lay behind the great cog, but his undeniable fatigue prevented him from voicing an objection. He fidgeted and groaned his way through a fitful sleep, waking with head pounding and his body wracked all over in protest at the previous day's exertions. It took a hearty swig of Green to banish his various aches and another before he became fully mobile.

"Lieutenant Sigoral," Hilemore said, having once again forbidden Clay from being first into potential danger. "When you're ready."

The Corvantine shouldered his carbine before taking a firm hold on the rope. He reached the gap in a few heaves of his athletic frame then paused to haul up an oil-lantern. He played the light over the gap for a short moment then carefully lowered the lantern inside.

"I can't see much," Sigoral reported to Hilemore. "Some sort of passageway, but it goes on too far to see the end."

"Stay put when you get inside," Hilemore instructed. "We'll join you shortly."

Sigoral nodded and unfurled another rope from his back, fixing the grapnel in place and casting the line into the gloom below the gap. The opening was an easy fit for a man of his proportions and he levered himself through in short order. After a short delay they heard his echoing shout of assurance.

"I'll go next," Hilemore said. "Then you Mr. Torcreek."

"What about the rest of us?" Braddon asked.

"We have no notion of what awaits us in there," Hilemore replied, drawing his revolver. He turned the cylinder a few times to ensure it hadn't seized in the cold, then holstered it. "I won't risk more lives than necessary. At least, not until we have a sound estimation of the dangers." He turned to Steelfine. "Lieutenant, you have command in my absence. Wait until tomorrow morning. If we fail to return, do not follow." He held the Islander's gaze for a moment until he received a terse nod.

"I c-can't stay out h-here," Loriabeth stated. She huddled between Braddon and Skaggerhill, both standing close to provide more warmth.

Hilemore seemed about to dismiss her with a reassuring platitude but stopped at the sight of her hollow and shivering face. It was plain to all present that another night on the ice might well kill her. "Can you climb?" he asked instead.

"To g-get out of this c-chill . . . I'd climb a S-seer-damn mountain."

"Very well. You follow me." He turned and started up the rope, reaching the top to clamber halfway in then waited for Loriabeth to follow. He was obliged to grab her arm and haul her the last few inches as her hands began to slip. After they had disappeared inside Clay took hold of the rope, then paused to address his uncle.

"The captain's right," he said. "Don't linger too long and don't follow." He glanced at Steelfine. "Regardless of what he does."

Braddon said nothing and Clay knew he had just wasted his breath. Neither his uncle, Skaggerhill nor Preacher would simply walk away if they failed to come back. He was also fully aware that Steelfine had no intention of following his captain's orders.

"Well, anyways," Clay said, starting to climb and grunting with the effort. "Here's hoping this damn thing ain't empty."

He dropped to Hilemore's side a few minutes later. Both the captain and Sigoral had lanterns in hand and were casting their light at the huge tube-like passage ahead. Loriabeth sat against the cog, deep breaths echoing along the passage-way. "You alright, cuz?" Clay asked.

"It's . . ." she began, then forced a smile, ". . . like a green-house in here."

In fact, the interior of the spire was only marginally less cold than the air outside, but even a small upturn in temperature brought welcome relief. "I'm guessing it'll feel a sight warmer the farther in we go," Clay said, helping her to her feet. "Where's your iron?" he enquired, putting a judgemental tone into his voice. "You still a gunhand or not?"

"Eat shit, cuz," she muttered, reaching into her coverings to extract one of her revolvers.

"If you're quite ready," Hilemore said.

"Lead on, Captain." Clay drew his own pistol and moved to Hilemore's side.

"I'll take the lead," the captain said. "Lieutenant, Mr. Torcreek, guard the flanks. Miss Torcreek, rear-guard, if you please." He hefted his lantern, the beam swallowed by the gloom barely twenty feet ahead. "Let's be about it."

Hilemore set a slow pace, continually playing the beam of his lantern from left to right. There were indentations in the walls every few yards and Clay soon understood that the passage had been fashioned from a series of huge rings placed end to end. Apart from the indentations, the walls remained as featureless as the exterior until Sigoral's lantern alighted on something that broke the monotony.

"Is that writing?" he said, pausing to let the light linger on a symbol carved into the passage wall. It was large, a good ten yards wide and twice as high. Clay saw no meaning in it but the way the form curved and entwined stirred immediate memories of the script he had seen in the city beneath the spike.

"Mr. Torcreek?" Hilemore prompted as Clay continued to stare at the symbol. "Do you have any notion of what this means?"

"It means we're in the right place," Clay said. "Beyond that, I got no clue."

They moved on, taking only a few minutes to traverse the passage before coming to an abrupt halt.

"No way the ice did that," Loriabeth said, eyeing the pile of rubble ahead. It seemed to Clay that one of the rings had collapsed, filling the tube from floor to ceiling.

"A blast of some kind, perhaps?" Sigoral said, crouching to scoop up a handful of dust from the floor. He let it fall through the beam of his lantern in a glittering cascade.

"Whatever it was," Clay said, "it was enough to turn this stuff to powder."

"Whilst we haven't been able to scratch it," Hilemore added.

Clay lifted his own lantern, playing the beam on the top of the piled rubble. "Can't see a gap."

"I'll find it," Loriabeth said, shrugging off her outer layer of coverings, "if there is one." She started to clamber up before they could protest, moving with a sure-footed energy that belied her former weakness. Clay found that his guess had been right; the air was definitely warmer now.

"Jammed," Loriabeth called down after a brief inspection of the rubble. "But I can feel air rushing from somewhere beyond this thing. Some of these boulders don't seem too heavy either."

"Guess I got some more work to do," Clay said, holding his hand out to Hilemore.

"Just enough to get us through," Hilemore said, handing over a flask of Black. "I'd rather the whole thing didn't collapse on us."

Clay told Loriabeth to come down and then had them concentrate their lanterns on one spot at a time. He used just enough Black to dislodge the topmost pieces, lifting several chunks clear and placing them carefully at the base of the pile until they had a decent-sized gap.

"Still blocked," Loriabeth said, having climbed up once more. "Think a decent push will see us through, though."

Clay clambered to her side, seeing the way ahead blocked by a large slab. He took a sip of Black and concentrated on the slab, finding it stuck fast. Another few sips and the barrier began to give, grinding against the enclosing rubble until finally tumbling free.

"Me first," Clay said, scrambling into the opening and pretending not to hear Hilemore's stern command to stop. He crawled through in short order, pushing his lantern ahead of him and emerging to be confronted by a black void. His lantern beam roved the darkness finding nothing for several seconds until it caught the edge of a narrow surface below. "Got a walkway here," he called over his shoulder before clambering down.

He moved to where the walkway met the edge of the rubble, tapping an experimental foot to its surface. "Seems solid enough," he said as the others climbed down to join him. Clay watched Hilemore's narrow gaze survey the walkway and assumed he was debating whether to bring the rest of the party inside before continuing.

"It's gotta lead somewhere," Clay said, fighting the impulse to simply stride off on his own.

Hilemore hesitated a moment longer then nodded. "Single file. Miss Torcreek . . ."

"Rear-guard." She sighed. "Yeah, I know."

The walkway didn't take long to traverse, though the echo birthed by their footfalls told of a very deep drop on either side and made for a nervous few moments. After thirty yards it broadened out into a round platform about twenty feet across. The only feature was a lone plinth about four feet high positioned where the walkway met the platform.

"We must be in a shaft," Hilemore said, his lantern revealing the platform to be the top of a cylindrical column that descended far into the void below.

"It's different," Sigoral said, stamping a boot to the surface of the platform and raising a dull echo. Clay lowered his gaze and saw the Corvantine's meaning. This platform had been fashioned from familiar stone, some form of granite by his estimation, rather than the impermeable material that formed the spire. The surface was formed of interlocking curved slabs, giving it a maze-like appearance that bespoke a remarkable precision in its construction. *Ain't seen nothing like it,* he thought, *not since the city beneath the mountain.*

He moved to the plinth, finding it also constructed from the same granite as the platform. There was an elegance to its form, almost as if it had grown from the stone even though closer inspection revealed it to have also been fashioned from interlocking bricks.

"What is that?" Loriabeth asked, stepping to his side and playing her lantern over the upper part of the plinth where it broadened out into a near-flat surface, in the centre of which sat a crystal about the size of a fist. Once again Clay's memories of the city stirred, recalling the statues and the floating crystals in the White's lair.

"Diamond maybe," Loriabeth went on, leaning closer to tap a finger to the crystal.

Both Clay and Loriabeth gave an involuntary yelp as a bright yellow glow appeared on the crystal, accompanied by a low, almost musical note that thrummed the surrounding air. The four of them stood stock still as the sound and the glowing point in the crystal faded away, all clutching their weapons and waiting. Clay saw the sweat shining on his cousin's skin and took some small comfort from the fact that at least they wouldn't freeze in here.

"It would be best if you didn't do that again, miss," Hilemore told Loriabeth, receiving an apologetic smile in response.

Lieutenant Sigoral moved to the edge of the platform and fished a small coin from his pocket. "A full crown," he said, tossing it into the void. "I trust you'll reimburse me in due course, Captain."

Clay counted off twenty full seconds before detecting the very faint note of the coin connecting with whatever lay below.

"That's quite a drop," Sigoral observed.

"Very well," Hilemore said, holstering his revolver and striding back towards the walkway. "I'll order the rest of the party to join us. We'll establish a camp in the passage-way and prepare for further exploration tomorrow."

"It'll take all the rope we have to reach the bottom," Sigoral pointed out.

"Then we'd best tie some strong knots." Hilemore strode onto the walkway and paused, turning to Clay with an impatient frown. "I'll have no argument from you on this, Mr. Torcreek."

Clay cast a final glance around the platform, his gaze lingering on the now-lifeless crystal gleaming dully in the plinth's surface. "You give the orders, Captain," he said, wiping sweat from his brow and flicking it away before starting after Hilemore.

They froze as the crystal sprang to life once more, the glass flaring bright and a series of notes filling the air. The light was of such intensity Clay found himself momentarily blinded. He blinked to clear his vision, finding that the crystal was shimmering now, flickering with a rapidity that brought an ache to his head. He moved closer, squinting through streaming eyes and making out the few dark droplets of moisture on the crystal's blazing facets. *My sweat,* he realised. *It felt my sweat . . .*

All semblance of rational thought vanished as the platform shuddered beneath his feet, and a vast echoing boom ascended from below. A near-deafening grinding cacophony filled the shaft, putting him in mind of the *Superior*'s engine room if its mechanicals were fashioned from stone rather than metal.

He reached for Loriabeth's hand, intending to drag her to the walkway, but the platform began to descend before he could take a step, plummeting down at such a rate it was a wonder it hadn't left them flailing in thin air. He managed to lock eyes with Hilemore for a second, standing on the edge of the walkway and staring down at them in impotent shock. But soon the captain's face was a dim pale speck, vanishing completely as the lights blinked out and darkness swallowed them completely.

CHAPTER 20

Lizanne

It was impossible to see the whole mine through the drifting clouds of smoke and steam, but Lizanne estimated the huge bow-shaped pit to cover a quarter-mile square. One side was formed from soil layered in steps where teams of Furies shovelled away at yellow patches of earth. The opposite side was solid rock, the surface shot through by dozens of shafts and encrusted in a web of scaffolding so haphazard in its construction that Lizanne half expected it to come tumbling down at any second. The floor of the pit was a brownish-yellow teardrop a hundred yards long where steam rose in constant billows from a small pool.

"Is that a hot spring?" Lizanne asked Melina as they paused at the top of the scaffolding.

"That it is," the tall woman replied. "It's where the sulphur comes from. I wouldn't be tempted to take a bath though. Water's hot enough to boil the flesh from your bones, if the stink doesn't kill you first. Here." She handed Lizanne a leather face-mask. "Best put this on till we get inside the shaft."

Lizanne examined the mask before donning it. It was a surprisingly ingenious design, large enough to cover the mouth and nose with slits on the outside and a thick gauze on the inside. "Tight-weave cotton soaked in old piss," Melina explained, pulling on her own mask, which muffled her voice somewhat but not enough to make it unintelligible. "Not pleasant but it's better than a lungful of powdered sulphur."

She moved to a ladder and started down without delay. They descended successive tiers of scaffolding, Lizanne finding she had to hurry to keep up thanks to her companion's long-legged stride. Melina exchanged nods and a few muffled greetings with the miners they met on the way. Most seemed keen to maintain a respectful distance although at one point she was obliged to pause and deliver a warning back-hand cuff to a bleary-eyed fellow who displayed an overly tactile interest in Lizanne. The man staggered backwards, blood staining the thin kerchief he wore as a mask, and would have tottered over the edge if one of his fellow miners hadn't reached out to steady him.

"Don't take it personal," Melina said through her mask as they continued to descend. "It's the mercury, plays havoc with a man's mind."

"Mercury?" Lizanne asked.

"That side is all sulphur," Melina replied, pointing to the stepped earthen banks opposite. "Dig out plenty on this side too but also cinnabar, which is mercury and sulphur mixed up in the same rock. They use it to make vermilion dye so it fetches a high price, but hacking it out is a nasty business. If a Fury misbehaves the Electress will set him to work on the cinnabar seams. Most don't last more than a year or two."

They proceeded down through successive tiers of walkway and ladder until Melina paused at a narrow shaft close to the base of the pit. The steam was thick here and, even through her mask, Lizanne could taste an acrid tint to the air. The shaft was unusual in being the only one Lizanne had seen with a grate over the entrance. The iron barrier was secured in place with a sturdy lock which, she noted in surprise, was only accessible from the inside.

"He doesn't like visitors," Melina said, reaching through the bars to pull the rope on a bell suspended from the shaft's ceiling. "Choosy about who he lets in."

"But he'll let you in?" Lizanne asked.

Melina said nothing for a few seconds, finally issuing a muttered response barely audible through her mask. "We're friends." She raised her gaze as a dim light glimmered within the dark confines of the shaft. "He's got an unusual manner," Melina said. "Can be aggravating if you're not used to it. No point getting angry with him though. He doesn't understand such things."

A young man about Lizanne's age appeared behind the grate, oil-lamp in hand. He was of average height, his slender frame clad in a set of standard prison overalls, heavily stained with grease and flecked with small burns of the kind Lizanne recognised as resulting from spilled chemicals. Unlike his clothing, his face was scrubbed to a level of cleanliness she hadn't yet seen in this place, and possessed of such aesthetically pleasing symmetry she was instantly reminded of Tekela's doll-like visage. But, whereas Tekela always had difficulty in preventing her features from betraying her emotions, this man exhibited none at all, regarding them both in placid and expressionless silence.

"Tinkerer," Melina said. "Need to have some words." She opened the sack in her hand and extracted a book, holding it up for inspection. "*Imperial Railways Locomotive Maintenance Guide, Volume Three.*"

Tinkerer shifted his blank gaze to Lizanne, still saying nothing.

"This is Krista," Melina said. "New arrival. She's like you, knows things. I thought you might get along."

Tinkerer stared at Lizanne for a long moment then set his lamp aside and began to fiddle with the lock on the grate. Lizanne saw that it had no keyhole and was secured in place via a series of cogs set into a cylinder. She had seen combination locks before, but they were an expensive rarity. Most relied on a six-cog cylinder, whilst this one had twelve, meaning even a Blood-blessed would find it practically impossible to pick. Tinkerer's fingers moved with an automatic speed, too fast for Lizanne to even approximate a guess at the sequence. He lifted the lock clear of the grate and pulled it open before retrieving his lamp and disappearing back into the shaft.

"Stay right behind me," Melina said, stepping into the shaft. "Step where I step. He's got contraptions rigged to discourage unwanted visitors, and you really don't want to find any."

"I thought he wouldn't hurt a fly," Lizanne replied, following her into the gloom.

"He wouldn't, lest any try to hurt him, then it's a different story. You don't live your whole life in Scorazin without learning a thing or two."

"His whole life? You mean he was born here?"

"So they say. The only inmate to have been born within the city walls to make it to adulthood. Newborns generally don't last long in here with the air the way it is."

After a hundred paces the shaft opened out into a circular chamber. Lizanne assumed it must have been a junction of some kind at one point, noting the three other passages that split off into different directions. The space was filled with dismembered machinery, cogs, wheels and chains all arranged in neat stacks alongside racks of tools. Tinkerer had taken a seat at a work-bench and begun working on some kind of device, his eyes narrowed in concentration as his nimble fingers made fractional adjustments to the workings with a screwdriver.

"What do you want, Melina?" he asked, not looking from his work. His voice was a curious amalgam of different Corvantine accents, the varying inflections no doubt picked up from the inmates over the years. But there was also a precision to it, as if each word was crafted with the same care he afforded his devices.

Melina took off her mask, nodding at Lizanne to do the same. She found the air inside the shaft musty but still a considerable improvement on the stench outside.

"Someone set off a bomb outside the Miner's Repose," Melina said, placing the book on the work-bench. "Bomb with a timer. Wondered if you had some thoughts on the matter."

"I do not make bombs," Tinkerer replied. "And have refused numerous lucrative offers to do so."

Lizanne's gaze roamed the chamber, eyes alive for anything familiar, any scrap of paper that might bear some resemblance to the work of the Artisan. At first glance it appeared simply a much more well-ordered version of Jermayah's workshop, but without a single document of any kind. *Not one doodle,* she thought, scanning the bare walls and finding the absence of blueprints or diagrams a stark contrast to her father's. Graysen Lethridge had an aggravating tendency to pin his designs to the wall of his workshop for any pair of thieving eyes to see.

"What are you looking for?"

Lizanne's eyes snapped to Tinkerer, finding him subjecting her to an intense scrutiny. She might have taken offence at the way he tracked her from head to toe, but for the lack of lust in his eyes. *Careful,* she cautioned herself. *This one sees everything you do.*

"A lever escapement modified to trigger a mercury-based detonator," Lizanne replied.

Tinkerer's mouth twitched in what Lizanne took to be a potential sign of irritation. "You imagine I would craft anything so inelegant?" he asked.

"Function is more important than elegance," she said, quoting her father.

"Not to me." His gaze flicked to Melina. "She is very dangerous. You should be careful."

"Always am, you know that."

"Not always." He turned back to his bench, picking up his screwdriver and device once again. "Otherwise you would still have both eyes."

Melina's face betrayed a grimace of accustomed annoyance before she forced a conciliatory smile. "You know we have to look around. If we don't the Electress'll send people who won't be so polite."

Tinkerer's lips twitched again but he voiced no objection, merely waving his screwdriver in irritated dismissal before returning to his task.

"Don't break anything," Melina warned Lizanne, moving towards one of the side passages.

The other chambers proved to be as spartan and well-ordered as his workshop, one contained a neatly arranged cot complete with precisely folded blankets, another held two buckets, one for ablutions and another for bodily functions, the contents sprinkled with lye to mask the smell. The third chamber was different and her initial sight of it provoked an excited quickening in Lizanne's pulse. *Books.* They filled the space from floor to ceiling, each arranged in stacks of equal height. Moving closer, Lizanne saw they were mostly technical manuals like the one Melina had brought. She angled her head to scan the spine of a book sitting atop one of the stacks: *A Treatise of the Correct Operation of Steam Condensers in Maritime Propulsion Systems.*

"Don't," Melina warned as she reached out a hand to pluck the book from the stack. "He gets awful agitated if he finds anything even a fraction out of order."

Lizanne shrugged and let her hand fall, continuing her survey and finding only the kind of reading that would have delighted Jermayah and her father but left her mostly cold. She might have inherited some of the famed Lethridge understanding of engineering matters, but none of the passion. Her studies of such things had always been driven mainly by need and rarely coloured by genuine interest.

"Where did he get all of these?" she wondered aloud.

"This is the sum of his wealth," Melina said. "He fixes things, pumps and winding-gear mostly, and trades the ore he earns for books supplied by the constables. Weird thing is, he only ever reads them once."

Although, I suspect he could recite every word without fault, Lizanne added inwardly, eyes tracking over each volume. She had hoped to find something related to the Artisan, but instead saw just more references to efficient drive-shaft alignments and differential gears. History, it seemed, was not amongst Tinkerer's interests.

"Waste of time," Melina said, drawing her gaze away from the library. "If there's anything to be found, it'll be here."

Melina stood with her arms crossed as she regarded a broad rectangular patch of the chamber wall. The surface differed from the others in being mostly smooth, Lizanne judging it to have been chiselled and sanded down over months or years to provide a usable writing surface. It was covered in a matrix of white chalk: lines, curves and numbers combined into an abstract and indecipherable jumble.

"What is that?" she asked, moving to Melina's side.

"The product of Tinkerer's mind," she replied with a slight shake of her head. "Keeps most of it in his head but even he has to let it spill out sometimes. See anything here that might be taken for your escapement thing-a-bob?"

Lizanne peered closer, eyes flicking from one calculation or grid pattern to another. Some of the lines were faded with time, whilst in other places the chalk was fresh and bright. It appeared Tinkerer felt no need to erase his prior work, simply overlaying it with new insights to produce this oddly fascinating but meaningless tapestry. She studied it closely for several minutes, eyes alive for anything familiar, or bomb related, but finding nothing. She was about to turn away when she glimpsed a very small diagram at the edge of the rectangle. Three overlapping circles of different sizes arranged so as to sound a chime in her head, a chime she hadn't heard since Jermayah's workshop in Carvenport. *Three circles . . . three moons. The Alignment.*

"Found something?" Melina asked with pointed impatience.

"Just a fragment of calculus I learned in school," Lizanne said, stepping back. "I suppose he must have picked it up from one of his books."

"More likely he came up with it himself. He does that a lot."

"You have been here long enough to establish my non-involvement in this matter." They turned to find Tinkerer standing in the chamber entrance, his gaze fixed on Lizanne once more with the same fierce scrutiny. "I want you to leave now."

His tone was as flat as before, but Lizanne noted the way Melina stiffened in anticipation of danger, though Tinkerer held no weapon. "Alright," she said, moving closer. "We'll be on our way." Lizanne saw her raise a hand to touch Tinkerer's arm, hesitate then lower it again. "It's . . . always good to see you."

Tinkerer kept his gaze on Lizanne. "I want you to leave now," he repeated, each word spoken in exactly the same tone as before.

The grate gave a loud clang as it slammed shut behind them, followed by the snick of Tinkerer reattaching the lock.

"Well that was a singular waste of time," Lizanne said, glancing back at the empty shaft before pulling on her mask. "What do we tell the Electress?"

"The truth," Melina replied, her one eye suddenly angry above her mask. "Trust me, love, that's the only thing you'll ever want to tell her."

Anatol's fist made a wet crunching sound as it slammed into the Scuttler's face. The force of the blow spun him around, the rope securing his wrists to the basement ceiling straining as he sprayed shattered teeth in a wide arc. The Scuttler sagged, all vestige of his former resolve now vanished from his swollen mask of a face. Blood dripped from his gashed lips as he moaned and bobbed his head in defeat.

"Three punches," the Electress commented through a cloud of cigarillo smoke. "I'm impressed. Most start babbling at two."

Lizanne had never found torture a particularly effective means of extracting reliable information. The threat of imminent death had a tendency to loosen tongues at a decisive moment but even then the results were often unpredictable. When Exceptional Initiatives needed detailed intelligence they favoured the more subtle approach of abduction and prolonged interrogation, usually augmented by judicious use of sleep deprivation and resistance-sapping drugs. Electress Atalina, however, proved to be an exponent of the more direct approach.

"Now then, Azarin," she said, rising from her chair to loom over the unfortunate Scuttler. She lowered her gaze to peer into his bleary, bloodshot eyes. "Let's start with Kevozan. Who's the Coal King been meeting with recently?"

Azarin exhaled a red vapour as he struggled to reply, the words a barely distinct sputter. "Never . . . meetsh anyone . . . outshide the Scuttlersh . . ."

"Yes, so I heard," the Electress said. "Leaves all the outside dealings to lickspittles like you. But I find it hard to credit he'd plan a move against me without a face-to-face with the assassin."

The captive spasmed as he tried to shake his head, succeeding only in dislodging a few more drops of blood from his face. "Washn't . . . ush . . ."

"Oh dear." The Electress moved back a little, drew deeply on her cigarillo then stubbed out the glowing tip on Azarin's eye. Lizanne was surprised at the strength evident in the scream he produced. "And I thought we'd reached an understanding. Anatol, let's try another three punches. To the body this time, if you please."

Three rib-cracking blows and some further questioning later it was apparent that if the Coal King had orchestrated the bombing, this particular lackey had no knowledge of it.

"Still a few breaths left in him," Anatol said, placing a hand on Azarin's barely moving chest. "You want me to take him to the pit?"

"No. Wait for nightfall then dump him outside that hovel Kevozan calls a palace. We need to maintain a clear line of communication." The Electress moved to the basement steps, gesturing for Lizanne to follow.

"I'm guessing this isn't your first dance," the Electress observed, casting a glance at Lizanne's unruffled features as they climbed to the inn's top floor. "Even Melina puked up the first time I had her stand witness to one of my little chats. But then, I didn't have Anatol in those days so it was more of a surgical exercise."

"I saw worse in Imperial custody," Lizanne said. "Though the Cadre's methods are a little more . . . artful."

"Really?" They came to the Electress's office and she sank into the chair behind her desk before reaching for an inevitable cigarillo. "And did they practice their arts on you?"

Lizanne allowed a short interval of grim-faced silence before replying, "Of course they did."

The large woman shook a match and smiled around a mouthful of smoke. "Then let's hope you learned a thing or two. Tomorrow you can take yourself off to the house of the Learned Damned. Make out like you're disgruntled, looking for a new home. Shouldn't be too difficult to win them over with your prior experience."

"If they've undergone anything like my prior experience they'll kill me the second I open my mouth."

"Oh, I don't think so. A fetching little morsel like you spouting all the right dogma will be hard to resist. They're all still idealists at heart, y'see. Delusion never really fades for the true believer, even in here. I trust you remember it all? Bidrosin's Credo and all that shit."

Lizanne made a show of smothering a sigh. "Yes. I remember it all."

"Good. Best get some rest for the morrow then, eh?"

Lizanne nodded and moved to the door, pausing as the Electress added, "The Tinkerer. You're sure he had no part in this?"

"As I said, I saw no evidence. And Melina vouched for him."

"Melina's overly sentimental when it comes to him. Saved her life, y'know, when she first got pushed through the gates. She was just a skinny slip of a thing then, didn't know better than to fight when they swarmed at her, did pretty well too but still ended up short one eye with no friends. She'd've starved if Tinkerer hadn't taken her in, though he was scarcely more than a boy in those days. Y'could say they grew up together, till she got tired of life on the margins and decided to make a real life for herself within these walls."

"She said he was born here."

"So they say. I've done fifteen years and he was here before me. Not many of us left from that time, I can tell you. The constables weren't so nice back then."

"His parents?"

The Electress shrugged. "Never knew 'em. Most likely he got squirted out by some poor cow pushed through the gates with a swollen belly. I expect she hated herself for not smothering the poor little fucker the moment he popped out."

The Electress winced and raised a meaty leg to the desk-top before tugging off her shoe to reveal a swollen and reddened foot. "Bloody corns. Send Makario in, will you? Time he put those fine fingers to some real use."

Lizanne spent the next few hours sketching in her room. She had traded a quarter of her soap with one of the second-floor ladies for a pencil stub and parchment. The pencil was too thick for this kind of work and the parchment rough, but she had little alternative. Scorazin was not well-supplied with stationery and she didn't want to arouse the Electress's attention by seeking out better tools. One of the traits she had inherited from her father was a facility for drawing, a skill honed by Exceptional Initiatives, who set great value in the ability to render detail from memory. Even so, she knew her sketch lacked the precision or the artistry of the original and had to trust it retained enough detail to serve as a recognisable facsimile. Once satisfied she rolled the parchment into a tight scroll and concealed it within a pocket she had sewn into the armpit of her overalls.

Nightfall in Scorazin brought a depth of darkness rarely seen in other cities. The lack of street-lights and the constant, moon-obscuring pall of smoke made for a depth of shadow she would normally have welcomed, had she any Green to enhance her vision. So it was with a considerable degree of care that she crawled from her window and out onto the roof-top, body flattened to the tiles and ears straining for unseen hazards. She lay still for a long time, hearing only the rumble of snoring whores and the faint regular grunts of Anatol and Melina's shared intimacy. Satisfied, she crept to the edge of the roof above the inn's north-facing wall and began her descent. She had chosen this wall for its sparsity of plaster, the bare brickwork affording a wealth of handholds, though finding them in the dark was a protracted business.

On reaching the street below she crouched and waited once more. The night-time streets of Scorazin had a legendary reputation for danger and even the most capable and well-armed folk tended to stay indoors. At night the streets belonged to the Creepers, the lowest rung on the prison city's ladder. These were the mad or deformed souls the Emperor had seen fit to send here, those denied a place in the gangs due to their appearance or erratic behaviour. Melina said even the mud-slingers and midden-pickers shunned them. *There's many a place to hide in here,* she said. *Those that don't starve find ways of getting by, come out at night to scavenge what they can, and they aren't picky about where their meat comes from.*

Lizanne made her way towards the sulphur pit, keeping to the darkest shadows and moving in a low crouch. She had her knife strapped to her ankle in case of emergencies but found it a scant comfort. Tonight she felt the absence of product more keenly than ever. In the event she only saw one Creeper during the journey. She had been about to vault a low wall at the corner of Breakers' Avenue when a soft, scraping sound made her freeze. She sank as low as she could as the sound grew louder, one hand resting on the hilt of her knife as she concentrated on keeping her breathing as shallow as possible. Instinct in times of danger was to hold one's breath but that had been trained out of her long ago. Lack of air caused the heart to race and sapped muscles of strength that might be needed in the event of discovery.

The scraping sound stopped on the other side of the wall, replaced by a series of harsh inhalations as someone sniffed the air. Lizanne was grateful she had resisted the temptation to indulge in a thorough wash with her precious scented soap for the sniffing soon faded and the scraping sound resumed. A few seconds later she saw a tall, stooped shadow emerge from the corner of the wall, moving away along Cable Lane. The silhouette was rendered indistinct by a cloak or other covering, but Lizanne could tell it was dragging something behind it. She waited a full minute after the shadow had merged with the surrounding gloom before vaulting the wall and continuing her progress to the pit.

The gloom faded as she neared the pit. The hot spring gave off a luminescence that added a yellow tinge to the billowing steam, the light reflected back onto the pit by the smoke banks above. There were some Furies about, cudgel-bearing guards set to ward off any intrusion or seizure by a rival gang. Lizanne was grateful to find them a lazy and amateurish lot, wandering the edge of the pit in groups of three or four with large gaps in their patrol pattern. It took less than an hour for Lizanne to establish their routine and slipping through the cordon proved almost laughably easy. Navigating the scaffolding with all its creaking infirmity was more precarious, she was obliged to hang from the edge of a platform when the squeal of a protesting joint drew a curious shout from one of the shafts. Luckily, the disturbed miner was either too tired or addled by mercury dust to investigate further and the rest of her journey to Tinkerer's refuge was free of interruptions.

He appeared as she crouched before the grate, knowing the combination lock was beyond her and pondering the best way to attract his attention. He stared down at her through the bars in silence for several seconds before asking in a faint, uninflected whisper, "Are you here to kill me?"

She shook her head, finding her professional curiosity too piqued to resist a question of her own. "Did you hear me?"

"I sleep only two hours per night and have very keen hearing. I believe it to be a necessary survival trait in this environment."

Lizanne nodded and rose from her crouch, raising and opening both hands before slowly reaching into her overalls and extracting the scroll. "I believe this will be familiar to you."

Tinkerer took the sketch and unfurled it, his gaze taking in the bulbous, propeller-driven contraption in a single, expressionless glance. He replied without hesitation, but for the first time Lizanne detected some colour to the tone, a slight quaver that told her the skills of this very special man did not extend to lying. "You are wrong. I have never seen this before."

Lizanne moved closer to the grate, managing to keep the smile of satisfaction from her lips. "Do you want to get out of here?"

He met her gaze, face blank but eyes suddenly very bright. "I have explored all possibilities. There is no means of escaping this city."

"Oh but there is, for me and any I choose to take with me. And I'll happily find a place for you"—she reached through the bars and tapped a finger to the sketch—"and him."

CHAPTER 21

Clay

He was never fully aware of how long it took for the platform to descend.
It could have been an hour or a few minutes, such was the pitch of his initial terror. When the first flush of panic began to abate his underlying
terror actually rose in pitch. Despite all he had seen he knew that whatever
awaited them below was far beyond his knowledge. For all its maddening
confusion, the vision born of the White's blood had at least engendered a
sense of certainty, an unwavering determination to bring himself to the
intersection between past and future. Now he was just one of three very
small souls snared in the innards of a vast mystery.

The terror finally subsided when the platform began to slow and it occurred to Clay that they weren't in fact about to die. Loriabeth's distress
took longer to fade. She kept clutching to him, jaw clamped tight to prevent
a cry escaping her lips. Clay could only hold her and cast the beam of his
lantern about. The light revealed a series of symbols carved into the wall of
the shaft, at first sliding past at too great a speed to make out but becoming
discernible as their descent continued to slow. Clay detected a pattern in
the symbols, their curving lines becoming less complex the deeper they
went. *Numbers,* he realised. *Counting down.* His mind kept flicking back
to the sight of the plinth and the beads of his sweat on the crystal. *Loriabeth
touched it and it just glowed,* he recalled. *One touch of my sweat and it took
us down.*

Lieutenant Sigoral had the stock of his repeating carbine jammed firmly
into his shoulder, fingers twitching on the trigger-guard. From the wild
cast to the man's eyes Clay judged his panic had been only marginally more
controlled than his own.

"Can't see anything to shoot at," Clay said. "Can you?"

The Corvantine's gaze jerked towards him and he flushed in momentary anger before straightening and lowering the carbine. "Did you do this?" he asked.

"Not on purpose."

The vast grinding of huge gears reverberated through the shaft once again and the platform gave a brief shudder before coming to a halt. For ten full seconds no one said anything as they stared in turn at the plinth, the carved symbol on the wall and the dimly illuminated shaft above. Clay fancied he could hear a faint voice calling somewhere and pictured Hilemore standing at the edge of the empty shaft shouting desperately into the gloom.

"We're alive, Captain!" he bellowed, tilting his head back to project his voice as high as he could. He had no notion if Hilemore heard him for the only answer was silence.

"We should touch it," Sigoral told Clay, pointing to the plinth. "Perhaps it'll take us back up."

"Or farther down," Loriabeth said.

"No." Clay pointed at the symbol on the wall. It was the simplest marking he had seen yet, a single unembellished form resembling a stretched tear-drop. "I think we're at the bottom."

"All the more reason to try," Sigoral said, moving to press a gloved hand to the crystal then stepping back. They waited. The platform didn't move and the crystal continued to cast out its glow without a flicker.

"You try," Sigoral said, gesturing to Clay with the butt of his carbine. From the hard insistence in his tone Clay decided this wasn't a time to argue the point. In any case, if it responded to his sweat it stood to reason the crystal might well do so again at the touch of his skin. He moved to it and tapped his forefinger to the stone. This time it gave off a pulse of more intense light and the low musical note sounded again. But still the platform failed to move.

Loriabeth tried next, producing no reaction at all. "Guess we should just wait it out," she said, peering upwards. "The captain's sure to be fetching rope . . ."

They whirled at a new sound to the left. It was the grinding gears again, but on a smaller scale, hidden mechanicals locking and unlocking as a section of the passage wall slid aside to reveal a rectangle of greenish-blue light. Sigoral raised his carbine once more and Loriabeth drew both pistols in readiness, however, nothing appeared in the opening.

"I think we're being invited in," Clay said, moving forward.

"Stop!" Sigoral barked.

Clay turned to find the Corvantine regarding him with implacable resolve. He also saw that the barrel of Sigoral's carbine was pointed at the centre of his chest. "I've no wish to cause you harm, Mr. Torcreek," he stated. "But you are not stepping through that door. We will stay here and await rescue . . ."

He trailed off at the sound of Loriabeth drawing back the hammers on both revolvers. She stood with them levelled at her sides, both pointing at the Corvantine and ready to unleash a salvo that would probably cut him in half at such close range. "I'll thank you to stop aiming a weapon at my cousin, sailor boy," she said, all trace of her previous distress vanished now.

"It's all right, cuz," Clay said, moving between them, staring hard at her until she lowered her guns. He cast a hungry glance at the opening then shook his head. "He's right. Once the captain fixes the ropes, we can get the others down here. I'll feel a lot better about venturing inside with more guns."

He turned to Sigoral, holding the man's gaze until he lowered his carbine. "I'm a marine," Sigoral told Loriabeth. "Not a sailor . . ."

His words died as a tremor shook the platform beneath their feet. Clay initially thought it was about to ascend, a conclusion dashed as the tremor continued, growing in violence with every passing second.

"Maybe we broke something," Loriabeth said, arms spread as she sought to maintain her balance.

A loud booming crash echoed down from the shaft and Clay looked up to see a very large, jagged shape descending towards them, too fast to allow for the slightest hesitation. He turned and sprinted for the opening, pushing Loriabeth ahead of him. They stumbled into the light, Clay barely having time to take in the new surroundings, a broad rough stone floor surrounded by tall columns, before Sigoral barrelled into him, sending them both sprawling.

The opening slid closed behind them just as whatever had fallen from above slammed into the platform. The sound of the impact died as the opening closed, but the tremor continued for at least another minute, Clay casting a wary eye at the surrounding columns in the fearful expectation they might topple over onto them at any moment.

Finally, the tremor faded, leaving them gasping in relief.

"And now we're trapped," Sigoral said, getting to his feet. "Wonderful."

"Ain't sure trapped is the right word," Clay said, getting to his feet and taking a good look at their surroundings for the first time.

They stood at the start of what appeared to be a concourse of some kind, the columns on either side forming an avenue that disappeared into a thick mass of trees some twenty feet away. Seeing the collage of light and shade that dappled the surface of the concourse, Clay looked up to see an interlocking canopy of tree-branches above. Through the gaps in the canopy he could see the pale blue of what he could only assume was sky. There was a faintly floral tinge to the atmosphere that put him in mind of the jungle, though the scent was decidedly more pleasant.

"What in the Travail is this, Clay?" Loriabeth demanded, her face riven with a mixture of wonder and fear.

"Not exactly certain what I was expecting to find down here, cuz," he replied. "But it surely wasn't this."

"It looks like the Imperial Swath," Sigoral said, eyes roaming the trees with deep suspicion.

"The what?" Loriabeth asked.

"The Emperor's private forest north of Corvus," the marine replied. "Three thousand square miles where only those of divine blood are allowed to hunt. I had the honour of escorting the Emperor's cousin on a boar-hunt once." He paused, peering through at the deep arboreal maze. "He was a very poor shot, truth be told."

They stood staring at the view for some time, Clay once again suffering the sensation of being dwarfed by discovery. He moved to one of the columns, finding it overgrown with a thick web of creeping foliage. Pushing the leaves aside, he saw the stone beneath to be rich in carved script, the symbols all reminiscent of those in the shaft and the city beneath the mountain. There was also a faint visual echo of the hieroglyphs he had seen in the ruins on the shore of Krystaline Lake. *Miss Ethelynne could read them,* he remembered, fingers playing over the swirling script. *Wonder if she could've read this too.*

"Look," Sigoral said, drawing Clay's gaze from the column. The Corvantine was pointing at something in the forest canopy above the now-closed doorway. Peering closer, Clay saw that the door was housed in the base of a very substantial structure. It possessed familiar architecture he had last seen bathed in the red glow of molten rock, all hard angles and interlocking blocks of stone that contrasted with the chaotic web of foliage that surrounded it.

"Military logic," Sigoral said, "dictates one should seek a vantage point when confronted with unfamiliar terrain . . ."

He trailed off as a high-pitched cry echoed through the forest. It lasted only a second, and was some ways off by Clay's reckoning, but both he and Loriabeth had no difficulty in identifying the source.

"What was that?" Sigoral asked, seeing them exchange tense glances before drawing their weapons.

"Green," Loriabeth said, eyes bright as she scanned the trees. They waited, peering into the myriad shadows of the forest, which seemed to have grown suddenly deeper. After several long minutes in which the Green cry failed to come again, Loriabeth holstered her guns and moved to the vine-covered stone fringing the door. "Sailor boy's right," she said, taking hold of a vine and starting to climb. "We need a good look-see at this place."

Clay hurried to follow as she nimbly ascended into the canopy. He struggled to keep her in sight as he clambered up the web of vines and into the trees. The branches were thick and became more twisted and difficult to navigate the closer they were to the structure. Clay could see numerous cracks in the stone where invading vegetation had gained purchase over what must have been many years' growth. It was hard to discern the true shape of the structure, but he gained a sense of sloping walls. Also, he could see no sign of any windows or other points of access.

He saw that Loriabeth had paused in her climb, having ascended above the canopy to perch on a narrow branch as she gazed all around.

"What you got, cuz?" Clay called to her.

Loriabeth left a long pause before replying, her voice rich in both amazement and despair, "You'd best see for yourself."

Clay clambered to her side and stopped, frozen by the scale and impossibility of what he saw. It took some time to fully comprehend it, and even then the sight was as baffling as it was spectacular. The forest stretched away on either side for several miles and to their front it continued on for about ten miles or so before giving way to what looked like a bare plain. Beyond that the landscape was too misted to make out any clear detail but he was sure he could make out the faint shimmer of water through the haze.

Looking left and right, he saw that the forest took on a gradual but definite curve where it met a vast featureless wall. It was dark, like the surface of the spire and Clay assumed it must be made of the same material. Turning completely around he found himself blinking in mystification at what appeared to be a great monolith rising from the trees. After further investigation he saw that it rose from the top of a tree-covered structure. *The shaft that brought us here,* he realised. As his gaze tracked upwards he expected to see the shaft meet a ceiling of some kind but the huge monolith faded from sight, occluded by a blue haze that grew thicker with altitude.

"Look," Loriabeth said, face raised. "Three suns."

Clay followed her gaze, blinking at the sight of a trio of blazing stars. The light they cast was sufficient to illuminate the entire landscape even though most of it was still obscured by the haze. He shielded his eyes, blinking in the glare as he tried to estimate the height and size of the three suns but it proved impossible. He also could see no structure that might be holding them in place. His memory returned once more to the White's lair and the crystals he had seen there, crystals that cast forth light and floated in mid air.

"They ain't suns," he muttered softly.

"Then what are they?"

Clay looked down to see that Sigoral had climbed up to join them, face flushed with exertion and a depth of unease that seemed even greater than Loriabeth's.

"Mechanicals," Clay told the Corvantine, deciding a full explanation would stretch the man's credulity a touch too far. "Of a sort. Set to keep this forest alive. Plants need light to live after all."

"Mechanicals need engineers," Sigoral said. "Meaning someone else must be down here."

"If so, they ain't seen fit to greet us." Clay took a final glance around and crouched to lever himself off the branch. "And we'd best move on if we're aiming to find them."

"Which way?" Loriabeth asked.

Clay paused to jerk his head at the plain beyond the forest. "Nothing behind 'cept a wall and we can't go up. Seems going farther in is the only option."

———

They spent a short while surveying the structure without identifying any way in. Here and there the stone was decorated with more carved script that provided no information or solution to their predicament. After an hour or so Clay called a halt and they started into the forest.

He took the lead with Loriabeth on rear-guard and Sigoral in the middle. The forest floor proved a tricky surface to navigate, featuring too many roots and constricted avenues to allow for a decent pace. Birds chattered in the trees above as they moved, a continual medley of different calls, the volume of which stayed constant despite a human presence. When they stopped for a brief rest a small red-breasted bird landed on the ground at Clay's feet, blinking the black beads of its eyes up at him in evident curiosity. Clay crouched and extended a hand to it. The bird hopped back a few inches but failed to fly away.

"No fear of man," Sigoral surmised as the bird darted closer to Clay's hand and jabbed its beak into his palm. It hurt more than he expected and left him sucking a trickle of blood from his punctured skin.

"So I see," he muttered.

"Why wouldn't it fear us?" Loriabeth wondered.

"I'd hazard that it's never seen our kind before," Sigoral said. "Nor have any of its kin for many generations."

"Sounds a little like Scribes, don't he?" Clay commented to Loriabeth, drawing a curious frown from the Corvantine.

"Who?"

"A friend lost along the trail," Loriabeth said in a tone that didn't invite further inquiry. She straightened and scanned the surrounding trees with a critical eye. "If he's right, it ain't good, cuz."

"Yeah." Clay flicked a drop of blood at the red-breasted bird, which finally took sufficient alarm to fly away. "Probably best if we try to move a mite quicker."

"Why?" Sigoral asked.

"We know there's Greens in here," Loriabeth replied. "Stands to reason they also got no fear of us. Not that the others we've met had much either."

They covered another four miles before Clay noted that the light had begun to dim. He found a gap in the canopy and saw that the glare of the three suns had faded. "Think night's about to fall," he told the others. "Time we made camp."

Sigoral chose a resting spot, a huge tree with a matrix of roots thick enough to create a raised platform. It offered only a marginally improved view of their surroundings but was the sole near by spot with any vestige of defensibility. They sat close to the trunk and shared what food they had, amounting to a few strips of salted beef and some jaw-achingly-hard ship's biscuits Sigoral had kept with him since disembarking the *Superior*.

"Not like that," he said as Clay came close to cracking a tooth on a corner of biscuit. "Soften it with water first."

He demonstrated, tipping a few drops from his canteen onto the biscuit. Clay tried a bite and found it chewable if hardly appetising. "I'm thinking we're gonna have to do some hunting before long," he said, swallowing a mouthful with some difficulty. "Plenty of birds about, and they won't be tricky to catch."

"Means we'd have to light a fire to cook 'em," Loriabeth said. "Greens can smell smoke from miles away. There's a chance they've already caught our scent anyways, but I'd still rather not send out an invite."

"We should sleep in the trees," Sigoral said. "Tie ourselves to the branches." He frowned as Clay and Loriabeth exchanged an amused glance.

"Greens climb better than people," Clay explained. "Tie yourself to a tree and you'll just be offering up an easy kill."

"Then what do we do if they come for us?" Sigoral asked.

"Shoot 'em," Loriabeth said, patting the butt of one of her revolvers. "Right in the head, sailor boy. Anything else is a waste of ammo."

"I told you, I'm a marine."

"What's the difference?"

Sigoral glared at her, face reddening. "Quite a lot, actually."

"We'll take turns on watch," Clay said, seeing his cousin bristle and hoping to forestall an argument. "Two sleeping, one watching. I'll go first." He glanced up at the dimming sky through the web of branches. *Pity they didn't craft moons to go with the suns,* he thought.

Sigoral woke him after a fitful doze that couldn't have lasted more than a couple of hours, but even so the shadows had lengthened and the air grown decidedly cooler. "I heard more cries," Sigoral reported as Clay shook Loriabeth awake. "They sounded a long way off, though."

"Let's hope they stay there," Clay said. He gulped water from his canteen, noting that it was now only a quarter full. "Gotta find a stream or something, soon," he said. "Has to be water here, else how does everything grow?"

The answer came a short while later. The rain arrived with no warning patter of droplets or change to the air, a heavy deluge falling unheralded from the sky with sufficient force to strip leaves from the trees. The ground turned to mud in an instant, forcing a halt as the three of them took shelter under the branches of a particularly broad tree Sigoral named as a yew.

"They live for hundreds of years," he commented, features bunched as rain-water streamed over his face. "From the size of it I'd estimate this one's at least two centuries old."

"No clouds," Loriabeth said, blinking as she peered up through the deluge. "So where's this coming from?"

Clay could fathom no explanation and the deluge stopped soon after, dwindling to nothing as quickly as it had arrived. They pressed on, slogging through mud and stumbling over slippery roots until the ground finally began to harden. He had hoped to be clear of the forest by the time the three suns faded but it was clear they would have to endure another night beneath the trees. Long, dark shadows had begun to merge and the atmosphere grew more chill with every passing second.

"Nothing else for it," he said, shrugging free of his pack. "Can't get through this in the dark."

"Do Greens hunt at night?" Sigoral asked.

"Depends on the pack," Loriabeth said. "Some are day hunters, some aren't. But any Green sees a damn sight better in the dark than we do."

They found another thickly rooted tree to huddle around, this one with a thinner trunk that enabled them to stay in sight of each other. The dark descended with an unnatural swiftness, reminding Clay that this wasn't actually night, at least not as he had always understood it. The light of the false suns didn't fade completely, retaining a slight glow that left glimmering pin-points of moisture on the leaves that seemed to shine like stars in the gloom.

"Don't s'pose you got any product about your person?" Loriabeth asked Clay in a chilled whisper.

"There's about a quarter of Black left in the flask the captain gave me," he replied. "And the Blue heart-blood. But I ain't touching either lest we got no other option."

"Are you sure about not lighting a fire?" Sigoral asked Loriabeth.

"Light one if you want," she replied. "But do it far away from me."

Sigoral grunted in frustration but stayed where he was. Clay could see a bead of moisture on the foresight of the Corvantine's carbine barrel, shimmering a little as it trembled in his grasp.

"I'm guessing you hail from warmer climes, huh, Lieutenant?" Clay asked him.

"Takmarin's Land," Sigoral said. "A large island bordering Varestian waters. And yes, it does get very warm there in summer months, though it's many years since I've seen it."

"No family waiting back there? Wife and young 'uns, maybe?"

"I enlisted as an Ensign of Marines at fourteen. It's Takmarin custom to give third sons over to Imperial Service. My father wanted me to join the army but had a prideful insistence I be an officer. However, commissions fetch a high price and his miserliness outweighed his pride. The marines are the only branch of the service to appoint officers due to merit rather than purchase of commissions, so that was that."

"Coulda told him to stuff it," Loriabeth commented. "Followed your own path."

"Respect for parental authority is a cornerstone of Corvantine society," Sigoral replied, though his stiff tone sounded a little forced. "A lesson you Corporatists would do well to learn."

"We're independents," Loriabeth returned. "Anything we get is earned, and my folks never tried to push me down a path I didn't choose."

"No, you all spend your lives grubbing for personal gain whilst unfortunates are left to perish in the gutter. I've sailed to enough corporate ports to know."

"Oh, fu . . ."

Her riposte was cut off by a piercing and familiar shriek, louder and closer than the one they heard before. It was quickly followed by another, this one farther off to the right, then another to the left.

"She's gathering the pack," Loriabeth whispered. Clay heard her shift into a crouch then the sound of iron sliding over leather as she drew her pistols.

"And fixing our gaze," he whispered in reply, drawing his own revolver and turning so that he and Loriabeth were back-to-back.

"What do you mean?" Sigoral demanded, shuffling closer.

"The noise is a diversion," Loriabeth said. "For every one you hear there's another you don't. Reckon it's time for you to light that fire."

"Won't it draw them to us?"

"They already know where we are, and we can't shoot 'em if we can't see 'em."

She kept watch as Sigoral and Clay moved about, gathering what fuel they could find on the forest floor. It amounted to a few bundles of twigs and fallen branches, which were swiftly snapped into smaller lengths and stacked close by.

"Hurry up," Loriabeth said as another trio of cries cut through the gloom, closer now.

Sigoral produced a flint from his pocket and struck sparks onto the stacked wood, which failed to catch. "Need kindling," he said. "Paper, something to catch the flame."

Loriabeth uttered a soft obscenity which was followed by the sound of a knife being drawn. "Here," she said, tossing a thick length of hair at them. Sigoral tried again, the cascade of sparks catching the bunched hair immediately. He and Clay piled on more wood as the flames rose, bathing the surrounding trees in an orange glow.

"They'd best turn up soon," Clay said, drawing his revolver once more and taking up position at Loriabeth's back. "This ain't gonna last more than a few minutes."

"What's your ammo like?" Loriabeth asked.

"Thirty rounds," Clay said.

"Lieutenant?"

"Six in the carbine, another forty-four in my bandolier."

"Me and Clay will fire first, you keep them off us when we reload. Remember what I said, gotta get 'em in the head."

They waited, eyes on the trees and the blackness beyond as the fire's glow dwindled by the second.

Clay had begun to debate the wisdom of retrieving more fuel for the fire when he caught a flicker of moving shadow. His gun hand snapped towards it instantly, arm straight and level as honed instinct kept the tremble from his grip. *It'll charge now,* he knew. *Once it knows it's been seen.*

He exhaled, finger tensing on the trigger in expectation of the beast's imminent rush. Instead the shadow he had seen paused for a second then shuffled closer. It was smaller than expected and for a moment he assumed he was seeing only the silhouette of the drake's head, but then it came fully into the light, yellow eyes blinking in the fire's glow. It was undeniably a Green, but unlike any he had seen before.

"I thought they were bigger," Sigoral said, training his carbine on the beast.

"They are," Clay replied, still staring at an animal that stood all of twelve inches at the shoulder and couldn't have been more than a yard in length.

The Green angled its head as it regarded him, a long pink tongue dangling from its open jaws as it hopped closer, issuing a short chirping cry.

"Is it an infant?" Sigoral wondered.

Clay's gaze tracked the Green from head to tail, finding numerous scars and wrinkles to its scaly hide. This was clearly an animal with many years behind it, and yet he had seen new-born Greens of far greater size. "I don't think so," he said.

The Green chirped again, bouncing on its stumpy legs and swishing its tail from side to side in puppyish animation.

"Looks like he wants to play," Sigoral observed.

"She," Loriabeth corrected. "And tiddler or not, it's still a Green."

"It probably doesn't even know what we are."

"Knew enough to hunt us." Loriabeth turned to her front, bringing both pistols level with her shoulders. "Just shoot it, Clay. Sooner we start this party, sooner it's over."

Clay trained his revolver on the beast's head, then hesitated as it continued to stare up at him in wide-eyed fascination. "Not so sure about that, cuz," he said, glancing over his shoulder at her. "Could be, we leave them alone, they'll . . ."

His words ended in a scream as the diminutive Green leapt forward in a blur and clamped its jaws on his leg, crunching through flesh and bone as it bit deep.

CHAPTER 22

Lizanne

"Take ten steps into the tunnel, then stop," Tinkerer said, pushing the grate open and moving aside. "Do not turn around."

Lizanne followed his instructions, counting off the required steps and coming to a halt. She resisted the impulse to turn on hearing the rattle of a reattached lock followed by the rapid clicks that told of a scrambled combination. "If you kill me," he said, moving past her, "you will be trapped here and Melina will kill you when she comes to check on me."

"Duly noted," Lizanne said. She followed him to the main chamber where he made his workshop. He paused to light a small oil-lamp of ingenious design, featuring a convex lens to magnify its glow. He moved wordlessly to the passage that led to his sleeping chamber and knelt next to the cot. Lizanne watched as he slid aside a panel on the plain wooden box that formed the cot's base, then reached inside. There was a loud clunk as he turned a hidden lever. Tinkerer stood back as the cot raised itself up to a thirty-degree angle, Lizanne hearing the rattle of chains somewhere in the walls.

"Very clever," she complimented him as he shined the beam of his lantern into the revealed hole, illuminating a steep flight of rough-hewn stone steps. "I must confess I detected no sign of this."

Tinkerer merely glanced at her, his pale, finely made features registering neither gratitude nor scorn for her praise. "You first," he said, keeping the beam of his lantern on the steps.

She hesitated. Slight as Tinkerer was, she recalled Melina's trepidation and found the prospect of turning her back on him for a second time decidedly unappealing. "You were right," she said, moving closer and meeting his gaze. "About how dangerous I am."

"If I wished harm to you it would already have happened," he replied and she took some comfort from the fact that his voice was free of the discordant note of dishonesty she had detected a few moments before.

"Very well," she said, inclining her head and proceeding down the steps. It proved a short climb, her feet finding a level surface after a dozen steps, Tinkerer's lamp revealing a broad tunnel as he followed her down. He passed her and moved on in silence, Lizanne following for several long moments until they came to a wide circular chamber. She drew up sharply as the lamplight flickered over the unmistakable sight of a corpse. She had only a brief glimpse before the beam moved away, but it was long enough to make out the bare bones and rags of a soul long dead.

"What is this place?" she demanded, stopping at the chamber entrance, one hand clasping the knife at the small of her back.

"The Artisan's Refuge," he replied. "Or so it was named to me eighteen years ago."

He stood in the centre of the chamber, turning slowly so the beam of the lantern tracked over the walls. Lizanne's unease deepened as the light illuminated more bodies, each one more desiccated than its neighbour. She counted fourteen before Tinkerer's light stopped on one particular corpse. It appeared older than the others, the clothing rotted away and the bones dark with age. Lizanne moved closer, still clutching the knife, and saw a rusted iron manacle on the skeleton's ankle. A length of thick chain traced from the manacle to a heavy bracket set into the wall.

"You came here to rescue a man who died one hundred and forty years ago," Tinkerer informed her, the beam flicking away from the corpse to illuminate her face. "What led you to the conclusion he could still be alive?"

"Take the light away from my eyes or I'll kill you," Lizanne commanded, gaze narrowed through the lamp's glare.

He lowered the beam and stood in silent expectation as she looked again at the now-shadowed corpse. "I am to believe that this is the Artisan?" she enquired.

"Your beliefs are a matter for you," he replied. "I state only facts."

She stepped past him and crouched next to the skeleton, eyes roaming the bones and the skull. The teeth were certainly those of an old man, many having decayed to stumps in his lifetime, the front incisors featuring the dark stains that told of an over-fondness for coffee. *So this was your fate?*

she asked it, peering into the black holes of the skull's vacant eye sockets. *Decades spent in adventure and invention only to die chained to a mine wall in the worst place in the empire.*

"What proof do you have that this is truly him?" she asked.

"Memory," Tinkerer replied.

"Of what?"

"Of his days in Arradsia. Of his many discoveries and the devices he crafted with the knowledge. Of the women he loved and the men he hated. Of what he saw beneath the mountain. Of the voice that called to him for most of his days and drove him to madness. Of the day he chained himself to this wall lest he succumb to the voice. The memories stop then."

Lizanne rose slowly, her gaze fixed on Tinkerer's placid mask of a face. "How?"

"Via the Blue-trance," he answered.

"You are a Blood-blessed?"

"As are you."

She ignored the statement and nodded at the corpse. "He died long before you were born. How could you have tranced with him?"

"I didn't." He trained the lamp's beam on the least desiccated corpse, the one she had glimpsed on first entering the chamber. "I tranced with him. He"—the beam moved on to the next corpse—"tranced with her. She"—the beam moved on again—"tranced with . . ."

"I comprehend your meaning," she broke in. "However, I have difficulty believing it."

"There is no other credible explanation. Failure to accept a conclusion supported by evidence is a fundamentally irrational position and indicative of mental instability."

"Has anyone, perchance, ever punched you very hard in the face?"

He blinked. "Only Melina. The day she left to join the Furies."

"I trust it hurt a great deal."

She moved back from him, wandering the chamber and searching for some clue that would either disprove or confirm his assertions. The idea that the Artisan might still be alive seemed outlandish to the point of embarrassment now. However, the notion that his memories could have been passed down through generations of Blood-blessed, all of whom had somehow fetched up in Scorazin, seemed scarcely more credible.

"You said you shared the memory of his inventions," she said after a long moment of consideration. "He once designed a solargraph. Describe it."

"A refinement of the sonic trigger he developed several years earlier, itself based on a design etched into a stone tablet he unearthed in a cave dwelling on the west Arradsian coast. The primary mechanism consisted of three cogs arranged so as to mirror the orbits of the three moons . . ."

"And the sketch I showed you?" Lizanne interrupted.

"A navigable aerostat. It was mostly his own invention but inspired by calculations he found in a tomb on the shore of the Upper Torquil Sea, which related to the lifting properties of hydrogen gas."

"Did he pen that sketch?"

"No." Tinkerer pointed to the most recently deceased occupant once more. "He did, among many others. He had developed an addiction to alcohol and would trade his drawings to the guards for wine. His memories are unpleasant to experience. I believe the sensation is referred to as bitterness."

"And it was he who passed the memories to you?"

"Yes."

"Meaning he must have had a supply of Blue."

"He did, and expended it in his final trance with me. Subsequently, he embarked upon a prolonged period of indulgence that I believe to have been the principal cause of his death."

Lizanne began to voice another question but it was Tinkerer's turn to interrupt. "You stated you could effect an escape from this place," he said. "How?"

"I need to know you're worth the trouble first," she replied. "And this"—she gestured at the surrounding bodies—"raises far too many questions for my liking. How did so many Blood-blessed come to be here?"

"Information loses its value once shared." Tinkerer's voice was as flat as ever, but Lizanne detected a glimmer of hard resolve in his gaze. "I deduce that you are an agent sent by a corporate entity to retrieve the figure known to history as the Mad Artisan. He, as you can see, is dead and all that remains of his mind now resides in me. If you want it, you will extricate me from this city."

"Keen to see the outside world, are you?"

"I believe there will be much of interest there. Also, the environment is likely to be more conducive to longevity."

"Then you may find it a disappointment," Lizanne muttered as images of Carvenport's fall flicked through her head. "There is a war," she added, "only just begun, but, I believe will grow to terrible proportions before long." She nodded at the Artisan's skeleton. "If you hold his memories, then you must know of the White Drake."

For the first time Tinkerer betrayed some true discomfort, a faint shudder running through his body, though his features remained impassive.

"I see that you do," Lizanne said, stepping closer. "Then you might be interested to know that it's awake, and very hungry."

Tinkerer stared at her in silence for some time, a slight frown on his brow and eyes taking on an unfocused cast. Lizanne thought he might be about to fall into some kind of seizure before understanding dawned. *He's calculating.*

"You came here in search of knowledge that might aid in its defeat," Tinkerer said finally. "I believe I have such knowledge. You already know the price."

She briefly considered trying to coerce more information from him, but knew it would be counter-productive, if not dangerous. Besides, anything he shared now would be of little use if she couldn't get them both out of the city.

"Very well," she said, turning and gesturing at the exit. "If you'd care to show me out, I'll begin preparations."

"And what is the nature of these preparations?"

"I shall need to make use of your skills, for a start."

"In what manner?"

Lizanne voiced a humourless laugh. Vile as this place was, she had a suspicion that the fate she was about to orchestrate for Scorazin might weigh on her conscience for some time to come. "Suffice to say, I intend to rekindle the flame of revolution."

"What is the true definition of money?" the man on her left demanded.

Lizanne supplied the required quote with only a slight pause for recollection, it being one of Bidrosin's better known pieces of naïvety. "'Money is best thought of as a shared delusion. An unspoken fraudulent compact between the rich and the poor ascribing value to worthless tokens in return for the illusion of societal security.'"

"Who commanded your cell in Corvus?" the woman on the right asked.

Lizanne sat on a chair facing a blank cellar wall, both her interrogators standing just outside her field of vision. They alternated, the man quizzing her on revolutionary dogma whilst the woman barked out more specific questions regarding Lizanne's fictional career as an insurgent. It was a subtler technique than that employed by Electress Atalina, however Lizanne suspected the Learned Damned weren't above resorting to more direct methods should she prove unconvincing.

She had eschewed a more contrived approach for simply walking up to the house they occupied. It stood at the western fringe of Apple Blossom Park, a three-storey mansion which, according to Makario, had been the residence of the city's richest mine-owner in the days before the Emperor chose Scorazin as his principal prison. Two young men moved to confront her before she could ascend the steps to the front door. A brief enquiry regarding the presence of any fellow members of the Correspondent Brotherhood had been enough to see her swiftly, and none-too-gently, conveyed to this cellar.

"I only knew him as Severil, he knew me as Valina," Lizanne replied, two names she had plucked from Hyran's head during their only trance, along with a wealth of intelligence on the Brotherhood the young Blood-blessed probably didn't know he had retained. "He's dead now," she added. "The Cadre paraded him in front of me before blowing his brains out. It happened in a cellar much like this one, actually."

"Just answer the question," the woman snapped. "Don't elaborate."

"What differentiates the peasant from the manufactory worker?" the man asked.

A trick question, and easily spotted. "'Only one's prejudice towards the other. In all other respects peasant and worker are essentially the same, only distinguished from one another by the methods utilised in their exploitation and enslavement.'"

There was a short pause before the woman asked her next question and Lizanne detected a partially suppressed reluctance in her tone. "What secrets did you betray in return for your life?"

She saw the trap in this question too. The impulse would be to proclaim her unwavering loyalty to the cause and eternal hatred of all traitors and informants. But they would know it a lie instantly, for no revolutionary could survive the Cadre's ministrations without talking, even if the only reward was to live out one's years in this miserable pit.

"Much the same as you, I imagine," she replied. "I gave them the names of my surviving cell members, and told them of the unlicensed printing-press in my father's basement. They killed him in front of me too."

The answer heralded a long silence, presumably as they reflected on their own betrayals. "Why are you here?" the man asked, a resentful edge to his tone. No one liked to be reminded of their weakness, after all.

"Electress Atalina sent me to spy on you," Lizanne said. "She suspects you may have aided in the recent attempt on her life."

She could sense the glance they exchanged and found she had to conceal a grin. Unexpected truth was often an effective tactic. "As for myself," she went on, "I couldn't care less if you cut the old cow's head off with a rusty saw. I am here on different business."

Lizanne felt the chill kiss of steel on her neck as the woman leaned close to whisper in her ear, "It would be wise for us to simply kill you now."

"Then you would be denying yourselves an opportunity such wretched souls as us are rarely afforded."

The knife pressed deeper then stopped as the man spoke again, "What opportunity?"

This time Lizanne allowed herself a smile. "Redemption, citizen. I believe the destruction of the Emperor's greatest prison would be a potent symbol. Wouldn't you agree?"

The woman's name was Helina, the man's Demisol. She was short, the top of her head barely cresting five feet, whilst he was tall and rake thin. They would have made for a comical pairing in other circumstances. However, at this juncture they appeared to be what they were, two jaded but undeniably dangerous people, made lean and hollow-eyed by a restricted diet. Lizanne took solace from the faint glimmer of lingering idealism she saw in their gaze. They would be of little use had their revolutionary fervour not survived the rigours of life within these walls.

"You're insane," Helina said after Lizanne had laid out her plan.

She sat opposite them on the other side of a broad mahogany dining-table that she assumed had been a prized possession of this house's original owner. The surface, which would once have gleamed with layers of polish, was now scarred from end to end by radical invective, quotes from Bidrosin and other ideologues etched deep into the wood as if in mockery of the servants who had once laboured to make it shine.

"Your little group seems to have a passion for defacement," Lizanne observed, running a hand over the table's coarsened surface.

"Thousands died in this place even before the Emperor made it a prison," Demisol said. "Toiling in the pits for a pittance and sucking poison into their lungs whilst their employer gorged himself at this table for years on end." He leaned forward to plant a finger on the table, running it over a list of scratched names. "Here, the names of the dozen workers he bribed the constabulary to hang when they tried to organise a union. Here"—his finger moved to another list—"the leaders of the uprising that killed the pig. They quartered his body and threw it in the sulphur pit."

"A fitting end," Lizanne said. "But, if my history is correct, the uprising ended in utter defeat, as well as provoking the Emperor into throwing a wall around the city and using it as a cesspit for the empire's worst scum."

"The Scorazin Uprising inspired the First Revolution," Demisol replied, flattening his hand to the table. "We do what we can to honour that memory, small gesture though it is."

More than just a glimmer, Lizanne thought, hearing the quiver of conviction in the man's voice. *All to the good.*

"I do not mock, citizen," she told him, stripping all traces of humour from her voice to lean forward, hands clasped together and meeting his gaze with grave intent. "My plan offers only a small prospect of escape, but will almost certainly result in the death of any who take part, and many who don't. But, if done correctly, perhaps we can once again light a fire that will spread throughout the empire. I was in Corvus not long before they brought me here. Riots were raging. The Emperor's failed war against the Corporatists has stoked the people's anger. The lives of so many sons spent on a madman's reckless gamble. Grief and rage will be the fuel for our fire."

Demisol closed his eyes for a moment, breathing deep, and Lizanne knew his lifelong passion for rebellion was at war with his reason. Finally, he turned to Helina, speaking softly, "Long have we sought such an opportunity."

"For escape," the woman replied, gaze dark as she stared at Lizanne. "Not suicide."

"By remaining here you are already committing suicide," Lizanne replied. "Just very slowly. I, for one, am not prepared to spend what years I have left stewing in this mire. We all have our ledgers to balance, do we not?"

Helina blinked and bit down on a retort as the words struck home. Her earlier reluctance in voicing the question of betrayal had revealed much about the depth of her own guilt.

"Your scheme has many variables," she said. "Much that could go wrong."

"Complexity will work to our advantage," Lizanne returned. "If one facet should be revealed it would take a mind of genius to work out the rest."

"The Coal King and the Electress are far from stupid," Demisol pointed out. "And Chuckling Sim is cleverer than both."

"Fortunate then that they are preoccupied with other matters. The attempt on the Electress's life, in particular." Lizanne leaned back, regarding them both in steady expectation.

"We will talk with our fellow citizens," Demisol said after another prolonged exchange of glances with Helina. "A vote must be taken. I expect the discussion will be . . . lengthy. Although most of us were Co-respondents, our group includes four Republicists, two Neo-Egalitarians and a Holy Leveller, amongst others, all of whom would happily have killed each other in the days following the collapse of the revolution. Old rivalries are normally set aside amongst the Learned Damned, but not forgotten. This scheme will be sure to reawaken previous grievances."

"And the risk of betrayal," Helina added. "Any fervent dissenters will have to be dealt with."

"And assurances provided," Demisol said, turning back to Lizanne. "Proof confirming the truthfulness of your intent. Remember, we do not know you. For all we know the Cadre sent you here."

"For what?" Lizanne enquired, a question which heralded another silence. "I'd best leave you to your discussions," she said, getting to her feet. "I'll return tomorrow with the proof you require. In the meantime, I shall inform the Electress that I have gained your trust and, whilst I could discern nothing that would confirm your involvement in the attempt on her life, I suspect there may be more to find. It would help if I had some small morsel of intelligence to share. It doesn't have to be true. As I say, I don't care if you tried to kill her or not."

"We didn't," Demisol replied. He paused then inclined his head at Helina. "Tell her."

"We were approached," the woman said, tone sullen with guarded reluctance. "Four months ago. A discreet and carefully oblique enquiry regarding any bomb-making expertise we might possess. The inquirer was sent on his way with a very clear warning not to return. This group has a strict policy of non-involvement with the various power struggles within these walls."

"The Coal King or one of his creatures, presumably," Lizanne said.

The woman responded with the first smile Lizanne had seen on her face, a smug little twist of the lips stirred by the pleasure of possessing superior knowledge. "Actually, no. It was the pianola-playing fop from that whorehouse you call home."

CHAPTER 23

Sirus

Majack died first, a bullet buzzing by Sirus's head to shatter the former soldier's remade features just as he jumped from the barge. He sagged into the water like a stringless marionette, his blood staining the surf red. Within seconds another volley of rifle fire came from the dark mass of trees beyond the beach. Sirus flinched as the bullets raised geysers from the surrounding water, felling three more of his company. He sent out a harsh thought-command to stem the sudden upsurge of confusion amongst his fellow Spoiled. Although their transformation made them resistant to panic, even the White's influence couldn't banish an instinctive fear of death. Their reaction was heightened by the shock of such unexpectedly fierce opposition. Their victories to date had often been hard-fought, but truly never in doubt, aided in no small part by the fact that so few Islanders possessed fire-arms. The tribe inhabiting this island, however, were clearly different. It was the largest and most populous island they had yet attacked. Its name translated from the local dialect as the Cradle of Fire, presumably due to the huge volcano that rose from the centre of the tree-covered land-mass. Thanks to their recent recruits, Sirus also knew it had earned another name in recent years: Kahlanah Dassan, the King's Cradle.

Keep moving! he ordered his company, raising his rifle and loosing a shot at the trees. *Fire back!*

They responded immediately, falling in on either side as he continued to wade towards the beach, firing and reloading with each step. Around them more barges were beaching on the sand-bar, disgorging their troops to add further weight to the advance. The Islanders in the trees, however, seemed uncowed by the sight of such an onslaught. They kept up an accurate and deadly fire throughout the three long minutes it took for Sirus to struggle clear of the surf, by which time he had lost fully half his company and the waves had turned a pale shade of crimson.

Lie down, Morradin ordered. *Harassing fire.*

Sirus duly had his company lie prone on the beach and fire at the muzzle flashes in the trees. His refashioned eyes made it easier to pick out the vague shapes of the island's defenders, counting at least a hundred directly to their front with more on either side. The fire of his company, all expert shots, took a steady toll as the rest of the assault force made a costly but inexorable progress to the beach. Some three thousand of them waded clear of the sea, leaving dozens of bodies bobbing in the swell around the barges. In accordance with Morradin's command they lined out on either side of Sirus's company, lying down to send a withering hail of bullets into the trees. For a few moments the air was filled with the cacophony of massed small arms, Sirus seeing numerous Islanders fall before Morradin gave another order.

Fix bayonets. Advance at the charge.

The entire line of Spoiled rose as one, steel glittering as they slotted their bayonets into place. There were no bugles or shouted exhortations to accompany their charge, just the sibilant rumble of many boots on sand and the now-intermittent crackle of the defenders' fire. Sirus could sense Morradin's excitement, glancing to see the large shadow of the Red drake that bore him as he swept low to witness the spectacle. Hoping for another fine old show.

They had closed to within thirty yards of the trees when the first cannon fired, the air around Sirus instantly filled with what sounded like a thousand angry hornets. He knew what it was thanks to the shared memory of a former soldier who had time to name the new threat before his torso was torn to shreds. Canister.

The five Spoiled charging on Sirus's left were transformed into a cloud of red mist and flensed flesh, whilst those to his right fared little better. He threw himself flat, this time needing no command from Morradin. He found himself face-to-face with Katrya. Like him, she appeared to be unscathed but the spines on her forehead were bunched in angry consternation. *Where did they get those?*

They ducked as another salvo of cannon fire blasted out from the treeline, cutting down those Spoiled who had resisted the instinctive urge to duck. Sirus could see that the whole line had stalled, their ranks broken by several large, red-smeared gaps. The defenders' rifles started firing with a new intensity, finding easy targets at such shortened range. Sirus could feel his fellow Spoiled dying around him. It was a curiously painless experience; like watching a hundred candles being snuffed by the wind one after the other.

Clever bastard, Morradin enthused from above. *Waited for the charge before revealing his guns. I'm liking this Shaman King more and more.*

Sirus watched the Red carrying Morradin angle its wings, aligning itself parallel to the tree-line. Another dozen Reds glided out of the sky to fall in behind as the beast flew lower, mouth gaping to breathe out a stream of fire that swept the trees. The following drakes followed suit, bathing the forest in flame along the whole length of the beach. Sirus looked at the inferno raging to his front, hearing the screams of the defenders above the roar.

Left you a gap, Morradin informed him, communicating an image of an untouched avenue through the forest a hundred yards or so to the left. *Renew the advance. There's some kind of fortification a mile inland. Surround it and wait for orders.*

The remnants of the assault force formed up behind Sirus as he led them into the trees. There were just over fifteen hundred left, some with wounds both minor and severe. It wasn't unusual for the White's Spoiled servants to keep fighting despite mortal injury. The Spoiled to his right, a petite young woman who would have probably been described as of delicate appearance in her human days, trotted along with one hand clamped over the wound in her stomach. Sirus could see a pink bulge between her fingers and a steady trickle of blood seeped from her mouth as she ran, her face betraying not the slightest twinge of pain.

They met further opposition upon leaving the beach, warriors charging out of the roiling smoke alone or in small groups, crying out their war cries as they hacked and stabbed. Sirus could pick out the words "Ullema Kahlan" amongst the furious babble as the Islanders were shot down or bayoneted. These suicidal attacks were costly but barely slowed the Spoiled advance, Sirus ordering a halt at the sight of Morradin's Red circling a large stockade.

Resistance continued as they surrounded the stockade, the Islanders eschewing their mad charges in favour of sniping from tree-tops. Sirus felt the rush of a passing bullet, which splintered the trunk of a tree a few inches from his head. His Spoiled-born eyes and reflexes reacted with automatic swiftness, picking out the dim shadow of the marksman perched atop a tall palm-tree, Sirus's bullet taking him between the eyes a half-second later. He ran to the body, retrieving the man's rifle for inspection. The words *Silworth Independent Arms Company Mark VI .422* were engraved in Mandinorian on the brass plate fixed to the stock, an image he instantly conveyed to Morradin.

Standard Protectorate issue, the marshal mused. *It appears Ironship have been making new friends. Explains where they got those cannon from.*

Sirus turned his gaze on the stockade, which was in fact a substantial fortress of thick wooden walls standing twenty feet high. *Meaning they'll have more in there,* he thought.

Of course they will. Sirus could feel Morradin's keen anticipation. *But that means they'll also have a great deal of powder. Continue to mop up the perimeter. See if you can actually capture a few. I sense our drake god isn't altogether happy with today's butcher's bill.*

The battery of cannon fired at once, muzzle flashes bright in the gloom as they cast their shells at the fortress. Sirus saw the projectiles strike home, each aimed with expert precision to impact on the same point. Over the past few hours repeated salvos had torn a large splintered rent in the fortress's south-facing wall, but as yet had failed to craft a breach. Morradin had initially intended to launch a massed assault, ordering the army to cut down trees and fashion scaling ladders, but then the White arrived.

Sirus could feel the great beast's simmering discontent as it soared high over the trees before finding a perch on the flanks of the volcano. Whilst the White would occasionally form thoughts into coherent words, for the most part its intent was divined through the emotions it conveyed. They consisted mostly of different shades of anger with the occasional pulse of satisfaction. So far the only joy the White exhibited came when it looked upon its clutch of infants and even then it was a dark, near-alien sensation; more like a swelling of sympathetic hunger as he watched the juveniles feast on yet another unfortunate captive. But now its feelings were far from joyous. The entire Spoiled horde stiffened as the White shared the sight of the many bodies littering the shore, colouring the images with a sharp note of dissatisfaction, most of it directed at Morradin.

So they set their ladders aside and brought up their small train of artillery to begin the long process of blasting a breach through the fortress's thick wooden walls. Morradin, unable to keep the stain of frustrated bloodlust from his thoughts but nevertheless keen to placate the White, ordered Sirus to take a third of the army and commence a hunt for captives. Most of the live Islanders they found were suffering from incapacitating wounds or severe burns. The unscathed or lightly injured proved a difficult quarry, fleet of foot and familiar with the many hiding-places offered by the island's dense forest and rocky coast-line. When cornered the fugitives were often suicidally unwilling to succumb to capture, several sinking a knife into their own throats as their pursuers closed in. By nightfall they had barely three hundred Islanders bound and awaiting conversion, less than a fifth of the casualties suffered in the initial assault and subsequent fighting.

The general lack of success resulting from this attack made Sirus consider the true level of the White's intelligence. It had been clever enough to spare Morradin and put his generalship to use, but was apparently unable to discern the particular characteristics that had once caused the marshal to be dubbed "The Butcher" by his own troops.

It is limited, Sirus realised, careful to accompany the thought with as many images of the day's slaughter as he could. He had learned that the more visual stimulus crowded his thoughts the less his fellow Spoiled were able to discern his reasoning. *It doesn't really understand us, any more than we understand it.*

Do you have to? Katrya asked, drawing back with a painful wince.

Sorry. Sirus muted his thoughts and she settled against him once more. They had found a resting-place near the cannon, a hollow created by the roots of a large tree that would offer welcome shade from the sun come morning.

He killed his wife, you know, Katrya mused as the cannon blasted out another salvo.

Who? Sirus asked.

Majack. Strangled her a few years ago when he was drunk. Thought she'd been tupping his sergeant. He wrapped the body in an old carpet and dumped it in the jungle for the Greens, told everyone she'd run off with a sailor. It'd been bothering him ever since. I think he wanted to die.

Then he got his wish. This particular memory of Majack's had escaped him as he had never felt the need to exchange more than the most basic thoughts with the former soldier. *He shared that with you?* he asked.

He dreamt it. Kept it buried deep down when awake, but you can't bury your dreams.

Sirus summoned another collage of imagery as her thoughts birthed an inevitable conclusion. But this time his memory shield wasn't enough.

Yes, she told him, entwining a scaly hand in his, *I see yours too, my darling. I see who you dream of every night. But I also see that, in your dreams at least, you see her as she really was. Not how you wanted her to be.*

A nother full day's pounding with the cannon and the breach was finally opened. It seemed far too narrow for a successful assault to Sirus, just wide enough for two men at a time, but Morradin's commands left no room for discussion. In common with previous assaults Sirus's company had been chosen to make the first attack. As he formed his troops into a narrow column Sirus allowed himself the suspicion that Morradin, driven by their mutual detestation, might well be attempting to orchestrate his death.

Not my choice, boy, the marshal informed him, reading his mind with ease. *It seems you hold the favour of our White god. The perils of having such a disciplined mind, I suppose. The rest of these morons don't respond half as quick as you.*

They crouched in the long grass that dominated the ground between the trees and the fortress, waiting for nightfall. The Spoiled had little difficulty seeing in the dark which gave them an advantage over the Islanders, although Sirus doubted it would count for much in the confines of the breach. Morradin's command came as the first stars began to twinkle in the sky. *NOW!*

Sirus rose and led his Spoiled forward at a run, covering the distance to the breach in less than a minute. He expected an immediate hail of rifle fire from the defenders on the walls but the charge was completely unopposed, the whole affair proceeding in an eerie silence broken only by the rasp of the grass as they ran. *Saving their ammunition,* Morradin mused as Sirus reached the breach. *It'll be any second now, boy. Best brace yourself.*

Sirus increased his speed, sprinting through the jagged fissure as fast as his monstrous body would allow, expecting a volley to come crashing down from above at any second. Instead, he cleared the breach in a few seconds and found himself standing amidst a scene of slaughter. The Is-landers lay everywhere, at least three hundred strewn about a broad inner courtyard, each one with their neck laid open.

Knew what they were in for, Morradin judged. *Didn't want to add to our numbers. It seems they're learning.*

Sirus crouched next to the body of a woman. She was young and tall, with the supple muscles and scars typical of Island warriors. Dark congealed blood covered her throat and the blade of the knife lying in her limp hand.

This happened hours ago, Morradin decided. *Search the place. Find him.*

They scoured the stronghold from top to bottom, finding only more bodies. *Any of the men could be him,* Sirus pointed out to Morradin. *None of the other Islanders in our ranks ever saw his face.*

No. Morradin was emphatic. *He's not here. Maybe he never was. Slipped away and left us to waste time and ammunition on this fortress of corpses.*

Eventually one of the Spoiled reported finding something in the bowels of the fortress. Sirus made his way down a series of wooden steps to a large, cellar-like chamber where one of his troops stood next to a narrow hole in the dirt floor. *A tunnel,* Sirus reported, crouching to inspect the find. *Recently dug.*

Follow it, Morradin commanded and Sirus leapt into the opening, find-ing he had to crawl on all fours to make his way along the passage. The tunnel's hasty construction was evident in the loose dirt that fell on him continually as he struggled along, expecting the roof to collapse at any second. It took the better part of an hour's crawling before he came to the tunnel's end. Sirus halted, eyeing the dim moonlight streaming down from a roughly hewn hole in the roof, drawing an impatient query from Morra-din. *What's the delay, boy?*

They didn't collapse the exit, Sirus replied.

Perhaps they didn't have time. Or perhaps there's an entire war-party waiting above to hack your head off the instant you pop up. We won't know until you do, will we?

Butcher indeed, Sirus muttered inwardly, squirming to take a firmer hold of his rifle and wiping the soil from the breech. A dozen Spoiled had followed him into the tunnel and he ordered them to clean their own weap-ons before crawling forward and rising to a crouch. The opening was four feet or so above his head, a leap beyond his former body, but well within the capabilities of this one.

He leapt as high as he could, clearing the hole and landing on his feet, rifle ready and eyes tracking the surrounding trees for enemies. Nothing. *Spread out,* he told his troops as they leapt to join him.

Sirus waited a moment to gauge his surroundings, seeing a mostly unremarkable patch of jungle, then his ears detected the sound of rushing water some way off to the left. He led his Spoiled towards the sound at a steady run, spurred on by Morradin's mounting impatience. After a hundred paces the trees thinned to reveal a large pool. The pool's surface lapped gently against the encroaching rocks, fed by a curtain of water that glittered in the moonlight as it fell from the edge of a high cliff. There were several large rocks rising from the water, each one featuring an ornamental stone of some kind. The few converted Islanders in their ranks had provided some insight into their spiritual beliefs, and Sirus knew these were shrines to the ancient spirits who were said to have first inhabited the Barrier Isles before the coming of man. His gaze soon went to the largest rock, a flat boulder upon which a small man sat, surrounded by bodies, all Island warriors of typically impressive stature. Like their brethren back at the fortress, they had all clearly died by their own hand, throats slashed open and their mingled blood seeping over the rock and into the pool in a billowing red cloud.

The Shaman King, if I'm not mistaken, Morradin mused as Sirus shared the image of the small man and his dead guards. *I thought he'd be taller, didn't you?*

The small man barely glanced over his shoulder at Sirus before returning his gaze to the shrine, head bowed and lips moving in some unheard prayer or invocation. He was certainly a contrast to the other Islanders, his limbs spindly and his back bent, though he possessed their usual fair colouring.

A new thought pushed its way into Sirus's head, far stronger and more implacable than Morradin's: *Not needed.* The White added a hard jab of urgency to his command that made Sirus shudder as he raised his rifle. He trained the sight on the centre of the small man's back where the bullet would be sure to shatter his spine before going on to pierce his heart. An easy shot at this range.

He had begun to squeeze the trigger when the entire surface of the pool exploded upwards. The water rose into a solid wall of white and red before blasting outward with sufficient force to send Sirus and the other Spoiled sprawling. He scrambled to his feet quickly, finding himself within a swirling maelstrom of raised water. Near by, he saw one of his Spoiled lifted off his feet and dragged into the enveloping wall of vapour. Through the confusion Sirus could see the vague shape of the body being dashed against one of the rocks in the pool before being cast away into the storm. Something hard slammed into Sirus from behind, throwing him flat once again. He looked up to see two more of his troops being borne high then slammed together, once, then twice, then once more before being flung aside. The bodies landed close to Sirus and he saw the force of the last impact had been enough to enmesh their part-shattered rib-cages, two pairs of lifeless slitted eyes staring at him in blank astonishment.

It appears the stories were true, Morradin observed dryly. *He is a Blood-blessed after all.*

Sirus could feel the other Spoiled dying around him as the Shaman King's invisible hand crushed them one by one. Their last agonies were a curious sensation, absent of fear but full of pain and confusion. He was also surprised to discover a small kernel of fear rising in his own breast, finding a perverse delight in the knowledge that at least he would die with some vestige of humanity remaining.

Oh no, boy. Morradin's implacable command brought him to his feet. *We have orders, don't forget.*

Sirus brought the rifle to his shoulder, aiming at the dim shape of the rock where the Shaman King sat, and fired. The maelstrom died immediately, the raised water transformed into a brief but heavy deluge, the weight of water enough to force Sirus to his knees. He shook the moisture from his face and looked up, finding the Shaman King on his feet now, staring at Sirus with a strangely sympathetic smile on his lips. Blood leaked from a bloody hole in his shoulder, though he gave no sign of pain.

Sirus worked the bolt on his rifle then reached into his ammunition pouch for another round. The rifle flew from his grip with a hard jerk then spun around, the butt striking Sirus on the side of the head. He fell, stunned and blinded by pain, scrabbling on the ground until his vision returned, and when it did it was to regard the sight of a large boulder lifting from the pool. Water trailed from its sides as it drifted closer, coming to a halt directly above where Sirus lay. The wonderful fear lurched anew, growing with every second he stared up at the hovering stone. He decided later that it was the fear that saved him, overcoming his pain and confusion to birth a final instinctive lurch to the side as the boulder fell.

He rolled upright as the rock slammed into the earth, whirling to see the Shaman King regarding him with what could only be described as amused respect. The small man sighed and crouched to retrieve a drinking-horn from the surface of the rock, pausing to utter something in his own language before drinking deep. He staggered as he finished, letting the horn fall from his grip, then straightened, his former humour vanished as he fixed Sirus with a dark, purposeful glare and the air around him began to shimmer with heat.

Red, Sirus realised, casting around for another weapon, hoping one of his unfortunate comrades had dropped a rifle near by, but there was nothing. His reborn fear compelled him to flee into the trees but he knew he would be burned to cinders before he made it. So he stood, watching the Shaman King summon the heat that would kill him, gratitude warring with fear in his heart.

A piercing cry sounded from above and a crimson streak descended onto the Shaman King in a blur of folding wings and flashing talons. The small man had no time to redirect his fire, barely managing to glance up before Katarias bore him down, claws pinning him to the rock. The huge Red gave a brief, triumphal screech and lowered its head to feed.

Sirus, finding he had no desire to witness this, turned away and walked off into the trees. The fear still thrummed in his chest, though it was lessened now. He clung to it, nurtured it with visions of recent horrors, for it was a precious thing he might have need of later.

CHAPTER 24

Clay

Clay screamed again as the dwarf Green worried at his leg, feeling teeth grind on his shin-bone. His finger closed convulsively on his revolver's trigger, blasting a hole in the earth a foot wide of the attacking drake. He tried to draw back the hammer for another shot, then spasmed as the Green clamped its jaws tighter still and a wave of the purest agony ripped through him from head to toe.

Sigoral's carbine gave a loud crack and blood exploded from a large hole in the Green's back. It jerked in response, tail thrashing and thick blood spurting from its wound, but still its jaws held tight.

"The head!" Loriabeth yelled, her words part drowned by a sudden cacophony of Greens crying out in challenge as they rushed from the surrounding trees. Clay heard her revolvers blast out a rapid salvo followed by a chorus of screams.

Sigoral crouched and jammed the muzzle of his carbine barrel into the corner of the drake's mouth, drawing another scream from Clay as the metal slid over his raw flesh. The carbine gave a muffled crack and the back of the Green's head dissolved in a blossom of gore and shattered bone. Clay gaped at the red ruin of his leg, fascinated by the sight of his exposed bone and the blood leaking in rivulets from severed veins.

Loriabeth's guns fell silent and Sigoral whirled away from him, bringing the carbine to his shoulder to loose off a rapid volley. Clay's gaze swung towards the Corvantine, blinking away a flood of sweat to watch him blast a Green's head apart in mid air as it leapt towards him. The sound of the shot was oddly dull, like a distant echo, and Clay's vision suddenly seemed to be bleached of colour, as if he were watching a moving photostat.

His head lolled as a great weariness descended, the world dimming further into a vague mélange of shifting grey. He would have passed out if a fresh flare of agony hadn't exploded in his leg, returning him to consciousness in time to catch sight of another dwarf Green clambering nimbly through the branches directly above. His reaction was purely instinctive and he later doubted he could have made the shot if he had tried. His gun hand came up in a smooth unhurried arc as his finger closed on the trigger, sending the bullet clean through the drake's head as it crouched to launch itself down at Loriabeth.

"Up . . ." he croaked, head swivelling towards his companions, who were now preoccupied with feverishly reloading their guns. "Look up!" Clay shouted, loosing another shot into the forest canopy.

Loriabeth was the first to react, her wide-eyed gaze turning to murderous fury as she raised it to take in the sight of a dozen or more Greens swarming through the branches overhead. She started firing as another wave of exhaustion swept through Clay, this time too overwhelming for any amount of pain to resist. His last glimpse before his vision slipped into utter blackness was of Loriabeth and Sigoral standing above him, guns blazing as they fired into the trees and Green after Green fell around them like over-ripe fruit.

A deep, persistent throb dragged him from the void, leaving him floating close to the surface of consciousness. He drifted in a fog of pain and confusion, wincing at the sound of distant thunder that he slowly realised were voices.

"Aren't we supposed to dilute it first?"

"He once drank the raw blood of a White and lived. I think he can handle this."

A burn on his lips, then his tongue, the taste familiar but also far more intense and acrid than he was used to. It invaded his mouth then burned its way down his throat as he gave a reflexive gulp. The pain lessened immediately, the throb subsiding into a slow, muted pulse that felt rather like being punched through a thick blanket.

"Cuz?" a faint voice asked from the far end of a long tunnel. "You hear me?"

Clay tried to open his eyes but still full awareness escaped him. He groaned instead.

"Gonna have to do something about your leg," Loriabeth's voice echoed to him and he could hear the note of grim determination it held. "Got no other option, Clay." A pause. "Soak it good. Alright, give it here. You'd best hold him down, he's apt to kick something awful."

Clay had begun to voice a query, which emerged as just another groan, when the void turned into a blinding white sky as a thousand hornets stung his leg as one. The pain was far worse than the Green's bite. A shimmering blade of fire sliced from his leg to his brain, birthing enough agony to wrench him back to consciousness.

He came to screaming obscenities into Sigoral's face, the Corvantine averting his gaze as spittle showered him. Clay tried to clamp his hands on the marine's neck, fully intending to choke him to death, but found they were confined, strapped to his sides by a thick leather belt. He thrashed instead, the foulest insults streaming from his gaping mouth as a shudder arched his back.

"It's alright, cuz!" Loriabeth's face swam into view. "It's us! Gotta do this to save your leg!"

"Fu-fuck you . . . !" Clay choked and screamed again. "Vicious . . . little bitch!"

"I'm sorry . . ."

He thrashed for a full minute, Sigoral's hands like vises on his shoulders, keeping him pinned until exhaustion finally claimed him once more. He drifted away to the sight of Loriabeth staring down at him, tears streaming from her eyes as she whispered pleas for forgiveness.

"You've looked better." She stood a few feet away, speaking aloud as she had in their only shared trance. She clasped the shaft of her spear with both hands, resting her weight upon it as she regarded him, the tattoos on her forehead bunching in amused appraisal.

"You're dead," Clay mumbled, then winced as a burning throb shuddered through his leg. "Go away."

Silverpin gave a pout of mock annoyance. "Of course I'm dead. You shot me, remember?"

"It was an accident," he muttered, casting his gaze around and finding himself in familiar surroundings. The cave in the Badlands where they found the infant White's nest. Also, the first time they made love. Clay decided he really didn't want to be here and made a determined effort to wake up. Nothing happened.

"This isn't a dream, Clay," Silverpin said.

Clay realised he was standing upright, his injured leg as straight and whole as before, though the pain it held was everything he expected. He turned around, taking in the surrounding environment, seeing none of the subtle or bizarre alterations a sleeping mind might make to a place plucked at random from the recesses of his brain.

"You shared the image with Miss Lethridge," Silverpin said. "So it remains fixed. Just like me."

"A talking memory?" Clay asked. "That's what you are?"

"We shared a very special form of trance, a deeper and more powerful connection than has been established between two Blood-blessed for centuries. There were bound to be consequences. What are people, anyway, if not just a collection of memories? I suppose you could say you made me." Her decorated brows bunched again in consternation. "Which kind've makes you my . . . father. Not sure I like that analogy."

Clay stared at her for a long moment, finding no flaw in her bearing or expression. She was as he remembered her, too real and vital to be just a collage of images moulded by his slumbering mind. "So," he said, "you're a ghost."

Her face grew sombre and she shrugged. "A murdered soul with unfinished business. A reasonable description, I suppose."

"How come I haven't seen you before?"

"It could be this portion of your mind was closed before now. Trauma can have a transformative effect on the brain. Or perhaps because you just didn't want to."

"Trust me"—he met her gaze, speaking in slow, unwavering tones—"I did not want to see you again."

Her blue eyes twinkled a little as she smiled. "There's no point lying in here. Can't lie to yourself after all." She glanced around at the gloomy interior, frowning. "This is boring. Let's go somewhere else."

There was no swirl of images like in his trances with Lizanne, just an abrupt shift from one location to another. This time they stood on the foredeck of the *Firejack*, steaming sedately down a stretch of the Bluechurn he recognised as lying south of Stockade. The hard report of a gun-shot drew

Clay's gaze to the starboard rail where a red-haired woman was educating a young man in the finer points of marksmanship. "Damn, kiddo. Woulda thought a Blinds boy would know how to shoot . . ."

Clay turned away, fixing his gaze on the river ahead. "I miss her too, on occasion," Silverpin said. "In fact, I miss all of them. However, thanks to you I at least get to see how they're doing. You do know your little quest is going to get them all killed, I assume?"

"No," he replied. "And neither do you."

"Remember what I said about lying?"

"We had no choice. If you've seen what I have, then you know that. That *thing* you woke intends to eat the whole world."

"No, only a large proportion of the people. And there truly is nothing you can do to stop it."

He gripped the rail at the prow of the boat, knuckles paling with the force of it. "We'll see. There had to be a reason for the vision."

"Did there? What makes you think that? You caught a fractional glimpse of the future and immediately concluded it amounted to a providential message. From whom, might I enquire? A Corvantine god perhaps?"

He shook his head, refusing to look at her. "It has to mean something."

"Everything *means* something. Water falling from the sky means it's raining, and that's all it means, whether you see it in the past or the future." She moved closer and rested her head on his shoulder before pressing a kiss to his neck. "Face it, Clay, you led a lot of people into certain death for no good reason. Though it wouldn't have been so bad if they'd had a choice."

He turned to find her offering him a sympathetic grimace. "Meaning what?" he demanded, then shuddered as the pain in his leg lurched once more into full agony. The surrounding mindscape took on an immediate misty appearance, water and jungle shimmering into a formless fog. Silverpin, however, remained complete and all too real.

"Clay," she said, shaking her head as the background faded into blackness. "Didn't you ever wonder why they were so willing to follow you on such an insane course . . . ?"

He came awake with a shout, or would have if Sigoral's hand hadn't been clamped so tightly over his mouth. "Quiet!" the Corvantine hissed into his ear.

Clay relaxed, as much as he could with the pain still raging in his leg. Sigoral removed his hand before turning away, the butt of his carbine tight against his shoulder and barrel raised high to point at a much-denuded forest canopy. The three suns were visible through the sparse branches, the heat they cast down more intense than before, drawing fresh beads of sweat from his already moist brow.

"Greens?" he asked in a murmur.

"No." He looked down to see Loriabeth crouched at his leg, gently pulling aside a heavily stained bandage to inspect the wound. She had positioned herself so as to block his view, but from the way she stiffened he concluded the news wasn't good.

"Festered, huh?" he asked.

She shook her head and turned, forcing a smile. "No, the Green we soaked it in seems to have warded off any infecting humours. You'll be up and walking in no time."

"Then let me see."

"You need to rest some more . . ."

"Let me see, cuz!"

She lowered her gaze and shifted out of his eye-line, affording him a clear view of the wound and why she hadn't wanted him to see it. A sizable chunk of the muscle on his lower right leg was gone or denuded, leaving bone and sinew exposed. It was the kind of injury he would have expected to see only on a corpse. His gaze shifted to his bare foot and he tried to wiggle his toes, an effort that provoked another upsurge of pain but left his toes unmoved. He stared at the wound for as long as he could, forcing himself to accept the reality of it, before a rising nausea compelled him to avert his gaze.

"Might've been best to just take it off," he said as Loriabeth knelt to replace the bandage with one from her pack. He tried for a jovial tone but it came out as a strained, tremulous gasp.

"I ain't no surgeon," she replied. "'Sides, I seen folk come back from worse. Remember that tail-strike laid me low at Stockade? And I'm still spry as ever."

She secured the bandage in place, Clay gritting his teeth against the pain and turning to Sigoral for a distraction. "If it ain't Greens," he said. "What're you on guard against there, Lieutenant?"

"Look at the lights," Sigoral said, maintaining his vigil.

Clay raised a hand to shield his eyes and squinted at the trio of crystal suns. At first he saw nothing then noticed the one in the centre dim a little as something passed in front of it, something with wings and long tail. "I'm guessing that ain't a bird," he said.

"Reds," Loriabeth said. "They're small, like those Greens, but they're Reds alright. And there's at least a dozen circling above. Ain't seen fit to come for us as yet."

"I think they're waiting for us to venture out there," Sigoral said, jerking his head to the left.

Clay turned, finding that the forest was mostly gone now, leaving a short stretch of widely spaced trees before giving way to the broad plain he had glimpsed from atop the overgrown structure. It was flat and mostly barren save for a few bushes. "How long you been carrying me?" he asked Loriabeth.

"Dragging more like," she said. "Three or four miles from where those Greens came for us. Night came and went. The lieutenant did some counting and reckons this place gets about ten hours of light and the same of darkness a day, if you can really call it a day."

"Why so short?" Clay wondered aloud, then grunted as Loriabeth tied off the bandage.

"Here," she said, reaching for two branches lying near by. "We cut crutches in case you woke up. No offence, cuz, but I ain't got the strength to drag you one more mile."

She made him eat before they set off. It transpired they had adopted his suggestion whilst he slept, catching several birds for roasting. They made for tasty fare, reminding him of the pigeons he had resorted to trapping during his early days in the Blinds.

"Been lighting fires without any trouble," Loriabeth said, turning a spitted bird over a healthy flame. "Greens've been content to leave us be."

"We killed many," Sigoral said. "Perhaps all of them."

"Or they just learn faster than these birds," Clay said, biting into a small drumstick as he cast a wary eye at the Reds circling above. "Have to hope this lot learns the same lesson if they try their luck."

Loriabeth had filled a whole canteen with product harvested from the pile of dead Greens they left in the forest. Clay tasted a little before they set off across the plain. The blood was heavily diluted with water but the effects made him conclude that, tiddlers or not, the blood of the drakes in this place remained just as potent as their larger cousins'.

Progress was inevitably slowed by Clay's infirmity. He soon managed to get the hang of the plant-and-swing motion needed to propel himself forward on his crutches, but his leg ached continually and the depredations of his injury forced him to halt every few hundred yards. Sigoral and Loriabeth displayed some muted frustration with his slowness but neither voiced a rebuke and, to his eyes, remained remarkably free of desperation or panic despite their circumstances.

Miles beneath the ice trapped in a giant cavern with wild drakes, he thought, watching Sigoral pause and raise his gaze to the Reds circling above. *And yet they never thought of leaving me.*

The notion stirred unwelcome thoughts of Silverpin's ghost. *Didn't you ever wonder why they were so willing to follow you?* He didn't want to think about the question overmuch, though it nagged at him as they inched their way across the treeless plain. He had convinced all the surviving Longrifles, half the crew of a Protectorate ship and a handful of Corvantine captives to follow him to the worst place on earth. All on the promise of something he saw in a vision, a vision only he and Miss Lethridge had seen. *I ain't never been that persuasive,* he knew, pausing to wipe a slick of sweat from his brow. *And yet they followed me here.*

The barrenness of the surrounding landscape drew his mind back to the Red Sands and that day they found the crater, the near-feverish need to find the White he had seen in his uncle's eyes, a need placed there by Silverpin. Images of the Longrifles' journey through the Arradsian Interior played out in his head as he stood, swaying a little on his crutches. *She birthed a hunger in them.* His gaze shifted to Loriabeth and Sigoral, both now halted and regarding him with deep concern. *What did I birth?*

"Clay?" Loriabeth asked.

He wanted to ask her if she had ever truly pondered their reasons for coming here, if the blind acceptance of so much danger ever gave her pause. And, if so, did those doubts disappear whenever she was in his company? *Have I doomed you, cuz?* he wondered, groaning as he looked away. He was pondering the wisdom of voicing his suspicions when his gaze caught something several miles ahead. The heat cast by the three suns produced a low hazy shimmer on the plain and he had to squint to fully make it out: a thin vertical line ascending from the tunnel floor into the black sky.

"You seeing this?" he asked, pointing. "Or did I pass out again?"

It grew clearer with every mile covered. A thin dark thread descending from the blackness above, slowly resolving into another shaft just like the one that had conveyed them to this place. Clay increased his pace as much as he could, but the effort soon left him gasping.

"We're stopping," Loriabeth decided as Clay came to an unsteady halt, head sagging and shoulders slumping between his crutches. She unhitched her fire-wood-laden pack and dumped it on the dusty ground. The lights had drawn ahead of them again and the trailing shadow lay only a short distance behind.

"Just a few more miles," Clay insisted, swinging himself forward and promptly falling over. He issued a profuse and enthusiastic torrent of profanity as his leg punished him with a fierce burst of pain. "Sonovabitching fucking thing!"

"You finished?" Loriabeth asked, bending to help him sit up.

"You should go on," he said, gritting his teeth as she settled a pack under his leg. "It's only a coupla hours away."

"Shut up, cuz," she muttered and went about building the fire.

"I mean it," he said. "Leave me here. Go see what's what . . ."

"I said shut up!" She glared at him, Clay suffering a fresh upsurge of guilt in the face of her implacable resolve.

"It's my fault," he groaned, head lolling as the guilt gave way to fatigue. "You followed me . . ."

"Made my own choice," she said, piling kindling cut from the stunted bushes found on the plain. "We all did."

"No . . ." he breathed, the world fading away once more. "You didn't . . ."

This time Silverpin failed to disturb his slumber, for which he was grateful. He blinked awake to find a large bug standing a few inches from his face. It was about three inches tall with six legs, fore-pincers and a tail tipped with a wicked-looking spike. The dim light gleamed on its black carapace as it maintained a frozen vigil for a few seconds before turning and scuttling off in a haze of dust. *More than just drakes to worry about in here,* Clay decided.

". . . under the ship?" he heard Loriabeth enquire, speaking in low tones so as not to wake him.

"And up the other side," Sigoral replied. "It's called keelhauling and is usually only reserved for the worst crimes. The barnacles on the keel will tear a man's flesh quite terribly, even worse so than flogging. I'd only ever seen it done once before I joined the *Superior,* and the miscreant in that case had been a drunkard who knifed a fellow sailor over a game of Pastazch. Captain Jenilkin, however, was much less discerning, keelhauling three men in as many months for petty infractions, one of whom perished. That was in addition to the numerous floggings he ordered. 'Peasants are beasts of burden, Mr. Sigoral,' he was fond of saying. 'And what beast doesn't respond well to the whip?' I swear, if that Corporatist shell hadn't taken his head off, the crew would have sooner or later."

"That how you got to be in charge?"

"No, that came later. The captain died in the Battle of the Strait. Our First Officer was killed when the Blues rose off Carvenport. He was inspecting the forward guns when one of the monsters stuck its head over the side and snapped him clean in two. We had no warning. In seconds it seemed as if the whole sea was on fire. When it was over I found myself the only officer still alive with a crew numbering a dozen men."

Sigoral fell quiet for a moment. When he spoke again his voice had taken on a note of forced briskness. "Still, doesn't do to dwell. Although, how we remained afloat long enough to sail to Lossermark is still something of a mystery."

"Only for us to come steal your ship out from under you." Loriabeth gave a soft chuckle. "Must've been a real pisser."

There was a pause before Sigoral replied, his voice coloured by a reluctant humour. "It was not one of my better days."

"How come you speak Mandinorian so well?"

"Takmarin is the principal centre for trade in the southern empire. I grew up hearing a whole host of languages, Mandinorian most of all since it's the language of commerce in all ports, regardless of what flag flies over the Customs House."

"Hardly heard anything but Mandinorian my whole life. Pa had a Dalcian in our crew for a while, bladehand before Silverpin. He taught me a few battle poems." She paused then recited a few lines of Dalcian. Clay heard Sigoral snort as he restrained an outburst of laughter.

"What?" Loriabeth demanded.

"Battle poems?" the Corvantine asked, still struggling to contain his mirth.

"Yeah. So?"

Sigoral took a deep inhalation and forced a neutral tone as he replied, "Nothing. Truly."

"Tell me."

"I'm afraid politeness forbids . . ."

"Just tell me, you Corvie prick!"

Sigoral took another deep breath before providing a carefully phrased response. "In Dalcian ports ladies of a . . . certain profession will stand in their windows chanting to attract . . . customers."

A long silence. "That bastard," Loriabeth breathed, provoking Sigoral into a restrained guffaw. "I was barely fourteen when he taught me that. Seer-damn pervert. Glad that Green pack roasted him now."

Sigoral's laughter increased in pitch then abruptly faded as a gust of wind swept over the camp, raising dust and causing Clay to reach for his revolver.

"You see it?" Loriabeth asked. Clay turned his head to find them both on their feet, weapons aimed upwards.

"Not even a flicker," Sigoral replied.

"He must've been lower this time." Loriabeth moved in a slow circle, arms held wide to cover as much of the sky as possible. "Twenty feet, less maybe."

"This time?" Clay groaned, shuffling into a sitting position.

"Happened twice before," she said. "Didn't wanna wake you. Skaggs told me about this. It's what they do when they're tracking a pack of Cerath across the plains. Trying to spook them into scattering so they can . . ." She cast a tense glance at him and trailed off, though it wasn't difficult to discern her meaning. *So they can pick off the weakest.*

Clay turned his gaze towards the direction of the shaft, now a thick straight vertical line edged by the burgeoning glow of the three suns. "Reckon there's another hour until the light returns in full," he said, stifling a pained grunt as he shifted his weight to reach for his crutches. "We'd best move on now."

"It might be better if we go back to dragging you," Sigoral suggested, watching Clay climb unsteadily to his one good foot, crutches splayed so he didn't topple over right away. "We can rig another litter . . ."

"I don't need dragging," Clay broke in. He replanted his crutches and swung himself forward, moving with all the semblance of healthy resolve he could muster. "Leave the fire burning," he said, swinging himself onward. "Might serve as a distraction."

"Well that's sure shit on our breakfast."

Loriabeth kicked some sand loose from the gently sloping shore-line, birthing ripples from the placid water beyond. It stretched out before them like a vast mirror, black around the edges and bright in the centre where the three suns illuminated an island. It was small, no more than a hundred feet from end to end by Clay's reckoning. Sitting in the centre of the island was a structure some thirty feet high with sloping walls of intricate construction. Clay assumed it to be much the same as the structure in the forest, except it was completely free of any encroaching vegetation. The shaft rose from the structure's roof, disappearing into the haze of the three suns several hundred feet above.

"A forest, a desert, now a sea," Sigoral mused. "It's as if someone built a miniature world in here."

"More of a lake than a sea," Loriabeth said. "But it's still too damn broad for my liking."

Clay blinked sweat as he peered at the island. "Maybe three hundred yards. Not an impossible swim."

"For us," Loriabeth said. "Not you. Anyways." She kicked more sand into the water. "Who's to say what's already swimming about in there?"

"If we had enough wood we could built a raft," Sigoral pointed out.

"Meaning a long walk back to the forest." Loriabeth looked at the Reds circling above. Their altitude had definitely reduced over the past hour, coming low enough for Clay to gain a full appreciation of their size. Although considerably smaller than an Arradsian Red, they were still of sobering proportions; seven feet from nose to tail with a wing-span even broader. Plus there were twelve of them, enough to overwhelm their guns if they came in a rush.

"We follow the shore," Clay said, nodding to left and right. "See what we can find." He chose the right on a whim and started off, glad for the swallow of Green he had taken earlier. He had been strict in rationing his intake, not knowing how much longer this journey would take, and didn't like to think about the inevitable moment when it ran out.

It was Sigoral who found it, his eyes being attuned to picking out objects of note in a body of water. It rose from the lake's surface some ten yards off shore, the faux-sunlight gleaming on the crystal it held. Another plinth, just like the one from the platform.

"Well," Clay said, swinging himself towards the water. "We know it won't work for either of you."

He saw Loriabeth swallow a protest before moving to his side, Sigoral falling in behind. As they waded into the water the circling Reds broke their silence for the first time, piercing shrieks cutting through the air as they swung lower still.

"I think we're making them angry," Sigoral observed, tracking a Red with his carbine.

"Hungry, more like," Loriabeth replied, pointing a pistol at the shore-line. "See how they won't venture over the lake's edge."

Clay glanced back, seeing she was right. The Reds, now barely twenty feet off the ground, were wheeling around at heightened speed but veering away every time they came close to the shore-line. *Something's keeping them at bay.* He immediately turned his gaze to the water, peering through the surface for any sign of danger but seeing only clouds of silt disturbed by his lumbering passage.

A sudden flare of agony in his leg brought him to a halt as the water seeped through his bandage and into his wound. He cried out, the crutches slipping from his armpits as he shuddered and would have fallen if Sigoral hadn't caught him about the waist.

"Green," Clay gasped, his body throbbing and sending white flashes across his vision that told of an imminent faint. It seemed to take several seconds of eternity for Sigoral to fumble the cap from Clay's canteen and hold it to his mouth. He drank deep, the undiluted product burning its way down his throat and squashing the pain into a small, pulsing ball at the core of his being.

"We gotta go!" Loriabeth said, her words accompanied by the snick of a cocked revolver.

Clay swung his gaze back to the shore, seeing the Reds had all now come to rest on the sand. They shrieked a continual chorus of frustrated hunger, jaws snapping as they fanned their wings, tails coiling like angry snakes. With every shriek they inched closer to the water as predatory yearning vied with fear. He turned back to the plinth and forced himself on, shouting with the effort. By the time he reached it the water was over his belt, and the drakes' cries had risen to fever pitch. He slumped onto the plinth, slapping his hand to the crystal. Nothing happened.

"Think you can get any from here?" Loriabeth asked Sigoral. They were following in Clay's wake, backing away from the shore in slow careful steps.

"One for certain," the Corvantine said, aiming his carbine. "Should I shoot?"

"Not yet. Might stir them up even more."

Clay grunted in frustration and slapped his hand to the crystal once more then swore as it failed to produce the hoped-for glow. "Seer's balls! Do something!"

The crystal blazed into life, the sudden flare of light enough to blind him for a second. He blinked tears, hearing a rush of displaced water. When his vision cleared he saw the surface of the lake rising in a huge elongated swell that stirred memories of Last Look Jack. *A Blue,* he thought wearily. *Of course.*

But it wasn't a Blue. The water fell away to reveal a long, narrow structure of algae-covered granite, extending from the shore to the island. *A bridge,* Clay realised with a laugh that died at an upsurge of squawking from the Reds. The appearance of the bridge seemed to infuriate them, overthrowing their last vestige of fear.

They rose in a cloud of dust, wings drawing thunder from the air. Three came straight at them, skimming low over the water, whilst the others split into two groups and swung out to left and right. Sigoral's carbine cracked and one of the onrushing Reds tumbled into the lake. Loriabeth's revolvers blazed, cutting down the other two. Their speed was too great to allow for head-shots, so they failed to die immediately, thrashing wings and tails churning the water white and crimson, distressed shrieks loud enough to pain the ears.

Clay whirled to the right, revolver raised to aim at a Red banking towards him. He fired as it levelled out. His reduced faculties made for a poor shot, raising a waterspout a good foot wide of the target. The Red shrieked in triumph, mouth gaping as it closed. Clay drew the hammer back for another shot, arm trembling as he attempted to aim down the beast's throat.

The water beneath the Red erupted into a white froth as something shot from beneath the surface, something with a long snake-like body and blue scales that glittered in the cascading water. The Blue's jaws clamped onto the Red's neck, plucking it from the air with a crack of breaking vertebrae. The Blue coiled in mid air, seeming to hang there for a second and affording Clay an opportunity to gauge its size. *Nine feet long,* he thought with an oddly amused detachment. *Just a tiddler.* Then the Blue was gone, scattering water and blood as it dived back beneath the surface with its prize.

"Come on, cuz!" Loriabeth and Sigoral appeared at his side, each taking an arm and dragging him towards the bridge. The remaining Reds seemed to have fled, leaving the sky empty, but Clay's attention was now fixed on the water. The appearance of the bridge had raised a great deal of silt from the lake-bed, leaving the water dark and pregnant with unseen menace.

They reached the bridge after a few seconds' struggle through the water, Clay expecting another Blue to come surging up from the depths at any minute. Sigoral climbed onto the bridge and took hold of Clay's arms, dragging him up and clear of the water whilst Loriabeth pushed from below.

Once successfully hauled clear, Clay lay at the edge of the bridge. The pain was now so acute his leg seemed to be on fire, sapping his strength so much that he could only lie there and watch Loriabeth offer her raised arms to Sigoral. Instead of reaching down to her, however, the Corvantine straightened, unslung his carbine and levered a round into the chamber. Clay raised a trembling hand as Sigoral lowered the barrel, croaking out an impotent "No!" as flame blossomed from the carbine's muzzle. He turned, expecting to see Loriabeth slumping lifeless into the water, but instead finding her staring at the bloody, thrashing body of a Blue barely a yard away.

"If you wouldn't mind, Miss," Sigoral said, crouching to offer her his hand.

CHAPTER 25

Lizanne

"Seems too small," Demisol said, peering at the spherical device she had placed on the defaced table. It was a little larger than an average-sized apple, constructed from a mix of iron and copper components. A small key lay alongside it, ready to be inserted into the slot on the top of the device.

"I'm assured it's more than adequate for the task," Lizanne said.

"So you didn't make this?" Helina asked, her perennial suspicion as yet undimmed by Lizanne's reappearance with the promised proof of her intent.

"I was fortunate enough to secure the services of someone sympathetic to our enterprise," she replied.

"The wider this plan is known the greater the risk." The diminutive radical stared down at the device for a long while before adding, "I know of only one inmate with the skills to construct something of this complexity."

"The Tinkerer?" Demisol asked Lizanne, who shrugged.

"What does it matter?" she said. "The device will work and he is in the process of producing more."

"We've had a few dealings with him in the past," Demisol said. "Enough to know he cares nothing for our cause."

"I promised him escape. He's not particularly skilled in detecting lies."

"But you are skilled in speaking them," Helina observed.

"What revolutionary isn't?" Lizanne nodded at the device. "Citizens, I require your decision. Once this is primed and placed there can be no turning back."

Demisol gave no immediate reply, instead moving to the head of the table and sinking into a chair where the owner of this house once sat and entertained guests. "What have you told the Electress?" he enquired.

"That you're reluctant to trust a new-comer," Lizanne replied. "However, whilst I have not yet discerned any evidence of your involvement in the attempt on her life, certain passing remarks lead me to conclude there is more to learn here. Also, you have intimated a desire to have me spy on her, as she would expect."

"So," Helina said, "you haven't given up the fop yet."

Lizanne gave a thin smile. "Play a high card at the wrong moment and you risk losing the pot."

"How does it work?" Demisol asked, nodding at the iron-and-copper apple on the table.

"Insert the key and turn it fully to the right. The delay is fifteen minutes. I will have a dozen more ready by next Ore Day, and a much larger device I'm assured will achieve our principal aim."

"And then," Demisol said softly, "Scorazin goes to war."

"Yes." Lizanne looked up, eyes tracking from one to the other. "Your decision, citizens?"

"We were obliged to . . . disenfranchise one of our number after putting your scheme to the group," Helina said. "The Holy Leveller, ironically. Despite a lifetime lost in religious delusion, he proclaimed the plan a murderous and insane folly. But the vote went against him."

"Unanimously," Demisol added, rising and coming around the table to retrieve one of the timepieces. "We're with you, citizen. It's time to wipe the blot of this city from the soul of humanity."

Earless Jozk was by far the worst gambler Lizanne had ever known. He would sit at her Pastazch table whenever he had money to spend, one hand twitching on his diminishing pile of chits as he peered at the hand she dealt, the value of which could be easily read in the various tics of his unwashed face. Tonight, the unalloyed glimmer of joy in his gaze told Lizanne he had drawn at least two cards of the Imperial Suit on the first throw of the die, a fact also plain to the four other players at the table who promptly folded.

"Cowards," the stocky Fury muttered, reaching for the meagre pot. Despite the poor haul, this was in fact the most Lizanne had seen him win in a single night. Usually he would sit playing out hand after hand until his chits were exhausted, whereupon he would disappear from the Miner's

Repose until labour in the sulphur pit earned enough to buy a chair at the table, and the entire fruitless exercise would be repeated.

"It's still a decent haul, Mr. Jozk," she told him as she gathered up the cards and shuffled the deck. "Enough for a full cup of the good stuff and an hour upstairs, if you'd like."

"I'm far from done," he growled in response. "Just work those dainty hands, m'dear. I'll decide how best to spend my wealth once I've cleaned the pockets of these craven dogs."

The other players gave voice to some restrained laughter, but no open mockery. Jozk had earned his name not from losing an ear, but from his habit of biting them off those foolish enough to rouse his temper past breaking point. To his credit, however, he never became violent at the table or fell victim to any unwise notions regarding Lizanne's person.

"Chits on the table or fold, please, gents," she said, dealing one card to each player. "Mr. Semper, first throw to you when you're ready."

Semper, a member of the Verdigris, was another regular at her table, drawn by a quickly acquired reputation for honest dealing. She could tell from his style of play that Pastazch had been his principal occupation before being consigned to Scorazin. He judged the odds with practised swiftness, never allowed emotion to colour his judgement and tended to leave the table richer than when he sat down. Unlike Earless Jozk, he had no aversion to spending his winnings on the ladies upstairs or on the establishment's most potent drink. Lizanne suspected such indulgence was due to a wasting illness that made his visage more cadaverous with every game and would surely see him cast onto the midden before the year was out.

Semper tossed his chit into the pot, glanced at the card she had dealt him then reached for the die with a bony hand. Some players liked to blow on the die before the throw, or offer it to Lizanne to do the same. "For luck," they said. Semper had no truck with such superstition and always threw without preamble, on this occasion turning up a four.

"Four cards to Mr. Semper." Lizanne dealt the cards and turned to the man on his left. "Your throw, sir."

The three other players all folded after their throws, leaving Semper and Jozk to battle over the pot. The Fury's throw earned him only two more cards, making this game a somewhat hopeless prospect, and yet his eyes betrayed the same excited gleam as before.

"Second throw," Lizanne said. Semper's next toss of the die earned him three more cards meaning Lizanne could only deal two in order to bring his hand up to the maximum of seven. Jozk's throw earned him one card, at which point his brow began to shine with sweat.

"Bet or fold, gents," Lizanne said.

The two men matched stares as the murmured voices from surrounding tables mingled with the lilting notes of Makario's pianola.

"You don't have it," Semper told Jozk, weary certainty colouring his rasp of a voice. Lizanne knew his meaning. There was only one hand in Pastazch in which four cards would be sure to triumph over seven; the rarely seen Imperial Quad.

"You don't know what I got," Jozk returned and pushed all of his chits into the pot.

"You had two Imperials on the last deal," Semper said, brows raised in an oddly sympathetic gesture. "The odds of having four in this one are . . ." He laughed and shook his head. "It's a poor time to choose for a bluff, Jozk. Take your money back and fold. I've no desire to make you an enemy."

"You won't."

Semper's gaze narrowed a little, Lizanne detecting a small flicker of uncertainty. *He doesn't have any Imperials,* she realised. *Meaning there's still a chance this is no bluff, however small.*

"As you wish," Semper sighed, pushing his impressive stack of chits to the centre of the table.

"Mr. Semper bets his entire stake," Lizanne said, reaching forward to count the value of the pot. "Mr. Jozk, you require . . ."

"Waiver," Semper cut in, offering Jozk a humourless smile. "Let's play it out. If this comes off it'll be one for my memoirs."

"Mr. Semper waives the matching bet," Lizanne said. "Gentlemen, show your cards."

A small crowd had gathered by now, a dozen or so patrons sidling closer to watch the outcome. Semper's slender fingers tapped his cards briefly before flipping them over, the onlookers voicing a collective gasp at the revealed hand.

"Seven-card flush," Lizanne said, raising an eyebrow. "Roses, no straight. Double points value makes for a total of one hundred and two. Mr. Jozk, you require one hundred and three points to take the pot."

Earless Jozk for once maintained an unreadable visage as he rested a hand on his cards, remaining still and silent as the moment stretched. Lizanne couldn't decide if he was enjoying the moment of triumph or contemplating his worst humiliation to date. She allowed him the time and let the tension draw yet more eyes to the table. A game like this had a tendency to stir the patrons up, making them more inclined to part with their chits, something the Electress always appreciated.

Finally a ghost of a smile flickered across the chapped lips of Earless Jozk's besmirched and prematurely aged face as he gave a wry shake of his head and began to turn over his cards.

Glass shattered off to Lizanne's right and something small and fast buzzed the air an inch in front of her nose. Her eyes instinctively followed its course, drawing up short at the sight of Jozk with a metallic dart embedded in his forehead. He met her gaze for a second, wet lips fumbling over final words no one would ever hear, then slumped face-first onto the table, leaking copious blood over the faded green baize. More shattered glass and the air was filled with a swarm of buzzing darts and the shouts of patrons.

Lizanne slipped from her chair and crawled under the table, watching men fall around her amidst a cacophony of panicked voices and stamping feet. One of her regulars collapsed near by, clutching at a dart in his shoulder. She watched as his hands spasmed and bloody foam began to seep from his mouth before he slumped onto his back, still twitching. *Poison on the darts,* she reasoned. *Clever.*

She realised Makario's music had fallen silent and looked up to see him still sitting at the pianola, gazing about at the unfolding massacre in wide-eyed bafflement. Lizanne rose to a crouch and scurried to the musician, feeling a dart flick through her hair. She grabbed Makario's arm and dragged him from the stool just as a dart embedded itself in the pianola, birthing a discordant howl of breaking strings.

"No," Makario breathed, rising and reaching out to the ruined instrument, face riven with grief.

"Don't!" Lizanne wrapped her arms around him and held him down as darts continued to streak through the shattered window above their head. Patrons littered the floor, dead or dying, whilst a thrashing knot of survivors jammed the stairwell in an effort to flee. Lizanne's attention was soon captured by the sight of Semper, standing upright as the darts thrummed around him. She could see one embedded in his arm and knew he wouldn't be long in joining the dead. He paid no mind to the injury, however, his gaze fully occupied by the four cards he held in his hand. Another dart slammed into his chest, making him stagger, but he stayed on his feet, his gaze slipping from the cards to find Lizanne.

"Emperor's balls!" he called to her in cheerful amazement, holding up the cards; the Chamberlain, the Landgrave, the Elector and the Emperor, all four cards of the Imperial Quad. "He actually had it!"

"What is it?" the Electress asked, looking over the device Anatol had placed on her desk. It consisted of two main components, a wooden stock joined at one end to a strip of sprung steel. The steel strip was curved thanks to the length of thick twine attached to both ends. The stock featured an ingenious modification that couldn't help but stir Lizanne's professional admiration.

"A cross-bow," she said. "But not a design I've seen before." She tapped a finger to the mechanical fixed to the stock. "A geared-lever arrangement and box magazine for the darts. The lever enables the user to draw back the string and reload in one movement, allowing for rapid fire. It would require a strong pair of arms to work, though."

"The Scuttler we found it on was strong enough," Anatol said. "Took three knife blows to bring him down."

"You get any more?" the Electress asked.

Anatol shook his head. "They were already running when we got there. Counted about a dozen, less the one who had this."

"Eight dead customers, and the loss of a night's takings, for one Scuttler." The Electress sank into her chair, match flaring as she lit the inevitable cigarillo. "That's a poor rate of exchange, I'd say." She looked at Melina and inclined her head at the cross-bow. "Tinkerer's work, would you say?"

"It's certainly clever enough for him," the tall woman replied with reluctant honesty. "But I'd say not. His mechanicals tend to have a more refined appearance. Besides, he never makes weapons. Not for anyone else, at least."

"King Coal must have gotten them from somewhere," Anatol said.

"Most probably from the same hands that crafted that bomb," Lizanne suggested. "I'm starting to think he managed to find himself a talented new-comer."

278 · ANTHONY RYAN

"Him and me both," the Electress replied, without much conviction.

"I'll gather the lads." Anatol started towards the door. "Time we finished this."

"I'd best go too," Lizanne said, moving to follow.

"You'll both do what the fuck I tell you to do!" the Electress snapped, smoke blossoming in an angry cloud. "When I tell you to do it." Her face took on a stony aspect as she calmed herself before turning to Melina. "What do you know?"

"A bomb went off in the Pit Number Three winding tower about three hours ago. Wrecked the gear and left two Scuttlers dead. Any coal they get from that seam will have to be hand-carted up from now on."

"Meaning most'll starve before long," Anatol said with a satisfied grimace. "The constables won't give two turds about their problems. No coal, no food. Saves us a good deal of killing."

A thin sigh escaped the Electress's lips as she closed her eyes and rubbed stubby, yellow-stained fingers into her temples. "Starving men are desperate men," she said. "And desperate men have no fear when it comes to a fight. Two Verdigris died here tonight, which means Chuckling Sim will feel obliged to respond, which means the Wise Fools will start itching to take advantage. When the whole city gets to fighting it's a safe bet the constables will have more than two turds to give."

She sat back, clasping her meaty hands together, brow furrowed in contemplation. "Send word to the pits," she muttered. "Triple guard tonight. Make sure everyone's armed up. No one sleeps. Now piss off downstairs and let me think."

Makario sat at the pianola, shoulders slumped as his finger tapped a dull thunk from one of the keys. The bodies had been cleared away, after a thorough looting, and efforts made to mop up the blood, though the worst stains still lingered on the boards. "I'm sure it's fixable," Lizanne said, moving to the musician's side. "Just strings and wood, after all."

His eyes flashed at her in momentary resentment, his normally fine features twisting into something she hadn't seen before. "What do you know about music?" he demanded in a harsh whisper. "You can name tunes, but what does your killer's heart really know?"

Some measure of surprise must have shown on her face for he sighed, closing his eyes and turning away. "I'm sorry," he said, splaying his delicate fingers over the keys. "It's just . . . She was a wreck when I found her, the last surviving pianola in the whole of Scorazin. It took months of work to nurse her back to health, make her sing again. The Electress's little project to bring music to the Miner's Repose. It kept me alive. Now . . ." He played a short melody, still recognisable despite the dull thud of keys on ruined strings. "What am I without her, Krista?"

Dead, Lizanne thought. *Like everyone else in here. But then, you always were.*

She was tempted to lean closer and whisper her knowledge into his ear; *I know what you did.* His reaction would be bound to reveal something useful, but she resisted. *Not out of sentiment,* she told herself, only partially feeling it to be a lie. *A card to be played when the pot's swollen to its fullest.*

She had been calculating the likely effect the bombing and subsequent massacre would have on her plan and knew the Learned Damned would be making their own calculations. It was possible, of course, that they had taken the bomb she gave them and put it to this unexpected use. However, she could see no reason why they would. *Wrong time, and the wrong kind of chaos. A gang-war avails us nothing since the constables will simply let us starve until it quiets down.* She considered slipping away to confer with Demisol and Helina, but knew it could well prove a fatal gamble. A dozen more Furies had been drafted in from the mines as additional security. They were a contrast to the slothful guards she had evaded to contact Tinkerer, experienced and keen-eyed veterans of gang-wars within and without these walls likely to notice her absence. So the Learned Damned would have to wait as she suffered the unwelcome sensation of being unable to influence events.

She let her hand fall to the keys, tapping out a tune and humming the accompanying melody, one she had last heard drifting out across shell-blasted trenches half a world away. "The Leaves of Autumn," Makario said, his lips forming a faint smile of recognition. "My old grandmamma's favourite."

"Do you know who composed it?" Lizanne asked, recalling that day in Jermayah's workshop when Tekela's ear for music led to the first fractional understanding of the solargraph.

"It's from the Third Imperium as I recall," he said, returning his fingers to the keys and tapping out a far-more-accomplished version of the tune, wincing all the while at the discordant clatter arising from the pianola. "The composer is believed to have been a member of the Empress Tarmina's Cloister, a group of young women hand-picked for their artistic gifts, many of comparatively mean station. The Third Imperium was a time of great change, often referred to as the Flourishing by historians, when the old feudal ways were being overridden by advances in the sciences, and the arts. The Cloister was destined to be a short-lived institution, being quickly disbanded by Tarmina's son when he ascended to the throne determined to cultivate a manly image free from feminine frippery. But for the best part of two decades they produced literature, paintings, sculpture and music. As is the way with art, most of the Cloister's works could be best described as mediocre, a good portion decidedly awful, and some . . ." His smile broadened as he closed his eyes and played on, his mind no doubt replacing the pianola's cacophony with something far more harmonious. ". . . quite beautiful."

"Do you know her name?" Lizanne asked as Makario's hands fell silent. "The composer."

"Not off-hand. It's probably buried in a book somewhere. I do know that she supposedly composed the piece whilst in the throes of a broken heart, a eulogy for a lover who abandoned her in order to seek adventure across the sea. He's a colourful fellow in his own right, actually, some mad genius said to have spent years wandering the Arradsian Interior before getting gobbled up by a drake, or some such. If so, it's a great pity he never heard the music he inspired."

No, he heard it, Lizanne thought, picturing Tekela tapping the probe to the solargraph's chimes. *And trapped it in a box before coming here to chain himself to a wall.*

A rhythmic thumping sounded through the ceiling, soon accompanied by the Electress's voice. "Melina! Time to call a parley!"

CHAPTER 26

Clay

Clay didn't remember crossing the bridge to the island, lost as he was in a mist of pain and exhaustion. Once again Loriabeth and Sigoral were obliged to drag him, clasping his arms across their shoulders to pull him along. His cousin had rigged a sling around his neck and under his thigh so his injured leg didn't trail on the ground, although his lack of comprehension was such he doubted he would have felt it in any case.

"Look," he heard Loriabeth say, her voice muffled as if spoken from behind a heavy curtain. "Door's open."

Clay felt the air change from warm to cool as they hauled him inside the structure they had seen from the shore. "Awful dark in here," Loriabeth observed.

"No platform that I can see," Sigoral added. "Must be farther in."

Clay felt hard surfaces press against his back and rump as they propped him against a wall. "Cuz," Loriabeth's voice, close to his ear. "You hear me?"

He tried to nod but could only manage a small jerk of his head.

"More Green?" Sigoral suggested.

"He's had a lot already. Not sure the raw stuff is that good for him after all. Besides, I'm thinking we'd best preserve what we got left. No telling how long we'll be in here."

"I'll take a look around. We need to find a way into the shaft."

"Not sure it's wise to split up."

"We can't drag him everywhere. And somebody needs to stay . . ."

Sigoral's voice subsided into a distant murmur then faded completely as Clay felt the void drag him down.

"She must have loved this place." Silverpin rested her hands on the balustrade and gazed out across the jungle at the distant blue shimmer of Krystaline Lake. "Such a wonderful view."

Clay surveyed the ruins below then confirmed his suspicion with a glance back at the shadowed room visible through the arch behind. *Miss Ethelynne's tower in the hidden city.* He was momentarily puzzled to find Silverpin here, she had never seen it after all. But then he had, and it appeared she enjoyed the freedom to roam his memory at will.

He sighed and closed his eyes, raising his face to let the warmth of the sun bathe his skin. *A single sun shining down from a blue sky,* he thought, enjoying the familiarity of it after so many hours beneath the false light of the three crystal suns. "Too much to hope you were gone for good, I guess," he said.

"That's . . . not very nice."

He blinked, turning to see what appeared to be genuine hurt on her face. Although, reading her expression through the mask of tattoos had never been easy. "You're the one who wanted to help a monster eat the world," he reminded her. "Lotta bodies weighing on your side of the scales."

"That was always going to happen." She turned back to the view, her voice taking on a reflective tone. "At least with me there would have been some . . ." She paused, mulling over the right word. ". . . not restraint, exactly. More pragmatism. The one he's calling to now." She gave a rueful laugh. "Let's just say, *she* is anything but pragmatic."

The one he's calling to now . . . Clay stared at her, silenced by the import of her words.

"Oh yes," she went on, angling her gaze as she enjoyed his shock. "You didn't think I was the only one, did you?"

"It needed you for something," Clay recalled, mind racing through his memories of the confrontation with the White, the rage it had exhibited when his bullet left Silverpin bleeding her life out onto the glass floor.

Silverpin didn't answer right away, instead turning from the view to enter the room where Ethelynne had spent so many years in study. Clay followed, resisting the urge to demand answers. There seemed to be no threats he could make, and he didn't know if any violence he might do here would have any effect.

"Year after year spent in feverish scribbling," Silverpin murmured, tracing a hand over Ethelynne's stacks of journals. "Page after page, and she never came close to even the most basic understanding. A wasted life really."

"Not to me," Clay stated. "And I'd hazard she knew a damn sight more than you did, on the whole."

"About the Interior, I've little doubt." She paused to pluck a book from one of the stacks, laughing a little as she opened it to reveal only blank pages. He had never read the journals so their contents were lost, something he now had bitter cause to regret.

"Never mind," Silverpin said, tossing the journal aside. "It's probably all still sitting here. Someone's sure to find it one day. Although, it'll most likely be a Spoiled in search of kindling for his fire."

"What did it need you for?" he asked, hating the desperation that coloured his tone.

"The same thing it needs *her* for." For a moment she held his gaze, a mocking smile on her lips as she revelled in his impotence.

"I used to feel bad about killing you," Clay said. "I think I'm over it."

Silverpin raised a tattooed eyebrow as her smile faded, her gaze moving to the bed, where it lingered. "Looks sturdy enough. What do you say? How about indulging in a little nostalgia?" She began to undress, pulling her shirt over her head and unbuckling her belt.

"I guess this really is more a nightmare than a dream," Clay said, making her pause, the hurt once again bunching her tattoos.

"You didn't use to be cruel," she said. "Selfish, at times. Overly prideful at others. But never cruel."

"Betrayal will do that to a man."

She moved closer, reaching for his hand, then closer still when he snatched it away. "Be nice to me," she said, backing him up against the wall. "Be nice to me and I'll tell you . . ."

He flinched as she pressed a kiss to his neck, hands moving to his belt. "I get so *bored*, Clay. Stuck in here. You'd think with so many memories to explore it'd be fascinating. But I can't change anything. It's like being trapped in a photostat forever . . ."

"If this is a trance," he said, a certain uncomfortable but tempting notion stirring in his mind, "then I have as much control over it as you do."

She stopped, drawing back, eyes narrowing in suspicion. "So?"

He pushed her away and concentrated, summoning every lesson Lizanne had taught him, re-forming the mindscape into a scene of his own choosing. Ethelynne's tower turned to mist around them, swirling into something much more impressive.

The White's roar filled the dome, blood leaking from its side as it whirled, scattering crimson droplets across the glass floor where a young woman lay. She shuddered as the blood spread out from the large hole in her belly, trying to stem the flow with hands that fluttered like pale birds.

"Stop it," Silverpin said. The memory blurred as she tried to take control, then snapped back into reality as Clay asserted his will. Shared trance or not, this was still his mind.

He saw that the dying woman's lips were moving, forming soundless words she could never speak outside of the trance. He crouched, peering closely at the shapes made by her lips, feeling her last breaths on his face. It wasn't hard to discern the word she spoke, just one, over and over until the light faded from her eyes. "Mother . . . Mother . . . Moth . . ."

"Stop it," Silverpin said again, the words emerging as a dry choking rasp.

"Why call for her at the end?" Clay asked, rising from the body. The White roared again and he froze the memory, killing the sound.

She stood with her head lowered, hugging herself tight. "Please, Clay . . ."

"Why call for a woman you enslaved and murdered?" he persisted. "I watched you kill her, remember? You laughed . . ."

"I WANTED HER TO FORGIVE ME!" Silverpin lunged at him, cat-swift and strong, bearing him to the floor, screaming into his face. "I wanted her to know it wasn't me! It made me! It made me do all of it!"

She fell silent, staring into his eyes as tears flowed from her own. "Except you," she said, her rage slipping away. She raised a hand to cup his face, smoothing her palm over his skin. "You were mine. The only indulgence it ever allowed me."

"Do you still feel it?" he asked. "Does it still command you?"

Her head moved in a fractional shake. "But I hear it, like distant thunder from a storm that never ends. I hear it . . . calling to *her*."

"Who is *she*?"

"The new me. The replacement. I have no notion of her name, but I see glimpses of her. Short visions of the world seen through her eyes, conveyed by the White, and they always show the same thing. Different victims, different places. But every vision is a vision of death and each one brings her closer to the White. And when she joins with it . . ."

"What?" he pressed as her words faded, grasping her shoulders hard. "What does it need from her?"

"More of what it got from me." She pressed herself against him, lips finding his, overcoming his resistance with desperate need. "Understanding . . ."

The chill woke him, leeching the warmth from his skin to leave him shivering in a clammy blanket of sweat. It took a moment to clear the lingering images of the trance, the feverish coupling with Silverpin at the scene of her death. *Wrong,* he berated himself, guilty repugnance mingling with desire. *Very, very wrong.*

He was huddled against the wall they had propped him against, the left side of his face compressed by the cold stone floor. The pain in his leg had lessened enough to be bearable, but still provoked a clenched shout as he levered himself upright, gazing around and blinking film from his eyes. The light of the suns had evidently faded on whilst he slept, leaving the structure in almost pitch-darkness save for a glimmer on the rectangular, inscribed pillars that supported the ceiling. It took him longer than it should have to register the most salient fact; he was alone.

"Cuz?" he said, speaking softly though it felt like a shout in the dark and silent confines of the structure. He saw Loriabeth's pack lying near by and reached for it, finding the remaining supplies intact, including the lantern she had carried from the shaft. A few moments fumbling for matches and he had it lit. The beam revealed a bare and dusty interior, but no sign of his cousin or Sigoral. He thought for a moment then called out, "Lori!"

The only response was the echo of his own voice.

Clay set the lantern down and reached for his canteen, steeling himself against the increasingly unappealing burn of raw Green. The blood had begun to coagulate and he had to force down three gulps of what felt like cold slime on his tongue. He waited for the product to drown the pain in his leg before attempting to rise. Fortunately, Loriabeth had retrieved his crutches from the lake-shore and seen fit to leave them close by. He was obliged to clamp the lantern's handle between his teeth as he rose precariously into his now-customary three-legged stance, swivelling his head about to illuminate as yet unseen corners. Starting forward, he saw the lake through the open doorway, the surface glittering in the distant glow of the three lights, a surface unbroken by any bridge. Whatever had raised it from the depths had subsequently seen fit to lower it.

"No way back, huh?" he mumbled around the lantern's handle, turning himself about to regard the deeper recesses of the structure. The lantern's beam played over a succession of pillars but failed to penetrate the gloom beyond. Lowering his head, he grunted in relief as the light revealed a line of footsteps in the dust. He didn't have his uncle's tracking skills but knew enough to discern two distinct sets of prints, one larger than the other. *Sigoral,* he decided, tracing the beam along the course of the tracks as they curved around the base of one of the pillars where they were swallowed by the shadows. *Decided to have a good look-see, but didn't come back. Loria-beth followed later.* He knew she wouldn't willingly have left his side except in dire need, and certainly not without waking him. *She must've tried and couldn't,* he realised with a reproachful sigh. *Too busy in the trance.*

Clay swung himself forward on his crutches, following the tracks and wincing at the echo birthed by the thud of wood on stone as the trail led him into the absolute dark of the building's innards. He soon came to a wall, the circle of the lantern's beam playing over a dense mass of script carved into the interlocking blocks of granite. Looking down, he saw that the footprints overlapped at this point, indicating both Sigoral and Loria-beth had halted here, just like him, before following the line of the wall to the left.

He moved on, keeping close to the wall until he came to a gap. It was broad, clearly an entrance of some kind, and carved into the stone on either side of it was a pair of identical symbols. Clay swayed on his crutches, gaze swivelling from one symbol to the other as a rush of recognition set his pulse racing. This one he knew; a circle between two vertical curved lines.

The upturned eye, he thought, recalling the symbol that had adorned the building where he had found the sleeping White. He hesitated, swinging the lantern to illuminate the gap, revealing a long corridor, the end of which was beyond the reach of the light. *Is it the White's sign?* he wondered, eyes tracking back to the symbol. *A warning, maybe? Stay out or get eaten.* It occurred to him that Silverpin might have the answer, but the thought of returning to the trance at this juncture was absurd. He couldn't slip back into unconsciousness and commune with a ghost whilst Loriabeth remained unfound.

Clay clamped his teeth tighter on the lantern's handle and swung himself forward. He counted his swings as he progressed along the corridor, reckoning each one to cover about a yard. After counting to thirty he stopped as a soft glimmer appeared in the darkness ahead.

Straightening, he fumbled his revolver into his hand, checking the loads and the action of the cylinder before returning it to the holster. He would have preferred to keep it drawn but needed both hands to grip the crutches. He moved with all the stealth he could muster, trying to place the crutches more softly on the floor and biting down on his grunts as he swung himself forward. Still, he doubted anyone with ears to hear would miss his intrusion.

The corridor came to an abrupt end after another twenty yards, the walls falling away to reveal a wide circular chamber. There were more pillars here, six of them arranged in a circle around a raised dais. Above the dais hung a slowly revolving crystal, floating without any visible means of support. A beam of soft white light issued from the base of the crystal to illuminate the dais where a curious object sat. It appeared to be fashioned from the darker material that had formed the spire and resembled a giant egg about twelve feet tall. Moving closer, he saw that it was split into three segments, revealing a hollow interior that gleamed with moisture. His gaze went to where a thin stream of liquid dribbled from the edge of one of the segments. *Just hatched,* he decided, eyes darting from one shadow to another. *Wonder what it held. That's no drake egg.*

Shifting closer he drew up short as two slumped, unmoving bodies came into view. Loriabeth and Sigoral lay on their backs near the segmented egg, still and apparently unconscious.

"Lori!" The lantern fell from his mouth as he called her name, its light snuffed out as it shattered on the stones. He started forward, stumbling in his urgency and coming close to falling. He cursed and forced himself on, though a sudden upsurge of exhaustion and a flare of pain in his leg forced him to collapse against one of the pillars. He sagged, dragging air into his lungs, eyes fixed on Loriabeth's immobile form. "LORI!" he called out, as loud as he could, but if she had heard him she gave no sign.

The panicked thought that she might be dead flicked through his head until he peered closer and saw the gentle swell of her chest. A glance at

Sigoral confirmed he was also still alive, though he remained every bit as unconscious as she did. Clay could see no obvious sign of injury on either of them, although it did little to quell his rising anxiety. Someone had brought them here and it was a safe bet they weren't far away.

He levered himself from the pillar, gripping the crutches with trembling hands as he swung himself to the edge of the dais. He was wary of letting the crystal's light touch his skin, so could only crouch to peer closer at Loriabeth for any sign of injury. She slept on, seemingly quite peacefully, and remained deaf to his entreaties to "Wake up, cuz, Seer-dammit!"

Clay straightened, his gaze drawn inevitably to the crystal floating above. His mind was filled with all he had witnessed in the city beneath the mountain, all the Briteshore Minerals folk standing and staring at the Blue crystal in the dome, every one of them somehow transformed into Spoiled. This crystal, however, wasn't Blue. In fact, as he squinted at its facets he saw that it seemed to hold myriad different colours within itself. "Whatever you're doing," he said, raising his revolver and aiming at the centre of the crystal, "chances are it ain't good."

He had begun to squeeze the trigger when he heard a soft thud at his back.

He whirled, losing his balance and staying upright only by virtue of colliding with the edge of the dais. A dim figure stood in the shadow cast by one of the pillars, a slender figure half-edged in white by the crystal's light. The figure stepped closer, the light catching its face, a female face, the eyes narrowed in shrewd appraisal. Her skin was a shade darker than his own, but so completely absent of flaws that he couldn't discount the thought that she was something conjured by his pain-addled mind. The sense of unreality was heightened by the fact that she was also completely naked but for a shiny silver belt about her waist.

Shoot her, you Seer-damn fool! instinct screamed as his eyes alighted on something in the woman's hand, something metallic with a short, stubby barrel. He had time to half raise the revolver before she shot him in the chest.

CHAPTER 27

Lizanne

The parley took place in a large ruined theatre occupying one side of Pitch-Blende Square. The building featured an ornate and mostly untouched frontispiece that mixed granite and marble to accomplished if overly elaborate effect. The words *Constellation Theatrical Emporium* were carved in classical Eutherian on a large marble lintel above the doors. According to Makario it was Scorazin tradition for negotiations to be held here, partly because the interior space was large enough to accommodate each party along with their escorts, but also due to the rats. "The place is riven with them," the musician explained. "It's why no one's ever claimed it."

Lizanne soon realised he hadn't been exaggerating. A large black rat sat on the front steps as she followed the Electress into the theatre, Anatol and Melina on either side with ten hand-picked Furies following. The rat continued to sit as they drew closer, regarding them with baleful disdain until Anatol stamped a massive boot at it. Even then it seemed to saunter away rather than scurry.

"Too much corpse meat in the diet," the Electress commented to Lizanne as they ascended the steps. "Makes 'em less afraid of us than they should be. Probably time we had another grand hunt. Have to every few years or they get too large in number, and too bold."

They proceeded through the doorless entrance into a foyer where a pair of once-opulent staircases ascended on either side, ready to convey an audience to upper floors that no longer existed. Beyond lay the auditorium with its long rows of seats, once plush with velvet and now grey with ancient mould. The stage and its massive curtain had subsided decades ago into a pile of decayed wood and fabric where a dozen or so rats moved about, apparently uncaring of the intruders. A thin drizzle fell from the occluded sky visible through the criss-crossed beams above, all that remained of the roof.

Lizanne saw that the Electress had timed her arrival well, as the other three delegations were already in attendance. Chuckling Sim and a retinue of Verdigris occupied a position parallel to centre stage. King Coal had placed himself off to the left and stood flanked by Julesin, his tall pale-faced lieutenant, with a dozen Scuttlers at his back. The leader of the Wise Fools stood to the right. Lizanne was surprised to find that Varkash had come alone, standing cross-armed with beads of rain shining on his thick muscled arms and the pyrite nose he wore.

"Fashionably late, my dear Electress," Sim said, offering a fair imitation of a courtly bow. He wore a well-tailored suit of dark cotton, his greying hair slicked back by oil and his face rendered white by a fine dusting of powder. Lizanne knew that powdered skin and oiled hair were both affectations of the Corvantine nobility that had fallen into disuse over twenty years ago. Had the leader of the Verdigris found himself in noble company his appearance would have made him a laughing-stock. Here, however, he was anything but.

Electress Atalina came to a halt halfway down the auditorium's aisle and replied with a polite nod of her head. "I'm sure you'll excuse a lady for exercising a time-honoured prerogative, Sim."

"Always, my dear." Chuckling Sim straightened from his bow, maintaining a welcoming grin as he surveyed the Electress's party, his gaze soon coming to rest on Lizanne. "And who is your delightful companion?"

"Krista," the Electress replied. "She kills people a lot, so best not to develop too much of an interest."

"Oh, at least let an old fool indulge a dream or two." The leader of the Verdigris came closer, Lizanne sensing her companions' sudden upturn in tension as he halted before her, bowing lower than he had for the Electress and extending his hand. "Jakisim Ven Estimont, at your service, my dear," he said, slipping into Eutherian that was a little too coarse to be the product of a noble upbringing.

"A pleasure to make your acquaintance, sir," Lizanne replied, placing her hand in his so he could press a brief kiss to it. She noticed a slight twitch in his composure as he released her, possibly due to the fact that her Eutherian was decidedly more refined than his.

"So accomplished a young lady," he said, his smile becoming sad. "Consigned to a place such as this. The capricious nature of the world never ceases to amaze, don't you find?"

"We are but leaves cast afar by the gales of life," she replied. It was an old Corvantine adage from the pre–Imperial Era, one clearly beyond Chuckling Sim's knowledge judging by the flush of annoyance he failed to keep from his gaze.

"Quite so," he said, reasserting his smile as he turned and strode back to his retinue. "We are called to parley by Electress Atalina, recognised leader of the Furies," he said, slipping back into Varsil and raising his voice to strident formality. "The rules of parley were in place long before any of us came through the gate, yet remain unbroken to this day, a tradition all present are expected to observe. Failure to do so will result in the other parties allying against them. Before proceeding we must agree on a moderator. As two of my brothers lie dead due to the agency of one party here present, I cannot claim impartiality in this matter." He turned and bowed to the leader of the Wise Fools. "Therefore, I nominate you, Brother Varkash."

"Seconded," Electress Atalina stated promptly.

All eyes turned expectantly to the leader of the Scuttlers, who stood frowning in silence for several seconds before shrugging. "What the fuck do I care?"

"Eloquent as ever, my liege," Chuckling Sim said, switching to Eutherian once again and casting a wink at Lizanne.

"And enough of that noble-pig talk," King Coal growled, hands shoved into a leather overcoat, presumably to conceal bunching fists. Seeing him at such proximity for the first time, Lizanne noted how the flesh of his face seemed possessed of a continual quiver, betraying a constant inner rage that threatened to erupt at the smallest provocation.

"Eloquent or not, he makes a fair point, Brudder Sim," Varkash said. He spoke in a low yet commanding voice that would have been much more impressive but for the nasal squeak that accompanied every hard consonant. Lizanne found it noteworthy that no one present felt inclined to utter the slightest sign of amusement as the Varestian spoke on. "Every word spoken must be clearly understood by all parties. Rules of parley."

"Of course, brother. I crave forgiveness." Chuckling Sim offered a florid bow to all present before moving to stand with his retinue.

"First order of business," Varkash said, striding to occupy the centre ground and turning to the Fury delegation. "Electress Atalina. You called dis parley. State your grievance."

"Unwarranted murder," the Electress replied, gaze steady on the Scuttlers' leader. "Done in my place of business without formal challenge."

"Challenge?" King Coal took a purposeful step forward, face flushed to a dark shade of crimson. He stopped when Julesin moved to his side, stooping to speak softly into his ear. Whatever counsel the pale man offered seemed to be enough for Kevozan to master himself, albeit after a few seconds' effort. "Where," he grated, addressing his words to Varkash, "was the challenge when this bitch bombed my winding house?"

"Our brother makes false accusation," the Electress stated with calm authority. "Show me evidence of a Fury's hand in the bombing and I'll happily cut it off and present it to you."

"Bombs don't leave evidence," King Coal replied. "Just useless mechanicals and blasted bodies."

"Much like the one that exploded outside the Miner's Repose not long ago," the Electress mused. "It seems we share common experience, brother."

"I'm not your fucking brother . . ."

"Accusation and counter-accusation," Varkash broke in as Kevozan's face began to flush once more. "Dis avails us nudding. We are not a court. Duh purpose of parley is to reach accommodation in order to prevent further bloodshed." He turned to Chuckling Sim. "You also indicated a grievance, brudder."

"Indeed." For the first time Sim's smile faded, not entirely but with an instant loss of humour and hardening of the eyes that told Lizanne much about his true nature. "Two dead," he continued, staring at the Coal King. "Well-liked men of industrious and loyal demeanour. Such men are hard to replace, and their loss stirs anger amongst their comrades."

"I also lost two men," Kevozan replied, a defiant glint in his eye which told of an unwillingness, or more likely, an inability to be cowed by the Verdigris leader. "And another last week," he added, turning his gaze on the Electress. "Left outside my place with his skull mashed in."

"If a beaten body lying in a Scorazin gutter is cause for war," the Electress said, "we would never have peace."

This provoked some laughter among all present, apart from King Coal, who silenced the chuckles of his own men with a glare. "I've got war aplenty," he said, eyes fixing on the Electress. "If you want it. You want formal challenge, you can have it here and now."

"Calm yourself, brother," Chuckling Sim said, his smile returning to its former fullness, though Lizanne detected an edge of warning in his voice. "We all remember the last unfortunate round of hostilities. The constables left us to starve for a full month as punishment, as you recall. I for one have no great desire to taste rat meat again. Besides which, since my grievance remains unresolved, a challenge spoken in the forum would apply as much to the Verdigris as to the Furies."

He fell silent, letting his gaze and his smile linger on the Coal King. Lizanne saw the quiver of Kevozan's features deepen into a shudder, his body tensed from head to toe with poorly contained anger. Once again it was Julesin who calmed him, his words too soft to catch but evidently carrying enough wisdom to stem his leader's rage. "I'm not making any settlement," he said, "until my winding-gear is fixed. Brother Sim worries about going hungry, so do my men."

"So fix it," the Electress said with a shrug.

"The only two fuckers who knew how are lying in pieces on the midden," King Coal returned. "I want the Tinkerer."

"Then perhaps you should hire him," Chuckling Sim suggested.

"Already tried, he said no." Kevozan's gaze roamed the Furies until it came to rest on Melina. "She can persuade him, though. Everyone knows he's sweet on her."

The Electress turned to Melina with a questioning glance. "If he's paid well enough," the tall woman said. "It'll take a lot of books, though."

"I'll contribute to the fee," Sim said. "Though it'll pain me to denude my library. Brother Varkash?"

"I don't have any books," Varkash said, before continuing with evident reluctance, "but I do have maps of duh south seas. Cost me six sacks each."

"Surrendering one to the cause of continued harmony would seem a reasonable exchange," Chuckling Sim said.

The pirate stood silent for a long moment, tapping a finger to his false nose in sullen consideration. "Very well," he said finally. "Duh fee for Tinkerer's services will be met equally by parties present. Speak now to voice disagreement."

Silence reigned for half a minute or so, broken only by a faint groaning Lizanne realised was the sound of Kevozan grinding his teeth.

"Agreement is reached," Varkash said. "Leaving duh madder of redress."

The haggling continued for another hour and by the end of it the Verdi-gris were richer to the tune of ten sacks of coal, five for each of their lost men. The Electress agreed to part with one tenth of the Furies' next food allotment to compensate the Scuttlers for their denuded income. In return she would receive a dozen sacks of coal as compensation for the attack on the Miner's Repose. Varkash was also provided with one sack each from the other parties in recognition for his wise moderation of the proceedings.

"Dis parley is concluded," the Varestian said in pinched but formal tones. "All parties will now give solemn oath affirming observance of duh truce agreed here today. By rules of parley, any who breaks their oath will be marked for death togedder wid any who stand in their defence."

"So affirmed," the Electress stated.

"Affirmed," Chuckling Sim said, adding in Eutherian as he favoured Lizanne with an arched eyebrow, "or may the gods rend my house asunder."

King Coal took longer to answer, his glowering gaze fixed on Atalina as a sheen of drizzle glittered on his still-quivering face. Lizanne wouldn't have been overly surprised to see steam rising from his shaven head as he gave a terse, guttural, "Affirmed," before turning and stomping from the theatre, his escort close behind. Julesin followed at a slight remove, his gaze sweeping across all the Furies as he passed by. He hid it well, but Lizanne saw the way his eyes lingered on her for the briefest second with a concentrated, detail-hungry focus unique to those of a particular profession.

"Could have been worse," Melina commented as they made their way back to the Miner's Repose. "One-tenth of the food will sting a bit, but it's hardly going to break us."

"You stupid bitch," the Electress muttered, the drizzle beading broad features set in a preoccupied frown. "That farce didn't change anything. At least now I know who's twitching that fuckwit Kevozan's strings." She stopped, turning and fixing Lizanne with a steady gaze. "Time you earned your keep, my dear. I want that pasty-faced bastard dead by Ore Day."

"It wasn't us," Demisol said as soon as the mansion-house door closed behind Lizanne.

"I know," she said. "It appears we have a competitor." She lifted the heavy sack from her shoulder and strode through the hall and into the dining-room.

"Competitor?" Helina asked, lowering her voice and closing the dining-room door.

"Someone intent on sowing discord," Lizanne replied. "Rather than destruction."

"Who?"

"As yet unclear, but I believe the Coal King's chief lieutenant may be at the heart of it."

"Julesin?" Demisol asked. "He's barely been here six months."

"And yet somehow managed to rise high in the interim. What do you know of him?"

"Well, he's a killer to be sure. Cut down three men his first day through the gate. All fair fights, and none were members of the main gangs."

"So he established his credentials early, and was careful about his targets." Lizanne concealed a faint grin of recognition. *An agent to be sure. But whose?* She recalled what the Blood Imperial had told her in Empress Azireh's crypt: *Sent my two best. The first one lasted three days, the second managed four . . .* She hadn't thought much of it at the time, but now the prospect of two presumably experienced and capable agents failing to survive more than a few days in Scora-zin seemed unlikely. Dreadful place though it was, she had come to understand that the greatest threats came from hunger or disease rather than other inmates. *Unless they were spotted by someone even more capable.* Also, they were both comparatively recent inmates whilst Julesin had arrived months before. *If he isn't Blood Cadre, then who is he?* She decided it was not a matter she could afford to spend too much time considering. *In a complex mission the straightest course is usually the best one.* Another lesson from her training days, one she had often found useful. *Cadre or not, he's an obstacle, and the Electress will be expecting swift results.*

"Do we delay?" Demisol asked.

Lizanne shook her head. "Delay invites discovery and adds to the risk of betrayal. Not to impugn the commitment of your fellow citizens, but the more time they have to dwell on the likelihood of their demise, the more their thoughts will slip towards survival."

"We've been emphasising the prospect of escape," Helina said. "Though our comrades aren't idiot criminals to be easily gulled."

"We have three days until Ore Day," Lizanne said. "Do everything you can to shore up their resolve before then."

"The main device?" Demisol asked.

"It'll be ready," she said, choosing not to share the news about the interruption to Tinkerer's work. She had visited him the night after the parley to collect the contents of the sack, finding him almost completely absorbed in his labour.

"Repairing the winding-gear will take only half a day," he had said, apparently incapable of raising his gaze from the large iron-and-copper egg on his work-bench. "Subject to provision of suitable materials." Such industriousness scarcely seemed possible to her but then Tinkerer, as Aunt Pendilla would have said, was cut from cloth of a different weave.

"And that?" Lizanne asked, nodding to the egg.

"Nearing completion." He reached for a cylindrical component and carefully slotted it into the egg's exposed innards, his slender fingers moving with an almost loving grace. "Mixing the compound will take longer, however."

"How many did you bring?" Demisol asked, nodding at the sack at Lizanne's feet. She hefted it onto the defaced dining-table and revealed the contents.

"Twelve in total," she said, as the two revolutionaries inspected the sack's contents. "Two with fifteen-minute fuses, the rest only three seconds so make sure your people know to throw them the moment they're primed. What other weapons have you gathered?"

"Knives and clubs, mostly. Though we have two citizens skilled with bow and arrow."

"Tell them to kill any gunners that survive. Just one blast of canister and our whole enterprise will be lost."

"We seem to be putting great faith in our fellow inmates," Demisol commented. "How do we know they'll respond as we hope?"

"We don't," Lizanne admitted. "But would you hesitate to risk your life for the smallest chance of escaping this place?"

She jammed a chair under the door-handle and sat on her bed, mouth wide as she inserted the pliers Tinkerer had grudgingly parted with. They left a metallic sting on her tongue before clamping onto the ceramic tooth. She had lost the original in a confrontation with a rival corporate agent some years before and Director Bloskin, never one to forsake an opportunity, had introduced Lizanne to the appointed dentist for Exceptional Initiatives. The procedure required hours in his chair and copious doses of Green but by the end of it she had a new tooth. It was fixed to the root of the original with a gold screw, meaning it could be removed and replaced. The ceramicist the Brotherhood found for her in Corvus had been exceptionally skilled, producing a near-perfect facsimile of an upper-right molar with a hollow cavity large enough for a small amount of product. The screw loosened after several seconds of uncomfortable effort as Lizanne tried not to damage her surrounding teeth. Blue flooded her mouth as it came free, burning as she swallowed, finding a certain joy in the sensation of recovered power. Life as an un-Blessed, she was finding, was not much to her liking.

Hyran's mindscape closed in immediately, in surprisingly accomplished and lurid detail. *At least he's been practising,* she thought, watching the pale youth in mid-cavort with a swirling cloud of naked female flesh. Glimpses into the carnal imaginings of fellow Blood-blessed were a frequent feature of the trance, usually tactfully ignored by unspoken understanding. However, she had yet to trance with someone who appeared to have crafted his entire mindscape from the stuff of adolescent lust.

Sorry if I'm interrupting. Lizanne put enough force into the thought to banish the swirl of phantom nymphs, but not before catching sight of their faces. All the same and all familiar. *It's heartening to learn you have such an acute visual memory,* she went on as the boy's image gaped at her, a frozen lanky thing in the suddenly confused mist. *In which case,* she added with a pointed downward glance, *I'm sure you can remember what clothes look like.*

The surrounding clouds flushed a deep shade of crimson, roiling thick enough to obscure Hyran's image. When they cleared he stood fully clothed and eyes averted, the shade of his mortification lingering in the clouds.

I . . . His thoughts stuttered, sending bolts of lightning through the clouds and for a moment it seemed as if his loss of concentration would shatter the trance.

Calm. She coloured the thought with a soothing memory, the day Aunt Pendilla pressed a damp cloth to her grazed knee and banished infant tears with chicken soup. *Focus. I don't have long.*

Sorry. The clouds were still pulsing red, though now shot through with the dark grey of his regret. *Been trancing every day . . . Tried building a castle or something, like you said. But . . . I got bored waiting.*

I'm here now. Are you in contact with Citizens Korian and Arberus?

Yes. We're only a few miles from Scorazin. Been gathering strength, like you wanted.

Show me.

He summoned the memory with surprising alacrity. It seemed his self-indulgence had paid off in tutoring him in efficient command of the trance. A dense patch of cloud swirled into the image of a campsite. Arberus sat close to a fire in the foreground, cleaning his revolver, prolonged tension clear in the depth of his furrowed brow. Beyond him Korian could be seen in animated disagreement with a cluster of young men and women. Fortunately, Hyran hadn't thought to summon the sound so she was spared the gabble of revolutionary dogma.

How many in total? she asked.

Two hundred and fifty-six, he replied promptly, causing her to assume Arberus had made him memorise the details of the small army. *All mounted and armed with repeating carbines. Two small cannon, also.*

Will any more be coming?

Korian expects another thirty by the end of the week. This is pretty much all that remains of the Brotherhood in this region.

It was hardly a force capable of storming the walls of Scorazin, but if her plan worked it wouldn't have to. *Tell them to move into a position where they can assault the guard-house at Scorazin. They need to be ready to attack in three days.* She felt the trance shudder around her as the Blue began to ebb. *I have to go. The signal will come an hour after midday. If it doesn't . . . tell Citizen Arberus this mission has failed and I believe he would be better employed in Feros than here.*

What will it be? The signal.

If this works, an earthquake strong enough to shake an empire.

"**M**elina said you weren't working tonight." Makario stood in her doorway, holding a bottle of wine in one hand and what appeared to be some form of musical instrument in the other. "Me neither. Seems I'm surplus to requirements without music."

"What is that?" she asked, peering at the curious thing he held, presumably the product of considerable effort over the three days since the parley. It appeared to be the result of an uncomfortable mating between a mandolin and a viola.

"My newest creation." He handed her the wine-bottle and took hold of the instrument, fingers stroking an unfamiliar but nevertheless pleasant note from the six strings strung along its narrow neck. "The bastard child born of my fevered mind, and the scraps of every instrument I could trade for within these walls." His fingers moved again, conjuring a jaunty tune she recognised as a Varestian sea shanty. "I doubt I could do justice to Illemont with it," he said, finishing with a flourish, "but I think it'll keep a roof over my head until we can repair my true love. I do need some practice, however. Perhaps you'd like to help."

She had adduced at their first meeting that Makario was unlikely to have much interest in her womanly charms, but now saw an entreaty in his gaze that went deeper than a desire for drunken companionship. "I have a prior appointment," she said, handing back the wine.

"Put it off," he insisted, summoning a poorly rendered smile to his lips. "Staying indoors is by far the safest course in such troubled times."

"Would that I could. But I also have to keep a roof over my head."

"I'm sure whatever errand our dear leader has you running can wait. At least for tonight."

"Why? What happens tomorrow?"

She held his gaze as the smile slipped from his face. *Best to subdue him now,* the professional part of her mind advised. *Extract what information you can. Break his neck and leave him at the bottom of the stairs for Melina to find in the morning, victim of a drunken stumble. And without the pianola what use was he anyway?*

Instead she just stood and watched as he retreated a few steps, face alternating between fear and charm. "I . . . really wish you'd stay," he managed finally, adding in a desperate whisper, "please!"

"It doesn't matter, Makario," she told him. "Whatever it is. Whatever you did. I'm sure you had your reasons and I really don't care. If you're in league with Julesin I assume you've warned him I'm coming, and that doesn't matter either."

Makario became very still, the neck of his hybrid instrument creaking under the strain of a suddenly white-knuckled grip. "I am not in league with him," he stated in a soft voice, each word spoken very precisely.

Lizanne sighed around a smile. "Best stay off the roof-tops tomorrow," she said, and closed the door.

She had spent the previous two nights reconnoitring the semicircular row of terraced houses on Prop Lane where the Scuttlers made their headquarters. The row curved around a patch of dirt that had once been a small park in the centre of which stood a large marble plinth, home to a long-vanished statue to some forgotten Scorazin luminary. A narrow alley opposite the park made for a useful vantage point. It was rarely visited by the Coal King's minions thanks to its proximity to a part-collapsed sewer drain. The stench was just short of unbearable but Lizanne's nostrils had an habituated resistance to the more repellent miasmas of life.

Her first journey here had brought another near encounter with the tall, cloaked creeper she had seen the night she made her way to Tinkerer's abode. She found a convenient corner to hide behind as the stooped figure passed by, once again dragging something. Given the legendary degeneracy of the night creepers she assumed it would be a body and was surprised to see it was in fact a sack, filled with something heavy that scraped filth from the cobbles as the figure disappeared into Keg Road. *Bones?* she wondered, but doubted it. *More likely stolen ore.* In either case it was a mystery she had no time or inclination to solve.

Julesin proved to be a fellow of unwisely regular habits. He would arrive from the coal pits at the same time, under heavy escort, whereupon he would enter the centremost house in the row. The windows in this house glowed brighter than the others, and the smoke rose more thickly from its chimney, making it easily identifiable as the Coal King's domicile. Whilst the king himself was never seen out of doors in the hours of darkness, Julesin would eventually re-emerge to make a tour of the guards. There were only two other Scuttlers with him as he made his way around the perimeter. He seemed to command great respect amongst the guards, or more likely fear since he was not shy in administering punishment. Lizanne saw him send one droopy-eyed unfortunate to the ground with a vicious back-hand cuff then stand by as his two escorts kicked the man unconscious. Consequently, she had little chance of evading detection here as she did regularly at the sulphur pits. There was only one point in Julesin's nightly routine that offered a workable opportunity. Having completed his tour he would linger on a bench alongside the plinth. The two escorts would retire a short distance whilst Julesin sat smoking a cigarillo, the tip glowing red in the gloom.

A decent aiming point for a ranged weapon, Lizanne decided on the second night. It was far less subtle than she would have liked, entailing a swift ground-level escape as the surrounding guards reacted. Still, she had no other options besides making use of one of Tinkerer's timed grenades and they were needed for Ore Day. Also, she would have had to explain to the Electress where it came from. Fortunately, King Coal himself had seen fit to provide the means by which she could assassinate his lieutenant.

She had been obliged to practise in the basement of the Miner's Repose, Scorazin being somewhat lacking in open spaces where one could loose a cross-bow without being noticed. At her request, Melina harvested the darts from the bodies left in the wake of the Scuttlers' attack, each wrapped with cloth to avoid contact with the poison that still lingered on the barbed steel-heads. The ingenious loading and drawing mechanism would have been easily operated with a drop of Green in her veins. Without it she found herself capable of loosing off only two darts before the strain on her limbs forced a pause. Realistically, this meant only one shot at Julesin. Gauging the effective range of the weapon had been a simple matter of arithmetic. The basement was fifteen yards long at its widest point and repeated practice shots at a wooden board revealed the darts would lose one inch of altitude for every six point eight yards travelled. Working out the correct angle of elevation for a kill-shot was therefore a relatively straightforward exercise.

She watched Julesin complete his nightly inspection then take his place on the bench, smoke blossoming as he lit his cigarillo. The gurgle arising from the exposed sewer provided enough noise to cover the sound as she primed the cross-bow, the string sliding back and dart slotting into place with a pleasing mechanical elegance. Whoever had crafted the weapon had seen fit to equip it with both front and rear sights, crudely fashioned from hammered tin but still accurate. She centred the front sight on the glowing tip of Julesin's cigarillo, meaning the dart would bury itself squarely in the centre of his chest. She took a shallow breath and squeezed the trigger as she exhaled. The cross-bow jerked in her grip as the string snapped forward, the dart streaking away. It covered the distance to Julesin's chest in a fraction of a second, whereupon it froze in mid air, an inch or two short of its target.

Julesin's cigarillo glowed brighter as he got to his feet, eyes fixed on where Lizanne lay prone in the filthy alley. It was obvious he could see her, and had most likely done so for the previous two nights. *Green and Black,* she realised, mind racing as she calculated her options. Julesin, however, didn't allow her the time to formulate an escape plan.

An invisible hand jerked the cross-bow from her grip, sending it spinning into the dark. She tried to roll away but the Black closed on her with suffocating force, lifting and dragging her from the alley. Julesin seemed to be in no particular hurry, standing still and continuing to smoke as he slowly drew her to him. He was evidently highly skilled in the use of Black, as he kept the dart she had loosed at him suspended in mid air. He halted her a few feet away, lifting her body so that she faced him. The dart flipped over and rose to hover parallel with her left eye.

Julesin stood regarding her in silence, head tilted in appraisal as the dart inched closer. Lizanne found she couldn't close the lid of her eye as the tip of the dart came within a hair's width of her pupil, where it lingered for a very long moment.

"Just joking," Julesin said, the dart making a loud ping on the cobbles as he allowed it to fall. There was an odd note of sympathy in his voice as he stepped closer, offering an apologetic grimace. "And, as one professional to another, I'm sorry about all this."

The Black closed in with increased force, clamping onto her throat, making her lungs burn and vision turn first red then black as the void claimed her.

CHAPTER 28

Clay

Clay came awake to a warm sensation in his leg, as if it were being caressed by a summer breeze. His eyelids fluttered over gritted orbs, harsh light birthing an instant ache in his head. He tried to move but found his entire body constrained somehow. More rapid blinking revealed him to be sitting on the stone floor of the chamber, his back pressed against something hard and unyielding. Looking down he saw ropes tightly bound across his chest and realised he had been tied to one of the pillars. He strained against the ropes, grunting with the effort, then stopped as an important fact rose to the forefront of his awareness: his leg didn't hurt any more.

Lowering his gaze, he found himself gaping in frozen disbelief. The bandage was gone and so was his wound. Not scabbed or scarred over, but gone. His denuded and ravaged flesh had been remade, leaving a hairless but otherwise whole segment of skin and muscle. The warm sensation he had awoken to was revealed as the result of a beam of light descending from above to bathe his leg in a soft, greenish luminescence. His gaze instinctively tracked along the beam to where it connected with the crystal floating above. It still cast a more intense beam down on the segmented egg but for some reason had seen fit to cast out another. The mystery and novelty of it provoked a laugh as his toes flexed and the movement failed to produce the expected blast of pain, a laugh that died as a voice spoke to him.

His head jerked up to find a slender figure standing a few feet away. Clay had no difficulty in recognising the woman who had shot him. She was now clothed in what he recognised as the spare trousers and shirt presumably taken from Loriabeth's pack, with the silver belt still fastened about her waist. It seemed to be formed of some kind of metallic material from the way it caught the light, and was bulky with several large pouches and an empty holster, presumably for the gun she had used to shoot him.

Memories of the gun caused him to look down at his chest, searching for any sign of injury and finding nothing. He couldn't even see a tear in his shirt, but there was a faint ache from a spot just above his sternum, not truly painful but present enough to signify a livid bruise. Whatever she had shot him with, it hadn't been a bullet.

He saw that she still held the gun, though now it was lowered to her side and he took some comfort from the fact that her finger wasn't on the trigger. Seeing it clearly, Clay wasn't sure "gun" was the right term. It seemed to be made of a combination of brass and steel, with a pistol-like grip that confirmed it as some kind of weapon. But it lacked a cylinder, and the barrel was too short and narrow for anything but the puniest projectile. There was a finery to the weapon's construction that was beyond Clay's experience, so many different components formed into a single device. He knew he was looking at something beyond the skill or knowledge of any gunsmith or artificer in the world above.

He tore his gaze from the weapon, heart leaping with relief when he saw Loriabeth and Sigoral still lying on the dais. Unlike him, his cousin and the marine remained unconscious. Also, his captor hadn't felt the need to tie either of them to a pillar.

He jerked as the woman spoke again, eyes snapping to meet hers. She had lowered herself into a crouch and regarded him with a level of scrutiny that bordered on the openly hostile. Their packs lay open near by, the contents disordered due to a thorough rummaging. Glancing at his bonds once more, Clay realised he was bound with the length of rope he had carried across the ice, and couldn't help voicing a rueful groan.

The woman spoke again, more insistently this time. Clay found the words meaningless, the cadence and prolonged vowels were all completely unfamiliar.

"Sorry, lady," he said, shaking his head. "Just Mandinorian, though I can just about get by bargaining in Dalcian."

The woman stared at him for a moment in obvious incomprehension then gave a deep sigh of frustration as she lowered her gaze and smoothed a trembling hand over her forehead. After a moment she calmed herself with a visible effort, breathing deeply and draining any emotion from her features. Clay estimated her to be scarcely older than he, though the flawlessness of her skin may have made her appear younger. Her hair was cut short, only a half inch or so from the scalp, and he saw no jewellery or other accoutrements on her person.

She turned to the packs and extracted Clay's canteen, the one half-full of diluted Green. She lifted the canteen, touching the cap to her lips as she mimed taking a drink, raising her eyebrows in an unmistakable question. *You drink this. Yes?*

Clay's gaze lingered on the canteen before tracking back to the woman, her expression now one of expectant surety. "Guess you know that ain't just water," he said.

The woman frowned and shook the canteen at him, making the contents slosh about as she asked a question in her unfathomable tongue. Clay stared back, saying nothing, unwilling to reveal so much to so strange a captor. He maintained his silence and they matched stares, her frown deepening into outright anger. She spoke again, voice raised as she moved towards the dais, stepping into the crystal's glow with pause. She halted at Loriabeth's side, raising the brass-and-steel gun to point it at his cousin's chest before turning back to Clay, a question and a threat evident in her gaze.

Clay strained against the straps, unable to contain his shout. "Leave her alone!" His anger provoked a small flinch in the woman's bearing but she didn't move, instead carefully placing her finger on the gun's trigger.

"Alright!" he shouted, nodding rapidly and hoping she understood the gesture. "I can drink the damn stuff."

The woman betrayed a small shudder of relief as she lowered the gun and returned to crouch at his side, reaching into his pack and extracting Scriberson's note-book. She leafed through it briefly, stopping at a particular page then crouching at Clay's side once more, holding it open. He recognised the page as an annotated sketch of Brionar, the ringed planet the astronomer had shown him through the telescope at the base of the falls. The woman tapped the sketch then made a scribbling gesture before pointing at Clay. *Did you do this?*

He shook his head. "No. That's the work of a dead man."

She grimaced in consternation, leafing through more pages until she showed him a table of some kind, rows of numbers set out in Scriberson's messy script below a much more neatly drawn diagram. It looked like one of the constellations to Clay, but his knowledge of Scriberson's work was meagre at best. The woman's finger moved over the page, tapping in certain places. It seemed she was particularly interested in the diagram and one set of numbers at the bottom of the table.

"Sorry, lady, I ain't never been no scholar," Clay said, shrugging as much as the ropes would allow him.

She seemed about to question him further but stopped when the chamber shuddered. A faint rumbling filled the space and the light cast by the crystal flickered as the shaking continued. Clay saw the woman tense as a thin stream of dust cascaded down from the shadowed ceiling. The tremor continued for about thirty seconds, after which the woman turned back to Clay, her face now set in a frown of hard determination.

He managed not to flinch as she leaned closer and stared into his eyes. He fought down an instinctive impulse to struggle against his bonds as her gaze lingered, unnerving in its intensity but also commanding, capturing his attention so completely he felt his fear fading away. Eventually she blinked and broke the stare, Clay's heart giving an involuntary leap as she hefted the brass-and-steel gun.

Her thumb depressed a small lever on the side of the chamber which duly sprang open with a kind of neat, mechanical efficiency that would have made any gunsmith envious. Clay let out a faint groan of self-reproach at seeing the chamber was empty. *She was never gonna shoot Lori,* he realised as the woman's free hand moved to the belt on her waist, opening one of the pockets to retrieve a small glass vial.

She held it up before his eyes, turning it so it caught the light. Clay was sufficiently familiar with the various shades of product by now to recognise the viscous liquid it contained. "Blue?" he said.

The woman slotted the vial into the gun and closed the chamber, muttering something before pressing the barrel to her forearm and pulling the trigger. There was a low hiss of escaping air, then she removed the gun from her arm, leaving behind a faint red welt.

"Oh," Clay said as she pressed the gun's barrel to his arm and pulled the trigger. "You too, huh?"

The trance closed in immediately, Clay finding himself on Nelphia's surface with the woman a few feet away. There was no sign of her own mindscape, which meant she either didn't have one or was skilled enough to keep it completely suppressed. She stood staring all around in patent awe, as if not quite capable of grasping what she saw.

Where's yours? Clay asked, causing her to turn, dust rising as she staggered a little in surprise. He raised his arms, gesturing at their surroundings. *I showed you mine,* he went on.

The woman stared at him for a moment then did something completely unexpected. She laughed. It was a genuine laugh, full of delight, continuing on as she went into a pirouette, raising more dust as she whirled. She moved with a fluid, practised grace that reminded him of Joya in the ball-room that time. He watched her dance, leaping and jumping before spiralling to her knees where she reached both hands into the moon-dust, laughing again as she cast it into the sky. It hung there, glittering like stars in the void.

You're making a mess, Clay told her, asserting his will over the mindscape and sending the frozen dust cascading to the ground.

The woman's laugh faded into a smile as she got to her feet, asking something in her own language. The words were meaningless, but in the trance language wasn't the barrier it was in the waking world. *You made this?*

The question baffled him. What kind of Blood-blessed would be so impressed by a mindscape? *Sure,* he replied. *It's still a little rough around the edges, though. Been awhile since I had a chance to work on it.*

The woman gazed all around, her wonder unabated. *So much detail. You can craft others?*

Not as fine as this one, but if I think hard enough, yeah.

She turned back and moved towards him, an unnerving amount of joyous anticipation on her face. He realised his estimation of her age may have been off by several years. She seemed almost childlike now, a near-desperate glint in her eye as she stopped and reached a tentative hand to his. *Show me,* she pleaded.

Clay took a step back, crossing his arms. *We gotta lot to talk about before I start sharing any memories.* He tapped a finger to his chest. *You shooting me, fr'instance.*

The joy slowly faded from her face and she took a backward step of her own, eyes downcast. *A necessary precaution.* The trance communicated her most prominent emotions with ease: bafflement and delight shot through with fear, but above it all a sense of grief, far deeper and more painful than even her displays of despair had indicated. Blood-blessed she might be, but she had no facility for concealing her thoughts. Clay suspected that if she had shared minds with Lizanne every secret would have been stripped from her in seconds. Such things were not within his skills, however, so he was obliged to wait for her to share.

The note-book, she said finally, thoughts leaking both reluctance and a sense of grim certainty. *The diagram in the note-book. Is it accurate?*

Couldn't say. But the fella who drew it was awful clever and exacting in his trade. Not the type to make a mistake when looking at the stars.

Is he here? Another member of your party?

Clay shook his head. *It's just the three of us. The man who wrote that book is dead. I carry it as . . . a souvenir, I guess. We were friends, for a short time.*

Are you . . . She paused, Clay sensing her thoughts churning as she sought to formulate the right question. *Part of a group? A large group?*

An army, you mean?

Feeling the pulse of incomprehension in her thoughts Clay conjured an image from a shared trance with Lizanne, the Corvantine forces massing outside Carvenport. He cast it into the sky, letting it play out as the woman stared at it. He felt her emotions shift at the sight of the memory, her despair returning along with a distinct note of disgust.

This happened recently? she asked, watching as the first cannon shot landed amidst the trenches.

Few months ago, he said. *Corvantine Imperial forces about to meet an ugly end, and I can't say I'm sorry.*

Who are they fighting?

The Ironship Protectorate, along with a whole lotta conscripts and Independent Contractors. That's what I am, by the way. An Independent.

Independent, she repeated, her puzzlement abating only slightly. *And what do the terms Corvantine and Ironship denote exactly?*

Clay frowned. *How long you been down here?*

She stared at him for a moment then broke into another laugh, shrill and only a note or two shy of hysteria. Eventually the laughter subsided and she turned her gaze to the battle in the sky. *I hoped the diagram was wrong.* Her thoughts were faint murmurs beneath a resurgent swell of despair. Clay found himself impressed by the way she mastered her emotions in the space of a few seconds, disciplining her thoughts with a kind of stern precision the equal of anything he had seen in Lizanne's mind. *What is your name?* she asked once the torrent of feelings had subsided into a tightly controlled ball.

Claydon Torcreek, ma'am, he replied. *Blood-blessed to the Longrifles Independent Contractor Company. You can call me Clay.*

Clay . . . She inclined her head in a gesture of greeting, though her eyes remained on the stars. *And you can call me Kriz.* Her shoulders shuddered as the ball of emotion threatened to burst, though she was quick to reassert control. *And, to answer your question, by my estimation I have been down here for just over ten thousand years.*

The trance vanished as quickly as it arrived, leaving him gaping up at her, still strapped to the pillar. "What?" he said.

She ignored the question and moved out of view. After a few seconds the rope fell away. Clay's hands immediately went to his leg, still bathing in the light from the crystal, fingers exploring the smooth, remade flesh. "You did this, I guess?" he asked as Kriz reappeared. She ignored the question and pointed to his pack then in the direction of the chamber entrance. The expression of pointed impatience on her face conveying clear instruction. *We have to go.*

Her meaning was given added impetus by the arrival of another tremor, more powerful this time and the flicker of the crystal's light more violent. Kriz motioned for him to get up as the tremor subsided, moving towards the dais.

"Thank you," Clay said, levering himself upright and marvelling at the absence of pain as he tested his weight on the leg. "I mean it," he persisted. "Really thought I was gonna lose it."

Kriz paused, thumbing the lever to open the gun's chamber once more, then glanced over her shoulder with a strained smile of acknowledgment. She gestured at the packs again and slotted another vial into the gun. Clay checked his pack, finding his pistol nestled amongst the contents. He checked the cylinder and found it fully loaded.

"Putting a lotta trust in someone you shot not long ago," he told Kriz, strapping his gun-belt around his waist. She gave no reply, instead pressing the gun's barrel into the flesh of Loriabeth's forearm and pulling the trigger.

Loriabeth came awake after a few seconds of spasmodic fidgeting. Clay rushed over to catch hold of his cousin's flailing arms as her wide, bleary gaze swung about before fixing on him.

"How you doing, cuz?" he asked.

She blinked up at him in incomprehension for several seconds, then jerked in fright as Kriz injected the same waking agent into Sigoral. "What in the Travail . . . ?"

"It's alright," Clay told her. "She's . . . friendly. Far as I can tell."

"Who is she?"

"Calls herself Kriz. She's a Blood-blessed. Seems she's been living down here for . . . a good long while. Beyond that, I can't say. Kind've a language problem."

Sigoral's awakening was considerably more violent than Loriabeth's, the Corvantine surfacing from his slumber with a flurry of kicks and punches. He continued to flail about on the floor, only abating when Clay pinned him down, though not before earning a hefty blow to the stomach.

"Hey!" Clay delivered a hard slap to the marine's face. "It's me, relax."

The sound of a handclap drew his gaze back to Kriz. She stood between two pillars, gesturing at the chamber door, her movements even more urgent than before.

"Who in the name of all the emperors is she?" Sigoral demanded.

Before Clay could answer the chamber shook again, sending a fresh cascade of dust down around them as a large rumbling crack sounded from above. Abruptly the crystal's light faded into a dim glow, leaving most of the chamber in darkness.

"That ain't good," Loriabeth said, scrambling to her feet.

"Get your gear," Clay said, rising from Sigoral and moving to the packs.

"Your leg . . ." Loriabeth said, staring at his uninjured limb.

"No time, cuz," Clay told her, casting a worried glance at the ceiling as ever more dust began to fall. He pulled on his own pack and lifted the others, turning to see Kriz disappearing through the chamber door, clearly unwilling to linger another second. "Come on!" he called to Sigoral and Loriabeth, starting after Kriz in a steady run. After a few steps he was gratified to hear the sound of them following.

He tracked Kriz through the corridor back to the shadowed interior of the building. Dust billowed down in ever-thicker cascades, the sibilant hiss of it punctuated by the thud of falling stone. Realising he had lost sight of Kriz, he came to a halt, Sigoral barrelling into him from behind.

"This place doesn't have much longer," the Corvantine observed, wincing as something large and heavy slammed into the floor close by.

"Got that right," Clay said, handing the marine his pack and tossing the other to Loriabeth.

"Where'd she go?" Loriabeth asked, eyes bright in the gloom.

A shout came from the left, Clay picking out the flicker of a shadow and starting towards it at a run. "Stay close," he told the others.

It took only a moment to find Kriz, standing in a faint patch of light cast down from above, apparently the result of a large slab of stone that had dislodged itself from the ceiling. Seeing them, she turned and started off again, sprinting now. Clay increased his own pace, yelling at the others to do the same. After a few seconds he saw Kriz's slender form outlined in the doorway. The three of them exited the structure just as a thunderous cacophony filled the space at their backs. Clay came to a halt and turned to receive a blast of gritty dust in the face. He blinked away tears and when he looked again he saw a jagged matrix of cracks appearing in the structure's outer surface. It seemed to sag in on itself as the cracks grew, issuing a terrible grinding roar as slabs of granite scraped against each other.

He felt a hard tug on his arm and found Kriz pulling him towards the right-hand side of the island. He lost no time in following, finding the prospect of remaining in this spot as the structure collapsed around them distinctly unappealing. Kriz kept close to the lake-shore, moving in a wide arc around the building to where a plinth rose at the edge of the water. She went to it immediately, slapping her hand to the crystal it held then turning an expectant gaze towards the water.

For a long moment nothing happened and Clay found himself casting increasingly nervous glances at the structure. The upper half of it had half fallen inward, the stone walls taking on a concave fragmented appearance whilst cracks continued to sunder the granite lower down. As concerning as its imminent collapse was, he was more afraid of what might happen to the monolithic shaft that rose from the building's roof. *If that comes down we're all done for,* he knew.

A rush of displaced water drew his gaze back to the lake, provoking a surge of relief at the sight of another bridge emerging from the depths. It was far longer than the one that had brought them to the island, disappearing into the mist a mile or so off shore. Kriz sprinted onto the bridge without preamble, pausing after a few yards to stare back at them as they failed to follow.

"Where's she taking us?" Sigoral said. He had his carbine in hand and seemed to view the prospect of following Kriz onto the bridge with only slightly less trepidation than remaining on the island.

"Wherever it is, it's gotta be better than here," Clay said, casting a final glance up at the shaft before starting towards Kriz at a dead run. Loriabeth followed without demur, Clay looking over his shoulder to see Sigoral following suit, his caution perhaps overcome by a fresh tremor that shook the island.

Kriz maintained a swift and punishing pace along the bridge that Clay soon found hard to match. His leg might have been healed but it seemed to possess some residual weakness from the drake's bite. He stumbled several times, coming close to pitching over the side of the bridge. Fortunately Loriabeth was there to steady him and he managed to keep going.

Kriz eventually slowed to a steady run, allowing them to catch up, then coming to a complete halt when they had covered perhaps three hundred paces. They all turned to regard the island, chests heaving. The tremors seemed to have stopped but the damage done to the structure was plainly irreversible. The upper half gave way completely, subsiding down to shatter the base, raising a thick cloud of dust that spread across the lake surface in a grey-brown fog. When it cleared Clay could see that the huge shaft had lost its base. It still hung there, impossibly huge as it seemed to float without any anchor to the earth. He turned to Kriz, finding her staring at the ruins with tears streaming down her cheeks. A sob rose in her breast and she turned away, lowering herself to her haunches and hugging herself tight. The despair had returned in full and she seemed resolved to surrender to it, at least for now.

He watched her sob for a time, motioning the others to silence when they couldn't contain their questions. Kriz exhausted herself after several long minutes and he reached out a hand to hers, touching it briefly. She opened her eyes to regard him with a gaze of utter desolation, as grieving a soul as he had ever seen.

He jerked his head at the shaft dangling above the vanished island. "Guess that was your home for an awful long time, right?"

She blinked wet eyes at him and rose from her huddle, breathing deeply before starting along the bridge with a determined stride.

"Where are we going?" Clay called after her. She paused, turning back to speak a single word in her own tongue. He knew from Lizanne that a shared trance did not bring immediate understanding of a previously unknown language. Such proficiency required repeated trances, but even a brief mental connection could engender a small amount of comprehension. So when she spoke the word he found he knew its literal translation, though its meaning remained as baffling as everything else in this hidden world.

"Father," she said before turning and striding off into the mist.

CHAPTER 29

Lizanne

"Spare me the performance, please," Julesin said, wood scraping as he dragged something across the room. "I know you're awake."

Lizanne pondered the wisdom of ignoring him, keeping her head slumped forward and torso limp within the mesh of ropes securing her to the chair. In fact she had woken only a few moments before, having managed a brief, blurred glance at her surroundings before hearing his footfalls on the steps. Feigning senselessness was a crude but occasionally effective technique in resisting interrogation. Any kind of response counted as engagement, the cardinal sin of the captured agent. However, the urgency of her predicament left little option but to abandon standard doctrine.

She raised her head, opening her eyes to see him perched on a chair placed at a sensible remove, giving him ample time to react should she contrive to get loose. *Taking no chances,* she decided, the thought bringing an uncomfortable realisation. *He's done this before.*

"I'll just keep calling you Krista, if you don't mind," Julesin said. "Not a lot of point in extracting your real name at this juncture. I wish I could say the same for the other information you hold."

Lizanne said nothing, eyes flicking around the room. It appeared to be an attic, possibly in one of the houses on Prop Lane, though something made her doubt it. There was no sound from downstairs and she felt sure the Coal King would have wanted to be present for her interrogation. Her cross-bow, knife and penknife were set out neatly on a table beside Julesin's chair. The sole window had been boarded up but she could see a dim glimmer of light through the cracks. She had no way of knowing how long she had been unconscious, but given the general lack of noise bleeding in from outside, she knew the Ore Day Promenade hadn't yet started. However, the most noteworthy feature of the room lay below the window, a huddled, slumped form she had initially taken for a bundle of rags but now saw, and smelled, it to be a corpse. The face was obscured by the rags that covered the body but she found herself annoyed by the worry that it might well be Makario.

"Three Cadre agents sent into this mire in such a short space of time," Julesin mused. "I'm afraid your colleagues were somewhat amateurish compared to you, but what they lacked in ability they made up for in dedication. One forced me to kill him and the other swallowed poison before we could have a chat." He reached into the pocket of his waistcoat and extracted a small white object. "This is fine work," he said, holding her false tooth between finger and thumb. "I was somewhat surprised to find it empty. Or perhaps"—he leaned forward, eyes intent on her face—"it held something other than poison? Something you already used?"

Lizanne met his gaze, finding herself reminded of another man of professional demeanour she had met aboard ship not so long ago. But then the circumstances had been reversed. "If I am what you think I am," she said, "don't you think the wisest course would be to let me go? If you have any interest in a long life, that is."

His brows rose in surprise as he leaned back in his chair. "Speaking so soon," he murmured. "I expected to have to at least pluck out an eye before we got to this stage. Why abandon protocol so quickly, I wonder?"

Lizanne cast a pointed glance around the attic. "I take it the Coal King is otherwise occupied? Or, does he perhaps have no idea that I'm here?"

"Angry men are rarely truly dangerous," Julesin replied with a shrug. "So easy to manipulate. I expect he's probably off beating one of the younger Scuttlers into a bloody pulp for a minor offence. He always likes that. And no, he has no notion that I have you, nor will he up until the moment I twist his ugly head from his shoulders."

Lizanne sighed, sagging a little in her ropes and using the gesture to conceal the act of testing the knots. In addition to the ropes binding her torso, her hands were bound together at the base of the chair-back and her ankles had been secured to the legs. Sadly, each knot felt too well tied to break without the assistance of product.

"You want information," she said. "Very well. Here is the most important intelligence I can impart to you at this juncture. You don't matter.

Whatever you're doing here doesn't matter. Let me go and you might live. That's the only promise I'll make."

He kept his face neutral, but she saw the faint twitch in his eye that told of an unexpected reaction. "People in your predicament usually have much more grandiose, not to say lucrative, promises to make."

"Really?" She inclined her head, smiling a little. "I recently heard about a treasure to be found at the bottom of a lake in the Arradsian Interior. I'll draw you a map if you like."

The bland neutrality on his face darkened considerably. "It's really not in your interests to mock me," he said, rising and moving to the corpse lying below the window. "Take this fellow for instance." Julesin dragged the corpse across the floor towards her, heaving it upright and pulling away the rags to reveal the face. Lizanne managed to conceal a wince at the sight of it, her alarm only slightly alleviated by the realisation that this wasn't Makario. The face was missing both eyes, two dark empty sockets staring at her above a gaping and mostly toothless mouth. The lank grey hair and deep lines in the face told of a man in his fifties, but she had no notion who the unfortunate might be until her gaze slipped to his hands. The left was whole but the right was missing two fingers, and it was an old injury.

"The bomb-maker, I take it," she said.

"Very good," Julesin conceded. "I never knew his true name either, so I called him Mr. Stubby on account of his fingers. I don't think he liked it. A fellow of many mechanical gifts, particularly when applied to the design of cross-bows and bombs. Sadly, such largesse of talent made him over-estimate his importance and attempt a renegotiation of the terms of his employment, little realising that his contract had already been fulfilled. I consider it poor practice to leave an aggrieved bomb-maker alive."

"Finding him in here couldn't have been easy," Lizanne commented.

"Ah." Julesin grinned as he shoved Mr. Stubby's corpse aside. "The point where you play for time by attempting to elicit information. Even though we both know how I found him." He stamped a foot on the floor, calling out, "Time for you to say hello!"

There was a short pause then the sound of ascending footsteps, Lizanne's experienced ears discerning the overlapping thuds which indicated two climbers. A creak of rusty hinges drew Lizanne's gaze to a trap-door in the centre of the room, finding little surprise in the face that appeared as it rose.

Makario studiously avoided looking at her as he ascended into the attic, keeping his gaze lowered as he shuffled to one side. The second figure to emerge was truly unexpected. A tall man in a long ragged cape, features hidden by the hood. *No sack this time,* Lizanne noted as the creeper slammed the trap-door shut and paused to regard her before turning to Julesin.

"We haven't gotten to it yet," Julesin said. "She's Blood-blessed, right enough, but I'd wager she's not Cadre. Meaning she's either employed by private interests within the empire or . . . something far worse. A true appreciation of her circumstances might loosen her tongue."

The hooded creeper stood in silence for a long moment then went to the table, a surprisingly strong and far from skeletal hand emerging from the cape to rest on her penknife. "I was sure you'd use this on yourself before you even made it through the grate," Constable Darkanis said, drawing back his hood to reveal familiar, broad features. "Must be losing my touch," he added with a humourless smile.

Lizanne replied with an equally bland smile of her own. "This, I gather, is your retirement plan?"

Darkanis shrugged. "Twenty years labour in the arsehole of the empire deserves more reward than a pittance of a pension." He paused for a moment, his hand moving from the penknife to take hold of her other knife, the one she had taken from Dralky. Darkanis stepped closer, all semblance of the affable professional she had met at the gate vanished now. She could see a deep well of fear in his eyes, the kind of fear that tended to override restraint or pretension to morality.

"Something worse, you said." Darkanis kept his eyes on Lizanne as he addressed Julesin. "What kind of something?"

"Ironship something," the Blood-blessed replied, Lizanne hearing the uneasy sigh he tried to hide. "One of their Exceptional Initiatives agents. The kind of trouble you're not paying me enough to deal with."

"Seems to me you dealt with it well enough," Darkanis observed.

Julesin moved into Lizanne's eye-line, looking down at her with an air of grim contemplation. "Exceptional Initiatives doesn't forget, or forgive. You can run for ten years, twenty even, and you'll still one day find yourself staring into the eyes of a Blood-blessed they sent to kill you, and they won't be quick about it."

"All true," Lizanne assured Darkanis.

"So you are Ironship," the constable said, leaning down so his face was level with hers. "Why did they send you here? Was it for this?" His hand disappeared into the folds of his cape and came out with a small fragment of rock. "Do they know about this?" He held the rock up before her eyes, turning it so the light caught something in its surface, a thin vein of white metal.

Not white, Lizanne realised. *Silver.*

"So, that's it," she said. "You found silver in the mines. Or rather, one of your informants found it and you failed to report it to your superiors. That alone would earn you the firing squad, but you didn't stop there, did you? Hiring Julesin here to run operations within the walls whilst you creep back and forth every night with your sack full of ore. Very clever. It does make me wonder why you'd go to the bother of trying to foment discord amongst the gangs. Getting Makario to find you a bomb-maker and so on. He's been working for you since he arrived, I assume? Another scared newcomer you steered towards the Miner's Repose."

"And very useful he's been." Darkanis glanced over his shoulder at Makario, still standing with his head lowered. "I wouldn't feel too bad," Darkanis told him. "This bitch would happily rip your balls off if her masters told her there was a profit in it." He turned back to Lizanne, looming closer. "It's time for a new dawn in Scorazin. Time to sweep away the gangs, institute some real order, profitable order. To do that, this place has to burn for a time."

"Leaving Julesin at the top of the heap when the fires die down." Lizanne inclined her head in reluctant admiration. "And free to mine the silver without interference from the gangs or the constables."

"Yes." Darkanis stepped closer still, Lizanne wrinkling her nose at the stench arising from his filthy cape. "They know, don't they?" he said. "Ironship. They know about the seams. That's why you're here."

"My employer neither knows nor cares about your petty corruption. We have larger concerns at the moment."

"You're lying!" He clamped a meaty hand on her throat and began to squeeze. Lizanne clenched her jaw to keep her neck muscles tensed against the pressure, but he was a very strong man. "This city sits atop the richest seams of silver anywhere in the world." Spittle flew from Darkanis's lips as he snarled into her face. "And you claim they don't care. I haven't spilled so much blood and risked everything to see it stolen from me now!"

Lizanne dragged air in through her nostrils as the constable lifted her up, chair and all, squeezing harder. He raised his knife in his other hand, poised and ready to slash at her eyes.

"What do they know!"

Grey mist began to creep into the edge of Lizanne's vision as Darkanis shook her, a rushing sound in her ears telling of an imminent loss of consciousness.

"You're wasting your time," came Julesin's drawl, faint and barely audible through the haze. "They're trained to resist such crude methods."

Another final squeeze and Darkanis let her go, the chair thudding to the boards and coming close to tipping over. Lizanne allowed herself a few convulsive gasps before reasserting control, forcing her hammering heart into a steady rhythm with a breathing sequence learned in her student days.

"See?" Julesin said to Darkanis. "You could take that knife to her nethers and she still wouldn't talk. I'm afraid a more invasive approach will be necessary. If you're determined to extract what she knows."

"You can do that?" the constable asked. "Get into her head?"

"Sadly no." Lizanne blinked water from her streaming eyes, seeing the Blood-blessed once again resuming his seat. "A trance would be possible, certainly. But her inner defences will be far too formidable, even for me." He offered Lizanne an apologetic smile as he reached into his jacket pocket and extracted a vial. "I'm afraid we've reached that point in the interrogation, Krista," he said, raising the vial to his lips. "Ever closed a blood vessel with Black?" He leaned forward to focus his gaze on her forehead. "There's a particular vein in the frontal lobe that, if pinched with the correct amount of pressure, produces a level of pain said to be truly unbearable. So unbearable in fact, the subject will do anything to ensure they never experience it again."

For a second Lizanne felt panic threaten to overwhelm her as the Black closed in, fixing her head in place. Julesin's control was impressive, allowing not the slightest movement in her skull, though her eyes were free to flick about as she tried to master her fear. Her gaze slid over Julesin's face, set in a frown of concentration, Constable Darkanis's bulky, filthy caped form and the spot where Makario had been standing only seconds before. Except now he was missing, and so, she noticed as her gaze flicked to the table, was her penknife.

Makario moved with a lithe economy of movement that made Lizanne conclude that he had also been tutored in dance as well as music. He leapt high, descending on Julesin and bringing the penknife's small blade down in a blur, sinking it deep into the join between the Blood-blessed's neck and shoulder. The grip of Julesin's Black vanished, leaving Lizanne sagging in her bonds, gasping for air as she tried to clear the throb from her head. The sounds of a struggle forced her gaze up, finding Darkanis slashing at Makario with her other knife. The musician danced back, evading the blade, then whirled to deliver a cut to the constable's hand, the resulting spasm of pain forcing him to drop the weapon. The bigger man roared and charged, head lowered and moving with bull-like ferocity. Makario tried to dance clear once more but the constable was too fast, his shoulder taking the slender musician in the chest and bearing him to the floor.

"I told you," Darkanis grated, grabbing Makario's hair in a meaty fist and slamming his head onto the floorboards. "Don't ever try to fuck me over!" He repeated the process, punctuating every word with another jarring slam. "Don't! Ever! Try! To! Fuck! Me! Over!"

Lizanne tore her gaze away, fixing it on Julesin who lay less than two feet away, gazing up at her with rapidly dimming eyes as blood pumped in rhythmic gouts from his wound. Makario might not have been the greatest of fighters, but clearly knew how to find the right vein.

Another slam as Darkanis vented his rage on a near-senseless Makario. Lizanne heaved herself back then forward, the chair legs squeaking on the boards as she built momentum. Three more heaves and it tottered so far that she feared it would send her onto her back. It hung there for a very long second then swung forward once more, Lizanne hurling her weight against the ropes to force it over. She toppled onto Julesin's body, squirming to manoeuvre her head closer to his wound. The severed vein was still pumping but with less energy now, blood coming in small, thick squirts, blood still rich in the Black he had drunk.

Lizanne struggled close enough to cover the wound with her mouth, fighting nausea as she sucked the blood down her throat, feeling Julesin die beneath her. The hot, iron-tinged flow slowed then stopped as the Blood-blessed gave a final twitch. Lizanne suppressed the reflexive need to vomit and raised her gaze to see Darkanis now standing over Makario. The musician flailed on the floor, arms moving in a spastic parody of combat. The constable had retrieved the knife and paused to laugh before he knelt, pressing the blade to Makario's throat, his mantra coming in a soft whisper now. "Don't ever try to fuck me over."

Seeing little point in prolonging matters, Lizanne summoned the Black, finding she had imbibed more than enough to crush the constable's head.

She used the last of the Black to free herself, finding she lacked the concentration to unravel the knots and settling for dismantling the chair. With the Black expended, she lay on the floor for a time, recovering strength enough to search Julesin's person. He had all four vials, presumably smuggled in thanks to Constable Darkanis, each about three-quarters full. Lizanne sniffed each in turn until she found the Green, managing to restrain the urge to gulp half the contents and instead rationing herself to only two sips, just enough to get her on her feet.

Makario and Darkanis lay side by side, the musician liberally spattered with the gory debris left by the constable's demise. Makario still moved his arms about, though with less energy, throwing feeble punches at nothing, an absent cast to his half-closed eyes. Lizanne knelt and lifted his head into her lap, checking to make sure Darkanis hadn't managed to crack his skull. She smoothed a hand over the musician's brow until some semblance of awareness returned to his gaze.

"Told you not to go out," he murmured, a small smile playing over his lips.

"What did Darkanis promise you?" she asked.

Makario swallowed and licked his lips, shoulders moving in a shrug. "Release, what else? New name, new life, far away from here. Once Julesin was in charge and the silver started flowing. Also gave me the components I needed, for the pianola. Music always was the quickest way to my heart."

They both winced in unison as a massive boom sounded from outside. It was perhaps the loudest explosion Lizanne had ever heard, louder even than the massed artillery at Carvenport. *It must have been quite a sight,* she thought, leaning over Makario as the building trembled, displacing a cloud of plaster and dust from the ceiling.

"What was that?" he asked.

Lizanne took the vial of Green and pressed it to his lips. "A chance at what you were promised," she said. "But I can't guarantee you'll live to see it."

CHAPTER 30

Hilemore

He stood on the walkway, frozen in the dark. The lights had disappeared only seconds after the platform began its plummet, leaving him alone in a pitch-black void, still staring down into the shaft even though there was nothing to see. Sigoral and the two younger Torcreeks gone in an instant. Hilemore clamped down on the rising swell of guilt and self-reproach. *You will always lose people,* his grandfather had told him once, sombre face veiled by pipe-smoke as he reclined behind his desk. *No matter how skilled a sailor or competent an officer you become, lad. Whatever you do, you will always lose people.*

They didn't fall, Hilemore reminded himself. *They may still be alive down there. Living souls can be rescued.*

Very carefully, he crouched and unslung his pack from his shoulders, undoing the straps by feel. It took a few moments fumbling to find the lantern and several more to light it, his impatience sending a succession of matches into the void before he finally touched a flame to the wick. He cast the glow about, crouching to illuminate as much of the shaft as possible, though of course the bottom remained far out of reach. Hilemore began to call out, hearing only the echo of his own voice, when the walkway shuddered beneath him. The tremor possessed sufficient violence to send him sprawling, his torso hanging over the edge of the void before he managed to lever himself to safety.

The shaking seemed to increase as he regained his feet, arms held out wide to maintain balance. The perilousness of his position was underlined by a sudden and very loud crack from above, accompanied by a cascade of falling dust. Hilemore didn't hesitate, keenly honed instincts acquired over the course of years at sea left little doubt in his mind that it was time to run.

He sprinted along the walkway, managing not to stumble as the tremor continued. As he reached the passage there came the thudding boom of something very large and very heavy impacting on the walkway. Hilemore paused for a second to turn, catching a glimpse of a huge slab tottering on the edge of the walkway for a second before tumbling into the shaft. *Living souls can be rescued,* he thought, teeth clenched in impotent fury.

Another violent shudder convinced him that this wasn't the time to indulge his guilt. He turned and raced along the passage, scrambling up the piled rubble and spending several frantic seconds navigating the gap Clay had created before tumbling out the other side. He fell repeatedly as he ran, the surface beneath his feet shifting with increasing energy. Finally he came to the great cog-like door, finding the rope still dangling from the narrow aperture they had used to gain entry. He cast the lantern aside and gripped the rope, hauling himself up as fast as the shaking would allow. Reaching the aperture and beginning to clamber out, managing to poke his head into the freezing air before another violent heave loosened his grip and he found himself slipping back inside.

"Captain!" Steelfine's meaty hand clamped onto Hilemore's forearm with a near-crushing force. The Islander heaved him through the opening, shouting with the effort, and Hilemore found himself lying winded at the bottom of the bowl-shaped crevasse they had blasted into the ice.

"Sir?" Steelfine crouched at his side as Hilemore dragged air into his lungs, momentarily unable to speak. The ice was shuddering too, he noticed, the energy released in the spire communicated to the surrounding sheet. He started at a sharp crack near by, gaze jerking towards the sight of a fissure opening in the ice a few feet from where he lay, white powder exploding upwards as the fissure snaked away. More cracks sounded all around, powdered ice rising in curtains to catch a rainbow from the sunlight.

"We..." Hilemore choked, forced more air into his lungs and got to his feet. "We have to get clear!"

They scrambled free of the crevasse and ran for the camp, Hilemore waving at the fur-covered figures rushing to meet him. "Back! Get back!"

"Where's my daughter!" Braddon Torcreek demanded as Hilemore made the camp. He ignored the Contractor, ordering the men to pile supplies on the sleds. His instinct was to order them to run, get away from this place as fast as possible. But without supplies they wouldn't last a day on the ice, regardless of what happened here. "Get your harnesses on! Quickly! "

"My daughter!" Braddon repeated, grabbing hold of Hilemore's arm and jerking him around. "My nephew. Where are they?"

Hilemore stared into the man's eyes, seeing fevered desperation and a burden of guilt that perhaps outweighed his own. "I believe them to be lost," he told the Contractor simply, tone as gentle as urgency allowed. "I'm sorry."

He tore his arm free and began to buckle on one of the harnesses. "We're heading north with all speed!" he called out to the men scrambling to follow suit. "No stopping until—"

His words were drowned by another series of cracks, louder and more numerous than before. For a second all was rendered white by the upsurge of powder and when it cleared Hilemore saw that the ice-sheet had fragmented. A complex matrix of cracks expanded out from the spire in all directions, as far as he could see. Tall geysers of vapour ascended from the widest cracks, one close enough to engulf one of his crew, a rifleman who had stood beside him at the Battle of the Strait. Hilemore watched in wretched fascination as the man was swallowed by the geyser, his screams brief but still terrible to hear. When the vapour cleared Hilemore could see the crewman's scalded red features amidst the swaddle of his furs before he fell into the crevasse left in the geyser's wake. *Steam*, Hilemore realised. *It's not being shattered, it's being melted.*

The ice beneath them pitched like the deck of a ship in heavy seas, sending the entire party from their feet. Hilemore watched as another man, one of the cook's assistants, slid across the angled surface, mitten-clad hands scrabbling and failing to find purchase on the ice before he slipped over the edge. Hilemore and the rest of the party might well have joined him had the ice not righted itself, heaving back and forth before settling into a more sedate rhythm.

Hilemore got unsteadily to his feet, gazing around at their refashioned surroundings. The sheet was now a dense collection of flat-topped icebergs, drifting in apparent haphazard fashion dictated by the currents of the churned and steaming sea below. He watched as the berg they stood on began to shrink, chunks of ice falling away as the heated ocean gnawed at its edges. All the surviving members of the party clustered together in the centre of the berg, piling supplies and warily eyeing their quickly diminishing platform.

Braddon was the one exception. The Longrifles' captain stood close to the berg's edge, staring down at the roiling waters below in indifferent stillness. Skaggerhill and Preacher rushed forward to drag him back seconds before the patch of ice he stood on sublimed into the sea. Braddon shook off their restraining hands and slumped down amidst the mess of upturned sleds and disordered supplies, his face a picture in abject grief.

"Skipper," Hilemore heard Scrimshine say in a tremulous whisper. He turned, following the smuggler's pointed finger to find that the spire had begun to break apart. The great monolith's pointed summit came loose amidst an explosion of dust as cracks appeared all over the spire's surface. It fell to pieces all at once, great jagged slabs of material shattering yet more ice as they toppled into the sea, producing a series of tall waves that threatened to capsize their refuge. Then it was gone, vanished within the space of a few seconds, leaving them alone and adrift in a shattered world.

Eventually the steam faded, by which time their new island home had shrunk to a platform twenty feet across at its widest point. *Not quite the smallest vessel I've yet commanded,* Hilemore reflected without much humour. *Yet still too small for even an eight-man crew.*

"Perhaps twelve days, sir," Steelfine reported in a quiet murmur, Hilemore having asked him to undertake a realistic appraisal of how long their remaining supplies might last. "Could stretch to fifteen, given we're not expending so much energy now."

"Thank you, Mr. Steelfine." Hilemore adjusted the pointers on his sextant and raised the instrument to the sky. One advantage the southern extremes offered the sailor was the clarity of the sky at night. He couldn't see even the slightest wisp of cloud from one end of the horizon to the other, making it fairly easy to gauge their heading from the stars.

"Two miles south of where we started," Scrimshine called to Hilemore with a strangely cheerful grin. "Am I right, Skipper?"

"Two point eight," Hilemore replied.

"I'm guessing all currents lead south at this latitude." The smuggler drew his hood back to cast his gaze about, shaking his head a little in wonder. "Will you look at all this. Could be the ice is melted all the way to the pole."

"It's certainly a possibility."

The gaps between the drifting bergs had increased considerably since the sea had stopped roiling, the nearest berg was at least fifty yards off and the distance showed no sign of lessening. Earlier he had risked dipping a hand into the sea, finding the water chilly but not numbing. He could only conclude that whatever processes had brought about this change were still continuing far below the surface. The kind of energies capable of returning so much of the ice-cap to the ocean in so short a space of time were far beyond both his comprehension and, he suspected, the comprehension of the finest scientific minds. The sight of the spire itself had been humbling enough but now he had an inkling of the vastness of the mystery they had come to investigate. *We were children,* he thought, his mind repeating the image of the platform taking Clay and the others into the depths of the shaft. *Rousing a monster we could never understand.*

"Reaching the pole would be something," Scrimshine went on. "Never been done as far as I know. One for the history books, if we ever get to tell anyone, o'course."

The man's cheeriness was both aggravating and puzzling. Hilemore, in common with the rest of the party, viewed their current predicament with grim comprehension, but this former convict seemed to find it a cause for levity.

"Didn't think I'd live to see anything else," Scrimshine said, perhaps in response to Hilemore's sour glance. "Besides the walls of my cell. Instead"—he spread his arms, baring his meagre teeth in a smile—"I got to see wonders. Can't say it's been an unfair shake of the rope."

"A creditable attitude, Mr. Scrimshine." Hilemore glanced over to where Braddon sat close to the edge of the berg, hunched and apparently indifferent to the bleakly concerned face of the stocky harvester who stood near by. "Even so," Hilemore said, turning back to Scrimshine. "I doubt anyone would take it amiss if you saw fit to once again beseech your ancestors on our behalf."

The smuggler pondered the notion for a moment before shrugging. "I think old Last Look may well have used up all my credit on that account, Skipper. But it can't hurt to ask."

Hilemore saw Skaggerhill hug himself tight and retreat from his captain. "Much appreciated, Mr. Scrimshine."

Braddon didn't turn as Hilemore approached, continuing to sit with his hood drawn back from his weathered features, staring out at the current-churned waters. Hilemore sank down next to him, drawing back his own hood. He didn't say anything. Commiserations would be redundant, as would apologies. However, if the fellow wanted to vent his anger at a man who fully deserved it, Hilemore wasn't about to stand in his way.

When the words came from Braddon's mouth, however, there was no anger in them, only faint curiosity. "Do you have a family, Mr. Hilemore?"

"I have a mother and two brothers," Hilemore replied.

"No. I meant a wife, children."

"No, sir. I was engaged until recently but fate decided the marriage wasn't to be."

"Fate, huh? In my experience it ain't fate that breaks a couple apart."

Hilemore gave a tight smile, acknowledging the point. "Very true. My fiancée is . . . was a lady of profound convictions and heart-felt principles. She considered my continued employment with the Protectorate to be incompatible with these beliefs."

"Gave you a choice, did she? Her or the Protectorate."

"Actually no. I don't imagine you know a great deal about the Dalcian Emergency, since Ironship's friends in the press were skilled in obscuring the details. Suffice to say that the reality of war rarely matches the image portrayed in the news-sheets. Lewella, however, has her own sources of information. I'll not pretend to have emerged from the Emergency with completely clean hands, but I was at least at ease with my own conscience. Lewella was not."

"Think she'll ever know about all this? You coming such a long way to die for no good reason."

"We had a good reason, Captain Torcreek. Perhaps Lewella would never have known my fate. Perhaps she would have found another man more suited to her outlook and forgotten me in time. I would be content to be forgotten if it meant she remained alive long enough to do so."

"My Freda would never forget. And she's lost more than just a husband. Turns out I'm a coward, Mr. Hilemore. Y'see, ain't nothing scares me more than the prospect of looking into my wife's eyes when I tell her I lost our daughter."

Hilemore didn't bother to institute rationing. The farther south they drifted it became clear that the cold would most likely claim their lives before starvation set in. So the crew occupied themselves with eating their way through the remaining supplies in between stomping about their limited environs in an effort to stave off the cold. Although the sea had warmed, the air was as chilled as ever. It had become an all-consuming presence now, adding a painful edge to every breath and a razor-like caress to exposed skin. Hilemore could see the beginnings of frost-bite on the men's faces, reddish patches appearing on noses and cheeks that grew more inflamed as the days passed.

Braddon Torcreek remained a mostly still and silent figure, eating only when Skaggerhill pressed him to it and then partaking of a scant few mouthfuls at a time. Hilemore couldn't help but be reminded of the man they had found frozen to death in the tunnels at Kraghurst Station. *Tends to happen when a fella loses all hope of deliverance,* Scrimshine had said. Braddon, Hilemore knew, could find no deliverance from his guilt.

They drifted for three full days, Hilemore diligently plotting their course with the sextant and estimating they had covered a distance of twenty-three miles from the spire. "Only another hundred or so to the pole then," Scrimshine observed. "We got a flag to plant?"

"Sadly, I was remiss in not bringing one," Hilemore replied, finding he truly did regret the oversight. It would have been good to leave some monument to the most southerly journey human beings had ever undertaken, albeit inadvertently.

"We could make one," Scrimshine suggested. "Break up the sleds to fashion a flag-pole, sew some tarps together for the pennant. Something to do at least, Skipper."

Hilemore saw wisdom in his reasoning. After their initial enthusiasm the party's exercise regimen had slackened off considerably, most sitting lethargic and preoccupied by their impending fate. He was about to start rousing them to the task when an unexpected someone called his name. Preacher hadn't said a word since they climbed Mount Reygnar, and precious little before then, so it took a second to recognise his voice. The tall cleric stood on the south-facing edge of the berg, pointing at something in the maze of bergs covering the horizon.

"See something?" Hilemore asked, moving to Preacher's side.

"A ship," the marksman said, still pointing.

"Can't be," Scrimshine said. "Probably just a trick of the light. No offence," he added quickly when Preacher turned his impassive gaze on him.

Hilemore saw the smuggler's point; no vessel could have sailed this far south through so many bergs, not in the few days since the sheet broke up. However, recalling that it was thanks to Preacher's eyes that they found the spire, Hilemore retrieved his spy-glass from the folds of his furs and raised it to his eye. It took some seconds of focusing the lens before he found it, a low dark shape just visible through a gap between two bergs, and rising from it the unmistakable sight of three masts.

"It seems," Hilemore said, lowering the glass, "the ice has one more wonder to show us, Mr. Scrimshine."

It transpired that they had to break up the sleds after all, but to build a boat rather than a flag-pole. Although the drift of their berg had brought them to within a few hundred yards of the mysterious ship, it had become clear that its course was unlikely to bring them any closer. Steelfine did most of the work, putting Island-born skills to use. Within the space of two hours he had crafted a bowl-shaped frame from the pliable struts, which was duly covered by a skin of hastily-sewn-together tarps. Hilemore forbade the Islander from taking charge of the craft, knowing this duty fell to him.

"I can't guarantee she'll make it all the way, sir," Steelfine cautioned. They had lowered the boat over the edge where it bobbed in the current, a small pool of water already sloshing in the bottom.

"I have every confidence in your skills, Lieutenant." Hilemore nodded towards the ship and the hump of an upturned life-boat visible on its upper deck. "She only has to last a few minutes."

He was obliged to use a rifle as an oar and it proved a clumsy implement, barely capable of ploughing a course through the swirling currents. Several times the tiny craft was spun about by an eddy before Hilemore managed to reassert control. They had fixed a line to the edge of the boat's hull, insurance against the life-boat on the ship proving to be unsailable. The men played out the line as Hilemore made his often-wayward progress towards the ship. It took an hour of arduous labour before he drew close enough to get a clear view of her hull. He was pleased to find it intact, the lower planks clad in iron and lacking any obvious damage or even overt signs of age, though this vessel was undoubtedly of antique construction. She lacked any stacks or paddles, the three masts telling of a ship built in the pre–Blood Age.

Hilemore was obliged to navigate a gap between two towering bergs, finding the current even more violent and difficult to traverse. By the time he made it through and the ship's hull towered above him, the once-shallow pool of water in the bottom of his makeshift boat had swollen to ankle depth. Hilemore unslung a rope from around his chest, taking hold of the grapple and preparing to throw, then pausing as his eyes caught sight of the ship's name-plate. The word had lost its paint long ago. Now he was close enough to read it clearly, he could make out a name set in Mandinorian letters rich in archaic flourishes: *Dreadfire*.

CHAPTER 31

Clay

The lake turned out to be more of a sea and the bridge more of a road. The crystals faded twice before they caught sight of another land-mass, an island even smaller than the one now home to the ruins of Kriz's home. So far their erstwhile captor and subsequent saviour hadn't provided any further information on her origins or explanation for the island's destruction.

She kept on striding along the algae-covered road, resting for short intervals and only stopping completely when the light of the three suns faded. She ate several of the sea-biscuits Clay offered her, but bunched her face in disdain when he proffered a strip of dried beef. After that she sat in silence, offering only vague shakes of her head to his repeated questions as she maintained a careful vigil over the surrounding waters. The reason for her caution soon became clear. Almost as soon as the darkness closed in the surface of the water was broken by a series of bright splashes. One flared only a few yards shy of the road's edge, Clay catching sight of gleaming scales and a long snake-like form before another splash erupted and it was gone.

"Stands to reason there had to be more Blues," he told an alarmed Loriabeth, now crouched to one knee, cocked pistol fanning back and forth across the water. "Seem to be just as titchy as the ones back at the shore."

He turned to Kriz, who seemed much less alarmed by the Blue's appearance than he might have expected. "Guess they just grow smaller here, huh?" he asked, elaborating by making a shrinking gesture with his hands. Kriz merely gave him a blank look before returning her gaze to the waters, the small brass-and-steel weapon clutched tight in her hand.

Their brief sharing of minds had increased the understanding between them so he found it increasingly easy to discern meaning in some of her infrequent words. He also suspected that she comprehended more of his conversations with Loriabeth and Sigoral than she let on. However, when he suggested, via some inexpert miming, that they trance again, she refused with a firm shake of her head.

Doesn't fully trust us yet, he decided. *Worried how we'll react to what she'll tell us, maybe.* He also suspected there might be another reason for her reluctance. *Could be she's more scared of what she might learn from me than what I might learn from her.*

"There's gotta be fish in here," Loriabeth commented a few hours into their second artificial day on the road. She paused to peer at the water below. "Like Krystaline Lake. The drakes there preyed on dolphins and such, Scriberson said." She turned to Kriz, making a flapping motion with her hand before pointing at the water. "Fish in here? Yes?"

Kriz returned her gaze for a moment, possibly contemplating if there was any danger in providing a response, then nodded. "Fishhh," she said carefully. "Yes."

"It would be nice to catch a few," Sigoral put in, chewing unenthusiastically on some dried beef.

"I'm all out of rods and nets, Lieutenant," Clay told him.

"You could go for a swim, sailor boy," Loriabeth suggested with a sweet smile. "See what you can catch."

Sigoral replied with a bland smile of his own and strode on.

A mile or so later they came to a fork in the road, a second walkway branching off to the right to disappear into the haze a hundred paces off. Kriz strode past the junction without pause, barely glancing at the alternative route and ignoring Clay's question about where it might lead.

"It seems she has a definite destination in mind," Sigoral observed.

"As long as it leads to a way out of here," Loriabeth replied. "Never thought I'd say it, but I'm sorely missing the sight of the ice."

They passed several more junctions before the light faded again, Kriz again ignoring each one. As the darkness descended and they made their customary halt for the night, Clay noticed a definite increase in the number of Blues disturbing the water on either side of the road.

"Gotta be double the number there were last night," Loriabeth surmised, squinting into the gloom.

"They hungry or just curious?" Clay asked Kriz.

He saw her fingers twitch on the brass-and-steel gun, a grim decisiveness colouring her gaze as she watched the Blues churn the water. "Hungry," she said, getting to her feet. "Yes."

She went to Loriabeth's pack, pointing at the lantern fastened to the straps. "Want me to light that?" Loriabeth asked, receiving a nod in response. Loriabeth struck a flint to light the lantern's oil-covered wick, Sigoral quickly following suit with his own heavier sailor's lamp.

"Look," Kriz said, gesturing for the two light-bearers to cast their beams out over the water on either side of the road. "Move . . . fast," she added, starting off at a rapid pace.

They marched through the darkness, Loriabeth and Sigoral constantly playing their lights over the surrounding waters. Clay noticed that the Blues seemed shy of the lights, diving down whenever one of the beams caught them on the surface. But whatever threat they sensed wasn't enough to force a retreat and the night air was constantly riven by the sound of multiple splashes.

An hour's rapid marching brought them to another junction and this time Kriz took the alternate route, branching off to the left. She moved with greater urgency as the journey wore on. Clay noted that the Blues were becoming bolder, rising close enough to the road to cast an increasing amount of lake-water over the party.

"Getting right feisty, ain't they?" Loriabeth commented. She moved with a pistol in one hand, the barrel aligned with the lantern's beam.

"I guess a meal like us don't turn up too often," Clay said, grunting a little with the effort of matching Kriz's pace.

Finally she slowed as a bulky shape resolved out of the darkness ahead; another island. It was much smaller than the last one, formed of a slab of rock rising to a height of perhaps fifteen feet from the water, lacking buildings or vegetation. They followed Kriz to where the road met the island, giving way to a series of steps carved into the stone. She started up the steps immediately, whilst Clay and the others lingered at the bottom. The water on either side of the road seemed to be roiling now.

"Gotta be fifty or more," Loriabeth said, her beam tracking from one shimmering form to another. "Reckon I could get a couple. Even from here." She drew back the hammer on her revolver, aiming carefully. "How's about it, Lieutenant?" she asked Sigoral, who duly raised his carbine in readiness.

"We got maybe thirty rounds between us," Clay reminded them. He turned as Kriz called to them from the top of the steps, voicing a phrase in her own tongue that sounded far from complimentary. "Come on, looks like we're wanted. I doubt she'd've brought us here without good reason."

They followed the steps to the bare flat crest of the island, finding Kriz standing beside another plinth. As she touched the crystal set into the plinth, Clay and the others started in surprise at a sudden thrum of grinding rock beneath their feet. A near perfectly square cloud of dust rose a few feet away as a section of the island's surface descended then slid aside. Clay felt a rush of wind on his skin and saw the displaced dust being sucked into the revealed opening.

"That's weird," Loriabeth said, levelling her revolver at the opening.

"Air filling a vacuum," Sigoral said, stepping closer to peer into the gloomy depths below the hole. "A hermetically sealed chamber of some kind."

Kriz motioned for Loriabeth to hand over the lantern then moved to the opening, playing the beam around until it alighted on a series of iron rungs set into the wall. She handed the lantern back and began to descend, soon disappearing from view as the three of them continued to stand immobile. After a pause they heard her call out an impatient summons.

"If she meant us harm," Clay said, watching Loriabeth and Sigoral exchange a suspicious glance, "we'd already be dead ten times over."

Moving to the opening, he lowered himself onto the ladder and started down. The shaft proved to be about a dozen feet deep, Clay stepping off the ladder to find Kriz waiting at the bottom, surrounded by darkness. He called to Loriabeth to toss down her lantern, catching it and casting the light around to illuminate a long tunnel-like chamber. The walls were lined with racks containing what appeared to be mechanicals of some kind. Some were long, others short and stubby and most featured handgrips set behind what were unmistakably trigger mechanisms.

Guns, he realised, noting how each device bore a similarity in construction to Kriz's stubby weapon. Steel and brass merged together in an intricate harmony that no manufactory he knew of could match.

"Looks like she's brung us to an armoury," Clay told Loriabeth as she climbed down.

"Don't look like no iron I ever saw."

His cousin stepped closer to one of the objects, a shiny black device about two feet long. It had a grip and trigger like the others, and a narrow cylinder fixed to its upper side. Loriabeth touched a tentative hand to the object before taking a firmer hold and lifting it clear of the rack. "Got a barrel, right enough," she said, turning the object over in her hands. "Small bore, though. And it don't weigh much for a weapon." She raised the device to her shoulder, a smile coming to her lips as her eye came level with the cylinder. "A spy-glass," she said, a certain anticipatory delight colouring her voice. "Could shoot out a pigeon's eyes with this."

"Not a speck of rust," Clay saw, running a hand over an identical weapon.

"Preserved by the vacuum," Sigoral said from the base of the ladder. "These could have been stored down here for a very long time."

Kriz moved deeper into the chamber and returned carrying a much larger device. It was longer than the one in Loriabeth's hands and had a barrel with a bore larger than any shotgun Clay had seen. Kriz paused to retrieve a drum-shaped object from a near by rack and slotted it into the weapon's underside with a loud clack. That done, she returned to the ladder and began to climb up.

"At least show us how this works," Loriabeth called after her, patting the weapon she held. Kriz failed to respond and Clay quickly followed her up the ladder, Sigoral and Loriabeth close behind.

He found Kriz standing close to the edge of the island's crest, the weapon raised with its stock at her shoulder. On either side of the road the lake continued to roil as the massed Blues thrashed their long bodies, making their positions easy to mark despite the gloom.

Kriz began firing almost immediately, the weapon making a percussive popping sound with every shot, six in all loosed off in quick succession. Clay saw six bright waterspouts rise up amongst the Blues. There was a one-second delay then the water beneath the surface blossomed into a bright shade of white before erupting upwards in a series of explosions. Clay could see flashes of red amid the rising water, and the sight of one Blue cut in half by the force of the blasts. The beast's two constituent parts trailed blood as they cart-wheeled amidst the spume before plummeting down to land on the road with a wet crunch.

As the lake becalmed into dark unbroken placidity Kriz lowered the weapon and favoured Clay with one of the few smiles he had seen on her face. "Not . . . hungry now," she said.

The weapon's stock gave a faint pulse against Clay's shoulder as he pulled the trigger, a ten-foot-high geyser of water erupting in the centre of the black circle visible through the spy-glass.

"Over four hundred yards," Sigoral said, eyebrows raised as he looked at the weapon in his own hands. "Barely any recoil, or smoke."

Clay saw that he was right, lowering the weapon to see a thin tendril of greyish vapour escaping the barrel. They had remained on the island until the lights came again, catching a few hours' fitful sleep. Come the dawn Kriz began to educate them in the weapons from the armoury. Loriabeth, as might be expected, took to the task immediately, quickly learning how to load one of the carbine-like guns with a surprisingly small box that slotted into its underside. Clay watched her fire off fifty rounds before the box emptied. The weapon was apparently capable of reloading its chamber without the need for cocking or levers. Also, unlike any other repeating fire-arm he had seen, it ejected no cartridges. When removed the box was empty.

"Ever see the like?" he asked Sigoral.

"There were persistent rumours of a self-loading rifle being developed in the Emperor's workshops," the marine replied. "But I doubt it could compare to this." He smoothed a hand along the weapon's stock. "This . . . is a thing beyond our time, Mr. Torcreek."

A cacophonous burst of gunfire came from the right where Kriz was acquainting Loriabeth with a different device. It was much larger than the carbine-like weapons, bearing a vague resemblance to a longrifle in the dimensions of its barrel and stock. The similarity ended there, however, for it quickly became apparent this weapon could outrange a longrifle by a considerable margin, and fire a great many more bullets. It also produced more smoke than the carbines and the calibre of its barrel was at least twice the size. It was loaded via a drum that contained at least two hundred rounds. But its most salient feature was the fact that it would fire continuously at one pull of the trigger, emptying its copious magazine in a concentrated stream lasting all of ten seconds.

"Well, how about that," Loriabeth said, a broad grin on her face as she lowered the weapon, smoke leaking from the barrel. "Could take me a whole pack of Greens with this."

In addition to the weapons the armoury also yielded an additional pack of ingenious design, resembling a rolled blanket in the way it curved across Kriz's back. It appeared to have been fashioned from the same material as her belt, as were the set of clothes it contained which Kriz had been quick to swap for her borrowed garb. The clothing consisted of a loose-fitting, all-in-one garment that covered her from shoulders to knees. A deep fold at the neck could be formed into a cowl to cover her head. The pack also contained a pair of shoes which at first appeared little more than flimsy slippers, but subsequently proved impervious to rigours of the road.

"Clean?" Kriz asked after a long day's march, brows furrowed in response to Loriabeth's query.

"Yeah, how do I clean it?" She hefted the large weapon Kriz had given her, miming running a cloth over it. "All guns need cleaning or they'll foul up."

This seemed only to baffle Kriz more and she replied with a shrug.

"Perhaps it requires no cleaning," Sigoral said. Although clearly impressed by the weapons, the Corvantine's unease was obvious. The cause wasn't hard to divine, for Clay shared much the same sentiment. *Beyond our time . . .* They were like the Spoiled now, primitives struggling to understand seemingly magical novelties. It wasn't a comfortable feeling.

"We need to trance again," he told Kriz, miming the motion of injecting Blue into his arm. She drew back a little at the hard insistence in his voice, but once again replied with a shake of her head.

"It appears she has secrets to keep," Sigoral observed, eyeing Kriz carefully. "What exactly she's doing down here, for instance. And where exactly we're going."

"She's in the same fix we are," Loriabeth said. "She needs to get out. Right, hon?" She turned to Kriz, raising her voice and pointing a finger at the featureless sky above. "You got a way out, right?"

Kriz's hesitation was slight, fractional enough to be easily missed, but Clay saw it and knew her next words to be a lie. "Out," Kriz said, smiling and nodding. "Yes."

They moved on, tracking back along the road that had brought them to the island then resuming the same route as before. No more Blues appeared to trail them and the unbroken, waveless water took on a tedious monotony. Clay began to wonder if this place would consist of yet more sea all the way to the end, if it actually had an end. The tedium was finally broken when

Sigoral trained the spy-glass of his carbine on the road ahead and reported the sight of land.

"Blessed be the Seer," Loriabeth said, moving to Sigoral's side. "How's it look?"

"Steep."

The cliff came into view a short while later, a dark grey wall rising from the surface of this strange sea to over two hundred feet in height. Clay trained his own carbine on the top of the cliff, finding a dense mass of tree-tops and beyond them, the unmistakable sight of a mountain slope.

The road ended at the base of the cliff where it met a series of stone steps carved into the rock. They ascended in a zigzag series of flights to a height of about twenty feet whereupon they disappeared. It seemed a section of the cliff-face had become dislodged at some point in the past, taking the upper two-thirds of the staircase with it. Although Kriz's command of Mandinorian was still limited, she had developed a fondness for certain words. "Shit," she sighed before raising her gaze to the cliff-top.

"We're climbing, huh?" Clay asked. This drew an exasperated glower from Kriz and he understood that, for the first time, she had no notion of what to do next.

"Shouldn't take more than a few hours," Sigoral said, surveying the cliff with a critical eye. "I can see three relatively easy routes from here."

"You're joshing us, right?" Loriabeth said.

"Certainly not, miss," the marine replied, stiffening a little. "I used to climb the bluffs on Takmarin all the time. It's a common pastime for children. Market traders would give you a quarter-crown for every dozen puffin eggs you brought back."

"No puffins here," Clay said, playing the spy-glass of his carbine over the cliff-face. "No drakes either, for which we should be grateful."

Sigoral led them to what appeared to Clay to be an unremarkable stretch of cliff. The marine divested himself of his pack and weapons before looping their one length of rope across his chest. "It should be long enough to reach," he said, hands exploring the rock for a moment before finding a hold. "I'll fix it up top and you'll use it to follow."

"What about the gear?" Loriabeth asked.

"We'll haul it up after us. Someone will have to wait here and tie them to the rope, though."

Clay opted to be the last up the rope, waiting as he tracked the others' progress with the spy-glass on his carbine. Sigoral's expertise was evident in the way he navigated the cliff, hands and feet moving with steady surety as he made an unhurried ascent, reaching the top in less than an hour whereupon he cast the rope down for them to follow. Loriabeth went next, her progress considerably less fluid and subject to repeated pauses, but still reaching the top after a lengthy effort. Kriz's climb was faster, the woman displaying a natural athleticism in the way she hauled herself up the rope and Clay found his spy-glass lingering on her slender form as she climbed.

Not a good idea, he reproached himself, head suddenly filled with visions of Silverpin. Something his uncle had once said came to mind as he lowered the carbine: *No room in my company for a man who needs to learn the same lesson twice.*

Once Kriz had crested the cliff-edge he slung his carbine across his back, tightening the strap over his chest before taking hold of the rope and beginning to climb. His years in the Blinds had provided ample opportunities to educate himself in the finer points of scaling a wall, but a cliff proved more of a challenge. The uneven surface and the length of the climb soon birthed an ache in his limbs. Although his miraculously healed leg stood up to the strain, it became apparent after the first fifty feet or so that he had yet to fully recover from the trauma suffered in the forest.

He forced himself up another dozen feet of rope before stopping to rest, sweat bathing his face as he slumped against the rock and tried to figure the best way of manoeuvring his canteen to his lips. It was then that he felt a hard tug on the rope followed by the deep, guttural rattle of an angry drake.

Clay splayed his hands against the rock and slowly eased his body away from the cliff-face, raising his gaze to find it met by a pair of slitted yellow eyes. The Black was perched on a ledge about eight feet above, its long neck curving a little as it moved its head from side to side, the angry rattle still issuing from its throat as it opened its mouth to display an impressive set of teeth. Although its body was hidden by the ledge, Clay judged from the size of the Black's head that it was considerably larger than the other breeds they had seen so far, as large as an adolescent Red in the world above.

A torrent of thoughts ran through his mind, principally concerning the prospects of getting a grip on either his carbine or the product in his wallet. He discounted the product almost immediately, as the beast would be upon him long before he could get a vial to his lips. However, he calculated the odds of bringing his carbine to bear in time as scarcely any better. Instead, he opted to remain completely still and continue to stare into the Black's eyes.

"I ain't your enemy, big fella," he told the drake in a whisper, searching its gaze in the faint hope of finding some measure of understanding. "Even made friends with one of your cousins up top."

The Black's eyes narrowed as if in consideration and they continued to stare at each other, Clay feeling a tremble creep into his limbs as the strain of clinging to the rope started to tell. The moment stretched and he began to suspect he would fall to his death long before the beast decided whether to eat him. In the event, his cousin chose that moment to resolve the issue.

"Seer-dammit, Clay!" she yelled. "Get clear of my sights!"

The Black jerked in response to the shout, head snapping to the top of the cliff. Clay seized the chance, bracing his legs against the rock and pushing clear of the cliff at an angle so that he swung out, body spinning. The Black gave an angry screech, fixing its gaze on him once again and flaring a pair of very broad wings, crouching as it prepared to launch itself clear of the ledge. Its mouth gaped wide, a dreadfully familiar haze appearing as it summoned the requisite gases from its gut. The flames blossomed at the same instant as Loriabeth let loose with a burst of fire from her repeating rifle. Clay had time to watch the Black's head dissolve into a thick mist of shredded flesh and bone before the fire it had breathed caught the rope a few inches above his hands.

He could only continue to hold on and stare at the flames licking over the tightly braided cord. He watched it blacken and turn to ash, glowing strands unravelling and fragmenting in a strangely captivating sight that put him in mind of fire-flies rising from a field at twilight. As the rope snapped and he began to fall, he considered that for a last thought, it really wasn't all that bad.

CHAPTER 32

Lizanne

The house Julesin had taken her to sat in the middle of Chandler's Row, a promenade of decrepit terraced houses a few streets west from Sluiceman's Way. Lizanne emerged to find a thick column of smoke rising above the roof-tops in the vicinity of the citadel. She could also hear a faint but constant crackle of rifle fire. A few confused inmates loitered near by in various states of indecision, mostly non-affiliated midden-pickers who must have fled the Ore Day parade when Tinkerer's bomb went off.

"The citadel will fall within the hour!" Lizanne called to the dazed unfortunates. "If you want out of here you'll need to fight for it. Spread the word."

She turned as Makario stumbled from the doorway behind her, blinking rapidly as he gazed up at the pillar of smoke ascending into the grey sky. The Green had banished much of the pain left by Darkanis's beating, but he was yet to regain his full senses. "Did you do that?" he asked in an oddly calm tone, one eyebrow raised to a quizzical angle.

"Yes," she replied. "And I'm about to do a great deal more. Come on." She took hold of his arm, hurrying towards Sluiceman's Way and pulling him along.

They found the broad thoroughfare wreathed in a thick pall of acrid smoke and littered with both corpses and rubble. People ran past in panic, some deeper into the city, some towards the cacophony up ahead where rifle fire mingled with the sound of many voices raised in anger or fear. Lizanne saw a bright yellow flash in the smoke ahead, followed a split-second later by the boom of a cannon. She threw herself behind a part-demolished wall and dragged Makario down beside her, flinching at the multiple high-pitched whistles of canister-shot rending the surrounding air.

"So they didn't manage to kill the gun-crews," she muttered, poking her head above the wall. Somewhere a voice was screaming in the fog, the diminishing pitch of their distress telling of a mutilated soul fast approaching death.

"Such wonders you have wrought, my dear," Makario said, Lizanne hearing the unrestrained reproach in his voice.

"I suspect we'll both have a great deal to atone for when this is done," she replied, tugging him upright. "Stay close. We need to move quickly."

They ran from corner to corner and doorway to doorway, crouching low as bullets and canister tore at the drifting clouds of smoke, threading their way through rubble and knots of panicked inmates, all babbling rumours and confusion.

"They've started killing us all . . ."

"The Furies are trying to break out . . ."

"The Emperor's ordered the Constables to execute everyone . . ."

"Might I enquire," Makario said as they huddled behind yet another part-demolished building to avoid a volley of bullets. "Where exactly are we going?"

"I have to meet someone," she said, moving on quickly and obliging him to follow.

"And then what?" the musician persisted. "Forgive me, but I doubt an easy stroll through the gates is on the cards just now."

She said nothing and ran on, resisting the impulse to shorten the journey with a gulp or two of Green. Makario wouldn't have been able to keep up. Besides, she would probably have need of every drop of Julesin's supply before long.

She gave a small sigh of relief at finding Tinkerer exactly where she had told him to be: the exposed basement at the eastern end of Pick Street. He stood alone, regarding her with typical impassivity as she jumped down to join him. She expected some nervousness at the sight of Makario but Tinkerer merely glanced at the musician before turning to her. "You're late," he said.

"Unforeseen difficulties." She jerked her head towards the river, away from the citadel and the continuing chorus of gun-fire. "Come along then."

She led them to the muddy fringes of the river-bank then towards the grate beside the outlet pipe where she had first made her entry to Scorazin. "You have your other devices ready?" she asked Tinkerer. He stepped wordlessly to the grate, reaching into a sack to extract what appeared to be a rough-hewn lump of fist-sized clay with a short length of wire protruding from the top. He fixed the lump to the barrier's heavy lock, working the still-soft clay around the contours.

"It's advisable not to look," he added before striking a match and touching it to the fuse, immediately stepping back and shielding his eyes.

Lizanne managed to turn away before the device ignited. Makario wasn't so lucky.

"Owww!" he squealed. Lizanne opened her eyes to see him clutching at his own, tears streaming down his cheeks. "Thank you very fucking much, sir!" he fumed at Tinkerer, rapidly blinking his reddened orbs. "As if this day hadn't been a sufficient trial already. What is that stuff?"

"A combustible copper-and-magnesium core with a dense silicate coating for insulation," Tinkerer replied, seemingly unruffled by the musician's ire. Lizanne looked at the grate, seeing a last guttering of sparks fall from the lock, which had been transformed into a steaming tear-drop of molten iron. She pulled at the grate, finding she had to give several hard tugs before it came free.

"Stay close and move fast," she told them, stepping into the gloom.

She took one of Julesin's vials from her pocket and sipped some Green to boost her vision before starting down the tunnel. Memorising the route to this entry point had been well within her expertise and following it out was a simple matter. They soon came to the second grate where Darkanis had left her that first day. Lizanne stood back, averting her gaze as Tinkerer affixed a second device to the lock. It was then that she noticed Makario was missing.

She hissed his name, enhanced eyes piercing the gloomy confines of the tunnels but catching no sign of him. Then her ears, also bolstered by the effects of Green, detected a faint scrabbling sound. *What is he doing?*

"Keep at it," she told Tinkerer. "Don't proceed without me."

She moved away, making for the source of the scraping sound in a crouching run. Makario came into view around the next bend. The musician was on his knees, clawing barehanded at some loose brickwork in the tunnel wall with an energy that put her in mind of a giant rat. He glanced up as she approached, blinking his still-bleary eyes at her, an eager grin on his lips.

"He couldn't risk taking it out through the guard-house," he said, turning back to pull another brick from the wall. "Not all at once. Only the tiniest bit at a time."

Lizanne crouched at his side, peering into the hole he had created. Despite the Green it was hard to make out the contents of this hiding-place, then she saw a dim patch of light catch the coarse weave of sackcloth. "Dar-kanis's silver ore," she realised.

"Yes." Makario grunted as he levered another brick from the wall. "Con-siderate of him to pile it all up in one place for us, wasn't it?"

Lizanne reached out and grasped his hand. "We don't have time."

She could see Makario's stricken, desperate face in the gloom. "Krista, there's enough for both of us. Enough to bribe every magistrate in Corvus. I can have a new name, a new life . . ."

His voice trailed off into a whine as she dragged him to his feet, keeping hold of his arm and making her way back to the grate. "Please . . ."

"Shut up or I'll leave you here," she ordered, suddenly infuriated by his greed.

They found Tinkerer standing beside the opened grate, a foul odour rising from the ruined lock. "I don't know how many constables will be waiting," she said, moving through the portal, still dragging Makario along. "Most will have been drawn to the fighting, but there will be others who'll have contrived to stay behind. Leave them to me . . ."

She fell silent and came to a halt as a new sound reached her ears. A deep, rushing sound that made the tunnel tremble from floor to ceiling.

"Run!" She turned and began shoving them both back along the passage. "They've flooded the tunnels! RUN!"

It took at most thirty frantic seconds to get clear of the tunnel, Lizanne exhausting her Green as she conveyed her two companions none-too-gently back through the first grate and onto the muddy river-bank. The water came rushing out a heart-beat later, a roaring torrent that sent the three of them sprawling into the mud. For a moment Lizanne entertained the grim notion that they might drown but then the torrent began to abate. She checked to ensure the others were still alive then began to pry herself loose from the mud, grunting with the effort.

"Don't!"

Lizanne's gaze snapped up to find Anatol standing atop the outflow pipe, eyes as hard as his voice. He held one of the cross-bows captured from the Scuttlers, the dull gleam of the bolt unwavering as he aimed it at her chest. Still imprisoned by the mud Lizanne could only lie still and watch as a bulky silhouette appeared on the bank behind Anatol.

"To think I was actually starting to like you," Electress Atalina said.

An expertly placed punch slammed into the centre of Lizanne's back, sending her face-first onto the hard floor of the basement. Air rushed from her lungs as something large and heavy pressed against her spine, pinning her in place. Lizanne bit down on a shout as the pressure increased, nostrils filling with a thick gust of cigarillo smoke as someone leaned low to whisper into her ear.

"Don't mistake me," the Electress said, speaking as if there had been no interval between their capture at the river and the short but punishing journey to the basement of the Miner's Repose. The inn itself had been ruined by a cannon shell, but the basement apparently remained open for business. "I always knew I'd have to kill you, just not so soon, and long before you contrived to bring the whole city down around us. Still, that's what sentiment gets you."

"I—" Lizanne's breath scattered grit across the floor as she fought to add her voice to the last vestiges of breath the Electress forced from her body, the words emerging in a garbled torrent, "I'm a Blood-blessed Ironship operative I can get you out . . ."

The pressure paused, then relaxed a little. "Ironship? You expect me to swallow that shit, dear?"

"It's true," Lizanne heard Makario say. "I watched her kill Darkanis."

"Your word isn't worth a rat's turd to me just now," the Electress told him. A brief pause for consideration then the pressure disappeared from Lizanne's back, leaving her gasping on the floor.

"Get up," the Electress commanded. "So much as twitch and Anatol will put a bolt through your skull."

Lizanne rose to her feet, keeping her hands out from her sides, fingers splayed. The Electress stood a few feet away in a state of bloody dishevelment. Never particularly elegant she now appeared almost monstrous, her face covered in dust save for the patch of congealed blood stretching from hair to jaw-line. She held a large oak-wood cudgel in one meaty fist. Lizanne saw fragments of bone sticking to the gore covering its gnarled head.

"Constable skulls crack just like any other," the Electress explained.

The basement roof had acquired a large hole and Lizanne could see Furies peering down at them, most bearing the minor scars and bleached features of those who have survived recent battle. She counted perhaps thirty in total, with one notable absence.

"Where's Melina?" she asked.

"Lying in front of the Citadel with half her head blown off," the Electress said. "Where the fuck d'you think?"

I'm sorry. Fearing Anatol's reaction Lizanne left the words unsaid, even though she was surprised to find her regret genuine. She also saw it mirrored in the slight stiffening of Tinkerer's posture; she had been the only friend he could claim in this place after all.

"The Learned Damned?" Lizanne asked, returning her gaze to the Electress.

"Holed up on the far end of Sifter's Corner, what's left of them. That bomb you had them hide in the ore made a right mess of the Citadel but left two of the cannon intact. They must've cut down a hundred or more trying to rush the breach. Then the whole garrison sallied out, shooting down everyone still standing. Your genius scheme has wrought a great deal of havoc, my dear. But I suppose that was the point. A nice big diversion to draw every constable in the gatehouse to the Citadel whilst you and Tinkerer sneak out through the tunnels." Her gaze shifted to the slender artificer, narrowing in consideration. "What's so special about him anyway?"

"He's worth a lot to my employer," Lizanne said. "Anyone assisting me in securing his safe passage from Scorazin will be handsomely compensated."

"Which means I may have need of him." The Electress's fingers flexed on her cudgel, her wide mouth forming a smile. "But not you."

"You need me to get you out."

Atalina surprised her with a laugh before replying in a precise, almost sympathetic tone. It reminded Lizanne of those card-players who enjoyed enumerating the mistakes of less expert opponents. "You silly, ignorant bitch. Didn't it occur to you that the Emperor's architects might have anticipated this? All the constables have to do is raise one sluice gate and the river will flood the tunnels. You were never getting out of here, and now half my people are dead." The Electress stepped closer, the smile fading from her lips as her eyes grew bright in anticipation. "So, as I was saying, I don't need you. And any day I get to kill a Blood-blessed is a good one. It's thanks to fuckers like you I'm in here."

"I can silence the cannon," Lizanne said, raising her voice so the onlooking Furies above could hear. "With the cannon gone the breach will be open, everyone will have a chance to escape."

She saw the onlookers stir at this, gazes previously filled with grim enjoyment of her imminent demise now lighting with fresh hope.

"The nearest Imperial garrison is less than two days' march from Scorazin," Lizanne went on, voice raised even louder. "And you can bet that a messenger will already be galloping towards them with a call for reinforcements. You know what will happen when they get here. Open rebellion cannot be tolerated. Our lives mean nothing, the Emperor can always find more slaves for his mines. We either escape or we die."

She met the Electress's gaze, seeing a lust for retribution vie with the career criminal's ingrained instinct for survival. "You've done impressive things in here," Lizanne told her, lowering her voice. "Think what you could do out there."

It took over two hours to gather what remained of the gangs and other survivors persuaded or coerced into taking part in this desperate gamble. Chuckling Sim and Varkash had both survived the initial massacre, along with about two-thirds of their affiliated members. King Coal, however, hadn't been so lucky. By all accounts the Scuttlers' leader had met his end in surprisingly heroic, if typically enraged, fashion, hurling himself into the advancing line of constables armed only with a half brick. It seemed Kevozan had managed to crush the skulls of no less than three constables before a volley of rifle fire ripped him apart from groin to chest. Lacking an obvious successor, the Scuttlers had fragmented into several loosely organised subgroups. Luckily, they hadn't required much persuasion before agreeing to lend their strength to the Electress's proposal. Neither had the Verdigris nor the Wise Fools for that matter, Chuckling Sim and Varkash both displaying a fatalistic awareness of their current predicament.

"We were all on borrowed time from the moment we came through the gate," Sim said with a shrug before favouring Lizanne with one of his overly florid bows. "I should thank this gracious lady for at least offering a chance to breathe clean air once more, however slender."

Varkash's response had been less eloquent, voiced in his nasal twang that now seemed markedly less comical. "A short death is bedder dan a long one."

The pragmatism of the criminal element, however, was not shared by those of a more political mind-set.

348 · ANTHONY RYAN

"Corporate whore!" Helina's left arm was constrained by a sling, but her right was both unharmed and possessed of an impressive strength and swiftness. She flew at Lizanne with knife in hand, obliging her to dodge aside but not before the blade had sliced open the sleeve of her overalls, leaving an inch-long cut on the flesh beneath. The diminutive woman's fury was such that it took several moments for Demisol and the two other surviving radicals to subdue her.

"Better get a leash on her," the Electress advised as Helina continued to thrash in her comrades' grip, spitting expletive-laden invective at Lizanne all the while.

"Lying, profiteering cunt!"

"You must admit she has a point," Atalina said to Lizanne before stepping forward and driving a meaty fist into Helina's midriff, which left her retching on the floor.

"Rest assured I share your sentiments," the Electress said, stepping back to address the radicals as one. "But we have little option but to trust this one." She nodded at Lizanne with a humourless smile. "Lying cunt though she is."

Demisol crouched at Helina's side, gathering her small form into a protective embrace. He shot a hate-filled glare at Lizanne before turning to the Electress. "What do you need from us?"

"A distraction," Lizanne said. "Do you have any explosives left?"

The Citadel resembled a cake which had been attacked by a greedy giant. Tinkerer's bomb had carved out a twelve-foot-wide breach in the wall as well as demolishing much of the inner structure all the way to the main gate. Lizanne could just make out the huge barrier through the gloomy crevice, less than three hundred yards away. With the guns still in place it might as well have been a thousand. After their first sally the constables had retreated into a tight perimeter around the base of the citadel, crouching behind rubble piled into a barricade and firing at any inmates who dared show themselves in the streets. The intervening ground was liberally dotted with corpses, victims of the constables' homicidal frenzy as they beat back the first disorganised rush of would-be escapees.

"Stay close to the Electress," Lizanne told Tinkerer. "If anyone is likely to make it through the gate alive, it's her."

They crouched together in the remains of a house opposite the breach.

The building had taken the brunt of the constables' cannon fire, providing some useful piles of shattered brick for cover. It was late evening now and the shadows were growing long. Torches fluttered atop the barricade and the raised walls flanking the breach. Lizanne watched Tinkerer complete the modifications to the only bomb remaining from the supply she had provided to the Learned Damned. She kept hoping to hear the tumult of confusion heralding the Brotherhood's assault on the outer keep, but so far there had been no sign of their arrival. She could only conclude the assault had already been launched and the Brotherhood defeated or, for reasons unknown, they hadn't yet arrived. In either case, it was obvious she couldn't rely on that particular diversion now.

"To clarify your meaning," Tinkerer replied, not looking up as his deft hands did their work, "you have calculated your own odds of survival as minimal."

Lizanne ignored his observation, taking Julesin's wallet from her pocket and extracting all three vials. "There may be friends of mine waiting on the other side," she said. "Members of The Co-respondent Brotherhood. Make yourself known to a man of military bearing named Arberus. He'll be the tallest one among them. He will convey you to my employers."

"Your tone indicates a suspicion this man may no longer be alive. In which case what course am I to follow?"

"Make your way to an Ironship holding by whatever means necessary. When you do, report to the company offices and tell them you have information for Director Bloskin. Mentioning my name will probably expedite matters."

"I do not know your name."

"Lizanne Lethridge." She concentrated her gaze on the barricade, judging the best angle of attack. "Pleased to meet you."

"A name shared by the inventor of the thermoplasmic engine," Tinkerer said. She detected a rare animation to his voice, a slight upturn in tone that could indicate he was actually impressed. "A relative of yours, perhaps?"

"My father, though he let my grandfather take the credit. It's a long and tedious story, best saved for another time." She turned to him, seeing the paleness of his complexion beneath the pall of dust. *He's terrified.* She almost laughed at the realisation, having thought such base emotion beyond him. "Do you have a name?" she asked. "A real one?"

"'Boy' when I was small. 'Tinkerer' when I grew."

"I'm afraid that simply won't do in civilised company. We'll need to think of something else when time allows." She turned back towards the Citadel, removing the stoppers from the vials. "When you're ready," she said, putting all three vials to her lips.

Tinkerer tightened a screw on the bomb's carapace and held it out it to her. "Three-second fuse."

She swallowed about half the vials' contents in a single gulp, fighting down the resultant wave of nausea at the acrid taste and the instant ache the substandard dilutions birthed in her skull. Despite the product's lack of refinement, its potency couldn't be denied, her body seeming to thrum as the Green flooded through muscle and sinew, bringing a much-missed focus to her eyes. She took the bomb from Tinkerer's outstretched hand, primed the fuse and hurled it at the barricade, the Green providing sufficient range to ensure it fell just beyond the barrier.

She heard a few shouts of alarm from the constables as the bomb landed in their midst, accompanied by some panicked firing in expectation of an imminent assault. The firing intensified when the bomb detonated, not with a blinding explosion but a dull boom. The smoke blossomed immediately, the result of a chemical concoction Tinkerer had derived from a mix of sulphur, salt and steamed milk. The yellow cloud soon covered about half the barricade's length, proving sufficiently dense to obscure the barrier from view, though Lizanne knew it would last only a few seconds.

"Remember, stay close to the Electress," she repeated before drawing her knife and vaulting over the ruined wall. She covered the distance to the barricade in the space of a few heart-beats. The smoke would have blinded her but for the Green in her veins, and the constables were not so fortunate. Some were coughing and stumbling about in confusion, others firing wildly into the haze. She leapt the barricade, killed the nearest constable with a single slash of her knife, the force of the blow sending him spinning like a top, blood spraying from the gaping rent in his neck. A rifle-bullet snapped the air an inch from Lizanne's ear and she whirled, lashing out with a round-house kick that sent the rifleman reeling.

She paused to finish him with the knife then took up his rifle, holding it by the barrel as she moved through the swirling yellow mist, clubbing down four more constables in quick succession until the weapon broke in two and she tossed it aside. The smoke had begun to thin now, revealing the breach and the walls on either side. The gun-crews were busily readying their pieces, Lizanne recognising the cylindrical shells being double-loaded into the barrels.

She chose the gun on the right and sprinted for the wall, leaping high and latching onto the brickwork before scaling the remaining distance in a rapid scramble that denuded much of her Green. A gunner appeared at the top of the wall just as she reached it, eyes wide with terror as he levelled a revolver at her chest. He was just out of arm's reach so she resorted to Black, plucking the revolver from his grip before unleashing a pulse that sent him flying backwards into the rest of the crew. She opened her hand to receive the stolen revolver and exhausted her remaining Green in eliminating the gun-crew, enhanced reflexes and vision combining to put a bullet in each gunner's forehead in less than four seconds.

She ducked at the sound of a barked command to her rear, bullets whining over her head to smack into the walls and the bodies of the fallen constables. Lizanne turned to see four gunners on the other side of the breach reloading their rifles. Beyond them a sergeant and two others were desperately manoeuvring their gun towards her. Lizanne turned her gaze to the gun standing a few feet to her right, an aged but serviceable six-pounder freshly loaded with two canister shells and a fuse already pressed into the firing port. She used her Black to push it around, raising the trail of the carriage to depress the barrel before unleashing a thin stream of Red to light the fuse.

The recoil sent the gun careening backwards with sufficient force to buckle its carriage and leave it lying on its side, but not before it had fired its payload directly at the other gun-crew. Lizanne got to her feet as the smoke cleared, finding that the other gun was intact, whilst what remained of its crew had been decorated onto the surrounding brickwork.

A great roar drew her gaze to the city in time to see what appeared to be its entire population rushing from the ruins. The Electress was in the lead with Anatol at her side and the surviving Furies at their backs. They were flanked by the Verdigris and the Wise Fools, clubs and makeshift spears waving and every throat voicing a cry so rich in blood-lust Lizanne found it pained her ears. Behind the three main gangs came the Scuttlers, their ranks swollen by the minor gangs plus those midden-pickers and mud-slingers who retained sufficient vitality to run.

The horde swept across the open ground like a dark tide, apparently immune to the bullets cast at it by the surviving constables, overwhelming the barricade in an unstoppable frenzy of rage and desperation. Those constables not killed instantly tried to run but were soon swallowed by the mob and torn to pieces. Within a few moments the barricade had disappeared, Lizanne seeing the impaled heads of several constables held aloft in jubilation as the river of unwashed criminality flowed through the breach and on towards the gate.

Lizanne paused to retrieve the revolver's holster and ammunition from the body of its owner before drinking a large dose of Green. After clambering down into the now-densely-packed throng below she was obliged to force her way through to the gate, shoving numerous inmates aside and being none-too-gentle about it. Her way became easier when constables appeared in the exposed walkways above and began to assail the crowd with rifle fire. Screams of pain and outrage rose as a dozen or more inmates fell to the first volley. In response many streamed into the corridors and doorways laid open by the Tinkerer's bomb, an animalistic cacophony echoing through the hallways as they hunted down the riflemen and exacted bestial revenge. Several uniformed bodies landed in Lizanne's path as she continued her journey to the gate.

She paused for a second at the sight of one constable's body, lying in a twisted tangle atop another corpse clad in unusually dapper clothing. She hauled the constable's body aside, revealing Chuckling Sim's bleached and frozen features. A bullet had removed much of his upper skull but somehow his lips had contrived to retain some vestige of a grin even in death. The resultant flare of guilt was a surprise; the man had been scum after all. *Like Melina, and the Learned Damned and every other wretch deservedly consigned to this place.* But still the guilt lingered as she pressed on. Scum or not, they would have lived if she hadn't come here.

A dense knot of inmates assailed the gate, the tree-sized cross-bar and huge iron hinges groaning under the pressure, but as yet showing no signs of giving. She found the Electress alongside Anatol and Varkash at the fore of the throng and was gratified to see Tinkerer had followed her orders and stayed at the Electress's side. His face remained as blank as ever, though there was a brightness to his eyes that told of unabated terror.

"Heave you fuckers!" Atalina yelled, pressing her own bulk against the door, the others all following suit. The huge barrier bowed under the weight of so many bodies, but once again failed to break.

"Move back!" Lizanne shouted, shouldering her way through the crowd. "I need room."

"Hoped you were dead by now," the Electress said, stepping back from the gate. Lizanne noted she had one hand firmly clamped onto Tinkerer's arm. A prize not to be given up lightly. She also noted that Anatol still had his cross-bow. "She played her part," he said, moving to the side and unslinging the cross-bow, blocky features hard with grief and a deep desire for retribution.

Seeing little point in discussion, Lizanne used Black to force the weapon up so that the bolt jabbed into the underside of Anatol's chin. His slab-like features twitched as he glowered at her, a thin trickle of blood staining the steel tip of the cross-bow bolt. "I'm sorry about Melina," Lizanne told him, hoping he could hear the sincerity in her voice. "But we have no time for this."

From outside came a tumult of gun-shots and raised voices, indicating that the Brotherhood had finally arrived to launch their assault. Judging by the intensity of the cacophony, it appeared they were facing much stiffer resistance than expected.

We're running out of time, she thought, releasing Anatol and retreating a few steps. *Too big to shatter or burn,* she decided, raising her gaze to the giant cross-bar above then reaching once more for Julesin's vials. She drank all but a small drop of the remaining Black, gritting her teeth against the queasy growl it birthed in her gut, then focused her gaze on the cross-bar. The first controlled release of power raised the bar barely a foot before it slammed back into place. Lizanne focused on one end of the bar and unleashed all the Black at once, the huge slab of timber tilting to the left then slowly sliding through the massive iron brackets before falling away, inmates scurrying clear as it tumbled to earth, scattering dust and rubble.

For a moment no one moved, all staring at Lizanne or the unbarred gate as if unable to comprehend the simple and obvious fact of their liberation.

Lizanne drew her revolver and strode forward, pressing her shoulder to the gate. "Best if you tell your people to gather all the rifles they can," she told the Electress. "There'll be more fighting to do outside."

CHAPTER 33

Sirus

"Dinish-kahr," Sirus repeated the name aloud, enjoying the novelty of hearing his own voice after such a long period of silence. "And the literal meaning?"

The Spoiled warrior regarded him with a flat gaze, not exactly hostile, but hardly welcoming either. Even within this army of joined minds differences persisted, social and cultural loyalties lingering among the transformed, and none more so than the tribal contingent. Sirus could share their memories at will, as they could share his, save for those he had learned to hide deep within himself. Despite this connection the indigenous Arradsians remained largely an enigma. Without context or a more fundamental understanding of their language and customs, the memories he took from them were often little more than a mish-mash of image and sensation containing no clue as to their significance.

"I know you understand me," Sirus reminded the warrior when he failed to respond verbally, instead conveying another enigmatic image from his memory, dark, capering figures silhouetted against a roaring fire. "Speak." Sirus underlined the command with a mental reminder of his authority. It was only a brief image of the White in flight but it tended to have a dramatic effect on the tribals.

The warrior spoke Varsal in slow deliberate tones, as if worried he might mispronounce the words, even though they were near perfect, albeit coloured by a lower-class Morsvale accent.

"Flame-dancer."

"This is your name?"

The warrior's thoughts betrayed fearful confusion, indicating the question was beyond his understanding. "Sirus is my name." Sirus patted his chest then pointed to the tribal. "Your name is Dinish-kahr? You are Flame-dancer?"

"Dinish-kahr." A glimmer of understanding rose in the warrior's mind as he mimicked Sirus's gesture then pointed at a group of fellow tribals standing near by. They all wore similar clothing, garishly decorated armour of hardened leather Sirus knew to be typical of the plains tribes, another example of cultural distinctiveness that continued to resist the unifying effects of their transformation. "Dinish-kahr," the warrior repeated as he pointed. "They are Flame-dancer." He stopped pointing then patted his chest again. "I am Flame-dancer."

Sirus glanced at the other tribals who all stood with heads tilted as they viewed the conversation, spined brows creasing in puzzlement. "You are all Flame-dancer," he realised. "You do not have individual names."

He sensed a new understanding take hold in the warrior's mind at that moment, the fellow issuing a grunt and stepping back, his slitted eyes narrowing. *You didn't know there was such a thing as an individual name?* Sirus enquired, slipping into non-verbal communication. *Did you?*

The warrior grunted again, his hand tightening on his war-club. His fellow tribals stirred in concert, hostility flaring in their minds.

The gift of knowledge is not always welcome, boy.

Sirus turned as Morradin strolled clear of the trees, a rifle slung over his shoulder as he dragged the corpse of a small deer behind him. *Best leave the savages alone, lest you attract the ire of our White god. I think he prefers them as they are, don't you?*

Sirus withdrew his thoughts from the warrior with a pulse of gratitude. The tribal failed to reciprocate, Sirus feeling him striving to close his mind as he returned to his companions. The group of tribals cast uneasy glances at Sirus as they retreated into the jungle. Like most of the indigenous contingent they preferred to live in their own groups at a remove from the main camps.

Might be the last one of these buggers left on this rock, Morradin commented, dumping the deer carcass next to his camp-fire. It had been a familiar story with every island they took, an abundance of game quickly denuded by so many hungry mouths. Since the fall of the King's Cradle they had begun a westward expansion of the White's dominions, taking six large islands in quick succession. The loss of their Blood-blessed king seemed to have had a demoralising and divisive effect on the Islanders. Individual settlements still resisted fiercely, many with modern arms provided by the Ironship Protectorate. But the disciplined and well-organised opposition they had faced at the Cradle was gone. Without appropriate training and tactics to make the best use of their weapons they could only delay the inevitable. Consequently, the White's army had soon made good its losses and begun to swell its ranks, despite the efforts of the Maritime Protectorate.

"Another bombardment this morning," he told Morradin, speaking in Varsal as a deliberate jab at the marshal's undiminished snobbery. "A sortie by three frigates against the encampments on the northern shore, all blood-burners. We lost nearly a hundred Spoiled until the Blues chased them off."

"I'm aware," Morradin replied in pointed Eutherian. "Nuisance raids only. If they were smart they'd cram every soldier in the Protectorate onto their fleet and send them to crush us. Instead they seek to moderate their expenses in the vain hope the Islanders will do the job for them. Typical corporate thinking."

Sirus detected an undercurrent of unease in the marshal's thoughts. Since his conversion Morradin had developed an ability to shield his mind from all but the most persistent intrusion, employing the mental discipline and rigidly organised mind of a career soldier to impressive effect. But even he couldn't suppress every emotion, especially his fears which Sirus found to be surprisingly potent for such a celebrated hero of the empire. Latching onto the unease, Sirus tried to probe further, stripping away the surface feelings of undimmed hatred of his continued enslavement to catch a glimpse of the deeper sensations beneath. He managed to capture only one image before Morradin clamped down on his thoughts with a snarl of rage.

"Who do you imagine you are, boy?" he grated, Sirus finding himself staring into the barrel of a revolver. Morradin's voice quivered with anger but his arm, and the pistol, remained steady. The marshal's emotions were raging now, ego-stoked fires of indignation burning so bright Sirus almost expected smoke to start pouring from his flared nostrils. "I have flogged men to death with my own hand for the merest flicker of insolence," Morradin continued in a strangled whisper. "And yet you paw at me with your filthy, vulgarian mind and expect no punishment . . ."

That's enough now, Mr. Marshal.

Sirus followed Morradin's gaze as it flicked to the right, finding Katrya standing with a rifle at her shoulder, the barrel levelled at the marshal's head. Sirus's entire company of two hundred Spoiled were falling in on either side of her, all raising their rifles to aim at the same target. Sirus felt a murmur ripple through the camp as the sudden discord spread from mind to mind. For a moment there was a swirl of uncertainty as each individual calculated their allegiance. Some former soldiers retained an ingrained sense of loyalty towards their one-time commander, but it was a grudging, resentful attachment to servile custom many were quick to discount. Amongst the Morsvale townspeople there was no such sentiment, long-held grievances and detestation of the Imperial yoke bubbling to the fore with rising heat. The Islanders, of course, had no sympathy of any kind for the marshal whilst the tribals regarded the whole episode with a confused indifference. Despite the joining of thousands of minds, it took less than a second for the decision to be reached and the decision was unambiguous. The army had chosen a new general.

Morradin staggered as the collective will bore down, groaning in pain as he slumped to his knees, the pistol slipping from his grip.

Kill him, darling, Katrya told Sirus, her mind shining with pride and exultation. She came to his side, proffering her rifle. *What use is he now, anyway?*

A shadow fell on them then, large enough to blot the sun as great wings beat the air to raise dust into a dense fog. As one the army subsided to its knees, forced into subservience by a will far greater than their own, bodies and minds seized by a vise of all-consuming fear. To his surprise Sirus found he had been spared and so stood staring up at the hovering form of the White, rendered black against the midday sun. Although the White had somehow contrived to exclude him from the wave of terror that laid his comrades low, Sirus was not immune to fear. The intoxicating rush of alarm that had seized him during his confrontation with the Shaman King returned now to birth a tremble in his limbs, though he managed to keep his eyes raised, unwilling to succumb to any craven inclination in what he fully expected to be his last moments.

He could feel the White's displeasure, poised like an executioner's blade, but coloured once again by the familiar sense of frustration. The small creatures under its sway were once again proving troublesome and it didn't understand why. Sirus grunted in disgust as the beast's mind touched his own, rummaging through memory and sensation with clumsy violence, soon fixating on his various interactions with Morradin, each one soured by mutual antagonism. The White issued a faint hiss that might have been a sigh, or another expression of annoyance, before withdrawing its intrusion from Sirus's mind. It paused for a moment and Sirus experienced a wave of confusion as it forced its thoughts into a comprehensible query, its attention now firmly fixed on Morradin's cowering form.

Still . . . useful?

The temptation to provide a negative reply was strong. Morradin was not a man who improved upon prolonged acquaintance and if this situation had been in any way normal Sirus would have felt scant regret at the man's death. But then, for all his faults, he and Morradin shared the same ignominy, and slaves could not revolt if they succumbed to disunity. He buried the rebellious notion by summoning a fresh wave of fear. Of all the various tricks he used to shield his mind, the Shaman's final gift was proving the most effective.

Useful, he confirmed to the White. *His mind is . . . unique.* Feeling the White's anger rise as it failed to grasp the unfamiliar concept Sirus went on quickly. *He has strategies, knowledge that will bring victory.*

The White hung in the air a moment longer, its wings maintaining a steady, majestic rhythm as its eyes glowed bright in the blank silhouette of its form. *Victory,* its voice repeated in Sirus's mind, accompanying the word with an image, the same image Sirus had plucked from Morradin's mind only moments before: an archipelago, the islands small clusters of green amid a vast blue sea, as if viewed from a great distance and considerable height. Sirus had never visited these islands but they were familiar to anyone who had ever viewed a map of the world. *The Tyrell Islands, where the entire might of the Ironship Maritime Protectorate has gathered to oppose us.*

Victory, the White repeated a final time before twisting its huge body about and flying away.

"Trying to break through the Protectorate fleet will be suicide." Since his loss of status Morradin insisted on communicating verbally, and then only in Eutherian. He kept his thoughts under tight control, allowing only rare bursts of outright hatred to escape his shields, much of it directed at Sirus. "Those confounded repeating guns of theirs will cut us to pieces," he went on. "And you can bet they've been busily manufacturing as many as possible since they lost their Arradsian holdings."

In the days since his elevation to army commander Sirus had formed the host's most astute minds into an ad hoc General Staff. His deduction that individuality was not overthrown by conversion had been proved correct. An unprejudiced search through the network of conjoined minds revealed some that shone like stars in a clouded sky. Consequently his staff was a surprisingly disparate group. A junior engineering professor from Morsvale Imperial College sat alongside an artillery sergeant who took evident satisfaction from his former general's diminished circumstances. The flogging the man had received as a boy soldier was often at the forefront of his thoughts. Next to him sat a robust woman of middling years who had run a dock-side tavern for the previous two decades, amassing a considerable fortune in smuggling revenue in the process. At her side sat a scrawny Islander girl a little over fourteen years in age who had somehow nurtured a remarkable gift for mathematics despite an upbringing devoid of formal education. The final member of this group was the most surprising, a veteran tribal warrior of impressive stature who stood apart from the others with his gaze averted. His sparse garb revealed him to be a member of one of the jungle tribes, all sharing a name which Sirus approximated as meaning Forest Spear. Unlike his indigenous brethren this man exhibited a growing understanding of his new comrades, his thoughts displaying a remarkable facility for language and a keen-eyed perception. However, the fellow's lifelong attachment to his tribal culture lingered like a dark cloud in his mind and each new insight was accompanied by a flare of guilt, as if enlightenment equated to blasphemy.

"The Blues can keep them bottled up in the harbour," Sirus said, speaking in Eutherian as a sop to Morradin's continued pique. It had been tempting to heap yet more humiliation on him, but he suspected it would prove counter-productive. He would need to succour all allies, however vile, if they were ever to escape this curious and terrible bondage. For now, however, the White's desire for victory was a constant ache, dispelling all other considerations.

And the Reds can attack from the air, the artillery sergeant added, summoning a map of the islands from memory. *Whilst our fleet lands the army on the beaches to the west.*

"Our mighty fleet," Morradin rasped, allowing his scorn to colour his thoughts, "is a rag-bag collection of merchant ships and barges. The Protectorate will be bound to have at least one flotilla patrolling the approaches to the islands. The Blues and Reds could see them off, to be sure, but the cost will be high and our White god is jealous of the lives of his fellow drakes. Even assuming we can break through their cordon, by the time it's done the full weight of the Protectorate High Seas Fleet will be bearing down on us, all bristling with repeating cannon."

A new thought crept into their collective, a faint image slipping from the mind of Forest Spear with reluctant insistence: a trio of Green drakes creeping through tall grass towards a solitary Green feasting on the carcass of some unfortunate animal. Sirus watched as the trio moved closer to the Green whereupon they stood up as one, the scaly hides falling away to reveal tribal warriors holding bows. They loosed their arrows in unison, the shafts sinking into the head of the Green, which flailed about for a time, casting flames which set the long grass ablaze.

Forest Spear let the image fade before sharing a final thought: *To kill a thing, become that thing.*

Sirus replayed the tribal's memory several times before turning to Morradin once more. "Where would you expect the Protectorate to launch their next raid?"

III

THE GATHERING CALL

FIERY DESTRUCTION
ENGULFS SANORAH DOCKS

Many Ships Burned and Sunk at Anchor

Riots Erupt in the Dockside

Identity of "Blessed Demon" Revealed by Our Correspondent

Last night saw our great city of Sanorah subject to a level of destruction not seen since the eruption of civil discord following the collapse of the Blood Bubble some eighty-six years ago. Whilst loyal readers of the *Intelligencer* will be familiar with this paper's tireless dedication to honest reporting, the exact series of events which resulted in last night's calamity have yet to be established and some of the confirmed facts are certain to arouse incredulity. We must, therefore, appeal to our readers' trust that they are being presented with the unalloyed truth.

At approximately fifteen minutes past the tenth hour on the 23rd of Rosellum a large conflagration erupted in the warehouse district abutting the Sanorah Dockside. The flames spread quickly from building to building, the intensity of the blaze being blamed, at least partly, on the fact that many warehouses had been stocked to full capacity. The crash in markets arising from what the Ironship Syndicate continues to refer to as the "Arradsian incident" has compelled many companies to hoard stocks of consumables against future shortages. Chief amongst these consumables are lamp oil and sugar, both highly caloric substances which undoubtedly did much to fuel the unfolding inferno.

By the eleventh hour at least two-thirds of the warehouse district was aflame along with a sizable portion of the Dockside buildings. Only valiant efforts by the Sonora Fire Watch, augmented by the City Constabulary, prevented the fire from spreading into residential environs. For a time it appeared that the blaze might be contained and the damage, whilst severe, would at least have been manageable. It is at this point in the narrative that your humble correspondent must ask his readers to trust the veracity of the subsequent account. Incredible though it may appear, I can only attest with simple honesty that what follows is the unexpurgated truth as witnessed by my own eyes.

Having been roused from my slumber at some point past the 10th hour by the general discord rising beyond my bedroom window, I proceeded, as all dutiful correspondents must, to the scene of the action. On reaching the Dockside my progress was impeded by a cordon of City Constabulary who were stringent in forbidding any closer approach. Fortunately, I espied a near by crane and duly made good my ascent to its topmost platform whereupon I found myself afforded a most excellent view of the dreadful spectacle below. A single glance proved sufficient to confirm the loss of most of the warehouses, the centre of the inferno blazing with such intensity that to look upon it pained the eyes. However, I could see the hoses of the Fire Watch hard at work on the fringes of the blaze and at that instant it appeared well contained and unlikely to pose further danger to the wider metropolis.

Then she appeared.

Regular readers will know well this correspondent's repeated scepticism with regard to the so-called "Blessed Demon" said to have conducted a fiery rampage through the Marsh Wold and beyond in recent months. It is therefore with great humility that I must now attest that this monster is in fact all too real.

She came striding out of the smoke that covered the wharf beyond the constables' cordon, tall and straight of back, one might even call her bearing elegant but for the rags she wore. The raging fire at her back cast her face in shadow but for a single instant. Just as she fixed her gaze upon the line of constables and called forth the fire in her veins, her face became clear and it was a face I knew well.

I know not whether it was the shock of recognition that froze me to the spot, or witnessing the horror of her unnatural flames consuming the servants of the law. In either case I must confess to a moment of absolute immobility in both mind and body as I stood and looked upon none other than Miss Catheline Dewsmine.

I should like to report that the face I looked upon was that of a madwoman—a cackling, wild-eyed hag bent on mindless havoc. But that was not the case. The countenance I beheld was not one of insanity, but serenity. In the past I had many occasions to look upon the face of Catheline Dewsmine and often felt there to be a certain artifice to those finely made features. Her smile strained a fraction, her eyebrow arched a little too high bespeaking a well-concealed contempt. I saw no such artifice now. The woman I watched commit mass murder was possessed of a contented certainty the like of which I have never witnessed in another human being.

She saw me as the last constable writhed his final agonies, glancing up to regard the solitary statue of a man standing atop a crane and pondering the imminence of mortality. I assume it was the certainty of my doom that unfroze me, a desire to meet my end with at least a semblance of dignity. So, standing as straight as I could I called down to her with the only greeting that came to mind: "Miss Dewsmine. Are you well?"

She stood regarding me in silence for some time, long enough in fact for a thick sheen of sweat to form upon my flesh as the inferno crept closer. Then she spoke, and I must report that as her face was absent any madness, so too was her voice. It was, in fact, the same rich, melodious voice I recalled from so many society gatherings.

"I am very well, thank you, Mr. Talwick," she greeted me in return. "And you, sir?"

"In point of truth, miss," I replied, somewhat startled by my own poise, "I must confess to a modicum of alarm at this very moment."

"Alarm?" she enquired, then gave a small laugh of realisation. "Oh yes, my little diversion," she went on, casting a glance at the encroaching flames. "I'm afraid I shall have to crave your forgiveness, sir. But necessity has spurred me to some . . . excesses of late."

"Necessity, miss?" I enquired, my gaze taking in the measure of her form. Underneath all the soot she remained as beautiful as ever, if noticeably thinner and clad in what appeared to be the torn and tattered remnants of a dress more suited to a high-status ball than a scene of wanton destruction.

"Yes indeed," she replied. "A most pressing and important matter." At this point she felt it appropriate to offer an apologetic smile. "One which requires me to cut this pleasant interlude short."

"I see," I said, standing straighter still and compelling my gaze to meet hers.

"Oh, don't concern yourself, Mr. Talwick," she assured me and I noticed a familiar arch to her brows, the form they adopted when she found herself in the company of one she knew to be her social and intellectual inferior. "I should like people to know, you see," she continued, waving an elegant hand at the blazing storm now barely ten feet from where she stood. "It's only fair after all."

"Know what, miss?" I enquired, my previous poise quickly eroding towards panic.

"Why, what's coming of course," she told me. "I believe it will make things so much more entertaining, in time. And with that, sir"—she gave a brisk smile and inclined her head—"I must bid you a fond farewell."

Then she was gone, transformed into a blur in the thickening smoke, no doubt the result of a recent intake of Green. Any hopes she may have vanished for good were soon dashed by the sounds of alarm rising from the harbour itself. I turned to see fire blossoming from the deck of a freighter moored twenty yards from my position. Then a few moments later a great gout of flame rose from the vessel's stack and a boom shook her from bow to stern, a boom that told of an exploding boiler. A few heart-beats later and another ship took light with similar results, then another until it seemed as if every vessel moored at the quay-side was wreathed in flame.

I cannot attest to the full horror of what unfolded in the harbour that night, preoccupied as I was with climbing down from my imperilled perch in order to make good my escape from the advancing conflagration. Suffice to say that the scale of destruction being wrought on those ships at anchor compelled the harbour-master to raise the gate and allow the surviving vessels to sail clear. This also had the beneficial effect of permitting the tidal waters to wash over the quay and extinguish the inferno before more damage could be done. Unfortunately, this in turn resulted in the flooding of dozens of homes fringing the Dockside District thereby providing an impetus for the riots that have been raging in our city for much of today.

No trace of Catheline Dewsmine has been found, although the appointed Protectorate investigators have assured this correspondent that exhaustive efforts are being employed to hunt her down. However, it is this correspondent's opinion that such efforts will prove fruitless, for I believe the "Blessed Demon" is no longer within their reach. Enquiries at the harbour-master's office reveal that six vessels were destroyed at anchor in Sanorah Harbour and twenty-three others are known to have escaped through the opened door. Of these only twenty-two have been subsequently accounted for. One vessel, the South Seas Maritime passenger liner the SSM *Northern Star*, has not returned to port and her whereabouts are unknown.

A full accounting of casualties has yet to be made public but it can safely be assumed to be in the hundreds. The Dockside District is now blackened wasteland and the cost in commerce and revenue so enormous as to defy easy calculation. And yet, your humble correspondent is forced to entertain the notion that what he witnessed the previous night was but a portent. Catheline Dewsmine, risen from death and rendered monstrous by means unknown has escaped this continent and gone to complete her "most pressing and important matter." It is this correspondent's grim duty to report his firm suspicion that we have not yet seen the last of her.

Lead article in the *Sanorah Intelligencer*—23rd Rosellum 1600 (Company Year 211)—by Sigmend Talwick, Senior Correspondent.

CHAPTER 34

Clay

His left hand scraped over ten feet of bare rock before finding purchase on a shallow fissure barely an inch wide. Clay shouted as the shock of his arrested tumble jolted through his arm to his shoulder, threatening to dislodge his grip. He gritted his teeth and dug his fingers deeper into the fissure, ignoring the pain and the wet rush of blood that told of a displaced fingernail or two.

He hung there, dragging air into his lungs and fighting panic. Loriabeth kept calling his name from atop the cliff, becoming more shrill with each plaintive cry. Clay's mind raced through various escape scenarios, none of which seemed to offer much prospect of success. The wallet containing his product sat in the right inside pocket of his jacket, meaning he would have to engage in some frantic manoeuvring to recover it. Even should he manage to retrieve it without separating himself from the cliff, the chances of getting it open and safely extracting a vial were remote. He considered attempting a descent, but a few careful probes with his dangling feet revealed an absence of ledges where he might find purchase. To add insult to his predicament the burnt and severed end of the rope dangled only a few feet above his head. Clay glared up at it in a spasm of helpless reproach, an emotion that soon turned to alarm when he saw a bright bead of blood swelling on the blackened stub. It wasn't his blood.

He could see the Black's severed neck dangling above, emitting a crimson cascade that coursed down the face of the cliff and inevitably found its way onto the rope. He watched as the bead detached from the rope and descended towards him, impacting on the upper side of his forehead. Had he been un-Blessed there would have been a hard jab of flaming agony as the blood met his skin. Instead, the undiluted substance produced just a warm wet tap, no doubt leaving a pale and permanent reminder in his flesh for the rest of his life, however short that proved to be in the current circumstance. Strangely, the bead's fall brought a new clarity to his thoughts, banishing the panic and allowing a certain realisation to dawn.

Black. He raised his gaze, watching another red bead swelling on the rope's ragged end. *Black for the push . . . But what to push?* The wild notion of employing Black to move his own body blossomed then died immediately. No Blood-blessed had ever successfully accomplished such a feat, and those that tried had merely gifted the world with a spectacular new form of suicide. It was an early-learned lesson for all those who shared the Blessing: Black never flows inward. *And there ain't nothing to push,* he concluded with a sigh, slumping against the unyielding rock, then frowning as another notion came to mind. *Nothing . . . 'cept the cliff.*

He levered himself back from the cliff-face as gently as he could, eyes exploring the rock. The fissure into which he had thrust his hand was part of a long crack that narrowed as it descended, Clay finding it extended nearly the length of his body. He could see it was in fact the edge of a narrow protrusion in the cliff, a thin slab of rock that might well come loose with enough prodding.

Another wet peck at his forehead returned his attention to the rope. It was now red from end to end, the blood winding along its braids in thick rivulets to birth a steady stream of droplets. Clay craned his neck and opened his mouth wide, letting the product flow down his throat. He had thought the taste of undiluted Green would be the worst thing ever to befoul his mouth, but it transpired that raw Black was an order of magnitude worse. He gagged as the thick, acrid liquid burned its way past his tongue and gullet before finding his belly, then shuddered at the instant upsurge of nausea. He forced himself to keep drinking, despite the spasm that began to make his whole body vibrate. He needed all he could stomach if this was to work.

He finally stopped when his guts threatened to throw up most of what he had drunk, closing his mouth and flattening himself against the cliff to avoid the continuing torrent of blood. After a few moments to recover his strength he eased himself back and concentrated his gaze on the crack in the rock just below his now-benumbed hand. He tried using just a small amount of Black to begin with, seeking to widen the crack just a little. The rock, however, proved unyielding and his efforts produced only a few flakes of displaced stone. Clay steeled himself against a new wave of fear and prepared to unleash half the Black in a single blast. *It's this or a long drop into nothing.*

The result was immediate, the fissure widening by a foot as a cloud of splintered rock erupted around him with a crack like the snapping of a giant's thigh-bone. The thin slab of stone came away from the cliff so fast it nearly proved fatal. Clay had no time to think, letting go of the slab as it came loose for just an instant as he reached out to grab it with the Black, then scrabbling to regain purchase as it hung in mid air. He held on with a light grip, uncertain of how the Black would affect an object subject to direct contact. He lessened the flow of Black, utilising every scrap of skill he had to concentrate the power on the centre of the slab then shifting his weight so that it slowly began to revolve. Sweat poured into his eyes as he fought to maintain the intense pitch of concentration needed to keep the slab horizontal. His body ached in protest as he slowly got to his feet, allowing himself a small grin of triumph. He was standing on a free-floating platform, a feat never before accomplished by another Blood-blessed, at least as far as he knew.

He looked up, finding the rope still out of reach. He tried using Black to elevate the slab to the required height but it gave an alarming shudder when he made the attempt. *Must be too close to it,* he realised. *Well that's a quandary.* It took a few moments pondering before the solution occurred, whereupon he crouched as low as he dared and jumped straight up, using Black to raise the slab to meet his feet before he descended. He had only ascended about a foot but it was better than nothing. Repeated jumps brought the end of the rope within reach, but he kept going for as long as the Black would allow, wary of grasping the blood-slicked lower end. Finally, as he felt the last vestiges of Black fade from his veins, he took a final jump and gripped the unbloodied stretch of rope just above the drake's headless corpse.

He watched the displaced slab of cliff tumble away below to shatter on the shingle beach, hearing the dim cheers of his companions above.

"Just hang on, cuz!" Loriabeth called to him. "We'll haul you the rest of the way."

"Wait!" he yelled back, turning to the dead Black. *Riches not to be ignored.* "Got something to do first!"

The Black's corpse lay on a broad ledge protruding from a deep cave in the stone. Recalling Skaggerhill's lessons, Clay punctured the vein at the join of the animal's neck and filled his canteen with the resulting torrent of product. Foul as it tasted, it was clearly a potent brew. Once full, he stoppered the canteen and began to reach for the rope once more, then found his gaze lingering on the dark interior of the cave.

Don't, he cautioned himself, nevertheless stepping closer to peer into the inviting gloom. "Dammit," he muttered, crouching at the cave mouth and knowing he would crawl inside. "A curious nature is surely the worst vice."

The interior of the cave was musty and remained a gloomy mystery until his eyes adjusted. A part-eaten animal of some kind lay in the centre of the cave. Clay thought it might be a cat from the blood-matted fur, but the mutilation was such he couldn't be sure. Beyond it he could see a small patch of light glimmering on something. Stepping over the unfortunate creature, he drew up short at the sight of an egg sitting atop a pile of fused animal bones.

Guess that's why she was so unwelcoming, he thought, sinking to his haunches and reaching out to smooth a hand over the egg. *Sorry young 'un. Mama's gone, and it's my fault.*

The sharp jab of regret was unexpected, Loriabeth hadn't had any choice after all. But still, his brief if tenuous connection with Lutharon, and the drake memories Ethelynne had shared with him back in the ruined city, left him with a new appreciation for the true nature of these animals. The Blacks, he knew, were not like the others. *They feel, they think.* If the evidence found in the temple was to be believed there had been a time when the original Arradsians lived in harmony with the Blacks. *Whilst all we've ever done is kill them.*

He took the egg on impulse, finding it weighing only a half-pound or so. An idea had begun to worm its way into the forefront of his thoughts, a notion stoked by his remembrance of Ethelynne and what she had done to survive the Wittler Expedition all those years ago.

Making his way outside, he consigned the egg to his pack then once again removed the stopper from his canteen. "Don't worry, young 'un," he said, taking a hefty gulp and wincing at the taste. "Mama's gonna make sure you get born after all."

They made camp a short distance from the cliff-edge, clustering around a fire as the lights faded. They were once again in a forest, though less dense than the first one. The trees were more akin in form to the jungle giants Clay was familiar with, although, like the drakes, these appeared to be stunted cousins.

"Looks like Green country to me," Loriabeth said as they made camp, eyeing the surrounding foliage with evident suspicion. "And you can bet there'll be other Blacks about somewhere."

Kriz tended to Clay's injured hand as they shared the first watch. He found himself blinking tears and swallowing profanity as she bathed the various small wounds with diluted Green. Seeing his discomfort, she took a vial from one of the pockets on her belt and loaded it into her needle gun. "This help," she said, pressing the muzzle to his neck and pressing the trigger to inject the substance. Clay gave a gasp of surprise as the pain abruptly vanished, the sensation transforming into a faint and not unpleasant tingle. Kriz completed her work by taking small bandages from her pack and fixing them over the ends of his two most badly damaged fingers.

"Well, that's surely something," he said, flexing the fingers and marvelling at the lack of pain. Whatever she had given him didn't seem to impair his senses the way laudanum or poppy paste might. "Guns and medicine of marvellous design. And all this." He gestured at their surroundings. "Your people were kinda special, huh?"

Kriz gave a faint smile, her gaze full of the same fascination she had displayed since they hauled him to the top of the cliff. It was an unfamiliar expression, one Clay had never thought might be directed at him, so it took awhile to place it. *Awe,* he realised. *And a touch of fear too.*

"How?" she asked now, flattening one hand whilst she danced her fingers atop the palm, miming a recreation of him jumping and raising the slab.

"It's a new trick," he confessed. "Seems like the more Black I use, the more tricks I can do."

She frowned and he realised that they were once again at the limits of their ability to communicate. Either that or she was being deliberately obtuse, still clinging to her secrets behind a veil of incomprehension. He had secrets of his own, of course. He hadn't told her or the others about the egg in his pack or the newly filled vial he had attached to the chain about his neck alongside the one containing Blue heart-blood. But he doubted his small subterfuge would alter their chances of survival, whereas her knowledge was certain to be of vital importance.

"Trance with me," he said, taking the wallet from his jacket and extracting a vial of Blue. He held it up before her eyes, tilting it to and fro so it caught a glimmer from the red glow of the cylinder. "Trance with me and I'll tell you all about it."

Kriz looked away, her face taking on a familiar mix of reluctance and refusal.

"Gonna have to happen sometime." Clay returned the vial to the wallet. "You know that, right?"

She didn't reply but he sensed she caught his meaning, in the tone if not the words. She kept her gaze averted for a moment longer then abruptly stood, gesturing for him to follow suit. "There," she said, pointing at something far off in the gloom. At first Clay could see only the jagged grey outline of the mountains beyond the forest, then saw she was pointing at something above the peaks: a thin pale line ascending into the black void. Some trick of the faux-sunlight must have concealed it when they scaled the cliff, but now it stood revealed as the distant glow caught its edge.

"Another shaft," Clay realised aloud. He turned to Kriz and laughed. "That's where you're taking us? Why didn't you say so?"

He began to give her an appreciative pat on the shoulder but she stepped back, features tense now. Her expression was harder than ever to read, fearful certainly, but also some guilt there in her eyes. It left him with the distinct impression that whatever awaited them at this new shaft, it wasn't a way out. "We . . ." Kriz began, speaking slowly and forming the words with care, "trance . . . there."

"And what's there?" he pressed, putting a hard insistence into his voice.

Kriz turned and resumed her seat, face set and unyielding as she muttered a soft response he knew would be her last word of the evening, "Father."

They saw no Greens as they made their way through the forest, nor any of the tell-tale marks the beasts were apt to leave on tree-trunks to mark their territory. But that didn't mean the forest was void of life. Small birds moved in darting flocks about the tree-tops whilst larger creatures lived in the trees themselves. Clay soon recognised them as belonging to the same species as the Black's part-eaten prey back at the cave. They were small monkey-like creatures with dark fur, stunted legs and long arms which they used to swing from branch to branch. They tended to make a righteous din upon sighting their party, screeching and hooting as they gathered into a protective huddle. Larger specimens, presumably the males, would be more active, bouncing on tree-branches as they bared an impressive set of teeth. One even threw twigs at them as they passed beneath the tree, screeching out a challenge.

"You ever see the like?" Clay asked Sigoral, ducking as the twig sailed over his head.

"I saw monkeys aplenty in Dalcia," the Corvantine replied, raising his carbine and using the spy-glass-sight to gain a closer look at the still-screaming creature. "Much the same size, though their heads were smaller and eyes bigger."

"Could bag a few," Loriabeth suggested, hefting her repeating rifle. "Some fresh meat certainly wouldn't go amiss."

"No!" Kriz moved to stand in front of her, then switched her stern visage to each of them in turn. "Leave . . . be. Not food."

"Alright, cuz," Clay warned his cousin as she started to bridle. "Reckon we got grub enough to last us to the shaft."

If Kriz didn't see the monkeys as food, it was not a sentiment shared by the local population of Blacks. They saw the first one a few hours into their trek, a male by Clay's reckoning given the breadth of its wing-span, which was much broader than the female Loriabeth had killed at the cliff. They watched the Black glide above the trees with something dangling from its claws, something that wriggled and screeched as it was borne towards the grey peaks beyond the forest.

"Might explain why there's no Greens here," Clay said. "Blacks won't tolerate the competition."

"Let's hope they tolerate us," Loriabeth said. "Leastways long enough to get where we're going."

Kriz led them on for another two days, eventually calling a halt when the forest began to give way to rocky hills. The mountains were looming ever larger ahead, as was the relentlessly inviting sight of the shaft. Clay could sense the impatience in Sigoral and Loriabeth, the growing desire to be gone from this place of wonder and ever-present danger. He shared their hunger for escape, but found his appetite for answers even more pressing.

It was what they came for, after all. He had followed the vision gifted by the White's blood in the hope that the spire might harbour some hope of defeating the beast's design. Instead, he had uncovered a maddening and complex enigma, one Kriz apparently felt no compulsion to unravel for his benefit, at least not yet.

He watched her scan the hills up ahead then straighten as she caught sight of something. A grin broke over her face and she began to run, scaling the rock-strewn incline with impressive agility and speed that left the three of them struggling to keep up. When Clay eventually caught up he found her standing before a plinth sitting alongside a huge boulder.

"Looks like she found us another treasure trove to raid," Loriabeth said, mopping her sweat-covered brow with a kerchief.

"I ain't too sure about that," Clay said, seeing the conflicting emotions play over Kriz's face as she regarded the plinth's crystal. Her grin had been replaced by a wide-eyed anticipation that abruptly turned to a grimace of trepidation. Clay moved to her side and nodded at the boulder. "Worried what you'll find in there, huh?" he asked.

She glanced at him, apparently understanding enough of his words to reply with a nod.

"Don't be," he said, putting a hand on her arm and hefting his carbine. "You got us backing you."

Kriz gave a brief, humourless laugh, closing her eyes and shaking her head. "No . . . need guns . . . here," she said, placing her palm on the plinth's crystal and stepping back. There came the now-familiar grind of stone and blossom of dust as a segment of the boulder's surface receded then slid aside. This time there was no rush of air, meaning whatever waited within didn't require a vacuum. The interior was completely dark which seemed to heighten Kriz's agitation. She motioned for Loriabeth and Sigoral to light their lanterns, peering impatiently into the gloom until they did so.

The lights revealed a narrow tunnel and a series of stone steps descending deep underground. Clay turned to Kriz, seeing that her trepidation had deepened, but there was also a steely resolve in her gaze. She said something in her own language, a brief muttered phrase that Clay fancied might have been a prayer of some kind, then took Loriabeth's lantern and started down into the dark.

CHAPTER 35

Lizanne

The assembled mass of convicts rushed through the gate with a roar of primal triumph, a roar that quickly faded as they were greeted by the thick smoke and thunderous chaos of battle. However, the combined weight of numbers and desperation ensured their charge continued, the close-packed throng streaming through the gate and spreading out to cover the cobbled parade-ground in front of the gate. A thin line of constables and Imperial soldiers had been hastily assembled to oppose them, but their volley was a ragged and pitiful thing against such an onslaught. The constables broke and ran after their first shot, the soldiers managing one more volley before they were swallowed up by the mob. Lizanne closed her ears against the brief but piercing shrieks as the soldiers fell victim to the fury of the escapees, keeping her gaze fixed on the Electress who, in turn, had her meaty hand fixed on Tinkerer's arm. She moved with a tight-packed body-guard of Furies led by Anatol. The giant had loosed all the bolts from his crossbow and now used it as a club, Lizanne seeing him bring the stock down to shatter the skull of a fallen sergeant before moving on with a steady and purposeful stride.

Opposition stiffened as they pressed on, rifle-bullets twitching the smoke with increasing frequency, soon joined by a cannon-shot that sent swarms of canister into the ranks of the inmates. The mob's speed had lessened now, people moving in a scuttling crouch as if caught in a heavy downpour. It was clear to Lizanne that someone of sufficient rank and composure had managed to organise an effective defence. She drank a small amount of Green and leapt, rising high enough to see above the smoke. Her enhanced vision revealed a full regiment of Imperial Cavalry, most dismounted and scurrying into a defensive formation. One battery of cannon had been set up in the centre of their line with another in the process of unlimbering on the right flank. Lizanne managed a quick headcount before gravity asserted its grip, and she found that the regiment was smaller than it should be by at least a squadron. Her second leap revealed the reason. Beyond the line of dismounts a thick swirl of dust rose as mounted troopers battled an unseen foe in a close-quarter contest of sabre and pistol. *The Brotherhood,* she realised. *It appears they arrived on time after all.*

Lizanne landed and rushed to where the Electress and the surviving Furies were crouched behind a row of upturned carts. The mob's advance had halted now as the troopers' massed carbine fire took an ever-increasing toll. Escapees clustered in knots or fled in panic, seeking refuge on the flanks which only exposed them to more accurate fire as they fled the concealing shroud of smoke. Lizanne saw one of the Furies clutching a rifle and tore it from his grasp, delivering a discouraging Green-enhanced slap when he bristled in protest. She checked to ensure Tinkerer was still unharmed, albeit remaining in the Electress's grip, then moved to Anatol's side. "Lift me," she told him, taking another gulp of Green and checking to ensure the rifle had a bullet in the chamber. Anatol just stared at her in naked animosity until the Electress spoke up, "Just do it. Can't lie here all day, now, can we?"

Anatol gave a snarl then grabbed Lizanne by the waist, raising her up above his head as if she weighed little more than a feather pillow. Lizanne allowed the Green to flood her system, her entire body seeming to thrum with the sudden injection of boosted strength and reflex. Time slowed as she brought the rifle to her shoulder, her pulse a faint, ponderous drum-beat as the drifting smoke stilled and the whine of passing bullets became a lazy drone. She trained the rifle on the regimental line, eagle-sharp eyes scanning for her victim. *Where are you, Colonel?*

She found him in the centre of the line, where a good commander should be. The colonel was mounted on a sturdy black charger and appeared the epitome of a Corvantine officer with his stern grey-moustached features and chest beribboned with an impressive array of battle honours. Lizanne thought he might almost have stepped out of a painting from the way he sat tall in the saddle, sabre resting on his shoulder as he boomed out encouragement to his men. A man that other men would follow anywhere, or despair at his passing.

Her bullet took him in the chest, ripping through his medal ribbons to find his heart. Impressive to the end he managed to stay in the saddle for a short while, gripping the pommel and continuing to shout his orders even as blood rushed from his mouth. Then, inevitably, he slipped slowly from his perch and lay still as his charger nibbled at his slack face.

Lizanne drew back the rifle's bolt to eject the spent cartridge and held out a hand to the Furies crouched below. "Ammunition please."

She killed the gunners next, picking off all but one of the battery in the centre. The final gunner took to his heels the moment his sergeant slumped dead beside him, leaving the twelve-pounder silent. On either side of the gun she could see cavalry troopers exchanging fearful glances, though they continued to maintain a steady fire at the prone and immobile mass of escapees. Their collective nerve only began to truly falter when Lizanne started to pick off the sergeants, obvious panic rising with every slain veteran. Open discord broke out on the left flank when she put a round into the head of a barrel-chested colour-sergeant bearing the company pennant. A squadron of troopers rose from their firing positions to begin an unbidden retreat, heedless of a vicious haranguing from a young officer. The panic soon spread to the neighbouring squadron, their line fracturing into confused knots as they saw their comrades succumb to fear. Within seconds the whole left side of the regiment's line was in disarray.

"That should do it," Lizanne said, slipping from Anatol's grasp and tossing the rifle back to its owner. She drew her revolver and caught the Electress's eye. "Unless you would rather lie here and wait for them to recover their wits."

She moved on without waiting for a response, draining all three vials of her remaining product before accelerating into a Green-powered run towards the disrupted regiment. A dozen or so troopers fired at her but she was moving too fast, the bullets whipping harmlessly at her back. She made for the cannon on the right flank, now fully unlimbered but still unfired as the crew dithered over what to do. Deciding not to allow them the time to reach a decision, Lizanne sprinted to within thirty yards of the cannon and leapt, unleashing a blast of Red as she sailed over the battery. The intense wave of heat ignited the crew's powder store, blasting them and their twelve-pounder apart in a bright orange fire-ball. The explosion had the added benefit of finally overturning what reserves of courage remained to the cavalrymen. The entire regiment broke as one, their line fragmenting as they turned and ran for their tethered horses.

Lizanne came to earth amid a party of stragglers, most of whom wisely kept running, although she was forced to shoot an overly dutiful corporal who felt obligated to aim his carbine at her. A growing, angry murmur drew her gaze back to the parade-ground. The escapees were rising, their ranks swollen by a steady tide of convicts still streaming through the gate. The mob's previous angry roar had changed now, the sound concentrated into a simmering, hungry growl. Dust rose as the horde cleared the parade-ground and swept over the dry grass beyond. It mingled with the drifting gunsmoke to obscure the dreadful spectacle as the citizens of Scorazin reached the milling ranks of Imperial troops, however the screams were ample evidence of vengeance being enthusiastically slaked.

Lizanne staggered a little as the last of Julesin's sub-standard product faded from her veins, leaving a residual nausea and weariness. She wandered back to the remnants of the cannon she had destroyed, slumping against an upturned gun-carriage. She knew she should be looking for Tinkerer amidst all this chaos but her fatigue was suddenly undeniable.

"Emperor's balls, but you look terrible."

She raised her gaze to regard a tall figure reining in a horse a few yards away. Arberus slid his bloody sabre into its scabbard before leaping from the horse's saddle. He rushed to her side, reaching out a steadying hand as a wave of fatigue threatened to topple her to the ground.

"You always say the sweetest things," Lizanne replied, raising a hand to brush away a patch of bloody grime on his chin. "Please don't feel compelled to apologise for your tardiness, otherwise I might find myself quite undone by your abundance of affection."

"Can't account for bad luck," he said, his gaze betraying a certain guilty defensiveness. "Seems the Thirty-eighth Imperial Light Horse stops by every few months to drop off their prisoners. They arrived just as we started our charge."

Lizanne cast a gaze around at the carnage revealed by the thinning smoke. Many convicts were either busily looting the troopers' bodies or squabbling over the spoils. Others could be seen rushing off in all directions, keen to put as much distance between themselves and Scorazin as possible. Most, however, stood around in loose groups, faces writ with confusion or fear. These were the gang members and veteran inmates, those who had spent years behind the walls and now had either no notion of what to do with their sudden liberty or a grimly realistic understanding of their situation. Winning freedom was one thing, keeping it was another.

"How bad was it?" Arberus asked, casting a dark glance at the city before moving closer to clasp her forearms.

He thinks I might have been raped, Lizanne realised with a pang of bitterness as she detected the reluctance in his tone. *How terrible for him.* "I achieved my objective," she said, disentangling herself. "Now I have to secure him. Do you have it?" She held out her hand, ignoring the hurt that passed over Arberus's face.

"Loaded with the finest product the Brotherhood could find," he said, reaching into his pocket to extract the Spider.

"I should hope so." Lizanne took the device and strapped it on, groaning in relief as she injected a dose of good-quality Green. "We need to gather the Brotherhood," she said, straightening and striding off. "I suspect a difficult negotiation awaits us."

"You can fuck right off, my dear." The Electress stood amidst a pile of gathered weapons, barrels and sundry valuables looted from the battle-field and the guard-house. The surviving Furies were arranged at her back, each now sporting a rifle or cavalryman's carbine. Anatol had taken up position on Atalina's left whilst between them stood the notably less substantial person of Tinkerer. The assembled ranks of the Brotherhood were drawn up behind Lizanne, along with Makario, who remained understandably nervous of placing himself in proximity to his erstwhile employer. Thanks to the losses inflicted by the constables and Imperial soldiery, the ranks of the Furies were somewhat thinner than Lizanne might have expected, meaning the two groups were roughly even in numbers.

"If this one's such a prize," Atalina went on, drumming her stubby fingers on Tinkerer's head, "it'd be awful foolish of me to just hand him over to you, don't you think?"

"The Ironship Syndicate will ensure you receive a substantial reward," Lizanne replied.

"Your syndicate isn't here," the Electress pointed out then nodded at the assembled Brotherhood. "All you have is this pack of rebels and it's sound odds they haven't got a pot worth pissing in. Besides which, what use is gold now?"

The Electress raised her thick arms, gesturing at the corpse-littered field and the guard-house, which the former prisoners had been quick to set ablaze after a thorough looting. "You said it yourself, they can't let this go unanswered. Right now there'll be messengers galloping to the nearest garrison. Within a week there'll be an army sweeping this province."

"Then hadn't you best be on your way?" Korian said, stepping to Lizanne's side. A freshly stitched cut leaked blood on the Brotherhood leader's cheek as he glared at the Electress. The injury and the comrades lost in the battle apparently left him in no mood for negotiating with those he plainly considered unworthy of his brand of liberty. "I'm sure there are plenty of farm-steads to pillage near by."

"Oh pipe down, boy," the Electress snapped. "You're in the same midden-cart as us, if you hadn't noticed. Whatever she promised you"—Atalina stabbed a blunt finger at Lizanne—"won't help now. The Emperor's soldiers will kill us all just the same. You let her take the Tinkerer and she'll have ghosted on her way by nightfall, leaving us to the slaughter."

Korian's cheeks bunched as he switched his glare to Lizanne, the innate suspicion of all things corporate rising in his gaze. "She makes a valid point," he observed softly. "What assurances can you offer that Ironship will provide the arms they promised? Our agents in Corvus tell us they're about to conclude a treaty with the Emperor."

"Merely a matter of convenience," Lizanne said, hoping her off-hand tone masked the insincerity. In truth she had no idea whether the Board would approve the contract with these fanatics, nor did she care. Their struggle was a distraction from larger concerns.

"She lies!" Helina's voice was shrill with what Lizanne recognised as the pitch of the recently mad. The small woman stood amongst the Brotherhood, clutching her wounded arm and staring at Lizanne with wild-eyed malice. Demisol and the rest of the Learned Damned had apparently fallen in the charge to the gate, leaving this crazed wretch as their only representative. "Trust nothing that issues from this whore's mouth!" Helina spat. "You would do the revolution a great service by killing her here and now!"

"You have no authority here, citizen," Arberus told Helina, pointedly putting a hand on the hilt of his sabre.

"And what authority do you hold?" she snarled in return. "By all accounts you are nothing but this whore's whore."

Lizanne resisted the temptation to forestall any further insults via the expedient of smashing every tooth in Helina's mouth, instead forcing a brisk but determined tone as she directed her words at Korian. "This avails us nothing. We have an agreement. Do you intend to honour it or not?"

"What if he doesn't?" the Electress broke in, Lizanne turning to find a grin on the woman's lips. It was a worryingly confident grin. "What if he tells you to fuck right off too? What will you do then, my dear? Use the Blessing to kill us all, perhaps? Got enough product for that?" She gave a meaningful glance to her right and Lizanne saw the reason for her confidence. Varkash was striding towards them from the direction of the blazing guard-house, a dense mob of Wise Fools at his back and a less orderly host of Scuttlers and sundry others on either side. Altogether, Lizanne estimated their number at well over three thousand people. *Too many to kill,* she knew. *Too many to flee from.*

"It seems to me," the Electress went on, now fixing her gaze on Korian but speaking with sufficient volume to ensure the encroaching masses heard her, "we have a limited set of options. We can scatter, take to the hills and forests and scratch a living through banditry. Some of us might live a few years, most will find themselves captured and dangling from a rope within a few weeks. Or we can wait here where we're certain to get slaughtered once the Emperor's army turns up. Or we move on. The port city of Vorstek lies two hundred and fifty miles due east. Where's there's a port, there's ships."

"You propose seizing an Imperial city?" Korian asked with an appalled laugh.

"I don't want to keep it." The Electress's gaze snapped to Lizanne. "Your Syndicate's got plenty of ships, I hear. More than enough to carry us all away to a nice safe Mandinorian port. Isn't that right?"

Lizanne watched Varkash come to a halt near by, the other escapees crowding in around to witness the scene. The huge Varestian crossed his arms and directed a steady gaze at Lizanne. He appeared to have emerged from the chaos without injury, and his gaze lacked the fury she saw in many faces. But there was an implacable purpose to it, a promise of inescapable consequences.

"Yes," Lizanne told the Electress, once again hoping her tone concealed the lie. "I can arrange that. Dependent on his safe delivery," she added, pointing at Tinkerer.

"Oh, Anatol will take very good care of him, be assured of that." Atalina pinched Tinkerer's chin. "As if he were a new-born babe."

"I fail to see why the Brotherhood should take part in this farce," Korian said.

"You get the arms she promised when the ships turn up," the Electress told him. "But you also get something far more valuable." She laughed and flung her arms out wide, encompassing the unwashed mob. "An army with which to relight the fires of revolution!"

"Two hundred and fifty miles," Arberus said, scanning the sprawling and disorderly camp with military disdain. "This lot will be lucky to manage another thirty."

"I wouldn't under-estimate the Electress's leadership abilities," Lizanne cautioned. "In any case we have little option but to follow her course, at least until this army meets defeat, as it surely must before long."

They sat atop a low hill a dozen miles or so from Scorazin where the Electress had ordered camp be made after a protracted and ill-disciplined march. The ranks had swollen to at least six thousand souls. This was substantially less than the population of Scorazin before the escape, so many having fallen and many others opting to take to their heels rather than join the Electress's expedition.

Scorazin had burned as they marched away. Although none of the army's principal figures had ordered it, every structure capable of burning had been put to the torch before the march began. Lizanne understood the instinctive desire that provoked the arson, the deep-set need to wipe this place from the earth thereby removing any chance they might be returned here one day. Inevitably the fires spread to the sulphur mines, birthing an inferno of such intensity it could still be seen on the western horizon.

"It might burn for years," Arberus mused, watching the yellow-orange glow flicker on the distant clouds. "At the very least the Emperor will have to find himself a new prison. You achieved that if nothing else."

"Is it true about the treaty?" Lizanne asked. "Is the Emperor close to an agreement with Ironship?"

"The Brotherhood has a few agents within the palace, but their reports are often contradictory. One day it appears the Emperor is entirely lucid and receptive to the delegation's suggestions, the next he's raving and executing guardsmen and nobles on a whim. But most agree that, mad or not, he will sign the treaty, if he hasn't done so already."

"Then we have a chance of opposing the White in decent strength, at least until we can unlock the secrets in Tinkerer's head."

"You're convinced he's that important?"

Lizanne thought back to the chamber Tinkerer had shown her, the circle of skeletons, each one a Blood-blessed. "I believe his presence in Scorazin is connected to the Artisan," she said. "And I doubt it was accidental. He has knowledge that can help us, I'm certain of it."

"You place a great deal of faith in a long-dead man and a pale-faced youth."

"In time faith may be the only thing that sustains us."

Something in her voice must have concerned him for he moved closer, putting an arm around her shoulders and drawing her close. She allowed herself to be embraced, her earlier pique lingering but not enough to push him away. "I hardly slept," he said. "The thought of you in that place . . ."

"Was better than the reality."

He winced at the hardness in her voice, drawing back a little. "It seems all I can do is say the wrong thing. What would you have me do? Just tell me."

"Find me a change of clothes for a start," she muttered, slumping against him, letting herself surrender to exhaustion. "And," she whispered as her eyes began to close, "a working and accurate timepiece."

In the morning Arberus presented her with a set of cavalry fatigues, presumably taken from the body of one of the more youthful troopers. Lizanne peeled away the filthy overalls she had worn throughout her time in Scorazin, uncaring of any witnesses to her nakedness. She tossed the garment on the camp-fire before dousing herself with the bucket of water Arberus had fetched from a near by stream. The chill of it was shocking, but also added a welcome tingle to her flesh which she realised had become increasingly numb during her imprisonment. She rubbed at her damp skin, scraping away the grime and stink of the place, but somehow knowing some vestige of the scent would always linger. *Blinds don't wash,* Clay had told her once in the trance. It seemed Scorazin didn't wash either.

Arberus had also procured her a mount, a russet mare with the sturdy proportions and broad, hair-covered hooves of a cart-horse. "The Brotherhood can't afford to be choosy over its mounts," the major explained as Lizanne looked the animal over. She regarded Lizanne with soft brown eyes, issuing a placid snort as she smoothed a hand over her snout.

"As long as she doesn't bite," Lizanne said, climbing into the saddle.

The Electress's army was already in motion, hounded to its feet by gang leaders turned captains. Varkash was most prominent among these enforcers of discipline, seemingly possessed of an ability to command instant obedience and quell grumbling with a glance. Despite their willingness to follow the Electress's course, these weren't soldiers and the host moved in a disorderly crowd, plodding east at an unimpressive pace.

"We've covered twenty miles since yesterday, I reckon," Anatol said as they assembled at the Electress's camp-fire come nightfall. Atalina seemed content to tolerate the presence of Lizanne and Arberus, despite the fact that they hadn't been summoned.

"More like twelve," Arberus insisted. "If that. These soldiers of yours move as if they're on a holiday stroll. And," he went on, nodding at a group of convicts near by who were busy squabbling over a bottle of wine, "many are too drunk to put one foot in front of the other."

The Electress glanced at Varkash, who promptly strode towards the squabbling group. They instantly fell into silent stillness at his approach, apparently too fearful to run as he took the bottle from one of them and slowly emptied the contents over the man's head. "Next time I'll piss in it and make you drink it," he said, smashing the bottle on the ground before walking back to the fire.

"Fear of him won't be enough," Arberus told the Electress. "Not when the fighting starts. If you truly want this to be an army, you'll have to make this lot into soldiers."

"How d'you propose we do that?" she enquired.

"Some proper organisation for a start. Divide them into regiments and the regiments into companies, each with its own captain. Each company will march together and camp together. Also, you need to take charge of the supply situation. At the rate this lot are consuming the food taken at Scorazin they'll be starving within two weeks. Gather the supplies into carts and appoint a quartermaster to ensure equal shares are rationed out. You should also start sending foraging parties out to gather more. And," he added with a glance at Varkash, "make sure any drunkenness is harshly punished."

"Seems sensible," the pirate said to Atalina in his nasal twang. "Haven't flogged a man in years. Preddy sure I can remember how, dough."

"No," the Electress said. "These people threw in with me on the promise of freedom. Start showing them the whip and they'll soon decide they might as well try their luck on their own. Still, getting rid of the booze is a good idea. Go through the camp in the morning, smash all the bottles you can find. Most'll still be too groggy to object. As for the rest of your suggestions," she said, turning back to Arberus, "I'll leave to you. It's your plan, you make it happen."

A rberus divided the army into five regiments of roughly a thousand soldiers apiece. Each regiment consisted of five companies of two hundred soldiers and tended to reflect the soldiers' prison-born allegiances. The First and Second Regiments were mostly Furies and Wise Fools whilst the Scuttlers made up most of the Third. The remaining companies had also been formed around a nucleus of survivors from the minor gangs. Those not allotted a regiment, mainly the older convicts and others unsuited to fighting due to infirmity, were organised into what Arberus called a logistics train of cooks, cart-drivers and medical orderlies. There were no qualified physicians amongst them but the pressures of life in Scorazin had produced a surprising number with hard-earned skills in the healing arts. Several were whores from the Miner's Repose, all familiar with various restorative concoctions and the tending of minor wounds. Arberus placed the perpetually rancorous Silvona in charge of the army's medical services. Being the oldest, and by far the most vocal, the others tended to defer to her in any case.

Arberus was also quick to establish a daily routine, having the companies roused shortly after dawn and attempting to educate them in basic drill before breakfast. There were several former soldiers in their ranks who found themselves quickly elevated to sergeants charged with forming the companies into a semblance of military order. Morning drill was followed by a short breakfast after which camp would be broken and the day's march commenced. Arberus insisted on organising the army into a column and ordered the sergeants to ensure no soldier wandered more than two yards from the line of march. He also set a punishing pace, marching them for two hours at a time before permitting a half-hour's rest. Inevitably, the sudden introduction of discipline produced an upsurge in grumbling and some outright dissent, though most of it died down after Varkash beat one man unconscious for throwing a handful of dung at Arberus's horse. Those not inclined to open disobedience, but also finding the strictures of military life not much to their liking, had taken the opportunity to desert during the second night, though not as many as Lizanne would have expected.

"Forty-four failed to answer the morning roster," Arberus reported at the Electress's nightly conclave.

"Send me after them," Anatol said to her with a murderous grimace. "Forty-four severed heads would be quite the lesson."

The Electress shook her head, puffing on one of the increasingly scarce cigarillos to be found. "What lesson? That I'm just as bad as the constables? No, Annie, old love, let them go. The Emperor's soldiers will find them soon enough."

"And learn our destination in the process," Lizanne pointed out.

"Can't be helped. There's too many to track down in any case, and we don't have time to be pissing about." She took a final draw on her cigarillo, wincing in regret as she inspected the smoking fragment before stubbing it out. "What else, General?" she asked Arberus, employing a title Lizanne noticed many were now using to address the major, and not all with the same ironic lilt.

"The supply situation is still worrying," he said. "Rationing has reduced wastage, but we'll need a great deal more if we're to make it to Vorstek."

"Yes, I've been thinking about that. Those buggers we killed back at Scorazin, the light-horsey wotsits."

"The Thirty-eighth Imperial Light Horse," Arberus supplied.

"Right. They must have had a base, I assume?"

"They were stationed at Hervus, a small garrison town to the south."

"Small, eh?" The Electress smiled. "Which means it'll now be mostly empty since we killed nearly all those bastards. Am I right?"

"They may have been reinforced by now," Arberus said, pausing for a moment's calculation before adding, "Although it's unlikely. Most of the Imperial troops in this prefecture are concentrated in the north to guard the approaches to Corvus."

"How far to Hervus?" the Electress enquired.

"Two days' march, if we push hard."

"Then push away, General." The Electress rose and stomped off towards her tent. "And let's hope they have some fucking smokes there, I'm gasping."

CHAPTER 36

Clay

Clay followed Kriz's slender form, outlined in the bobbing glow of the lantern as she descended the stairs with a sure-footed swiftness. He suspected she was unwilling to let herself stop, as if the slightest pause would undo her determination to confront what lay below. It took several minutes to reach the bottom, Kriz striding through the narrow opening they found there with the same purposeful lack of hesitancy. Clay followed her then came to an unbidden stop at the sight that greeted him.

They were in a large chamber, most of it shrouded in darkness but he was able to gain an impression of its size as Kriz's lantern beam swept around. He heard her stifle a choking gasp as the light caught a bulky shape near the centre of the chamber. She rushed towards it, the light revealing a curved form that stirred an instant note of recognition. Moving closer, he saw it was a large stone slab that possessed a vague resemblance to a segment of orange. Full recognition dawned when Sigoral followed Loriabeth into the chamber, his sailor's lamp adding enough light to afford a fuller view of the chamber.

Not an orange, Clay thought, his gaze picking out the outline of an identical segment near by. *An egg.* It was the same as the huge segmented egg back in the structure where they had encountered Kriz. That one had been wet and, he now understood, recently opened. This one, however, was dry and covered in pale yellow dust.

"More over here," Loriabeth said, tapping the toe of her boot to another slab several feet away. Clay scanned the chamber, seeing numerous slabs all lying in their dusty shrouds. He did a quick count and estimated there were enough segments to make a dozen eggs. But it was clear that whatever had been waiting to hatch had done so a very long time ago.

A soft keening drew him towards the centre of the chamber where he found Kriz on her knees, hands playing over the dust-covered surface of a different object. This one was smaller than the eggs, with a more jagged appearance. As Kriz smoothed some of the dust from its surface he saw how it caught a bright gleam from her lantern.

"Crystal," he murmured, moving closer. It was much the same dimensions as the glowing rock from in the island structure, but this one lay dark and lifeless on the chamber floor.

A stream of words issued from Kriz's mouth in a rapid jumble, too fast to follow but Clay was sure one of the words translated as "alone."

"She lost her mind?" Loriabeth asked.

"I don't think so," Clay replied, then nodded at the surrounding shapes. "I think there was something here she hoped might still be around."

"This is a tomb," Sigoral said, rubbing dust between his gloved fingers. "All bodies will turn to dust with sufficient time."

"I don't think she was expecting to pay her respects to the dead." His mind ransacked the evidence, coming up with an unpalatable but undeniable conclusion. *The opened egg back at the island* . . . "*Ten thousand years* . . ." "It was a storehouse," he went on. "Or a barracks, depending on how you look at it." His gaze tracked from the crystal to one of the sundered eggs. "She slept in one of these for a very long time, not knowing she'd be all alone when she woke up."

"Slept?" Sigoral asked, clearly finding the notion absurd.

"We've seen a lot since we got ourselves trapped down here," Clay replied. "Folk who could build this place, and everything else, ain't too much of a stretch to imagine they could contrive a way for people to sleep for years at a time."

Kriz let out a sob, so full of pain and loss he gave an involuntary shiver. The sense of being observed was strong here, as if the silent scrutiny of those gone-to-dust souls were pressing in from all sides.

"Guess something went wrong at some point," he went on, moving to rest a hand on Kriz's shoulder.

"Father . . ." Kriz's voice was a whisper. She remained huddled on her knees, tears dripping from her face, but there was a sibilant anger to her tone that hadn't been there before. "Father . . ." she repeated, forming the words with care, "went . . . *wrong.*" Without warning she threw her head back and screamed, "FATHER!"

The scream echoed through the chamber like thunder, full of rage and accusation, then slowly faded without reply.

"We, uh . . ." Loriabeth began after a short interval during which Kriz subsided back into herself, slender shoulders moving in gentle heaves. "We should go."

Once outside Kriz didn't pause, striding away from the opening without a backward glance. A few times she faltered, succumbing to brief bouts of grief that saw her choking down sobs. Clay made no attempt to talk to her. The depth of sorrow on her face made him doubt she could hear him just now. She only seemed to regain full awareness when Loriabeth spotted an unusual feature in the landscape ahead.

"That smoke I see?" she said, pointing at a large opening marring the otherwise smooth surface of a cliff some ways off to the left. Clay surveyed it through the spy-glass on his carbine, finding it dark and weathered but with a hard-edged quality that made him doubt it was a natural feature. *If anything in here could even be called natural,* he thought, watching a thin but continuous stream of grey smoke rising from the opening.

"Could climb up and take a look," he mused aloud, turning to Sigoral. "Feel up to it, Lieutenant?"

"No!" Kriz moved to Clay's front, shaking her head. Her grief seemed to have evaporated for the moment and her voice was hard. "No climb!"

Clay's gaze lingered on her emphatic frown for a second before tracking back to the opening. "Something bad in there?" he asked. "More long-dead folks turned to dust?"

She ignored the question, flicking her gaze about as if searching for something in the surrounding rocks. "We go," she told Clay, moving off with a rapid stride. It seemed clear to Clay that this time she had no intention of waiting to see if they followed.

"We'd best move on," he told the others with a final glance at the smoking hole in the cliff. "If something's got her this spooked it's probably not a good idea to linger."

Kriz led them on through ever-steeper country for another hour before calling a halt atop a broad rocky shelf overlooking a shallow canyon. "Kinda lacking in cover for my liking," Loriabeth said, casting her gaze at the gathering gloom above. "Nowhere to shelter if a Black comes calling, and this is their sorta country."

Clay surveyed the surrounding landscape. The trees had all but vanished now, leaving them in a region of rock-covered hills he knew would soon become mountains. "Can't see much of an alternative," he said. "We'll keep double watch just in case."

Kriz had perched herself on the edge of the shelf, legs dangling as she gazed down at the canyon below. Clay and the others sat around and finished off some sea-biscuits whilst Kriz continued her silent vigil.

"Can't be more than thirty miles off," Loriabeth said, turning to regard the silver line of the shaft. "That's a two-day march in country like this."

"Then you'd best get some rest, cuz," Clay told her, having opted to share the first watch with Kriz. Sigoral had already settled down for the night, using his jacket as a blanket and pack as a pillow, as was his custom. His eyes were closed and his face slack in slumber, though he still had a firm grip on his carbine.

"Pops off in seconds, every time," Loriabeth said, covering herself with her duster. "Must be a sailor's habit." She paused a second before correcting herself. "Marine's habit."

"Must be."

Clay waited until his cousin was safely asleep before moving to sit at Kriz's side. The faux-night had come on fully now, casting a silver outline over her profile, which barely twitched as he joined her. It was evident her earlier grief had returned, at least partially.

"Sorry about your folks," he said, failing to produce a response. "I'm guessing that was your folks back there, or at least people you were close to."

Kriz's slim shoulders moved in a listless shrug, giving no indication of understanding or interest in his sympathy.

"Seemed awful aggravated at your pa," he forged on. "That I can understand. My pa was a worthless, headhunting shit-pile and I ain't felt a moment's sorrow over blowing his brains out, mostly anyways. That what you're planning on when we find your father? Got an account to settle?"

Kriz turned to him, features bland and eyes dim, a soul sunk deep into sadness. "Can't . . . talk," she said, then added, "now." With that she turned away and lowered her gaze to the canyon once again where the faint light danced on a stream winding its way through the rocks.

"Those markings back at the island," Clay persisted, reaching out to take her hand when she didn't respond. She tried to pull away but he held her in place. He used his finger to trace the two lines and the circle on the back of her hand then pointed at his own eye. "I've seen it before," he told her. "In a place far to the north of here. Another hidden place. Did your people build that too?"

Kriz gave an annoyed grunt and succeeded in tugging her hand free. She got to her feet and stalked away, Clay following at a cautious distance lest he provoke her to violence. "You lost your people," he said. "Your world too, I guess. But there's another one, up there." He moved into her eye-line, pointing to the black sky. "My world, and something's fixing to tear it all to pieces. You understand?" He stepped closer, speaking in an urgent rasp. "We came here for a reason. You got answers and I need them."

He reached for his wallet and extracted the Blue vial. At the sight of the product Kriz shook her head and stepped back from him, arms crossed in stern refusal. Clay bit down on a shout of frustration, fighting the urge to grab her and force the product down her throat, an act he suspected would see one of them nursing an injury or two.

"People are dying up there," he said, letting the anger leech from his voice. "Thousands are dead already and there'll be thousands more before this ends. And it's my fault, 'cos I woke it up." He blinked and felt tears trickle from the corners of his eyes. "Please," he said, his voice a thin croak as he held the vial out to her. "Please."

Kriz maintained the same posture for some time, arms tight about her chest, though he saw her gaze track the tears coursing down his face. "You . . . not . . . understand," she said, Clay detecting a wince of apology as she tapped a finger to her head. "What I . . . show."

"Think I'm too dumb to grasp it all, huh?" He grunted a laugh and wiped the tears away, still holding the vial out to her. "I'll try to follow as far as my dimwit's brain allows."

Kriz closed her eyes for a second, taking a short breath as if summoning some reserve of strength, then reached to take the vial.

The scream split the air like an axe blade, rebounding from the surrounding rocks to produce a piercing echo that made it impossible to discern the source. Loriabeth and Sigoral came awake instantly, surging to their feet with weapons raised. An unspoken instinct drew the four of them together so that they stood back-to-back, eyes straining against the encroaching dark as the scream faded.

"Black," Loriabeth breathed. "Leastways, I think so. Never heard one so loud, though."

"No," Clay said, a dreadful recognition churning his stomach. He found his hands trembling as he tried to keep his carbine steady. "That's a White."

CHAPTER 37

Lizanne

Arberus spent several hours formulating a detailed plan for the seizure of Hervus. The Brotherhood's riders were sent to scout the approaches and the regiments were drawn up to assault the town walls in several places at once. The army's two cannon would be used to pound the bastion that housed the main gate, principally as a diversion whilst the assault parties scaled the walls with hastily constructed ladders. So it was with some small amusement that Lizanne noted the disappointed frown on Arberus's face when they approached to within a mile of Hervus, finding the gates standing open and a truce-flag flying above the bastion.

"Never mind," Lizanne told the major with a grin. "I'm sure it would have worked."

She attached herself to the delegation accompanying the Electress as she made her way to the gate. Atalina bounced gracelessly on the back of a massive dray-horse she had named Dropsy. Lizanne thought the woman made a defiantly impressive sight as she dragged her mount to a halt a few yards short of the town's gate, the impression of bulk and purposeful aggression overcoming any humour aroused by the otherwise unedifying spectacle she made. Lizanne watched her take in the grisly spectacle that greeted her at the bastion; six naked bodies hanging by their ankles from the arched entrance. The corpses were perhaps two days old by Lizanne's reckoning, the blood dried on their flesh into brown stains and their skin not yet begun to blacken. Their wounds were clustered around the chest and abdomen in a pattern Lizanne knew well. These men had died by firing squad. Beneath the bodies stood a cluster of young men wearing the uniforms of mixed Imperial soldiery: short-jacketed cavalry troopers, infantrymen in their grey-green long coats and blue-jacketed artillerymen. The motley group numbered twenty in all, fidgeting in silence under the Electress's scrutiny until she deigned to address them, "Who the fuck are you lot?"

One of the young men stepped forward, trying and mostly failing to put some stridency into his voice as he provided a clearly pre-rehearsed response, "Elected representatives of the Council of Free Soldiers." He coughed and pointed to the corpses dangling above his head. "This town has been liberated and those who held us in bondage subject to just execution."

"So I see," the Electress replied. "These your officers?"

"Those that failed to join us when we raised the standard of freedom." The young soldier had gained some confidence now and straightened his back as he resumed his prepared speech, "Too long have the honest soldiers of this empire borne the yoke and the whip of the officer caste. It's time for a new army, a people's army . . ."

"Alright, give it a rest, lad," the Electress said, wincing at the youth's increasing volume. "How many of these newly free soldiers have you got in there?"

The soldier's composure faltered a little but he held himself in place with what Lizanne thought was commendable self-control. "Enough to defend this station," he said. "Should it prove necessary."

"Balls," Atalina replied, smothering a yawn. "We killed most of your lot at Scorazin. That's where we're from, if you hadn't guessed. Me and all my friends." She turned in the saddle, gesturing at the assembled ranks of the army drawn up some two hundred yards short of the gate. "Cutthroats, bandits and killers," she said turning back and favouring the young man with a surprisingly sympathetic smile. "And that's just the nice ones. Does this really have to get unpleasant, lad?"

"We want no trouble," the youth replied, his face paling and voice taking on a thin, reedy quality. "In fact we wish to negotiate an alliance. News of your victory was the second spark to our rebellion."

"Nice to know. I'm sure we'll get on famously, 'specially if you've got any cigarillos going." The Electress groaned and climbed down from Dropsy's back before stepping forward to offer the young man her hand. "Name's Atalina, but you can call me Electress." She gave him a conspiratorial wink. "I didn't inherit the title, but don't tell anyone, eh?"

"Jarkiv," the soldier replied, grimacing as he shook the proffered hand and no doubt suffered a demonstration of brute strength. "Corporal Jarkiv."

"That won't do." The Electress released his hand and clapped him on the shoulder. "Smart lad like you should be a captain at least. Make a note will you, General," she called, waving Arberus forward. "Captain Jarkiv and the First Free Soldier Brigade welcomed into our ranks on this day."

Lizanne followed as Arberus walked his stallion closer and dismounted, offering Jarkiv a smart salute, which the youth returned in an automatic reflex. "Welcome, Captain," Arberus greeted him in brisk tones. "I'll need a full accounting of your numbers and supplies."

"Yes, sir!" Jarkiv saluted again, the cluster of soldiers at his back all snapping to attention and following suit. Lizanne suspected that, for all his revolutionary rhetoric, Jarkiv and his comrades were too steeped in the military mind-set not to welcome the arrival of competent authority, however unexpected the source.

"Excellent," Arberus said, glancing up at the bodies hanging above. "And let's get this mess cleaned up, shall we?"

"Very good, sir."

"The second spark," Lizanne said, making Jarkiv and the others pause as they turned to follow their orders.

"Ma'am?" he asked with a cautious glance at Arberus and the Electress.

"You said our victory was the second spark to your rebellion. What was the first?"

Jarkiv frowned at her in bafflement. "You mean you don't know? We assumed it's what sparked your own uprising."

"Know about what, lad?" the Electress said.

"The Emperor," Jarkiv told her. "The Emperor's dead."

The Electress had been quick to take possession of the offices once occupied by the colonel who had commanded this station. After securing the town and its precious supplies she convened a council of the army's captains where Jarkiv related what he knew of the momentous event. Atalina reclined behind the fallen officer's desk, a contented grin on her broad lips as cigarillo smoke leaked from her mouth and nostrils.

"A Blood Cadre agent brought the news ten days ago," Jarkiv said. "Apparently, the Emperor suffered a fit and drowned in his bath."

Lizanne exchanged glances with Arberus, finding his sceptical frown a mirror of her own. "If he drowned, it wasn't due to a fit," she said, experiencing an unexpected pang of regret for the passing of poor mad Emperor Caranis Vol Lek Akiv Arakelin. His delusions had been entertaining, if nothing else. "Has an heir been named?"

"The Emperor died without issue," Jarkiv replied. "The Cadre agent told our major that Countess Sefka Vol Nazarias has convened a Regency Council to exercise power pending a decision on the succession."

"Sefka . . ." Lizanne whispered. *To think I persuaded Caranis to let her live. The Blood Imperial won't be happy about her elevation, if she hasn't had him killed yet.* "It was a coup," she said, raising her voice to address the room. "I expect in a few days this Regency Council will find a convenient puppet to place on the throne or the countess herself will miraculously discover a blood line linking her to the Imperial family. Which doesn't bode well for anyone with a legitimate claim."

"Prince Reshnik is Caranis's closest living relative," Arberus said. "But he's seventy years old and, reputedly, a simpleton."

"Countesses, emperors, princes," Korian said, voice rich in scorn and an excited gleam in his eye. "The great aristocratic circus doesn't matter now. The nobility has always been a pestilential snake coiling itself around the heart of this empire, and now it's headless. We have never had a better opportunity."

"To do whad?" Varkash enquired. He stood at the Electress's left, arms crossed and a stern frown on his brow.

"To win of course," Korian replied, turning about to address them all, voice trembling a little. "Think of it, brothers and citizens. The road to true freedom lies open, we need only take it."

"My men didn't join up for a revolution," Varkash pointed out. "They were promised ships and passage off dis blighted land. As for myself, I have bidness in Varestia and couldn't give a sea-dog's cock for your freedom."

"Your homeland will be freed from the perennial threat of invasion once we are victorious," Korian insisted then turned to point at Jarkiv. "This man and his fellows have shown how fragile the Regnarchy's grip has become. They will not be the only soldiers to rise against their officers. This will not be the only town to wrest itself free of its chains. There were riots in Corvus before the Emperor's death. Now the city must be in ferment. We should strike north in the morning, begin a march on the capital that will capture the hearts of thousands . . ."

"We come up against one decent-sized and well-organised force and we're done," the Electress broke in, speaking quietly but firmly as she stubbed out her cigarillo and immediately reached for another. "Right, General?" she added, raising an eyebrow at Arberus.

"In all probability," Arberus said, face set in hard contemplation. "But that presupposes such a force exists to oppose us. If Citizen Korian is correct, the road to Corvus would be open."

Lizanne found she didn't like what she heard in Arberus's voice, the echo of that revolutionary zeal that had birthed so many arguments. "And what would we do when we got there?" she enquired.

"What many of us have dedicated our lives to," he replied, turning to meet her gaze. "We put an end to the tyranny that has been the bane of this empire for centuries."

I thought you had progressed beyond this, she wanted to say. *I thought I had made you . . . more.* Instead she hid her disappointment with a shrug and turned her attention to the Electress. "There are too many unknown factors here," she said. "Clearly there will be a measure of chaos, but to imagine that we could march all the way to Corvus unopposed is lunacy."

The Electress glanced at her before clasping her hands together in a familiar contemplative gesture. After a long moment of calculation she turned again to Arberus. "What're our numbers like now?"

"With the addition of Captain Jarkiv's men, close on six thousand," he replied.

The Electress nodded, face expressionless as she pointed a stubby finger at the door. "Everyone out, I need to think about this for a bit. Not you, dear," she added, as Lizanne made to follow the others from the room. "We're overdue for a proper chat."

"The last woman to betray me begged for death." Atalina had ordered a bottle of wine brought to her rooms and sipped at it as they sat opposite each other beside the fire-place. Lizanne noted that the tray holding the bottle held only one glass. "The last man who betrayed me couldn't," the Electress went on, "on account of how I'd stuffed his balls in his mouth."

"Yes, you're a very frightening person," Lizanne said, offering a bland smile. "Consider me suitably intimidated."

"'Cept you're not, are you? Faced worse than me in your time, I'd guess. I'd also guess they're all dead now. Am I right?"

Lizanne's mind flashed to Madame Bondersil's last moments, the helpless fluttering of her arms before the Blue drake jerked its head and swallowed her whole. "Is this relevant?" she asked.

"We need to properly understand each other, if we're to forge a common purpose."

"I thought we had already done that."

"Hah." The Electress gave a brief chuckle. "You think I don't know that the moment you get a chance to sneak off with Tinkerer you won't take it? You do a pretty good job of hiding your thoughts, but the mask slips a little when our radical friends start talking. Got no stomach for their babble, have you?"

"Wilful naïvety is irksome."

"And General Arberus? He irksome too?"

"He has his ideas, I have mine."

"Then I'm sorry to say I can't see much've a future for you two. It's how it was with my old man, before I killed him. We ran a profitable smuggling operation together in northern Kestria. We were young in those days, but we'd been brought up in the smuggling trade and knew the ropes well enough to get by. The purges after the First Revolution had killed off the older breed and much of the competition, so we had a pretty clear run for a few years and got very rich in the process. By the time I was twenty we lived in the finest house in town and had all the ornamentations to go with it. You should always be wary of wealth, my dear, for it'll make you soft and brave at the same time.

"Came the day the Emperor saw fit to appoint a new Provincial Governor who had a mind to triple the annual bribe we'd paid his predecessor. My husband wasn't having any of it, grown brave in his wealth, like I said, but arrogance is its own brand of weakness." She paused to breathe out a nostalgic sigh. "If ever I actually loved someone, it was him. Broke my heart when I slipped the mandrake into his supper. Had no choice, y'see? We could fight another gang, but not the empire. So, I did what needed doing and paid up."

"And yet you still ended up in Scorazin," Lizanne noted.

"Things rolled along pretty well for everyone for a good few years. With my husband gone I was able to bring a certain efficiency to the business, doubled our profits soon enough. Then the old governor died of gout. His replacement was some cousin of the Emperor's, a real stickler with a rod up his arse who thought accepting a bribe was beneath one who bore the Divine Blood. He set his constables to seizing our shipments, after hanging a few who'd been a bit too free with their bribe money. Even then we might have survived, kept things at a low level and waited for the bastard to sod off back to Corvus, but it turned out he had the favour of the Blood Imperial. Once that old fucker sent his agents into Kestria, it was only a matter of time before I found myself at the end of a rope or in Scorazin. Spent a good deal of my life behind those walls. Not saying I didn't deserve at least some of what I suffered there, but by no means all."

She raised her eyes to Lizanne's, holding her gaze for a long moment of silence.

"Oh dear," Lizanne groaned in realisation as the woman's intent became clear. It was odd, but her disappointment in the Electress was almost as great as her disappointment in Arberus. Although as dreadful an example of the criminal class as Lizanne had ever expected to meet, she nevertheless had nurtured a deep respect for the woman's pragmatism. "You actually intend to march on Corvus."

The Electress shrugged her broad shoulders. "We've all got scores to settle. Besides which, with this empire in chaos, who knows what opportunities might happen along? Sailing away to some corporate holding has a certain appeal, if you'd've actually kept your side of the deal, which I have my doubts about. But I don't know the corporate world like I know this empire and its people. Like you said, I could do great things here."

"Arrogance is its own brand of weakness," Lizanne reminded her, expecting to arouse the woman's anger and so was disappointed when she only laughed.

"I've never been arrogant in my life," she said. "But I've also never been one to turn my back on an opportunity, or an unpaid debt."

It took a moment for Lizanne to understand her meaning, and when she did she voiced a brief laugh of her own. "The Blood Imperial. You want revenge for what he did to you."

"Seems like the only occasion in this lifetime I'm likely to get the chance. But it takes a Blood-blessed to kill a Blood-blessed."

"Meaning me, I assume."

"Meaning I'm renegotiating our arrangement. You want Tinkerer, I want that old bastard dead when we get to Corvus."

"There's a fair chance he's dead already."

The Electress shook her head. "Done my research over the years, gathered every scrap of knowledge I can about the Blood Cadre. I think we both know the Blood Imperial will have survived this coup. Perhaps he even had a hand in bringing it about."

Lizanne thought back to her meeting with the Blood Imperial, the old man's deep-set cynicism and ingrained facility for intrigue certainly indicated a soul capable of engineering Caranis's downfall. But she also recalled his attachment to the established order. *It's an absurd and ancient pantomime, and it works.* "I find that unlikely," she said. "It's probable that he will be paying lip-service to Countess Sefka's authority for now, but they've been enemies for years. Conflict between the Blood Cadre and the new order is most likely inevitable, meaning he will be more use as an ally than an enemy."

"You talk like someone who knows him."

"I do, although our acquaintance was brief. It was thanks to his intelligence I came to Scorazin."

"Suffering a great deal of privation and risk just so you could bring out Tinkerer. I think it's time I knew why he's so important."

"Suffice to say, if you don't permit me to take him to an Ironship holding nothing that occurs in this empire will matter a jot."

"Yes, I gather plenty has happened since I went away. A lot of wild tales to be heard in this town, about how the empire and the corporates got kicked out of Arradsia by a bunch've drakes and deformed savages."

"Sadly all true."

"Which means no more product for you and your kind. If we wait long enough the Blood Cadre will have exhausted its stocks and won't be able to oppose us."

"By which time you'll be facing something far worse than the Cadre."

"Then it's in your interest to ensure our victory is a swift one, my dear." The Electress paused, eyes narrowing. "You really think the Blood Imperial will throw in with us?"

"Only in extremis. It's more likely he'll do everything he can to crush us. You can expect to face his Blood-blessed children before long."

"How fortunate then that I have you, and that Brotherhood boy, what-sisname."

"Hyran. He's far too inexperienced to face combat with a Cadre agent, Blessed or not."

"Best get to training him then."

"This is madness," Lizanne told her simply. "Countess Sefka can still muster enough loyal troops to defeat us, even without the Blood Imperial's help. You can't expect this rabble to stand against regular, veteran soldiers."

"You should have more faith in our general. I'm expecting great things of him."

The Electress levered herself out of her chair and nodded at the door. "Think that gets it said, don't you? You could take yourself off of course, can hardly stop you. But this is the deal now, you get the Tinkerer the day you lay the Blood Imperial's head at my feet on the steps of the Sanctum. In the meantime, go within a dozen feet of the Tinkerer and I'll have Anatol slit his throat."

The army moved out after a three-day halt at Hervus during which time Arberus did everything he could to transform his rabble into soldiers. To Lizanne's surprise there had been no sudden upturn in desertions following the Electress's announcement that their ultimate objective was now Corvus instead of Vorstek. The ease with which Hervus had fallen seemed to embolden the recruits, even attracting a few more volunteers from the surrounding towns and villages as word spread. Recruitment increased further after the Brotherhood began proclaiming Arberus's true lineage. They sent riders from town to town spreading the news that the grandson of Morila Akiv Bidrosin herself had emerged from the shadows to lead the march to freedom. By the time they began the march the army's ranks had swollen to almost ten thousand people, although to Lizanne's eyes they still displayed only a vague semblance of military order.

"At least we have something like a decent artillery train now," Arberus commented as the army assembled itself for departure. In addition to Jarkiv and his somewhat grandiosely titled Free Brigade, the fortified town had yielded a dozen cannon and substantial stocks of ammunition. Fortunately, the garrison's gunners had been amongst the most enthusiastic mutineers, meaning each gun was fully crewed by experienced hands.

"It won't be enough," Lizanne said. "One regiment of Household troops will put this lot to flight in a matter of minutes."

"That supposes Countess Sefka will be able to spare a regiment. Our new recruits brought news of rioting in Corvus, more mutinies in the northern garrison towns. Korian is right, we'll never have a better opportunity."

Lizanne watched him survey his army, seeing the zealous gleam in his eye. She knew her disdain was unfair. Arberus had been steeped in revolutionary dogma since birth and this unexpected turn in events could be said to be the culmination of his life. Even so, the swiftness with which he appeared to have abandoned their mission stung more than she cared to admit.

"Come with me tonight and we'll take the Tinkerer," she said. "We'll be far away by morning and safely aboard an Ironship vessel within ten days. Leave these fools to their mad endeavour."

He didn't look at her, though she took a crumb of comfort from seeing his zealousness subside into a regretful frown. "I can't," he said. "Not now. Not when we're so close."

"Is this my fault?" she wondered aloud, addressing herself more than him. "If I had been . . . less myself would you be so quick to throw away what we shared?"

"Did we ever really share more than a purpose?" he enquired, turning to her with a sad smile. "Was I ever more than a useful convenience?"

Lizanne began to answer then stopped, appalled to find the words halted by a catch in her throat. *This thing has weakened me,* she decided, turning away. *And I can no longer afford weakness.*

"I see." Arberus swallowed a sigh and extended a hand to point out the slight form of Tinkerer amongst the busy throng. The artificer stood directing Anatol and his brace of guards as they placed a collection of tubular devices in the back of a wagon.

"The Electress let me put him to use," Arberus said. "There's a foundry here, I thought he might be able to produce a thumper or a growler if I gave him the designs. He said it was impossible in the time available, but he did come up with another less complex device that might prove equally effective."

Lizanne straightened a little at his tone and the note of intent it held. She paused to swallow away the catch in her throat, straightening her back and draining all emotion from her response. "So, I assume you wouldn't want him to go suddenly missing."

"Or you. We need you both. We have a chance here to do something great . . ."

"Spare me. You know what we face, you saw it with your own eyes at Carvenport. This trivia"—she waved a hand at the untidy ranks of the sluggishly assembling regiments—"is a distraction."

"Sefka and the Blood Imperial have no interest in anything beyond their own power," Arberus countered. "An empire freed from the corruption and incompetence of the ruling nobility will be far better placed to resist the White's onslaught."

"Such inventive rationalisation does you credit, General." Lizanne turned her mare about and trotted away, knowing she would pitch her tent far from his come the evening and that he would make no effort to seek her out.

"Beautiful," Makario said as Hyran fell silent, clasping his hands together and a small tear rising in his eye. "Simply beautiful."

The youth flushed a little and gave a modest shrug. "Just an old choral piece Ma and Pa taught me," he said. "Music was a big part of their faith. Said it gave voice to the soul."

"So you know others?"

"A dozen or so. There are more, but the Cadre burned all the holy books, so I s'pose they're gone for good."

"Yet another Imperial crime to be punished in full when we get to Corvus." Makario sighed and stepped closer to Hyran, placing a hand on his chest and another on the small of his back to ease him into a more upright pose. "Posture is important, my boy. Raise your chin and let the words soar. Contrary to popular belief the voice comes from the stomach, not the throat."

"If you're quite finished," Lizanne said, impatience adding an edge to her tone. The army had made camp for the night and she had sat watching Makario tutor Hyran in the finer points of vocal performance for nearly an hour now. The musician had remained close to her since the escape, pitching his tent beside hers every night and rarely straying more than a few yards from her side. He had escaped Arberus's training regimen by appointing himself Assistant to Miss Blood, though his duties in that regard seemed minimal to Lizanne's eyes.

Miss Blood. The name had re-emerged during their time in Hervus and soon spread throughout the ranks of the army. She suspected Arberus might well have had a hand in resurrecting a title she thought left behind in Feros. Perhaps he sought to cement her position in this unwise expedition whilst also publicising the fact that the army boasted at least one Blood-blessed in its ranks.

"We have work to do," she told Hyran, rising and plucking a vial from the Spider.

"Oh can't you leave him be?" Makario implored, striking a somewhat theatrical pose as he placed himself protectively between her and Hyran. "I seek to educate him in the arts of life, whilst all you do is mire him in the arts of death."

"You've been waiting all day to say that, haven't you?" Lizanne enquired.

Makario gave a sullen frown and slouched aside. "Actually, I only thought of it a moment ago."

"Black," Lizanne said, tossing the vial to Hyran. "Just a drop. We need to husband our supplies."

So far these nightly training sessions had done little to bolster her faith in the youth's abilities. His lack of experience and limited exposure to product made him a slow student, barely capable of more than a first-year girl at the Academy. He tended to exhaust any Green he imbibed in a matter of seconds, proving repeatedly incapable of suppressing the exhilaration that accompanied the rush of vitality. His use of Red was clumsy to the point of danger, not least to himself as evidenced by the long scorch-mark on the sleeve of his jacket. However, he did at least display some facility for Black, managing to exert an impressive level of control over the objects he grasped, though his choices were a trifle obvious.

"Smaller is often better," she told him as he slammed a large boulder against the trunk of a near by oak. The great tree shuddered at the impact, shedding leaves that cascaded around them in a green rain. The boulder itself shattered on impact, sending stone shards in all directions, one of which found the back of Makario's hand.

"Have a care, if you please!" he huffed, mopping at the bleeding scratch with a kerchief. "These"—he raised his hands and twiddled his fingers—"are my fortune, after all."

Lizanne ignored him and pointed to a small stone lying close by. "Try that one," she said. "See if you can set it spinning before you throw it. It'll fly straighter."

Hyran frowned and focused his gaze on the stone, raising it to eye level where it hovered and shuddered as he attempted to add the spin.

"Just one hard shove at a single point," Lizanne advised. "Like flipping a coin. Momentum will do the rest." The stone lost its shudder then abruptly began spinning so fast it blurred. "Focus on the target." Lizanne nodded at the oak. "Remember, the quicker you do this the better. Product is always finite."

The stone vanished and Lizanne initially thought Hyran had exerted enough force to crush it, but then saw a plume of powdered bark and wood blossoming on the centre of the oak's trunk. "Faster than a bullet," she told him, gratified by the mingled surprise and satisfaction on his face. "Send a swarm of them into the closed ranks of an advancing regiment and the results can be impressive."

"I'll try a load at once," Hyran said. He raised the vial to his lips then frowned in annoyance when she reached out to tug it from his grasp.

"Sorry," she said. "I'm afraid this is your last lesson. We can't afford to expend any more product. Not if we're to have any chance against the Blood Cadre."

"You're sure they'll turn up then?" He tried to hide it but Lizanne could see his fear. *At least he has enough wit to be afraid,* she thought.

"I regret to say I'm quite certain of it."

Her gaze was drawn to a commotion in the camp, soldiers clustering around Arberus and the Electress as buglers blew an inexpert rallying signal. Near by Lizanne could see Korian and a cluster of mounted Brotherhood scouts, the steaming breath of their horses indicating a recent arrival after a hard ride.

"And perhaps sooner than expected," she added. "I do believe we are about to have some Imperial company."

CHAPTER 38

Clay

The White's cry faded after a few seconds, leaving the four of them standing back-to-back in primed and silent vigilance. The surrounding gloom seemed suddenly impenetrable, compelling Clay to enhance his vision with a swallow of Green.

"You see it?" Loriabeth whispered as he scanned the landscape, finding only yet more rocks each one of which possessed an uncanny ability to resemble a crouching drake.

"No," he whispered back, "but it's out there for sure."

"Too much to hope you might be mistaken, I suppose?" Sigoral enquired in a tense mutter.

"It's not a sound I'm ever likely to forget, Lieutenant."

"Felt close," Loriabeth said, the butt of her repeating rifle braced hard against her shoulder. "Musta' seen us."

"It saw us," Clay assured her, his gaze flicking from one rock to another. Although Green enabled his eyes to pierce the dark to a high degree, there were still shadows of sufficient depth to conceal a full-grown White. The sense of being observed was strong and he could imagine the beast lurking in a rocky nook as it gazed upon the strange two-legged intruders into its domain. *What's it waiting for?* he asked himself. He knew this beast would be smart, a drake that understood much of what it saw, and perhaps what it heard. *If it's waiting it has a reason.*

A faint breeze chilled his scalp and he jerked his gaze upward, eyes roving the blank sky until he saw it, a broad-winged silhouette thirty yards above, moving in a slow circle. Clay gauged its size as a little larger than the fully grown male Reds he had seen in the Badlands. He raised his carbine and trained the optical sight on the silhouette. The range was well within reach of this weapon, but he had severe doubts the carbine's ammunition could pierce the hide of a White. Also, even with Green in his veins the chances of making a head-shot against a moving target were minimal.

"I'll follow your aim," Loriabeth said, raising her repeating rifle. "Aim for the wings. Once it's down I can make the kill-shot."

"If we miss it'll be on us in seconds," he replied. "Ain't a good idea to provoke one of these things."

"Since when did they need any provocation?"

A loud clack snapped his gaze to Kriz, finding her standing with the bulky form of her bomb-thrower raised high and her face set in a fiercely determined grimace.

"Don't!" he shouted, reaching out to push the weapon aside just as it gave a loud cough and a bright plume erupted from the muzzle. The projectile gave a faint whistle as it arced into the air before exploding in a blaze of white fire that banished the gloom in an instant. The flare dangled from a small canopy of some kind, casting forth a blazing light that painted tilting shadows over the surrounding rocks as it swung about. The White screeched in response to the sudden illumination, revealed in full as it angled its wings and swept towards them. Clay was struck by how thin it seemed in comparison to the full-grown cousin he had confronted beneath the mountain. This one had a neck that seemed more bone than flesh, its wings thin and ragged as was its hide. He stood in frozen surprise as it flew closer, his eyes picking out the mottled patchwork on its scales, before Loriabeth and Sigoral opened fire in unison.

The White twisted as bullets rent the air around it, swooping low then high in an effort to avoid the stinging rain of metal. Sparks flew from the rocks as they chased it across the half-lit landscape, the staccato rattle of their guns soon joined by the percussive boom of Kriz's bomb-thrower. The White jerked left and right as the bombs exploded around it, Clay seeing one come close enough to blast a hole in its wing. It landed as his companions emptied their weapons and the gun-fire died.

They began to reload with feverish energy, Clay keeping his gaze locked on the White as it crawled towards them across the rocks, covering the distance in a skittering blur, mouth gaping as it summoned its fire. He fumbled for his vials, gulping down Black and stepping forward just as the flames started to blossom. He had intended to hold the beast in place but the urgency of the moment made him clumsy. Instead of freezing the White the unleashed wave of force blasted it to one side. The gout of flame streaming from its jaws went wide, though not before leaving a patch of flame on the sleeve of Clay's duster. He ignored it and tried again, reaching out with his invisible hand to grab the White so Loriabeth could put a bullet through its brain. Once again it evaded him, leaping to the side as the Black cracked rocks to powder.

Clay sank into an involuntary hunch as gun-fire erupted again, Loriabeth and Sigoral moving to his side and blazing away with their reloaded weapons. The White screamed under the lacerating barrage. Clay saw several impacts on its flesh, though no evidence it had suffered serious damage. It leapt high, wings scattering shards of rock into their faces as it sought the air, then jerked spasmodically as one of Kriz's bombs struck it square in the chest. The White's wings folded as it plunged back down, smoke rising from a glowing orange spot on its chest. It began to thrash, tail whipping and wings fluttering, issuing an enraged scream along with an intense stream of fire.

Kriz stepped to Clay's side, her face still fixed with a determined rage. He watched as she switched the drum on her bomb-thrower, slotting a new bulkier one into place. "What is—?" he began then stepped back in alarm as she lowered the angle of her weapon and resumed fire.

The first bomb struck the White just below its neck. Instead of the explosion Clay expected it gave a dull, popping hiss as it blossomed into a ball of flaming sparks, so bright his eyes flooded with water and he had to look away. Kriz continued to fire, emptying all six bombs in the drum in as many seconds. When he looked again, squinting from behind shaded eyes, he saw the White writhing in a bath of pure flame. It gave a final screech before succumbing to the inferno, the tail, now scorched and mostly denuded of flesh, rising to coil like a somnolent snake before subsiding into the all-consuming heat.

"Well," Loriabeth said, giving Kriz an appreciative hug. "I guess that'll do it, hon."

He found a pool of the White's blood in the lee of a large boulder. It was shallow and part congealed, probably the fruit of one of Loriabeth's bullets. In the gathering light of the false dawn the blood appeared almost black and deeply uninviting. Clay well remembered his only previous taste of raw White blood and had no desire to repeat the experience, but they had come here in search of answers. Sighing he dipped an empty vial into the pool and scooped up a portion of the blood, careful not to get any on his fingers. He washed the excess away with his canteen and consigned the vial to his wallet before moving to join the others.

They stood around the blackened patch of rock which marked the White's passing. The fire unleashed by Kriz's weapon was evidently the result of some clever chemical concoction for it had reduced the beast down to a collection of blackened bones. Its skull was a cracked and wasted thing, though enough of it remained to form an eye socket. Clay couldn't prevent his gaze from straying to that empty hole.

What did you know? he wanted to ask it, his gaze lost in the dark recess of the skull. *Did you have the same purpose as your friend up top?*

"The Wittler Expedition powdered up the bones," Loriabeth said, poking a toe into the ash.

"Then went crazy and killed each other," Clay reminded her, finally managing to tear his eyes from the White's skull. "Think they're best left where they lay, cuz."

"At least we know they're not invincible," Sigoral said. "If we've learned nothing else here, there's that."

"This one wasn't whole," Clay said, shifting his gaze to Kriz. She stood regarding the beast's remains in silence, apparently lost in thought. He recalled the animal's comparatively spindly appearance and the mottled nature of its hide. Also, fast as it had been it was still sluggish compared to the only other White he had met. "Something was wrong with it. Had it been full-grown and healthy, we'd likely be the ones all burnt up. Right?" he asked Kriz, raising his voice and pointing to the White's remains, speaking slowly. "It . . . was . . . sick."

She met his gaze and gave a brief nod, frowning as she struggled to formulate a response he would understand. "New . . ." she said, grimacing in annoyance then trying again. "New hatched."

Clay's mind immediately went to the opening in the cliff they had found the day before. *Too regular to be natural and coughing up smoke.* "Hatched," he repeated, pointing at the ground. "Hatched down below, right?"

She nodded, offering an apologetic smile as she gestured to the remains. "This is . . . one. There are . . . many."

"Well ain't that just fine," Loriabeth said, casting a wary gaze around.

"We go," Kriz said, moving away to gather up her pack. Clay wanted to object, compel her to wait so they could finally trance. But he knew she was right. If there were more they couldn't linger.

"I'll take the lead," he said, donning his own pack and unslinging his carbine. "Lori, follow at a twenty-yard interval. Lieutenant, guard the rear if you please. Keep an eye on the sky. We push hard from here on. No sleep till we reach the shaft."

They covered perhaps another five miles without incident, their progress inevitably slowed by the increasingly steep landscape. The hills had now become mountains and they were climbing rather than walking. Clay soon felt obliged to surrender the lead to Sigoral, who possessed a keener eye for the most efficient route up the successive slopes, each one more treacherous than the last. Almost all greenery had vanished now, save for the occasional patch of moss. Also the air grew noticeably colder with every passing mile, so that their breath soon began to steam in the chill.

"At least there's no snow," Sigoral observed during a brief rest stop. They were required to clamber from one rock to another, putting Clay in mind of children scaling a staircase. After a few hours his leg had begun to ache once more and his chest burned from exertion.

"Guess whoever made it wasn't overly keen on being too authentic," Clay replied, taking a long pull from his canteen. He resisted the urge to take another gulp. Their canteens were becoming increasingly light and he hadn't seen another stream since leaving the ledge where the White met its end.

"Which once again raises the question of who made it and why." The marine met Clay's gaze for a second before his eyes flicked towards Kriz, who had perched herself on a boulder a few feet below. "Questions that require answers, Mr. Torcreek."

"She says we'll trance again at the shaft. Guessing we'll get our answers then."

"If we can trust she intends to keep her word to a bunch of savages."

There was a bitterness to Sigoral's voice that Clay didn't like, and a certain resentment in his expression as he regarded Kriz. "Why don't you just throw down your scrip, Lieutenant," Clay said.

Sigoral frowned at him. "My scrip?"

"Old Blinds expression. Means say what you gotta say."

The Corvantine inched closer, lowering his voice. "I catch her expression sometimes when she thinks we're not looking. My old captain had a similar look in his eye when he surveyed his crew, but he didn't bother to hide it. Contempt, Mr. Torcreek. That's what she thinks of us. To her we are just useful primitives. Which raises the question of what happens when she's done with us."

"Or maybe she worries what we'll do when we're done with her."

"A question we also should be pondering."

Clay held the marine's gaze for a second longer then looked away. "We'll keep a keen watch on her," he said, his tone short. "Best get moving," he added, jerking his head at the slope ahead.

"I was there when the drakes rose off Carvenport." Sigoral straightened, shouldering his carbine. "I know what is at stake here. We both have a duty to perform. Rest assured I will perform mine, regardless of how unpleasant it becomes."

"Then you'd better hope we see things the same way when the time comes." Clay met his gaze again, holding it for longer this time. Eventually Sigoral's mouth formed a faint grin before he gave a shallow nod and resumed the climb.

By the time the light began to fade they had reached a point less than two miles from the shaft. It had swelled to monolithic proportions now, rising into the black void beyond the reach of the lights. The urge to press on through the dark was strong, but the route that confronted them forced a pause. They had ascended to the top of a plateau to find that there was only one remaining peak to scale. It was a broad mountain with an artificially flat summit where a building of familiar construction sat. Viewed through the optic of his carbine Clay found it to be a much larger version of the structure on the island, standing at least twice as high, its broad base covering most of the mountain top. The shaft rose from the structure's roof in all its weird majesty and irresistible promise of escape. However, between them and the mountain stood a ridge no more than five feet across at its widest point. Clay could make out signs of construction along the ridge as it wound its way towards a point less than a few hundred yards from the mountain's summit. The ridge was littered with patches of flat stone and disordered brickwork bespeaking a once-impressive construction.

"This was a road once?" he asked Kriz, who nodded.

"Very old," she said. "Need to . . . walk with care."

"It would be wise to wait for first light before starting across," Sigoral said, casting an uneasy eye over the steep sides of the ridge. "This is not a place to lose one's footing in the dark."

"But we're so close," Loriabeth said, nodding at the shaft. "Just an hour or two more."

"We keep going till it gets dark," Clay decided, striding forward. "Camp in the middle if we have to."

"It's too exposed," Sigoral contended, gesturing at the sky with his carbine. "If there are more Whites . . ."

"Look around," Clay replied, taking his first steps onto the ridge. He concealed a sigh of relief when the slabs beneath his boots failed to crumble away. "There's no more cover to be had here anyways." He moved on, hearing their footfalls as they followed after a long moment of hesitation.

The track atop the ridge did indeed prove precarious, even treacherous at times. More than once the apparently whole stone slabs on which they walked revealed deep cracks at the mere touch of a boot. Kriz was obliged to save Clay from one near-disastrous tumble down the near-vertical slope after a slab turned to fragments under his foot. She managed to grab hold of his pack in time, dragging him back as they collapsed together.

"Thanks," he said, his hammering chest adding an unmanly tremble to his voice.

She grinned and nodded, then frowned as her hand pressed against his pack and detected the large round object within. "What this?" she asked.

"Just a souvenir," he replied, getting to his feet and turning away.

"Egg," she said, her voice hardening as she rose and hurried after him. "You take egg."

"Killed its ma. Seemed the least I could do."

"It hatch. Kill us all."

Clay's hand went to the vials around his neck, playing over his growing collection of heart-blood. *Only three more for the set.* "I don't think so," he said. "Besides, without the waking fire it ain't hatching anytime soon."

She fell silent though he could sense a lingering discontent. For the first time it occurred to him that Kriz harboured a real hatred for the drakes inhabiting this strange world. The joy she had taken in killing the Blues back at the ocean and the fierceness in her gaze when she took aim at the White told of something more than just the triumph of survival.

He came to a halt, surveying the ruined brickwork around them. It had clearly been a substantial piece of construction in its time, now it was just old stone gradually crumbling to dust. "Wasn't always like this, huh?" he said, turning back to Kriz. "This place. Something went pretty badly wrong once upon a time. What was it?"

Her face took on a familiar guarded aspect and she merely returned his gaze, saying nothing.

"The drakes," he realised. "This place wasn't made for them. It was made for you. They took it over, didn't they?"

Kriz's brow creased as she pondered the right response. "Made . . . for both," she said finally. "They took all . . . as I slept."

"Uh, Clay," Loriabeth said. He saw she was standing close to the edge of the ridge, peering at something far below. Clay followed her gaze, eyes scanning the mist-shrouded depths. At first he saw nothing then noted a shimmering through the mist, as if the fading lights had caught the course of a fast-flowing river. Then he saw that it was growing, the shimmer fragmenting into many different points of light glittering on a rising dark tide. He heard the screams then, echoing up to assail his ears with grim familiarity. It was a sound he hadn't heard since the temple back in the jungle bordering Krystaline Lake, the frenzy song of massed Greens.

They emerged from the mist in a wave, scrabbling over the rocky flank of the ridge. Clay raised his carbine for a closer look and soon realised these were not the pygmies of the forest but similar in size to full-grown Arradsian Greens. They were still different, however, their limbs and tails possessed of the same spindly quality as the White. Also, their hides had the same mottled appearance, something the carbine's optic revealed to be glistening wet sores in their flesh. *None too healthy,* he realised, lowering the carbine as the rising mass of Greens swept closer. *Still plenty fast enough, though.*

Loriabeth started firing, her repeating rifle sending lengthy salvos into the advancing horde and sweeping a dozen or so off the ridge to tumble back into the gloomy depths.

"More here!" Sigoral called, Clay turning to see him standing at the opposite side of the ridge. The marine put his carbine to his shoulder and began to fire, sweeping the barrel from side to side in order to hit as many targets as possible. Kriz moved closer to the edge, her palm slamming a lever on the stock of her bomb-thrower and a now-familiar hatred marring her features.

"Forget it!" Clay said, reaching out to grab the strap of her pack. "There's too many!" he called to Sigoral and Loriabeth as they continued to blaze away. "We gotta go! Now!"

He paused just long enough to ensure they were following then turned and started to run. His earlier caution was forgotten now as he sprinted across near-vanished walkways and leapt over stunted walls. The frenzy song of the Greens seemed to thicken the air at his back, pushing him on and banishing the ache in his leg. A Green scrambled over the edge of the ridge just ahead, tail whipping as it whirled to face him, jaws gaping. Clay kept running, raising his carbine and letting loose with a stream of bullets as he closed with the drake. The concentrated burst of gun-fire tore into the Green's forelegs and shoulders, vapourising flesh and bone into a red cloud. The beast screamed and writhed, spraying blood from its myriad wounds. Clay fired again as he neared the thrashing drake, a short burst of fire that blew its head to pieces. He vaulted the corpse and ran on.

The end of the ridge came in view after what seemed a few seconds, by which time the exertion was finally starting to overcome his fear-born energy. His momentary elation died at the sight of the deep crevasse between the ridge and the flank of the peak beyond. Too wide to jump for anyone but a Blood-blessed with Green in their veins. He didn't pause, stumbling onward and dragging his wallet from the inside pocket of his duster. He gulped down as much Green as he could, covering the final few yards to the end of the ridge in a blur and leaping high. He overshot the gap by several yards, thumping into the side of the mountain with enough force to have shattered several bones but for the Green. He slid to the narrow ledge opposite the ridge and rolled quickly to his feet, finding the three of them gaping at him from the other side. The sense of betrayal on Loriabeth's face was particularly striking, although Sigoral's grimace of fury displayed little surprise. Kriz spared him only a glance before she turned about and started firing bombs at the onrushing swarm of Greens. They now covered the ridge from end to end in a dark roiling mass that barely seemed to notice the bombs exploding in its midst.

Clay extracted the vial of raw Black and drank down half the contents, fighting the convulsive retch as the product made a fiery progress to his gut. He took Loriabeth first, lifting her over the gap and depositing her close by. The urgency of the moment left little room for finesse and she gave a pained grunt as she landed on her rump. She shot him a reproachful but nevertheless relieved glare before getting to her feet and taking aim at the Greens. He returned his attention to the far side of the gap where both Sigoral and Kriz were firing furiously at the on-coming drakes. Clay hesitated, the Greens were so close now and it was possible he couldn't save them both. *I need answers,* he decided, fixing his gaze on Kriz. *Sorry, Lieutenant.*

At that moment, however, Sigoral's carbine fired empty. The Corvantine immediately began to reload but it was clear the Greens would be on him before he managed it. Clay acted through instinct, reaching out with the Black to snare the marine and drag him across the divide. His landing was even harder than Loriabeth's, slamming into the ledge at a shallow angle and rolling away with unnatural speed thanks to the momentum conveyed by the Black.

Clay immediately refocused his gaze on Kriz. She stood facing the Green horde with her bomb-thrower held limp at her side, apparently empty. The Greens were only yards away now and she gave no sign of panic or even concern as they came on, flames blossoming from the jaws of those in the lead. Clay lifted her clear of the horde just as they reached the end of the ridge, leaping and snapping at her dangling feet. A dozen or more tumbled into the crevasse whilst the rest milled about on the ridge-top, screaming their frustration.

Clay turned Kriz about as he carried her over the gap, looking up to find her smiling down at him as she floated closer. It was a smile he hadn't seen on her face before, possessing a genuine regard, even affection. He found it so surprising and captivating he failed to notice the Red until it was almost upon her.

CHAPTER 39

Lizanne

"The Emperor's Ravens and the Iron Watch," Korian said. "Plus three batteries of artillery and a full regiment of dragoons. That's just the vanguard. There are at least three other regiments of conscripts a few miles behind."

The Electress had convened a council to hear the Brotherhood leader report the results of his most recent reconnaissance. She had purloined a command tent from the stores at Hervus which was large enough to accommodate the army's captains. Lizanne was unsure if she should be reassured or worried by the fact that Atalina had made a point of ensuring Miss Blood attend this meeting.

"Pretty much the entire Household Division," Arberus mused. "Or what's left of it after the Scarlet Legion were destroyed at Carvenport. It appears Countess Sefka doesn't want to take any chances."

Lizanne found his reflective tones somewhat odd given Korian's report. Together, the Emperor's Ravens and the Iron Watch comprised the elite infantry of the Corvantine Imperial army, each possessing a fearsome reputation equal to that of the now-extinct Scarlet Legion.

"At least six thousand men in the vanguard and another nine thousand following," she said. "We may have gathered plenty of recruits in recent days but not that many."

"Numbers aren't everything," the Electress stated, her words accompanied by a glower that warned against any further unasked-for opinions. "Where?" she asked, turning back to Korian.

"Fifteen miles north-west as of this afternoon. Looks like they're keeping to the Corvus Road."

"So they'll already have encamped for the night," Arberus concluded. "And won't be too hard to find, even in the dark." He straightened, addressing his next words to the Electress. "We should break camp, a night attack offers the best chance of success."

Lizanne managed to contain her appalled exclamation but others present were not so restrained. "Are you fucking mad?" Varkash asked. "Dis lot against the empire's finest troops? In duh dark?"

"Better the dark than daylight," Arberus replied. "The Household Division is a formidable enemy, it's true. But having fought alongside them, I know their strength lies in the rigidity of their discipline. In close ranks with a clear field of fire they could prove unbeatable, but such discipline comes with a price. The Ravens and The Watch are like automata, responding to orders without thought or individual initiative. Confusion will be our ally, and darkness breeds confusion. Also," he added after a moment's pause, casting a reluctant glance in Lizanne's direction, "all manner of terrors."

Lizanne's gaze moved from him to the Electress, who now wore a broad smile. "Miss Blood," she said, "will be our key to victory."

"I cannot work miracles," Lizanne stated flatly. "And there may well be Blood Cadre in their ranks."

The Electress's smile broadened further. "Best kill them first, then."

"Even wid her, it's too much of a risk," Varkash persisted, his objection soon echoed by Captain Jarkiv and a few others.

"This is what you fuckers signed up for!" Atalina's voice cut through the rising babble like an axe blade. She rounded on them, teeth bared and shoulders hunched as if about to charge. "What did you think? It'd be a gentle stroll all the way to Corvus? We paid in blood to escape Scorazin, now it's time to pay again, but this time we escape the biggest prison of all. Defeat the Household Division and people will flock to us. An ocean of people that'll sweep all the way to the Imperial Sanctum."

She stood, glowering at each of them in turn, daring any to raise an objection. They all looked away as her gaze fell on them, except Varkash, who stood returning her glare in equal measure. "If I'd had more of my Fools left after Scorazin . . ." he began.

"You didn't," the Electress cut in. "Take your people and go if you're determined on it. But know that once we bring down this empire the books they'll write in the aftermath will make full note of Varestian cowardice. Is that really the name you want to carry back to the peninsular? Varkash the shiny-nosed coward, Shame of the Seas? If so, good luck finding another crew."

Varkash straightened, fists bunching and the slabs of muscle on his bare arms tensing. Lizanne entertained some hope he might launch himself at the Electress, the ensuing chaos facilitating a swift exit from the tent whereupon she would find Tinkerer and make good their escape. Sadly, the threat of a coward's name evidently outweighed the pirate's fury. After a long moment of simmering rage he crossed his arms and gave a short nod.

"So then, General," the Electress said, turning back to Arberus. "What's your plan?"

"Remember, where their ranks are thickest. The Tinkerer's new toys lack accuracy." Arberus held out a revolver, a long-barrelled model presumably scavenged from an unfortunate cavalryman's corpse at Scorazin.

"This will do, thank you," Lizanne said, patting the short-barrelled constabulary pistol in the holster under her arm. "Besides, I doubt any amount of arms will make much difference this night."

"If there was another way . . ."

"Oh, spare me . . . General."

She turned her back on him and gestured for Hyran to follow her to the edge of the copse where they had secluded themselves to await nightfall. Like her he wore all-black clothes of loose cotton and was armed with a pistol. His hands played over the weapon, twitching a little as he clicked the cylinder. "Stop fiddling," she told him. "And don't fire that unless we're discovered. Until then product is your principal weapon."

He forced a smile, face pale in the gloom, and consigned the pistol to its holster. "Just wish we had more of it."

Seeing his wan, tense features, she suppressed the urge to leave him behind. Tonight she would have need of all allies, regardless of ability. "Before this night's out," she said, forcing a brisk reassurance into her tone, "I suspect there'll be product aplenty for both of us."

She lowered herself into a crouch and moved into the sparse bushes beyond the reach of the trees, motioning for him to follow. "Now?" he whispered.

"I see little point in delay," she muttered back. "Do you?"

She paused to survey the ground ahead, finding it frustratingly free of cover all the way to the Corvantine picket line. Luckily, it was a lone-moon night so at least the shadows were deep. She cast a glance back at the copse where Arberus waited with the Brotherhood and the hundred or so other mounted troops in the army. A few hundred yards to the rear of them waited the entirety of the Electress's host, no doubt still tired from the rapid forced march along the darkened Corvus Road. Lizanne considered it a minor miracle no Corvantine scout had discovered their approach. She harboured a faint hope such good fortune might result from an over-confidence on the part of whoever had command of the Imperial expedition. *They most likely can't believe a rag-bag collection of convicts and peasants would attempt something so foolish,* she decided, fighting down another flare of rage at Arberus. *Not without good reason.*

"Green?" Hyran suggested, eyeing the intervening distance with palpable unease. "We could cover the ground in only a few seconds."

"Raising dust and drawing the pickets' gaze in the process," Lizanne replied. She lowered herself into a prone position and motioned for him to follow suit. "It'll have to be the laborious approach, I'm afraid. Stay two feet behind me. Move as I move and stop when I stop."

She started forward, covering the first hundred yards in a steady crawl. As the glow of the Household Division's camp-fires began to grow she lowered herself to her belly and inched her way through the grass in slow, careful increments. She could see the picket line now, tall men in black uniforms patrolling back and forth. *The Emperor's Ravens,* she concluded. They were also known as the Black Hearts thanks to the numerous atrocities ascribed to them in the Wars of Revolution. She could make out the face of the closest sentry, finding the stern-eyed, weathered visage of a veteran. Clearly there were no easily scared conscripts to be found in this camp.

She came to a halt and watched the veteran make a slow progress across her path, rifle unslung and held low as his eyes scanned the grass. His gaze swept over the patch of shadows where she lay then moved on, paused and moved back again. Lizanne stifled a curse as the man's features tensed, well-honed soldier's instincts no doubt warning of something out of place. He began to move closer, his thumb easing back the safety lever on his rifle with a soft click.

Lizanne heard Hyran give a sharp intake of breath and saw the veteran's eyes widen in alarm. She depressed the third button on the Spider, injecting a half-second burst of Black and reached out to clamp the soldier in place just as he opened his mouth to call out a warning. She rose to her haunches, looking left and right to check on the position of the other pickets. Fortunately, both had just completed their regular turns and were moving in opposite directions.

Lizanne nudged Hyran to his feet and led him around the frozen veteran in a huddled run. She saw the man's eyes track her as she moved past him, full of frustration and fury, but also the knowledge of his impending fate. She turned around and back-pedalled, keeping her gaze on the unmoving sentry until they were safely concealed by shadow cast by a large tent. She waited a moment, crouching in the dark until satisfied no other pickets had witnessed their intrusion, then unleashed the last of her Black in a concentrated burst to snap the veteran's neck. She watched him collapse into the grass then turned and tugged on Hyran's sleeve, leading him deeper into the camp.

"We don't have long," she said, depressing the Spider's second button. "Drink half your Green and be ready with your Red."

Lizanne reasoned her quarry would most likely be found close to the centre of the camp. Accordingly she led Hyran in a series of rushes from one shadow to another. It was vital they get as close as possible to their objective before the inevitable hue and cry resulting from the discovery of the sentry's body. It came just as she found the correct tent. It was large but otherwise nondescript and she might well have passed it by but for the man who stood outside the open flap smoking a cigarillo. A man wearing plain dark clothes instead of a uniform, with a silver pin on the lapel of his jacket. Thanks to the Green the Imperial crest was easy to make out. The man stiffened as the alarm sounded from the southern pickets, frowning and peering into the dark before turning to call to his companions in the tent. Lizanne hoped they were few in number.

"Red," she told Hyran, pointing him to the rear of the tent. "Set it aflame as soon as you can."

"What about you?" he asked.

Lizanne drew her revolver and pressed the other two buttons on the Spider, closing her eyes to steady herself against the rush of product. "I'll take care of this," she said. "If I die, I leave it to your conscience as to whether to continue with this unwise escapade."

He gaped at her for a second then gave a jerky nod before crawling away.

Lizanne crouched lower and watched as two more Blood Cadre operatives emerged from the tent, a man and a woman. She saw that all three were young, several years her junior in fact. She remembered the fiercely skilled and deadly Blood Cadre agents she had faced at Carvenport, concluding that misadventure must have cost the Blood Imperial many of his most capable children. *At least I'll have the advantage of experience,* she thought, trying to quell her impatience as she waited for Hyran to do his part.

The flames blossomed as the three agents began a lively discussion regarding their response to the continuing alarm. Bugles were sounding throughout the camp and soldiers running to retrieve their rifles from neat conical stacks. The woman evidently wanted to investigate immediately whilst her two male companions were decidedly more cautious. It was therefore an easy decision as to which one to shoot when Hyran lit their tent on fire.

All three turned to look as the flames rose, engulfing the rear of the tent and providing a back-drop that rendered them easy targets. The woman dropped as Lizanne put a bullet into the centre of her back. The two men whirled, their inexperience evident in the fact that neither began to reach for their product. Lizanne shot the taller of the two then switched her aim to his companion. This one, however, managed to recover from his shock in time to dive to one side, rolling away with unnatural swiftness as Lizanne's bullets tore at the earth around him. *He didn't drink,* she realised. *He has a Spider.*

Voicing a soft curse at the many betrayals of Madame Bondersil, Lizanne leapt high as the Cadre agent let loose with a blast of Black. It was a hasty and poorly aimed response, but the wave of force was wide enough to catch her foot before she managed to get clear. She spun end over end, landing hard amidst the flaming remnants of the tent. She used Green to spring to her feet, blasting the encroaching flames away with Black then leaping aside as the Cadre agent opened fire with his revolver.

Over-eager, she judged, ducking under the salvo of bullets as the agent blazed away with more enthusiasm than skill. *Red would have been a better choice.*

She watched as he managed to assert some measure of control over his actions. Resisting the impulse to fire his final round as his fingers twitched over the buttons of his Spider. Lizanne didn't allow him the time, reaching out with Black to bend his arm, doubling it over so that the revolver pointed at his face. A final flare of power compressed the bones in his hand with sufficient force to squeeze the trigger, the bullet transforming the agent's features into a bloody pulp.

Lizanne rushed towards the body of the woman she had shot, keen to retrieve her product, then ducked as a fresh volley of bullets tore the air around her. The speed afforded by the Green in her system was enough to evade the rifle fire, Lizanne dropping and scuttling to the side as dust plumes rose around her. A harsh tumult of shouts sounded and four of the Emperor's Ravens came charging out of the gloom, rifles lowered, each one tipped with a gleaming bayonet. Lizanne began to summon her Black but stopped as a series of high-pitched whines sounded above her head. All four charging soldiers dropped immediately, jerking as blood erupted from small holes in their tunics. She turned to find Hyran emerging from a cloud of cinders rising from the remnants of the tent. "Smaller is better," he said, grinning as he held up a thumb-sized stone.

"Come here," Lizanne instructed, turning back to the female agent's body. "Roll up your sleeve."

She quickly removed the Spider from the woman's limp arm and strapped it onto Hyran's outstretched limb, all the time casting wary glances around for more soldiers. A steady crackle of rifle fire could be heard from the southern perimeter, indicating Arberus's mounted skirmishers were busy compelling the Imperial troops into their disciplined ranks. *It's working,* she thought. *So far.*

She tightened the straps fixing the Spider onto Hyran's arm and pointed to each button in turn. "Red, Green, Black, Blue. The vials are full. The longer you depress the button the more product it delivers."

She turned back to the Cadre agent's corpse, rummaging through her jacket pockets until she found the wallet containing the rest of her product. "Here," she said, handing it to Hyran before running to the body of the first man she had shot. His wallet proved equally rich in product, as did the vials of his Spider. She managed to consign it all to her own pockets before a fresh bout of shouting sounded near by. She recognised the source of the voice, if not the name of the owner. *A sergeant, whipping his squad into shape.*

"Time to go," she told Hyran, rising and running towards where she expected to find the Corvantine artillery. "Now's the time for some Green."

They moved through the camp in a blur, tearing through canvas and camp-fires. Fortunately, most of the Ravens had already answered the call to muster in ranks so there were only a few stragglers about, none of whom reacted swiftly enough to do more than cast a few useless shots in their wake. The artillery-park was busy with movement as Lizanne brought them to a halt on its fringes. Gunners were hard at work readying the cannon for line deployment whilst others carried powder and ammunition to the wagons. However, most of the powder barrels were still piled in three separate stacks in the centre of the formation.

"Red, I assume?" Hyran asked, flexing his fingers over the buttons of his Spider.

"Not just yet." Lizanne's gaze quickly found a squad of gunners heaving powder-bags onto the back of a wagon. "There," she said, pointing. "Feel free to use your revolver from now on."

Lizanne eliminated three of the gunners around the wagon by the simple expedient of freezing them in place before shooting them in the head. Hyran dealt with the remaining two in less tidy fashion, managing to hold one still long enough to shoot him in the chest but allowing sufficient time for his companion to sprint off into the darkness.

"Leave that," Lizanne told him as he sent a flurry of shots after the fleeing gunner. She turned her attention to the wagon, using Black to lift one of the powder-bags clear. She raised it a good twenty feet into the air before injecting a small amount of Red and setting a very small fire burning on the corner of the cotton sacking. She waited for the flame to lick along the bag's seams then gave it a precisely judged shove, sending it in a high arc towards one of the stacked barrels of powder. The bag detonated a split-second after impacting on the stack, birthing an instant fire-ball and a blast wave of sufficient force to kill any gunners in a thirty-foot radius. Flaming debris landed on the neighbouring stacks resulting in near-simultaneous explosions of equal size and ferocity. Gunners fled in panic as flames spread to the wagons and further explosions added yet more thunder to the general din.

"That will do," Lizanne commented as the inferno spread throughout the camp. "Now for the hard part."

They resumed a stealthy approach towards the rear of the Corvantine battle-line. The bulk of the Emperor's Ravens and the Iron Watch were drawn up in three rigidly ordered lines, unwavering despite the continuing chaos at their backs which would surely have sent conscripted troops into a panicked rout. Lizanne and Hyran concealed themselves beneath a wagon and watched as sergeants and officers paced along the line of troops, calling out stern exhortations. The words "traitorous scum" seemed to be most favoured, along with promises that any captives would be available for "sport" in the aftermath of inevitable victory.

After a short interval a series of orders swept along the line followed by the sound of thousands of rifles being cocked at once. A ripple went through the formation as the first rank knelt and the second switched their rifles to port arms, indicating the first volley was imminent. Lizanne raised her gaze to the dark sky above, injecting Green to enhance her vision as she searched for the first of Tinkerer's new toys to make an appearance.

She saw it just as the Corvantine officers called out the aim order, a rapidly growing cluster of sparks in the night sky. It rose to a height well over a hundred feet before beginning a downward plunge. Lizanne judged its trajectory would bring it to earth well to the rear of the Corvantine line. She waited until it had descended to less than fifty feet then unleashed a concentrated wave of Black. Unfortunately, the fact that she hadn't had the opportunity to practice this manoeuvre made this first attempt a clumsy one, the force wave proving too powerful and causing the device to explode in mid air some ten feet above the point where the Ravens' line joined that of the Iron Watch. Despite this lack of success, the effect was still impressive. Her Green-boosted eyes afforded a clear view of the rocket just before it exploded. It was far larger than the signal rockets used at sea, the case fashioned from iron tubes and packed with small metal shards around a core of black powder. Tinkerer had formulated a propellant capable of projecting such a heavy object through the air to a range of half a mile, but the means of guiding it to a target with any accuracy still apparently eluded him, hence Arberus's decision to send her on this less-than-palatable mission.

The rocket exploded with a thunderous boom, louder than any cannon shell, sending its deadly cargo down onto the neat ranks of Corvantine soldiery below. Lizanne estimated at least a whole platoon were killed instantly, with double the number wounded. The line rippled in response to the blow, but didn't break. Sergeants swiftly hauled the dead and maimed away and hounded the survivors into a semblance of order. The middle of the Corvantine line had thinned, but not broken.

Lizanne had more success with the second rocket, reaching out to push it with a series of gentle shoves rather than a single application of force. The results were somewhat spectacular, the rocket exploding just as the tip of the warhead made contact with the earth barely a foot in front of the centre of the Corvantine line. This time it broke, hacked in two by the blast that left a smoking red mound of sundered men in its wake. The complete destruction of almost an entire company in less than two minutes was bound to disorder even the most elite soldiers and Lizanne saw a number of Ravens turn and run. They were quickly shot down by pistol-wielding officers but it was still an encouraging sign.

She brought the next two rockets down on either side of the bloody mound, and within seconds the two regiments stood separated by a gap at least thirty feet wide. A tumult of shouts and discordant bugle cries sounded in the gloom beyond the now-wavering Corvantine line, indicating Arberus had no intention of passing up this opportunity. She could see the charging horde through the gap in the Corvantine ranks, a dense mass of people rushing from the dark, those in front firing their rifles as they ran. She recognised them as a mix of recently recruited townsfolk and ex–Scorazin inmates from the lesser gangs. Apparently Arberus didn't want to commit his best troops to the first assault.

A volley crashed out from the Corvantine line, ragged and poorly aimed by the standards of regular infantry, but still potent enough to cut down at least a hundred attackers. Lizanne raised her gaze once more, finding three more rockets in the sky, all descending fast. She managed to bring one down close to where an Iron Watch officer was attempting to rally his unnerved company, vapourising the man and sending most of his troops to flight. The other two rockets landed beyond the line without material effect, though the proximity of their explosions proved sufficient to disorder the entire left wing of the line just before the rebel charge struck home.

The two sides came together with final sputter of rifle fire, soon swallowed by the chorus of growls and shouts that told of people engaged in savage close-quarter combat. Whilst a good number of Ravens and Watchmen had fled, there were enough stalwart regulars remaining to put up a stiff fight, but not enough to close the gaping rent in their formation.

As she expected, Arberus was first through the breach, his stallion at full gallop and sabre raised high. His hundred or so mounted troops were close behind, wheeling left and right to assail the Corvantines from the rear. In most engagements of this size an attack by so small a contingent of cavalry would have had little effect, but with the Corvantines stripped of their artillery and beset by determined if inexpert infantry, the charge quickly proved decisive. Soon the Imperial troops had fragmented into a dozen close-packed pockets of resistance, battling desperately against the seemingly unending rebel tide still streaming out of the darkness. The toll on the attackers was high, the Corvantine troops were veterans after all and Lizanne reckoned each accounted for at least three rebels before they fell.

She turned as Hyran stirred at her side, seeing his gaze fixed on a particularly stubborn knot of Watchmen who had gathered into a defensive circle a hundred yards away. The ground surrounding the Watchmen was continually littered with rebel bodies as they fired disciplined volleys into the ranks of the onrushing horde.

"Don't!" she warned, reaching out to grasp Hyran's sleeve as he began to crawl from beneath the wagon. "We did our part."

He shot her a look that was part disgust and part disappointment. "These are my people," he said, tugging himself free. Lizanne watched him sprint towards the encircled Watchmen, revolver raised and fingers pressing the buttons of his Spider.

Now would appear to be the time, she concluded, taking in the unfolding carnage beyond her hiding-place. Freed of encumbrances, she could make her way to where Tinkerer tended his infernal devices. Anatol would most likely be guarding him, but the battle would provide ample cover for a well-placed shot. She began to shuffle free of the wagon then paused as a figure caught her eye, a slender figure running through the smoke with a rifle in hand. Makario's eyes were wide and he yelled as he ran, more she assumed in panic than martial enthusiasm. Even so, he pelted towards the still-battling knot of Corvantines with an unfaltering stride, a cluster of rebels at his back.

"Sentiment," Lizanne muttered, checking her revolver and filling her veins with product, "will surely be the death of me."

CHAPTER 40

Clay

The Red swept around the flank of the mountain, wings angled to catch the air-current. It was full-grown but sickly like the Greens and the White, but still moving too fast for Clay to shift Kriz clear of its talons. She spun as a claw tore into her side, arching her back and casting out a spiral of blood. Kriz issued a brief, convulsive scream as Clay set her down before turning his gaze to the Red.

The beast fanned its wings and whirled about, tail whipping as it angled its body for a second attack. Clay reached out with the Black to clamp the animal's head in place. Its body coiled and thrashed as he raised the carbine, centring the glowing circle of the optic on its forehead. His doubts about the power of the weapon's ammunition proved unfounded as a single bullet between the eyes was enough to render the animal lifeless. He used the last of the Black to throw the sagging corpse against the side of the mountain. It impacted with bone-cracking force and slid to the ground a few yards away, blood streaming in thick rivulets from its pierced skull.

"Clay!" Loriabeth was at Kriz's side, pressing a bandage to a bleeding gash in the woman's side. "She needs Green."

Clay crouched next to Kriz's head, taking a vial from his wallet and holding it to her lips. She gazed up at him, eyes dull as he tipped the contents down her throat. They brightened as the product did its work, banishing a good deal of her pain and adding much-needed vitality to her body, but it couldn't do anything to stem the blood streaming from her wound.

"Gotta stitch this up," Loriabeth said, blood seeping through her fingers from the already soaked bandage. "She'll bleed to death in moments otherwise."

Clay's gaze snapped to the Red's corpse. He rushed towards it, taking an empty vial and scooping up a portion of the blood leaking from the animal's skull. His first try at drinking it left him retching with such force he abandoned the attempt. Raw Red, it transpired, was even fouler than raw Black. Cursing, he took his canteen and added a few drops of water to the vial, shaking it to dilute the contents. He steeled himself against the reaction and forced the whole lot down in one swallow, clamping a hand over his mouth to stop his body immediately rejecting the noxious brew.

"Clay!" Loriabeth said.

He staggered as the Red seemed to explode in his gut and would have fallen if Sigoral hadn't caught him about the waist. "I'm alright," he said, shrugging free and stumbling back to Kriz. Loriabeth moved aside as he slumped to his knees, pulling away the bandages she had applied to the wound. The sight of the deep, oozing rent in Kriz's flesh nearly had him retching again but he managed to contain his gorge long enough to summon the product.

"Hold her tight," he told Sigoral and Loriabeth. "This'll hurt."

He placed his hands at one end of the wound, pressing the lips of the cut together then unleashing a thin stream of Red. Kriz shuddered and let out a lacerating scream as her skin blistered under the intense heat, releasing a sickening stench that forced Loriabeth to turn away and heave up the contents of her stomach. Clay continued to work, tracking his gaze slowly along the length of the wound and leaving a hideous track of puckered, smoking flesh in its wake. But it was flesh that no longer bled. By the time he was done Kriz's screams had faded into a faint whimpering and her body lay slack, her breathing shallow and skin cold.

"Mr. Torcreek," Sigoral said with quiet urgency. Clay glanced up to see him aiming his carbine at the quickly darkening sky. Just visible in the gloom were three winged silhouettes, growing closer by the second.

"Go . . ." Kriz said in a barely audible whisper. Clay looked down to see her bright eyes meeting his as she smiled. "Leave . . . me."

"Fuck that." Clay took out another vial of Green and drank it all before gathering Kriz into his arms and rising to his feet. "Stay close," he told Loriabeth and Sigoral, turning and starting up the slope towards the building at a dead run. "Keep them off us."

Kriz sagged in his arms as she lost consciousness. Clay fixed his gaze on the building ahead and gave full vent to the product in his veins, resisting the urge to turn as the guns of his companions barked into life. Drake screams and blasts of heated air chased him up the slope, all the way to the building, which, he saw with a plummeting heart, appeared to be undamaged and lacking any obvious point of entry.

He sagged against the building, laying Kriz down before turning about just in time to see Loriabeth hack a Red out of the sky with a concentrated burst from her repeating rifle. The beast crashed to earth a dozen feet away in a tangle of wings and dying flame, twitched and lay still. The other Reds screamed and wheeled away, weaving to and fro as Sigoral's bullets tracked them across the sky. They retreated out of range of the guns and began to circle, calling out their piercing cries all the while.

"What are they waiting for?" Loriabeth wondered.

Clay's enhanced vision picked out a distant shape above the jagged peaks. At first he took it for a cloud, then realised his mistake. Beyond the occasional patch of mist, this was a world without clouds. The shape soon grew and his unnaturally keen sight left no doubt as to its true nature. *Reds. A whole flock of Reds.*

"Reinforcements," Clay told his cousin, turning and casting his gaze around. *Where is it?* He found it at the corner of the building, a free-standing plinth identical to the others. Rushing towards it he slapped his palm to the crystal, sighing in explosive relief at the grind of stone as a section of wall slid aside to create an entrance. He gathered Kriz into his arms and rushed inside, the others following quickly. They moved into the cool dark interior then stopped, turning to regard the open entrance.

"How do we close it?" Sigoral asked.

Clay's frantic gaze searched the surrounding gloom, finding no sign of another plinth. "Don't think we can," he said. "Guess when they built this place they weren't overly concerned with locking their doors behind them."

"Cuz." Loriabeth stood staring at the fast-approaching flock of Reds, less than a mile off now and closing quickly.

"Take her," Clay said, placing Kriz in Sigoral's arms then rushing towards the entrance. He ran outside and moved to the plinth before taking out his wallet and extracting the vial of raw Black. He could hear the Reds now, the flock voicing a collective cry rich in hungry malice. He drank all the Black, swallowing with hard jerking gulps as it coursed down his throat to his gut. The burn of it provoked an agonised shout and he fell to his knees, gasping air into his lungs then pressing his hand to the crystal.

He sprinted for the entrance as the grinding rumble rose again, the section of wall sliding closed with aggravating swiftness. He lashed out with the Black just as it came within a few inches of closing. The huge stone slab resisted the pressure at first, the hidden mechanicals pushing it were strong, but the Black was stronger. Clay maintained a steady pressure, widening the gap to an inch, then another, sweat coursing down his forehead as he felt the Black diminish with alarming rapidity.

He could see Loriabeth and Sigoral on the other side, hands clutching the slab as they tried to widen the gap. Loriabeth called his name, the sound of which was barely audible above the rising fury of the Reds' hungry chorus. Clay kept his gaze locked on the edge of the door, pushing and pushing until the gap widened to almost a foot.

Feeling the last vestiges of Black fade from his veins, he lunged forward. Sigoral caught his arm and hauled him through just as the door slammed shut behind, sending a booming echo through the structure.

Clay spent a few moments on his knees, dragging air into his lungs before he regained the strength to stand. He rose, surveying the building's interior as Loriabeth lit her lantern. They were in a broad central chamber, the surrounding walls interrupted by several entrances. Clay moved to the closest one, peering at the symbols carved on either side but finding them unfamiliar, resembling a curved diagonal cross.

"Look for something that looks like an eye," he told the others, gulping Green and moving to the next entrance. His boosted sight found it a few moments later, the upturned eye flanking a corridor, the depths of which were lit by a soft glow. "This one," he said, rushing to gather Kriz into his arms.

They hurried along the corridor and out into another larger chamber. Loriabeth and Sigoral drew up short at the sight confronting them, although Clay had little time to wonder at the crystal floating above a huge stone egg. Like the chamber where they had found Kriz, the egg stood on a raised dais, bathed in the soft white light cast by the crystal.

"Cuz?" Loriabeth asked, voice heavy with uncertainty as he moved swiftly to the dais.

"It healed me," Clay said, stepping into the crystal's light. "It'll heal her."

He gently set Kriz down on the dais, settling her onto her side so that her ravaged back was presented to the crystal. "Come on," he implored in a whisper, stepping back, gaze locked on the slowly rotating stone. "Do it . . . Do it!"

The crystal continued its serene rotation for several long seconds then Clay detected a subtle flicker deep in its facets. A new beam lanced out from the crystal to envelop Kriz. She groaned in response, limbs twitching and features tensing. Clay resisted the impulse to pull her clear of the light, focusing on her wound. After a few seconds he saw the redness surrounding the ragged puckered line in her back begin to fade. He kept watching to ensure it wasn't some trick of the mind, finally letting out a relieved laugh as the redness faded almost completely. Soon the glistening blistered flesh around the cauterized wound had begun to re-form itself, smooth skin replacing raw tissue.

"How'd you get it to do that?" Loriabeth asked, moving closer, eyes wide in fascination.

"I didn't," Clay said, staring up at the crystal. "I think it'll heal any wounded body that comes into range of its light. It's what it does." He lowered his gaze to the egg, still bathed in the crystal's light, which hadn't faltered with the appearance of the second beam. "It keeps things alive," he added in a soft murmur, eyeing the tightly sealed joins in its side where the segments fit together.

"Back here!" Sigoral called from the far end of the chamber, voice high with uncharacteristic excitement.

As Loriabeth answered the Corvantine's call, Clay knelt to check Kriz's breathing, finding it smooth and regular. Touching a hand to her forehead, he found the skin warm but free of fever. The only sign of distress was a slight flutter to her eyelids.

"Might wanna come see this, Clay!" Loriabeth called, just as excited as Sigoral.

He found them standing next to a plinth several yards away from the dais. It sat close to the edge of a twelve-foot-wide circular indentation in the floor. Hearing the echo birthed by his footsteps, Clay looked up. The shaft rose into the gloom above, the length of the echo indicating it went a very long way up.

"We made it, Cuz," Loriabeth enthused, coming closer to hug him tight. "We're finally getting out."

"We need to know it works first," Sigoral said, gesturing at the plinth.

Clay disentangled himself from his cousin, giving the plinth a brief glance before turning back to the crystal. "All in good time," he said.

"Mr. Torcreek," Sigoral said, stepping into his path and jabbing an insistent finger at the plinth.

"Not quite ready to try it yet, Lieutenant," Clay replied, stepping around him. "Kriz ain't fully healed. And we don't have what we came for."

"I'm afraid I must insist, Mr. Torcreek," Sigoral stated in an unambiguous tone of command. Clay turned to find the Corvantine regarding him with a steady, determined gaze, the butt of his carbine against his shoulder.

"I ain't on your crew, Lieutenant," Clay reminded him. "And I didn't come all this way to leave without answers. We ain't done here."

"*I* am done here." Sigoral raised his carbine, centring the sight on Clay's chest.

Seeing the hard, implacable determination in the Corvantine's gaze Clay recalled the words of Silverpin's ghost. *You led a lot of people into certain death . . . it wouldn't have been so bad if they'd had a choice.* But whatever compulsive power she alluded to didn't appear to be working on the lieutenant just now. *Just like hers didn't work on me.*

"Thought you had a duty," Clay said.

"My duty is to return home and report everything I've seen here."

"And what good's that gonna do if no one understands it? Do you? Got any answers to share? Some great insight the rest of us missed, maybe?"

"Enough of this shit," Loriabeth said, moving to wedge herself between them, pushing Sigoral's carbine aside.

The Corvantine met her gaze, jaw clenching as he tensed. "I have no desire to see you hurt, Miss Torcreek," he said. "But I have to get out of here. *We* have to get out of here. You know I'm right. It's only a matter of time before some fresh horror appears. And I suspect our luck is wearing thin."

"Like my patience iffen you don't lower that weapon," Loriabeth grated, returning his glare in full measure.

"No . . . way . . . out."

They turned at the sound of Kriz's thin, croaking voice. She was on her feet, leaning heavily on the curved flank of the huge stone egg. Although the crystal's healing light continued to bathe her, she regarded them with bright, pain-filled eyes, features pale and slack from blood loss.

"What?" Sigoral demanded, the muzzle of his carbine moving to point at her.

"No . . . way out," Kriz repeated, raising a hand in a weak fluttering gesture at the shaft above.

"This will take us out," Sigoral insisted, stepping closer to her. "It leads back to the surface."

"Not . . . now," she told him, her hand falling limply to her side. "Too much . . . ice."

"Ice?" Sigoral's face took on a reddish tinge as he moved closer to Kriz, speaking through clenched teeth. "Enough riddles. Tell me exactly what you mean."

"Ice . . . less when we . . . built it all," Kriz replied, then winced as a spasm of pain wracked her. "Not any more. So many . . . years."

"What?" Sigoral demanded, moving closer still.

"The ice," Clay said. "She means it was thinner in her day. Guess it's built up over the years to cover this whole place. The spire was the only bit of it still visible." He glanced up at the shaft. "Even if we get to the top of this, there's no way out."

"Then why," Sigoral grated at Kriz, finger twitching on the carbine's trigger, "did you bring us here?"

Kriz blinked her too-bright eyes and turned towards the egg, running her hand over the surface. "To see . . . my father."

CHAPTER 41

Hilemore

". . . and so I commend my soul to the King of the Deep," Hilemore read. The logbook lay open on the desk before him, just as he found it on entering the cabin occupied by the *Dreadfire*'s captain. "I avow my firm knowledge that He, alone amongst all the gods, will afford me the most fair and careful judgement. To any who may one day read these words know that I die with the greatest contrition burning in my heart. I have lived as a pirate, but I perish as a penitent. Signed Arneas Bledthorne, Master of the *Dreadfire*, on this day 17th Termester in the Queen's Year 1491."

"Pretty way with words for a pirate," Skaggerhill observed.

"Yes." Hilemore scanned the finely rendered script flowing across the page. "I suspect Captain Bledthorne may well have been a fellow of some education."

"Fat lot of good it did him," Scrimshine muttered, casting a glance at the corpse lying on the cabin's only bunk. Despite the many decades since his death, the cold ensured Arneas Bledthorne's body retained a fair amount of its flesh, desiccated and blackened though it was. His stiff, grey hands lay on his chest, one of the fingers still lodged in the trigger-guard of an antique flint-lock pistol. A large hole in the top of the captain's skull provided further evidence of how he had contrived to make his exit from the world. Before undertaking his final repose Bledthorne had clad himself in a fine set of well-tailored clothes, the cuffs and lapels braided with gold in the manner of an admiral. So far this was the only gold they had found aboard the *Dreadfire*.

"Don't s'pose he makes mention of where he stashed his treasure, Skipper?" Scrimshine asked Hilemore, brows raised to a hopeful angle.

"If he had any treasure he didn't feel compelled to record it here."

Hilemore leafed through the log, noting how each entry grew shorter as the voyage progressed towards its fateful conclusion. It told a tale of thievery, murder and mutiny, all recorded in Bledthorne's unwaveringly elegant script and eloquent phrasing. It appeared the *Dreadfire* had encountered a full squadron of Royal Mandinorian Navy ships after an abortive attempt to seize a freighter off the south-east Arradsian coast. In response Captain Bledthorne embarked upon a series of desperate navigational gambles in an effort to evade his deserved meeting with the hangman. The farther south they sailed the more fractious the crew became, forcing the captain to resort to what he termed, "Mortal punishment, undertaken with the barbed, three-tongued whip, for it creates the more lasting impression on the weak-minded." After that the log became a grim litany of repeated mutiny and bloody murder until Bledthorne found himself sailing alone in icy waters, reduced to a mere passenger on a ship he had no crew to sail. Hilemore doubted the judgement afforded by the King of the Deep would have been as merciful as Bledthorne hoped.

Hilemore looked up as a heavy hand knocked on the cabin door. "Enter."

Steelfine came in, standing to attention before the desk and saluting smartly. "Inspection complete, sir."

"Excellent, Number One. In what state do we find our new command?"

"The hull is intact below the water-line, sir. Benefit of the iron-cladding, I assume, else the ice would have crushed her long ago. There's cordage aplenty too, though we'll have to spend time thawing it out before it's of any use. Life-boat's intact and fully oared. The sheets are more of a concern."

Hilemore nodded in sober acknowledgment. The *Dreadfire*'s masts were bare of canvas, the sails no doubt having been torn away by the polar winds over the course of many years. "Do we have any?"

"There's spares in the hold, sir, but not enough for every mast. I'm confident she'll make headway, but it'll be a canter rather than a gallop."

"You are familiar with the intricacies of sail then, Mr. Steelfine?"

"My first ship was all-sail, sir. Some things you never forget."

"Very good, Number One. I hereby appoint you Sailing Master of the newly acquired Ironship Protectorate Vessel *Dreadfire*. Mr. Scrimshine will undertake the duties of helmsman. Mr. Skaggerhill, I request you act as the ship's physician and quartermaster for the time being. Supplies will have to be strictly rationed from now on. Also, Green will be administered at your discretion."

The harvester gave a cautious nod. "Happy to do my part, Captain. Probably a good idea if you ask Preacher to take the crow's nest, put those eyes of his to good use."

"A fine suggestion, sir." Hilemore glanced down at the log once more. "All appointments to be recorded in the ship's books just as soon as I find something to write with. Mr. Steelfine, let's get those sheets unpacked."

"Aye, sir." Steelfine saluted again. "There was just one other thing, sir. Something you should see, in the hold."

Hilemore saw Scrimshine straighten immediately, eyes suddenly agleam with interest. "Don't be telling me you found the treasure, Mr. Steelfine."

The Islander turned to the former smuggler and Hilemore saw the corners of his mouth twitch just a little. "Oh, it's treasure to be sure. And plenty of it."

"I estimate three tons altogether."

The cargo filled approximately half the hold and Hilemore quickly intuited the contents from the construction of the barrels. *Wooden braces and pegs, no metal of any kind.* "Three tons of powder," he said.

"Not quite, sir." Steelfine went to the nearest barrel, the lid of which he had already levered open. Hilemore moved closer, seeing that the contents were concealed within in a tight oilskin wrapping. Steelfine pulled the covering aside to reveal what appeared at first glance to be a dense mass of fragile, fibrous linen.

"Whassat stuff?" Scrimshine enquired, leaning closer with his lantern raised then stepping back as Steelfine placed a firm hand on his chest.

"Gun-cotton," Hilemore said. "An accelerating agent possessing six times the blasting power of black powder."

"Not used on a Protectorate ship for near twenty years," Steelfine added. "Since the unfortunate incident in Feros harbour."

"Is it still potent?" Hilemore asked.

"Seems likely, sir. The wrapping will have kept out the moisture and the cold'll kill any corrupting agents in the air."

"Best sling it all over the side, Skipper," Scrimshine said, taking another step back holding his lantern out behind him. "One spark'll tear this whole ship to splinters."

Hilemore ignored him and turned to Steelfine. "The state of the ship's guns, Number One?"

"A dozen eight-pounders on the upper deck, sir, all undamaged with twenty iron round shot each. The firing mechanisms are archaic and unfamiliar but I'm pretty sure I could reckon out how to get them working."

"See to it once we're underway. I shouldn't like to run into any Blues without guns."

"Aye, sir."

It took another day to get the sails rigged. The task was prolonged by the need to thaw out the dense, frozen mounds of rope required to affix the sheets to the masts. The stove in the galley, fortuitously stocked with a decent supply of coal, was duly fired up and the cordage piled around it. By morning they were able to start the rigging. At Steelfine's insistence the mainmast received the bulk of the sails, with the fore and mizzen afforded the remaining canvas. Hilemore had some familiarity with sailing-ships, the basics were still taught to cadets at the Maritime Protectorate Academy, but it was clear that Steelfine's knowledge of this fast-disappearing art far outstripped that of every man on board. Consequently, Hilemore felt it prudent to leave the handling of the ship to the Islander whilst he busied himself with an inspection of the charts bequeathed him by the unfortunate Captain Bledthorne. They had consigned the pirate's remains to the deep following a brief ceremony the previous evening, mainly to allay the perennial superstitions of the men. It went against custom to deny the King of the Deep his due.

Hilemore's study of Bledthorne's charts swiftly led him to the conclusion that, whatever the man's failings as both pirate and human being, his navigational skills had been of a very high order. The charts were all of the finest draughtsmanship and each of the *Dreadfire*'s course changes carefully plotted to within the nearest fifty yards. Bledthorne had also been scrupulous in annotating his charts with items of navigational interest, such as previously unrecorded reefs or dangerously swift currents. It was therefore a simple matter for Hilemore to track the course of the ship all the way from its luckless encounter off the south-western Arradsian coast, across the

Myrdin Ocean and into these frozen wastes where she found her temporary grave.

He was surprised to find that the final position plotted by Bledthorne put the *Dreadfire* over one hundred miles to the north-east of her current situation. Hilemore's finger traced along the dotted pencil-line through a blank section of chart. In Bledthorne's day the southern polar region had received only minimal exploration and it was common practice for cartographers to leave large tracts of the southern reaches empty save for the words "Unknown—Navigate at Own Risk."

Got her through the bergs in high summer, he mused, tapping the black circle at the terminus of the dotted line. *But didn't have the hands to sail her out again. Winter came and the ice closed in to claim its prize, dragging her ever farther south.* Bledthorne had kept hold of the vessel's original registration documents which revealed her to be an armed merchant trader named the *Pure of Heart,* apparently one of the first vessels beyond the Royal Mandinorian Fleet to be built with an iron-clad hull. *The pirate was right about one thing,* Hilemore thought, running a hand over one of the ship's thick oak beams. *Tough old bird like you deserved a better name.*

They got underway around midday, Steelfine's shouted order to unfurl the sails easily carrying the length of the ship. In response the men in the rigging undid the bindings and the sails fell free to billow in the stiff breeze blowing from the south-west. "Won't be able to keep true north at this gauge, Skipper," Scrimshine warned, steadying the *Dreadfire*'s massive wheel with practised ease.

"As long as you keep us pointing away from the south and clear of any bergs I shall be well satisfied, Mr. Scrimshine." Hilemore's gaze tracked over the sails. The breeze was sufficient to put them in motion but he doubted the *Dreadfire* would manage more than two knots with such meagre canvas aloft.

"Could throw all unnecessaries overboard, sir," Scrimshine suggested, reading Hilemore's expression. "Lighten the load. That blasted cotton stuff would do for a start."

"I'd sooner throw you over the side," Hilemore told him with a brisk smile before moving to where Steelfine tended to an eight-pounder gun on the starboard mid-deck. "Reckoned it out then, Number One?"

"Not a lot to reckon, sir," the Islander replied. He used a small penknife to scrape frost from the weapon's touch-hole then leaned down to blow the powder away. "Pack in a measure of gun-cotton, ram the shot home on top of it, fill the touch-hole with powder then set it off. It'll go bang for certain, just not sure what state the gun will be in afterwards. So many years in the freezing air can't have been good for the metal."

"We'll undertake a test-fire when she's ready, use only a small amount of propellant."

"Aye, sir." Steelfine glanced up at the partially rigged masts above, lowering his voice, "Permission to speak in candid terms, sir?"

"Of course, Number One."

"Barring a miracle we're more likely to starve before we see another Blue. At this speed we'll need three weeks to reach open water, and we only have food enough for one."

"I saw food barrels in the hold."

Steelfine nodded. "Corn meal and salt-beef. But after so many years I find it hard to credit it could still be edible."

Hilemore made a show of inspecting the cannon's wheeled carriage for the benefit of any men who might be watching. "As far as the crew are concerned," he said. "It's all edible thanks to the miraculous preserving properties of the polar climate. But we'll stick to our own supplies for now. Might as well use it up, eh?"

"Very good, sir."

After two days' sailing Hilemore estimated they had moved a little under ten miles in a generally northern direction. *Only five miles south of where we found the spire,* he mused, studying the chart he had kept since starting this voyage. In addition to the lack of sail and anaemic winds, progress was further slowed by the need for Scrimshine to navigate around the bergs drifting continually into their path. The ice, fragmented by the mysterious forces that had warmed the region's waters, was an unpredictable foe. The air was often riven by the thunderous sound of bergs colliding or collapsing under their own weight and more than once Scrimshine was obliged to spin the wheel into a blur to counter the effect of the resultant waves.

"Report from the crow's nest, sir," Steelfine's voice called from beyond the cabin door. Hilemore went out onto the deck, looking up to see Braddon

Torcreek pointing to the north. The Contractor captain had been an almost entirely silent presence since they found the *Dreadfire*, the grief etched deep into the lines around his increasingly hollow gaze. Consequently Hilemore felt a certain guilty relief when the man joined Preacher in the nest on the first day, opting to remain aloft ever since.

Hilemore strained to hear Braddon's shouted report, grimacing in frustration at the vagueness of it, "Think you'd best see this yourself, Captain." He went to the mainmast and began the arduous journey up the rigging to the crow's nest, a task he hadn't been obliged to undertake since his days as a junior lieutenant. Diminished rations had left him in a poor state for such exertions and he found himself concealing an embarrassing wheeze as he hauled himself into the nest.

"A few points west of due north," Braddon said, handing him a spy-glass and pointing towards the horizon. Hilemore found it quickly, his heart leaping at the sight of what first appeared to be the tell-tale plume of smoke rising from the stack of a ship. This delusion was quickly dispelled, however, when he gauged the size of the ascending column and its overly dark colour. It rose from a position just within the curve of the horizon and he didn't need his chart to discern the source.

"Mount Reygnar," Hilemore said. "Come back to life. Which would explain a great deal." He lowered the glass, taking in the sight of the fractured ice-shelf surrounding the smoking mountain. The sea was clear at the peak's base, forming a wide circular lake free of bergs. Tracing southwards in a zigzag course, a comparatively clear channel wound its way to the *Dreadfire*'s current position. "There must be a fissure running along the sea-bed," he mused aloud. "The mountain is but a part of it. Beneath us a great deal of molten rock is leaking through the earth's crust."

"Seems awful coincidental it would start leaking so when it did," Braddon said. Hilemore took some gratification from the slight animation to the man's voice, a sign that perhaps he might not succumb completely to grief after all. "Clay . . ." Braddon faltered for a moment, then swallowed and carried on. "Clay said the city he found beneath that mountain in the Coppersoles was built atop a lake of molten rock. If the same folks built the spire, could be it was connected to this fissure in some way."

"It could," Hilemore conceded, once again experiencing the uncomfortable sensation of being dwarfed by the enigma of their discoveries. "In any case, at least we know the way ahead is clear, perhaps all the way to the Chokes."

"Where your lady-love will be waiting with the *Superior*."

"Captain Okanas is not my lady-love." Hilemore's tone was curt and he bridled a little until he saw the faint glimmer of humour in Braddon's eye. Hilemore coughed and raised the spy-glass once more. "I shall need to sketch this," he said. "Plot a more efficient course."

"So we don't starve to death in the meantime, you mean?"

"We have provisions in the hold . . ."

"Which raises the question as to why we're still on rations," Braddon interrupted. "Perhaps it's time to break open a few of those casks. I'm willing to risk my guts on a bite or two. Something I learned in the Interior; even the most reliable folk are unwilling to follow sound orders when true hunger sets in."

Hilemore spent a moment studying the winding channel through the ice. Even with the benefit of a tightly plotted course their existing supplies would be exhausted long before they came in sight of the Chokes. Over the last two days he had been increasingly preoccupied with Scrimshine's tale of his previous journey across the ice. *You'll be surprised how fast a man starts to resemble a side of pork* . . . Although his own career had yet to bring Hilemore to such extremes, seafaring history was rich in similar tales of marooned or becalmed crews pushed to bestial measures by hunger. That men under his command would ever find themselves so far removed from humanity was an uncomfortable notion, but as his own hunger grew he began to see an unpalatable truth in the smuggler's story.

"I believe you're right, Captain Torcreek," he said, handing him the spy-glass before leaning over the rope cage ringing the nest and calling down to the deck below. "Number One! Lay anchor, if you please! All crew to report to the galley!"

The crew looked on with stomachs growling at varying intensities of volume as Skaggerhill did the cooking. The harvester mixed a measure of cornmeal into a thin gruel, seasoning the concoction with some salt from the large jar the *Dreadfire*'s long-vanished cook had seen fit to leave behind. Once spooned onto a tin plate the result had a grey, watery appearance but Hilemore found he had never seen or smelled anything so appetising in his life. Steelfine had all but forbidden him from taking the first meal, volunteering himself instead. "I think Mr. Scrimshine is more deserving of the honour, Number One," Hilemore told him, a sentiment which met with the helmsman's immediate enthusiasm.

"It'll do for me, alright," Scrimshine said, having wolfed down the entire plate in a few scrapes of the spoon. He held his plate out to Skaggerhill in expectation then scowled when Hilemore told him to wait awhile. After a somewhat tense fifteen-minute interval, during which the helmsman signally failed to keel over with stomach pains or display any other sign of an unfortunate reaction, the crew gave a relieved groan when Hilemore ordered Skaggerhill to dole out the rest of the gruel.

"What about the meat, Skipper?" Scrimshine asked Hilemore after his third helping.

Steelfine immediately started to rise, face darkening but stopped as Hilemore shook his head. He was learning that too tight a leash might not be the best option for a crew in crisis. "Best left be, at least for now," Hilemore told Scrimshine. "The corn should suffice until we rendezvous with the *Superior.*"

In truth, he had serious doubts the *Superior* would still be waiting. Faced with the break-up of the ice, Zenida may well have opted to haul anchor and head north at the best possible speed. *Not that I would blame her,* he thought. The crew, however, didn't need to hear him voice his suspicions. Artifice was also valuable in a crisis.

He watched the crew eat, taking heart from the instant lift in their spirits brought on by something as basic as a decent meal. A hum of quiet conversation soon filled the galley, the men sitting straighter as previously gaunt faces took on new colour, even breaking into a smile or two, all of which came to an abrupt end as the sharp crack of a rifle-shot sounded through the decking above their heads.

"Preacher," Braddon said as the crew surged to their feet and made for the ladders. The marksman had opted to stay in the crow's nest as they ate, fortuitously as it transpired. Hilemore could see him outlined against the pale sky, standing with his rifle aimed towards the east. A yellow flame erupted from the rifle's muzzle as Preacher fired again, Hilemore following the line of shot in time to see water cascading down some two hundred paces off the starboard bow. He could find no target for the marksman's bullet and was about to call up to him when he saw a swell around the point of impact. The water frothed briefly as a set of spines broke the surface, Hilemore glimpsing a speck of blue before the drake dived deeper.

"Is it him?" Scrimshine asked in a panicked rasp.

"No," Hilemore said, taking out his spy-glass and training it on the spot where the Blue had broken the surface. "Spines were too small."

He lowered the glass and barked out a series of orders. Soon the crew were all armed and lining the rails, both port and starboard as there was no telling where the beast might appear. They waited for several very long minutes, the surrounding waters remaining placid all the while.

"Maybe he's just swam off," Skaggerhill suggested. "Didn't take kindly to being shot at."

"The guns, Number One?" Hilemore asked Steelfine.

"One prepared, sir. Got a packet of gun-cotton ready for the test firing."

Hilemore's jaw clenched as he rebuked himself. *Should have seen to this earlier.* "It appears we'll be undertaking a battle-field test. Make it ready, if you please."

"Aye, sir." Steelfine saluted and ran to the eight-pounder, calling a pair of men to assist as he began to drag the gun-carriage back from the port.

"Wait!" Scrimshine said. "Quiet for a moment." Hilemore turned to find him standing with his head cocked, a frown of deep concentration on his face. "Y'hear that, Skipper?"

Hilemore motioned for Steelfine to halt his preparations and called for silence. He felt it rather than heard it, a faint tremor thrumming the deck timbers beneath his boots. He had to strain to hear the actual sound, a faint rhythmic keening from under the ship that put him in mind of whale-song, though the pitch was much more shrill.

"Blue-hunters call it the Gathering Song," Scrimshine said, his face losing much of the colour gained during the meal. "That's how they hunt 'em sometimes, capture a young 'un and torment it so it'll call out to its pack. The ocean carries sound a far greater distance than the air. The big 'uns come running to answer the call from miles away, smack into the nets strung betwixt the ships." He gave Hilemore a weak smile. "Don't s'pose we got any nets aboard?"

"No," Hilemore said, moving to the rail and staring out at the drifting bergs beyond. "No we do not."

CHAPTER 42

Lizanne

Arberus found her at first light, smiling despite the scowl she turned on him as Makario stitched the cut to her forearm. The bodies of the last valiant Watchmen lay around them, burnt or blasted into a near-unrecognisable state. Hyran sat near by, knees drawn up to his chest and an unfocused cast to his eyes.

"Come to report a glorious victory, General?" she enquired of Arberus, which made his smile falter a little.

"Victory is never glorious," he replied, casting a glance around the grisly field. "But we have one nonetheless. The Iron Watch and the Emperor's Ravens are no more."

"What about the dragoons?" she enquired. "And all those conscripts?"

"The dragoons were stubborn, the conscripts were not. The Electress is talking to them now. It seems most of their officers had their throats cut last night, and those who didn't are currently fleeing back up the road to Corvus. A road that now lies open."

"Congratulations." She gritted her teeth as Makario drew the suture tight on her cut. "The great General Arberus cements his reputation. I imagine someone is already planning a statue."

"If so, it's more likely it'll be of you than me. The army is abuzz with talk of Miss Blood and her selfless courage."

"You have Hyran to thank for all this." She jerked her head at the surrounding corpses, adding inwardly, *And Makario to thank for the fact that I'm still here.*

"Even so," Arberus said, "every revolution requires its heroes. Legends inspire, truth does not."

"If you quote your grandmother at me again I swear I'll shoot you."

She watched his smile fade completely and knew any lingering hopes of salvaging their intimacy had gone. *Did we ever share more than a purpose? Apparently not.*

She forced a smile of gratitude at Makario as he snipped off the suture and mopped the last of the blood from her cut. "Come along, young man," the musician said, moving to Hyran and tugging him to his feet. "I'm sure somewhere amongst this rabble someone is cooking an approximation of breakfast."

Hyran merely blinked at him as he allowed himself to be guided from the field, empty eyes tracking over the carnage he had helped create.

"The first taste of battle is always bitter," Arberus observed. He moved to sit at Lizanne's side but she rose and turned away, crossing her arms and taking some small sadistic pleasure in allowing the silence to play out to an uncomfortable length.

"When this is over . . ." he began.

"You won't be returning to Feros," she finished. "Yes, I had already divined that."

"Victory in Corvus won't be the end of this war. An empire that has lasted a thousand years doesn't just slip easily from tyranny to freedom. Building the republic will be the work of years, decades even."

"Republic?" She raised an eyebrow in grim amusement. "Bidrosin's great vision made flesh, at last. Tell me, just how much sympathy does the Electress have for your cherished beliefs? I'm sure her views on revolutionary philosophy make for a fascinating discussion."

"She is committed to victory, as am I. As to what might happen next . . ."

"She'll kill you." Lizanne stepped closer, looking directly into his eyes so there would be no mistaking her certainty. "Once she's done slaking her thirst for vengeance on the Corvantine nobility, she'll kill you and anyone else who might pose a threat to her power. To her this empire is just Scorazin on a larger scale. If you think otherwise you're a bigger fool than I took you for."

"If the Electress also considers me a fool then I'll enjoy the advantage of having been under-estimated." His gaze was as steady as hers, his tone suddenly hard. "The true revolutionary does not get to wield power. Their role is to ensure power is transferred to those who were once its victims. Leonis used to say that the world we wanted to build would not welcome us, so steeped were we in blood and deceit. I have been doing this all my life, Lizanne. I know what the Electress is, as I know what I am, and so do you."

Lizanne dropped her gaze, suddenly weary as the exertions of the previous night bore down on her, demanding sleep. "Everything that happened since I returned to Arradsia has . . . changed me," she said. "Morsvale, Carvenport, Scorazin, all of it. Like hammer-blows beating me into a new shape. I cannot be who I was, even if I wanted to. I had hoped the same might be true of you."

"It is," she heard him insist softly as she walked away. "But it seems the shape I was beaten into is not the one you want."

The casualties suffered by what was now being termed "The People's Freedom Army" during its first major victory amounted to some two and a half thousand dead and wounded. The losses were immediately made good by the addition of the mutinous conscripts and the steady stream of civilian volunteers, a stream that became a flood as they resumed their northward march. A host of willing recruits emerged from every town and village they passed on the Corvus Road, so that within a week the army had risen to over sixty thousand people. The new recruits were a decidedly mixed bunch. Older veterans of previous revolutions marched alongside eager sons and daughters, their zeal fired by years of secret education in radical doctrine. As the march towards Corvus continued Lizanne began to see a partial vindication in the Brotherhood's faith. It seemed the spark of revolution had met willing tinder after all. However, it soon became apparent that the path to the capital would not be the unopposed victory march the Electress envisaged.

"Selvurin clansmen," Arberus said, skewering the ground with a captured sabre during the Electress's regular evening council. The sabre's blade was several inches longer than a typical cavalry weapon with a distinctive tassel of eagle feathers dangling from the pommel. "Attacked some Brotherhood scouts in the woods to the west around noon, made off with six heads by the time reinforcements arrived. We only caught one. He didn't survive questioning."

"So Countess Sefka's relying on northern mercenaries," the Electress mused, angling her head to inspect the sabre. "Probably paying them by the head."

"I thought the northern provinces hated the empire," Lizanne said.

"That they do, dear," the Electress replied. "But there's always loyalists in any province. A few of the horse clans sided with the crown during the revolutions. Settled old scores and got rich into the bargain. The fact that they've turned up so far south might actually be a good sign. Could mean they've been driven out of the north, or the Countess is getting desperate."

"Desperate or not, they're a fearsome enemy," Arberus said. "The finest horsemen in the empire, given to worshipping gods that reward the kin of any who fall in battle. You can be sure we haven't seen the last of them. We're having to gather supplies as we move, and I don't have enough mounted troops to cover every caravan. If they start raiding in earnest it will seriously impede our progress."

"Clansmen are hunters," Varkash said. "Like wolves, or eagles," he added, nodding at the tassel on the sabre. "Every eagle has a nest. We have but to find it."

Lizanne sighed as all eyes in the tent turned to her. "I'll need a faster horse," she said.

From the high quality of its tack and comfortable saddle she divined the horse had been captured from a fallen Dragoon officer. It was a dappled-grey stallion several hands taller at the shoulder than her cart-horse and considerably faster. Nevertheless it took her two days to find the main Selvurin camp. She started at the scene of their most recent attack, a raid on a supply caravan that left all the drovers headless and their wagons burnt or empty. She followed the tracks for several miles until they disappeared into dense woodland some ten miles west of the Corvus Road. The clansmen were evidently skilled in concealing their tracks, which made finding them a tortuous business.

Lizanne rode west at a steady pace, stopping at regular intervals to inject Green which allowed her enhanced hearing to catch the distant sound of voices through the trees. She found a number of smaller encampments but steered clear of them, pushing on until the whisper of voices revealed by the Green grew to a steady murmur. As Lizanne drew closer her nose proved more useful than her ears thanks to the rising scent of dung, both horse and human. When it grew into a stench she dismounted and climbed the tallest tree she could find, thin tendrils of rising smoke soon revealing the whereabouts of the clansmen's den.

Lizanne checked her timepiece and settled herself as comfortably as she could into the tree's branches, watching the camp below. In total she estimated this clan to number close to three thousand individuals. They had concealed themselves in a broad clearing deep in the forest. Conical shelters of animal hide clustered around camp-fires as riders came and went. She could also see women at work about the camp and, running between the shelters, a large number of children at play. The Selvurin, it seemed, took their families with them when they went to war. In a circle in the centre of the camp were a number of wooden stakes arranged into a circle, each topped with a round object. Lizanne didn't need to enhance her vision to know what those objects were.

Savages, she thought, as she watched the infants play among the impaled heads. *Savages with children.*

At the allotted hour she injected a short burst of Blue and slipped into the trance. *I see you've been busy,* she observed to Hyran, taking note of his refashioned mindscape. The swirling carnal mélange had been replaced with what appeared to be the interior of a shop. A tall bank of small drawers rose behind the gleaming oak counter and the words *Robian and Sons Fine Spices* were painted in mirrored Eutherian on the window. From what she could see of the exterior the shop was situated in the main commercial district of the capital and the street outside busy with people, though they were indistinct, ghostlike wisps.

My grandfather's shop, Hyran explained, one of the many drawers opening and the face of an old man rising from the powdery contents. It was a kindly face, but also very sad. *He took me in when Ma and Pa were killed. Did his best by me but the Cadre always watching the place didn't do much for custom. When he died the bailiffs took it all.*

I'm sorry, she said. *It seems a . . . pleasant place.*

Smell's what I remember most. All those different spices mixed together. Haven't managed to make it yet.

Memory requires context to be truly vivid. Think about the first time you came here, that's when your mind formed the dominant impression of this place.

The shop shimmered around her as Hyran concentrated, the drawers opening to form more powdery images; the kindly old man, this time sinking to his haunches to offer a sweet to a skinny boy. The shimmer stopped and the images faded, leaving behind an aroma that brought a tingle to the nostrils whilst also conveying a sense of comfort.

Yes, Hyran thought. *That's it. Thank you, miss.*

My pleasure. She summoned a memory of her own: the Selvurin camp and a mental sketch of its location in relation to the army, along with the position of the outlying smaller camps. *Tell the general he'll need to move quickly.*

I will. He asked that you remain in place, to guide the rockets. The Tinkerer should have his devices in a firing position by nightfall.

The rockets . . . She stilled her whirlwinds as they took on a ragged, distressed appearance. *Very well,* she told Hyran.

Are you alright, miss? he asked, meaning his perceptive powers in the trance had improved more than she liked.

Quite alright, thank you. Please assure the general of my willing co-operation.

She blinked in the sunlight as the trance faded, her vision soon clearing to reveal the Selvurin camp. The children were still playing amongst the small forest of impaled heads, laughing as children do.

"Oh bother!" she grunted and began to climb her way down from the tree.

S he reined in on the edge of the clearing and waited. Selvurin pickets were not long in detecting her presence, the nearest coming on at full gallop with his sabre drawn only seconds after she appeared. Lizanne let the clansman get within ten feet before blasting him from the saddle with a surge of Black. He connected with the ground in an untidy tumble, Lizanne hearing the crack of at least one broken bone before he came to a halt. His five comrades, who moments before had also been charging towards her at full pelt, dragged their mounts to a swift halt. After exchanging a few shouts of puzzled alarm they began to draw rifles of antique appearance from the leather sheaths on their saddles.

"Don't!" Lizanne shouted in her perfect Selvurin. "Unless you wish a coward's death!"

The sound of their own language, spoken by a Blood-blessed no less, sufficed to give them pause. Her study of the northern empire had been limited mostly to linguistics but she did possess a rudimentary knowledge of clan customs and traditions, one of which included a lingering attachment to superstitious notions regarding the Blessing.

"If this rabble has a leader!" she went on. "Bring him forth or let him be forever known as Piss-britches!" She wasn't entirely sure she had phrased this insult correctly. However, it seemed to carry sufficient gravity for her would-be assailants to respond with the expected glowers, though they made no further move to attack her. One of them growled something to another, who turned his mount around and galloped towards the camp. Lizanne turned her back on the remaining clansmen and waited. She knew them to be an intensely status-conscious people and one so exalted as her did not acknowledge an inferior unless necessity required it.

It didn't take long for the clan leader to respond to her challenge. Within minutes a retinue of two dozen riders raised a tall column of dust as they came galloping from the camp. They were led by two men, one young, one old. The younger of the two rode partially in front of the old man who, Lizanne saw, carried a gourd of some kind which he held tight to his chest.

The pair reined in a short distance from Lizanne, their followers spreading out on either side. She made note of the fact that they had all drawn their sabres. The younger rider was lean almost to the point of thinness with the pale complexion and dark hair typical of the northern provinces. He wore a short beard and moustache waxed into spear-points that contrasted somewhat with the unconstrained chest-length beards of his clansmen. In all other respects, however, his appearance was every inch that of a leader of a horse clan. He was clad in leather britches and vest, arms bare to reveal his scars and a red-silk scarf on his head braided in silver.

He returned Lizanne's scrutiny in full before trotting his horse forward and coming to a halt barely six feet away. Unlike his men he hadn't drawn his sabre, nor did he share their evident trepidation at being confronted by a Blood-blessed. "'Piss-britches,' eh?" he asked her in finely spoken Eutherian, grinning a little.

"I needed to talk to you," she explained, also slipping into Eutherian.

"And what would the famous Miss Blood have to say to me, pray tell?" His grin broadened a little as her face betrayed a tic of surprise. "Oh yes, I know your story. We wrung it out of some radical shit-eater a few days ago. He said something about you wreaking justice upon our barbarian souls, before we cut his tongue out, that is."

Lizanne resisted the sudden urge to forget her good intentions, kill this savage with a lashing of Black and ride off into the forest. But she could see the other clan-folk gathering to watch this diverting exchange, children chattering excitedly amongst the throng. "You need to leave this place," she said. "Abandon whatever arrangement you have with Countess Sefka and go home."

"Fifty crowns per head," he said. "That's our arrangement and so far it's proving highly lucrative. Can your rebel friends match that? If not, it seems we have little to discuss."

He turned and gave a nonchalant wave to the old man, who duly trotted his mount closer. Although he did his best to hide it behind a fierce glower, Lizanne could see he was markedly more nervous of her than his clan leader. It was there in the way his bony hands twitched on the gourd held close to his chest, a gourd she could now see was inscribed all over with runes.

"This is Tikrut," the younger man said in Selvurin. "Blood Shaman to the Red Eagle Clan. See his mighty power and tremble, foreign witch." The sardonic lilt to the clan leader's voice indicated a less-than-serious attitude to this confrontation, a sense of ritual performed for the sake of appearance.

The old man managed to maintain his glower as he met Lizanne's gaze, though his bony neck bulged as he began to speak in a low guttural chant. The words were gibberish to Lizanne's ears, some form of archaic tribal tongue she suspected no one else present could decipher. Tikrut raised the gourd above his head as he spoke, shaking it back and forth so Lizanne could hear the liquid contents sloshing about.

"He invokes the Blessing of the gods," the clan leader said as Tikrut chanted on. "The divine brew is potent, formed of drake blood fermented over the span of centuries and imbued with the gods' essence."

"Really?" Lizanne enquired, refreshing her reserves of Black with the Spider before reaching out to snatch the gourd from the old shaman's hands. She plucked it out of the air and turned it over in her hands, Tikrut sputtering all the while, this time in Selvurin. "Blaspheming witch! Prepare to burn! The gods will not tolerate so vile an insult . . ."

He trailed off as Lizanne found a stoppered opening on the underside of the gourd. She pried it open and dipped a finger inside. "This is water," she said, after tasting the contents. "Fresh too. I expect he refills it quite regularly." She replaced the stopper and tossed the gourd back to Tikrut. He failed to catch it and the receptacle duly tumbled to the ground, much to the gasping shock of all present, apart from the young clan leader.

"You useless old bastard," he told Tikrut as the shaman scrambled from his saddle, fumbling desperately for the holy gourd. Upon grasping it the shaman immediately began his chant once more, sinking to his knees and raising the gourd to the heavens in the hope, Lizanne presumed, the gods might see fit to smite her with a thunderbolt or two.

"Been hearing about his remarkable powers my entire life," the clan leader said, switching to Eutherian as he turned to Lizanne. "But never seen him do a damned thing, except eat and drink all the offerings my people piled outside his tent. Nice to have one's suspicions confirmed, even if it is by an enemy. Name's Ahnkrit, by the way. Tenth of his name, slayer of a hundred men and leader by the gods' will of the Red Eagle Clan." He inclined his head, turning his horse about and trotting back towards camp. "Nice to meet you, miss. Come and have a spot of lunch, why don't you?"

"It's all a matter of honour, I'm afraid," Ahnkrit told her, sipping wine as he reclined on a cushion of wolf pelts. "I assured Sefka I'd have my lot visit their barbaric worst on your rebellious swine, you see? It's just not done to break a promise to an old friend."

"Old friend?" Lizanne enquired. She had been provided with a generous plate of undercooked venison and a large goblet of wine, neither of which she had touched. Despite the clan leader's sudden affability, she couldn't discount the possibility of poison.

"Oh yes," Ahnkrit replied. "You could say we went to school together. I was but a toddler when dear old papa sent me off to the Imperial Court. Officially as a guest but in actuality a hostage to his continued loyalty to the crown. Sefka was one of the few high-born brats who bothered to talk to me. Fifteen years of courtly etiquette and noble education did wonders for my manners, as you can see. However, it did make for a slightly troublesome home-coming. Papa had been busy siring bastards in my absence, none of whom relished the prospect of surrendering the first saddle to a youth who spoke Eutherian better than he did Selvurin." Ahnkrit's face clouded a little in sorrowful nostalgia. "It's a hard thing to kill one's own brother, I must say. But, like anything else, it got easier with practice."

Lizanne's gaze went to the shelter's entrance where the light had begun to dim. "I would have thought survival would trump honour," she said. "And as for promises, I can promise that you and most of your people will be dead come morning if you don't break camp and leave now."

"A less enlightened man might take that for a threat." Ahnkrit sat up, leaning forward to regard her with intent scrutiny. "But that's not it, is it, my dear Miss Blood? Is it all the little kiddies? Worried what may become of them, are we?"

"I've seen a great deal of death this past year," she replied. "Dead children included. And I believe I've seen enough."

"My people do everything as one, including going to war. Nor do we spare our young the horrors of the world, for they will have to face them soon enough. Custom, you see. Like silly old Tikrut and his magic gourd. I am a prisoner of custom." He proffered his forearm, pointing to a fresh cut behind the wrist. "I blessed my sabre with my own blood and swore I would lead this clan to riches in the southlands."

"Riches?" Lizanne asked. "Rather than victory?"

"What care we for your revolt? Win it or lose it, we'll make treaty with whoever comes out on top. Pragmatism is also a custom in this clan. But I cannot simply pick up sticks and march off, not just because some foreign witch rides into my own camp and makes a fool of my shaman, a nice gift though it was."

Lizanne concealed a sigh of frustration, her brow furrowing in consideration until a singular notion popped into her head. *Riches trumps victory.* "There's a place," she said. "A burning city to the south. Scorazin. You've heard of it?"

"The Emperor's prison city, recently brought low." Ahnkrit shrugged. "What of it?"

"There is a great deal of silver waiting to be dug out of it. Rich seams as yet undisclosed to any outside authority."

The clansman's lip curled in disdain. "My people are not miners, miss."

"You don't have to dig it out, just be in possession of the city when the war ends. Whatever regime holds power will be in dire need of funds and willing to negotiate, I'm sure. I also know the location of a hidden cache of silver ore, if your people require a more immediate incentive."

"Scorazin is still burning."

"Only the sulphur mines. Or is the Red Eagle Clan afraid of a little smoke?"

Ahnkrit's face took on a still, expressionless aspect, his dark eyes half-lidded. She couldn't tell if he was pondering her proposal or suffering her insult. "This People's Freedom Army," he said finally. "Would I be wrong in thinking that your attitude towards them is uncoloured by any radical notions?"

"You would not," she replied. "But you would be wrong in thinking I might be enjoined to betray them."

"I do not require your betrayal, miss, only your honesty. Give me your unbiased and unprejudiced opinion, if you would. Do you believe they will actually win?"

Lizanne's mind traced through everything she had seen since arriving in Corvus, all the people she had met, from Hyran to the Electress. She recalled the day Scorazin fell, and what had since been dubbed the Battle of the Road when a mob of criminals and barely trained civilians had over-run the best troops in the empire. *Caranis died and the great pantomime died with him,* she thought. *Now all that's left is for the audience to give their verdict on the performance, and it is far from favourable.*

"Yes," she said. "I do believe they will."

"In that case"—Ahnkrit leaned closer, smiling the brisk smile of a born trader about to strike a fine bargain—"I'll agree to your terms. I'll take my people off to find this silver, on the understanding that, witch or not, no corner of this earth will hide you should your words prove false. I'll hold the smoking ruins of Scorazin until adequate compensation is paid to my clan, thereby leaving the road clear for your rebels to march on Corvus. But"—his smile became cold, his previously affable tones transforming into something entirely serious—"I require you to perform for me an additional service. And it is not a matter for negotiation."

CHAPTER 43

Sirus

He could feel the Red's hatred, it seemed to emanate from beneath its crimson scales like a constantly stoked fire. *You want nothing more than to eat me,* Sirus observed, allowing the thought to slip free of his shields. *Do you?*

He wasn't entirely sure of the degree to which the lesser drakes could discern the thoughts of the White's enslaved minions. Communication between drake and Spoiled was limited to the exchange of images, shorn of nuance or deeper understanding. He had made some tentative attempts to connect with the animals' minds, finding the experience akin to hearing a distant echo spoken in an alien tongue. But, although a true joining of minds appeared to be impossible, the beast's emotions were easily read. This ability Katarias at least appeared fully capable of mirroring. A shudder of revulsion ran through the Red's huge form from end to end and it opened its jaws to cough out a thick cloud of foul-smelling, yellow smoke. The rushing air-current swiftly conveyed the noxious miasma directly into Sirus's face, leaving him choking for several seconds as he clung to the spines on the beast's neck.

When I free this army your death will be my delight, he thought, careful to cloud the vow in a thick covering of fear. Katarias gave another shudder, as if sensing the emotion behind the thought, a loud rumble issuing from its throat. Sirus couldn't escape the notion that if a drake were capable of laughter, he may have just heard it.

Katarias had carried him about fifteen miles north of the Isles, describing a zigzag course across the sky until their quarry appeared beneath. Following close behind was a pack of ten more Reds, all large specimens capable of carrying heavy loads. In addition to the lone tribal Spoiled on their backs they all clutched another, bulkier cargo in each of their talons.

Sirus could see the ship now, its wake a bright spear-point in the dark expanse of the ocean. Although he knew this to be a blood-burning frigate the ship moved under steam power at less than a third of its top speed.

After conceiving his plan and communicating it to the White, the Reds had kept a constant watch on the northern coast-lines of those islands held by the Spoiled army. At Sirus's instruction numerous camp-fires were lit along the coast, giving the impression of greater numbers and hopefully providing a tempting target for the Maritime Protectorate's raiders. The frigate below had been the first to take the bait, steaming in close to shore at sunset to pound one of their decoy camps with a brief but intense barrage. The ship had then turned about and steamed due north, using her blood-burner for close on an hour as her captain no doubt assumed such speed would deliver her from any pursuing Blues.

Spying the ship, Katarias drew in his wings and descended at a dizzying velocity. The air-stream became so intense Sirus found himself clutching ever tighter to the Red's neck spines. At little under thirty feet from the waves Katarias flared his wings and they levelled out, gliding towards the frigate's stern at a shallow angle. The Red reared up as they came within a few feet of the stern, dipping his head so Sirus could jump clear. He performed a slow somersault as he descended towards the frigate's deck, pulling the weapons from his belt, a broad-bladed knife in one hand and an Islander's war club in the other. He also had a pistol holstered under his shoulder but, if all went as planned, he wouldn't need it. There were two sailors stationed on the stern, both standing in open-mouthed shock at the sight of a Spoiled landing on the deck of their ship barely a few feet away.

Sirus moved in a blur, making full use of the capabilities of his remade body. The war-club shattered the skull of the sailor on the right and the knife opened the throat of his companion, the warning he had begun to shout choking into a wet gargle as he slid to the boards. Sirus whirled in time to see Katarias open his claws to deposit his additional cargo on the frigate's upper works before lashing out with his tail to skewer the look-out in the crow's nest. With that, the huge Red angled his wings and glided off into the gloom.

Sirus crouched and waited, eyes fixed on the ship's bridge. The screams were not long in coming, short, piercing shrieks as blasts of flame lit the windows. He looked up at the sound of rushing air, seeing Forest Spear leap from the back of a Red to land at Sirus's side. The Red swept on, releasing the Greens in its clutches over the prow of the ship. More Reds followed in quick succession, tribal Spoiled landing on the stern and Greens on the works and the fore-deck.

Sirus could sense the tribals' lust for combat, the legacy of a life lived as warriors. Nevertheless, he held them in check until the screams emanating from the rest of the ship rose to a crescendo of panic and fear, punctuated by the occasional gun-shot.

Take the bridge, he told Forest Spear and three others, who immediately sprinted off. He led the remainder towards the hatch he knew led to the engine room. Amongst the army were several former Protectorate sailors possessing valuable knowledge. *Down the ladder, follow the corridor to midships, take the ladder on the right to the lower deck.* They encountered little resistance, save for a clumsy lunge with a fire-axe from a teenage ensign who scarcely seemed strong enough to lift it. Sirus side-stepped the axe and tapped the war-club against the lad's temple, knocking him unconscious. The White would be expecting new recruits from this endeavour.

He found the engine room in chaos. One stoker lay on his back shrieking as a Green savaged his legs. The Chief Engineer and a clutch of others were backed up against the far bulkhead, trying to fend off another Green with their coal-shovels. *We need the engineer,* Sirus told the tribals as they charged into the fray. *Spare the others if you can.*

It was over in seconds, the engineer clubbed down and bound along with two of his men. The remaining three proved overly aggressive and were left to the attentions of the Greens.

The captain died, Forest Spear's thought came from the bridge. *We have the First Officer.*

Sirus went to the bulky mass of the ship's auxiliary power plant, shutting it down with a few deft shoves to the requisite levers. There were several engineers in the army in addition to sailors. *Secure all captives on the fore-deck,* he instructed Forest Spear. *Then search the ship for survivors. No more killing.*

Sirus turned to the Chief Engineer, who stared up at him with a mixture of revulsion and defiance. The man's craggy, oil-streaked features spasmed in impotent rage at the diminishing screams of his men as the Greens feasted on the fruits of victory.

"What is the name of this ship?" Sirus asked the engineer as the last of the screams faded.

The man blinked in surprise at the sound of a Spoiled speaking his own language, then clenched his jaws tight and shook his head in refusal. One of the tribals stepped closer and dragged the engineer's head back by the hair, pressing a knife to his throat. Still the man refused to speak, instead casting a thick glob of spit in Sirus's direction, his steady gaze conveying a clear invitation for Sirus to do his worst.

"The *Ultimate Sanction*!" one of the stokers rasped out, voice pitched high in terror. "She's called the *Ultimate Sanction*!"

"No, that won't do." Sirus paused for a moment's reflection. "She is hereby renamed the *Harbinger*."

They sailed back to the Isles where the surviving crew were duly converted. The ship's Blood-blessed had managed to emerge unscathed from the battle but, as was becoming gruesomely routine whenever they discovered one of his kind, was not so fortunate when he met the White. Once again the great beast undertook a close inspection of the captive, a corpulent fellow who displayed an admirable resolve in the face of what he must have known to be imminent death.

"When our full fleet sails," he growled at the White as it leaned closer, nostrils flaring, "your pestilent horde will be rent to nothing."

The White betrayed no obvious reaction to the words, continuing its inspection for several seconds before issuing the customary huff of annoyance. Despite his courage, even this resolute fellow couldn't help but scream upon being tossed to the ever-hungry clutch of juvenile Whites.

Sirus seized another three ships in less than a week. With the renamed *Harbinger* under their control it proved a relatively simple matter to approach a Protectorate warship once its location had been revealed by patrolling Reds or Blues. Once the vessel hove into view signal flags requesting urgent assistance were raised and the ship's speed reduced to a crawl. Only one paddle was left turning and the engine room ordered to make smoke to convey the impression of a damaged vessel. The smoke had the additional advantage of concealing the features of the *Harbinger*'s crew until her well-intentioned comrade had drawn alongside, by which time their fate was sealed.

Grapples were hurled to lash the vessels together and gang-planks lowered to bridge the gap whereupon two hundred Spoiled emerged from hiding to rush across and seize the prize. The fighting was usually fierce but short-lived, and the complement of sailors to man the White's growing fleet grew with every capture. Sirus ensured that no more Blood-blessed were found alive. He concealed his purpose by personally hunting down the Blood-blessed on each vessel and masking the swift death he gave them with a burst of fear. As yet, the White didn't appear to have detected his merciful subterfuge though the members of Sirus's ad hoc staff proved more perceptive.

We can't fire the blood-burners without Blood-blessed, Veilmist, the mathematical girl-genius pointed out. Her thoughts tended to lack all but the most subtle emotion, possessing a singularity of focus that Sirus suspected had been there long before her conversion. He had convened a council of war in the *Harbinger*'s ward-room. Although remade into something other than human, they were still compelled by the strictures of human custom, including a ritual obeisance to hierarchy.

"The auxiliary engines will suffice," Sirus replied, speaking aloud in Eutherian as had become his habit at these gatherings. "Your calculations please. And talk, don't think."

Veilmist replied in Varsal, her lilting Island accent counterpointed by the precision with which she enunciated each word. "In the event of a direct assault and given the strength of the Protectorate garrison in Feros we can expect a casualty rate of forty to forty-five percent. Assuming the attack is successful, however, and factoring in the likely death toll amongst the civilian population, the overall strength of the Army will at least double."

"And assuming we can fight our way past the naval cordon," Morradin said. "Four ships won't be enough." The marshal's simmering rage at his loss of status hadn't abated. But, like all of them, the White's need for victory left no room for dissent. Also, Sirus could sense the man's innate inability to resist a military challenge.

"We won't be fighting our way in," Sirus said. "At least not at first. And, the casualty estimate is too high to justify a massed assault on the harbour."

He had a map of the Tyrell Islands spread out on the ward-room table. It was another sop to ritual since they all shared the same visual memory. "Feros sits at the end of an isthmus on the southern coast of Crowsloft Island," he said, pointing to the city's location. "And no inland fortifications to guard against an overland assault."

"Because they've never had to worry about it," Morradin replied. "There aren't any viable landing sites on the isthmus. But there is this." He jabbed a stubby finger at a small inlet to the west of Feros. "The Corvantine Imperial General Staff had a plan for an invasion of the Tyrell Islands, to be undertaken following the conquest of Ironship's Arradsian Holdings. We identified this bay as the optimum landing point. The beach is usually too broad for a successful attack, being overlooked by cliffs all around, but it's a different matter during a three-moon tide. What was a muddy mile-long tract enclosed by impassable cliffs becomes a short beach fringed by easily climbed slopes."

"The next three-moon tide is in eighteen days," Veilmist said.

"An achievable time-scale," Sirus said, tapping a finger to Morradin's proposed landing site. "We land the main force here and Feros is no more than a six-mile march away. Night will provide additional cover as well as confusing the defenders, since they don't enjoy our advantages in the dark."

"The General Staff also intended a simultaneous attack on the harbour," Morradin said. "Considered vital to disrupt the enemy defences and divide their forces." He shot a brief, malicious glance at Forest Spear. "Send the savages. They're nothing if not expendable."

Sirus was obliged to still Forest Spear's upsurge of anger with an implacable pulse of command, freezing the tribal in place as his hand flew to the knife on his belt. *Only this man could breed disunity in an army of joined minds,* Sirus thought, turning a hard gaze on Morradin.

"Kill him," Avris, the former artillery sergeant said. The memory of his flogging was a permanent dark stain on the man's memories and this was not the first time he had made this suggestion.

"He weakens us, darling," Katrya said, moving to Sirus's side and smiling sweetly in Morradin's direction. "Why do you keep him?"

"Because he remains useful," Sirus replied simply, sending out another thought pulse that forbade further discussion on the subject. He returned his attention to the map, mind churning over the plan, drawing pertinent detail from the wealth of knowledge acquired over recent months. He could see plenty of risks, for war was always risky, but no obvious flaws. It was tempting to send Morradin to command the attack on the port itself, squeeze some more use from him whilst hopefully orchestrating his death in the process. But there was another factor to consider, one he was careful to conceal.

"Marshal Morradin will command the landing force," he said. "I will lead the assault on Feros."

Katrya's anger was fierce, making her thrash and scratch at him as they coiled together in the captain's cabin on the *Harbinger*. Had he still possessed a fully human form her attentions might well have been fatal; as it was they were merely painful, if irresistible.

"Do you hate me?" she asked as her passion finally began to subside, her tongue licking along the cut she had left on his scaled brow.

"Of course not," he told her, sharing a memory of their time together in the Morsvale sewers. For all the terror of those days he still preferred them to this enslavement.

So you want it to end? she persisted, returning to thought-speech. *You think death will bring freedom?*

The White wants its victory. The attack on the harbour has a greater chance of success if I lead it. It was a carefully constructed lie, possessing enough truth for plausibility but shot through with sufficient uncertainty to conceal the deception. At least, he had hoped so. Katrya, however, was not so easily fooled.

It's her! Her thoughts lashed at him and her steel-hard nails added another cut to his face as she tore herself free of the bed. *Isn't it? You think you'll find her there!*

He saw no point in denial. Simply sitting up to regard her in silence as the blood coursed down his face.

"She's dead!" Katrya hissed at him, elongated teeth gleaming in the darkness. "The little bitch is dead!"

No she is not. He let the thought bubble to the surface of his mind. His investigations had been cautious, surreptitious intrusions into the minds of those captured at Carvenport. Those taken alive when the city finally fell amounted to barely a dozen people, all but four considered too old or infirm to be worthy of conversion. But there was one, a former stevedore whose pistol had misfired when he attempted to kill himself after a valiant stand at the docks. The man possessed a vivid recollection of the day Miss Blood's rag-tag fleet had sailed from the harbour to fight their way through the blockade of Blues. She strode onto the deck of a warship to greet the captain and, at her side, a disconcertingly pretty young woman of diminutive stature. Her bearing was different, less stiff and formal than he remembered, her face lacking the scowl of one in constant search of something worthy of criticism. But it was undoubtedly her, Tekela, still alive and about to sail to safety in Feros.

"So she's alive," Katrya said, speaking aloud in clipped, angry Varsal. "Think she's waiting for you? Think she's dreaming of the day you come knocking at her door? If you were beneath her notice before, what do you imagine she'll think of you now?"

"A monster," he said and shrugged. "And she would be right. Soon this will be a world of monsters. I would spare her that, if I could."

Katrya's rage subsided at that, the bestial grin fading and her claws becoming hands once more. *You intend to kill her,* she thought, her mind roving through his thoughts as he lowered his barriers. *Like you killed those Blood-blessed.*

Even a monster can be merciful.

She came to him, leaning down to kiss his wounds before taking hold of his hand and pressing it to her belly. *Soon there will be three of us. When you look upon our child will you see nothing more than a monster?*

He wanted her to be lying, but he could feel it in her thoughts and her body. A new life grew inside her. A life they had made.

A life made in love, she said. *Slaves we may be. Monsters we may be. But if we can be merciful, can we not love too?*

CHAPTER 44

Clay

"That's enough, Seer-dammit!" Clay grabbed the barrel of Sigoral's carbine and forced it up. Sigoral tried to tug the weapon free but the Green lingering in Clay's veins wouldn't allow it. The marine's rage at Kriz had come close to overturning his reason and he spent several seconds swearing at her in Varsal, his trigger-finger twitching continually until Clay decided to forestall any unwise actions. They stared at each other, Sigoral refocusing his rage on Clay, removing a hand from the carbine's stock to reach for the pistol at his belt.

"Don't!" Loriabeth said, moving closer to clamp a hand on the marine's arm. "Won't do no good," she added in a softer tone, holding on until he turned to her, the rage fading from his gaze.

"I told you we couldn't trust her," he said, voice coloured by weary resignation. Clay released his grip on the carbine and Sigoral pulled free of Loriabeth before turning away.

"So," Clay said, moving to Kriz's side and nodding at the egg. "He's in there, right? Your father."

She nodded and sagged, Clay reaching out to catch her before she fell. "How do we open it?" he asked, holding her upright.

She drew the small needle gun from her belt and looked up to meet his gaze with a weak smile. "We . . . trance."

"There's not much left," Clay said, eyeing the vial resting in the needle gun's chamber. He snapped it closed and turned to Sigoral and Loriabeth. "Don't know how long we'll be under. Or what I'll find," he added, glancing at the egg.

"Your point, cuz?" Loriabeth enquired.

Clay turned to Sigoral, gave a bland smile which drew a quizzical frown from the marine, a frown that turned to alarm as Clay quick-drew his pistol and levelled it at the Corvantine's head. "Point is, I ain't keen on leaving my cousin in such uncertain company," he said, gaze locked on Sigoral's. "I'll thank you to remove your gloves, Lieutenant."

Sigoral stood stock still for several seconds, then his face betrayed a flicker of grim amusement as he slowly pulled off his gloves. "Let's see it," Clay ordered and the Corvantine extended his hands, turning them over. It was hard to spot in the gloom but Clay found it, a small pale mark on the palm of the marine's left hand.

"Blood-blessed," Loriabeth breathed, gaze narrowing as she stepped to the side, raising her rifle.

"How did you know?" Sigoral enquired.

"General demeanour," Clay said, unwilling to elaborate in front of Loriabeth. "And you never took off your gloves. You're Blood Cadre, right?"

"Certainly not," Sigoral responded with a disdainful sniff. "I am an officer in the Marine Division of the Corvantine Imperial Navy. I also happen to be the appointed Blood-blessed to the INS *Superior*."

"So the ship's Blood-blessed didn't really die off Carvenport. That's how you got her all the way to Lossermark. Guess you ran out of product during the voyage, huh?"

"All but a few drops of Blue. I intended to report your arrival in Lossermark to the Imperial Fleet Command the very night Captain Hilemore seized the *Superior*. For obvious reasons I chose to be somewhat economical with the facts when telling him my story. Otherwise he might not have been so willing to allow me to join this very interesting expedition. My men knew their duty and kept quiet as to my true nature."

"Have you tranced since? Told your bosses what we're up to?"

"I attempted to, when we reached the ice. There was no one to receive my communication, something so unheard of it forces me to conclude the empire may have suffered some form of calamity."

"Horse shit," Loriabeth said. "He's lying. For all we know he's got orders to kill us and steal whatever we find here."

"My cousin makes a good point," Clay told Sigoral. "Seems the smartest thing would be to kill you now."

"Yes it would." Sigoral slowly let his hands fall to his side. He regarded each of them in turn, expression free of any fear, and also any defiance. "A servant of the empire must hold to his duty. But, for what it may be worth, I bear you no ill will and am proud to have made this most enlightening journey in such company."

"Journey ain't over yet," Clay said. "You got any product on your person?"

"A small amount of Green, harvested in the forest when Miss Torcreek's attention was elsewhere."

"Best wait on using it till you really have to." Clay holstered his revolver and turned back to Kriz. "My own supply is pretty low."

"Cuz?" Loriabeth said, gaping at him.

"Got a better chance of getting out of here with two Blood-blessed in our party," Clay told her. "And if killing us was his object, he'd have done it long since."

He went to crouch at Kriz's side, pressing the needle gun's muzzle to her forearm. "Ready?" he asked.

Kriz had recovered a great deal thanks to the crystal's healing light but he could see the lingering pain in her red-tinged eyes. Nevertheless she nodded, forcing a smile. "Ready."

Clay squeezed the trigger, pushing half the Blue into her veins, then pressed the gun to his own forearm, pausing at Loriabeth's softly spoken question, "What if you don't come back?"

He looked up at her, smiled and nodded at Sigoral. "Try not to hate him too much. It'll be awful lonely for you down here otherwise."

She replied with a scowl that slowly softened into a tense smile. "You don't come back I'm gonna spend what time I have left killing all the drakes I can find. *He* can do what he likes."

"Uncle Braddon . . ." Clay began, then faltered, struggling for the words. "Reckon he'd be right proud, seeing you now. First Gunhand indeed."

Her smile broadened a fraction and there was a catch in her voice as she replied, "Reckon he'd be proud of both of us, Clay."

He nodded, closed his eyes and pulled the trigger.

They looked out upon mountains bathed in the light of the three moons. At first Clay thought they were in the Coppersoles, but soon saw differences in the landscape. These mountains were not so tall, their dark flanks largely free of snow or frost. This was a place he had never seen.

"I don't have your skills," Kriz said. She stood near by, close to the edge of the promontory on which they stood, spreading her arms to encompass the view. "Still a little fuzzy around the edges."

Clay scanned the mountains once more, seeing a subtle shift to the peaks and valleys, as if it swayed in some mighty wind, though the air was completely still. "It's not so bad," he said. "Should've seen my first mindscape." He raised his gaze to the sky, eyes taking in the sight of the moons. Nelphia and Morphia were slightly overlapped with Serphia drifting off to the right. "Got the moons right, anyways," he said.

"I remember them very well. This"—she nodded at the mountains—"this I never saw. Nor has anyone else for twelve thousand years."

Clay frowned at her, watching a grim anticipation settle over her face as she also raised her gaze to the heavens. "If you never saw it, how'd you make it?" he asked.

"There are . . . were paintings, sketches. This is my best guess. I needed something suitably impressive to help you understand."

"Understand what?"

She gave a small jerk of her head, Clay seeing a small glimmer of light swelling in her eyes. He followed her gaze to find a new light in the sky, a bright orange ball trailing fire across the faces of the moons. "My father called it the Catalyst Event," Kriz said as the fiery ball grew ever larger. "One moment that forever altered the destiny of this planet."

The fire-ball made a silent descent towards the mountains, streaking down to slam into the peaks a few miles away. The entire range shimmered as a huge blast wave spread out from the impact, ancient stone transformed to powder in the blink of an eye as the sky turned black with displaced dust. For a second the mindscape disappeared, swallowed by the dark, and when it returned Clay found himself standing in a crimson desert.

Something Skaggerhill once said came back to him as he gazed about at the rust-coloured dunes stretching away on either side: *Educated fella I knew in Carvenport said it must've been a mountain range once . . . thousands a years ago some great catastrophe turned it into a desert.*

"You know this place?" Kriz asked, stirring pink dust as she came to his side.

"Been here once," he replied. "We call it the Red Sands."

"My people called it the Iron Wastes, though those of a more spiritual outlook termed it the Cradle of Divine Rebirth. All that remains of a range of peaks that stretched across the centre of this continent, brought low by something beyond human understanding, at least at the time."

She pointed at something on the crest of a near by dune, a tall figure swaddled in thick clothing, face covered against the dust. The figure strode across the sand towards them, giving no indication of registering their presence. It stopped a few feet away, crouching low to scrape at the iron flakes with a rag-covered hand. The covering on the figure's face came loose as he crouched lower to peer at what he had uncovered. Clay half expected to find himself looking upon a Spoiled, but instead saw the face of a man. Dark-skinned and weathered with long-healed scars marring his skin, but undoubtedly a man.

"We believe there were at least half a million people living on this continent at the time of the Event," Kriz said as they watched the scarred man dig in the sands. "Within the space of a century the population had fallen to barely ten thousand. The planet suffered a hundred-year-long winter, so much debris had been cast into the atmosphere it obscured the sun. Whole species were wiped out, the larger animals went first, followed by the predators that preyed upon them. It's no exaggeration to say that all life on this continent stood on the brink of complete extinction. The Event came within a whisker of destroying us, so ironic then that it also brought the key to our prosperity."

Clay watched the scarred man scrape away another handful of flakes to reveal the glassy, multi-faceted surface of a crystal. "How these people came to know enough to make use of them is lost," Kriz said, as the crouched figure pressed his hand to the crystal. "We do know they thought them to be gifts from the gods, a few ancient texts call them the Divine Seeds. And so, the people of this continent began to recover, their entire culture forever transformed. But"—she turned away from the crouching man, nodding at something scrabbling in the dust a short way off—"they were not the only thing to change."

It was small, smaller even than the Green that had bitten him, no more than a foot long from nose to tail. Its skin was mostly hidden by a thick pall of crimson dust, but as the beast shifted Clay saw the light catch on gleaming black scales. The drake gave a small, almost kittenish squawk then convulsed, jumping in alarm as a small but intense gout of flame erupted from its mouth.

"This is just supposition," Kriz said as the tiny Black coughed out some more flames, its wings flaring in excitement. "We never really discovered how exactly it happened, but somehow a small, reptilian species survived the Event and it . . . changed them. The ability to spit venom became the ability to breathe fire and they grew in size with each generation. Some theorised that crystals disintegrated during the Event and the fragments fused with the drakes. The power they held seeped into their being."

"And their blood," Clay said, squinting at the drake in wonder. "Guess it didn't take long before folks found out what it could do."

"Actually, no." Kriz turned away from the drake, closing her eyes in concentration. "That took a very long time."

The Red Sands disappeared, fragmenting into a million shards that in turn shattered into sparkling motes of dust. They swirled about him like fire-flies, the glow they cast slowly increasing as they came together to form a new scene. When it was done he thought at first she had taken him to another mountain range, so tall were the structures that slid by below.

"We're flying," he realised, looking around to find himself in an oval-shaped cabin of some kind. Wide circular windows ran along the walls, affording a clear view of the mountains below. *Not mountains,* he thought, looking again as the summit of the structure passed beneath. It rose to well over a hundred feet in height, a greatly enlarged version of the buildings he had seen in the city beneath the mountain. It was connected by branching walkways to similar buildings on either side and they in turn connected to others so that the city resembled a jungle fashioned from stone. He could see people on the walkways, a great many people.

"Much can happen in two thousand years," Kriz said, appearing at his side. From the smile on her lips it was clear she was enjoying his amazement.

"What is this?" he said, gesturing at the oval-shaped room. "A cable-car?"

"No." She frowned, clearly struggling with an explanation, then shrugged. "You'll see soon enough."

The sound of laughter drew their gaze to the front of the room where a tall man and a little girl stood watching the city pass by below. They were both dressed in clothing that resembled the garb Kriz had found in the armoury, the white fabric contrasting with the darkness of their skin. Clay knew instantly they were father and daughter. It was there in the tall man's gaze, the pride in his eyes and the indulgent smile on his lips as the girl pressed both hands to the glass.

"So many people, Father," she said. "I didn't know there were so many in all the world."

The tall man hesitated before playing an affectionate hand through the girl's short-cropped hair. When he spoke Clay heard Kriz murmur the words in unison, "So many people, Krizelle. And none so special as you."

The room shifted then, Clay's stomach lurching a little as whatever carried them aloft began to descend. It was less alarming than riding on Lutharon's back but still disconcerting. He saw buildings and walkways slide past the windows, as the craft banked then levelled out. The little girl squealed and jumped in excitement at the sight of another building looming ahead, the tallest one yet.

The tall man placed a calming hand on the girl's small shoulder, crouching to meet her gaze, his expression intent. "Do you remember what I told you, Krizelle?" he asked her, provoking a roll of her eyes.

"Don't speak unless directly questioned," she said, her tone rich in the bored annoyance of a child repeating a frequent lesson. "Do not lie, do not exaggerate, demonstrate only as instructed. There will be ignorant and angry people, ignore them."

"Very good." The tall man cupped her cheek and Clay saw how he strove to conceal his trepidation behind a confident grin. "This will all be over soon. Then we'll get to go home."

The little girl gave an aggrieved pout. "But I want to see the city."

"You will." The tall man pulled her into a brief embrace then took her hand, rising to regard the tall building which now filled the window. "But only for a little while."

For a time it seemed they were about to collide with the building, but the speed of their approach soon slowed. The craft carrying them gently descended towards a circular platform extending from the tall building's sloping flank. A slight bump indicated they had come to rest.

"Come along now," the tall man said, clasping his daughter's hand tighter as unseen hands levered open a hatch in the floor. A ladder was hoisted into place and the two of them duly climbed out, Kriz and Clay following close behind.

Once clear of the ladder Clay turned around and backed away, looking up to find a large bulbous object obscuring his view of the sky. He was obliged to retreat a good distance before gaining a full view of the craft. A two-deck gondola was fixed by means of a dense mesh of ropes below a large ovacular balloon. Protruding from either side of the gondola were two mechanicals, the rear of which was fitted with what appeared to be three-bladed fans. Clay immediately recalled Lizanne's trance memory of the propelling mechanism she witnessed in Morsvale harbour. That had been used to push a ship through the ocean so it seemed reasonable to assume these would push this thing through the air.

"So your people have no aerostats," Kriz observed, reading his expression.

"Heard of balloons being used to carry folk aloft," he replied. "Seen pictures in books and such. Nothing like this though."

"It was a recent innovation, truth be told," she said, glancing back at the craft before turning her gaze towards the little girl and her father. "One of many, in fact."

The pair were being greeted by a small delegation, all older people wearing more elaborate garb than Clay had seen before. There was a robe-like formality to the clothing that told him these were people of some importance, a fact confirmed by the sudden deference evident in the posture of the girl's father.

"Were they your Board?" Clay asked Kriz, drawing a bemused frown. "The folk in charge," he elaborated. "Y'know, like a government."

"In charge?" she mused, starting forward as the delegation concluded their greeting and led the little girl and her father into the building. "Sadly, yes they were very much in charge."

They entered the building through a tall pointed arch, proceeding along a wide corridor to a huge tiered chamber. It had a flat circular centre which gave way to a series of wide terraces which ascended to form a great bowl. There were a great many people sitting or standing on the terraces, with more crowding the flat space in the centre. The air was filled with a loud growl of energised conversation, all of which came to an abrupt end when Krizelle and her father followed the delegation into the chamber.

Kriz abruptly froze the memory, Clay turning to find her standing with her arms crossed tight over her chest, eyes closed. "Something wrong?" he asked.

For a second she said nothing, then murmured, "Don't you think it's a curse sometimes? This . . . *thing* we can do. Every memory lingering in your head, ready to be played out in all its detail. Aren't there things you'd rather forget?"

"Sure. Then there are memories I never want to lose. That's just what happens when you live a life."

Clay resisted the urge to encourage her to restart the memory. Although he worried over how much Blue they had left, he also sensed she needed a moment to steel herself for whatever she was about to show him. Biting down on his impatience, he scanned the chamber, eyes roving over all the statue-like figures and finding a peculiar absence. *No guards,* he realised. These people were all dressed much the same as the greeting party, though the colours varied and some were much more elaborate. What struck him as most odd, however, was that no two people were dressed alike.

"No uniforms," he murmured. "No guards. No need for a Protectorate here, I guess."

"Protectorate?" Kriz enquired, the trance communicating her puzzlement at the concept.

"Army, police, soldiers. Folk employed to keep the peace, defend this place."

"Ah." She nodded in understanding. "We'd fought our last war decades before then. Not long before this city was first constructed. The world beyond this continent might still be steeped in tribalism and savagery, but here peace is the norm. However . . ." Her face darkened as she scanned the crowd and her gaze came to rest on one figure in particular, a thin woman of middling years dressed in the plainest robe of any present. "Unfortunately, we had yet to shrug off the lingering taint of superstition."

Clay noted how the thin woman's frozen features were set in an odd expression, somewhere between a disdain and hunger as she stared at the little girl clutching her father's hand and staring at the surrounding assembly with fearful eyes.

Kriz unfroze the memory, the thin woman's strident voice cutting through the silence a half-second later. "So," she said, shifting her narrowed eyes from the girl to her father, "Philos Zembi finally deigns to answer our summons."

"I received a request, not a summons," Krizelle's father replied in a carefully mild tone. "And I came as soon as I was able."

"Ah yes," the woman replied, her own tone much less civil, "you are so busy crafting fresh horrors in that mountain fortress of yours."

"The Philos Enclave is not a fortress, nor is it mine," Zembi replied, Clay seeing how he struggled to keep any animosity from his voice and bearing. "And I fail to see how the many gifts arising from the science practised there could be considered horrifying. Why, the very building we stand in could never have been constructed without the engineering genius of the great Philos Menzah, founder of the Enclave."

"Brick and stone," the woman replied, her voice rising as her gaze snapped back to Kriz, "not flesh and blood to be stolen and twisted into something that offends the very sight of the Divine Benefactors."

"This child has not been twisted into anything," Zembi said, a certain heat creeping into his voice. "Merely nurtured, educated and the gifts she possesses studied."

"Gifts?" The thin woman grated out a humourless laugh. "You talk as if she merely has the ability to compose a tune or paint a pretty picture. In truth"—she raised a bony arm to point at Krizelle—"it is no exaggeration to say she could kill every soul in this assembly if the whim took her."

"Devos Zarhi," a new voice cut in, deep and pitched just below a boom. Clay turned to see a stocky, barrel-chested man emerge from the crowd. He wore a grey-blue robe with short sleeves that revealed thickly muscled arms. Noting his straight-backed bearing and the way the surrounding people made way for him, Clay suspected that he might be the leader here, or at least capable of commanding the most respect.

"This assembly," the stocky man said, lowering his voice a little though it still easily filled the chamber, "is a venue for calm reflection and reasoned decision. Philos Zembi has done us the courtesy of responding to our request. And so"—the stocky man smiled at Krizelle—"has this young lady. I bid you Welcome, Krizelle. Your presence honours us greatly."

Devos Zarhi gave a loud huff at this but remained quiet as the stocky man came forward, sinking to his haunches in front of Krizelle. "I am Veros Harzeh, Speaker of the Chamber," he said. "I believe you have prepared a demonstration for us."

Krizelle raised her small face to her father, Zembi squeezing her hand with an encouraging smile before reaching into a pocket in his robe to extract two objects. "I assume all present possess a basic familiarity with crystalline science," he said, raising his voice and holding up one of the objects, a small crystal little larger than a pebble. "Even the smallest shard gifted to us by the Event is incredibly dense and contains more internal facets than can be counted with the naked eye. Although they have enabled us to craft great works, the true nature of the power they hold still eludes us. But now"—he turned a fond smile on Krizelle—"providence and science have combined to provide us with the key to unlocking their secrets."

He held out the second object to her, a small glass bottle containing a viscous and instantly recognisable substance. "Black?" Clay said, glancing at Kriz and finding her attention entirely absorbed by the unfolding scene.

Krizelle hesitated before reaching out a small hand to take the bottle, removing the glass stopper and drinking the contents. Her face flushed as she swallowed, staggering a little as the product took hold. She straightened quickly and nodded at Zembi, features set in a frown of concentration.

Zembi reached out his hand, the pebble-sized crystal resting in his palm, and gave what Clay thought to be a pause of overly theatrical length before abruptly turning his hand over. The crystal fell several inches then stopped, freezing in mid air as Krizelle reached out to seize it with her Black.

From the vast gasp that filled the chamber, and the subsequent explosion of amazed chatter, Clay deduced this was the first time the vast majority of these people had ever witnessed such a thing.

A small ticking sound drew his gaze back to the crystal, seeing it shudder as Kriz modified her stream of Black. It gave another tick as a new facet appeared in its surface, quickly followed by two more. The crystal abruptly expanded to twice its previous size, new facets appearing so fast it was as if the stone blurred. The ticking sound grew into a continual almost melodic accompaniment to the crystal's transformation. It grew to a fist-sized ball then flattened into a disc, the edges of which began to bow outwards then subdivide into thin overlapping shapes. An irregular cylinder grew from beneath the main body of the crystal, extending for several inches before resolving itself into what was clearly some kind of plant stem, complete with thorns. The ticking sound stopped as Krizelle reduced her Black to a thin stream, letting the newly made crystal rose spin slowly in the air.

Clay gaped at the spectacle. It was the most accomplished and detailed use of Black he had ever seen, outshining even the murderous precision of the dread Black Bildon, the famously skilled assassin from the Blinds.

"Well . . ." he breathed, turning back to Kriz. "That was surely something."

She gave no reaction, instead watching the assembly's reaction. Clay saw amazement, fear and delight on many a face and, in the singular case of Devos Zarhi, naked outrage. Her eyes seemed to glitter as she stared at Krizelle and hissed something through tightly clenched teeth. The words were lost amidst the continuing babble, but he doubted it was anything pleasant.

"You were the first," Clay said to Kriz, laughing in realisation. "The first ever Blood-blessed."

"No," she whispered back, a tear swelling in her eye as she looked upon her younger self, "I was the first abomination."

CHAPTER 45

Lizanne

"Scorazin wasn't yours to give!" The Electress hunched in her saddle, broad features taking on a dark red hue as Dropsy shifted beneath her, perhaps sensing her mistress's growing rage. "Now I have to bargain with a bunch of horse-shagging savages just to buy back a city that's mine by right."

"They're gone," Lizanne replied, meeting Atalina's gaze and speaking in a placid, unrepentant tone. "The threat is removed, without bloodshed I might add."

"She has a fair point," Arberus said. He sat atop his own horse close by, a squad of mounted Brotherhood guards at his back. Lizanne had noticed he never went anywhere without an escort now, as did the Electress. "An intact horse clan with no unsettled blood-feud will be more inclined to join us after Corvus falls," Arberus continued. "It's time we started looking to the future."

The Electress glared at Lizanne a moment longer then slowly straightened, calming Dropsy with a scratch to her ears. She turned to regard the Corvus Road stretching out ahead, a near-straight line of gravel fringed by untended fields, empty all the way to the horizon. "You're lucky I still have need of you, dear," she muttered before kicking Dropsy into motion. "Don't forget our agreement," she added, starting up the road with her body-guard of Furies following close behind.

Arberus guided his horse close to Lizanne's and they sat in silence for a time, watching the People's Freedom Army pass along the road. Varkash's command were first in the marching order, moving in tidy companies now. The uniformity of dress adopted by the Wise Fools in Scorazin had been modified into something that resembled military order, though they still felt obliged to tear the sleeves from the captured uniforms they wore.

"Sentiment?" Arberus asked after a lengthy silence.

They had children. Lizanne left the thought unsaid. Honesty was another thing they no longer shared.

"What was it?" Arberus pressed, apparently undaunted by her silence. "The agreement you struck with her?"

"Just another murder." Lizanne stroked her heels along the grey stallion's flanks, spurring him to a walk. "What else?"

The country grew more populous the closer they drew to Corvus, outlying towns yielding ever more recruits. Local militias either melted away or summarily executed magistrates and senior constables before proclaiming loyalty to the revolution and falling into line. Organised opposition flared intermittently, Imperial officers marshalling hastily assembled loyalists in order to block the road. Some were little more than poorly armed groups of nobles and Imperial functionaries and tended to flee at the first sight of Tinkerer's rockets. Others were much more formidable, usually formed around a hard core of cavalry officers whose troopers were proving to be the least likely conscripts to switch sides. These formations were also more numerous, some numbering close to ten thousand troops and volunteers and requiring an organised assault before being overcome or set to flight. The fighting could be fierce, those with the most to lose in the impending fall of the old regime proving capable of desperate resistance. But numbers always told in the end. By the time Corvus appeared on the horizon the People's Freedom Army counted over two hundred thousand souls in its ranks, and an unbroken line of victories at its back.

"Fires are burning out of control in several districts," Korian reported to the army council after returning from a reconnaissance to the capital. "Though most of the actual rioting seems to have died down. In the aftermath the city divided itself into warring factions. As you might expect the richer the neighbourhood the more likely it is to remain loyal to the crown."

He turned to the map of Corvus spread out on the Electress's desk, his finger making a circular motion around the outer suburbs. "We've managed to make contact with Brotherhood agents in most of the outlying slums. We're confident they'll join us when the army enters the capital. They're lacking arms and ammunition but so are the loyalists." His finger moved to the central districts, hovering over the Imperial Sanctum. "There were some initial attempts to storm the Sanctum when the riots broke out, all bloody disasters. It appears the Blood Imperial has gathered every Blood Cadre operative he can to defend the heart of the empire. In addition, our agents estimate Countess Sefka has between six and ten thousand troops, all well supplied with artillery. Added to that"—his finger moved east to where six large crosses had been pencilled within the confines of the Corvus harbour—"there are two Imperial cruisers and three destroyers at anchor and most of the city is within range of their guns. We can thank the Arradsian disaster there aren't more."

"Quite a formidable knot," the Electress mused, tapping a stubby finger to her chin before turning to Arberus. "Untangle it for us, will you, General?"

Arberus studied the map in silence for some time, gaze narrowed in calculation. "Given the weight of opposition," he said eventually, "siege might be a better strategy than direct assault."

"Starve them out," Varkash said, grunting in approval. "Seems preferable to anodder blood-bath."

"The Sanctum's vaults are copious," Korian said. "And we have reports from all over the empire of loyalist forces marshalling for a march on the capital. It will take months before Sefka's forces are weakened by siege, by which time we could be facing a loyalist army equal in size to our own."

"What other intelligence do we have on these ships," Arberus said, pointing to the harbour. "Just how keen are their crews to fire on their own people?"

"The Imperial Navy has always been a bastion of loyalty."

"To the Emperor, yes. But he's gone, and his mad excursion to Arradsia can hardly have endeared him to the rank and file. They have to come ashore for supplies. Send agents to contact the sailors when they do, the ordinary seamen not the officers. See if we can't foment some discord."

Lizanne's gaze lingered on the harbour and the pencilled crosses. "You said five Imperial ships," she said to Korian. "I count six."

"That's not an Imperial ship," he replied. "Your people, it seems, have either opted to stay or been forbidden from leaving."

"The *Profitable Venture* is still there?"

"And possessing enough fire-power to blow every other vessel at anchor out of the water," Arberus pointed out, meeting her gaze. Although their intimacy might not have survived the revolution, they still possessed a facility for unspoken communication.

"It seems I have another mission," Lizanne said.

The sailor stationed at the *Profitable*'s aft-anchor mounting gaped at her for a full two seconds before fumbling for his rifle. A half-formed challenge died on his lips as Lizanne reached out with Black to pluck the weapon from his grasp. "Exceptional Initiatives," she told him, climbing down from the anchor chain and shaking the less-than-fragrant harbour water from her hair. "Please tell the Duty Officer to rouse Director Thrift-mor and inform him of my arrival."

Thriftmor was a markedly less composed figure than the unruffled diplomat she remembered. His hair was tousled from what Lizanne judged to be an unsettled sleep and his somewhat sagging, red-eyed visage told of a man beset by unaccustomed worries. "So, you're alive," were his only words as Lizanne was conveyed to the ship's ward-room.

"And good evening to you, Director," she replied, casting her gaze around the room to ensure they were alone.

"I find I have little appetite for petty niceties these days," Thriftmor replied. He went to the drinks cabinet in the corner and poured a generous measure of brandy into two glasses. "Ice?" he enquired.

"No thank you."

Thriftmor carried the glasses to the ward-room table and sat down, Lizanne moving to join him. The brandy was an excellent vintage and the finest liquor she had tasted for some time, fine enough for her to resist the impulse to drink it all at once. Director Thriftmor was not so restrained, gulping down the entire contents of the glass before asking a hoarse question, "Your mission?"

"Still progressing. I require your assistance to ensure its success."

"Assistance?" Thriftmor gave a humourless smile and rose to pour himself some more brandy. "What possible assistance could I provide? I assume you have some awareness of our current situation?"

"Yes. You sit aboard the most powerful warship in the western hemisphere doing precisely nothing whilst the empire that has long been our enemy crumbles to pieces."

"The Regency Council has formally ordered this ship not to leave the harbour. If we attempt to do so Countess Sefka has assured me hostilities will resume immediately."

"War with the Syndicate is the last thing she wants just now. Her plate being somewhat overflowing."

"It is Syndicate policy not to interfere in Corvantine internal disputes."

"Yes. Curious then that I have spent much of my career doing just that. For decades the entire corporate world has been hoping for the day this empire faces its ultimate collapse. Now it's finally here, do you really intend to do nothing?"

"We have an agreed treaty with the late Emperor. Countess Sefka has given assurances it will be ratified once the current criminal insurgency is dealt with."

"Why wait?" Lizanne took an oilskin-covered packet from her pocket and tossed it onto the table.

Thriftmor lingered at the drinks cabinet, regarding the packet with grave suspicion as he polished off another full glass of brandy. "And what is that?" he asked, reaching once again for the bottle.

"A Mutual Assistance Agreement between the Corvantine Republic and the Ironship Syndicate, signed by all members of the Interim Governing Council. They will consider the agreement fully valid once your signature is added."

Thriftmor gave a short, high-pitched laugh as he poured more brandy. "You expect me to formally and publicly support this rebellion on my own initiative?"

"Yes. And having done so, you will order the captain of the *Profitable Venture* to place his Blood-blessed under my authority and stand ready to fire upon the Imperial Sanctum at a time of my choosing."

He gaped at her, brandy trickling from the upended bottle, spattering onto the floor as it missed his glass by a wide margin. "You are patently quite insane," he said.

"If so, you are alone in a room with a Blood-blessed agent of the Exceptional Initiatives Division who also happens to be mad." She placed her left arm on the table, the sleeve of her shirt rolled up to reveal the Spider, holding his gaze. "Just sign the document, Director," she said with a bland smile. "Once you've introduced me to the captain I'll let you go back to bed."

The *Profitable Venture* had two thermoplasmic engines, each requiring its own Blood-blessed to operate. Lizanne met the pair of them in the captain's cabin, the man himself having gone to oversee his ship's surreptitious transition to battle stations. At first Lizanne took the two Blood-blessed for brother and sister, so similar were they in colouring, both with striking red hair and pale freckled skin. They also both had similarly narrow noses and eyes of dark green, so it was a surprise when the male Blood-blessed made the introductions, "Zakaeus Griffan. This is my wife Sofiya."

"Sir, madam," she greeted them both. "The captain has advised you of your change in circumstances, I trust?"

The two of them exchanged an uneasy glance. "We are to follow your instructions," Mrs. Griffan said in a cautious tone.

"You are indeed." Lizanne gestured at the captain's desk where a pair of revolvers had been placed along with thirty rounds of ammunition. "Please arm yourselves. Product will be provided once we reach our objective."

Neither of them moved, eyes tracking from the guns to Lizanne. "I . . ." Zakaeus Griffan faltered, coughed and tried again. "I didn't catch your name, madam?"

"I didn't give it."

"Even so." The man licked dry lips, forcing himself to meet her eye with a stern resolve. "Never having met you before, my wife and I cannot simply . . ."

"Standard Ironship Maritime Contract Number Seventy-four," Lizanne cut in. "Pertaining to the employment of registered Blood-blessed aboard Protectorate Vessels. Clause Ten, sub-clause Twelve-B: All contracted Blood-blessed shall consider themselves subject to the orders of any Exceptional Initiatives agent who identifies themselves to the ship's commanding officer. Failure to comply will be considered a breach of contract and result in forfeiture of all payments set out in this agreement, formal removal from the Register and a period of no less than ten years in an Ironship custodial facility."

She forced down the spark of pity in her breast as she watched them clasp hands, Mrs. Griffan's features tensing with the onset of tears. "I find myself with recent experience of prison life," Lizanne told them, maintaining a stern tone. "I assure you it is far from pleasant."

Zakaeus squeezed his wife's hand, meeting Lizanne's steady gaze with one of his own. "I will serve in my wife's stead . . ."

"Unacceptable. I require both of you." Lizanne moved to the desk, retrieving the revolvers and pushing them into the Griffans' arms. "I'll allow you five minutes of privacy," she said, moving to the door. "After which I shall expect your presence on the fore-deck."

They slipped ashore in the morning, disguised as crew members on the small launch the *Profitable* was permitted to send to the docks for supplies. Sofiya Griffan fidgeted continually as the launch neared the wharf, her face even paler beneath the peak of the cap under which her red locks had been concealed. Watching her Lizanne wondered if it might have been better to accede to her husband's request. For all their gifts, Blood-blessed were people like any other and fortitude was a far from universal trait.

"Stop that!" Lizanne said in a harsh whisper, reaching out to grip the woman's forearm as her hands began to tremble.

"I can't . . ." Sofiya hissed back. "I can't fight! I don't know how!"

"I do not require you to fight," Lizanne returned, casting a cautious glance at the Corvantine marines on the wharf.

"Then why drag us into this?" the woman persisted.

Lizanne watched the Protectorate sailors toss ropes to the marines. "In war the illusion of strength is as valuable as the reality. Now clench your fists and keep your gaze lowered. Do not say a word."

As per his orders the Protectorate officer in charge of the shore party began to loudly harangue his coxswain for poor helmsmanship as soon as the gang-plank was lowered into place. He continued the diatribe as the sailors trooped onto the wharf, much to the apparent amusement of the onlooking marines. The sailors closed in on either side of Lizanne and the Griffans, shielding them from any curious glances as they made their way to the stacked crates containing the supplies.

"They may have counted us off," a petty officer warned Lizanne as she moved to the far side of the crates.

"If they attempt to impede your return, kill them," Lizanne replied, removing her sailor's cap and tunic. "Try to be quiet about it."

"We'll be seen," the man insisted. "Within seconds the whole harbour will be on alert."

"Your captain has clear instructions should that occur. In a few hours it won't matter anyway."

Lizanne gestured for the Griffans to follow and made for a shadowed alley between two warehouses. "Both of you stay within three feet of my person at all times," she told the couple as the shadow swallowed them. "And leave any talking to me."

Lizanne was obliged to share some Green with the Griffans to enable a sprint past the outer cordon of Corvantine marines guarding the docks. A few shots were fired in their wake but their speed made it a waste of ammunition, not that Zakaeus seemed to appreciate the ease of their escape.

"You're going to get us both killed!" he raged at Lizanne, pulling his wife close after she concluded a short bout of fear-induced vomiting.

Lizanne ignored him and turned her attention to the broad square ahead. They had taken shelter behind a huge tumbled pillar of bullet-pocked marble, part of the front edifice of the Corvantine Customs House, now transformed into little more than rubble. The square, once a small park of neat lawns and flower-beds, had become a shell-cratered patch of corpse-littered earth. Smoke rose in thick columns above the surrounding roof-tops and rifle fire echoed intermittently in the distance. Corvus, it appeared, was now more battleground than city.

Lizanne led them in a circuitous route around the square, keeping to the rubble piled on the fringes. Challenges came from various barricades as they followed a westward course through successive streets. Lizanne gave no answer to the shouted demands and for the most part those manning the barricades were content to let them proceed on their way. One, however, proved excessively keen for confrontation.

"Proclaim yourselves as true citizens!" a tall man called from atop a mound of loose brick and piled furniture, the Imperial flag flying from the pole he carried. He wore the besmirched clothing of a well-to-do member of the middling sort, this district lying at a decent remove from the dock-side slums.

"Proclaim or perish!" the tall man added, the others manning the barricade echoing what was evidently a newly born battle-cry. They were an ill-disciplined lot, evidenced by the volley of shots that rang out to accompany their exhortation. Lizanne dragged the Griffans behind an upturned coal-wagon as the bullets impacted around them like angry lead bees.

"Come out!" the tall man ordered. "Come out and procla—"

His words died as Lizanne injected a burst of Green, drew her pistol and darted out from behind the upturned wagon to slot a bullet between his eyes from a distance of thirty yards.

"I am a Blood-blessed soldier in the People's Freedom Army!" she called out to the now-silent barricade. "And you've seen what I can do! Put down your weapons and go back to your homes!"

Lizanne hauled her companions to their feet and pushed them ahead. She wasn't sure what effect her words might have had, but they made their way clear of this district without further incident.

"This is all?"

Besides Hyran, there were five people gathered in the basement of his grandfather's long-abandoned shop, three men and two women. They were all much the same age, about twenty-five by Lizanne's estimation, and also shared the ragged and besmirched appearance of those who had spent days in combat. They also had a hollow-eyed aspect that told of a lack of Green to stave off the consequent exhaustion.

"Every surviving Blood-blessed to have joined the Corvus rebels," Hyran replied. "The empire takes all but a few into the Blood Cadre at a young age, so parents with radical notions tend to hide the true nature of any Blessed children."

"What of the agents Arberus sent to the harbour?"

"It seems they found more willing ears than expected. Being cooped up for weeks hasn't done much for morale and there's many a sailor with family in Corvus. The general's confident we can seize at least three ships when the time comes."

"You're *her*, aren't you?" one of the Blood-blessed spoke up, a slender young woman with a bandage around her forearm. "Miss Blood?" Lizanne found herself discomfited by the gleam of awe in the young woman's eyes. It seemed her legend had flown far wider than she thought.

"Just 'miss' will do," Lizanne replied. "And you?"

"Jelna, here in the name of First Republic." She cast a sour glance in Hyran's direction. "The only true voice of revolution."

"And the first to abandon the cause," Hyran replied, which provoked Jelna into a combative snarl.

"Your Brotherhood has as much blood on its hands as the Regnarchy. You betrayed Bidrosin's legacy . . ."

"Enough!" Lizanne broke in, her impatience with their radical feuding adding a hard edge to the command. *They still can't forget their petty squabbles even in the midst of all this.* She took a moment to calm herself and nodded at the bandage on Jelna's arm. "How bad is it?"

"Bullet graze." Jelna shrugged, a cautious hopefulness creeping into her gaze as she eyed the satchel on Lizanne's shoulder. "Stings a bit. A spot or two of Green would go down nicely."

Lizanne placed the satchel on the floor, opening it to reveal the contents. "Courtesy of the IPV *Profitable Venture*," she said. The captain had been none-too-happy about parting with almost the entire contents of the ship's product safe. Consequently Lizanne had been obliged to issue a reminder of his obligations and the likely reaction of Director Bloskin should he fail to meet them. She shared the product out equally, Zakaeus and Sofiya accepting their vials with a reluctance that contrasted markedly with the enthusiasm of their new colleagues.

"Got enough Red here to burn down the whole fucking Sanctum," one of the men commented. He spoke in coarse Varsal rich in the accent of the slums and wore a cavalryman's coat, dark with dried blood and marked by several poorly stitched bullet-holes.

"This is Kraz," Hyran introduced the man. "Besides me, the only surviving Brotherhood Blood-blessed in the city."

"Luckily, burning down the Sanctum in its entirety shouldn't be necessary," Lizanne told Kraz. She reached into the satchel and extracted the two additional Spiders she had taken from the fallen Blood Cadre agents at the Battle of the Road. She handed one to Jelna and the other to Kraz before spending a few minutes educating them in the correct operation of the devices.

"Do you have any more of those?" Zakaeus asked, peering into the satchel.

"No," Lizanne replied. "They're only for fighters."

She extracted her timepiece and did a rough mental calculation of how long it would take to get to the outer walls of the Sanctum. "We need an unobstructed route," she said, realising they would be unlikely to reach their objective if required to traverse more barricade-ridden streets.

"Could try the sewers," Kraz suggested.

"Most have been flooded," Jelna said. "The Cadre learned a lot of lessons after the last revolution."

"If we can't go down," Lizanne said, slotting a fresh vial of Green into her Spider, "we'll have to go up."

The roof-tops of Corvus were fortuitously rich in tiled slopes and broad ledges, which made traversing them at Green-enhanced speeds a relatively simple matter. Lizanne led the way, the others following her route as she sprinted and leapt from one roof-top to another. A few snipers, both rebel and loyalist, had taken to the upper levels of the city. Most just stood and gaped at the momentary intrusion into their domain, but a few possessed sufficient reflex and resolve to cast some shots in their direction.

"We're on your side, you silly fucker!" Kraz admonished one unfortunate marksman whose bullet had added another hole to his already ragged garment. Fortunately it had passed through the Blood-blessed's sleeve without finding any flesh, not that this cooled his anger any. Having injected a burst of Black he seized the sniper, marked out as a rebel by the Brotherhood symbol stitched onto his jacket. The fellow struggled vainly as he was lifted, legs dancing in thin air.

"Thought . . . you was . . . Cadre," the man rasped out through a rapidly constricting throat.

"Leave the poor sod alone, Kraz," Hyran said. "We ain't got the time."

Kraz's face bunched in frustrated malice and he cast the sniper aside, tossing him end over end to land on the opposite roof-top amidst a cloud of shattered tiles.

"We're just about there," Jelna said, pointing to where the rows of streets came to an abrupt end. Beyond them lay the band of green fields surrounding the Sanctum. Lizanne went to the edge of the roof-top, eyes tracking over the expanse of well-maintained grass and shrubbery she remembered from her coach ride with the unpleasantly aromatic Chamberlain Yervantis. It was much the same but for the numerous bodies lying in a line of blackened, dismembered clusters all the way to the outer walls of the Sanctum.

"It would've fallen on the first day but for the Blood Cadre," Jelna said, face dark as she stared at the piled bodies below.

Lizanne checked her timepiece once more and turned to the south, her boosted vision making out the dark mass of people streaming into the Corvus suburbs. The progress of the People's Freedom Army was swift but not unopposed. Cannon shells exploded here and there along with frantic flurries of small-arms fire, but the loyalists were far too few in number to successfully contest the advance. Within minutes the rebel throng had reached the dense streets of the slums where their numbers swelled amidst an upsurge of cheering.

"Four minutes," she told the others before injecting more Green and commencing a swift descent to ground level.

She had them form a line then led them across the fields in a sprint, raising a cloud of churned earth and shredded grass in their wake in an unmistakable sign of their nature. Lizanne brought them to a halt some four hundred paces from the wall, extreme range for a rifle-shot but not a cannon. A salvo of shells was launched almost as soon as they came to a halt.

"Remember," Lizanne said to Hyran. "Just like I showed you."

She injected a second long burst of Black and raised her gaze, finding the plummeting shells easily thanks to the Green in her veins. A concentrated burst of force was enough to explode three of the shells in mid air, Hyran taking care of the remaining two a split-second later. After that the cannon fell silent.

"We're just going to stand here?" Zakaeus demanded. Lizanne turned to see he and his wife had edged back a little, faces slick with sweat.

"If you run," Lizanne told Zakaeus in a flat, sincere tone, "I'll break your spine and make you watch whilst I disembowel your wife. Now stand still and shut up."

She turned back to the wall, eyes scanning the battlements as she felt the timepiece tick away in her pocket. *Where are you, you old bastard?*

It took perhaps a minute for the first Blood Cadre agent to appear, a man of slight build but with the age and bearing of a veteran. Lizanne's unnatural vision picked out the gleam of the Imperial crest against the dark fabric of the man's tunic. He was soon joined by more agents, dark-suited figures shoving soldiers aside as they crowded onto the battlements to view their enemy. Seeing the animosity on their faces, Lizanne was reminded of something the Blood Imperial had said in Azireh's tomb: *Many of my children want justice for their murdered brothers and sisters.* Whatever the truth of that, it appeared he hadn't deigned to join them in administering justice, for she couldn't find any sign of him.

"This is . . ." Sofiya managed before choking into a terrorised silence.

"Madness," her husband finished. "We can't possibly fight so many."

"I told you," Lizanne said, raising her gaze to the sky as her ears detected a familiar, droning whine, "I do not require you to fight."

The *Profitable Venture*'s captain had assured her that the required precision was well within the capabilities of his gun-crews. "A large static target," he sniffed. "Just a matter of trigonometry, miss."

It proved no idle boast. The first shell impacted directly atop the battlements some fifty yards to the left of where the Blood Cadre had assembled. Some were killed outright by the blast and the shrapnel, others reacted with impressive swiftness, leaping clear or sprinting in the opposite direction with Green-facilitated strength. It wasn't enough to save them. The next four shells landed in quick succession, making the ground quake with every impact. The section of wall where the Blood Cadre had gathered dissolved into a storm of flame and shattered stonework. The bombardment continued for five minutes, the fall of shells pausing a few times as the gunners adjusted their aim so as to carve a breach in the wall a hundred feet across.

Hearing a growing, angry murmur at her back, Lizanne turned to see the vanguard of the People's Army emerging from the streets fringing the fields. They came streaming over the green expanse, convicts from Scorazin, turncoat conscripts and thousands of rebel townsfolk all making for the smoking breach in the wall with no Blood Cadre to oppose their charge.

"I consider your contract fulfilled," Lizanne told the Griffans. "Feel free to return to the ship, though I would advise hiding out for a few hours first."

She hefted her revolver and glanced at the five rebel Blood-blessed who stood regarding the ruined wall with equal parts delight and anticipation. "Shall we?"

CHAPTER 46

Clay

A strange, guttural gasp rose from the crowd as they moved closer, jostling each other in their desire to gawp at the crystal rose crafted by the impossible powers of a little girl. The initial awe had given way to a collective hunger, as if the mere sight of something so incredible had transformed them all into children desperate to get their hands on a new toy.

"Stop this!" The voice cut through the crowd's rising tumult like a knife. It was Devos Zarhi, standing apart from the encroaching throng, her arms raised and eyes lit with a manic light that put Clay in mind of Preacher in one of his rare talkative moments. "This . . ." the thin woman hissed, lowering her arms so both hands were pointed blade-like at the gently rotating crystal rose. "This vile corruption of the Benefactors' gifts offends all who hold to the divine. Do not imagine they are blind to this!" She turned to the crowd, voice raised in shrill conviction. "Do not delude yourselves they will allow such interference in their design to go unpunished! Do not—"

"Oh, cease your prattle you ignorant fool!" It was Zembi, his face full of an anger that gave the lie to his studied mildness from only a few moments before. He had moved to place himself between Krizelle and Zarhi. Whilst not quite so imposing a figure as Veros Harzeh, he was still a substantially built man and his hunched bearing carried an obvious warning. "This girl is not a corruption of anything," Zembi went on, addressing the crowd now. "Her gifts are innate, revealed only through blind chance. No one made her this way. My daughter is as much a gift as the crystals . . ."

"She is not your daughter," Zarhi cut in, voice lowered now to a sibilant hiss. "You stole her."

The rose stopped spinning, trembled for a second then fell to the floor.

"Father?" Krizelle asked, moving to tug at Zembi's robes. "What does she mean?"

"Oh yes," Zarhi said, her features taking on a sympathetic grimace that didn't alter the animosity still shining in her eyes. "Didn't you know, little one? You share no blood with this man."

"Liar!" Krizelle said, tears blooming in her eyes as she lunged towards the thin woman. Zembi caught Krizelle in a tight embrace, lifting her and carrying her away.

"This man stole you!" Zarhi called out. "Your real parents ache for your return . . ."

"LIAR!"

Clay winced at the thunder-clap sensation of a large amount of Black being released at once. Devos Zarhi was blasted off her feet like a twig caught in a gale. She slammed into the crowd, the crack of breaking bones mingling with a chorus of panicked shouting. The remaining throng retreated, some more resilient souls coalescing to resist the fleeing tide whilst others went to aid the pile of groaning bodies surrounding the crumpled form of Devos Zarhi.

Kriz froze the memory as Zembi ran for the exit, Assembly members fleeing from his path, the little girl in his arms staring over his shoulder at the carnage she had caused.

"I didn't kill her," Kriz said, moving to peer at the twisted and inert body of Devos Zarhi. "Though I'm told she never walked properly again. To my shame I find this does not trouble my conscience."

"Was it true?" Clay asked. "About him stealing you?"

"Adopted is more accurate, albeit an adoption ordered by the Assembly. I have no memory of my parents. Zembi told me only that they were farmers . . . and that they feared their daughter greatly. Apparently a pack of Reds attacked the farm when I was an infant, descending out of the night to pick off the livestock. One got into the house and found me in my crib. My father shot it before it could eat me, but its blood got on my skin, in my mouth. And yet I didn't die, but I did burn down the house. Fearing me subject to some curse sent by the Benefactors, they took me to the local Devos, a man far wiser than Zarhi here, who had a long-standing friendship with Philos Zembi, famed genius of the Enclave. Clearly I was far too important to be left in the hands of simple farmers."

"And you never found out till that moment?" Clay asked.

"My education and co-operation were easier to achieve if I grew up believing we had a familial bond."

"Still a shit thing to do."

Kriz turned away from Zarhi to regard her father, staring at his tensed, determined features as he bore her younger self away. "I suppose so," she said. "But I've come to understand that he was a man beset by many troubles. It's often the way with those who dare to make their dreams a reality."

She was older in the next memory, Clay guessing her age at somewhere between fifteen and eighteen. This Krizelle stood on a lawn of well-tended grass alongside a large crystal structure Clay quickly realised he had seen before. It was a sculpture of a man holding both arms aloft. His hands appeared unfinished, frozen in the act of growing fingers. A quick survey of their new surroundings confirmed it, the vast granite wall of the mountain's interior lit by a soft orange glow from below, the same hard-angled buildings with their balconies, bridges and stairs, so many stairs.

"The city beneath the Nail," he said in a soft murmur, gaze tracking over the successive stairways that had taken him to his confrontation with the White.

"Welcome to the Philos Enclave," Kriz said, stepping into view and frowning at the recognition evident in his face. "You've been here before."

"That I have. It was . . ." He paused to gaze around at all the people crowding the various staircases and terraces. ". . . quieter then."

"You mean empty," she said with grim certainty. "Lifeless."

"Not exactly. There was something living here alright."

"What . . . ?" Kriz's question died as a child's cry of frustration sounded across the lawn. Clay saw the younger Krizelle going to comfort a boy several years her junior engaged in furiously kicking the mangled crystal ring at his feet.

"Won't do what it's told!" the boy fumed as he kicked.

"Come now, Hezkhi," Krizelle said, laying a calm hand on his shoulder, taking a firmer grip until he stopped kicking. "What have we learned about anger?" she asked him.

The boy's lips formed a momentary snarl as he prepared a scornful reply, but something in Krizelle's kind but implacable gaze made him re-consider. "Anger is the barrier to clarity," he mumbled.

"Quite so." Krizelle knelt and retrieved the twisted crystal ring from the grass, holding it up for critical inspection. "What were you trying for?" she asked Hezkhi.

"A snake," he said, affording the ring a sullen, accusatory scowl. "It ate itself."

"Too many facets." Krizelle ran a finger over the surface of the misbe-gotten snake. "You're trying for too much detail. Remember these shapes are grown, not crafted. You have to let them find their own way." She reached into the pocket of her robe and came out with a small vial. "Try again. I'll guide you."

"Blood-blessed," Clay realised, watching the boy drink the product. "Zembi found another one?"

"Not just one." Kriz nodded to her right, Clay turning to see a dozen or so more children near by, all engaged in the same activity. He estimated their ages varied from as young as seven to thirteen and their attempts to produce crystal sculptures weren't much better than Hezkhi's.

"Despite the . . . unfortunate incident at the Assembly," Kriz said, "or perhaps because of it, Zembi was granted authority to seek out others like me."

"He adopt them too?" Clay asked, seeing the obvious affection on her face as she gazed at the Blood-blessed youngsters.

"No," she said. "But they still called him Father, nevertheless."

A loud chiming sound came from above, Krizelle and the children all looking up towards the city's summit in response. "It appears Father needs me," she said, giving Hezkhi a final pat of encouragement before moving towards the nearest flight of stairs. "Stay here and finish the lesson. I'll see you at supper."

"He must have finished another monster," the boy said, dropping his misshapen artwork to the grass and starting after her. "Let me come, Kri-zelle. I want to see."

"No!" Krizelle's tone was sharp enough to freeze the boy in place. "And they're not monsters," she added, in a softer tone, then pointed at the fallen sculpture until Hezkhi sulkily went to retrieve it. "Remember, let the crys-tal find its own way," she reminded him before starting up the stairs.

Kriz and Clay followed her as she ascended successive tiers, exchanging numerous greetings with the people she passed. Although Clay saw none of the fear exhibited by the Assembly members, there was a notable deference in their demeanour, as if Krizelle, despite her youth, held some kind of authority here.

"Were you in charge or something?" he asked Kriz as they climbed.

"No, I held no formal position, except as tutor to the children. But informally . . ." She trailed off, face clouding as she watched her younger self turn a corner. "The more Father lost himself in his studies the more remote he became. Sometimes he wouldn't appear for weeks. Since I was the only one to see him with any regularity, I became a conduit of sorts, his link to the rest of the Enclave."

He guessed where Krizelle was leading them before he saw it, the unadorned rectangular building rising from a broad plaza of tiled stone. He was immediately struck by how different it looked, not just the people but the light. The orange glow of the lower tiers had disappeared, replaced by a soft white light cascading from above. Raising his gaze, he saw a crystal, far larger than any he had seen before, slowly revolving above the summit of the city.

"So you had your own sun here too," he said, pausing to shield his eyes as he took in the sight. Despite all he had seen the wonder of it was still jarring. "How do they do that?" he asked Kriz. "Just hang there like that."

She halted the memory, freezing the crystal's slow rotation. "Would you like the scholarly explanation or the simple one?" she asked.

"Simpler would be better."

"Very well. I don't know. None of us did. Not even Father."

Clay squinted at her. There was a faintly sheepish smile on her lips, eyebrows raised as if she were confessing a minor lapse of some kind. "What d'you mean?" he said. "Your people built all this. Built that place beneath the ice. How can you not know?"

"We didn't make the crystals, Clay. We found them. We knew only what they did. We knew that if they were placed in proximity to a powerful heat source they would float in the air and exude a light that could both heal and nourish vegetation. That's how we recovered from the Event, the crops grown with the crystals saved us and the settlements that cultivated them became the foundation of our civilisation.

"We also knew that, if subjected to sufficient force, the crystals could be persuaded to adopt different shapes. And we knew that they had fundamentally altered drake, and as it transpires, human biology. But how they did it." She shrugged and turned away, unfreezing the memory and following her teenage self towards the building. "That we never knew. I sometimes think that's what made Father . . . become what he became. For him, an unsolved mystery was always the worst torment."

As they approached the building the familiar symbol above the entrance came into view. "What does it mean?" Clay asked, pointing at the upturned eye. "Keep seeing it everywhere."

"The emblem of the Philos Caste. Philos meaning knowledge in the ancient pre-Event tongue."

"And Devos and Veros?"

"Devos is the archaic collective term for the pantheon of pre-Event gods. In our time it's become synonymous with those who serve the Benefactors. Veros, which translates literally as Overlord, now pertains to those who ascend to senior roles in the Assembly."

They followed Krizelle into the building and down the deep stairwell to the chamber with the three domes. Once again it was different, the domes were there but the light that emitted from the apertures in their roofs was all the same colour. Krizelle led them towards the largest of the three domes, Clay feeling his heart quicken as they approached even though he was pretty sure he would find no White in residence this time.

"Are you alright?" Kriz asked, sensing his distress.

"Yeah," he said, marvelling at his ability to sweat in a trance. "I'm just fine."

The dome interior was not how he remembered it either. Instead of the glass floor there was a matrix of walkways, some level, some sloping down to the vast space below. In Clay's time the space below the dome had been filled with drake eggs, but now it was sectioned off into a honeycomb-like series of glass-roofed, hexagonal rooms. He could see shapes beneath the glass, four-legged, long-tailed shapes. Some prowled back and forth whilst others lay unmoving.

Drakes, Clay realised, seeing the unmistakable form of a Green languidly coiling its tail below. It was smaller than its modern cousins, but still substantially larger than those he had encountered in the forest.

"Breeding pens," he said. "This is where you harvested your product."

"Yes." Kriz spared a brief glance for the drakes below. "I assume you must have something similar."

"Yeah, not so clean though."

They came to a halt as Krizelle paused up ahead, her gaze drawn to something directly beneath the walkway. Clay moved closer to view the object of her interest. The glass roof of the room below was smeared with something dark, making it hard to discern the exact shape of what lay behind it. However, he could see that it was far larger than the others, its long tail coiled around a slumped, inert body.

"What is that?" Clay asked Kriz.

She continued to stare at the shape beneath the smeared glass. "For now, just another failed experiment."

"Krizelle!"

They turned to watch Krizelle approaching a place where the various walkways converged to form a wide central platform. Zembi was waiting alongside Veros Harzeh. The intervening years had affected both men differently. Zembi's hair had become noticeably thinner, as had his frame. Also his features now exhibited the gaunt, hollow-eyed look of a man who slept little. By contrast Veros Harzeh had become an even more substantial human being, his frame several inches wider and a large, grey-flecked beard covering his chin.

"So good to see you again," Harzeh told Krizelle with a broad smile.

"Speaker," Krizelle greeted him with a respectful nod. Clay noted that she exchanged no greeting with Zembi.

"Not for much longer," the stocky man replied.

"Veros Harzeh comes with news," Zembi told Krizelle. "Unwelcome if not unexpected."

"Devos Zarhi won the plebiscite," Krizelle said with a heavy sigh.

"I'm afraid so," Harzeh said. "I'm sorry. But you know what this means . . ."

"It means our society has surrendered itself to fear, ignorance and superstition," Zembi cut in. "A surrender I am not prepared to accept."

"Zarhi will take over as Speaker within the year," Harzeh said. "When she does . . ."

"The Philos Enclave will fall. Everything we have worked for will be destroyed. Decades of progress lost." Zembi's gaunt features spasmed in barely controlled fury before he mastered himself. "Fortunately, the Philos Caste has long anticipated this moment and we have not been idle." He took an apple-sized crystal from his pocket and held it out to Krizelle. "Show him."

Krizelle took out a vial and drank before reaching out with Black to pluck the crystal from Zembi's hand. The ticking sound rose again as she began to transform it, first flattening it into a wide disc. A few seconds later the facets began to form themselves into a miniature landscape; rivers, valleys, mountains appearing in concentric circles. It reminded Clay of a shooting target, a flat outer ring, followed by an indentation that bespoke a body of water which in turn gave way to a mountainous region in the centre.

"What is this?" Harzeh asked, peering at the crystal model as Kriz finished crafting the last mountain.

"A new enclave," Zembi said. "A whole world in microcosm. Self-contained and far removed from the petty superstitions that would impede us."

"You want to build this?"

Clay saw Zembi exchange a glance with Krizelle. "We already have," he said.

Harzeh voiced a loud, incredulous laugh then sobered when he saw the sincerity on Zembi's face. "How?" he demanded. "Where?"

"You recall the southern polar expedition five years ago?" Zembi asked. "Its purpose went far beyond mere exploration."

Harzeh laughed again, a soft gasp of bitter realisation. "So you lied to me, and to the Assembly."

"Yes," Zembi said, a fierce note of conviction colouring his voice. "And I'd tell a thousand more lies to achieve our goals. We are so close, old friend. You know how vital this is." He moved closer to Harzeh, voice lowered to an intent murmur. "I intended to complete the transfer over the course of the next two years, but with the Assembly in the hands of that delusional woman time is no longer a luxury we enjoy. We need your assistance. The sun crystals still need to be transported, as do the children. Just three aerostats. That's all I ask."

Harzeh ran a meaty hand over his greying beard, frowning at the model. "Why so elaborate?" he asked.

"Drakes don't flourish in captivity," Krizelle said. "We lose more than half of every generation hatched here, and those that survive infancy tend to live only a few years. Father believes we have corrupted the blood lines. A fresh start is needed if we are to breed stock with sufficiently potent blood. A sealed environment simulating their natural habitat will achieve that."

"Think of it, Harzeh," Zembi said as the Speaker continued to ponder the model. "Within a few generations we will finally achieve convergence. Is that not a prize to risk everything for?"

Harzeh closed his eyes, drawing in a deep breath. "We live in an age so wondrous it would have made our ancestors weep to see it," he said. "Sometimes I wonder if the Zarhis of the world don't have the right of it. Should we not be content with the Benefactors' gifts?"

"You may call it contentment," Zembi said with hard certainty, "I call it blind indolence. You remember why we started this, old friend. Humanity once came within a whisker of extinction because we were too mired in ignorance to develop the means to deal with so great a calamity. Convergence will ensure that never happens again."

Harzeh opened his eyes, gave the crystal model a final glance before nodding to Krizelle. "Thank you, child," he said, turning and starting along the walkway towards the exit. "The aerostats will be here within the week," he added without turning. "It will be my last act as Speaker before Zarhi calls for my exile. Be sure to use the time well."

The memory broke up as the stocky man walked away, the dome swirling into mist then re-forming into a familiar landscape. It was the cliff-face from their trek through the mountains, but now partially covered with some kind of wooden scaffolding. A glance at the sky revealed the three crystal suns shining bright above it all.

Clay watched Krizelle navigate the scaffolding with the practised ease of an oft-performed task, descending a series of ladders before entering the wide opening in the cliff. She descended a long narrow passage then followed a winding course deep into the rock. The passage was lit by a soft orange glow that grew brighter the deeper they went. A five-minute journey brought them into a large cavernous chamber where a single walkway led from the passage to a large central platform. Beneath the walkway a series of stepped terraces descended towards a bright, fiery red circle. Clay had to squint at it to make out the sight of roiling lava. On each of the surrounding tiers lay eggs, hundreds, perhaps thousands of eggs all bathing in the glow of the lava pit.

"The crystals need thermal energy to work," Kriz explained. "The greatest source of continuous natural heat in this world comes from beneath the earth's crust. It's why this site was chosen. The entire construct rests atop an active lava-stream."

"They hatched," Clay said, nodding at the eggs. "That's where that sickly White came from, and all those Greens and Reds."

"It seems the stream and the fault-line that produced it have become more active in recent years, hence the tremors. The increase in temperature must have caused a mass hatching."

A soft voice drew their attention to the central platform where Krizelle was greeting an older and thinner Zembi. He stood at the edge of a large circular pit in the floor of the platform. A faint huffing sound came from the pit, along with the scrape of something hard on stone. Whatever lay below seemed to absorb Zembi's complete attention and he failed to turn when Krizelle entered. Clay noted she came to a halt several yards from the edge of the pit and seemed distinctly disinclined to venture any closer.

Krizelle stood in silence for a time, watching her adoptive father with an expression that veered from frustration to concern and back again. To Clay's eyes she seemed to be the same age as the Kriz he knew, meaning whatever was about to occur had taken place shortly before she began her centuries-long sleep.

"Hezkhi's back," Krizelle said, causing Zembi to stir from his reverie, though he barely glanced at her.

"And?" he said, a slight irritation to his voice.

"You were right. The Philos Enclave is abandoned. He flew on to the city, seeing burning buildings . . . people rioting in the streets. Then he landed in the desert and walked to a settlement. The people there were full of stories about abominate children born with vile powers. They say Speaker Zarhi launched a purge of these abominations, and for her pains one of them assassinated her three years ago. Since then . . ." Krizelle shrugged, repeating softly, "You were right."

Zembi gave a vague nod and returned his attention to the pit. Clay saw Krizelle bite down some angry words before forcing herself to step closer. "Still no response?" she asked.

"Your sister tried again this morning." Zembi waved a hand at something lying near by. "Nothing."

Clay turned to the object, finding it to be a crystal, one of four in fact. They were shaped differently from the other crystals he had seen in Kriz's memories, with jagged spines that gave them a star-like appearance. They gave off no illumination but he was able to discern that they were all different colours: red, green, blue and one so dark it seemed to swallow the light. His mind immediately flew to the domes and the crystals he had seen there, the blue one that had so entranced the Spoiled Briteshore miners.

"You should destroy it," Krizelle said, drawing his gaze back to the pit. She had edged closer to Zembi, but still kept several feet between herself and the edge. The expression on her face as she leaned forward to peer at the occupant was one he had seen before, back when she blew up the pack of Blues with her bomb-thrower.

"Premature," Zembi muttered in response. "She still has much to show us."

Krizelle let out a sigh and removed her gaze from the pit. "Father, the situation at home . . ."

"This is your home." The old man finally turned to face her, a vestige of a paternal smile on his lips.

"My own kind are being persecuted. Hunted like animals . . ."

"And what fate do you imagine awaits you if you return? I built this place to be a refuge for you and your siblings, a place to shelter from the storms I knew were coming. The world changed forever with your birth, and change is never easy."

"You expect us to just live out our days in this . . . pretence of a world? Some of the others have started calling it a prison, and consider you their gaoler."

Zembi let out a sigh of his own, though it was more of a resigned groan. "Then it's time," he said, starting towards the walkway.

"Time for what?" Krizelle called after him.

"To sleep," he said, voice echoing in the cavern. "You always knew this day would come. We will sleep and, fate permitting, awaken to a better world . . ."

His voice faded away, leaving Krizelle in silent contemplation. She remained still for some time, arms folded tight across her chest, then started as a loud, rasping roar came from the pit.

"Be quiet!" Krizelle shouted, moving to the edge of the pit where she stared down at the occupant in unabashed hatred. After a second her face softened to a resentful mask and she stepped back again. "It's unfair of me to despise you so," she said. "We have so much in common, after all. Like you, it appears I should never have been born."

As she turned to go Clay stepped forward, looking down and finding himself staring into the eyes of a White Drake. It was about a third the size of a full-grown adult, its scales marked by ugly wet patches like the one they had killed on the mountainside. His pulse began to race as he continued to stare into the beast's eyes, bright with understanding and dark with malevolent promise. *Knows it's in a cage,* he thought. *And doesn't like it.*

"Father's greatest achievement," Kriz said, moving to Clay's side. "The product of decades of cross-breeding and chemical interference. It was supposed to be the key to convergence, a great and precious gift that would change everything."

"You made it," Clay said, his thumping heart slowing as a cold anger built in his chest. "You brought it into the world."

There was a tightness to her gaze now, her features clenched against something it took him a moment to recognise: shame. "You didn't know, did you?" he asked. "What it was capable of. You had no idea."

Kriz stared at him for a moment, frowning in incomprehension until the realisation hit home. "The threat you spoke of," she whispered. "The thing you woke up. Is this it?" Her voice rose as she stepped towards him, gripping his shoulders, demanding. "Did it get loose . . . ?"

She trailed off as a shudder ran through the trance, the surrounding cavern taking on a misty appearance. "What's happening?" she said.

"The Blue's starting to thin," Clay said. "Whatever you brought us here to do, you need to do it now."

She cast a frantic gaze down at the now-shimmering form of the White. "But there's still more to show you, more to explain . . ."

"We ain't got time. You said we needed to trance to open that thing. How do we do it?"

Kriz grimaced in frustration then tore her gaze from the White. "Very well," she said, and the memory vanished, leaving them in a pale grey void. Clay looked around, seeing white flecks in the void that bespoke an imminent loss to the trance connection.

"One of Zembi's better notions," Kriz said, staring straight ahead and frowning in concentration, "was to bond drake blood with the crystals at a molecular level. When Blue was used it enabled a meeting of minds, even between those who don't have our gifts."

Clay watched a misty white form shimmer into being just in front of Kriz. It flickered and expanded for several seconds before settling into a vaguely human shape. "So you can trance with Zembi?" he asked. "Even though he's not Blood-blessed?"

"The connection is limited, but enough for basic communication." Kriz continued to focus on the shimmering form. "I just need to—"

She choked off into silence, sagging in his grasp, a dark jet of blood erupting from her mouth. Clay gaped as she collapsed, still choking, his gaze finding the knife buried to the hilt in the back of her neck.

"Were you under the impression," Silverpin asked as she strode towards them across the grey void, "that I *wasn't* the jealous type?"

CHAPTER 47

Hilemore

"Don't look like near enough," Scrimshine said, peering at the contents of the barrel sitting open on the mid-deck. A fist-sized bundle of gun cotton sat in the barrel surrounded by a mixture of loose chain and nails.

"A submerged explosion carries far more force than one in the open air," Hilemore replied. "And I'd rather not handle this material in any larger quantities than we have to."

Scrimshine gave a wry shake of his head and seemed about to speak again but fell silent as an irksomely familiar vibration thrummed the deck. "Will that bastard ever shut up?" he wondered in a soft but shrill mutter.

They had continued to sail north since encountering the Blue, covering another eight miles throughout the succeeding day and night. All the while the beast prowled the waters beneath the hull, casting out its gathering call. So far, however, none of its brethren had seen fit to answer. The tension evident in the crew ratcheted up with every passing hour and none had slept except in short, shallow naps brought on by sheer exhaustion. The two dozen modified barrels on the mid-deck had been conceived by Hilemore as much to occupy the men's fear-wracked minds as to provide some meaningful defence against the inevitable Blue assault.

Each barrel was stocked with a dense ball of gun-cotton, packed with whatever scrap metal they could find and the top covered by a circle of waxed canvas. In addition, a string of stoppered, empty grog bottles had been tied around the waist of each barrel. Manufacturing it all had taken several hours of labour that served to distract the men from doom-laden notions, but no amount of work could completely banish their fears.

With the barrels completed, and in need of something more to occupy the crew, Hilemore followed Scrimshine's suggestion and had them begin throwing all excess weight overboard. Half the cannonballs went first, followed by all the guns save the one Steelfine had managed to get into working operation. After that he ordered every spare stick of furniture over the side and instructed Steelfine to identify any further fittings not essential to sailing the ship. He wasn't sure if any of this actually increased their speed, but he fancied the wake left by the *Dreadfire* in the otherwise placid waters had begun to broaden a fraction, which at least was something.

The alarm call finally came two hours past noon, just as Hilemore had begun ordering the wall planks stripped from the captain's cabin. He rushed onto the deck, looking up to see Braddon Torcreek standing alongside Preacher in the crow's nest. The Contractor captain pointed east and opened his hand, spreading the fingers wide. *Five of them.* "A mile off!" Braddon added, shouting through cupped hands.

Hilemore kept the dismay from his features, striding forward and casting out a string of orders, sending the crew rushing to follow a pre-rehearsed drill. "Furl sails! Drop anchor fore and aft! Mr. Steelfine, to your gun, if you please! Deck crew stand by to deploy mines!"

The deck crew consisted of Scrimshine and Skaggerhill at the starboard rail and Hilemore and another crewman on the port. They waited until the anchors bit the sea-bed, bringing the *Dreadfire* to a dead stop, then began hauling rope through block and tackle.

"Gently, man," Hilemore cautioned as the first mine was lifted off the deck. They hauled it a good few inches clear of the rail, then slowly swung it out over the side before lowering it into the water. The temptation to rush the task was strong but Hilemore was wary of how the gun-cotton would react to any sudden movements. The barrel sank into the water two-thirds of its length before floating free of its enclosing mesh of ropes. Hilemore took an oar and gave it a soft shove, provoking the crewman at his side to take a deep breath and hold it until the device bobbed its way out to a safe distance.

"Only another twelve left," Hilemore told the man, clapping him on the shoulder and moving to the stern.

It took fully ten minutes of nerve-stretching labour to float off the mines, during which time Scrimshine contrived to jerk his rope a little too fast, causing the device to tumble free of its ropes. The entire crew froze and stared at the tottering barrel spinning on its base until coming to a juddering stop.

"Slipped me grip, Skipper," the smuggler said with a weak smile. Some of the crew were vociferous in calling for Hilemore to "tip that bilge-scum over the side," to which he replied, "We're short-handed. Draw your rifles and stand ready. I suspect we're in for some hot work today."

By the time one of the deck crew called out a sighting the *Dreadfire* sat surrounded by a floating ring of mines. Hilemore craned his neck and called up to the crow's nest. "At your discretion, gentlemen!" Braddon replied with a wave whilst Preacher simply crouched and put his rifle to his shoulder.

"Leave the mines to the Contractors," Hilemore repeated to the crew in a soft murmur as he paced along the deck. "Aim at any drake that shows itself above water and then not unless they're at pistol-range. Aim for the eyes. Anything else is a waste of ammunition."

He completed his tour and moved to where Steelfine and Skaggerhill crouched at their only cannon. They had crafted a raised platform from the few bits of furniture that hadn't been tossed overboard. The twelve-pounder sat atop it, the barrel at full elevation and packed with both ball and chain-shot. Steelfine touched a match to a taper as Skaggerhill packed a wad of gun-cotton into the touch-hole.

"Hardly a rifled pivot-gun," Steelfine commented as Hilemore came to his side. "Hauling her about won't be easy. But she'll do."

She'll have to, Hilemore said inwardly, turning his gaze to the water. The surface remained placid but for the occasional swirling eddy and the ripples caused by the bobbing barrels. A hush settled over the ship, the stillness made more ominous by the realisation that the Blue beneath their hull had stopped its call. *The pack is gathered,* Hilemore thought. *Now all that remains is the kill.*

The first attack was so swift it almost proved disastrous, a Blue rearing up twenty yards off the port bow, mouth gaping to deliver its fire. The flames had already lanced out towards the hull when Preacher fired his longrifle, detonating the barrel just to the left of the beast. The resultant explosion dispelled any doubts as to the efficacy of their invention, and also made Hilemore wonder if they hadn't overdone it with the gun-cotton. The ship shook from end to end, heaving on the swell birthed by the blast. Fortunately the anchor cables held and she stayed in position. Hilemore staggered across the swaying deck to the rail to gauge the effect on the Blue, seeing it coiling in a spreading red mist. The explosion had almost cut it in two, its mouth opening to deliver a pathetic final stream of fire before it slipped into the depths.

Another shot sounded from above and an explosion erupted thirty yards to starboard. Again the *Dreadfire* shuddered, shifting to port as the blast wave caused her to drag her anchors. "Got the bastard!" Scrimshine yelled, pointing to a large slick of gore on the rippling surface.

Preacher and Braddon detonated two more mines in quick succession, one blasting a drake into several large pieces a short distance from the prow, the other without obvious result though it did appear to herald a lull.

"Scared them away good and proper, sir," a crewman commented to Hilemore, face flushed with relief and triumph.

"Look to your front!" Hilemore snapped. "This isn't over yet."

For a time it appeared the Blues intended to prove him wrong, launching no more attacks for a full quarter hour. "Any thoughts, Mr. Skaggerhill?" Hilemore asked the harvester quietly as the calm dragged on.

"Not my speciality, Captain," Skaggerhill replied. "Could write volumes about land drakes, Blues're something else." His craggy features bunched in consternation as he scanned the water. "Were they Greens I'd hazard they're waiting for nightfall."

Hilemore looked up, seeing the first glimmer of stars in the darkening sky. Night came early and fast in polar climes, something the Blues were certain to know. "Light the lanterns!" he called out. "And rig torches, all you can make!"

By the time the sun began to dip the *Dreadfire* was brightly lit from bow to stern, making Hilemore grateful for the fact that he hadn't tipped any oil over the side. The mines had begun to drift farther away as the minutes dragged by, coming close to the edge of the glow cast by the lights. Hilemore ordered two small rafts fashioned from the planks they had ripped from the walls of the captain's cabin. Empty barrels were lashed in place for buoyancy before the small craft were piled with oil-soaked rope and set adrift to port and starboard. Torches were thrown to set the rafts alight and the mines flickered back into view, along with something else.

The spines cut the water just beyond the ring of mines, wakes bright in the glow of the burning rafts. Hilemore's gaze swept around, seeing spines knifing through the surface on all sides. The Blues were circling the *Dreadfire*.

"Shoot them!" Skaggerhill shouted, casting his voice up at the crow's nest. "They're gonna rush us all at once! Shoot the mines!"

As if in response a set of spines immediately turned and slipped below the surface, an action mimicked by the drakes on either side. "Open fire!" Hilemore ordered, calling out to every crewman on deck. "Aim for the mines!"

Water spouted all around the ship as the crew obeyed, the crackle of rifle fire joined by the deeper blast of Preacher's longrifle. Three mines exploded in quick succession, two to starboard and one to port. Realising there was scant cover at the stern, Hilemore retrieved the spare rifle he had slung over the wheel and rushed aft. He could see a mine bobbing on the surface thirty yards off, raised high by the swell as something very large passed beneath it. He put the rifle to his shoulder and fired, missing by several inches. Hilemore cursed, reloaded, took a shallow breath, held it and fired again. The mine blew, transforming the surrounding water into a cascade of white, shot through with red. He caught a glimpse of the Blue's snout, snorting blood into the air before it sank.

Three more explosions shook the ship, causing her to heave to and fro at alarming angles. Hilemore was pitched from his feet, his head connecting painfully with the deck. He lay there dazed for several seconds, vision clouded and ears filled with a high-pitched buzzing, a buzzing that transformed into screams as the confusion faded. He scrambled upright and turned to the bow, finding much of the forward rigging in flames. A Blue was in the process of hauling itself aboard, huge coils bunching and thrashing as it forced its bulk out of the water, fire spewing from its gaping maw all the while. One man writhed on the deck, covered all over in flames. Hilemore saw another leap over the side, hands scrabbling at the blaze engulfing his head and shoulders.

The Blue's flames died as it shifted its bulk, shattering timber and rigging in an effort to gain purchase on the ship. A flurry of rifle-shots cracked out and the beast reared, screaming as blood spouts erupted around its eyes. Hilemore cast his rifle aside and drew his revolver, charging across the deck and firing, a bestial roar erupting from his throat. As if recognising a challenge the Blue focused on him, one eye narrowing whilst blood and viscous fluid leaked from the other. It hissed, its crest flaring as it reared up, mouth gaping as the heat-haze formed around its maw.

Hilemore suddenly found himself in the air, propelled off his feet by a fresh explosion on the fore-deck. Time seemed to slow as he flew backwards, enabling him to enjoy the sight of the upper half of the drake's body disintegrating into red-and-blue pulp. Its severed head turned end over end, casting out a crimson spiral before disappearing over the side.

Hilemore landed with a jarring impact that left him winded and immobile. He lay there, chest heaving as he tried to will strength into numb limbs. "C'mon, Skipper," Scrimshine grunted as he put Hilemore's arm over his shoulders and hauled him upright. "Not quite time for bed."

The twelve-pounder lay on the mid-deck, smoke rising from the barrel which had shattered down to the breech. Steelfine stood next to the remnants of the gun platform, his taper still in hand and much of his clothing hanging from his massive frame in charred tatters. As Hilemore limped closer he saw that the Islander's face was blackened and his eyebrows appeared to have been singed away.

"All right, Number One?" Hilemore asked him, drawing a blank gaze, Steelfine's eyes blinking in the ashen mask of his face. "A little deaf perhaps?"

"Apologies, sir," Steelfine replied in a hoarse bellow. "You'll have to speak up. I think I may be a little deaf."

Hilemore grasped his shoulder briefly and moved away, straightening his back and forcing the limp from his leg. "Let's get some buckets over the side, lads!" he called out. "I want this blaze extinguished in five minutes!"

Morning brought still waters and no sign of any drakes. Incredibly one mine had survived the night, bobbing indifferently on the surface a short way off to starboard. "Got 'em all, d'you think?" Scrimshine wondered, cocking an ear towards the deck. "No call that I can hear."

"I'd prefer not to wait and find out," Hilemore said, raising his voice to a moderate shout as he turned to Steelfine. "Unfurl the sheets, Number One."

Damage to the fore-deck was severe but not fatal, leaving the *Dreadfire* with a blackened prow and partially denuded deck. The loss of two more crewmen was of far greater concern, not least in the fresh wave of guilt it left in Hilemore's breast. *To have followed me such a long way and receive an ugly death as their only reward.* Added to the guilt was the inescapable fact that they now had two less bodies to work the rigging. Hilemore considered it an odd piece of good fortune that they didn't possess more sails since working a fully rigged vessel of this size would have been impossible with so few hands. Even so, progress was painfully slow, every course change a trial of frantic rope pulls and hands made raw by hauling canvas.

They gave the burnt body of their crewmate to the King of the Deep after they had been underway for a good few hours. Hilemore entertained the faint hope they had denied the fellow's flesh to any Blues that might have lingered at the scene of the battle. The fiery spectacle of Mount Reygnar grew on the horizon as they followed the winding channel through the ice. Hilemore trained his spy-glass on the volcano to watch the red-orange gouts of lava cascade over the lip of the crater to flow in sluggish rivulets down its flanks to the sea. The base of the mountain was perpetually shrouded in mist now, the waters raised to the boiling-point by the continuing tide of lava.

"Pondering the question as to how we'll get by that thing?"

Hilemore turned to find Braddon had joined him at the prow, his shrewd gaze focused on the blazing mountain. They could hear it as well as see it now, crying out with a throaty, booming roar every time it spewed up another gobbet of molten rock.

"We'll keep to the fringes," Hilemore said. "It'll take some careful sailing, but I think we're equal to the task."

"More worried about the gas. There's volcanoes in south-west Arradsia given to coughing up all manner of foul humours."

Hilemore knew that the Contractor was right but also knew they had no alternative. "I'd appreciate it if you didn't share this knowledge with the men, Captain Torcreek," he said.

Braddon gave a small shrug. "As you wish . . ."

His brow furrowed and his shoulders took on an involuntary hunch as a boom sounded from astern. From the length of the echo Hilemore judged the source to be a few miles off. He and Braddon hurried aft, Hilemore training his glass on the distant maze of bergs. "That a cannon?" Braddon wondered.

"No." Hilemore's glass stopped as it alighted on something between two large bergs. Something large jutting out of the water to a height of at least twelve feet. "It was the mine we left behind." He watched the huge spine slip below the water. *It didn't kill him,* he thought. *Of course it didn't.*

"Captain!" Preacher called down from the crow's nest, pointing to something off the starboard bow. Hilemore didn't require the glass to find the object of the marksman's alarm. The water some twenty feet across appeared to be boiling, though there was no steam. Huge bubbles rose and burst on the surface, which soon began to swell as something very large rose from the depths.

"Last Look Jack brought a friend," Hilemore murmured, a wry, despairing grin forming on his lips. *I should have had them make more mines.*

CHAPTER 48

Clay

This is impossible. Clay held Kriz as she shuddered, blood still pouring from her mouth in a dark torrent. *This can't happen.*

Silverpin gave a soft laugh, Clay looking up to find her standing with her arms crossed and a triumphant grin on her lips. "If we can fuck in here," she said, "why do you imagine we can't kill too?"

Clay clamped down on his burgeoning rage, returning his gaze to Kriz and seeing the light begin to dim in her eyes. "The trance," he said, pulling her closer. "End it."

Kriz just stared up at him in agonised incomprehension, her convulsions coming in shorter, weaker spasms now.

"Feel free to leave if you like," Silverpin said. "But she stays. Her mind thinks this is all real, you see. Shock I expect."

All real . . . "No," he grated. "Nothing here is real."

He closed his eyes and concentrated, the grey void around them transforming into Nelphia's dusty surface. *My mindscape,* he thought, turning Kriz over and taking hold of the knife embedded in the back of her neck. *I decide what's real here.* He pulled the knife free with a quick jerk of his wrist and concentrated on the gushing wound left by the blade. *It's not bleeding.* He summoned the image of Kriz, healed and undamaged, willing it into being. The blood faded away and the wound vanished, Kriz letting out a moan of agonised relief, though she still lay limp in his arms.

"Oh no," he heard Silverpin say in a hard, intent voice. "I don't think so, Clay."

He took a firmer hold of Kriz and surged upright, raising dust as he whirled away with unnatural speed. Silverpin cast a brace of knives after them, aiming for Kriz. He summoned a blast of wind to deflect the spinning shards of metal and sank into a crouch, Kriz still clutched in his arms.

"My mind," he told Silverpin. "And I don't remember inviting you."

He raised a hand, summoning a gun to fill it, the Stinger he had lost within the mountain. Silverpin leapt as he fired, tumbling across the mindscape like a surface performer as the bullets raised dust in her wake. She came to a halt as the Stinger clicked empty, laughing again in the face of Clay's rage. He could feel the trance fading fast, cracks appearing in Nelphia's surface.

"Your mind is my mind too," Silverpin called to him. "My home, you could say. Call me greedy, but I've never been fond of sharing."

"I don't want you any more!" Clay shouted, rising with Kriz held tight in his arms.

"If that was true I wouldn't be here." Silverpin's face became suddenly sombre, sad almost. "You saved me, Clay. Kept this part of me inside you. Looks like we're stuck with each other for a very long time."

"I don't want you any more!" he repeated, teeth clenched as he willed truth into the words. In response another crack appeared in the ground between them, broader than the others and emitting a deep orange glow. Clay looked down to see lava bubbling in the bottom of the newly created chasm. It was darker than the molten lake he had seen beneath the mountain, the fiery soup shot through with streaks of blood red.

Guess that's what rage looks like, he thought, raising his gaze to Silverpin. "I . . . don't . . . want . . . you . . . any more!" he told her in a harsh, grating whisper and had the satisfaction of watching the surety fade from her face.

"Without me what are you?" she demanded, tone edged in desperation. "You're like a child lost in the jungle, fumbling around, trying to find a way to defeat something you can't even understand. The White remembers and it doesn't forgive. When it comes for you . . ."

Her words died as Clay shattered the ground beneath her feet, sending her tumbling into the depths of the chasm. She screamed as she fell, all the way down to the molten river where she screamed some more until falling blessedly silent.

"End the trance," Clay said, taking hold of Kriz's face, shaking it gently to bring some life into her eyes.

"Father . . ." she whispered, a glimmer of focus returning to her gaze. She angled her head, once again summoning the shimmering human shape.

"Forget him!" Clay told her. The trance was crumbling around them as the last few drops of Blue faded. They had only seconds before waking. "None of this is real," he told her in a gentle murmur. "Just a bad dream and it's time to wake up . . ."

Clay staggered as the trance vanished, finding himself staring into Loriabeth's concerned face. He realised he was drenched in sweat, his heart hammering in his chest. "Started to think you'd stay in there forever, cuz," she said in a voice laden with relief.

A harsh guttural moan drew his gaze to where Kriz lay, body jerking as it had in the trance, albeit without the blood pouring from her mouth. He crouched to embrace her, holding her until the spasms ceased. "It's alright," he said softly, watching her eyelids flutter. "We're out. Y'gotta wake up now."

She gave a plaintive groan, like a child reluctantly roused from sleep, opening her eyes to regard him with a fearful gaze. "Who was that?" she asked in near-perfect Mandinorian.

"Somebody best forgotten."

A loud grinding rumble filled the chamber and Clay looked up to see a thin line had appeared in the egg's surface. As he watched the line widened into a gap, the grinding growing louder as the four segments that comprised the egg slid apart, unleashing a brief torrent of pale, greyish liquid. Clay helped Kriz to her feet and the four of them backed away. The light emanating from the crystal had altered, becoming more intense whilst also taking on a pronounced flicker. Beneath it the four segments ground to a halt, revealing something small and hunched. The crystal flared even brighter for a second then faded into a soft glow.

"Father!" Kriz said in her own language, starting forward.

"Wait." Clay tried to catch hold of her arm but she was too quick, rushing towards the huddled form on the dais, then drawing up short at the sight that greeted her.

The hunched figure shuddered and as it did so the damp scales on its back glittered in the light from the crystal.

"Seer-damn Spoiled!" Loriabeth cursed, pushing Kriz aside and levelling a pistol at the huddled figure.

"Don't!" Clay warned, though he had his revolver drawn as he approached the huddled and shivering Spoiled. "Guess this was something else that wasn't s'posed to happen, huh?" he asked Kriz.

She said nothing, continuing to stare at the naked Spoiled in dumb shock. Finally she swallowed, blinked tears and said, "Father?"

The Spoiled's shudders ceased, freezing in what might have been terror. *Or he's getting ready to spring,* Clay thought, half-raising his revolver.

"Father," Kriz repeated. "It's me. It's Krizelle."

The Spoiled issued a low groan and shifted in response, arms unfolding to reveal two long-nailed hands that were more like claws. It raised its hairless, spined head and blinked yellow eyes up at Krizelle. Even by the standards of the Spoiled, Clay had never seen a more deformed face. The once-human features had been completely submerged beneath a thick covering of leathery scales, the brows ridged with gnarled protrusions and a line of twisted, needle-like spines traced back from the forehead to the base of the neck. He could recognise nothing of the man he had seen in Kriz's memories, but apparently she could.

"Father . . ." she breathed, sinking to her knees and extending a hand.

"Best you don't get too close, hon," Loriabeth cautioned.

Kriz ignored the warning, reaching out to touch her fingertips to the Spoiled's forehead. "I know . . . your eyes," she said, choking out the words as tears slipped freely down her cheeks.

Zembi recoiled from her, shaking his spiny head in warning as he shrank back. It was then that Clay saw he had something on a chain around his neck. Something long, shiny and very sharp.

"Back!" Clay lunged for Krizelle just as Zembi surged upright, the long sharp object clutched in his claws. His deformed features were set in a raging mask and a roar of animalistic fury erupted from his throat. He was fast, the shiny spike in his claw blurring as he stabbed towards Kriz's chest, but Loriabeth was faster.

The pistols thundered in her hands, muzzles flaming as she emptied all twelve chambers, displaying a speed and accuracy Clay doubted even the late Miss Foxbine could have matched. Zembi spun as the bullets struck home, blasting holes in his glittering hide and sending spirals of blood across the dais. Kriz screamed as the guns fell silent and he collapsed, spasming on the stones in a spreading pool of blood.

Kriz rushed to kneel at his side, hands fluttering over his wounds. "How?" she sobbed. "We were supposed to wake . . . to a better world . . ."

Blood gouted from Zembi's mouth, his scaled lips twisting over elongated teeth as if in a snarl. Clay stepped forward, ready to put a bullet in the ancient Spoiled's head should he lunge at Kriz, then saw that Zembi was trying to speak. Kriz leaned closer to catch the faint, sibilant words, each one accompanied by a plume of blood. Clay couldn't make sense of any of it and quickly realised Zembi was speaking a language different from the one he had learned in the trance, a language Kriz had evidently chosen not to share. Her sobs faded as she listened, her face transforming from grief into a hard angry resolve.

Zembi fell silent, his clawed hands fumbling for the spike on the chain about his neck. Clay stepped forward, thumbing back the hammer on his revolver, then stopped as Kriz waved him back with a raised hand. Zembi guttered out another word as he held up the spike, which Clay now saw was in fact a narrow shard of crystal. Kriz gave a sombre nod, lifting the chain and crystal over Zembi's head and placing it around her neck.

"You were perhaps the greatest man who ever lived," she said, dropping back into her more familiar tongue as she smoothed a hand over Zembi's deformed brow. "And the worst."

Zembi's lips formed what might have been a smile as he shuddered for the final time, slumping into death with an inhuman rattle.

"What language was that?" Clay said as Kriz continued to kneel at Zembi's side, her fingers twitching on the crystal shard.

"The ancient tongue," she murmured, not lifting her gaze from the body.

"What did he tell you?"

Kriz didn't reply, instead raising the crystal shard and staring into its many facets. Clay was about to demand an answer when the floor suddenly shifted beneath his feet. A deep, muted rumble filled the chamber as the tremor continued, the floating crystal taking on a rapid flicker.

"The fault-line is shifting," Kriz said as the tremor subsided. "We don't have long."

She gave Zembi a final, damp-eyed glance before wiping her tears away and getting to her feet. "To answer your question," she said, switching to Mandinorian as she turned to address all three of them, "he told me the way out."

She gathered up her pack and moved towards the rear of the chamber, Clay and the others hurrying to follow suit. The tremor rose and fell in intensity as they made their way onto the circle where the plinth lay. Clay noticed how the crystal's flicker seemed to match the tremor, the stronger it was the dimmer it became.

"Fluctuations in the energy flow," Kriz explained, dropping back into her own language as she hurried towards the plinth. "The Philos geologists estimated the fault would remain stable for at least another twenty thousand years." She winced as an even more powerful tremor shook the chamber and a booming crack came from the shadows. "It seems they were overly optimistic."

"What's she saying, cuz?" Loriabeth asked.

"We need to get out of here," Clay replied, side-stepping a stream of powdered rock that came cascading down from above. "And damn quick, by the sound of it."

Kriz pressed her hand to the crystal embedded in the plinth, which failed to respond with the expected flare of light. Cursing, she tried again, this time the crystal producing a faint, fluttering glow. The stone beneath their feet gave an alarming jerk, the circle revolving as it dislodged itself from the floor and began to ascend.

"What about the ice?" Clay asked Kriz, peering into the murky heights above.

"I suspect it's partially melted," she said. "However the exit is likely to still be submerged."

"So we swim out?"

Kriz's expression brought to mind Sigoral's suspicions about her viewing them as little more than useful savages. "No," she said after a moment. "We fly."

They ascended for what seemed an age, the platform continuing to shake as fresh cascades of dust and grit fell all around. The shaft grew so dark that Sigoral and Loriabeth relit their lanterns, though, when they turned the beams upwards they failed to reveal the top of the shaft.

"This thing ever gonna stop?" Loriabeth wondered, the lantern swaying as she fought to maintain her balance. The beam alighted on Kriz for a second, Clay noting how her face seemed strangely free of alarm. Instead she wore a preoccupied frown, her hand clutching the crystal shard about her neck.

"What is that?" he asked, moving closer to touch the shard.

She stepped away, a sharp scowl of warning on her brow as she gave a terse reply, "Memory."

The platform juddered and began to slow, the lanterns revealing a fast-approaching ceiling. It resembled the giant cog-like door on the exterior of the spire, revolving and sending yet more dust down upon them as it slid aside. A great rush of wind whipped around them, Clay feeling himself being partially lifted as air was sucked into the opening above.

"Another vacuum," Sigoral shouted above the wind.

The wind died as the platform rose to fill the opening, leaving them standing in a large darkened chamber. The tremors continued unabated. If anything, Clay sensed an added violence to the shaking, his alarm increasing with every booming crack that echoed through the chamber. *This place is coming down soon.*

"There," Kriz said as Loriabeth's lantern beam caught the edge of a large curved shape several yards away. She started forward at a run, Clay and the others following.

"What in the Travail is that?" Loriabeth said as the lanterns revealed more of the shape, the massive elongated ball, the enclosed boat-shaped gondola beneath and the two propelling engines on either side.

"Aerostat," Clay said in Kriz's language which drew only a baffled glance. "A flying machine," he explained. "Like a balloon, except you can steer it."

"And where are we supposed to fly to?" Sigoral asked.

"To be honest, I ain't too sure."

A clanking sound came from the right, the lanterns swinging towards it to reveal Kriz's slender form climbing into a hatch in the gondola. After a second her head poked out of the hatch, staring at them with stern impatience. "Well, come on then," she said before disappearing back inside.

"Cuz . . ." Loriabeth began with evident unease, then fell silent as another tremor came close to tipping them from their feet.

"We're all out of options, Lori," Clay said, moving to the hatch. He clambered inside, finding Kriz standing before an array of levers and small wheels sprouting from a panel at the front of the gondola. The panel also featured several dials and Clay was surprised to find he could read a good portion of the symbols they displayed.

"'Pressure low,'" he said, peering at the largest dial where the arrow-shaped indicator hovered over a red-coloured symbol. "What's that mean?"

"It means we're in for an eventful flight," Kriz replied, her hands flying from one lever to another with automatic familiarity. "You best secure yourselves." She jerked her head at the six seats arranged along both sides of the gondola's interior, each rigged with straps.

"How do we get out?" he asked, lingering to peer through the window at the darkened chamber beyond. "Can't see no door."

Kriz's hand darted out to touch a small crystal in the centre of the panel, which immediately lit up with a familiar chime. After a short delay a curving white line appeared in the gloom outside the window, expanding into a gap that flooded the chamber with light. Clay blinked moisture from his eyes at the sudden glare, then found himself squinting at the mountains they had traversed to get here.

Kriz spun a wheel which caused the arrow on the pressure dial to move away from the red symbol. Clay felt the gondola shift as it lifted from the floor, the widening gap outside tilting to and fro before Kriz took hold of the largest lever. She hauled it into a central position, the craft levelling out in response. "Go sit down," she ordered, in a tone that brooked no argument.

Clay nodded and started towards the seats then paused as he saw her expression change, the frown morphing into a surprised grimace. Clay followed her gaze, seeing the expanding light reveal the bulbous form of another aerostat thirty or so yards away.

"What is it?" he asked Kriz as she continued to stare at the craft.

"Only one other aerostat," she said, turning back to the panel. "There were supposed to be two."

She gestured impatiently at the seats where Sigoral and Loriabeth were already strapped in. Clay took the nearest seat and buckled on the straps, watching Kriz hesitate as her hand reached for two other levers, both placed in close proximity on the panel presumably so they could be pushed at the same time. She closed her eyes as her hand continued to hover, making Clay wonder at the true scale of the risk they were about to undertake. Whatever qualms she had were overcome when another boom sounded from outside, the loudest so far. Clay saw a large chunk of masonry tumble past the window, quickly followed by several more.

"I'm thinking it's time to go!" he called to Kriz, who needed no further encouragement. As she pushed the two levers the aerostat lurched forward, Clay finding himself forced back into his seat by the acceleration. The gap beyond the window widened to fill his field of view, then they were out, the shadows vanished to leave them in the light of the three sun-crystals.

Clay's surging relief evaporated when the aerostat promptly tilted forward into a steep dive. The mountain tops disappeared to be replaced by the sight of the rapidly approaching ground. "Kriz . . ." he said, voice suddenly reed thin. Sigoral and Loriabeth were more vocal, both issuing loud and, in Loriabeth's case, profanity-laden cries as the aerostat plunged towards the earth.

Clay watched Kriz's hands dance over the controls, pushing levers and spinning wheels with feverish energy. The aerostat's descent slowed, much more gradually than Clay would have liked, but within a few seconds the mountain tops swung into view once more as the craft settled into a level flight.

"The envelope was only six-tenths full," Kriz explained over her shoulder, pulling back on the central lever to gain altitude. "We're at full capacity now."

Clay unclamped his white-knuckled hands from the edge of his seat, breathing deep as he undid the straps. "So," he said, moving to stand at her side. "What now?"

Kriz eased back the two levers that controlled their speed, the aerostat slowing to a lazy drift as the landscape revolved beneath them. Seeing it from this height, Clay was struck by the similarity to Kriz's crystal model in the trance, the central hub of the mountains surrounded by the vast circle of the artificial sea and the outer ring of dense forest. Much as he longed to be gone from this place, the scale of ambition and achievement it represented was staggering. Kriz's people had truly lived in an age of wonders.

The shaft swung into view and Kriz steadied the aerostat into a hover, keeping it in the centre of the window. "We wait," she said, her gaze fixed on the great monolithic rectangle. It seemed to blur around the edges as the tremors continued to assail it, a growing plume of dust billowing from the opening through which they had made their escape.

"It's stood for centuries," Clay said. "And yet a few tremors can bring it down."

"It's not the tremors," she said. "The outer shell and the shafts were constructed from a crystal-infused compound. The strongest building material ever created, but reliant on a continual energy source to maintain its integrity. The interruption in the flow of energy from the fault-line has fatally weakened the whole structure."

"Clay!" Loriabeth called, voice flat with urgency. He turned to find her and Sigoral staring through the gondola's port-side windows, both with weapons gripped. "Seer-dammit," Clay cursed softly, moving to Loriabeth's side and seeing the dark, rapidly approaching cloud.

"Gotta be a hundred or more," Loriabeth said, hefting her repeating rifle.

"Does this thing have weapons?" Sigoral demanded of Kriz, who shook her head.

"We never thought we'd need them."

"What tremendous foresight your people had, madam," the Corvantine observed with a bitter sigh.

Kriz ignored the jibe and pushed the accelerating levers all the way forward, the shaft looming in the window as the aerostat lurched into motion. Kriz angled the large central lever so that the craft swung to the right, steering them around the shaft in a wide circle.

"They're still gaining," Loriabeth reported from the port-side window.

"We need to open the hatches," Clay told Kriz. "Can't shoot 'em otherwise," he added when she hesitated. Kriz pulled another lever on the panel and the gondola's hatches all opened at once. There were four in all, two at the front and two at the rear.

"Lieutenant, take the starboard side," Clay told Sigoral, having to shout above the sudden torrent of invading air. "Lori, cover the rear." He hefted his own carbine, taking up position at the forward port-side hatch.

He took a firm grip of the edge of the hatchway before leaning out to cast his gaze towards the rear of the aerostat. The pursuing drakes were spread out in a ragged, undulating line. Clay raised his carbine, using the miniature telescope on top to survey the drakes. They were mostly Reds but here and there he caught sight of a White, flying higher and faster than the others. He put the range at perhaps three hundred yards, which his cousin evidently took as a challenge.

From the rear hatch came the rapid thump of Loriabeth's repeating rifle followed by the sight of a Red spiralling down from the pack, one of its wings flailing as it vainly tried to catch the air with the other. Her success, however, didn't seem to deter the others and Clay soon gauged the intervening distance to have shrunk to under two hundred yards.

"Hold still, dammit," he hissed, aiming the carbine one-handed at a White. He could see the animal's hide through the scope, mottled and sickly like the others, but its wings were still strong and powerful enough to draw it closer with every beat. His first shot missed as the beast veered left, but his next two struck home on the White's neck, producing two satisfying crimson plumes, although the animal barely seemed to slow. His subsequent attempts to put a bullet in its head proved fruitless as the White swung high and low, neck coiling as it seemed to discern his intent.

Clay cursed and withdrew from the hatch, casting about until he caught sight of Kriz's bomb-throwing gun lying next to her pack. She held to the steering lever with both hands, maintaining a tight circular course around the still-trembling shaft.

"How much longer?" he asked, bending to retrieve the bomb-thrower.

"There's no way to tell. A few minutes, perhaps."

Clay studied the shaft for a second. The dust that bloomed from the opening was growing thicker all the time and chunks of masonry were cascading down its sides. He tore his gaze away and turned back to the hatch, pausing as she reached out to flip a brass switch on the bomb-thrower's stock. "Safety catch," she explained.

Poking his head outside, Clay found the White was no longer flying level with the aerostat. It had closed the distance to fifty yards and ascended, wings sweeping in mighty arcs before flaring and twisting its body in preparation for a dive that would bring it close enough to cast its flames at the gondola. The bomb-thrower bucked in Clay's hands as he pulled the trigger, the bomb leaving a thin vapour trail through the air as it arced towards the White, passing within a few feet of its torso before exploding a good distance behind.

Although uninjured, the blast seemed to infuriate the White, its jaws opening to scream out a challenge as it folded its wings and began its dive.

Clay fired again, the White twisting in the air to evade the projectile, streaking down like a huge pale arrow.

A burst of fire came from the rear hatch, Loriabeth unleashing a stream of bullets that lashed the White from neck to tail. It abandoned its dive, wings flaring and flames gouting from its mouth less than thirty yards away. At that range Clay couldn't miss.

The bomb exploded in the White's chest in a cloud of black smoke and vapourised flesh. Its wings folded up and it plummeted towards the earth, flames still pouring from its mouth.

"Well," Clay said, fixing his gaze on the remaining mass of drakes. "That's one."

He could hear Sigoral's carbine chattering from the other side of the gondola, meaning the drakes were attempting to assail them from both sides. The bulk of the pack was less than sixty yards off now, Reds weaving through the air to avoid Loriabeth's bullets whilst the Whites flew above. Clay aimed for the densest part of the pack and fired off three bombs in quick succession, grunting in satisfaction at the trio of explosions that sent several Reds tumbling towards the ground. But still the rest came on.

"Clay!" Kriz called, her voice almost immediately drowned out by a loud roar, too vast and deep to be a drake's cry. He swung himself back inside, finding Kriz staring at the shaft which now seemed to be wreathed in dust from summit to base.

"It's happening," she shouted above the roar, which he realised was the sound of the shaft breaking apart. "We need to close the hatches!"

He nodded, setting the bomb-thrower down and moving to the rear of the gondola. "Leave it, cuz," he told a sweat-covered Loriabeth, teeth gritted as she unleashed another salvo at the encroaching drakes. She was so intent on her work he was obliged to clamp a hand on her shoulder and drag her back from the hatch. "Looks like we're about to get out of here," he explained in response to her aggrieved glare before turning to Sigoral. "Lieutenant, time for a cease-fire."

Sigoral glanced over his shoulder, nodding as he lowered his carbine. The Red must have used the momentary distraction to latch onto the underside of the gondola, rearing up to thrust its head through the hatch just as Sigoral turned to face it. Clay dove forward as the beast's jaw gaped wide. He caught the Corvantine about the waist, pulling him aside as flames cooked the air. Sigoral let out a scream as Clay bore him to the deck, high and childlike in the agony it conveyed, and mercifully swallowed by the rapid thud of Loriabeth's repeating rifle. Clay looked up in time to see the headless Red tumbling free of the gondola before Kriz closed the hatches.

A fiery ache in Clay's foot drew his gaze to the patch of flame eating at his boot and he spent several frantic seconds stamping it out. Looking up he saw Loriabeth clutching a writhing Sigoral, smoke rising from the ruined flesh around his right eye. Clay fumbled for his canteen of Green and held it to Sigoral's mouth, forcing the liquid past his clenched teeth as he continued to struggle. He gradually calmed as the Green found its way down his throat, banishing much of his pain, a calm that was short-lived as Clay tipped the last of the canteen's contents over his burns. Skaggerhill had once opined that Green could take the infection from burns but had only a marginal effect on the scars. Loriabeth held Sigoral tight as he thrashed, a torrent of what Clay assumed to be profanity issuing from his mouth in harsh Varsal.

"No way to talk in front of a lady, Lieutenant," Loriabeth told him, continuing to hold on until the Corvantine's shudders subsided.

Clay looked around, hearing a thunderous pounding assail the gondola's hull. The drake were swarming the aerostat, Red after Red crowding the windows, clawing and biting to get at the meat inside.

Clay dragged his gaze away and helped Loriabeth get Sigoral into one of the seats, his cousin strapping him in before turning her attention to his wound. "Can you open it?" she asked, peering at the mottled flesh around his eye. Sigoral grunted and choked down on a scream as he forced his eyelids apart.

"Is . . . it there?" he rasped. "Can't see . . . through it."

"Looks whole," Loriabeth said, sounding more confident than she looked. "Probably be fine in time. Just the glare of the flames."

Clay left her to tend him and moved to the front of the gondola. "He'll live," he told Kriz.

She didn't seem to hear, her gaze fixed on the shaft. The drakes hadn't yet reached the front of the gondola and they had a clear view of the great structure's final moments. The gondola appeared to be completely sealed so Clay watched the spectacle unfold in eerie silence. The whole structure gave a final shudder as a thick rain of shattered stone fell from above. Incredibly, it stayed upright for several seconds, swaying back and forth until another tremor sent it toppling over like the trunk of a giant, limbless tree, trailing dust as it fell. Clay moved closer to the window, watching the shaft slam down onto the mountains below, shattering along its length all the way to the shimmering flatness of the lake where it birthed two huge waves. Clay moved closer to the glass for a better look, fascinated by the sight of the waves sweeping across the distant shore, then reared back as a Red butted its head against the window.

The beast hissed at him, wings thumping in excitement as two of its companions landed close by.

"Don't suppose this thing's fire-proof?" Clay asked Kriz. She seemed oblivious to the drakes, staring upwards at the dark void left by the fallen shaft.

"Actually, it's flame-resistant," she replied softly. "But I don't think that will be an issue."

There was no warning of what happened next, no gradually increasing trickle, just a sudden vast torrent of water descending out of the sky in a white blur. A blast of displaced air hit the aerostat as the torrent struck the ground, clearing the drakes from the windows as they took flight in alarm.

Clay stepped close to the glass once more, watching the deluge swamp the mountains below before flooding the foot-hills and the forests where the strange monkeys made their home. Soon it had all vanished, the mountains, the lake with its matrix of roads, the desert and the forest all submerged in a matter of minutes by an ever-rising tide.

"This is the way out?" Clay asked Kriz, hearing the half-hysterical humour in his voice, which felt at odds with the sudden calm he felt. It all seemed like some huge joke now; her promises of escape, their pointless trek through this place of wonder and terror. A prolonged piece of theatre so they could watch it drown, and them along with it.

Kriz turned to him with a weak, apologetic shrug. "I never said it would be easy."

CHAPTER 49

Lizanne

The Blood Cadre agent descended through the smoke, blazing away with a revolver in his left hand. Lizanne had time to notice that his right arm was missing, presumably lost in the bombardment, before lashing out with Black to sweep him out of the sky. He landed amidst a ruined gun-position a short way off, struggled to his feet then fell dead as Kraz put three bullets into his chest.

"Loses an arm and keeps on fighting," he said in reluctant admiration.

"They know what fate awaits them," Jelna replied, voice rich in righteous fury. It was clear to Lizanne she had been looking forward to this day for a very long time. "Even a cornered rat will fight."

They had charged through the ruined wall at blurring speed, wreaking havoc on the scratch force of Imperial soldiery hastily assembled to cover the breach. The lingering pall of dust and drifting gunsmoke soon made the whole enterprise an exercise in confusion and unseen threats. One of their number had already fallen to a stray bullet and another had been cut down by a wounded Blood Cadre agent. Despite being pinned by a fallen chunk of masonry the fellow managed to cast forth a torrent of Red-born fire. Kraz set the agent's head alight with his own Red and they left him to burn.

Ten minutes of confused fighting brought them to the Blue Maze where they found numerous Household troops fleeing across the ornamental bridges, whilst others flailed in the canal waters having been thrust aside by the crush.

"If I were given to believing in the old gods," Jelna said, depressing the first three buttons on her Spider, "I think I'd be offering thanks just now."

She sprinted forward and leapt, ascending in a high arc over a series of bridges, casting a wave of Red and Black down at each one in turn. Kraz leapt to join in, moving deeper into the maze, flames and human wreckage rising in his wake. Men burned and were blasted away, bodies tumbling into the canals, which soon began to run red. Seeing Hyran start forward, grimly determined to take part in the unfolding massacre, Lizanne reached out to restrain him.

"Leave the slaughter to the mob," she told him, casting a pointed glance over her shoulder at the vanguard of the People's Freedom Army now streaming through the wall. "We have an objective."

They refreshed their product and she led him on through the Blue Maze, leaping high to avoid the main concentrations of fleeing troops and cutting down only those who tried to bar their way. These stalwarts were few in number, mainly officers or veteran sergeants unwilling to shirk their duty even now. But the panic of the rank and file told an inescapable truth no amount of dutiful courage could deny; the Corvantine Empire would fall this day.

Having traversed the maze, they sprinted through the ring of ornate temples to long-dead Emperors, making for the central palace complex. There were fewer troops this far into the Sanctum, most of the people they encountered being courtiers and chamberlains. Some reacted with outright terror at the sight of them, whilst others could only stand and stare, either in shock or fatalistic acceptance. Spying a familiar face, Lizanne came to a halt, Hyran sliding to her side amidst a cloud of displaced gravel.

They had reached the Horse Parade where the Household Cavalry once staged their equine displays for the Emperor's pleasure. It was mostly empty now save for a few fleeing courtiers and one rather plump man who stood still and straight-backed, sweat shining on his bald pate as he faced towards the fast-approaching rebel tide.

"Chamberlain Yervantis," Lizanne greeted him with a bow of appropriate depth.

"Miss Lethridge," he replied in a surprisingly well-modulated tone, meeting her gaze. She noted that his evident resolve was undermined slightly by the need to blink the sweat from his eyes.

"It would have been better if you had found somewhere else to be today," Lizanne told him.

He inclined his head. "Logic with which I find it hard to argue, madam."

"I take it then that you are prepared to survive the empire's fall?"

His gaze flicked towards the temples where Kraz and Jelna were enthusiastically destroying a band of die-hard troops. "I wasn't aware that might be a possibility."

Lizanne stepped closer to him, looping her arm through his and guiding him towards the palace. "All things are possible in the new republic, good sir. For example, were you to tell me where I might find Countess Sefka it will transpire that you have been a Brotherhood agent for years now, as my young friend here will be happy to attest."

Countess Sefka had secluded herself on an artificial island in the centre of the Sanctum's broad ornamental lake. Lizanne recalled strolling the lake-side with poor, deluded Emperor Caranis not so long ago and couldn't suppress a pang of amused regret at the man's inventive insanity. *Sethamet's Bane,* she thought, judging the distance from the shore to the island. *Returned to seek justice for the Guardians' murdered servant. If he had lived he might actually have been useful.*

"Surely it's too far to jump," Hyran said. "Even for you."

She nodded and started to wade into the water. "Take Chamberlain Yervantis to the general," she told Hyran, waving him back when he attempted to follow her. "I'm sure he has a wealth of intelligence to share."

"But the countess . . ."

"Leave her to me." Her voice held a note of implacable command that stopped him dead and she held his gaze until he retreated from the edge of the lake. "I'll find you later," she said, softening her tone and trying to quell the rising guilt at the trust she saw in his face. The task she had to perform here would not be easy.

It took a few minutes to swim to the island, a half-second burst of Green making it an easy matter. The island took the form of a domed temple of ancient design and was fashioned entirely from white marble. Various scenes from Corvantine history and legend were etched into the stone and Lizanne considered she would have found it a fascinating place on another occasion. Today she found the ostentatiousness of it somewhat aggravating, another example of how the Corvantine ruling class had indulged themselves whilst their beggared people grew to hate them more with every passing year.

She levered herself out of the water and onto the island's flat outer surface, eyes scanning for enemies even though Yervantis had assured her the countess was unguarded. "Every Cadre agent in the Sanctum was dismissed this morning," the portly chamberlain explained. "She just . . . sent them all away."

Lizanne's gaze settled on a slim figure seated on a plain marble bench beneath the temple dome. Countess Sefka failed to turn as Lizanne approached, even though she made no effort to conceal the sound of her steps. *Fight,* she thought, coming to a halt directly behind the soon-to-be-deposed head of the Regency Council. *Fight me, you bitch!*

"This must be a great day for you," Countess Sefka said, failing to turn as Lizanne lingered at her back. Her tone was much as Lizanne remembered it, full of strident surety and uncoloured by the fear she had hoped for.

"Actually," Lizanne replied, "I find it a singular disappointment."

Sefka's slim shoulders moved in a shrug. "Oh well. I had hoped to hear a few choice declarations. A final jibe or two. Were our positions reversed I assure you I would have rehearsed a speech."

"You are not me. And I, much to my lasting pleasure, am not you."

"No. I tried to save an empire, whilst you destroyed one."

"That was never my mission." Lizanne stepped closer, eyes fixed on the countess's neck beneath her tied-up auburn hair. The skin was bare and unadorned, the so very fragile bones visible beneath the alabaster skin. "I should like to know," she said, "did you kill Emperor Caranis yourself or leave it to one of your creatures?"

Sefka's head moved in a small laugh. "Neither. He was certainly becoming more mad by the day, but I lacked the support needed for a successful coup. The Blood Imperial, however, decided to precipitate matters. The Emperor had resolved to kill him, you see, and all his precious Blood-blessed children. Apparently Caranis got wind of the silly old bastard's plan to assassinate you upon your return from Scorazin. How was it, incidentally?"

"Improved immeasurably by its destruction."

"I expect so. Anyway, it seems Kalasin was very keen to get his grubby hands on whatever you had dug out of that dung-heap. Caranis couldn't risk any harm to Sethamet's Bane, nor any revenge from the Blood Cadre. So he signed the purge order and went off for his nightly bath where the agent Kalasin had concealed in the ceiling stopped his heart with a gentle application of Black."

"If you know all this why wasn't Kalasin executed?"

"A simple matter of practicalities. The two Cadres that serve this empire are like conjoined twins that hate each other, forever trapped in conflict knowing all the while that if one dies so does the other, and then so does the empire."

"Do you know where Kalasin is? An associate of mine is very keen to see him."

"Spirited himself away the moment your rabble reached the suburbs, I expect. A rat always finds a hole to crawl into."

Sefka slumped a little then, her only sign of weakness so far, raising a hand to her forehead before forcing herself once again into a pose of rigid elegance. "So, what is your intent, pray tell?" she asked, voice as calm as before. "Some prolonged torture before you hand me over to your radical friends? Or just a nice, tidy assassination? I do know an awful lot of ugly things about your Syndicate, after all. Things I'm sure you wouldn't want heard in public."

"It doesn't matter." Lizanne sighed, tired of repeating this particular mantra. "Why do none of you understand how little any of your intrigues and your wars matter now? There is only one war that matters."

"Oh yes, your monsters are coming to eat us, aren't they?" Sefka gave a girlish giggle, swaying a little. Lizanne stepped forward, looking over the countess's shoulder to see the small empty bottle that lay in her upturned hands. "Heard you sploshing about," Sefka said, turning to her with a pouting grin, like a child caught in a minor transgression. "Sorry, but I couldn't face the show trial. The torture I think I might have withstood, but not the trial . . ."

Lizanne grabbed Sefka about the shoulders, forcing her off the bench and onto her back. Sefka struggled feebly, groaning in annoyance as Lizanne held her down with a knee to her chest and pulled the Green vial from her Spider.

"No!" Sefka's struggles became fiercer, jerking her head away as Lizanne pressed the vial to her lips. "Not fair! You won . . ."

Lizanne clamped a hand on Sefka's face, forcing her mouth open then pouring the Green down her throat. Lizanne pushed the woman's jaws together, pinching her nose to force her to swallow. She convulsed for a short while, Lizanne feeling her heart slow, the pulse fading almost to nothing before returning with a strong, poison-free thump.

Sefka stared up at her as Lizanne stood back. "You vicious, hateful bitch!" the countess hissed, eyes and voice alive with hate.

"I've never been vicious," Lizanne replied, leaning closer to deliver a hard tap with her fore-knuckles to Sefka's temple, leaving her unconscious on the floor. "But I will admit to hating you a great deal."

She found a boat moored on the leeward side of the island. After rowing to shore Lizanne hefted Sefka's body over her shoulder and made towards the ring of temples. Smoke was rising from the palace complex itself where, as she expected, the bulk of the People's Freedom Army were busy ransacking the once-sacred seat of Imperial power. Consequently she enjoyed an uninterrupted journey to the temples, attracting little attention as there were plenty of others carrying wounded away for treatment. The bodies of Household troops and palace courtiers littered the ground whilst others had been used to decorate the many trees dotted about the palace grounds. Lizanne passed an acacia with branches sagging under the weight of dismembered body parts.

Victory is never glorious, Arberus had said and, for all his radical nonsense, she knew there was wisdom there too.

With so many riches to be had in the palaces the bare stone temples had so far attracted little attention from the mob save for some minor vandalism. She knew that would change in time, such a visible reminder of the Imperial pantomime would inevitably face destruction, but for now it provided a useful refuge.

The door to the tomb of Empress-cum-Emperor Azireh lay closed and locked on this occasion, but the lock was unable to resist a blast of Black. Lizanne kicked the part-ruined door aside and carried Sefka into the tomb, dumping her on the floor.

"Have you brought me a gift, love?"

He was much as she remembered him, standing stooped half in shadow, cane in hand and face veiled by slack grey hair.

"It's more of a peace offering," Lizanne replied. "A gesture of goodwill, you might say."

"And what would you want with my goodwill?" Behind the grey veil she saw cracked lips sliding over yellow teeth in a hesitant parody of a smile. The tension in him was obvious in the way his bony hands rested on his cane, veins standing out and gnarled knuckles turning from red to pink. Unlike Sefka, he was far from accepting of his fate.

"Nothing," Lizanne replied. "But you have information I require. Tell me what I want to know and you can have her"—she nudged Sefka's limp form with her toe—"and I'll allow you to escape through the passage-way concealed beneath this tomb."

"What passage-way?"

Lizanne returned his smile with one of her own. "You wouldn't have risked being seen coming here the night we met. Not with so many of Sefka's people watching your movements. I expect Azireh had it built, somewhere to hide her treasure perhaps. She did hide something here besides that scroll didn't she?"

Kalasin's forced smile broadened, hair swaying as he gave a slight nod. "It transpired the Empress and I shared an interest in the Artisan, she being his contemporary. Upon achieving the throne she began to amass all the artifacts and documents she could, hiding them here in the hope that some worthy soul might discover them one day."

Instead, it was you. Lizanne resisted the impulse to voice the thought. *Let the old man talk. The more he talks the less potent the product in his veins.*

"There was a vault where she kept it all," the Blood Imperial went on. "I suppose that's where my little hobby really started. Who knew it would lead to all this?"

"And the passage-way?"

"Built it meself, with a little help from my children. Took a long time but eventually I had a convenient means of getting about and beyond the Sanctum without being seen."

"Which begs the question of why you linger here instead of making your escape."

"Where the fuck d'you imagine I would go, love? Besides"—his hands twitched on the cane—"I was really hoping to see you again."

He was quick but she was ready for him, unleashing her Black a fraction of a second after he lashed out with his. The competing waves of force met, birthing a thunder-clap that sent them both reeling. Kalasin proved the illusory nature of his infirmity by scrambling to his feet in an instant, whirling to face her with no sign of a stoop. But, spry as he was, he was still several decades Lizanne's senior and it was clear to her he hadn't faced combat with another Blood-blessed in years.

She injected a burst of Green and sprang aside as he summoned Red, casting out a stream of fire. Lizanne rolled across the dusty floor as the flames flashed overhead before sliding over the walls, then replied with a second burst of Black. He dodged, moving with speed that told of a heavy ingestion of Green, but was fractionally too slow. The force wave caught his shoulder, spinning him around to collide with the wall. Lizanne heard the dry crack of breaking bone as the old man rebounded, a shrill gasp escaping his lips.

Lizanne cast her remaining Black out like a whip, snaring Kalasin in an unseen vise, holding him in place as she got to her feet and moved towards him. "You're out of practice," she observed.

He snarled at her, all pretence of humanity vanished from a face now revealed in full. Seeing the deeply etched lines and liver-spotted skin of his hate-filled visage, Lizanne realised that he was far older than she first thought. "Excessive and prolonged use of Green," she said, marvelling at the amount of product he must ingest on a daily basis, "is not a good idea, even for a Blood-blessed."

Kalanis strained against his invisible bonds, spittle leaking over his age-cracked lips, an odour fouler than the Scorazin midden rising from his mouth.

"The countess said you intended to kill me on my return," Lizanne went on. "And seize what I had worked so hard to retrieve. What were you going to do with him?"

The Blood Imperial said nothing, his ancient features hardening into a defiant mask. Lizanne summoned a small amount of Red, igniting the tip of one of his lank tendrils of hair, letting it curl up towards his face. "Unlike you I do not revel in cruelty," she told him. "But do not imagine I will baulk at this. What were you going to do with the Tinkerer?"

Her Green-boosted hearing saved her, detecting the metallic scrape of the cross-bow's lock just before the bolt was launched. She dropped, feeling the projectile flutter her hair before finding a target in the Blood Imperial's forehead. He hung in the grip of her Black for a second, a small trickle of blood making its way from the embedded steel dart into his eyes, which blinked once before all light faded away.

Lizanne whirled, taking Kalasin's body with her, swinging him around like a club as Anatol cast his cross-bow aside and charged from the tomb's doorway, a large knife shining in his fist. The giant managed to cover only a yard before the Blood Imperial smashed him into Azireh's sarcophagus with sufficient force to displace the lid, Lizanne hearing the multiple dry-wood crackle of shattered bones.

She loosed her hold on Kalasin's corpse and drew her pistol, moving to stand over Anatol's broken form. He glared up at her with a hate she knew to be far more justified than the Blood Imperial's. This she had earned.

"I said I was sorry about Melina," she told him.

"Sorry . . ." Anatol spat blood at her and tried vainly to stand, sinking back down with a shout of frustration. "What is . . . sorry to me? Or to . . . her?" he replied in a series of pain-filled grunts. "Sorry meant . . . shit in Scorazin. Means shit now."

"Did the Electress send you or was this your idea?"

He angled his head at her, glowering and saying nothing.

"Promised you would get your chance when the Sanctum fell, I expect." Lizanne bent and retrieved his knife from the floor. "Do you mind? I need to borrow this."

Sefka came awake after a few hard slaps, blinking in grim realisation at the sight of Lizanne's face. "Didn't expect you to do this yourself," she said, eyeing the knife in Lizanne's hand. "I rather assumed you would hand me over to your rebel friends to play with."

"Get up," Lizanne told her. She went to the sarcophagus, standing on tip-toe to peer down at the contents. As expected there was no sign of Azireh's bones, just a series of steps descending into deep gloom.

"You really are settling a lot of old scores today, aren't you?" Sefka asked, Lizanne glancing over to see her peering at the Blood Imperial's corpse. "I do wish I'd been awake for that."

"It's time for you to go, Countess," Lizanne said, stepping back and nodding at the open sarcophagus. "I'm afraid you'll probably have to do a fair bit of wandering about to find it, but I'm reliably informed there's a passage down there that will take you beyond the walls."

Sefka stared at her, unmoving. Lizanne doubted this woman was capable of such mundane emotions as surprise and her reaction was more likely a symptom of well-justified suspicion. "You're just going to let me go?" she said, voice laden with doubt.

"Clan leader Ahnkrit and I reached an agreement regarding your future," Lizanne told her. "You'll find him at Scorazin. How or if you manage to get there is not my concern, but I'm sure it's a task well within your capabilities."

"Ahnkrit," Sefka repeated softly, pursing her lips. "Mother used to beat me if I wasn't kind to the other children at court. Now I see why."

"A certain degree of urgency is required," Lizanne said, her voice growing hard.

Sefka inclined her head then paused to crouch at the Blood Imperial's side. "Good-bye, Kalasin," she said, teasing the slack grey tendrils from his face. "It was a singular displeasure knowing you." She tugged the cane from his stiff fingers and straightened. "You'll allow me a souvenir, I hope," she said to Lizanne, hefting the cane as she moved to the sarcophagus.

Lizanne said nothing and Sefka shrugged, hauling herself onto the edge of the marble box and swinging about. "You really should kill me, you know?" she said before slipping from sight.

Lizanne listened to her footsteps fade away before replying. "I know."

The Blood Imperial's head gave a soft thud as it landed on the steps of the Imperial palace. The Electress stood with her fleshy arms folded, regarding the grisly trophy in expressionless silence for some time. Her band of Fury body-guards stood behind her, all impressively festooned with jewellery and fine clothes looted from various palaces. Lizanne could see Tinkerer standing amongst them. She hadn't been this close to him since Scorazin and saw that, whilst his clothing had changed from a besmirched set of miner's overalls to a long, deep-pocketed coat, his demeanour hadn't. He greeted her with a short nod as Lizanne met his gaze, face betraying neither fear nor anticipation at the prospect of release from the Electress's clutches.

At the base of the steps Arberus looked on with what appeared to be the entire Co-respondent Brotherhood arrayed behind him in loose but attentive order. A large number of the army's rank and file were also present, although most were too preoccupied with looting or vandalism to afford this meeting much attention. Arberus was flanked by Hyran and Kraz, with Jelna standing a short way off. Lizanne could see Makario loitering on the fringes of the Brotherhood and felt some measure of relief at finding him only lightly wounded, standing with his arm in a sling as he waved at her with his free hand.

"Anatol?" the Electress asked, glancing up from Kalasin's bleached, sagging features.

"Sleeping in the Tomb of Emperor Azireh," Lizanne replied. "I dosed him with Green, he should heal in time."

"Unusually nice of you. Where's Countess Sefka?"

"I haven't the faintest idea."

"Lying bitch."

Lizanne gave a bland smile and nodded at the object lying at Atalina's feet. "Our contract is fulfilled. I require payment."

The Electress replied with a smile of equal blandness, looking over her shoulder at Tinkerer. "His value's gone up since. Those marvellous toys of his really do make a difference and I'd hazard that I'll have more than a few battles to fight soon."

"That is not my concern. And I have no inclination to bargain with you further." Lizanne flexed her fingers over the Spider. "So I'll make it very simple for you. Give him to me or I'll kill you and take him."

"In front of this army?" The Electress raised her heavy brows in mock surprise. "*My* army, love."

"Really? You imagine it's you they followed here." Lizanne cast a pointed glance at Arberus. "Or do you imagine they don't know the debt they owe Miss Blood? How do you think they'll react when they find out you tried to assassinate me on this day of victory? Some will no doubt seek to avenge your death, but far from all and unless you have some Blood-blessed to call on at this juncture I'd say you have no more cards to play."

Lizanne shifted her gaze to Tinkerer, raising her hand to beckon him from the midst of the Electress's guards. He started forward after a moment's hesitation, stopping when the Furies began to reach for their weapons.

"Leave it!" the Electress barked, her gaze still fixed on Lizanne. "Let him go."

The Furies parted ranks, allowing Tinkerer to walk free. He moved towards Lizanne in a wide arc, well clear of Atalina's reach.

"Any chance you might finally tell me why he's so fucking important?" Atalina asked.

"He's going to save the world." Lizanne raised her gaze to the smoke rising from a large blaze in the palace roof, then lowered it to survey the corpse-littered grounds and the hordes of rebels rushing off with their bundles of loot as if worried someone might snatch it away. "Such as it is," she added, inclining her head at the Electress and turning to descend the steps with Tinkerer in tow.

"I'll escort you to the docks," Arberus said as she paused at his side. He was unharmed but heavily besmirched from the battle, his uniform torn and stained with loyalist blood. Even so it seemed to her he had grown even taller now and, when future artists inevitably came to record this scene on canvas, he would be the principal subject.

"I think you had better stay here," she replied, glancing over her shoulder at the Electress, still glowering away at the top of the steps. "Remind the new regime of its treaty obligations. They might feel they've scored a great victory, but all they've won is the right to stand against the White's onslaught, and it is coming. Make sure they know that."

She stepped closer, raising herself up to plant a kiss on his cheek, knowing it would be the last they ever shared. "Don't let her live another night," she whispered before stepping back.

"The Blood Imperial is dead," she said, turning to Hyran and extending her hand. "Perhaps they'll name you his replacement, though Blood Republican doesn't scan so well."

He ignored her hand and enfolded her in a tight embrace, murmuring, "Please stay."

"I can't." She eased him back then turned to Makario, gesturing for him to follow as she led Tinkerer away.

"Where might we be going?" the musician asked, hurrying to catch up as she strode from the palace grounds.

"To the docks where we will take a ship to Feros," she replied. "My father has an old pianola that hasn't been played in years. And I believe I will require an accomplished musician to complete this mission."

CHAPTER 50

Sirus

Katarias roared as Feros appeared through the drifting clouds below, an exultant blast of anticipation echoed by the huge flock of Reds filling the sky on either side. Sirus could see the waves roiling against the harbour wall in a white froth, driven by the three moons that provided ample light with which to view the city. It seemed so small at this height, just a cluster of pale blocks and dark lines fringing the wide bowl-shaped bay that formed the harbour. *She must be sleeping somewhere down there,* he thought as his gaze tracked to the bright wakes of the main assault force to the south. *And I have come to rouse her to a nightmare.*

Katarias angled his wings and began to slowly circle the isthmus below, the other Reds all following his lead. They maintained their current altitude lest any vigilant Protectorate sentry spot their approach, although Sirus thought it unlikely. *Who would think to seek a threat from above this far north?*

Transporting so many to within flying range of the Tyrell Islands had been a difficult and costly task. The animals clearly detested having to perch on barges and ships in such close proximity to so many Spoiled. During the voyage the White's army had lost almost a hundred soldiers to sudden lunging bites or tail-strikes as drakes, both Red and Green, vented their irritation. The fleet moved in tight formation to lessen the chance of detection, their four captured Protectorate frigates in front followed by the civilian craft captured in Morsvale, each one towing at least two barges laden with Spoiled or drakes. Blues proceeded ahead of them in a broad mass covering several miles of ocean, reporting any sightings of enemy craft to the White. It had made a nest for itself atop the bridge of the *Harbinger* and seemed to take little interest in the intense activity all around, instead spending the voyage fussing over its clutch of juveniles.

Sirus was struck by how large the infant Whites had grown in a relatively short time, each one now possessing similar bulk to a full-grown Green. They had also begun to fly with greater regularity and soon adopted a favourite sport of swooping low over the fleet and selecting a meal at random from the close-packed ranks of Spoiled. Two or three of the beasts would descend on the unfortunate and pluck them from the deck of a barge or ship, sometimes tearing their prey apart in mid air and tossing the pieces to each other in an obscene game of catch. On other occasions they preferred to carry the victim back to their nest, stripping the flesh from the carcass in a frenzy before dismembering the skeleton. They would then weld the bones into the growing stack in the centre of their nest, coughing up bile to cement the remains in place. Sirus found he had to give full vent to his fear whenever this happened, lest his simmering rage boil high enough to draw the White's gaze. Somehow the whole ghastly ritual was made worse by the absence of screams. The victim and onlooking Spoiled alike remained completely silent throughout every ordeal.

They had encountered two Protectorate vessels during the journey, one a small coal-burning patrol boat easily overwhelmed by the Blues. The second had been a much more formidable enemy, an old but fearsomely armed cruiser. The White communicated the sighting to Sirus, who immediately ordered the four frigates to increase speed, sending one on a north-westerly course and another north-east to catch the lumbering vessel in the event she tried to escape. The ship, named as the IPV *Rate of Return* by the elegant Mandinorian script embossed on her hull, obligingly hove to and reduced speed upon sighting the approach of two friendly vessels. However, some keen pair of eyes in her crow's nest evidently spotted the White Drake perched atop the *Harbinger*. Sirens sounded the length of the cruiser and a full complement of heavy guns sprang to life, her paddles churning the sea white as she attempted to gain speed. *Pity,* Sirus thought as plummeting shells raised tall spires of water all around. *It would have been nice to capture her.*

Either due to hasty gunnery or sheer luck, none of the cruiser's shells found a target. The Blues, suddenly loosed from their restraint by a command from the White, surged from the sea surrounding the *Rate of Return*, bathing her in flame from bow to stern. The old ship continued to fight on despite terrible damage, the repeating guns on her upper works claiming four Blues before she was finally borne under by sheer weight of drake flesh, leaving a slick of mingled blood and oil to mark her passing. Night followed soon after and they enjoyed an uninterrupted approach to the southern shore of Crowsloft Island.

Another Red swooped closer to Katarias as they continued to circle, Sirus seeing Katrya waving atop its back. He had wanted to leave her behind in deference to her condition but she reacted to the notion with violent defiance, keen as ever to do the White's bidding. He had come to realise that her attitude was far from unique in the army. With every passing day this host of remade souls grew more willing to accept its lot. Some, especially the Islanders, continued to rage inwardly at their enslavement but the mood amongst the less recently converted was gradually subsiding into one of unreasoning loyalty. There were even some who seemed to rejoice in their inhuman state, mainly those of dull intellect or inherent cruelty.

Change and growth, Sirus remembered his father saying in one of his lectures to archaeology students at the Morsvale Museum. *The two constants in the history of human civilisation. As our circumstances change, so do we, and we always prosper in the changing.*

As Katarias swept round for the second time Sirus lowered his gaze to gauge the progress of the fleet. He could see the wakes of the frigates separating as they came within a mile of the bay where Morradin had promised a successful landing. Sirus sent the marshal a questioning thought pulse, receiving one of fierce anticipation in return.

The tide is high and not a corporate swine in sight, Morradin reported. *The Greens will go ashore first. They'll be raising an appropriate level of havoc in the outskirts of Feros in the space of a quarter hour. I'll have the whole army off and advancing towards the isthmus in two hours.*

No killing once the Protectorate forces have been dealt with, Sirus reminded him. *We'll need to make good our losses.*

Tell that to the drakes, Morradin answered, his thoughts coloured by grim amusement. *So many days at sea seems to have riled them a great deal. Can't you feel it?*

Sirus could indeed sense the blood-lust in the surrounding flock of Reds and knew it to be mirrored in the Greens and Blues below. It went beyond just the endless hunger of the natural predator, more a collective feral need shot through with a depth of enmity he might once have imagined beyond a non-human soul. Although their minds remained out of reach, his continual exposure to these creatures left him in no doubt that their mental faculties were far more developed than any naturalist had previously guessed. *They do not think like us, but they do think. And they remember.* He found he had to summon an upsurge of fear as the knowledge that Feros was about to suffer the full vengeance of the Arradsian drake brought Tekela's face to mind. *Please just sleep on,* he implored her silently. *Don't wake up.*

He saw the first fires appear in the northern suburbs a few minutes ahead of Morradin's schedule, blossoming like bright yellow flowers in the dark earth. There would be screams, he knew, and gun-fire. Constables would be sounding the alarm and the Protectorate garrison roused from its slumber. Within minutes companies would be formed and sent towards the scene of chaos, away from the docks.

It's time, he told Katarias, colouring the thought with an urgent sense of command the beast couldn't fail to understand. A low, rattling growl emerged from the huge Red's throat as he dipped his head and drew in his wings. They descended towards the harbour at a near-vertical angle. Only the strength of Sirus's refashioned body enabled him to stay in place, so fierce was the air-current. He glanced back to ensure the other Reds were following, seeing them all streaking in Katarias's wake, the flock dense enough to obscure the pale disc of Serphia beyond.

In accordance with the plan the flock split apart after descending to a point some five hundred feet above the docks. A dozen smaller flocks veered off to assault specific gun-positions whilst a dozen more made for the warships anchored within the harbour. Some repeating guns started up as the flock descended the final few hundred feet as shipboard gunners overcame their shock. The smaller guns growled as they cast glowing streams of bullets into the air, soon joined by the more percussive thump of the larger cannon. Sirus saw several drakes tumble into the harbour waters, but not enough to stem the onslaught.

Katarias banked low over the western mole, spewing flame at the sailors positioned atop it, lashing out with both tail and talon as he flared his wings and brought them down on the quayside. Sirus leapt clear of the drake's back, war-club and knife in hand. He cut down a dazed Protectorate rifleman who stood staring at him with smoke rising from a half-melted face, then ducked as Katarias's tail flashed overhead, scything into a squad emerging from a near by blockhouse. The tail spike cut one clean in half and left the other four slumped against the wall of the blockhouse, gaping in shock at the blood leaking from their gashed flesh.

The Red gave a brief squawk of triumph before turning about and launching itself from the quay, wings blurring as it sought the air. Another dozen Reds descended a heart-beat later, rolling over to deposit their riders on the dockside. Forest Spear landed close by, soon joined by Katrya and ten more Spoiled. They were hand-picked fighters, tribals, Islanders and former soldiers, all chosen for their battle prowess.

Before leading them from the docks Sirus cast his gaze over the harbour. The battle was far from over, rifle fire cracking continually, but most of the repeating guns had been silenced. Fires seemed to be raging on every ship and he saw burning men cast themselves from the decks whilst others attempted to make a stand. Officers hounded groups of riflemen into defensive knots only to suffer a blast of flame as Reds swooped down from above before rolling over to cast their Spoiled riders into the smoking confusion. Despite the apparent success of this attack Sirus also saw the truth in Veilmist's calculations. Many wounded Spoiled and Reds thrashed in the water, the drakes crying out their death calls as they sank from view. In contrast Sirus felt the final moments of the Spoiled as a silent, sputtering scream.

They encountered a full platoon of Protectorate infantry a few streets from the harbour. They were led by a youthful, pale-faced officer who wasted precious seconds gaping at them in shock rather than ordering his men to open fire. Sirus drew his revolver and shot the officer dead as his chosen Spoiled tore into the troops, knives and war-clubs blurring. It was over in seconds, all but a handful of riflemen lying dead or close to it, the survivors casting their rifles aside as they pelted away in terror.

Just boys, Katrya observed, angling her head to inspect a young soldier who lay on his side, hands feebly attempting to gather his spilled intestines back into his belly. Sirus saw she was right, this fellow couldn't have been much older than sixteen.

It seems the Protectorate is becoming desperate to fill its ranks, he commented, gathering his Spoiled and leading them on.

Bodes well for victory, Forest Spear added. Like Katrya his mind was perennially lacking in any suggestion of doubt or disloyalty, a common trait amongst the tribals.

The cacophony of multiple repeating guns firing at once erupted as they pressed deeper into the town, intersecting lines of flaming bullets arcing up into the sky. Sirus spied a gun emplacement on a near by roof-top, one of the heavy four-barrelled cannon. As he watched the gun loosed off a burst of fire, the shells streaking upwards to impact on a Red, blasting it apart.

Deal with it, he ordered Forest Spear, the tribal immediately charging off with five Spoiled in tow. Sirus didn't wait to witness the gun's destruction, instead making for a broad avenue that sloped up towards the Artisan's Quarter. The army had plenty of minds with intimate knowledge of Feros and he knew this district was home to one Professor Graysen Lethridge, famed inventor and father of the equally famed Lizanne Lethridge, better known as Miss Blood, Defender of Carvenport.

They encountered numerous fleeing townsfolk upon entering the quarter. They appeared to be from the outlying neighbourhoods, many running past clad in night-clothes, eyes wild in panic. Most were so intent on flight they failed to register the fact that they were running towards greater danger. However, one woman stopped in midstride to stand pointing at the Spoiled, screaming out an incoherent warning that sent her fellow townsfolk scurrying in different directions.

Sirus could see Greens in the streets up ahead, either feasting on their kills or pursuing prey through alley and courtyard. Several fires were raging whilst the boom of artillery to the north indicated the lead elements of Morradin's army were now engaging the Protectorate garrison.

Sirus found a pack of eight Greens feasting on a body at the wide door to a structure that was part workshop, part house. He could see a large bulbous shape of some kind above the edge of the roof-top, bobbing slightly in the wind. The Greens snarled at him as he drew nearer, then shrank back, revealing their prey as a thin woman of middling years in an ankle-length nightgown. A key lay next to her part-eaten hand, Sirus's gaze tracking from it to the heavy padlock on the workshop door. The words "Lethridge and Tollermine Manufacturing Company" were emblazoned across the door in fresh white paint.

Sirus turned to the largest of the Greens, assuming it to be pack leader due to its size, and sent it a mental image of melting metal. The Green snarled again, lowering itself in preparation to lunge, as if pained by the intrusion into its mind. Sirus added an image of the White to the thought and the Green stopped snarling, huffing as it turned to the door, an action mimicked by its pack. They opened their jaws at the same instant, eight streams of fire lancing out to engulf the lock, continuing to breathe out flame until it had been transformed into a blob of dripping slag iron, the door smoking but not yet fully aflame.

At Sirus's command the Greens quelled their flames and launched themselves at the door, shattering it and streaming through into the workshop with a chorus of hungry screams. He followed close behind, pausing at the sight of a large wooden scaffold in the centre of the workshop, his eye drawn upwards to a raised platform, whereupon he froze.

It wasn't the sight of the moons through the missing roof or the huge elongated balloon that froze him, but rather the young woman in overalls standing on the edge of the platform and staring down at him in shocked recognition.

Tekela's eyes were wide, her expression one of sheer amazement rather than dismay or, he saw with a pathetic flare of gratitude, disgust. He wanted to say something but found his mind suddenly void of all words. Instead it was there again, reborn and undeniable, that same all-encompassing devotion to this girl.

The Green pack leader leapt and latched onto the platform. Splinters flew as it started to claw its way up, followed by the rest of its pack. Sirus's gaze went to Tekela, who, he noticed for the first time, was holding something. It was a squat object with a blocky base from which six narrow cylinders protruded, arranged in a circular cluster. A drum-shaped box was fixed to the side of the object's base, which, Sirus saw, was throbbing rhythmically in the manner of an engine.

Sirus threw himself aside as Tekela lowered the object and the cylinders began to whir, belching out a flame a yard long and birthing a sound that seemed to rip the air apart. He had time to witness four of his Spoiled being torn apart as he fell, rolling away with all the strength and speed his monstrous form would allow. The sound died for a moment and he looked up to see Tekela adjusting her aim, lowering the device and firing again, moving the whirring barrels back and forth to sweep the Greens from the scaffold. They seemed to fall apart as the stream of bullets met them, scattering the remains across the workshop in bloody chunks.

Sirus watched in grim fascination as the bullet stream snaked towards him across the floor, raising a curtain of shattered stone. He tensed for a leap, knowing he wasn't fast enough and, despite the compulsion to abide by the White's will and survive, finding himself content to die at her hands.

The last bullet impacted an inch from his face and the miniature repeating gun fell silent. Sirus looked up to see Tekela lowering the weapon, smoke rising from the barrels. "Out of bullets," she told him with a shrug.

"You always were a nasty little bitch!"

Katrya stepped from the doorway, her pistol raised, elongated teeth gleaming in a hungry smile. Sirus could feel it shining within her: a deep, joyous sense of triumph. *He's mine and you're finally dead! I win! I . . .*

The pistol jerked in his grip, the bullet shattering Katrya's skull, silencing any dying thoughts she might have shared. He watched her fall, feeling the last fluttering of her mind fade like the ripples of a pond after the rain. She sighed, giving a final shudder as life left her. *Two lives,* he reminded himself, knowing that if his will were his own he would certainly have put the pistol to his own head and pulled the trigger.

"Tekela!"

He returned his gaze to the platform where Tekela still stood, staring down at him. She turned at the sound of her name, looking up at a stocky man hanging from a rope ladder above her head. The ladder was suspended from what appeared to be a row-boat, itself attached to the elongated balloon by a complex net of ropes. Sirus saw another man in the boat, a tall fellow in a long coat busily fiddling with some form of engine fixed to the boat's stern.

"Tekela!" the stocky man repeated, extending his hand.

She nodded, hefting the repeating gun and placing it in his outstretched hand before taking hold of the ladder. She started to climb up then stopped, turning back to Sirus. "Come with us," she called to him.

"That thing is not . . ." the stocky man began then fell silent as Tekela turned a fierce glare on him.

"Please," she said, beckoning to Sirus.

Sirus could feel the White's will like a fire burning away his resolve. Whether it witnessed or even knew of this encounter didn't matter. These people were valuable. He *needed* to capture them, or kill them if he couldn't. Sirus summoned all the fear within him, unravelling every nightmare he could remember, reliving all those brushes with death, suffering again the attentions of the Cadre's torturers. It was enough to keep him from raising his pistol. But only just.

"I . . . can't!" he grated, spittle flying from between tight-clenched teeth. "You . . . go! Now!"

He saw a spasm of deep sorrow pass across her face before she resumed her climb.

"Where is Pendilla?" the tall man in the boat asked as Tekela clambered aboard.

"Dead," she replied shortly.

The tall man stared at her for several seconds, face and body frozen until a pat to the arm from the stocky man set him in motion once more. He pushed the lever on the engine, which immediately coughed into life, a set of blades fixed to its side whirling into invisibility. Tekela and the stocky man cast a number of sandbags from the boat and the balloon rose.

Sirus found the White's will diminished as the balloon ascended higher, removing all chance of preventing their escape. "Head north!" he called out, the strange contraption now reduced to toy-like proportions. "There will be fewer Reds there!"

Whether they heard him or not he couldn't tell as the craft sailed from view.

Sirus cast a final glance at Katrya's body before walking from the workshop, making for the docks where the babble of voices in his head told him there was more work to do.

CHAPTER 51

Clay

A lone White made a final, desperate attack as the waters rose to within a hundred feet of the roof. The three sun-crystals had slipped beneath the tide by now, their light dimmed but not extinguished, though they flickered continually. It made for a somewhat nightmarish spectacle as the White streaked towards them, skimming the water and spouting flame like a demon glimpsed in the chaos of a lightning storm. The flames swept over the gondola's windows without apparent effect before the White crashed into the exterior, its claws leaving deep scars on the glass, which failed to break despite the fury of its assault. It continued to batter the gondola with claw, tail and flame as the waters rose ever higher. Finally, as the top of the aerostat met the roof and water began to lap at the lower edge of the windows, it collapsed in exhaustion, gasping out a final unheard shriek before slipping into the depths.

"This thing ain't likely to leak is it?" Clay asked Kriz as the water crept higher over the glass.

"I've sealed the air-intakes," she replied, eyes focused on the dials. "Hopefully we won't be submerged long enough for it to matter."

She waited until the water had completely covered the windows before pulling a lever on the side of the panel. A loud hissing sound came from above and the aerostat immediately began to sink, the view beyond the window transformed into a murky fog, thick with floating debris. Kriz started the engines and used the central lever to guide them towards a distant column of dense bubbles.

"We need to wait for the flow to stop," she said.

"A craft that can fly and move below the waves," Clay said, shaking his head as he peered at the flickering blue-grey haze outside. "Your people really were something."

Kriz slowed the craft as they neared the column, waiting until the bubbles thinned then disappeared completely. "Hold on to something," she said before taking a deep breath and reaching for the steering lever. She restarted the engines and retracted the steering lever to tilt the aerostat on its back at a sharp angle. Clay saw a dark, jagged shape slide into view above: the hole left by the shaft's collapse. It grew larger as Kriz fed more power to the engines, taking them into the newly made portal.

The darkness closed in swiftly, leaving them in pitched darkness but for the faint glow of the small crystal above the panel. Clay began to worry that the passage might be closed, choked with fallen rubble, but then saw a small glimmer of light far above. It swelled as they rose higher, Clay's relief swelling with it, then fading as the aerostat slowed to a stop.

"What's wrong?" he asked Kriz, who was busy pushing her palm hard against the engine levers.

"The engines weren't designed for this," she said, sighing in frustration as her free hand moved to another, smaller lever at the base of the panel.

"What's that?" Clay asked, seeing how her hand trembled.

"Rear main valve," she said, still hesitating. "I can vent all the remaining helium at once, it might provide enough thrust to get us to the surface."

"Might?"

The moist helplessness in her eyes told him all he needed to know about their chances. "Can't stay here, that's for sure," he said, hauling himself forward. Reaching out he closed his hand over hers, placing it on the lever. "And I got no intention of going back."

She gave a tight smile and nodded. "You better strap in," she said, waiting until he had manoeuvred himself back into his seat and buckled on the straps.

"Best hold on tight back there!" he called to Loriabeth, glancing back to make sure she had secured herself and Sigoral. The lieutenant appeared to have fallen into a fever, either through shock or the lingering pain and sat slumped in his seat, the meagre light glistening on his burns. Clay watched Loriabeth fasten her own straps before turning back to Kriz. "Ready when you are."

She took a firm grip on the steering lever then flipped the valve lever with a quick flick of her wrist. The effect was immediate, Clay finding himself pushed back into his seat by the force of the acceleration. The dark confines of the passage blurred as the aerostat sped through it, Kriz somehow managing to keep the craft on track as it veered about. Then they were out, the light that had been a distant glimmer broadening into a shimmering plane of blue.

The aerostat continued its rapid ascent, the blue shimmer filling the forward window then disappearing in an explosion of white as they broke the surface. Clay found himself floating in his straps as the aerostat reached the top of its arc, then felt a bone-jarring thump as it slammed back down onto the water. The force of the impact jerked Kriz off her feet, Clay reaching out to grab her arm as she tumbled towards the rear of the gondola.

The gondola bobbed on the surface for a second then slowly keeled over onto its port side. Water lapped at the starboard windows but for the moment the craft showed no sign of sinking and Clay found himself gaping at the clear blue sky above.

"That's a welcome sight alright," he whispered.

"Something's out there."

Clay twisted in his seat, finding that Loriabeth had unbuckled herself and was crouched atop one of the starboard windows, peering at the murk below. He heard it then, a faint high-pitched moaning from outside. It wasn't one he had heard before but the pitch of it was dreadfully familiar.

"Blue," he said. "We gotta get out. Now."

Kriz slipped free of his grip and clambered towards the panel whilst Clay undid his straps and went to help Loriabeth with Sigoral. They carried him to the front of the gondola where Kriz waited at the hatch.

"You might want to brace yourselves," she said before taking hold of the lever on the locking mechanism. The hatch tore itself free of her hand as soon as she turned the lever, Clay wincing in discomfort as all the air inside the gondola seemed to rush out at once, birthing an aching whistle in his ears. When it cleared he looked up to see Kriz clambering outside. He went next, climbing onto the outer hull then crouched and reaching back inside to grab hold of Sigoral's arms. Some animation seemed to be returning to the Corvantine's features and he grunted out a few short phrases in garbled Varsal as Clay and Kriz hauled him clear and set him down.

"Didn't truly think I'd ever see it again," Loriabeth said, poking her head through the hatch, eyes raised to the pale blue sky above.

Clay's grin of agreement died at the sight of something cutting through the becalmed waters. It was a good distance off but still recognisable, and growing larger by the second. *Hilemore was right,* Clay decided as the huge spine of Last Look Jack drew closer. *We didn't kill the bastard after all.*

"The bomb-thrower," Clay said to Loriabeth, who promptly ducked back inside, returning a few seconds later with the chunky brass-and-steel weapon.

"You better take it," Clay said, passing the weapon to Kriz. "Got more practice."

Loriabeth retrieved the packs and the rest of the weapons before clambering out to join them on the hull. Clay looked around, seeing they were in some kind of channel perhaps a half-mile wide fringed by dense drifts of icebergs on either side.

"Cuz!" Loriabeth said, rifle trained on the fast-approaching spine. Clay moved to her side, reaching into his pack for a fresh carbine magazine.

"Sh . . ." Sigoral slurred, causing the gondola to rock as he attempted to rise.

"Settle down, Lieutenant," Clay said, reaching out to calm him.

"Shhip!" Sigoral said, glaring at him with his one good eye and pointing. Clay followed his outstretched arm, at first unable to make out anything of interest amongst the backdrop of icebergs which seemed like just a jumble of angular shadows. Then he saw it, the long dark hull and tall masts of a sailing ship. *Not just a ship,* he realised, his eyes picking out the sight of people lining the rail. He raised his carbine and trained the optical sight on the ship's rail, almost immediately alighting on the bearded, gaunt but still-familiar face of Captain Hilemore and, standing at his side, Uncle Braddon. They were waving with furious energy, breath steaming as they called out desperate warnings.

"Seer damn me to the Travail if that ain't something to see," Clay said, lowering the carbine.

"People you know?" Kriz asked.

"Family," he said. *But too far away to be any help.* He returned his gaze to the front of the gondola, keen to keep an eye on Last Look Jack, but found the huge spine had vanished.

"Went under a coupla seconds ago," Loriabeth reported, tracking the muzzle of her rifle across the water. "Gone too deep to make out."

Clay spent a fruitless few moments scanning the water, a hard, chilly certainty gripping his guts. "Is there any way to move this . . ." he began just before the sea exploded.

There was a moment of weightlessness, as if he were floating in a rainstorm, then he realised they had been cast into the air. Through the cascading water he saw sunlight glitter on blue scales before it caught a gleam from something large and yellow, something shot through with red veins surrounding a black slit. *Eye to eye with Last Look Jack,* he thought, doubting he would ever get to tell the story.

His limbs flailed as he fell, slamming into the water with enough force to dislodge the carbine from his grip. Although the sea had been heated sufficiently to melt the ice, it was still shockingly cold, birthing an instant flare of pain in his chest and head that threatened to drag him into unconsciousness. He could see his companions struggling in the water near by whilst the gondola sank a short ways off. The craft raised itself up on one end before sinking from view, leaving a diminishing patch of foaming water to mark its passing.

The huge spine circled the four of them at an almost leisurely pace for a few seconds then, as if sensing the cold was about to rob him of his prize, the Blue reared up out of the ocean. It rose to at least twenty feet above the surface, though most of its bulk remained hidden from view. Jack began to open his jaws then jerked as something impacted on his skull, producing a bright plume of blood. The monster turned towards the ship, a rattling growl of irritation issuing from his throat. Clay could see a tall, familiar figure in the Crow's Nest, raising his longrifle for another shot. Jack, however, didn't betray any particular concern as he once again lowered his massive head towards his prey, jaws opening wide and the haze of new-born fire rising from his gullet.

If there was ever the right time, Clay thought, his hand going to the vials around his neck. Thumbing the stopper from the vial of Blue heart-blood, he raised it to his lips and drank.

CHAPTER 52

Sirus

Veilmist calculated the total death toll resulting from the capture of Feros as amounting to just over forty-five thousand people, plus eight hundred drakes, mostly Reds and Greens. Despite predictions, fighting had been fiercest and most costly north of the port where Morradin's forces met with well-organised, often savage resistance. The Protectorate Commander had taken the ruthless, if undeniably correct, decision not to reinforce the city itself following the assault on the harbour. Instead he consolidated his re-maining forces atop the surrounding hills from where his artillery could pound the attackers with relative impunity, much to Morradin's delight. "Always more satisfying to defeat a commander who knows his business," he stated with uncharacteristic cheerfulness the morning after the initial assault. "No sport in it otherwise."

It required a complex assault by air and land over the course of two days to take the hills, a victory that yielded barely three hundred prisoners, and most of those wounded. Even then the fighting wasn't over.

The Carvenport refugees used the time purchased by the Protectorate's stand to construct a redoubt amidst their cluster of hovels. Commanded by a man named Cralmoor, and assisted by a small coterie of Blood-blessed, the makeshift fort managed to fight off a dozen assaults before being over-run by a massed charge of Greens. In the aftermath it became clear that this had been a delaying action designed to allow the refugees' children to escape. A rag-tag fleet of fishing-boats and small steamers had set sail from a fishing-port a few miles up the coast whilst the battle raged. The White seemed indifferent to the escape of so many and the Blues were not sent in pursuit. Children were no use as soldiers after all.

More useful were the prisoners taken at the headquarters of the Ironship

Syndicate, yielding numerous senior managers with heads full of valuable intelligence and two members of the Board itself. Of the three other Ironship Board members known to be in Feros during the attack, two had died in the fighting and the third committed suicide rather than face capture. He had been a large bearded man who somehow contrived to keep his pipe in his mouth even after blowing his brains out with a revolver.

In all the White's army had lost over half its strength, losses that might have crippled a human force, but the surviving residents of Feros provided ample reinforcements. The conversion process was much more protracted than in the Isles. So many captives required days of close guarding before they could be forced to take their turn at the crystal. Riots and escape attempts were common, particularly amongst parents desperate to find their vanished children. Sirus had been assiduous in ensuring the slaughter of the infants took place far from the sight of the adults, aware such a spectacle might produce a riot no amount of cruelty could contain. Instead the children were crowded together in a valley beyond the northern hills and left for the sport of the drakes, the White's dreadful brood taking particular delight in such easy prey.

Throughout it all Sirus kept a corner of his mind open for any report of a strange, balloon-like craft seen flying away from the city during the first attack. So far it seemed that if any Spoiled had witnessed such a thing the knowledge had died with them.

Come with us, she had said. Sirus believed this may have been the only occasion where she genuinely seemed to want his company.

The sight of Katrya's slumped, lifeless corpse also lingered in his mind. *Was I her Tekela?* he wondered in quieter moments, thinking how much he wanted to claw his way into his own past and make a different future for both of them.

He was at the docks overseeing the conversion of the last few hundred captives when lookouts on the eastern shore reported the approach of a ship. Sirus began to order one of the patrolling frigates to intercept the intruder but stopped at a sudden command from the White. *No,* it told him, Sirus sensing an eager anticipation beneath the thought. It seemed that whatever was coming was expected.

He went to the outer mole and ordered the harbour door raised. The tide was low enough that it posed little danger but they had kept the door lowered since the city fell lest any escapees attempt to steal a ship. The White's fleet now stood at fifteen frigates and six cruisers plus a number of smaller craft and several civilian freighters. They would all be very useful in the months ahead.

Sirus watched smoke rise on the eastern horizon as the ship steamed closer, his inhumanly keen eyes revealing her as a mid-sized two-paddle passenger liner. She seemed to him to be in a poor state of repair, the hull streaked with smoke and cast-off waste, a tangle of flags and ropes hanging from her single mast. The SSM *Northern Star*, he read as the ship came fully into view. *A corporate vessel.*

The liner steamed towards the harbour mouth at an excessive speed, forcing her to reverse paddles in order to make her way beneath the door. Sirus could make out the dim shape of the helmsman behind the besmirched glass of the wheel-house, but the only other passenger was a tall young woman standing on the fore-deck. He walked along the mole as the liner entered the harbour, keeping pace with her as she steamed towards the wharf. The young woman wore a ragged dress of some kind, torn and scorched in places to reveal much of her body, though she exhibited no sign of concern at her near nakedness. The woman's gaze roamed the harbour and docks, a fierce expectant scrutiny on her face as she searched for something. Sirus saw the scrutiny turn to outright, unalloyed joy as a large shadow swept across the harbour.

As the White flared its wings and landed on the prow of the ship the young woman put her hands to her mouth, and Sirus saw tears streaming from her eyes. *As if greeting a lost love,* he thought. The liner's engine died and the paddles stopped turning, a deep hush settling over the entire harbour so that Sirus could hear the woman's whispered greeting to the White.

"You called to me . . ." she said, rushing towards the beast with her arms outstretched, ". . . and I answered."

And the White spread its wings wide, raising its head to roar out a welcome of fire.

APPENDIX I

Dramatis Personae

IPV Viable Opportunity

Wulfcot Trumane—Captain of the IPV *Viable Opportunity*.

Corrick Hilemore—First Officer and acting captain of the IPV *Viable Opportunity*.

Dravin Talmant—Junior Lieutenant IPV *Viable Opportunity*.

Naytanil Bozware—Chief Engineer IPV *Viable Opportunity*.

Steelfine—Barrier Isles native and First Officer of the IPV *Viable Opportunity*.

Claydon Torcreek—Unregistered Blood-blessed and member of the Longrifle Independent Contractor Company.

Braddon Torcreek—Uncle of Claydon Torcreek. Captain and chief shareholder of the Longrifle Independent Contractor Company.

Loriabeth Torcreek—Daughter to Fredabel and Braddon, apprentice gunhand to the Longrifle Independent Contractor Company.

Cwentun Skaggerhill—Chief harvester to the Longrifle Independent Contractor Company.

Preacher—De-anointed cleric to the Church of the Seer and marksman to the Longrifle Independent Contractor Company.

Zenida Okanas—Blood-blessed and former captain of the pirate vessel *Windqueen*. Contracted Blood-blessed and navigator to the IPV *Viable Opportunity*.

Akina Okanas—Daughter to Zenida.

Feros

Lizanne Lethridge—Blood-blessed. Full shareholder and covert agent of the Exceptional Initiatives Division, Ironship Trading Syndicate.

Jermayah Tollermine—Technologist and employee of the Ironship Trading Syndicate.

Professor Graysen Lethridge—Estranged father of Lizanne Lethridge. Freelance technologist. Son of Darus Lethridge, inventor of the microscope and co-inventor of the thermoplasmic locomotive engine.

Pendilla Cableford—Aunt to Lizanne and housekeeper to Graysen.

Tekela Akiv Artonin—Orphaned Daughter to Corvantine noble Burgrave Artonin. Lizanne's ward.

Arberus Lek Hakimas—Former Corvantine Cavalry Officer and Major of Imperial Dragoons. Covert member of the radical Co-respondent Brotherhood.

Fredabel Torcreek—Wife to Braddon and co-owner of the Longrifle Independent Contractor Company.

Cralmoor—Barrier Isles native, prize-fighter and former head of the Blinds underworld.

Gloryna Dolspeake—Chair of the Ironship Syndicate Board of Directors.

Taddeus Bloskin—Ironship Syndicate Board member and Director of Exceptional Initiatives.

Admiral Heapmire—Head of the Ironship Syndicate Sea Board, overall Commander of the Maritime Protectorate.

Electress Dorice Vol Arramyl—Former Corvantine captive and Blood-blessed. Later Imperial Ambassadress to the Ironship Syndicate.

Corvantine Empire

Emperor Caranis Vol Lek Akiv Arakelin—Divine Emperor of the Corvantine Empire, first of his name.

Viscount Caled Vol Kalasin—The Blood Imperial to the Emperor's Court, Commander of the Blood Cadre.

Countess Sefka Vol Nazarias—Commandant of the Imperial Cadre, second cousin to the Emperor.

Chamberlain Avedis Vol Akiv Yervantis—Courtier at the Imperial Sanctum.

Korian—Leader of the Corvus cell of the Co-respondent Brotherhood.

Hyran—Blood-blessed and member of the Co-respondent Brotherhood.

Kraz—Blood-blessed and member of the Co-respondent Brotherhood.

Jelna—Blood-blessed and member of Republic First.

Benric Thriftmor—Ironship Syndicate Board member and Director of Extra-Corporate Affairs.

Zakaeus Griffan—Contracted Blood-blessed of the IPV *Profitable Venture*, husband to Sofiya.

Sofiya Griffan—Contracted Blood-blessed of the IPV *Profitable Venture*, wife to Zakaeus.

Scorazin

Electress Atalina—Leader of the Furies.

Makario Bovosan—Pianola player and member of the Furies.

Anatol—Member of the Furies, body-guard and chief enforcer to Electress Atalina.

Melina—Manager of the Miner's Repose, lieutenant to Electress Atalina and inmate of Scorazin.

Devies Kevozan—Leader of the Scuttlers, known commonly as King Coal.

Julesin—Member of the Scuttlers, chief enforcer to King Coal.

Jakisim Ven Estimont—Leader of the Verdigris, known commonly as Chuckling Sim.

Varkash—Former Varestian pirate and leader of the Wise Fools.

Tinkerer—An artificer of aggravating manners.

Darkanis—Imperial constable stationed at Scorazin.

Others

Sirus Akiv Kapazin—Former curator Morsvale Imperial Museum of Antiquities.

Katrya—Former maid to Sirus.

Myratis Lek Sigoral—Junior Lieutenant of the Imperial Marines, acting captain of the INS *Superior.*

Scrimshine—Convicted smuggler and inmate of Lossermark gaol, later helmsman to the IPV *Superior.*

Madame Hakugen—Comptroller of the Eastern Conglomerate Port of Lossermark.

Attcus Tidelow—Captain of the SSM *Farlight.*

The Rules of Pastazch

Pastazch is played with a deck of 60 cards and a six-sided die by up to five players. A standard Corvantine deck consists of four suits of 56 numerical cards and four "Imperial" cards. The numerical cards are divided into the following four suits of fourteen cards each—Roses, Swords, Stars and Crowns—each card in the suit possessing an incremental numerical value, for example the One of Roses is worth one point whilst the Fourteen of Crowns is worth fourteen points. If a player's hand is made up entirely of cards in the same suit, the value of the hand is doubled. The four Imperial cards possess the following values:

Chamberlain—30 points
Landgrave—40 points
Elector—50 points
Emperor—60 points

At the start of the game the pack is shuffled and each player is dealt one card. At this stage each player must make a bet equal to a previously agreed amount or fold their hand. Each player then rolls the die and is dealt more cards according to the value of the throw, for example a throw of three will earn three cards from the deck. Once the cards are dealt, each player will then either bet or fold. Each player will then roll the die once more and will choose from the following options according to the value of the roll: replacing one or more of the cards in their hand, adding to their hand up to a maximum of seven cards, or sticking with their existing hand. There will be no more rolls of the die for the duration of the game. Therefore the minimum number of cards in a hand is two and the maximum is seven.

The first player on the dealer's left will then bet and each player will then bet in turn, matching or exceeding the previous bet or fold their hand. Betting will continue until the pot reaches a previously agreed maximum value or all available funds have been added to the pot. At this point the remaining players will show their hands and the player with the highest-value hand will take the pot.

READ ON FOR A SPECIAL PREVIEW OF

THE NEXT DRACONIS MEMORIA NOVEL,

THE EMPIRE OF ASHES

COMING JULY 2018 FROM ACE!

Clay

It was like drinking liquid fire, the heart-blood sending a searing bolt of agony through him the instant it touched his tongue. Somehow he managed not to lose his grip on the vial, keeping it pressed against his lips until the entire contents had made a fiery progress from his throat to his gut. He convulsed as the pain blossomed, thrashing in the water as it grew, banishing all other sensation, turning his vision grey, then black. He wondered if the pain would kill him before Last Look Jack could send a stream of flame down to boil him as he thrashed. Either way, he knew with absolute certainty he had barely seconds to live.

Then it was gone. The pain vanished in an instant. Clay blinked and the black void filling his eyes cleared. He was still in the water, floating weightlessly below a shimmering surface. The water was cold but the chill was muted somehow, a distant thing beyond the confines of his body, a body he quickly realised had grown to huge proportions. The view ahead was a mélange of colour, cool azure shades shot through with smudges of orange and the occasional small flutters of deep red. *They see heat rather than light,* Ethelynne Drystone had said when she shared memories with him in the ruined amphitheatre. Once again, he was seeing the world through the eyes of a drake.

He saw that these colours were not so vibrant as those captured by the doomed Black all those centuries ago, but any sense of limited vision was more than dispelled by the sound that filled his ears. It was a constant vibrating echo, varying in pitch from one second to the next. It meant little to him but he could sense an understanding somewhere in his mind, an instinctive knowledge possessed by the one who had captured this memory.

The conclusion was as inescapable as it was terrifying. *I'm trancing with Last Look Jack.*

The view shifted as the soundscape changed, a sharp, pealing cry cutting through the echo. The shimmering surface above blurred as Clay was propelled through the water, moving with a speed that was beyond any human engine. He could feel the great drake's pulse quicken from a steady, ponderous thrum to a rapid drum-beat as the pealing cry came again. It was plainly a distress call, shot through with panic and terror. Clay could sense Jack's increasing alarm as they raced through the water, the understanding afforded by the trance enabling him to recognise it as parental concern. Somewhere his child was suffering.

Abruptly the distress call rose to a scream, piercing enough to send a shiver of pain through Clay's mind; then it was gone, cut off in an instant. Another sensation seeped through his consciousness as the scream faded, not a sound this time, a scent. It was a smell that would usually stir hunger in the belly of this monstrous predator, but now stirred only despair. Blood, but not prey to be hunted down or a drifting whale carcass to be scavenged. This was the blood of a Blue drake.

Last Look Jack gave voice to a cry of his own then, a deep throaty roar of grief that seemed to shake the sea. His speed remained undiminished, however, his massive body coiling with furious energy to propel him on. The scent of blood grew more intense until Clay saw a dark, billowing red fog ahead, cooling to pink as the warmth leached into the water. Jack slowed as he neared the cloud, Clay making out a dark matrix amidst the billowing warmth, a net stretched tight around something large and limp. He could see the dark barbs of several harpoons jutting from the dead Blue, a juvenile, judging by its size. Blood bloomed with fresh intensity as the net shifted and the body rolled in its snare as it was drawn up towards the surface. Jack's gaze followed the black lines of the hauling ropes, finding two long dark shapes interrupting the surface above. He knew these shapes, knew they brought danger and normally the sight of them would have caused him to dive for the security of the depths. But not today.

He tore the net apart first, triangular, razor-like teeth tearing it to pieces, freeing the slaughtered juvenile inside. Jack paused to regard the slowly descending corpse, falling away into the cold black depths in a shroud of blood. A new memory filled Clay's mind. A small Blue struggling free of her mother's womb to coil against her father's massive flanks as he curved his body around them both in a protective embrace, voicing a soft song to soothe her distress.

The memory faded and Clay found Jack's gaze had returned to the two dark shapes above. He roared again, his despair merging with rage. It was a rare emotion for a Blue, conserved for the mating season and defending territory from aggressive young males. Now it bloomed to unprecedented heights, filling every fibre of Jack's body. Clay felt something give in Jack's mind, a jolting shock that banished his last vestiges of reason. The great Blue's roar died. He had no need to voice his rage now. He was rage.

The two dark shapes had begun to move, the water on either side of them frothing white and a rhythmic thrum sounding through the ocean. Clay saw soft yellow globes burning in the centre of each shape as the Blue-hunter's engineers stoked them high. Unnerved by the sudden loss of their catch, these sailors had clearly opted not to linger. It wouldn't save them.

Jack made for the shape on the left, making a steady but unhurried approach from below. Although the rage still boiled in his mind, his predatory instincts held true and he knew the wisdom of preserving his energy for the final rush. When he was some fifty yards from the spinning blades of the Blue-hunter's starboard paddle, he struck. A single thrash of his massive tail shattered the paddle-blades into splinters, causing the ship to veer off in a ragged circle, tilting from the force of Jack's blow. Small, dark figures plunged into the water around him, sailors cast from the deck of the stricken vessel. Jack took his time, snapping each struggling figure in half and spitting out the remnants, finding he disliked the taste of these tiny monsters. Their blood was bitter and their flesh too full of bones. In any case, he was not here to feed.

He thrashed his tail again, an explosive release of power that propelled him free of the sea. The ship passed beneath him as his massive body soared over it, sailors gaping up at him in terror, then screaming as he opened his jaws wide and unleashed a torrent of fire. The flames swept the ship from stern to bow, incinerating men and fittings alike, flooding the holds and setting light to anything that would burn.

Jack plunged back into the welcoming chill of the ocean, circling the ship as it burned and killing the charred and barely alive sailors peppering the surrounding waters. A sudden, hard vibration pulsed through the sea as something gave in the ship's vitals, probably a stock of gunpowder, from the size of the explosion. Jack watched it break in two and slowly subside into the depths, trailing a dark cloud of blood from its sundered holds. The scent of his kin's blood stoked Jack's rage to even greater heights, Clay feeling the already fragile structure of his mind crumble yet further.

The huge Blue returned to the surface, raising his head above the waves to see the second ship several miles to the north, smoke billowing from her funnels and paddles churning as she piled on the steam. It wouldn't save her.

The trance fragmented then, Clay experiencing a jolt of pain as the shared memories flitted through his head in a kaleidoscope of wrecked ships and slaughtered sailors. Jack's existence had evidently become an unceasing epic of vengeance, days and nights consumed by the hunt, the endless search for more monsters to kill. He preyed upon whales or giant squid only when his hunger grew into pain; otherwise, he scoured the oceans for ships, destroying all he could find, but there were always more.

Then came a change, a shift in the torrent of rage and tireless hunting. Jack had shunned the company of his own kind for years, ignoring their songs of greeting whenever he passed close to a pack. He knew on some basic level he was no longer one of them; their songs of bonding and play or the joy of the hunt were echoes of something forever lost. Jack had only one song: the rage song. But then came the day he heard something new, not a plaintive cry drifting through the depths, but a song within his mind.

Clay felt another jolt of pain as the song enveloped him, alien and dislocating, and yet dreadfully familiar. *The White.* The depth of malice was unmistakable, although he found it impossible to fully comprehend the intricacies of the beast's thoughts. But he could feel them, the new sense of purpose seeping into Jack's mind, merging with his rage. Clay could sense the Blue struggling against this intrusion. He had a purpose of his own and wanted no other, but the White would not be denied. Soon a fresh torrent of images accompanied the sensation, another ship viewed through the eyes of another Blue. This ship was different, however, a warship judging by its guns. Also, it had no paddles. *The* Superior, Clay realised, watching a young woman raise a pair of revolvers on the deck below. *Loriabeth, the day the Blue attacked us.*

The image changed as Loriabeth's bullets struck home, filling it with a red mist that obscured much of what came next, although Clay was able to discern the sudden halt in movement, recalling how he and the Varestian Blood-blessed had used Black to hold the Blue in place whilst Captain Hilemore and Lieutenant Steelfine readied the cannon. There was a flash amidst the red mist and the vision turned instantly to black.

The sense of purpose flooding Jack's mind altered, becoming an implacable command as the image of the *Superior* reappeared. This time Clay was able to discern a clear meaning in the White's thoughts: *Go south . . . Kill them.*

Clay reeled in shock as Jack's memories swirled around him. *It sent him after us. It knew where we were going. How?* The answer dawned swiftly, accompanied by a tinge of self-reproach at his failure to realise it sooner. *Silverpin.* The remnant of her consciousness had been living in his head since her betrayal and death beneath the mountain. *It followed her scent, forced poor mad Jack to hunt us down.*

Another tumble of memories: Jack finding himself part of a pack once more, although the Blues he swam with sang no songs. The destruction of Kraghurst Station and his repressed but still-evident relish at the sight of so many small monsters burning. Jack chasing the *Superior* through the channel between the Chokes and the shelf, the crushing weight of the huge wedge of displaced ice bearing him down to the depths, so far down the pressure threatened to crush his mighty body like paper. But he hadn't died, somehow struggling from under the descending weight and straining damaged muscles as he sought the surface. Soon exhaustion claimed him, leaving him limp and drifting on the current. He would have subsided back into the depths had the pack not found him, coming together to bear him up to the surface and the salvation of the air. Still, he was wounded, needing time and sustenance to heal. The other Blues brought walrus and whale-meat, starving themselves so he might eat. Had he still been capable of such things, he would have sung the song of thanks. But they were not truly his pack and such songs were a distant murmur of who he had once been.

He ate, he healed, he waited, and then came the great upsurge of heat from below, fracturing the ice and allowing him to hunt down the monsters that had wounded him. He marshalled his silent pack, sending them out into the newly sundered ice, ranging far until one found his quarry. A new ship, one with no bloom of heat within its hull, but with monsters roving its deck. Jack, though mad, was far from stupid. Having recently suffered at these creatures' hands, he opted for a more cunning approach, sending his pack to bear the brunt of their terrible, unnatural defences. He watched the sundered, flailing Blue bodies fall one by one, clamping down on his rage, forcing patience into his damaged mind. Only when the last of his pack had slipped into the depths, trailing a cloud of gore from the rent in its neck, did he determine to strike.

Then a new distraction, a fresh bloom of heat from below accompanied by a great cloud of bubbles as something rushed towards the surface. Jack had no notion of what this thing was, his vision unable to penetrate the hull to discern any heat sources within. But, as it bobbed to the surface and he watched four monsters clamber out, he knew he had found his first easy prey for a long time. A shallow dive, then an upward rush was enough to leave the creatures struggling in the water. Jack made for the closest one, grunting in momentary pain as one of the monsters on the ship cast something at him, small but possessed of enough speed to tear a hole in his scales. But it was a familiar sting—his scales bore the scars of many such irritations—and with the prey so close he paid it scant heed.

The creature struggling in the water below stared up at him with its tiny bead-like eyes, its claws fumbling for something about its neck. A weapon, perhaps. As if anything so small could threaten him . . .

Clay watched the image of himself struggling in the water freeze and then shatter, leaving him in a formless multicoloured fog. Mist swirled around him, coalescing into dense, vibrantly hued clouds, then breaking apart. Here and there he caught glimpses of firmer memories, Blue bodies drifting, dismembered sailors, burning ships. This, then, was the mindscape of Last Look Jack. Beneath the horror Clay could feel a deep weight of confusion pressing in on his own consciousness, shot through with a growing anger.

You can feel me in here, can't you? Clay asked, hoping the drake could discern some meaning in his thoughts. The surrounding mist shimmered, reddish forks of lightning crackling as evidence of Jack's burgeoning rage. *Well, you're stuck with me, for now at least. So let's talk.*

Photo by Anwar Suliman

Anthony Ryan is the *New York Times* bestselling author of the Raven's Shadow novels, including *Blood Song*, *Tower Lord* and *Queen of Fire*, and the Draconis Memoria series, including *The Waking Fire* and *The Legion of Flame*. He lives in London, where he is at work on his next book. Visit him online at anthonyryan.net, facebook.com/anthony ryanauthor and twitter.com/writer_anthony.

Ready to find
your next great read?

Let us help.

Visit prh.com/nextread